"LOOK, LON~~~ ~ ~~~~
A PROPOSITI~

D0564828

Thorne reached in his shirt pocket and handed me five one-hundred-dollar bills. My eyebrows crinkled. "What's up?"

"You're on the list. You're going to get laid off next Wednesday."

He put his hand on my thigh. Was he saying that if didn't give it up he'd fire me? Or was he suggesting that if I gave him some, I'd keep my job and the five hundred bucks?

I flicked my hair over my shoulder and looked him in the eye. "So what are you saying?"

"I'm just saying that my dog needs walking and I'm willing to pay you for it." He reached down and whipped out something large and hard from his pants. "London, meet Bear."

My body immediately began to pulsate. It had been a while since I had a piece. I looked at the money in my hand and at the king-sized candy bar pointing at me. I wrapped my hand around him. "Does this mean I keep my job?"

"I can't promise you that. I'm offering you a job as a well-paid dog walker."

My mind was telling me that this was stupid but my body was saying something completely different. I wrapped my arm around his neck.

ALSO BY CANDICE DOW

We Take This Man by Candice Dow and Daaimah S. Poole

Feelin' the Vibe

off the chain
CANDICE DOW

GRAND CENTRAL
PUBLISHING

NEW YORK   BOSTON

Grand Central Publishing
Hachette Book Group
237 Park Avenue
New York, NY 10017

www.HachetteBookGroup.com

Printed in the United States of America

First Edition: June 2011
10 9 8 7 6 5 4 3 2 1

Grand Central Publishing is a division of Hachette Book Group, Inc.
The Grand Central Publishing name and logo is a trademark of Hachette Book Group, Inc.

Library of Congress Cataloging-in-Publication Data
Off the chain / by Candice Dow.
     p. cm.
   ISBN 978-0-446-17953-9
   1. African American women—Fiction.   2. Escort services—Fiction.
3. Prostitution—Fiction.   I. Title.
   PS3604.O938O34 2011
   813'.6—dc22

ACKNOWLEDGMENTS

I would like to thank God for all his many blessings. Big thanks to my family for supporting me in my dreams. To my little man, Ali, you are definitely the greatest and I'm so happy that I'm your mommy. To all my friends, thanks for always giving me something to write about. To book clubs and readers everywhere, thank you for selecting my books and for promoting them to others. Special thanks to my agent, my editor, and the entire Grand Central team.

Love,
Candice

PROLOGUE

I remember my first escorting experience like it was yesterday. The driver parked directly in front of the Roosevelt Hotel on West Hollywood Boulevard. It was the first time I'd been to LA during Golden Globe weekend, so I was smitten by the various celebrities jumping in and out of cars. They were dressed in the best designer clothes to mix and mingle at all the major parties. Various magazines and production companies were hosting parties for LA's A-listers. No parties for me. I had other business to handle.

My heart pounded loud enough for the driver to hear. The concept of selling my body had been proposed to me just hours earlier, packaged in a bunch of encouraging words, travel opportunities, and networking possibilities. I should have taken more time to decide but not many entry-level jobs were offering those perks, so I agreed. I felt somewhat cheap for being so easily enticed into the forbidden profession. I had arrived at the place where I would first sell my soul.

When I stepped out of the limo, the warm February night breeze blew through my fresh weave and I tossed my hair over my shoulder. My large sunglasses were propped neatly on my slim nose, mainly for me to remain incognito because it was close to midnight and the sun had long gone. My

hands ironed over my slinky black spaghetti-strap cotton
dress. The black-and-cream snakeskin-print stilettos I wore
made my legs look long and lean.

My initial steps were reluctant and nervous, but the perfectionist side of me warned me that if I was going to do
it, I should do it with confidence. My stride became more
determined and assured, as if I'd been doing this for a while.
I had to hype myself up.

I stepped into the palatial lobby: A huge antique chan-
delier hung and comfortable sofas were strategically placed.
I paused momentarily, looking for the elevators. Finally I
spotted them across the lobby. I caught a glimpse of myself
in the mirror. My full lips were glossy and my copper skin
glistened like it had been buffed and polished. The absence
of a bra caused my C-plus breasts to bounce just enough
to still look sexy and give my already slim waist the illusion of being smaller, which made my round butt look even
rounder. My hair was long and straight with a part in the
middle. I patted the sides to make sure there were no strands
out of place. I winked proudly at the reflection staring at me.
My one dimple, on my right cheek, winked back. The black
suede vintage Chanel tote bag propped on my shoulder was
stocked with essentials: toothbrush, ponytail holder, underwear, condoms, and a change of clothes.

I stepped into the elevator and headed to room 714. The
hallway was empty when I stepped off and was greeted by
another mirror for one last check. I lifted my shades to get
a good look. Then I read the sign posted on the wall and
headed in the direction of the room. In seconds, I was about
to knock on the hotel room door. My life would never be the
same again. Several breaths and a bunch of affirming words
later, I knocked. I wondered if he'd been at the door the

entire time, because it opened immediately. I was shocked to see an older white man cheesing at me. He stretched out his hand. "Mr. G."

I smiled. "Tammy."

I didn't think it was wise to tell a stranger that my name was London. My eyes cased the room, searching for anything suspicious. He was a trusted client and, although it was my first time, he'd been with many of the other girls from what I'd been told. He placed his hand on my waist, ushering me to the wet bar.

"You need something, Tammy?" he asked, swirling his dirty martini.

"I'll have what you're having."

I leaned in front of the bar as he shook my drink. I watched him. His energy was relatively calm and relaxed. I sensed a bit of arrogance but in a harmless sense. He was an accomplished movie director, and I could see he didn't need anyone's approval by the shameless expression on his face. I sat on the bar stool and tried to psychoanalyze him, wondering about his story, his likes and dislikes. As a dog walker, I do the same type of observation with a new dog. He walked around the bar and kissed my neck. "Glad you could make it tonight."

As I ran my fingers through his mixed gray comb-over, his large belly poked me. He made growling sounds, mixed with heavy breathing; I assumed this was a result of his weight.

I said, "What would you like?"

He grabbed my knees and yanked them apart. Several fingers shoved inside me at once as he bit and slobbered on my neck. It seemed like we'd gone from freezing to boiling in a matter of ten seconds.

"Oh, baby," I whined as if I were enjoying his sudden aggression.

He yanked my dress straps off my shoulders and reached back to unzip the dress as he continued kissing me.

"Call me King," he said out of nowhere.

"Don't hurt me, King."

I hoped that my submissive words would be a calming gesture and assert that he was in control and there was no need to be so aggressive. The rapid finger-thrashing inside me slowed as he licked inside my ear. "I won't hurt you."

He touched my face softly and repeated, "I won't hurt you. I promise."

He opened his tuxedo shirt in what appeared to be one quick motion. It was almost magical as he exposed a rug hiding underneath. His chest was covered with thick salt-and-pepper hair. *Yuck.* But I continued to pretend he was the most attractive man alive.

He carried me to the bed and lifted my dress over my head, pulling off my thong. Standing at the bottom of the bed, he looked like Fred Flintstone in a pair of black boxer briefs. He spread my legs apart and said, "Kiss my chest."

Ugh. I hesitated, but for a thousand bucks an hour, surely he expected to have no complaints. I sat up at the edge of the bed and ran my fingers over his chest, searching for his nipples underneath the forest. Once I found them I pushed the surrounding strands away from one and twirled it while putting the other in my mouth. I closed my eyes and imagined he was my ex-boyfriend, because I probably would have vomited picturing the man in front of me.

He begged to enter me. So I reached over and grabbed my bag to pull out a condom. I pulled his shorts down and his medium penis protruded, a bit shy of his belly. Quickly rolling the condom on, I asked, "Which way do you like it?"

He sat on the bed and lay back. "Get on top?"

After pushing his stomach up I climbed on top of him and twirled my hips vigorously, and in about twenty minutes he was satisfied. He asked me to lie beside him. After a brief rest, he was ready for one more round. When we finished, we chatted a little about the weather and movies; pretty much a superficial exchange. Shortly after, his eyelids became heavy and he finally said, "Thank you."

My job was done and it didn't seem so bad. I looked at the clock; I'd been there for nearly two hours. It felt like the easiest two stacks I'd ever earned. That was the last time I wondered where I'd get my next dollar. Before I knew it I was in too deep, taking on multiple clients per week, making men feel like the leader of the pack.

It's funny how time flies because seven years had passed and I couldn't turn around if I wanted to. As I sat in a hotel room, watching the spring rain drench the windows, I had no one and nothing to show for all the men I'd made happy through the years. I wish life came with a rewind button.

1

Every call girl, prostitute, hooker, or whatever you choose to call the sex-for-hire professional finds something to help her cope; something that allows her to disconnect from reality and convinces her that there is absolutely nothing wrong with the career path she's chosen. My love for dogs and my quest to make them all happy was all I ever needed to completely escape myself during the act, because men were nothing more than intellectually superior canines.

It was probably my sophomore year at Georgetown University when it dawned on me that they were one and the same. Men like to be praised and petted. They protect their pack. They bark when you interrupt them or let's say when you nag them. They hate doing tricks in front of your friends. They don't give a damn what you look like as long as you let them hump you. And despite what women think, men are actually dedicated creatures.

From as far back as I can remember I have had a natural gift with dogs and it was only natural that I would want to be a veterinarian. I majored in biology and was almost certain that with my good, not great, grades and charming personality, it would be a breeze getting accepted to my veterinary school of choice. Wrong! Not only did I not get accepted into the

high-ranking schools, I didn't get into any school. The consensus was that my grade point average in my major was not
high enough, nor was my personal statement strong enough to
override that. Let's face it, how many black female vets do you
know? They should have accepted me on my demographics
alone. What the hell was I supposed to do now? I asked that
question over and over for the remainder of my senior year and
still came up with nothing. I didn't really have a plan B. There
was always the option for me to retake many of the science
courses, continue working with dogs, and reapply the following year. That seemed too much like hard work for me to face
the possibility of not being accepted again. I wasn't sure my
heart could handle another disappointment like that.

Unfortunately, with a degree in biology, even one from
Georgetown, there isn't much you can do except teach. You
have to get a professional degree and, from the looks of
things, that wasn't happening for me, at least not when I
wanted it. And I didn't plan to be in someone's classroom
dealing with a bunch of damn kids. I'd always related better
to animals than to people anyway. Reluctantly I began to
search for a *real* job, in between partying like it was 1999.
Actually, it was. It was the spring of 1999. I was weeks away
from a purposeless degree. I'd broken up with my boyfriend
and had no job offers. Practically, I was shit out of luck.

Returning home to my mother wasn't an option. Not
only did I not want to have her nagging me, she had moved
clear across the country. I grew up in Arlington, Virginia,
right outside of DC, the mecca of the black elite. And when
I moved onto campus, her job offered her a promotion in San
Francisco and she bolted out of the area like lightning. I went
to visit once and it wasn't my type of town. So that was out
of the question for more reasons than one.

The other reason is that my mother and I never really saw eye to eye anyway. Even the thought of living with her was like a natural disaster. Our relationship had been strained from as far back as I can remember. We were complete opposites. She had adopted me as a baby and I couldn't tell you why, but we just didn't click. I'm thinking that during the time a woman carries a baby in her womb, she develops into a mother. Then there are special women who instantly become mothers whether they adopt or give birth. I think my mother was one of those women who needed nine months of pre-bonding before my arrival. Not to mention that less than two months after the adoption, her husband told her that he wasn't in love with her.

She obviously thought I would bring them closer; instead I made their weak marriage crumble. It's possible he would have left anyway, but I think she often looked at me as the primary reason. He went from our home straight to his mistress's house. Adding to the injury, he subsequently married the other woman and they had three or four children together. Still married, I believe.

My presence probably didn't help her heal because it seemed like she was an eternal man-hater. She busted her ass as a corporate VP of a cosmetic company so she'd never have to consciously or unconsciously depend on another man again. I don't remember her dating, or even flirting for that matter. She never showed anybody much love at all. There was a bitterness that lingered around her, making her already bland personality stink. It was never clear to me if this was a result of her ex-husband's betrayal or if it was just the way she was. If it was the latter, I could see why he left her.

She gave me a plush life, she sent me to the best private schools, she fed me, she took me on a yearly vacation, she bought me a car at sixteen, but I can honestly say I never really thought there was much love there. Never saw her cry. What kind of woman doesn't cry?

When I was seventeen my concerns about her love were validated. Her then-forty-year-old brother was at our home visiting from New Jersey with his family for a weekend. Uncle Leo was an accountant and he always had a square, calculated way about him. I liked when they visited because it made my mother smile, something I never did because I was always in some kind of trouble. She somehow thought my mischievous spirit was a result of something she did or didn't do. She was always calling an expert to psychoanalyze me and make me conform to her mold. I was always the type to go against the grain and I think that made her more unhappy.

I'll never forget. It was a Saturday afternoon and Uncle Leo's wife and my mother had gone out shopping. I walked out of my room wearing shorts and a tank top. Uncle Leo startled me as he headed toward the guest room in the upstairs hallway. His eyes burned through me in a somewhat predatory way. He had small, sneaky eyes anyway so I tried to shake the feeling of him inspecting my curves. He was wearing a pair of yellow shorts, a yellow-and-gray plaid shirt, and one of those yellow golfer's hats tilted to the side. The bright color combo made his dark skin look like midnight hiding from the sun. Although I'd always known him to be a professional man, he looked like a city slicker that day. After passing me, he paused.

"Give me a hug, Niece."

Something in the pit of my belly hesitated, but I reached out to give him one anyway. What I thought would be a kiss on the cheek turned into his tongue down my throat. I snatched away, and before I could even rationalize what had just happened I said, "You're a pervert?"

I spoke softly as if I was confused, because I honestly couldn't believe what he had done. I backed away slowly. My facial expressions probably condemned him. I wondered if he'd tried some young girl before, because he stood there paralyzed like he was stunned that I had responded in such a way. Did he think I'd just oblige? Did he really think that I didn't know any better than to allow my uncle to kiss me? For God's sake, I had been sexually active since I was fourteen years old and I knew his advance was inappropriate.

He stepped toward me and tried grabbing my arm, pleading with me to keep this between us. I looked over the banister at the foyer one story below, wondering what would happen if I pushed him over there. After a short struggle he let go. I rushed into my bedroom and slammed the door.

Though I'd always been slim, I'd always had that lean thickness that men like. I started getting breasts and booty probably by the age of twelve. It seems that most women get one or the other. I've always had a perfect portion of both and a tiny waist to match. My mother always tried to make me feel uncomfortable. She would say, "Stop walking like that. Stop batting your eyes. You're fresh. You need to cover up." She practically convinced me that I was doing something to entice men. It wasn't my fault that grown men were attracted to a damn teenage girl.

I called my then-boyfriend, crying. I cried because I somehow felt guilty, like maybe I did actually do something to turn my uncle on. Uncle Leo called for me at my bedroom door. He kept calling my name in an apologetic manner. I cringed at the sound of his voice as I whispered on the phone with Glenn McCall. He didn't know what to say, he kept questioning whether I had misinterpreted my uncle's actions. As I defended myself on the phone with him, I became more concerned that no one would believe me. I felt alone and finally I hung up because Glenn was only making it worse. In retrospect, he was just a little boy and I had called him with an issue way above his intellectual capacity.

I didn't want to talk to anyone else about it. I wanted to forget it had ever happened. All I really wanted was for Uncle Leo to go home. I stayed in my room until my mother came back and I planned to tell her right away. Instead, I couldn't find the words and I didn't want to be blamed for the shorts I was wearing. So I said nothing. I let the incident boil inside me while we ate dinner. Uncle Leo looked at me like he'd shoot me if I said something. So I didn't.

For several days and weeks after I tried desperately to push it out of my mind. But each time I thought about it I cried. I cried because I wasn't sure who was at fault. Finally, nearly a month after it happened, I walked into my mother's bedroom holding my puppy Snuggles in my arm. I stood at the foot of her queen-sized bed. I said, "What would you do if I told you someone touched me inappropriately?"

She removed her chestnut-framed reading glasses and put her book on her platinum satin comforter. Then her eyes returned to me, as I stood there in a Mickey Mouse nightshirt rubbing Snuggles. She looked through me. My heart pounded because her initial response made me feel like she would condemn me. I said, "Never mind."

As I turned to leave her room, she said, "London, if you have something you want to tell me, I suggest you do it."

I paused and considered telling her that I was joking, but I knew her well enough to know she would not let it go so easily. I got it out as quickly as the words would come. "Uncle Leo tried to kiss me that day you and Aunt Linda were shopping and—"

Her hand gestured for me to stop. Mid-sentence, my mouth hung open. She smirked. "London."

That was the way she said my name when she accused me of stretching the truth. I said, "Honestly, he put his tongue down my throat."

Her big eyes bulged from her chubby brown face, demanding that I shut up. Her wide nostrils spread and she pursed her full lips. She didn't speak. She just kept looking through me. Her reaction made me wish I could eat my words. She took a long, deep breath and put her book back on her lap like she was done with the nonsense I was talking. Her non-response left me shattered. Even Snuggles whined a little. I shook my head and headed to my room. I sat on my bed and muffled my cries with my pillow. Snuggles lay beside me, licking me, trying to make the wound all better. Without words, Snuggles expressed her love to me and my mother couldn't even say anything to make me feel safe. I hated her and a part of me thought she hated me too.

That was the summer before my senior year of high school and I was accepted to Georgetown that December. When she packed me up the next May to live on campus, it felt like she was relieved. She'd committed to raising me and I'd gone as far as getting into a prestigious college. Her job was done and she acted like it. While my other friends' parents called frequently, she called about once a month.

As my college graduation approached and my mother discovered that I didn't have any plans for the future, she was livid. She wanted me to find a corporate job, but I didn't think that was for me. She made an offer for me to come and stay with her, but I decided I'd starve to death first. She explained to me that if I didn't follow her advice, she would not be able to help me. I guess the threat was supposed to make me listen, but I didn't. Finally she told me that it was time I made my own way. I guess she'd spent enough money on a child she didn't love. She told me that she was proud of me, but in the same breath she said she would not be my crutch. *A woman can never have it all. Something suffers.* That was her motto. She really thought that women were put here to suffer. She would always tell me that a woman's life is hard. We carry the burden of the world. It was my turn.

2

Many of my college friends were moving out of DC after graduation and on to graduate school or jobs. I was glad when my close friend Kari decided to accept a position as a DC city schoolteacher. Kari was tall, somewhat awkward, and pale, with ear-length curly hair. I didn't understand her strong desire to be in a classroom towering over the little kids, but her parents were filthy rich and Kari wanted to give back.

When Kari was young her family lived in Saudi Arabia for six years because her father was an executive at an oil company. By the time they came back Kari was thirteen and her family was financially set for generations to come because of her father's choice to work in a war zone. If it had been my choice my entire family would be broke, because we wouldn't have been over there. But from what Kari tells me, their life there was pretty plush, with drivers, cooks, and nannies. So to say the least she was pretty much a privileged, sheltered girl. I think that's what I liked most about Kari, though: She was untainted. And despite her upbringing and wealth, she was really down to earth and in touch with her sista side, unlike many of the other black chicks at Georgetown, who suffered from an identity crisis.

Kari offered to let me move in with her until I could figure out what I was doing with my life. Her parents were footing the bill for a one-bedroom luxury condo in Dupont Circle on N and Twenty-first streets. She said there'd be more than enough room for both of us to stay. She had her parents buy a pullout couch for the living room. It was a nice brown rustic leather sofa from Jennifer Convertibles. She upgraded the mattress so that her good friend would have a comfy place to sleep. I never understood how I'd hooked up with this sweet, charitable girl with so much compassion for people. I would never be labeled the most compassionate chick on the block, because I feel like people have enough sense to make their own way. I have compassion for dogs, though, because they don't have logic. They can't rationalize why they do or don't love you. Either they do or they don't. They don't overanalyze what they feel and they don't feel obligated to do anything they don't want to do. People, on the other hand, can never be trusted, because you never know what their motives are.

Aside from Kari, I was extremely careful about who I let into my inner circle. I partied with the best of them, but there were only a few people who knew the real me. I was always able to determine how far a friendship or relationship would go almost instantaneously after meeting someone. I tried to approach people with the same sense of awareness as a dog. I'd be lying if I said that it always worked for me, but when I ignored my first impression of someone, it almost always came back to bite me. Every living thing naturally emits energy, but humans are the only beings who try to rationalize an uncomfortable feeling. We tell ourselves whatever we need to say to make people out to be what we want them to be. Not only do I not trust people, I don't fully trust myself when it comes to analyzing someone's character.

Kari kept encouraging me to apply to DC schools and I just couldn't do it. Teaching just wasn't in my nature and I was completely convinced of that. I wanted to make a living for myself but I wasn't willing to sacrifice my happiness in the process. The only thing that I loved more than partying was dog sitting. Since my little Snuggles had moved to San Francisco with my mother, I was always eager to keep someone else's dog. I really wanted one of my own, but being that my life was in limbo, I couldn't afford or commit to one.

Kari and I had been living together for nearly a month. She was funding pretty much everything, aside from the charitable one hundred dollars my mother would deposit in my account from time to time. It wasn't consistent, though. Kari never complained: When she ate, I ate. When she hung out, I was with her.

One evening Kari came into the apartment after her summer teaching workshop. She looked tired and drained. I was chilling on the couch, eating a caramel sundae from McDonald's. It was a rare expression, but she looked at me almost as if I was irritating her. I smiled. "What's up?"

"So, how much longer you planning to act like we're still in college?"

My neck snapped back, not so much that I was offended, but more because the comment had come out of left field. We had just been out drinking and partying the night before, and she had told me that she had me until I figured things out.

"London, basically what I'm saying is that you need to really start thinking about what you want to do. You don't even talk about plans. It's like you're content living off of me."

"Well, Kari, you know I'm going to reapply to vet school."

"But that's in the fall. What are your plans for right now?"

She was agitating me as she began to sound like my mother. I was figuring things out and she had offered to help. Yet she was standing there treating me like I wanted to be a loser. I said, "Kari, do you want me to get a job?"

"I want you to try and do something. I don't like coming home from a long day and you're asleep on the couch."

"You think I'm just chilling."

"London, you are just chilling."

I didn't like her busting me out like that but I guess technically I was. "I'm going to look for a job tomorrow," I said, with very little excitement.

Kari said, "Actually, I was thinking you could be a dog walker. I saw a girl earlier with five dogs walking down N Street. And when she noticed me looking at her like she was crazy, she said, 'I'm a dog walker.'"

I asked, "Well, how much does something like that pay?"

"She said they usually pay for a thirty-minute walk, two times a week for one dog, it's about twenty bucks and she gives a discount for multiple dogs in the same house."

I began to smile and it made Kari smile too as she continued: "And I thought, dang, my girl could do that."

I hugged Kari. "That's a great idea."

"I thought so," she said as she wriggled out of my bear hug.

"So, what? You gonna help me get started?"

"How am I supposed to help you?" She rolled her eyes. "I'm helping you enough as it is."

I could tell by the frown on her face that she had no intention of walking one dog. I laughed. "Silly, I mean you're creative. Help me make some flyers to put into people's mail-boxes and all."

"Yeah. I can do that because I can't afford to keep taking care of you."

She said it jokingly, but I could tell that she'd reached her threshold. Kari was extremely mild-mannered and sweet as pie. So for her to say that, she really had to be feeling it. I gave her another hug. "Don't worry. One day I'll make enough money to take care of you."

Kari was in what I called a teachers' boot camp for the summer. I thought they did all kinds of teacher activities to prepare them for the next year, but when she got home the next day she had a stack of flyers printed out on neon green paper. She plopped the stack on the table. "All right, get your shoes on. We have to go pass out flyers."

My neck snapped back. There was no question about my drive; I just needed to find something that I wanted to do. I had no plans for just turning my wheels, just for the sake of doing something. Maybe it was a pipe dream, but I had always imagined loving my job. I shook off my irritation, because she had been supporting me and maybe enough was enough.

We left the house at around three in the afternoon. We went into every high-rise apartment building in the neigh-borhood, posting flyers. We handed them out to people we saw walking dogs. It was a hot, steamy August day and I remember looking at Kari. There were red patches on her face and her acne looked more irritated than usual. Sweat beaded on her forehead and nose, but she was passing out flyers like her life depended on it. I thought, *That's my girl.*

When we were out of the one thousand flyers that she'd risked her job to print, she said, "Let's get a drink."

We rolled up into a neighborhood bar, sweaty and probably stank. There was an after-work crowd there and we stuck out like a bad breast lift. We didn't care, though, because we'd just worked our asses off too. I hoped it would pay off. We sat down, ordered a pitcher of draft beer, and chatted about the next step for me.

When we headed home I pulled out my cell phone and was happy to find about three strange numbers on the call log. We were both slightly intoxicated as we pinned our heads together to listen to the first message: "Hello. I'm calling to get information about your dog walking service."

I didn't even hear the end of the message, because we both screamed simultaneously. We jumped up and down in the middle of Dupont Circle as we listened to the subsequent messages. All were inquiries about the service. I decided to return the calls in the morning, when I was sober.

The first thing I did when I woke up was get my rate sheet together. I decided on ten dollars per half hour and five dollars extra for any additional dogs in the same household. Clients interested in daily service would get a weekly ten-dollar discount. I called Kari to see what she thought; she agreed. The next call was to my first potential client. She asked to meet me and if I would mind getting a background check. I frowned at the phone. *A background check?* She went on to say, "You will have access to my home and my last walker was a referral."

Not that I had anything on my record, but that was a possibility we hadn't considered. I was happy this woman was willing to go as far as getting one done, because if this was a referral-type business it was probably going to be a slow start. My lips were poked out far enough to hit the television across the room as I sat Indian-style with my hand cupping my chin.

"Well sure, I'm totally open for a background check. What do you need?"

"I'll just need your name and license number. I have a form that you'll need to fill out. We can do that when we meet."

"Sounds good. When would you like to meet?"

"Can you meet on New Hampshire and Twentieth?"

"Certainly, what time?"

"Around five o'clock this evening? I'll be wearing a floral skirt and white shirt."

I felt pressure to say what I would be wearing too. But the truth was I had no clue, because I was in the house on my butt. Luckily she gave me an out. "Oh yeah, I'll have two Labradors with me, one chocolate and the other yellow." She chuckled as she spoke of her dogs. "They're adorable."

"I'm sure they are. I'll see you at five."

She added, "This is my cell phone number if you need to reschedule."

I didn't have anything else to do, so that wouldn't be happening. I said, "Okay, thanks."

Shortly after, I decided to return my mother's phone call from a few days prior. It was close to eight West Coast time, so, I figured she'd just be getting in to work. That usually meant she was too busy to talk, but at least there would be a record that I had returned the call, which was really all that mattered. She wanted to talk to her deadbeat daughter as much as I wanted to talk to my overachieving mother. The phone rang three times. As I waited for the voice mail I heard some fumbling and finally she said, "Hello?"

"What's up, Mom?"

"I think I ate something I shouldn't have eaten. I'm feeling a little sick."

"Are you at work?"

"No, I'm taking the day off."

Shit. I had to at least try to make small talk. "Oh yeah, you should."

"How's the job search?"

Damn, I thought. I had figured that at least we could beat around the bush for a minute before discussing that, but I guess not. I took a deep breath. "Okay."

"London, you're going to have to pay back your loans starting in December."

"And it's August," I snapped.

"You shouldn't wait for things to pile up on you. You have to be proactive."

"I'm being proactive. I've decided to start a dog-walking service."

She laughed. "Honey, how many times do I have to tell you? You can't make a living off of hanging out with dogs."

"Just trying to make extra change, Mom."

"Are you really only interested in making change? You have a hundred-thousand-dollar education and you want to walk dogs." She made me angry as she went on, "If you're not getting into vet school, you need to come up with something else."

"I told you that I'm going to apply again next year."

"And what are you going to do in the meantime?"

I shouted, "Walk dogs!"

"Dogs are pets, London. Not a profession."

"Mom, let's talk about something else."

"London, you have expensive taste and I just don't know how you plan to make a living walking dogs."

"Mom," I said, more agitated.

"And what's the plan if you don't get into school, again?

What's your backup plan? It seems like you don't have one and you're not interested in trying to find one either."

"Why would you say that?"

"You get defensive every time I say something to you. Do you think I want you to have a real career for your own good or mine?

I took a deep breath. It was as if no one understood my quest to find myself before plunging into some backup career only to wake up miserable ten years down the line. Contrary to what she believed, I was smarter than that. Sure she made a good living, but I can count how many times we'd shared a good laugh. I didn't want to be like her, making a living just to be making a living because it was something I was supposed to do. I wanted to live! Didn't all these unhappy people realize that the American dream was an empty one? I was searching for the thing that would bring me ultimate happiness. I didn't understand why no one respected that. Maybe misery loves company.

As I wandered off into visualizing the life I desired, she snapped, "That wasn't a rhetorical question. Do you think I want you to get a job for you or for me?"

"I don't know."

"London, you can't survive without income. Sometimes you have to do things that may not be ideal in order to eat."

"Mother, I am eating and I haven't asked you for anything."

"That doesn't make me proud. If you need something, I'll give it to you, but I want to see some effort on your part."

"Like what?"

I thought she'd shout back, but she didn't. She spoke calmly. "London, I still have a lot of contacts in DC. If you want a job that will support your champagne taste just until you can get into vet school, I can help you."

"I'm okay, honestly."

"Don't be stubborn. Let me help you."

I took a deep breath. "What do you have in mind?"

"I'll call a few people to see if they can get you an admin assistant job somewhere. That shouldn't be too much of a hard job."

It irritated me that she thought I really didn't want to work hard. I just didn't want to get stuck in a job I didn't like. A free-spirited person like me would feel suffocated, but she was so structured that she could never understand. I agreed to let her help me and accepted that because everyone else thought it was a good idea maybe I should just conform and get a dumb job.

Later that evening I headed out to meet my potential dog-walking client. As I walked up Twentieth Street I noticed people in their work clothes walking their dogs. I calculated in my mind what I could earn if only half those people needed my service. Finally I noticed a thirtysomething white lady with red hair standing on the corner with ebony and ivory Labradors on a leash. I smiled anxiously as I approached.

Reaching out my hand, I said, "Hello, I'm London."

It appeared that she was shocked to see me. Maybe it surprised her that I was a black girl, but it took her a second. Finally, she said, "Nice to meet you, London. I'm Lynn." Looking down at the well-behaved dogs that were nicely sniffing me, she continued. "These are my boys, Peter and Paul."

I stooped down to the friendly little guys and they playfully licked my hands. "Hey, little fellas. How are you?"

Their tails wagged and their ears were relaxed. Lynn said, "Looks like they like you. My guys are very weird. They don't like everyone, but I'm really busy. I travel a lot, so I need someone I can depend on."

I stood back up and said, "Well, I'm your girl."

She smiled. "Hopefully. Well, let's walk down here to this pizza shop so that I can get your information."

The dogs brushed up against the sides of my legs as we headed to the pizzeria. They were both quite hefty. I wondered if I'd be capable of walking them with other dogs. I figured it was best if I secured this client and then decided how I'd handle multiple clients.

We sat at the table outside the pizzeria and Lynn pulled out a long application. My thoughts must have been written on my face. She said, "The background app is pretty long."

"I see."

"If you want, you can fill it out now and I'll wait. Or you can take it home and fax it back to me."

I shrugged. "I'll do it now if you don't mind."

"Oh no. I prefer you do it now."

I dug in my purse for a pen and finally Lynn handed one to me. As I filled out the application for the background check, she continued talking to me. *Listen, lady, I can't think and talk about two different things at once.* Instead of saying this I smiled and entertained her as I jotted down my information. It took quite a while longer than it should have, but I think that in the process Lynn became comfortable with me.

After I signed, both Lynn and I stood to leave. I petted the dogs and headed back home. On my way I was thinking that I'd closed the deal. And considering there was nothing in my background that would interfere with her wanting to hire me, I was certain she'd be calling in a week, after the investigation was done.

I was light on my feet as I headed back to the apartment. Then it struck me: I'd given a stranger all my personal information and there was no guarantee that she really needed my service. I didn't have her address or even her last name. I walked into the apartment looking like I'd seen a ghost. My heart was pounding, because I thought I might have made a big mistake.

Kari frowned back at me. "What's wrong with you, chick?"

"Ah, I just gave her all of my confidential information and now I'm thinking that was stupid."

"Like what?"

"Well she wants to do a background check on me and she needed this information and I gave it to her, but now I'm second-guessing myself."

"London, I'm sure it's fine. She's just trying to protect herself. You wouldn't let any stranger into your home without a background check. Would you?"

"I guess not."

"Don't worry. It'll be fine. She'll run the check. It will come back flawless and you'll be on to walking hundreds and hundreds of dogs. You'll be DC's most successful dog walker."

Kari made me blush as I tried to envision it. My shoulders relaxed as I thought how blessed I was to have a friend like Kari. She was always so encouraging. It was as if she saw great possibilities in every person she met. That sometimes worked against her, especially when it came to men, but she always had the right words to pull me through a rough patch.

"You're right. It's gonna be fine."

"So what about the other people? Do they all want background checks?"

I covered my mouth and gasped. I had been so excited about my first call that I completely forgot about calling anybody else.

"I don't believe you. Call them now," she said, shaking her head.

I called the two other potential clients. One guy wanted to know when I could start and didn't mention anything about my background. The other lady also asked for a background check. I arranged to meet them both.

Later my mother called back to let me know she had an interview set up for me. Ugh! I hadn't asked her to step into my life. I knew that if I didn't go I would never hear the end of it. From the looks of things, I'd begun to wear everyone down and no one was going to support me as I searched for my destiny. So I had to give a little in order to get a little empathy.

3

The next day I whipped out the interview suit that my mother had bought me for vet school interviews and headed downtown to Quinn Forrester. I was scheduled for an interview with William Thorne, a senior investment banker. He was a friend of a friend of my mother's. She'd given me the rundown prior to the interview. He had a billion-dollar portfolio and was in need of additional administrative help. He'd made more money for Quinn Forrester in eight years than some brokers make in their entire careers. His clients were CEOs, entertainers, and athletes.

I opted to leave my Toyota Camry parked in the building's garage and caught the Red Line downtown to the Quinn Forrester building. Shortly after, I was standing in front of a tall glass building, thinking, *I don't feel like working for some investment firm.* I walked in and stood in front of the guard, requesting William Thorne. The guard called up to the office. After getting approval, he directed me to catch the elevator up to the twenty-third floor and told me that a receptionist would be to my left.

I followed his directions and stepped off the elevator into a sleek office space. There was a nice sitting area in front of the receptionist's desk. A television tuned to CNN Money hung from a ceiling mount. The décor was in earth tones: butter-soft beige leather sofas, brown accent chairs, and a chocolate coffee table. A gorgeous gigantic abstract painting was on the wall, which looked to be covered in an ivory houndstooth fabric. I stood there absorbing the scenery and I smiled, thinking, *I could sit right here and transfer calls all day long.* That didn't seem too challenging, and in between receiving calls for Quinn Forrester I could develop and organize my dog-walking service. But I guess they only needed one person to do that and it looked as if that seat was taken. Slightly disappointed, I said, "Good morning, I'm here to see William Thorne."

The receptionist was a twentysomething white girl with a snazzy short bob cut and a skunk stripe of platinum blond in her brown hair. She was dressed more like she worked for *Vogue* as opposed to at a desk. When she ushered with her right hand toward the waiting area, I assumed she was asking me to have a seat. When I sat down there were a bunch of financial magazines sprawled across the coffee table. Just as I lifted one up a young lady walked out through the glass doors that separated the lobby from the other side of the office. She came up to me and shook my hand. "Hello, London. I'm Amanda."

"Hi, nice to meet you," I said, standing and adjusting my skirt.

She was wearing a black pin skirt and a yellow short-sleeved poet shirt with the ruffle bib type of thing. Her hair was pulled up into a knot on top of her head. She wore minimal jewelry, but I noticed a large rock on her left hand.

"You can follow me."

I did and as she opened the glass door she said, "I'm Thorne's first-line administrative assistant, which means that when I'm here I handle all customer service issues. Because of the magnitude of the business that Thorne has, he needs two assistants. The second assistant is responsible for making sure Thorne has everything he needs, like printer paper, coffee, writing pads, confirming calendar appointments, and things like that."

I nodded. That didn't seem too challenging. I was definitely capable of that. It was pretty much like common sense. We arrived at another glass door with THORNE FINANCIAL GROUP written on it.

Before she opened it I asked, "I guess we're going in here?"

"Exactly."

I first noticed when I walked in the office that the art on the walls mainly contained the colors yellow, red, green, blue, and black. The walls were dark and seemed to be a major contrast to the rest of the company's office space. Immediately I assumed that Mr. Thorne was a rebel. The small waiting room had European-style black leather chairs and a glass table.

William Thorne's office door was closed and Amanda scooted behind the desk on the left side of the office. She told me to have a seat as she picked up the phone. I heard several beeps. Finally she said, "Your eleven o'clock is here."

After hanging up the phone she pointed to the desk directly opposite hers and said, "If you get the job, that's where you'll be sitting."

Almost five minutes passed before William Thorne's office door opened. It seemed like a bunch of attractive guys in suits walked out. Maybe they weren't attractive, but they all looked like they had money to blow. I wasn't sure which one was Mr. Thorne. They chatted calmly in front of me for a few more seconds. Finally Mr. Thorne said, "Yeah, we'll talk later. Glad you guys were able to come."

"Thorne, you know we can't come through DC without checking up on our man. I gotta stay on your radar, because I can't miss out on any business ops."

Thorne laughed. "Man, I told you that investment wasn't something you guys are into."

The other man said, "Look, if I'm getting one hundred percent return in a year, it's something I'm into."

They all laughed hard, shook hands, and gave the pat-on-the-back type of hugs. Thorne said, "I'll keep that in mind."

"Yeah, do that," the man replied.

The three men left and he focused his attention on me. I stood up to shake his hand. He was just about as tall as I am with heels on. I estimated him to be about five foot eight. Standing eye to eye, we both smiled. His small eyes felt like they were serenading me as he said, "William Thorne. Pleasure to meet you."

His smile was almost perfect and his facial structure was strong, but handsome. He wore black wire-framed glasses. His goatee was artistically shaped, almost neurotically aligned on both sides. My eyes directed their attention to his nicely shaped full lips, which were slightly darker, more pigmented than his cinnamon complexion. I was practically speechless as I stumbled to say, "London Reed. Pleasure to meet you too."

His handshake was painfully strong and overconfident. He said, "C'mon in the office."

His style was professional preppy. He wore stylish suspenders on his slacks. I guessed that he was about forty. As he walked in before me, I noticed his broad shoulders and could practically see the definition of every single muscle in his back. His torso was vee-shaped and his nice butt looked perfectly round in his pants. He was the finest businessman I'd ever seen and there had been plenty in my mother's network. He appeared a lot younger than most of my mother's friends.

He sat down behind his desk and I handed him a copy of my résumé. My previous employment had been grooming dogs at a pet store for two summers. The other was as a receptionist at a vet clinic. I shifted in my chair, because I didn't have much experience or interest in corporate America. He tossed the résumé to the side and said, "So, tell me about you."

Tell me about you, handsome. Luckily, not everything I thought came out of my mouth. I paused and finally said, "I'm a recent college graduate and I'm looking for a job that will allow me to use my skills and abilities to advance in the company."

He leaned back in his chair and laughed. "So what book told you that's what employers want to hear?"

"Well, not a book per se, but the placement office at my school had different workshops."

"Judging from your résumé, that doesn't seem like what you want. You can relax and be honest with me. This isn't a serious interview. One of my best clients called to see if I had work for you. I'm just trying to get to know you, not necessarily interviewing you. So be real with me."

"Well, let me say this. Right now, that's what I want

because I have bills. I like nice things. I like to go out. And I need to sustain those things."

"You like to travel?"

"I love to travel."

"Where'd you go last?"

"My friends and I went to Jamaica after graduation."

"Cool. So tell me about your love for animals."

My eyebrows scrunched. And he explained, "Well, it's clear from your résumé that you've spent a lot of time with animals."

I shrugged and looked around his office, trying to figure out if he too was a dog lover. There were pictures of a beautiful wife and three sons, but no dogs. I pressed my luck and proceeded to go through the long journey of how I had planned to be a vet, but the admission process was grueling. He said, "You should never give up on your dream."

"I'm thinking about applying again in the fall. And I've decided to open a dog-walking service in the process. I hope that will make my application look better."

I lied. The dog-walking service had been a spur-of-the-moment decision.

"You're more like an entrepreneur."

"I guess."

"No, you are. Here's the thing, administrative assistants come and go. So I'm always prepared for that. You have a bigger future than this place ahead of you. So here's what I'm thinking, come work for me for a while. During that time you can be applying to school and running your service. As long as things are on the uncertain side, you stay. If anything pops off, you let me know and I'll give you my blessing."

Nodding anxiously, I said, "Yeah, that sounds like a plan."

"Good. My client speaks highly of your mother and it seems to me that she's raised a focused young lady."

"Thank you."

He proceeded to tell me more about what I'd be doing as his second assistant. He had a cool older-guy swagger that made me blush whenever he spoke. Finally, when we were done, he stood and so did I. He escorted me all the way out to the floor lobby. When the elevator chimed, he lightly touched the small of my back. Chills ran up my spine as I stepped inside. He smiled. "I'll see you next Monday."

"You bet."

The doors closed and my eyes rolled. He would make coming to work a whole lot easier. Though he had a somewhat stocky build, it looked like he didn't have any body fat.

I needed to call my mother and let her know that was the hookup, but I couldn't sound too excited. She'd be worried that I would like the job too much. Something was wrong with that lady. She had something against people who wanted to enjoy life.

I called her once I got back to the house.

"So, how did your first interview go?"

"Pretty good. He offered me the job."

"And this is the investment banker. Correct?"

"Yes."

"Maybe you can work your way into the field. They make great money. Did he make it seem like he'd mentor you in any way?"

"Yes," I said, lying.

"Great. So that's one thing I don't have to worry about anymore. Are you sure you want to work for him or do you want to go on these other interviews?"

"No, I'm sure."

I wasn't interested in going on a bunch of interviews. Really I just needed to make some meantime money. She tried to advise me differently, suggesting that I didn't want to make a decision with just one option. *Whatever.* I had a job and that still wasn't enough for her.

4

By the time I started work the next week, I had booked three clients with a total of five dogs. Luckily the other three were smaller- to medium-sized dogs and I would be able to walk them all together. I went to get my big boys, Peter and Paul, later.

Thorne asked about my dog-walking schedule on the first day. He told me that as long as I got my eight hours in and he had everything he needed, I could come in as early as seven and leave at three. I was sold on that schedule. All of my clients were concerned about their late work schedules and wanted me there at least by five for the evening walk.

Corporate America wasn't as bad as I had imagined it to be. The hardest part of working was dealing with the crowded subways and standing in heels all day. Many women would just slip into their tennis shoes after work, but I never found that look attractive. I felt like I looked like a bum. On days when I was late picking up the dogs, I took them out in heels when I didn't have time to change into sporty clothes. My mother had been so anal about everything that the dress-clothes-and-sneakers look just didn't feel comfortable.

By October I'd gained some clients and lost others. What I learned was that owning your own business took diligence.

There were no guarantees. You could have ten clients one week and two the next. The thing I liked about working for a company was that if you showed up every day there was a paycheck coming every other week. There were weeks when my own business paid more, but the very next it would pay very little. In addition to being a dog walker, I felt like I was a promoter, advertiser, and anything else it took to get my name out to potential clients.

I found myself throwing away most of my dog-walking money on shopping. Of the money I earned from work, I would give some to Kari to help with bills. I suggested we move into a two-bedroom, but she didn't want to. She said it was too easy to let her parents pay for everything and that I should try to keep my money. So we continued to make my sleeping on the couch work. I was a neat freak so it also helped that with my room being the living room, the house stayed clean. Kari, on the other hand, could give a hoot about junk. The entire place could be filled with it and she wouldn't notice. That drove me crazy and she claimed I was driving her crazy by moving her things each time she set something down. That was our primary argument. She didn't get ticked off about much but when she couldn't find something she'd go on a rampage.

I would remind her that she should put her stuff away. She'd never say this out loud, but I could feel that she was thinking, *This is my damn apartment.* Most of our issues were solved over a good drink. Being that we lived near any type of bar you wanted to go to, our disagreements were short-lived.

We argued in the morning because I had moved her paperwork and she couldn't find her grade book. When I came in the house that evening from walking the dogs, she had changed her clothes and was ready to go. I said, "We going out?"

"Of course we are. So get ready."

As I showered, Kari proceeded to tell me that we were meeting some guy that she had met on the Internet. I said, "Are you crazy?"

I had no plans of being a part of that. It just wasn't in style at this time. I tried to convince her that she didn't need to go, but she was determined, and if she was going, then by golly, I had to go. We went to a spot not too far from the house, and found Mr. Internet sitting at the bar. He wasn't at all attractive. His head was supposed to be bald, but there were remnants of hair left, probably a result of dull clippers. His gray dress shirt looked dingy. He had droopy eyes, a wide nose, and soup-cooler lips. *Nasty.* I wondered if Kari had seen any pictures before dragging me out. He introduced himself as Eric.

"Nice to meet you, Eric."

We spoke in unison. He joked, "The Bobbsey Twins, huh?"

Kari sat beside him and I sat beside her. He was a teacher also. They talked about the school system and how bad the kids were. I knew for sure that he wasn't Kari's type and I was hoping we could just bounce. Then Eric asked what I did for a living. I told him about my job and that I was a dog walker.

He added, "Yeah, that's all right. Nothing like trying to do your own thing."

"I guess. It's very hard. It's hard getting over the hump and getting your name and your business out there."

"Yeah, I know. I have a landscaping service."

I opened my mouth. I was quite surprised, considering the

weeds sprouting from his full beard looked like they hadn't been trimmed in weeks. It shocked me that he would care enough to keep anyone's lawn tamed.

We went off on a tangent, discussing starting a small business and maintaining it. The conversation went on for way too long. When I looked at the clock, I thought it was almost time to turn in. I guess when you're running your own thing you can't stop talking about it, because an entire hour had passed. I yawned and looked at Kari. "You about ready?"

She smirked. "Are *you* ready?"

"Yeah, whenever you are."

I stepped away and went to the bathroom so they could say their goodbyes. When I came back I stood a few steps away so they could have their privacy. Finally Kari stood up. She and Eric shook hands. I said goodbye to Eric as well. On our way out of the bar, Kari seemed to be walking briskly in front of me.

Outside, she practically threw his business card at me. "Here, he said to give him a call sometime."

She was acting angry and I just didn't understand. "Kari, what is wrong with you?"

She stopped and her neck was rolling. "What's wrong with you? Why do you always have to push up on guys I'm interested in?"

"Kari, you definitely were not interested in that guy," I said, pointing back at the bar. "And damn if I was pushing up on him."

"London, you do it all the time."

"Do what?"

"You bat your eyes. You smile seductively and you make them forget that anyone else is in the room. I'm tired of it."

There is no way she really believed that I had been pushing up on that guy or any guy she'd ever been interested in.

"You are tripping. This is all in your mind."

"It's not in my mind. You've been doing it since I met you. I've just never said anything."

I grabbed her arm. Whatever I was doing wrong, I wanted to make it right. "Kari, trust me. I'm not doing anything intentionally to hurt you. Please believe me." She had tears in her eyes. I said, "I really didn't think you liked that guy and I was just talking to him to pass time. Honestly, you have to believe me."

"But wherever we go, the moment I put my eye on a guy, you start talking to him."

"Have you ever done that with someone you said you were interested in?"

"I never get a chance."

"I'm really sorry. I'll try to be more conscious of it."

She took a deep breath, and I could see in her face that she wasn't done with me yet. My apology wasn't enough to convince her. She said, "And when I bring guys over to the house, they all tell me how cool my roommate is and they never call me back."

"Kari, guys are jerks. But don't take it out on me. If there is something I'm doing, I'll work on it. Men aren't worth losing good friends." She nodded and I said, "Hugs."

She embraced me but it wasn't wholehearted. I didn't like that she felt this way. I wanted to fix whatever it was she thought was preventing her from getting what she wanted.

The next morning Kari woke me up around five-thirty. She sat on the side of my bed and said, "You know, two women can't live in the same house."

My heart plunged because I knew what she was trying to say.

"I think that it's time for you to find your own place."

Her issue with me was obviously bigger than Mr. Internet. She'd been feeling this way for quite some time and last night had pushed her over the edge. I'd never had problems communicating with men, and something that was so easy for me was a challenge for her. And in her mind she felt that it was a direct attack. The most tragic part about it was that probably 99.9 percent of the men she was talking about, I wasn't even interested in. I said, "Kari, thank you for everything. I understand how you feel. And I hope that one day you'll see that I wasn't trying to hurt you."

"London, I don't think you're trying to hurt me. I just think you're not even conscious of it."

She believed she was right and I believed I was right. Because I was living in her place, it didn't matter who was right, she wanted me to leave. I said, "Kari, I appreciate everything you've done for me and I'll start looking for somewhere else to live today."

"I think that's a good idea."

She got up and went into her bedroom. I stayed in bed until she left the house. It put me a little behind schedule but it would have been too uncomfortable for us to be fumbling around in the bathroom at the same time. I sat up in bed after she left the house. *Damn.* We weren't living in the cheap part of town. All my clients were in the neighborhood. I had to figure out how I was going to swing paying rent on a one-bedroom.

5

I moved into a studio apartment in a building directly across the street. It would do in the meantime. I thought a studio wouldn't be that bad because I'd been staying in a living room for almost five months anyway. Kari willingly helped me move, but our relationship took a hit after that night. I think she realized that she really didn't like me, because every attempt I made to make it better, she resisted.

So we were quite estranged. There was nothing left for me to do. I missed her every evening when I came in from walking the dogs. I wished it hadn't ended that way but there is no way to fix a relationship if someone is no longer interested in being around you.

Not having company made the desire to get a dog that much stronger. I had always planned on getting one but I wanted to be sure I was stable first. I applied to school again, now adding to the application that I ran a dog-walking service, and making my personal statement more intriguing. I hoped the candidates wouldn't be as strong as the year before. As the new year approached, the rejection letters began to pour in. I was slightly depressed, but I figured nothing could fix it except an energetic puppy to come home to.

I contacted a breeder who had recently had a litter and

the pups were weeks away from being ready to live with an owner. I put a beige pug on reserve. When I drove out to Manassas, Virginia, to pick up my puppy, I was so excited. I was prepared with everything he needed. I decided to name him Bruno. I wasn't sure how we'd manage in the small space we called home, but I knew that I needed him.

I went to work after Bruno came home, bragging about my new dog. Thorne, as everyone in the office called him, asked me to come into his office. He said, "I've been meaning to tell you that I'm sorry about school."

I shrugged. "Well, all I can do is try. Maybe it's not meant for me."

"Don't give up."

"I guess."

"So tell me more about your new dog."

I went on to tell him as much about Bruno as I knew. There was something so smooth and effortless about Thorne. I loved talking to him. We connected and I loved all his advice. He was wise for no good reason at all. It was no wonder he could get people to effortlessly give him millions of dollars to invest.

When I was done with my doggy dilemmas, Thorne removed his glasses and wiped the sweat from between his eyes. There was an abnormally distressed look on his face. "So, London, tell me this. How do you plan to really get your dog-walking service off the ground?"

I shrugged. "I don't know."

"The reason I'm asking you this is because I was honestly hoping you got into school, and if that's no option, you really need to begin focusing on your service."

"I agree, but it's kind of hard when you have to pay rent and buy clothes and yada, yada, yada. I guess it's just easier to come to a nine-to-five."

"Unfortunately, a nine-to-five is not a guarantee. Whatever you do, you always have to have a backup plan."

I nodded, slightly unsure of where he was going.

"Anyway, the staff meeting I just left. We heard some bad news."

"Really, like what?"

"Like there are going to be layoffs next week."

I blurted out, "Next week?"

"Yes, next Wednesday. They are going to be laying off a large portion of the staff."

I'd become quite comfortable with my job and this news had my head spinning. I'd been shopping with business money and paying bills with work money. I didn't have a backup plan or a homegirl who would let me live on her couch. This was devastating news. I sat there for a few minutes with my lip hanging. Finally, I said, "Thorne, can't you put in a good word for me?"

"I can only request to keep you. It's possible they'll listen, but from what I'm hearing these cuts are going to be deep. I'm sorry, London, the admins go first."

Tears welled up in my eyes. "This is too much for me to deal with."

"Have you been saving?"

"No. I don't have a lot of money to save."

"What about your business money?"

"You mean my dog-walking money?"

"Yeah, don't you make good money doing that?"

"About two hundred a week on average. Sometimes a little more and often a lot less. You just can never tell. One day someone will want your service. They come home late and find that the dog has peed on the floor; they blame you and then they don't want your service anymore. I can't depend on that money."

"How much do you think you can make if you did it full time?"

"I don't know. It's not consistent. Like I said, people fall in and out. Some weeks I make nothing."

"That means you're not running your business right."

"I do the best I can do while working."

"Run your business first. Work second. You can't build wealth working a job."

I was confused. It seemed like everyone I knew who ran a business was broke and everyone with a job lived a comfortable lifestyle. Thorne continued to school me and told me that a job's salary had a ceiling, but running a business you could make as much as you were determined to make. He explained that although he worked for Quinn Forrester, he pretty much ran his own business unit and could make as much as he wanted. He began putting things in my head that I had never even considered, like making my clients sign a contract. If they broke it without certain reasons stated, they would owe me for the term of the contract. He also suggested I consider running a doggy day care and having other walkers work for me.

It was sad that after I had been faced with losing my job, he was offering all this business knowledge. He said, "And by the way, do you come as far as Rockville to walk dogs?"

"Not really, because I don't like to incur traveling expenses. Most of my clients are right in Dupont Circle."

"I do understand, but my wife and kids are away this weekend and I need someone to walk my dog for me. You think you can help me out?"

"I guess I can break the rules for you," I said with a smirk. "I never heard you mention a dog. What kind of dog do you have?"

He smiled sneakily. "What kind of dog does it look like I would have?"

"I don't know. A poodle, maybe?" I said jokingly.

"A black Rottweiler. His name is Bear."

We laughed and I agreed to go to his house the next afternoon to meet Bear. He promised that he'd pay me well for my travel and I was looking forward to it. Also, I hoped he'd give me some more of that business advice. If anyone knew how to make someone rich, he was the one, and it was time I used my resources.

6

When I turned into the long entrance to Thorne's home, I was in awe. It was practically a mansion. The top of the driveway was circular and there was a small round pond with a little frost glazed over it and what looked to be a small water sculpture inside. I bet it was gorgeous when it was warm outside. The Colonial-style house had a golden-beige stone exterior with extra-large brown double doors with polished brass handles. I was almost scared to ruin the scenery by parking my blue Camry out front.

When I got out, I looked at the acres on his property. He could have just let the dog run out in the yard. I rang the doorbell. Seconds later he opened the door wearing a pair of jeans, a button-down Ralph Lauren shirt, and a pair of tennis shoes. I smiled. "This was a long ride," I joked.

"It's right around the beltway. It should only take fifteen minutes," he said, placing his hand on my shoulder and massaging gently. He invited me into his family room. "Have a seat."

Where is the dog? I wondered. He pulled a case from an armoire and opened it. There were different types of cigars in there. I waved my hand to decline. He picked one out. "Here, try a petite one. You'll like it. Cigars are calming."

"I nearly choked to death when I first tried a cigarette. I know I can't smoke a cigar."

He sat down beside me and clipped the end of the cigar. "Smell that," he said, waving the cigar in front of me.

He continued, "Cigarettes are like the chitterlings of tobacco. Cigars are like a premium pork loin. You should try one."

I felt like I was on a peer pressure commercial. He lit the cigar and inhaled. "Best feeling in the world. This is how I spend my time when I'm not working."

"I thought you always worked."

"Pretty much."

He inhaled and exhaled like the cigar was sex. Finally I agreed because he made it look so inviting.

"See, this is a Cohiba from Cuba," he said, handing it to me. "Don't take a long drag, just inhale slowly, keep it in for a minute, then exhale."

I followed his instructions and surprisingly didn't choke. I nodded, "Not bad."

"You want to help me finish?"

I shrugged. He'd told me previously that sometimes you have to try a potential client's hobby in order to seal the deal. I wasn't sure what the deal was, though.

We finished that cigar and just as I began to mellow out, I remembered the purpose of my being there. "Where's Bear?"

He scooted close to me and turned the speaker volume up. Jazz music played as he began to talk. "Look, London, I have a proposition for you."

I scooted a little farther away from him because I wasn't certain where he was going. He reached in his shirt pocket and handed me five one-hundred-dollar bills. My eyebrows crinkled. "What's up, Thorne?"

"You're on the list. You're going to get laid off next Wednesday."

He put his hand on my thigh. Was he saying that if I didn't give it up he'd fire me? Or was he suggesting that if I gave him some, I'd keep my job and the five hundred bucks?

I flicked my hair over my shoulder and looked him in the eye. I wanted him to clarify what I'd be getting out of this deal. "So what are you saying?"

"Really, I'm just saying that my dog needs walking and I'm willing to pay you for it."

He reached down and whipped his large hard penis from his pants. "London, meet Bear."

My vagina immediately began to pulsate. It had been a while since I had a piece. I looked at the money in my hand and looked at the king-sized candy bar pointing at me. I wrapped my hand around him. "Does this mean I keep my job?"

"I can't promise you that. That's not up to me." He looked down at himself. "I'm offering you a job as a well-paid dog walker."

My mind was telling me that this was stupid but my body was saying something completely different. It was commanding me to take the job. He must have noticed the confusion in my eyes as he leaned over and stuck his tongue down my throat. I obliged and wrapped my arm around his neck. He ripped my shirt open and buttons flew all around the room. He kissed my neck and I returned the favor. I felt obligated to over-perform.

I took his pants down and said, "Do you have condoms?"

He pulled one from his pocket. I grabbed the packet and opened it and proceeded to put the condom on him.

He seemed to get a thrill from the touch of my hands as he panted in anticipation. He lay back on the floor and rested his hands behind his head. I stepped out of my pants and climbed on top of him.

I slowly lowered myself on his pole and began to grind. He started giving me instructions. "Go up and down slowly. Kiss my chest and flex your hips at the same time." I felt like I was in Sex Education 101. It was taking the joy out of the moment. When we finished he said, "You'll be a pro in no time."

I didn't read much into it, but I wanted to know what our arrangement was and how long I could expect it to last. I rested beside him because I'd begun to feel bad about what I had succumbed to. I said, "I never got paid for sex before. I feel kinda slimy."

He reached over and stroked my hair. "Why? Do you feel bad when your dog-walking clients pay you?"

"No, but I provide them with a service..."

"And you're providing me with a service."

I laughed. He said, "Whether you see it as a service or not, it is. And I plan to pay you for it."

I rose up on my elbow and rested my head in my hand. "Why would you do that?"

"It's simple. I get what I want. You get what you want. No lies. No telling you that I plan to leave my wife. All men need a side item, but most of them don't have the means to pay for it, so they mislead you."

Maybe this was his effort to make me feel better but I felt like shit. I wondered if I'd rather be misled. He massaged my shoulder. "London, in business, always use your mind, not your emotions."

"I guess. So when you get tired of this side item, you just stop calling."

"Let today take care of today."

I lay back on the floor and stared up at the complex ceiling fan hanging above us. "So am I done for the day or what?"

"I'd like you to stay awhile longer."

We had a peaceful evening, smoking cigars and having sex. Before I knew it, it was one in the morning and we were cuddled up in his first-floor guest room. I was enjoying him and I wanted to know how long this would last, but he kept it professional.

I woke up the next morning and climbed out of bed. I wondered if I should wake him up. Instead I went into the bathroom and showered. I kept hearing him tell me this was business and I should save any miscellaneous income like this so that a job loss would be nothing. When I questioned him about what I should do when the miscellaneous came to a halt, it shocked me when he explained that if a woman isn't in a committed relationship, she should always get paid well for sex.

7

When I got home, I was confused and uncertain about what I'd just done. I needed someone to talk to. I looked at Bruno as I cleaned up the mess he'd made in his crate, thinking he wouldn't do. Kari and I didn't talk much and I hadn't really been able to get her to come around. It had been nearly three months, and when I stepped out of my building to take Bruno on a quick walk, I looked over at her building wishing we were still close and praying that I could erase my flirtatious spirit to make her comfortable. As soon as I stepped back into my apartment, I pressed my luck and I dialed Kari.

"Hey, chick, what's up?"

"Hey, London," she said hesitantly.

"I miss you a lot."

"Yeah, I kinda miss you too."

We'd been through too much and I was sincerely sorry and I really missed her. I wanted to tell her what I had just done, but since my flirtation had ruined our friendship, I didn't think it was wise. I just wanted to hang out and chat for a minute. I needed girlfriend therapy.

"Good, so you can come over for a drink."

"Okay, I'll be over soon."

By my giving her space and letting her deal with her issues

with me on her own, I think Kari realized as much as I did that we were good friends. When she got there she opened her arms to hug me.

"I'm sorry about all the mean things I said to you."

"It's okay. We're not even going to go back to it. I really miss hanging out with you. So what's been going on?"

She pouted slightly. "Nothing, just dating."

Kari wanted a relationship badly and it seemed as if men were running away like she had a disease.

"So how's it going?" I asked.

"Not so good."

"What do you mean?" I stood up. "Wait, let me pour you a drink first."

"Yeah. Do that. I went on a date last night with a guy I met online."

I rolled my eyes. She laughed. "Exactly. Anyway, we had a pretty good conversation and all. He was a little older. Very nice-looking. He ordered a two-hundred-dollar glass of wine."

"Okay, that sounds good."

"Wait, I'm not finished. When the bill came, he said he had to go to the bathroom." She dropped her head. "Thirty minutes later, I realized that he wasn't coming back."

I was so shocked by what she'd told me that I dropped the martini glass on the floor. We laughed, but it was obvious Kari was in pain. I resisted the urge to immediately sweep up the glass. Instead I went over to the bed and wrapped my arms around my friend.

"Kari, your time will come."

"But when?" she asked.

"Stop looking. It's a man's job to find you."

"I'm just not sure he will."

"He will, trust me. Just because you try hard to find a guy doesn't mean that you'll find the right guy. It just means that you'll kiss a lot of toads before you find your prince. But if you wait for your prince to find you, you avoid all the toads. Basically what I'm saying is the right guy isn't coming until it's the right time and no matter how much you date before he comes, he ain't coming any faster."

"But it seems like I've never had a boyfriend."

"And that means you don't have any baggage either."

"I wouldn't say that."

"We all have a little."

She said, "And I didn't even tell you."

"What?"

"I crossed over."

"Crossed over? As in to white guys or females?"

She pushed me. "Silly, white guys."

"And how'd that work out?"

"Not so good."

"What happened?"

"Well I was seeing this guy for about a week and we went out to eat. The waiter asked if we wanted to see the dessert menu. And I said yes. Girl, when the waiter left he told me that he didn't think I needed dessert, trying to insinuate that I was fat."

Kari was pretty slim to me. The fact that this guy even made it a point to say that was ridiculous. I hugged her again. "Kari, stop dating for a little while. It's stressful. You just don't need the headache."

"I think you're right."

It was ironic that I had called Kari at a moment when she needed me as much as I needed her. We spent the rest of the day together, watching a bunch of romantic comedies.

Hopefully they inspired her to believe that when it's meant to happen it will. Kari went home close to midnight.

Listening to her dating drama made me feel better about what I had done as I reflected on Thorne's words. "If a woman is not in a committed relationship, she should be earning something for her services." That was probably the best advice I'd heard in a long time. He knew how to make money and just about anything as far as he was concerned could be a business. And poor Kari was dealing with these losers free of charge.

As I prepared for work, I was empowered. At least I wasn't dealing with any bullshit. I had earned a few dollars to spend an evening with a gentleman. It wasn't until the next day when it was time for work that I began to feel sleazy. I stepped into the office and opened Thorne's *Wall Street Journal* on his desk, like I did every day.

It was around noon when Thorne came into the office. "Afternoon, London," he said, just as casual as a week before.

My heart pounded, but I smiled. "Afternoon, Thorne. There are two urgent messages on your desk."

"Cool. Yeah, had to wait for the wife and boys to come in from vacation this morning."

I looked across at the other assistant and she curled her lips. My eyes shifted. I began to wonder why she had done that. Had she been with him in the same way that I had? She mouthed, "He probably overslept."

I smiled tightly. "Probably."

Thorne stepped out of the office about an hour later and handed me a phone message: HYATT. ROOM 724. 3:30 P.M. TODAY. I didn't read it until he stepped away. My heart dropped. I wasn't sure what the frequency of our arrangement would be but I hadn't expected it would be daily.

When he returned to the office from the restroom, he looked at me for a response to his note. I nodded. He smiled and told Amanda, "I'm going to be in a meeting this afternoon."

He looked at me. "Monday is your early day. Right?"

"Yes, sir."

"Well, I'm going to be skipping out of here around two. So, Amanda, hold down the fort."

"Always," she said, smiling.

I hoped she hadn't noticed our exchange, and I wondered if she knew something about Thorne that I didn't know. What if this was what he did with all his second assistants? He definitely had a high turnover. I racked my brain with questions, but I kept reminding myself that we didn't have that type of relationship. I shouldn't even want to know these things.

Around three-thirty I began to gather my things and headed out of the office. I knocked on the hotel room door around quarter to four. When he swung the door open, he had a stern look on his face. I smiled, and he barked, "You're late."

"Yeah, I know. I had to send out some e-mails and..."

He covered my mouth. "Being punctual is important. Are you ever late for work?"

I felt like he was taking this business thing a little too far. "I'm here now. That's all that matters."

"What's your hourly rate?"

My neck snapped back. "Whatever you give me."

"So if I only have an hour to spare, should I give you three-fourths of your money?"

I walked up to him and kissed him on the mouth. "Is that worth my fifteen minutes?"

I untied his robe and began to bite his nipples. "Is this worth my fifteen minutes?"

He said, "Take your clothes off."

As I undressed, he helped me and pushed me onto the bed. He rammed his penis inside me. He pounded rapidly. It was far from the passionate experience we had shared on Saturday. As he quickly released and pulled out, I felt like a slut. He walked into the bathroom and I heard the shower running. This wasn't what I wanted. No money was worth that feeling.

Why did I want to pretend I could handle this? I had always been able to completely forget about a guy after sex, but it was my choice. There was an unhappiness brewing inside of me from this quickie and his lack of affection afterward. He stepped out of the bathroom and began to put on his clothes. He walked over to the bed. "You, okay, London Bridge?"

I shrugged. He was in front of the mirror fixing his tie and looking at me in the reflection. I was still naked, sitting on the bed Indian-style.

He began to talk. "Sex minus emotion. Can you do it or not?"

"I don't think so."

After he tied his tie, he sat on the bed. "Paid sex is not always sensual. Every dog you walk isn't well trained, is he?"

I pouted a little and hung my head. He lifted my chin with his finger. "The only reason I did what I did today was to remind you that this is business. There are going to be days when I need to get in and get out. And you'll have to respect that. The quicker you see it the way I do, the better we'll be." He stood up and grabbed his jacket out of the closet. "Or maybe you're not the businesswoman I thought you were."

I just looked at him. He extended his hand to shake mine. There were five one-hundred-dollar bills clasped in between our grip. "London, a fair exchange is no robbery."

I'd made one thousand dollars in less than three days. It would take me four weeks of walking dogs to make that kind of money and two weeks of my gross salary. Emotionally, this definitely didn't seem like the ideal profession. Financially, it seemed brilliant, almost too good to be true.

Just as he was about to leave, he said, "We cool?"

"Yeah, we cool."

As he turned the doorknob, he added, "Do you have a passport?"

"Yes, why?"

"We may have some opportunities abroad."

Abroad? I looked in the mirror, thinking, *This is better than a real job any day.* After he closed the door behind him, all the discomfort and confusion from the quick boom-boom bang-bang he'd just served was now discounted and I was wondering what would be next.

8

When I arrived at work on Pink Slip Wednesday, people were crying as they were escorted out of the building. My mother always taught me not to wear my heart on my sleeve. "Dress up stress in the best garments you own," she'd say. I walked into the office wearing a knee-length stiffly tailored trench coat from Banana Republic, a short black skirt, and a plum silk three-quarter-length-sleeve fitted button-up top from J.Crew. I wore silver accessories and a pair of black Nine West pumps. I sashayed through the doors like I knew I still had a job.

On normal days the brokers strolled in between the hours of nine and eleven. Everyone was there by seven-thirty. The brokers were responsible for breaking the news to the unlucky members of their teams. When I walked in, Amanda appeared shocked by my positive energy. I smiled. "Hey, you."

Looking at me suspiciously, she responded slowly. "Hey..."

I asked, "Did he talk to you yet?"

Almost apologetically she nodded.

I smiled. "Okay, so..."

"I'm still here," she said in a guilty tone.

"It's okay, Amanda."

"But I think…"

"You think I'm gone. I think so too, but it's okay. I'll find something."

She reached out for a hug. While we embraced, she said, "I'm sorry, London."

"Don't be, sweetie. I'll just walk more dogs until I find something else."

I almost laughed out loud. Before I could get to my desk, Thorne came out of his office and asked me to come in. Amanda mouthed, "Good luck."

I curled my lips, thinking *Don't be phony*. We both knew that one of us would go and if it wasn't her, obviously it was me. Inside Thorne's office there were two human resources representatives.

Thorne sat in his chair uncomfortably, like it was a challenge to find the words to let me go. He grimaced before speaking. "London, I regret to inform you that there have been major budget cuts in the last quarter and as a result your position has been eliminated. As of five o'clock this evening you will be escorted out of the building and asked to return any of Quinn Forrester's equipment and/or belongings."

While handing me a black folder, he continued, "There is an exit checklist enclosed to assist you in the departure process. Do you have any questions?"

"No, not really."

One of the human resources representatives spoke up. "Also, you'll note in your departure letter, you are eligible for two weeks of severance for each full year of service." She looked down at a form in front of her. "So you get one week. It's prorated," she said, smiling as if that was something to be excited about. After a week, then what? I was out of a damn job. Being that I was no longer gainfully employed, I planned to walk Thorne until his paws fell off. I loved having my own place and my own money. Although it had been only a few months, I was so far beyond struggling and living on Kari's sofa. Also, Kari had made it clear that she did not want me back.

When I walked out Amanda's face was beet-red. I smiled. She said, "What happened?"

"Take a wild guess."

"I'm so sorry."

I shook my head. "Don't be."

It was interesting that there were Office Movers boxes strategically placed on the wall adjacent to my desk. I couldn't recall if they had been there before I went into Thorne's office or not, but suddenly a feeling of rejection came over me. I didn't like it, so to avoid letting this get to me I proceeded to pack my things in the boxes. Amanda kept trying to make small talk but I practically tuned her out.

I stepped out for lunch to get some fresh air. I went down the block to a deli. After I ordered my food, and a double shot of espresso in my caramel latte, I sat on a stool in front of the counter facing the large glass window so that I could people-watch. I daydreamed momentarily. Finally a server came to bring my food. He grabbed my number off the table and slid the tray in front of me.

"It'll get better."

Slightly taken aback, I said, "Oh, I'm fine, but thanks."

He nodded. "Good, enjoy your lunch."

And I did just that. My lunch lasted longer than normal. There was no reason to rush back only to be escorted out in a few hours.

When I returned to the office I sat around, doing nothing.

There was no real reason to be there in my opinion, except that I got paid for those hours. As I sat at my desk doodling on a notepad, Thorne walked out of the office looking exhausted. I asked, "Are you okay?"

"Are *you* okay?"

"I'm fine. Just on to the next thing, whatever that may be."

He sat on my desk, which he'd never done before. Quickly I looked up to see if Amanda was watching. He slightly lifted his hands up in a defenseless gesture. My assumption was that he was trying to let me know this was out of his control.

"You know, London, I know an entrepreneur when I see one. This isn't for you anyway."

"Are you saying that you got rid of me because you want me to focus on my business?" I asked, laughing.

He nodded. "Exactly."

"Whatever."

"Do you need any help getting this stuff home?"

I shrugged.

"You catch the train to work, don't you?"

"Yes, I probably should've driven today."

"I'll drive you home since I had to do the ungentlemanly thing and lay you off."

"How nice of you."

Amanda said her goodbyes close to three. She promised to keep in touch and to let me know about any other opportunities that she heard of. I didn't believe her, but I said, "I'm going to hold you to that."

She said, "I'm going to miss you. It's been fun."

We hugged and she rushed out of there like she was trying to avoid the close-of-business drama that would probably occur.

Shortly after four-thirty, Thorne came out and asked if I was ready. I looked at the boxes atop my desk and said, "Looks like it."

"I'll take a box with me and I'll meet you at the seventh-floor exit in the garage. You can put the other two on a mail cart."

He grabbed one of the boxes and walked out. I stood up thinking, *Damn, this* was *a pretty good first job.* I had realized that not all of corporate America was completely stuck up. Unfortunately, nothing lasts forever. It could have at least lasted longer than six months, though. I turned the lights down and pulled the door closed for the last time.

I opened the door to Thorne's Benz S500. I loaded the boxes in the back and pulled the mail cart back into the building. When I sat in the passenger seat, I asked, "So did you fire me so that I could be your mistress?"

"You're not my mistress."

"We're sleeping together. So what am I?"

"We're two people in business. We are exchanging goods. I thought we settled this the other day."

We headed to my apartment. When we arrived I invited him in. Without hesitation he dropped the boxes off in the lobby. "I'm going to find a parking space and I'll be in in a second."

He knocked on my door within minutes. When he first walked in, Bruno started barking aggressively. He probably sensed Thorne's authoritative energy and felt he had something to prove. He was locked in his crate and I knew he wanted to get out and sniff Thorne, but he had to wait a moment while I entertained. Thorne walked in a small circle around my one-room apartment and nodded. "Very nice for a first apartment." He continued scoping. "Someone has OCD."

"What?"

"Obsessive-compulsive disorder."

I laughed. "No. I just really like a clean place. And not to mention, this place is only like four hundred square feet, I have to keep it clean or it can get really junky, really fast."

"Damn. I mean, everything is in order like you're a serial killer or something." He laughed. "You hiding something, London Bridge?"

"Whatever, it's not that bad."

"You're crazy, I have a cleaning lady and my house isn't nearly this clean."

"But you have kids."

"Yeah, but it's like a damn operating room in here."

"Well, I'm in the job market if you need to replace your house-keeper," I said, laughing as I hopped up on the countertop in my kitchenette. He walked up and stood in between my legs.

"London, are you really trying to work for me?"

"One part of me says yes, but the other side says no."

He kissed my neck on each side. "Where's the no side?"

"It's just that I don't know about being a random booty call whenever you feel like it. What happens when you start looking for something else on the side? Am I going to be out here searching for a job?"

"What if I told you that you had a guaranteed weekly salary?"

"Will you give me two weeks' notice when the job is coming to an end?"

"What makes you think it will end?"

"All good things come to an end."

"If you learn how to manage good things, they can last forever."

"You think?"

"I know."

He unbuttoned my shirt and I twirled his tie in my hand. He leaned in for a wet, sloppy kiss.

"Yeah, London. Walk this dog."

I yanked his tie harder. He bit softly on my neck. Bruno growled as he watched on. Thorne lifted my skirt over my hips and cupped my vagina, massaging vigorously. He yanked my tights down. "You like it like that, mommy."

I panted heavily, wanting him to shove himself into me. He unbuckled his pants with the other hand and pulled a condom out of his pocket just before he let his pants fall to the floor. He placed the condom on the counter beside me. With his penis poking proudly through his boxers, my eyes quickly focused on the beautiful structure inside his underwear. He smiled and grabbed my hand, guiding me to stroke him. He said, "Get down."

I hopped down from the counter and stood close to him, with his penis in my hand. He looked deep in my eyes. "Put it in your mouth."

The sound of loud screeching brakes rang in my ear. I wasn't sure I wanted to do this with a man that I wasn't in love with. Sex is reciprocal, but oral sex is a service. Sure we'd discussed this whole exchange of services, but concept is one thing. Reality is another. I didn't want to come across as immature and unequipped to handle our arrangement. When I felt the pressure of his hands on my shoulders, a piece of me felt like I had no choice. Being that I had already succumbed to him, it was too late to start pleading my morality. Slowly, one knee at a time, I knelt before Thorne. As if my mind were free of all apprehension, I opened wide and let him push back until he was in my throat. Maybe it was my strong attraction to him or maybe it was what I had to convince myself of to get it over, but he smelled almost like a watermelon Jolly Rancher. My tongue slipped and slid up and down his candy stick. His fingers were tangled in my hair as he groaned with pleasure.

He reached for the condom on the counter and ripped the packet open. "Get on the counter," he demanded.

I wiggled out of my tights and underwear, then jumped on the counter and scooted my hips to the edge. His height put him in a perfect position to just slide right in. My jaw muscles relaxed as his throbbing penis filled me. My neck fell back and my eyes closed as he stroked. My hands rubbed up and down his chiseled back, touching his tight ass.

"Talk dirty to me, mommy."

At first I didn't say anything. Then he began instructing me, telling me to repeat after him. I started to repeat after him. Then he would demand, "Say it like you mean it. Say you love this dick."

And so I did. I said everything like I meant it, even if I didn't. I performed to the best of my ability while Bruno acted like a fool, barking angrily in his crate. When we were done Thorne was satisfied. He carried me to the bed and we lay across it together.

He rubbed my stomach and said, "You have the perfect body. Do you know that?" After a short pause, he said, "Honestly, you're definitely the full package."

"Is that why you picked me to work for you?"

"Not necessarily. Every woman with the perfect body and perfect face isn't equipped for this type of work."

"So what about me makes you think that I can handle this type of arrangement?"

"Remember when you first started working in my office and I asked you about your life and your hobbies?" I nodded, and he continued, "Well, I knew then that you were an emotionally detached person and that's not all women."

"I don't think I'm emotionally detached."

"Let me say this, I think you have the potential to be emotionally detached and that's a plus. You may never have to work a real job in your life if you master that."

I looked up at the ceiling, wondering why he'd picked me and how many women he'd picked before and what they were like.

"When I first saw you, I thought to myself, *He's a dream man.* I mean, a dream black man. You're attractive, you're smart, you're rich, and every day since Saturday I keep thinking, *Why me?* Why is sex with me worth so much to you?"

He began to speak and than he stopped. "Let's say this. You'll understand me and what I do better after this weekend."

"What happens this weekend?"

"I want you to go to LA with me."

"Really? What's in LA?"

"Number one, the Golden Globe Awards is this weekend. That's the bulk of my clientele in one place at one time. You have to mix and mingle with the money if you want to stay at the top of your game. It's not always your reputation that takes you to the top, it's your representation."

I squinted and he clarified. "You have to be at all the right events. People gauge if they want to get to know you or if they're interested in doing business with you based on where they meet you. If you're at the right events, you're obviously in the circle. So they want to work with you just because of what they *think* you represent."

He paused for a reaction and then changed the subject. "Do you have a business bank account?"

"No. I just use my personal account."

He frowned at me. "London, is your business even registered?"

I felt slightly stupid as I shook my head no. I hadn't worried about that part yet. For me, walking dogs was a hobby that I got paid for. He told me to register my business as soon as possible, as in it should be the first thing I did in the morning. He suggested that I put at least half the money I earned from him into my business account.

He advised, "When you own your own business, only you get to say what you earn."

"But I don't make a lot of money walking dogs."

"Let's say you continue to work for me. You want to report those earnings as business income, so that you can build your credit and be able to purchase things like houses and cars. What good is making money under the table if you have nowhere to shelter it? Always remember, you are your recorded income, anything that's not recorded is nothing."

It was a lot of information to take in, but it made a lot of sense.

"The government doesn't really care where you get the money from; all that matters is that you pay taxes on it. I've been doing this since college."

I wasn't exactly sure what *this* was, but I nodded as if I understood. He continued, "I've always had a business, and anything I make on the side from the odds and ends I record as business earnings. You'll never get caught that way."

"Get caught?"

He sat up on the bed and leaned over to kiss me. "Yes, get caught. Let me get out of here."

He stood up and walked toward the kitchenette and I lay on the bed feeling overwhelmed with information and uncertain about what was going on between me and Thorne.

He walked back toward the bed buttoning his shirt. "Yeah, and your plane leaves at seven-thirty Friday morning. I'll e-mail your itinerary tomorrow."

"Wait. Am I going to be with you?"

"No. I'll meet you in LA. I'm leaving tomorrow."

"Okay," I said hesitantly.

"And make sure you handle your business tomorrow. Register your company. It'll take about thirty minutes. If your name search is cleared, you'll have a confirmation right there and you need to go straight to the bank and get an account in your business name."

"But I don't have a name."

He smiled. "The Dog Trainer."

"But I'm not a trainer."

"Not yet, but you will be," he said with a smirk.

I said, "You really think so?"

"Yeah, that's enough for one day," he said, tossing his suit jacket over his shoulder. "I'll meet you in LA."

"So will I talk to you before then?"

I stood up and walked toward him. He placed his hand on the knob. "Oh, and one last thing, we need to upgrade your apartment."

I definitely wanted an upgraded place to stay, but I needed to be sure this income was consistent before I agreed to that. I called a few of my clients to let them know that I wouldn't be available for the upcoming weekend. I explained that I had a last-minute engagement and apologized for any inconvenience. It was almost a definite that I would lose one or two as a result. Dog owners are so temperamental.

While I was out walking Bruno, it dawned on me that Thorne hadn't given me any money. I wondered if it was an oversight or if it was intentional. Did he think I should ask for it? I didn't know, but I did know that it concerned me. It was possible that this so-called working-for-him was shady.

When I got back home I immediately turned on my computer and started updating my résumé. I needed a backup plan in case this alternative way of making a living wasn't all it was cracked up to be.

Bruno and I stopped over to visit Kari and to ask if she would keep an eye out for my pup over the weekend. She reluctantly agreed. I told a little white lie, claiming that I needed to visit my mother because she wanted to see me after she found out about my job loss.

The next morning I woke up early and headed to the Department of Consumer and Regulatory Affairs to register my company. I was one of the first people in line to fill out my paperwork. While Thorne had schooled me on starting a business, he hadn't given me full details on the type. So I had to ask one of the customer service representatives. I would be applying for a limited liability corporation. The name search was successful and The Dog Trainer was available. When asked about the description, I basically listed all dog services from kenneling to walking to training. It was Thorne's suggestion that I look at the bigger picture. And just like that, I owned my own business. I left the building feeling accomplished. Despite the fact that I'd been a dog walker for almost six months, something about having the papers listing me as the owner/founder made me proud. I headed straight to the bank with five hundred dollars of the money that Thorne had given me and opened my business account.

9

I arrived in LA around noon. Assuming Thorne would meet me, I anxiously headed for baggage claim. Instead I was greeted by a man in a black suit carrying a sign that read LONDON REED. *For me?* But without reservation I walked up to the guy holding the sign and said, "Hi, I'm London."

He was a middle-aged Hispanic guy. "You have your bags?"

"Not yet."

We walked to the conveyer belt and I pointed out my bag. After he grabbed it we headed for the car. There was a black Lincoln waiting outside and he opened the door to let me in. Then he tucked his head in with me, showing me the drinks. Soda. Champagne. Wine. He told me that he'd open the champagne if I wanted. Why not live it up? Thorne didn't know what he was creating, because just from sitting in the limo I was certain this was the type of life I deserved to live. The driver popped the champagne and the bubbles spilled from the bottle as he poured it into the flute. He placed the bottle back on ice and closed the door. I downed what he'd poured. It was a little bitter, but I liked the taste and the mere thought of sipping bubbly in the back of a limo was quite appetizing to me.

I rested my head back and thought, *What did I do to deserve this?* My phone rang and before I even checked I knew it was Thorne. I answered, "Hey, how are you?"

I heard a lot of giggling in the background, but he said, "Just waiting on you."

"I guess I'll be there shortly."

"See you soon."

I poured more champagne when I hung up, hoping to be nice and toasty by the time I arrived. When we rode down Sunset Boulevard the driver pointed out the famous shops on the Strip. We then headed to Rodeo Drive and there were more television-popular spots. I couldn't wait to spend my money. I'd been turning the pages of *InStyle* magazine since my last year at Georgetown, hoping that one day I'd be able to dress like the girls on them. I'd always liked expensive things. They seemed to fit my shape better. It's possible it was all in my mind, but I really didn't think so. I couldn't wait to get where I was going, settle down, and get back out on the Strip to shop.

We traveled up a mountainous road off of Rodeo Drive; each home was nestled and gated behind beautiful greenery. Finally we turned into one of the driveways and the driver spoke into the intercom. The large steel gates opened and granted us access. A beautiful multi-tier home with a brown stucco exterior awaited us. Large windows enclosed most of the house and a stone walkway led to the entrance on the second tier. The driver pulled my luggage from the car and we headed to the door. He rang the bell and Thorne opened the large French doors with shiny brass accessories. His muscular arms spread, welcoming me to the castle as he stood there looking even more fine in swim trunks and baring his abs of steel. My mouth watered. I liked him a lot and luckily he liked me enough to want to pay me for my goodies.

I stepped into the home, which was decorated in a contemporary style. Nice artwork adorned the walls. There was a sleek crème leather couch in the living room with two accent chairs. A multicolored rug with a geometric pattern was in the middle.

After hugging me tightly for many seconds, Thorne said, "Welcome to my LA home."

"Thank you. Very nice."

"I'm glad you like."

It sounded like someone was in the kitchen mixing drinks and I could hear noise coming from the back patio. I said, "Is there a party here?"

"Something like that. Let me introduce you to everyone."

I followed him into the kitchen, where an attractive girl with long curly hair, wearing a bikini, was blending margaritas. "This is Jasmine. Jasmine, London."

I reached out to shake her hand, but she offered a hug. "Hi, London. Welcome aboard."

Aboard? A strange greeting but I smiled it off. We proceeded out through the sliding glass door into a breathtaking landscape of huge stones, green bushes, and waterfalls surrounding a medium-sized pool. At least six to eight women, each one in tip-top shape, jumped in and out of the water, splashed each other, and appeared to be having a blast. Thorne walked me around, introducing me to each girl.

I didn't know what the hell I had walked into. Did *all* these girls work for him? Was he paying us *all* to sleep with him? There was no way one man could have this much energy. Thorne noticed the perplexed look on my face and told me to follow him into the house.

He first poured me a drink and told me that he was going to take me up to the room I'd be staying in. We walked upstairs into an artfully decorated room with a queen-sized bed and no headboard. Thorne sat on the bed and gestured for me to stand between his legs. He rested his head on my stomach and looked up at me. "Did you have a good flight?"

"For the most part, yes."

"Did you do everything I asked you to do yesterday?"

"Yes."

"Good, because you can potentially make a lot of money this weekend. I mean, it depends what you're down for."

I slouched down beside him and looked him straight in the eye. I was tired of his evasiveness. "Why are all these girls here? Are you paying them all?"

"No, technically they're paying me."

"What do you mean?"

He took a deep breath. "When I asked you to work for me, I don't know if you thought you'd only be working directly for me or not. But I need to let you know, that's not the case."

My heart pounded, because that had been my understanding. I thought he was paying me to be his mistress, but from the tone in his voice and the look in his eyes, I knew this was definitely something else.

"So you expect me to sleep with different men for money."

"Only my clients. They're not random. I only deal with men that can afford what I charge for my women. Every one of my girls is hand-selected."

He made us sound like nothing more than pieces of meat. I felt like he'd taken advantage of me, or better yet misled me. "Why didn't you just tell me you wanted me to be a prostitute? I could have told you no before you wasted your money and flew me to LA."

He stood up and closed the bedroom door. "London, you probably would have said no. And you would have said no because of the negative stigma associated with being a call girl. But let me ask you something, what were your plans for the weekend?"

"What does that have to do with anything?" I snapped.

"We all like to have sex. We all need to have sex. Why not get paid to do something that you're going to do for free anyway?"

"I wouldn't sleep with strangers for free."

"Exactly, but you'd have sex with some knucklehead for free because he promises you fidelity?" He paused for a response and I looked away. He continued, "So can you tell me what's so bad about sex with a stranger for a premium fee? It affords a lifestyle that most girls only dream about."

"A life of a prostitute?" I said, with my lips curled because I couldn't fathom how this could give me some dream life.

He smiled. "The correct term is *call girl*. My girls are all quality."

My eyes squinted and I sighed in frustration. "I just don't get it. You're a millionaire banker. Why do you do this?"

"I have well-respected clients that look for a service and I provide it. To me it's just another business. I get paid off the top and everyone is happy."

"So you'd get a cut of my five hundred?"

He laughed. "Five hundred? London, that was nothing more than a love offering to test your willingness. My clients pay on average about three thousand per night for regular sex and a premium for multiple girls and/or kinkier things."

My mouth hung open. I mouthed, "What the fuck?"

He smiled. "Quite the commodity, huh?"

"Are you serious? What do the men get out of it?"

"Drama-free stress relief. I mean, you have to understand I only deal with clients that have money to throw away. A few thousand dollars here and there won't break the bank."

"But why? Why do you feel like *you* need to do this?"

"This business opportunity actually found me when I was at Wharton."

My eyes stretched and he noticed. "That's where I went to business school."

"Oh no, I know. I'm just shocked that's where you started."

"Anyway, I had a class studying business modeling and what professions were recession-proof. The subject of prostitution surfaced and as we talked about it, my mind began to wander. I thought that selling sex would be too stressful. I actually made the comment out loud. And a white chick in my class said, 'That's only if you're sloppy. If you run it like a business, you could probably get rich.'"

He chuckled as he continued to reflect on it. "And it just sparked a nerve in me. I started my own personal science project, asking other men if they would pay for sex. And if so, what would they expect. Then I started profiling women and asking if they would accept money for sex. Before I knew it I was swept up in a whirlwind. The more successful I became as a banker, the more successful my client base became and the price for the sex skyrocketed. It became too lucrative to quit and I think somewhere along the way I got addicted."

"Why is it so addictive?"

"It's so easy. I mean, you have a little drama here or there, but for the most part all I do is matchmake."

"Do you think you'll ever stop?"

"I've tried a time or two."

I longed for a better explanation but I could tell by the

look on his face that was all I was getting. My chin lowered. I was confused. It sounded good, but I was scared. Not everything that looks good is worth it. He reached into my jeans and his fingers crawled down my panties. "I'll protect you. I promise."

I wasn't sure I was up for it, but then again I wasn't sure that I wasn't. Where else could a chick with a bachelor's degree in biology make that kind of money? Maybe I'd do it a few times and get out. Then again, maybe not. I took a deep breath. My head was pounding and my palms were itching. It was the battle of common sense versus morality. My hand ran over my face. "Can you give me a moment to think about it?"

"Sure. And talk to some of the other girls about their experiences. That's why I wanted to bring you out here this weekend. The girls here this weekend are my best girls. They only work for the highest-paying clients. So talk to any of them. They'll give you the 411 from their point of view. But I'll say this: I already have people requesting you."

"Why me?" I thought out loud, meaning *as compared to all the other beautiful girls downstairs.*

"You have a platform. All men want to be trained, Ms. Dog Trainer." He opened the door. "Get some rest, and when you're up for it I'll have one of the girls come talk to you. Deal?"

"I guess." I sighed, before plopping back on the bed.

My veins pumped with anxiety. I knew this wasn't right, but Thorne made it sound sensible. My balled fists covered my eyes and I let out a sigh of frustration. Then I stood up and walked to the window that faced the pool. I looked out and watched the girls swimming, wondering how they had gotten there and how being a call girl had become an acceptable profession. I sat back on the bed wondering if I was wrong for even being interested. Was I stupid for agreeing to let Thorne pay me? I decided to sleep on all my decisions and indecisions, because I was too confused to do anything else.

I heard a soft knock, and my head popped off the pillow as I sprung from a deep slumber. For a moment I didn't know where I was. My heart raced as I took in my surroundings. A calm voice called out, "London."

"C'mon in."

I raked my fingers through my fresh weave, and the girl named Jasmine came into the room. She smiled. "Hey, Thorne told me to come talk to you. He said you were having second thoughts."

"Second thoughts, huh? I'm not sure I agreed to anything in the first place."

"I understand. It's very different than you can probably imagine. The biggest thing I had to learn is not to ask why. You'd be surprised at our clientele. Celebrities. Athletes. Businessmen. Politicians. It's not like streetwalking and sleeping with slimy old perverts." Her body shivered like the thought repulsed her, and she continued, "I can honestly say that every man I've been with was respectable and possibly someone I'd want to date anyway. I mean, like look at Thorne."

"I'm sure they aren't all as attractive as Thorne."

I was slightly leaning toward doing this, but I wasn't going to believe that I would be paid to sleep with some fine man every night. If that were the case, there probably would be more women agreeing to it.

She said, "No, they don't all look like Thorne, but most of them are financially stable like him. Some are attractive.

Some are not so attractive, but trust me, after your third encounter, it won't even matter what he looks like. Then it's just a well-paying job."

"So three's the magic number?"

She laughed again. "That seems to be the consensus around here."

"So everyone had reservations at first?"

"Everyone." She paused. "I mean, I'd say at least all of the girls here. Thorne usually recruits the non-typical girl. He likes cultured girls with class and usually they're a harder sell, so it took some convincing for most of us, but I think what gets us all is that nothing rakes in money like this. I don't care if you're a damn surgeon; most people don't make a couple of thousand dollars in one night. Depending on what you're trying to gain from this, you could work once or twice a month." She shrugged. "That's all I do."

"Do you work?"

"Yes, and I also have two small children at home."

"Wow. How do you manage it all?"

"I've been doing this since medical school."

"You're kidding me, right? You're a doctor?"

"Yeah, an emergency medicine physician."

"And this still is worth it to you?"

"Listen, London. I'd have to work about a week to make what I make in one night doing this. I don't do this all the time. I moved to Chicago after my residency, so I only have Chicago clients. And I'll come out to do an event weekend like this. When there are a lot of players in one city, Thorne makes sure he has a bunch of girls on tap and I'll usually come through."

"If you don't mind me asking, are you married?"

She smiled. "Yes, I'm married. I guess you're curious how

I manage it. Well, I think of it like this: Most women have two lives. Maybe not to this extreme, but there are two sides to every woman."

"So you're not afraid of your husband finding out? I mean, don't you feel guilty?"

"No, this is a business. When you remove the emotion, it eliminates the guilt."

Jasmine helped me come to terms with what I was about to agree to do. At least I'd give it a try. One way or the other, I would know if I was cut out for this or not. If I felt grimy afterward I'd fly back to DC and leave this world behind. Jasmine and I talked for several more hours. She walked me through her first time and her last time and the time before the time before that. After a few cocktails I told Thorne to close the deal. And before I knew it I was dressed in pantyhose, garters, and a black cotton dress, knocking on a room door at the Roosevelt Hotel.

10

After thanking me, the snoring man in the bed managed to tell me that the money was in an envelope in the top right drawer of the dresser. I stepped out of the bed and turned on the shower before going to confirm that the money was there. King, as he had asked to be called, was practically comatose. It had been a two-hour job, but it seemed that time had gone really, really fast. King knew just how long he needed because the envelope was stacked with two thousand dollars cash.

By the time I stepped into the shower the water was hot just like I like it. As the water poured down my face I was disturbed because for sure I should feel slimy, but I didn't. I didn't feel anything. It was weird because although I tried to control my thoughts by telling myself this was just work, I didn't feel good about actually believing it. While I scrubbed my skin of my first client's scent, I wondered if Thorne knew what he'd done to me. I really couldn't see working for the average dollar again if this was all I had to do. I thought about Jasmine and how even though she was a physician she still did this on the side. It was too easy. Even working a couple of hours once a week would be equivalent to a six-figure salary. I wrapped a towel around me and called the driver before coming out of the bathroom. After drying off and putting on lotion, I slipped back into my dress.

It was crazy how he'd charmed me into the business, I thought as I rode back to the house. We drove up the winding driveway and the lights were still on. I rechecked the time, making sure it was as late as I recalled. It was definitely three in the morning. When I opened the door the other girls clapped like I'd just been inducted into a sorority. They cheered loudly and I felt bashful. I covered my face and Jasmine stood up and grabbed my arm. She said, "It wasn't bad at all. Was it?"

Initially, it popped in my mind to say, "Hell no, not for two thousand dollars." But then I recalled Thorne telling me to keep the financials confidential because each girl was paid differently based on the level of requests. I laughed and said, "Nope, not at all."

A few of them screamed and comments were made. "It's the easiest thing you'll ever do." "It becomes fun after a while." "Wait until you get used to it."

I was slightly excited but the other piece of me wondered if I'd done a good job. Thorne sat up from lying on the couch and yawned. My attention immediately went to him. He stood up and groggily walked over to me, offering me a pat on the back. "Did you do a good job, London Bridge?"

For the sake of not lying, I shrugged. I felt like I'd done my job. I felt like the guy was satisfied. He'd even told me that I was good, but I wasn't totally confident that he'd request me again. Thorne ignored my concern. "I'm sure you did well. Go ahead up and get ready for bed."

I stepped away from him and headed up the stairs. It was as if he were the father of the group and he pimped out all his daughters. I noticed that each girl pretty much did what he said and yearned for his approval or praise. He seemed to treat everyone with sensitivity, certainly a gentleman across the board. I wondered if he'd always be so kind or if that was only during the initiation phase, but the fact that some of the girls had already been working for him for some time made me believe that despite selling sex, Thorne was the perfect guy.

After changing into my nightclothes, I lay in bed looking at the ceiling fan and out of nowhere I felt engulfed by guilt. I felt like I'd gone against some morality code, but I couldn't say I would refuse to do it again. While I flipped around trying to get comfortable emotionally and physically, I heard a knock at the door. "London?" Thorne said softly.

I quickly sat up and said, "Yes?"

He turned the knob and walked into the room. I moved over in the direction of the sliding glass window, hoping he'd climb in, and he did. I faced away from him and curled into a fetal position. He spooned me, wrapping his arm around my waist. After pushing my hair away from my neck, he began kissing it.

"You okay?"

"I'm not sure."

"It's normal to feel that way."

"You sure?"

"Yes. I'm going to hold you to make it all better. A'ight, London?"

I nodded and he pulled me tighter and closer to him. His arms removed my feelings of guilt, leaving me with the conclusion that a woman just needed to feel connected to someone after sex, not necessarily the man she'd shared her body with.

"So how do you make money? Am I supposed to give you a portion of what I make or what?"

He laughed as he softly kissed on my shoulder. "I'm more like a booking agent instead of a pimp. I make my money straight off the top. So whatever they give you is your money. I give them a rate, and for booking I get a flat fee of one half hour of that hourly rate. At minimum they will pay the stated rate, but if you exceed their expectations they may give you more. I have nothing to do with that."

"That makes sense."

"Always."

The room-darkening window treatments made me feel like it was the middle of the night, but when I finally awoke it was eleven-thirty. I sat up in bed and rubbed my eyes. Thorne wasn't beside me, but I didn't feel abandoned. In fact, I felt fulfilled and peaceful. The range of emotions was frightening. I got out of bed, grabbed my case of toiletries, and headed to the bathroom.

After I put on some clothes I headed downstairs. A lady was cooking brunch for everyone in the house. I automatically searched for Thorne, but they told me he'd gone out. Although Jasmine and the other girls seemed friendly, I wasn't sure that I wanted to be around them 24-7. I didn't know them that well. I asked them if I could call the same limo driver so I could go shopping. Jasmine told me Thorne kept a car there and she'd tell me where to go.

I pulled the convertible Benz out of the garage and headed to the Beverly Center. Shopping was always a stress reliever. I took an initial walk through the mall to scope out the stores. Everything was screaming my name and the money in my pocket was telling me to answer, but I kept thinking, *What*

if I get no more requests or what if I decide I can't do this? I opted
to hold on to my money and just try on the nice things as
an incentive to keep doing it if there were interested clients.
In a way it seemed like fate: As I was going back and forth
with myself standing in the Dior store, my cell phone rang.
It was Thorne.

It seemed like he didn't hear me say hello, but he began to
speak. "What's your availability this evening?"

I was thinking he should know better than me. My flight
didn't return to DC until Monday morning, and as far as I
was concerned I was on his schedule. I said, "Uh, I guess free.
I don't know."

He laughed. "Okay, you have an appointment at twelve.
You down?"

Standing in the mirror, looking at the form-fitting leather
jacket with a two-thousand-dollar price tag, I said, "Yeah,
I'm down."

It was at that moment that I knew this lifestyle would be
the only way to afford items like the one I was wearing. For
some reason, looking at expensive clothes and trying them
on made me feel like this was where I belonged.

I left the Dior store and headed to Louis Vuitton. I had a
few Louis bags that I had scraped up money in college to buy,
but I wanted a new one. As I stood there, posing in the mirror
with my bag, 650 bucks didn't seem like a large amount to
pay after what I'd made in one evening. I copped it and felt
like I was walking on air as I headed out of the store.

Once the buying bug bit I was ready to spend more money.
Maybe I needed to splurge to console myself and make me
feel like my new career was worth it. A pair of Gucci shoes
and a denim Dior jacket later, I left the mall with 120 dollars
in my pocket.

When I got to the house it was around three and no one was there except Thorne. I sashayed in, carrying my bags and feeling proud of myself. He frowned at me and I smiled. "So what's up?"

"The photographer will be here to take your head shots in about two hours. The makeup artist and hairstylist should be here any minute."

"A photographer?" I asked, with a perplexed stare.

"Now that you're in the club..." He paused. "You are committed to being in the club, right?"

With all the money I just spent, I thought, *how can I not be in the club?* I nodded. "Yeah, I'm in."

"Good, I'll need to put you in the portfolio."

"Portfolio?"

"Yeah, grab the one on the island in the kitchen on your way up. It's outdated, but you'll get a clue of what I include for my clients' perusal."

He seemed short with me, but I didn't know what that was about. Maybe we'd transitioned into the more professional phase of the process. I didn't like it but I had to handle my business. As I headed up the stairs I tried psyching myself out. *This is a job. Thorne is your boss, not your friend.*

Before jumping in the shower I browsed through the portfolio. Each girl had her own profile with several head shots, a summary of her likes and dislikes, her measurements, her educational level, and her profession. It simply amazed me that some of these women had doctorate degrees and professional jobs, many were business owners, but they still chose to do this. It made me feel almost honored. It seemed like almost every girl had at least a bachelor's degree. I'd been looking at it as just sex, but the clients obviously had requirements.

Apparently any old girl would not do. They were willing to pay the price for the pedigree Thorne offered.

I took a quick shower and put on the brand-new robe that was lying on my bed. When I headed downstairs the family room had been transformed into an all-out spa. There was a massage table in the middle of the floor. The makeup artist introduced herself to me. After wiping her hands with an alcohol towelette she began touching my skin. She asked, "What type of skin regimen do you have?"

I shrugged. "Neutrogena, witch hazel."

She laughed. "You have pretty skin, so you can get away with that for a while. If you don't mind me asking, how old are you?"

"I'm twenty-three."

She nodded like she could tell my age. "As you get older, your skin won't shed the dead skin cells as much. So you need to adopt a healthy skin regimen now. A facial every two months or so will have you flawless."

She explained that prior to making up my face she was going to give me a therapeutic facial. I lay on the table and it felt like she was doing some sort of wax-on-wax-off with creams and scrubs. My mother got facials at least monthly and it never seemed to do much for her skin or her attitude. I lay there thinking this was a huge waste of time. After the makeup artist was done she handed me the mirror and said, "Look at the difference in your skin."

I rolled my eyes, feeling a little doubtful. I didn't believe that a difference would be immediately apparent, but I was shocked by my reflection. My skin felt like a baby's bottom and my complexion was completely blemish-free. I kept touching it and she laughed.

I said, "Oh my goodness, it feels great."

She told me that she would apply the makeup once my hair was done. Shortly after, a flaming gay guy stormed in. I assumed he was the hairstylist and it was confirmed when he introduced himself. He stood behind me and hesitantly picked through my hair.

He said, "Oh, honey, we got to do something about these glued-in tracks."

Neither the makeup artist nor the hairstylist was making me feel pretty. If I'd been asked twenty-four hours earlier about my cute factor, I would have rated it pretty high, but I was feeling pretty subpar as Lenny continued to critique me. "Where did you get this hair, honey?"

"The hair store," I said apprehensively, because the frown on his face stated that wherever I got it wasn't the right place.

He laughed. "Once I'm finished with you, you'll never go back to a homemade weave."

I never considered my weave to be homemade. I'd actually gone to a professional stylist and I usually got a lot of compliments. Frowning, I said, "Probably not."

He said, "Trust, honey."

It was clear that Lenny knew he was the hair king. In the portfolio all the girls looked like models, and certainly, if I wanted to increase my clientele, I needed to be sure my pictures represented me appropriately or at least made the best of what I had.

Lenny literally ripped all those tracks from my hair and left me touching my scalp wondering if any of my own hair remained. After giving me a treatment, Lenny cut much of my hair. That was fine because it had been a long time since I'd worn my own hair, so that length didn't bother me. He blew the short mushroom hairstyle out and the roots felt bone-straight. He began sewing in tracks in strategic places throughout my hair. After he trimmed the hair he let me touch it.

"Feel that, honey. See, that glue stuff is played."

I smirked slightly, but it felt good and quite natural. The long hair flowed down my back. It was light and bouncy. His technique was certainly better than what I'd had. I wanted Thorne to see me but I hadn't heard his voice the entire time I was getting polished.

The makeup artist came back to the family room with a large suitcase full of makeup. I was thinking, *That's a lot of face painting.* She sat me down in a brightly lit place and quickly got down to business. It felt like she was literally putting layers and layers of mud on my face. I began to feel uncomfortable, wondering if I looked like a cake face, but I assumed that this was the same beauty team Thorne had used many times before. Knowing him to be a perfectionist, I was certain that if I didn't look right, he wouldn't have a problem asking to have my face redone. Finally, after what seemed like an eternity, she told me that she was done. I stood and walked to the bathroom. I stared in the mirror at a beautiful stranger. I had never known that I was capable of looking so flawless. It felt like I should be on someone's runway instead of in someone's bed.

As I admired myself, I heard Thorne's voice. "Where's London? We have to get a move on. The stylist is here. Let's go!"

I rushed from the bathroom. "I'm ready."

"Go in that room right there."

When I walked in I saw a white English bulldog in a cage. "Hey, buddy," I said, stooping by his cage.

He lazily looked up at me and Thorne came in the room.

"Hey, I'm glad you two are getting along. Your shoot is going to be done with Oscar."

Speaking to a young lady with a real earthy, Zen vibe, Thorne said, "Nori, get her clothes on."

Her Afro was about ten inches high and she wore an entire arm of metal bangles. How the hell did granola girl become *my* stylist? She removed the cover from a rolling rack of clothes and grabbed a cream-colored straight-cut three-quarter-length trench coat with a butterfly collar and large gold buttons. Handing the hanger to me, she said, "This is your first look. We can go in this room right here."

When I walked into the bedroom, there were large gold accessories lying on the table and gold platform shoes on the floor. I dropped my robe and asked the stylist, "Should I keep on my underclothes?"

"Just your panties," she said, as she held the coat out for me to put on.

As I unsnapped my bra I felt a little bashful. When I looked at her this-is-just-business expression, I quickly pulled it off and slipped into the coat. She hooked a gold slave choker around my neck. Then she grabbed the bracelets. "Here, put these on."

She stepped back and looked me up and down. Her face squinted like there was something not quite right. She unsnapped the necklace. "Let it hang off of you a little."

It was as if I were a three-year-old being dressed by my mother. Considering that I think of myself as relatively stylish, it was a bit of a challenge to let this lady have complete control over me. Finally, after she swiftly switched and swapped accessories, she nodded. "Okay, you're good."

She opened the door and I said, "Can I look in the mirror?"

"Go ahead, but we have to move fast. We don't have all day."

Trying my best to ignore her frigid demeanor, I pranced over to the mirror and offered her a partial smile. She smirked with an arrogant shrug, like she was thinking, *I know I'm bad.* I was looking good thanks to Thorne's glam clan and I knew it. I strutted out of the bedroom and into the room where the photographer had set up a studio. Lights. Camera. Action.

There were a white backdrop and huge studio lights in the roomy space. Thorne entered the room with Oscar, who seemed to be quite calm. He lifted the heavy dog and put him in my arms. I nearly toppled over. "Wow, he's solid."

As the photographer instructed me, I sat down and lay down on the floor. Lenny rushed over to fix my hair to make it spread out like a fan. Thorne placed the well-trained Oscar on top of me, almost like a baby resting on its mother's breast. The photographer stood over us and took several shots. With each snap of the camera the energy in the room seemed to increase, and everyone nodded with approval. We then moved to the fireplace, and the photographer had me stand with my legs apart and Oscar at my feet. Then he took some shots without the dog.

We moved to the next outfit, black lingerie with leather trim and thigh-highs. I posed in various positions with a silver dog chain. As I knelt on all fours with the dog chain in my mouth, the photographer turned on a fan that made my hair blow. Thorne clapped. "That's the money shot."

A part of me hoped that meant we were done. Unfortunately that wasn't the case. I changed clothes two more times and the photographer took what felt like a thousand more shots. I was exhausted and irritated with people shouting instructions at me by the time we were finished. I really just wanted to go upstairs and take a damn nap.

Before everyone rolled out, I headed up to my bedroom to prepare for the night. I sat on the bed thinking that if I could just snooze for fifteen minutes I would be good. It was thirty minutes later when Thorne knocked at the bedroom door. I popped up and looked at the clock on the nightstand. My heart raced as if I were doing something wrong. I rushed to open the bedroom door and a weird-acting Thorne entered.

He had seemed strange all evening, but I assumed it was because he was in business mode while conducting the photo shoot. Clearly there was something on his mind, as my smile was greeted with a raised eyebrow and a disappointed expression.

"What's up?" I asked, letting it roll slowly off my tongue.

He kicked aside the bags sitting on the floor as he sat down on the bed. "Is this what you plan to do with your money?"

"No. I just picked up a few things."

"London, I want you to be smart. It's easy to get caught up in this lifestyle and want to spend every dollar you make, but that's not the point. You want to secure your future doing this. Always save a portion of your money. In a couple of months you'll have the spare change to splurge on foolish things. But if you're doing it with the little money you just made, you'll always be working just for today."

There was nothing I could really say, but no matter what he said, I had needed that shopping spree to rationalize my actions. I said, "I understand."

"Did you spend all of your money?"

"No, not all of it."

"Keep your mind on your money. That's why I told you to shelter your money in a business account. If you don't, mark my words, you'll wake up at forty wondering where all the money and time went."

I hoped to have more self-control in the future. He gave me the details and location of my appointment. Then he left the room without his extra affection, and it left me longing for one of his hugs or kisses on the forehead. It didn't feel good, but work never does.

11

The only information Thorne provided me about client number two was that he was a professional football player. He had selected me from a snapshot that Thorne provided him. The driver pulled up to the W Hotel in Westwood. My heart raced a bit faster than the evening before. It seems like the first time you do something outlandish it's easier. I slowly stepped out of the car, wondering if it was too late to turn around. Did I really have the gall to do this night after night? Could I wake up to a stranger every day? Would the money always be enough to keep me going? With each step I contemplated, but came closer and closer to the hotel room door of my second client.

To reduce the anxiety spilling out of my pores, I rubbed my hands together and gently cupped them over my nose and mouth in a prayer-like gesture. I took a few deep breaths and finally tapped gently on the door. A few seconds passed. *Maybe I should just leave.* Just as the thought entered my mind, *he* opened the door. I prayed that my expression did not reflect what I felt inside. *Utter shock.* As I stood there looking at one of the most popular football players in the league, I scrambled to find what I was supposed to say or do next. What were the chances that I would get the opportunity to be with a man I loved on my second encounter? I was starstruck. One side of me was honored, but the other side was nervous as hell. I didn't want to mess up. With him, I felt like I had something to prove.

I smiled because I didn't know what else I should do. The door opened wide to reveal all of him. He wore nothing except a white towel wrapped around his waist. He was taller in person than he appeared on television and his muscular arms looked like works of art. His chest was rock-solid. Tattoos spanned the length of his arms, although I could barely make out any of the symbols. His skin was the color of onyx and it glistened as if he had just taken an oil bath. I instantly wanted to slip and slide all over him. He was fresh, clean, and smiling back at me as I entered his suite.

"Hello," I said, brushing past him.

As the door slammed shut he grabbed my arm and pulled me to be face-to-face with him. "What's up, ma?"

"You," I said, as his sensual scent captivated me.

Getting down to the reason for my visit, he dropped his towel and guided my hand to touch him. My hand struggled to surround the circumference of his endowment. It felt like he had implanted a can of Lysol in place of his penis. As I stroked up and down, I thought maybe Thorne should implement a size pay scale: Anyone over a certain length should be required to pay a bonus.

"Take this shit off," he said, referring to my dress.

I raised it over my head and stepped out of my heels. He backed up and sat on the bed. I knew what he wanted next, but I wasn't sure I was capable of stretching my mouth that wide. As if he could see the hesitation, he looked down at the stiff monster protruding from him and said, "Kiss it." I coaxed my brain to crave him so that I could produce enough saliva to manage the task at hand. Slowly, reluctantly I knelt down and began handling my business. There was absolutely zero pleasure for me, just jaw pain and irritation, yet I pretended to be indulging in a tantalizing treat. I prayed he would climax so I could just stop. Finally, he said he wanted to feel me. I yanked off my panties and grabbed a condom from my purse. He said, "Naw, I got my own condoms."

He grabbed a condom from a pile on the bed and quickly rolled it on.

"Lay on your back."

He climbed on top of me and looked into my eyes as he attempted to fill me to capacity. He made distressing facial expressions, and I took deep, long breaths. Finally I received him. He ground passionately and I studied his every move. I hoped, I wished, I wanted to be pleasing to him despite the torture for me. I screamed and talked dirty. We moved from position to position. I stared at the clock, wondering how much longer.

Finally he humped rapidly and I kissed on his chest, hoping that yes, this was it. When he collapsed on me I was like *Thank you*. He rolled onto his back and we both faced the ceiling in the dark room. He turned over on his side and propped his head up on his hand. He slung his other arm over and began to play with my nipples. It was awkward because I wasn't sure what we should be talking about. I wondered when he'd ask me to leave. He sat up and grabbed another condom.

"Get on top?"

You have to be friggin' kidding me. He was serious, though. In less than ten minutes, this man was ready for another round. I climbed on top of him and went to work, hoping to put him to sleep, but he showed no signs of fatigue. Round two lasted longer than the first. Not only did he endorse an energy drink, he obviously overdosed on it too. I was completely worn out, but that didn't seem to matter to him as we had rounds three and four. It was no wonder he had to pay for sex. I couldn't imagine that anyone would volunteer for this abuse. I hoped I'd still have some left after being with him.

Finally he began to snore. *Please don't wake up*, I prayed. After about twenty minutes passed I assumed he was done. I tried to slide out of his strong embrace to shower, but when I moved, he moved. I didn't want to wake him, so I lay there looking at the sunrise. My mind went back to my conversation with Thorne. This was not free money, because I had earned every penny that night. I planned to find a way to make my money work for me.

He got a wakeup call at around eight in the morning, less than two hours after he had dozed off. *Ugh!* I was so irritated and exhausted. I lay there praying he didn't want any more and that he would just let me rest. He sat up on the side of the bed and walked over to pull the curtains back. The sun beamed right into the room. I stretched and turned in the opposite direction.

"Good morning, soldier."

Assuming he was talking to me, I said, "Good morning."

"You up?"

As a rule, you stay until the client asks you to leave. I hoped that was next as I sat up, yawning. "Yes, I'm up."

He scrambled in his luggage. "You good?"

Aside from my vagina being chafed, my legs muscles being sore, and my head spinning from the lack of rest, I was okay. I nodded and offered a fake smile. *Just say thank you so I can leave!*

He headed toward the bathroom. "I'm ordering breakfast. You want something?" He tossed the room service menu onto the bed. "Here you go."

As I perused the menu he told me what he wanted and asked me to call it in whenever I decided. He walked into the bathroom and turned on the shower. I wasn't sure if he wanted me to spend the day there, but I was ready to go. I wanted to shower and take a nap. Instead I picked up the phone to order breakfast.

"Good morning, Mr.—"

My heart skipped a beat as if I were doing something wrong. I said, "Ah, yes, I'd like to place an order."

She confirmed the suite number and took the order. I don't know why I was nervous when he was the one who had suggested I call. Obviously he didn't care that the hotel attendants knew he had a woman in his room. I would think someone of his caliber would have to be more cautious, but I guess not.

After he got out of the shower, I headed in. When I came out of the bathroom my client was watching ESPN and our food had arrived. He was sitting on the bed, eating from the tray, which was set nicely with white linen. I walked over and lifted the cover from my food. He reached over and grabbed one of my turkey sausage links. "These joints are slammin'."

I smiled and he said, "What's wrong? You don't want my fingers in your food?"

"Oh no, you're cool."

"So, you new at this?"

I wasn't sure what Thorne had told him and I didn't recall that years of service were listed in any of the other girls' profiles. I asked, "What makes you say that?"

"You seem a little shy." He laughed. "Not in the sack, though."

"I'm not shy."

"It's like you don't know what to say to me."

It wasn't that I didn't know what to say to him. It was more that I was one of his biggest fans and I was sure he heard that all the time. Why should he pay for sex with a groupie? So I kept my composure and tried to remain businesslike. Apparently I'd overdone my job and appeared too standoffish, because he was probing me for more.

"No, I'd rather you lead the conversation. I'm at your service."

His hand rose, requesting a high five. "That's what I'm talking about, ma. I like that."

From the pleased expression on his face, I had scored big with that response. He continued, "Yeah, I really enjoyed last night."

"Good."

"Dudes need that."

"I bet."

"I'ma be honest. Sometimes you just want to spend a night with somebody. No questions. No drama."

"I understand."

"You're probably not like that with ya man, though."

My neck snapped back. I wasn't sure if I was supposed to have a man or not. I laughed. "Why you say that?"

"I don't know, y'all get all crazy once you snag something."

I shook my head. "That's not true."

"Y'all be like, 'Gotcha! Now I can nag your ass to death.'"

"Is that what you think?"

"That's what I know. I've been married for six years."

He said it so carelessly, as if there were nothing wrong

with my being there with him. He was open and waiting for me to open up. So I did. "So you're telling me that your wife nags you to death."

"Damn right, and every married man I know is going through the same thing."

I shrugged. "So why get married?"

"I got married 'cause I owed her that. She been riding wit' me since high school, but that still don't mean she don't get on my goddamn nerves."

Shaking my head, I laughed. He started laughing too. "You see what I'm saying."

"Yes, I see what you're saying. Women are a pain in the ass."

"Yeah, that. Plus y'all manipulative as hell too," he said, laughing. "Y'all can't be taken at face value."

I looked him in the eye. "Do you really believe that?"

"Hell yeah. You fall in love with Cinderella and wake up one day to the damn Wicked Witch of the West."

"It's not that bad."

"Man, even my daughter is manipulative. I feel like my wife is teaching her how to manipulate and that shit ain't right."

"I think women have to be manipulative for our survival."

"That's what I'm talking about. At least you're honest about it. I can tell you every woman I talk to about this tries to act like I'm crazy. If y'all do it for survival or not, it's still manipulation."

"Yeah, it is," I said to appease his philosophy.

"Y'all call us dogs but women are the sneakiest creatures alive."

"I agree."

He put his fist out to give me dap. "See, I like that. You are real. Most women are so self-righteous, they would never admit. At least you're real about it. I appreciate that.

"You really are the dog trainer," he said, nodding his head slowly. "Teach a nigga some new tricks. Have him reevaluating what he thinks about chicks."

I blushed. I really didn't deserve that much credit, but if he wanted to give it to me I was going to accept it. We talked for a while longer before he had to leave. He pulled out a stack of cash and handed it to me.

"This should take care of you."

I took the money and put it into my purse. After kissing him on the cheek, I headed to the door. He walked behind me and said, "See you again."

"You know how to reach me."

I hoped he would want to see me again. The next time I would know to sleep the entire day before. Inside the taxi I counted the money and was shocked to discover that he had given me ten thousand dollars. Thorne had told me that I would earn one thousand dollars an hour, but I hadn't known every hour counted. I guess men like that could throw that kind of money away at the bar, so why not spend it on good sex, good company, and good conversation?

12

Thorne and I caught the same flight back to DC on Monday morning at five forty-five. The ride to the airport was the first time since I'd brought those shopping bags in the house that we'd spent any quality time together. He placed his hand on my thigh and said, "I'm proud of you."

It was as if I'd been waiting for his approval because a wide smile spread across my face. He continued, "What are your plans when you get home?"

"Nothing. Are you coming over?"

"London Reed. It's family time. I've been out of town for a while. It's time to spend time with the wife and my boys."

I nodded. I really wasn't sure what to say because it seemed oxymoronic to me that he could speak so endearingly about his family, yet be running a sex-trade empire at the same time.

"So does your wife know?"

He smiled. "Know what?"

"About this. About what you do on the side."

"In order to protect her, I think it's best that she not know."

"So what do you tell her when you're out of town or handling the phone calls?"

He took a deep breath, seemingly irritated by my questions, but I planned to get as much as I could get out of him.

He said, "Well, she knows I'm a businessman and she has always given me space to do what I had to do. She doesn't work, she has no plans to work, and she trusts that I'll make a way for her to live in a lavish home, have a beach house, drive a nice car, and that there will be money in the bank to buy whatever she wants. So she doesn't stress me. She never has."

I envied her. What did she do to deserve that lifestyle? A piece of me felt Thorne and I were growing closer and I wondered if she'd worked for him before they fell in love.

"So where did you guys meet? Were you in *this* business?"

"Absolutely. We met a few years after I got involved in this."

"Did she ever work for you?"

"Nope. Never," he said, definitely.

I smiled tightly, not sure what I wanted to say next. There was a lump in my throat as I searched my soul for why he had bribed me into working for him but not her.

"So did you know you wanted something different from her when you met her?"

The expression on his face softened like he was visualizing her. "Not really, she was just different."

"Did you try to get her in the business?"

"I tried, but she didn't bite."

"I thought you said that almost all women will bite, especially if you present it right."

"*Almost* is the key word. I didn't think I could convince her."

My heart raced like he'd just smacked me. What about my character had made him think he could convince me?

After noticing the disappointment in my face, he said, "London, some girls do. Some girls don't, but one isn't better than the other."

He softly pinched my cheek. "No big deal."

I smirked. Certainly he was bullshitting me, but what could I say? I'd fallen for his proposal and not only had I fallen for it, I was convinced it was a great opportunity. Maybe he'd taken advantage of my adverse circumstances. Maybe I'd had a FOR SALE sign stamped on my forehead. Whatever the case, I wondered what was so special about her and I knew it was too late to prove that I was special too.

"So what are you going to do with that large sum of money you got this weekend?"

I was agitated that he was trying to change the topic, so I said, "I'm not sure."

"I would think you'd get somewhere larger to stay."

"Well, I do have another nine months on my lease."

"You can get out of that, you know. Always remember, every contract has a way out."

"What are you saying?"

"I believe you'd just have to pay two months' rent and give a thirty-day notice. Most leases have a cancellation clause. You should never sign one without it because you never know what can happen."

"I'll have to see if my lease has one."

"I hope it does and if not, don't ever sign another without it. You have the right to see the lease before your actual move-in day so that you can make sure it meets your needs. If you wait until the day you're scheduled to move in, you already have movers and helpers lined up. That puts you in a desperate situation and you'll sign anything. Never sign a contract out of desperation. Always with clarity and calm."

"Yeah, when I moved into that place I was definitely desperate. So it's likely anything could be in that lease," I said with slight chuckle.

"Yeah, that's in the past, but no more of that." Raising one eyebrow, he said, "Got it?"

I nodded. "I got it."

"Nine times out of ten, contracts are not written in your favor, so always cover your ass."

"I agree. I guess you just assume that some things are standard."

"Assume nothing. Know everything whenever you sign your signature."

"That's good advice."

He put his hand on my knee and said, "Always."

"You're funny."

"I'm not trying to be," he said with a smile. "For real, though, back to the lecture at hand, that dog of yours definitely needs his own space. It just ain't cool having him growling like that while you're getting it on."

"But I thought you told me that no one would ever come to my house."

"I was just joking about that. Seriously, though, when you do your taxes, you can write off the portion of your home that you use as office space. It's calculated by square footage. You don't have much to write off when your entire living space is four hundred feet, now do you?"

"It's closer to five or six hundred."

"You're missing the point. Make your business work for you. You can afford it now."

We arrived at the airport and the driver took our luggage to the skycap. After we checked in, we headed to our gate. Shortly after, we were boarding the plane. Luckily we were in first class. The flight attendant offered us drinks while the other passengers boarded. Thorne said, "Mimosas for the lady and me."

When she brought the drinks, Thorne raised his glass. "London Bridge, you really handled your business. Keep up the good work."

As I tapped my glass against his, I wondered what type of feedback he had received. I gulped down my drink. Within minutes both Thorne and I were asleep. I didn't know when the plane took off.

When we arrived in DC I felt abandoned once we got our luggage. Thorne waved goodbye as if I were a stranger he'd met on the plane and headed toward the town car waiting for him. My pockets were full, but I felt empty as I watched him walk away, detached and carefree.

By the time I got home, after sitting in traffic for what seemed like forever, it was a little after five. Bruno, his crate, and his food were gone. Kari must have decided it was easier to just take him home with her instead of going back and forth. I quickly searched for my lease to see if moving was a possibility. As I read through it, it appeared I could upgrade my apartment in the same building without penalty and with only a nominal transfer fee. It was just about ten minutes to six and the leasing office was about to close. I rushed downstairs and into the office.

I smiled at the leasing agent. "Hello."

He smiled politely. "Hello. Can I help you with something this evening?"

"Well, I moved into a studio in November and I was looking to upgrade because it's a lot smaller than I realized. I was wondering—"

He smiled. "You wouldn't believe this. I got a letter today from a tenant who won't be renewing the lease. It's a two-bedroom on the sixth floor. Do you think you'd be interested?"

"What's the rent?"

"Sixteen hundred."

"Yep, I'd love to see it."

"We don't have any two-bedrooms available to see, but I can show you the floor plan. All the appliances are the same. Hardwood floors, et cetera."

"Cool, when can I move in?"

"If you're interested, you can move in on March fifteenth."

"Okay, so what do we need to do?"

"You will have to put your intentions in writing and my manager will have to agree to it, and she will. Then you pay the transfer fee and we'll be set for March."

I nearly hugged him, but I shook his hand. "Sounds good to me. I'll get that letter to you tomorrow."

"Okay, cool. What's your name and apartment number?"

I gave him my information and headed across the street to get Bruno. I called Kari just before walking into her building.

"You home, chick?"

"No, Bruno and I walked down to the Starbucks on M Street."

"Oh, well, I'll meet you guys."

"No, it's okay. I'll just bring him home when I get back."

She probably had a blind date at the coffee shop, so I backed off. If I'd been on some of the horrific dates she'd been on, there would be no way I'd keep hopping on the dating treadmill. Some people are fine with disappointment.

I would just wait for a guy to find me instead of being on the prowl 24-7.

I went back home and stretched across my bed. Kari knocked on my door about an hour later. When I opened it Bruno nearly attacked me, sniffing me like crazy. Kari struggled to control him before handing the leash to me. I sternly shouted, "Sit!"

He whined a little before sitting. Finally I hugged Kari. "Thanks so much."

She said, "Anytime, girl. So how was your visit?"

She'd caught me completely off guard. I hadn't thought about what I would tell her about my visit with my mom. I smiled. "Surprisingly, it was pretty good."

"Your hair looks good."

"I know. I went to her stylist and he hooked me up."

"I like it. It looks so natural."

"You trying to say my other hair looked cheesy."

"No, not at all. It always looked good, but you could tell it was fake. This looks like it's coming out of your roots. You look Hollywood."

My heart skipped a beat because I wondered why she had picked that term. I quickly looked at my luggage and hoped she didn't pay attention to the baggage claim sticker. It was time for Kari to go. The past weekend had too many secrets and I hadn't fully figured out what I planned to tell her.

I petted Bruno and said, "I'm glad you like the new hair. I am so sleepy; I don't know what to do."

She said, "I bet you are. Let me go."

"Thanks again for keeping my baby."

"Anytime, he was a lot of company."

"Good."

As she approached the door, she said, "Your mother must have been feeling really sympathetic."

"Why you say that?"

My eyes looked in the direction she was looking. My new purse sat on top of my luggage.

"I see she bought you a brand-new Louie. Or was that just her way of trying to convince you to apply to medical school?"

I laughed. "Probably."

We exchanged a hug and Kari was gone. I was consumed with how I planned to live this double life. How long would I be able to keep this from Kari? How could I explain all the new designer clothes when I'd just gotten fired? How could I explain my late nights? I didn't have any answers, just questions and uncertainty.

13

The next day Thorne asked to meet me for lunch. We had an early afternoon meeting not far from his office. I stopped at the bank to deposit half of my earnings just before hooking up with him. When I walked in the restaurant, I looked around and spotted him in a booth in the corner. How can you miss someone you don't really even know? I wanted to skip over there and hug him. Instead I headed in his direction, trying to suppress my schoolgirl excitement.

As I was about to sit on the bench across from him, he patted the seat beside him. When I sat down I leaned over to kiss his cheek. It was as much of a surprise to me as it was to him. He blushed. "Thank you. I needed that. I've had a crazy day at the office."

"You're welcome."

He pulled out his laptop and said, "I have something amazing to show you."

"Amazing?"

"Absolutely," he said, as he began to start up his computer.

Before turning the screen so that I could see, he continued, "I told you that my team works fast. My graphic artists touched up your shots and uploaded them to the website last night."

"Those pictures are on the Web?"

"Calm down. The website is secure, everything is encrypted. Nobody is going to see these pictures who isn't supposed to see them. You can't download or copy them. You know me, London. Whatever you're concerned about, I've already handled."

"I believe that."

He opened a folder titled THE DOG TRAINER and my jaw dropped to the ground. I covered my mouth, slightly flattered but mostly puzzled.

"Thorne, I hope you don't plan on showing these to clients. They'll be disappointed when the real me shows up."

He laughed, "London, what makes you think you look any different in person than you look in these pictures?"

"I look in the mirror every day and I certainly don't see her."

"Listen, you're too hard on yourself. I'm a man and I'm telling you that you look exactly the same."

"If you say so, but I'm not comfortable with you showing these."

"Too late, you've gotten a bunch of requests in the past twenty-four hours."

My palms started to sweat. I felt pressured by the image he was selling. It was like false advertisement.

"Thorne, I just don't know."

"Look, I've been doing this for a long time. You'll be fine. So let's talk about your schedule. How often do you want to work?"

"Twice a week, I guess."

"London, you don't have a job, you can do better than that."

"I just don't want to wear my body out, if you know what I mean."

He laughed. "I've never had that problem."

I smiled to appease him but I didn't find that funny. He'd lured me into this using his body and I wondered if that was how he recruited everyone. I wondered how many women he slept with in one week and how he could in turn trade them for sex. He was no doubt a damn Rottweiler.

"At this time, I would prefer no more than two, maximum three a week."

"I gotchu. I was just messing with you. You tell me how much you want to work and I'll take care of the rest."

"I understand."

"I have someone on hold for tomorrow. You up for that?"

I shrugged.

"Listen, let me know."

"I guess so."

He typed into his laptop. "Okay, that's at six tomorrow evening. Downtown. Also, the football player wants to see you again."

"Really?" I said, blushing momentarily, as much work as a night with him had been.

"He'll be in Miami this weekend if you don't mind flying down. I have to talk to him, but I think it's a two-day job."

"So how does that work?"

"What, the two-day job?"

"I mean, am I supposed to book my own flight and am I supposed to stay with him for two days?"

"They pay for travel. I book it through my travel agency. You just show up. If they request multiple days, the assumption is they are taking care of you. You're staying with them or in a room they provide."

He sure knew how to milk every dime out of every angle of a transaction. It amazed me how organized he was with everything.

"So is the booking fee more for multiple days?"

He looked at me, shaking his head, and seconds passed before he spoke. "London, you ask a lot of questions. If I didn't know any better, I would think you wanted my job."

"No, I'm just curious."

"I like curious. And to answer your question, I get a little more off the top for multiple days."

After a long pause he said, "So, can I book you for this weekend?"

I wasn't too excited about being stabbed with the football player's machete for forty-eight hours straight. Taking a deep breath, I said, "Let me think about that for a minute."

Raising his eyebrow, he demanded a confirmation. Although that guy was hard to handle, he certainly compensated well. So I agreed.

The next evening I headed downtown to meet a man by the name of TC. Thorne didn't tell me his profession, but I trusted that I was in good hands. When I arrived at the small boutique hotel on Massachusetts Avenue I decided to take the stairs to the room. After checking my hair and makeup in the hallway mirror, I knocked softly on the door. My lip gloss glistened just like I liked it. The door swung open and I was surprised to be greeted an overly uptight man. He was stiff in every sense of the word. It was quite shocking because my first two clients had been just like animals and it had been no surprise to me that they would pay for sex. This man on the other hand looked like he went strictly by the book. His nervous energy was instantly transferred to me. While I almost tensed up, I quickly thought, *What would I do to make a nervous dog feel comfortable?*

I ran my hand softly down his jawline and smiled. Speaking in a soft voice, I said, "Hey."

In a quivery tone, he said, "How are you?"

His dialect was proper and his thin red lips almost appeared not to move. If I had heard him before seeing him, there is no way I would believe he was a black man. His light-colored face was sprinkled with brown freckles. He had short brown hair and was about six feet even. His thin frame looked like it had been years since he'd seen food. He was neglected, but obviously very successful. I reached out to hug him and I don't know why that was my first reaction. He did the stand-steps-away-and-pat hug. I pulled him toward me so we could be chest-to-chest. He was hesitant, but after holding him tightly I could feel his limbs relaxing.

"Thank you," he said, pulling away.

There was something quite innocent about him. I pinched his cheek and he blushed. When I noticed he'd had a drink on the nightstand, I asked what it was. He smiled, "Ah, it's Rémy. Do you want some?"

I'd never tasted Rémy but I anxiously nodded yes. He poured a little in a glass and handed it to me. I reached for his hand to interlock my fingers. I swallowed, and the liquid filling my mouth felt like gasoline. I tastelessly spit it out. My tongue hung out of my mouth. He completely loosened up as he laughed at me losing my cool. We hugged each other and he said, "First time drinking Rémy?"

"Yes."

"I guess we're both experiencing firsts tonight."

He confirmed what I already knew. I tilted my head and looked into his small eyes. "It's your first time, huh?"

A piece of me wondered why Thorne hadn't sent a bodyguard with me like he'd promised he'd do when I served new clients. Then, as I looked into the timid eyes of this man, I wondered if Thorne assumed he was harmless too. He said, "Yes."

"What made you decide to do this?" I asked before sitting on the bed.

I reached out for his hand, requesting that he sit beside me. He slouched down. "Stress."

I massaged the nape of his neck. "It's okay. Whatever it is. You know?"

He nodded. "I owe a lot of people a lot of money."

Why the hell would you blow the money you have on a one-night stand? "Are they after you?"

"No, not right now. I'm going to make the money back. Somehow."

His head hung like that of an honest man ashamed of what he'd done. I stroked his earlobe, a relaxing technique that I use with dogs. "I'm sure you will. I believe you can do it."

He perked up and looked like he wanted to lick me for the praise. I smiled graciously back at him. "Watch. This time next year, promise me that you'll meet me here again and tell me how you made the money you owed back."

Laughing, he asked, "Do I need to wait until next year to see you again?"

"Of course not, you just have to make the arrangements and I'll be here."

"Wow, I really needed that."

"What? To know we can hook up again?"

"No, the encouragement."

"Oh, that comes with the deal."

It seemed like a dark cloud hovered over him again as he began to speak. "It's been a long time since my wife said anything positive to me."

"What do you do, if you don't mind me asking?"

"I'm an attorney." He paused. "And promise me your secrecy."

"That's a part of the deal too," I said, trying not to sound too eager to know more.

"I'm also a politician."

"So are you concerned about the people you owe or your reputation?"

"Both."

I placed my hands softly on each side of his jaw. "Don't worry. Everything is going to be okay." I waited for him to look in my eyes and repeated, "Okay."

He smiled bashfully. "You think so?"

"I know it will."

TC looked at me with such gratitude and said, "Thank you so much."

"It's nothing." I could just feel that he was a good guy and he cared what people thought of him. So I said, "You seem like a really great guy and when you do your best, things always work out."

"I wish someone would tell my wife that."

"You want me to call her?" I asked jokingly.

"Please don't. She would never let me live this down. No matter what I do, it's just never good enough."

"I think you're good enough. The fact that you care about what people think makes you good."

"Yeah, my wife used to feel that way too."

"Really?"

"When we first met, she'd always tell me that I was the good guy. And good guys always end up on top."

He blushed as he reminisced. I said, "I bet she still feels that way."

"Naw. Not anymore."

"If you don't mind me asking, how long have you been married?"

"Twenty-six years."

"What? When'd you get married? At sixteen?"

He smiled. "No, I'm fifty-two years old."

"Wow, you don't look a day over forty," I said, lying.

While I'm certain he was flattered, he dismissed my compliment. "Sure. Anyway, I'm certain she thinks I'm a jerk."

"Why do you think that?"

"She thinks that she's the brains behind my success. Her parents funded my law degree. She's pretty much the reason we have all that we have and she never lets me forget it."

"I'm sure you had something to do with it."

"Sometimes I feel like I'm just a puppet."

"No, you seem strong and smart to me."

"Thanks. I really needed that."

"Do you still love her?"

"I don't know."

"Do you think she still loves you?"

"Probably not. It seemed like she did until both of the kids left for college."

"How long has that been?"

"Three years ago. It seems like she was pretending to respect me while the kids were there because that's what she was supposed to do, but when my son went to college, she seemed to take out all her extra anxiety on me. I think before then she was busy with the kids so she didn't pay me much attention. Now all she sees is what I do wrong and if this dilemma I'm in ever comes to light, she'll never let me live it down."

"Why don't you relax?"

I loosened his tie and told him to lie back on the bed. I lay beside him and unbuttoned his shirt. As I ran my hands across his bird chest, I tried to tell him everything would be okay.

He continued to talk. "Everything we have, we built it together. All of our businesses have been joint ventures."

"I understand."

"But if you ask her, I would have nothing without her."

"I bet that's not true."

"Hell no, it's not true."

That was the first time since I'd been there that TC had expressed any aggression. He was tired and he was frustrated.

"I understand. It's going to be okay. You just have to make her respect you again."

"How do I do that?"

"You know dogs have a clear understanding of which dog is the leader of the pack and they respect that dog's role. But there are times when the leader is challenged by a dog in his pack, a dog that feels like he deserves that role. The alpha dog either puts that dog in his place or the other dog has to go. You're going to have to start carrying yourself with authority. She doesn't respect you because you're not acting like a pack leader but you want to be treated like one."

"But I've never been extremely aggressive."

"So how'd you become a politician?"

"I ran a campaign. But she was the brains behind it."

"And you were the face of it. Don't minimize your role. You guys are a team, but right now she's the team leader. If you want to get your respect back, you have to demand it."

I wasn't certain if I was giving this man the right advice, but it seemed to be making him feel better. And that was my job, to make him feel like a leader even if he could never live up to the role. He thought he just needed a fling, but clearly he needed female encouragement. He'd been beaten down for way too long. I stood up and asked if he wanted me to top off his drink.

I made vodka and orange juice and he sat up to sip the drink I'd made him. He continued to open up to me. I could tell he felt a strong connection to me as he revealed more and more of his secrets. I vowed that I would never tell and obviously I'd done a pretty good job gaining his trust.

We lay back on the bed and he wrapped me in his fragile arms as we talked for several hours longer. Finally he held me tighter and said, "I had the best time that I've had in a long time."

"But we didn't even do anything," I said.

"You know it's hard to really find someone you feel comfortable talking to. Sometimes you get tired of living a lie. Sometimes you just want to tell the truth. Sometimes you want to say you're scared."

"Are you scared?"

"Scared that if I fail or if people find out the truth about me that I will disappoint so many people. That's very scary."

"I can imagine, but I don't think there's anything wrong with the real you. You're probably harder on yourself than anyone."

He leaned in for a kiss. "You're probably right."

I stroked his back, assuming he was about ready to get it on. He said, "It's been a complete pleasure."

He stood up and walked over to the dresser. I sat at the edge of the bed and he handed me some money. That was a typical sign that the date was over. I was confused. "Are we done?"

"Yes, and thank you so much."

Not that I was really interested in doing anything further, but I needed to be clear on this. "But nothing happened."

"Everything that I needed to happen happened."

He reached for a hug and held me tightly like I was his

best friend. I'd been everything he needed for the few hours I was there. I wondered if a platonic date had been his intention from jump. We embraced for what seemed like five minutes and I kissed his cheek. He walked me to the door and looked forever grateful for my visit. That's when it first dawned on me that while sex is a priority for some men, there are many others who despite all the money in the world don't have anyone to confide in. It was my first of such encounters, but not my last.

Those were the ones who gave my job reason. It made me feel like I was helping people. I went home that night feeling like I'd done something worthwhile and I was excited about my next experience. The different personalities I had experienced in just three short dates left me hungry to learn more about men and how easy it was to train them.

14

Thorne e-mailed the itinerary for Miami the day before I was supposed to leave. He hadn't even called to find out if I'd made it home from my last date. Nor had I been able to get him on the phone. It felt as if I had been coerced into the situation with gentle words and affection; now I was being treated like just another employee. I quickly responded to the message: "Hey Thorne, am I supposed to check into the hotel using my credit card or am I supposed to call him when I get there?"

My phone rang barely five seconds after I pressed SEND. Thorne cleared his throat before speaking. "London Bridge... how are you?"

"How are you?"

"Why do you sound like that?"

"No reason. I called you earlier."

"I was busy."

"How did you know I didn't need anything?"

"London, we're not about to turn this into an interrogation. Now if you have questions about this weekend, I'm all ears."

A huge lump sat in my throat because I wasn't sure I could swallow his ice-cold tone. "So when I get to Miami, what should I do?"

"Go to the hotel. Give your name at the front desk and your room should already be taken care of. If not, just give me a call."

"Okay," I said, letting the word linger a little longer than necessary.

"You good?"

"Yeah, for the most part."

"I'm on my way to a meeting. If I don't talk to you, have a safe trip."

After he hung up I held the phone in my hand, staring at the blank screen. Our conversation felt almost like he was trying to pull away from me. It didn't feel good.

As if he knew that I was questioning going and if I should even continue in the profession, Thorne called about an hour before I was supposed to be at the airport.

"London Bridge," he said cheerfully.

"Hi, Thorne."

"You need a ride to the airport?"

"No thanks. I'll just park in satellite."

"Okay. You sure?"

"Positive."

"Let's hook up when you get back."

I assumed Thorne dedicated a lot of time to the prey of the week, but once he caught it was on to the next one. As I packed the last of my things, I concluded that maybe that was just the nature of the business. How could I expect him to spend countless hours with me? He'd been doing this long before he met me.

I didn't want Kari in my business so I didn't ask her to keep Bruno; instead I headed to the kennel to drop him off. When we arrived he began whining as soon as we entered. He was trying to pull me back toward the door. As I was signing him in, the girl at the front desk came around to pet him and he seemed to settle down. That made me feel a little better as I prepared to hand my baby over. It was the first time he'd been with strangers. Finally I walked backward toward the door and she took him to the back with the other dogs.

When I stepped off the plane the warm air smothered me as I walked through the tunnel into the terminal. It felt weird not having anyone to call to say that I arrived, so I just headed to baggage claim. I wasn't sure if there would be a car waiting for me or not. I looked around and didn't see my name on any of the signs. That was my cue to hail a taxi to South Beach.

It was mid-afternoon and Ocean Drive was packed with people of all colors and ages. The taxi pulled up to the Shore Club hotel. I put my sunshades on before stepping out of the car. The driver rolled my small luggage around to me. For a moment I stood there. I felt nervous. The building looked just average, not what I would expect of a baller. When I entered, my opinion immediately changed.

The lobby was art deco with sleek white leather couches scattered around. I tossed my hair behind my ear and removed my shades. I walked to the front desk and the bubbly receptionist greeted me politely with a strong Brazilian accent.

"I'm checking in."

"Your name?"

"London Reed."

She typed into the system and nodded. I began to open my wallet because I wanted to be ready just in case. She placed the keys in a small silver envelope.

"You're in one of our poolside bungalows, number six. If

you walk out here toward the pool you'll see the bungalows on the left."

I headed to my room, unsure of what to expect. I was trying to figure out if my client was going to call me or was already in the room. When I opened the door to the two-story little cottage I said, "Hello."

When no one responded I assumed I was there alone. So I went into the bathroom and turned on the shower. Thorne had given me limited instructions, so I figured I would just hang out until the next clue. After I showered I put on a bikini and stepped onto my private patio.

I flagged down one of the waiters hustling around the pool and asked for a menu. After ordering a piña colada and chicken quesadillas, I stretched out with my head at the foot of the lounger to face the pool. It wasn't too crowded, but there were a good number of people lounging around the pool.

When my food came, I sat up to eat, looked across the pool, and there he was. He wore a pair of red swim trunks and had a bare, chiseled chest. He carried two drinks in his hands. I could barely concentrate to sign the receipt for my food as I watched his every step, none of which was in my direction. He stood over a lady lying by the pool and handed her the drink. He straddled the lounger with her and I noticed that she was wearing a ring. Could that be his wife? Why would he invite me here with his wife?

There was no way this was occurring. I had a hard time keeping my eyes off of them. Two little boys jumped out of the pool and ran toward them. He put more sunblock on them and proceeded to rub his wife with the excess. My bottom lip was hanging; I was confused and baffled. Were they also in the bungalows? There were only a few, about six or seven, and that would be too close for comfort. They talked and laughed as my food sat in front of me untouched. Finally I figured I would snap out of it and pretend to be ignorant.

I started eating and just couldn't shake the thought. I waved the waiter down for another drink. There was no way I could participate in this drama with a sober mind. After I began to feel a buzz I headed back inside. I wanted to call someone, but I didn't have anyone I could share this with, so I paced the floor.

Knock. Knock. Knock. I nearly jumped out of my skin. After taking a deep breath, I went to the door. He came in, still in his swim trunks. "I'm glad you made it, ma."

"Is that your wife you're with?"

"Don't talk," he said, as he stuck his tongue down my throat. While untying my bikini, he said, "I know you got condoms."

"In my purse..."

He rammed his fingers inside me as we stumbled over to the sofa where my purse sat. I quickly pulled out a condom and he yanked the monster from his shorts. This man required no foreplay, he was always ready. He bent me over and entered me from behind. It didn't hurt as much as the first time. Maybe it was the excitement mixed with the fear of being caught by his wife that turned me on, because I was prepared for him. He held my waist as he pounded into me. As he commanded me to say I loved it, I looked at the open patio door and didn't say anything. He pulled my hair and I screamed. He kept doing it. My pain was giving him pleasure as he groaned behind me. He turned me around and plunged deep in me. I wiped the sweat dripping from his face as he panted aggressively on me. Finally he released.

I'd learned the last time that that didn't necessarily mean we were done. I took a deep breath when he rolled over and sat beside me, but I didn't move. I waited for his second wind to kick in. He rubbed my thigh.

"I like that."

"What?"

"You can handle me." He laughed. "All of me."

He stood up and went into the bathroom. Not sure if he rinsed off while in there, but he came out with his shorts back on. He headed toward the door.

"I'll meet you back here around one in the morning."

My eyes circled as I said, "Okay."

I still wanted to understand the arrangement but it was obvious that he wasn't offering any explanations. I was just here to provide a service. The rest was none of my business.

"You got two keys?"

I handed him my other key and sat on the couch, feeling slightly used and even more confused. After he left I went into the bathroom to shower and decided I should sleep on this situation.

When I woke up it was close to eight and the sun had started to set. I looked out my patio door and there weren't many people left at the pool. I put on some clothes and headed to the hotel lounge.

It was quite empty, so I sat on the slim leather bar stool in the middle of the bar. The bartender spun around, passing me a bar menu as I studied the royal blue tiled backsplash.

I smiled at him. "That looks nice."

"I wish I could take credit for it but I think the interior designer picked it out."

I laughed. "I figured that, but I just thought I'd let you know I really like it."

He was an ultra-tanned white guy with spiked hair, but he was cute. I smiled flirtatiously when he winked.

"Can I get you something to drink?" he asked.

"You sure can. Give me a dirty martini."

I was in one of those moods. I heard some heels coming toward me. She looked different dressed up, but it was definitely her. His wife marched toward me almost as if she were about to approach me. Had she still been at the pool when her husband came to my room? Did she hear us?

Her long, curly black hair was pulled back into a ponytail and she had on a short fuchsia dress that hung off one shoulder. The rest of her dress looked melded onto her flawless copper skin. I quickly turned in the opposite direction because I didn't want to give her the impression that I knew her or her husband. She would have to prove that she knew it was me first.

She plopped down a stool away from me. While shaking up my drink the bartender said, "Good evening, Mrs. Rick Picasso. What can I get you?"

"Malibu and pineapple juice," she said politely.

My back was slightly turned in her direction when the bartender set my drink in front of me. She leaned over and tapped me. *Oh shit*, I thought as I slowly turned in her direction. She offered me the most pleasant, peaceful smile. Her teeth were so white and straight they almost made her look like a portrait.

"What's that?" she asked.

"Oh, this is a dirty martini."

"That looks strong."

"It is," I said, laughing.

The bartender asked, "You want one?"

"Certainly not. You know I don't drink like that."

How in the world could she have sex with her husband without heavy drinking? He was a beast and she was taking it with nothing for the pain. I checked out her wedding ring and it was huge. She deserved every karat she got for satisfying his appetite.

The bartender handed her the drink.

"Thank you. I needed a little something. We're about to go on a boat ride."

"Really? Just you and hubby or the kids too?" asked the bartender.

"Absolutely not. Those rug rats are with the nanny. Rick will be down in a minute. After he finishes polishing every inch of his skin with oil."

She laughed and it made me smile. I didn't want to give her the impression that I was familiar with his vanity. She shook her head at me.

"Men. You gotta love them."

"That's true," I said nicely, but I really wasn't trying to be overly friendly.

The bartender said, "And what are you ladies trying to say?"

She touched my shoulder. "I don't know about her man, but my man is a piece of work."

She certainly wasn't lying. That was the best way to describe him.

The bartender spoke passionately. "Your man is supposed to be a piece of work. He's the best wide receiver in the league."

"Okay, and..." she said, with her neck twirling.

He raised his hands defenselessly. "And I'm done."

She seemed to be extremely carefree and offering information without reservation. Since she was clearly trying to strike up a conversation with me, I decided to oblige her.

"They all are a piece of work, girl."

"You can say that again."

"What kind of boat ride are you going on?"

"One of my husband's friends is having a birthday party." She paused. "I want to go like I want a hole in my head."

"Why? It should be nice."

"Honey, the groupies always find their way to the so-called private parties and it's just irritating. You can't even go out and have a nice time with your husband without having to claw chicks off of him."

I felt bad, because I might have been in that groupie category. Or was I different because he had found me? I didn't know, but as I sat there looking at this lady, sympathizing with her, I didn't feel like there was a difference.

"I could imagine that being pretty irritating."

"It is, but the sad part about it is, if they really got him, they would ship his ass right back on the first train smoking."

She laughed and I laughed with her. There was something so sweet and happy about her. He didn't deserve her and she didn't deserve the drama.

"Things always look good from the outside looking in," I said.

"How old are you?"

I was kind of shocked by the question, but finally I said, "Twenty-three."

"You are smarter than most women ten years older than you. What you see is not always what you get."

The lounge door opened and he walked in our direction with a perplexed look on his face. I wanted to crawl under the bar because I didn't want him to think I'd approached her. He stood a few steps away from us.

"C'mon, baby."

He acted like he didn't even notice there was another person at the bar as he shook the bartender's hand. After signing her check, she scooted off the stool and extended her hand. "Nice to meet you...?"

"London."

"Okay, London, I'm Sandi."

"Good to meet you."

I peeped at the check to see which room they were staying in and if they were close to me as they headed out of the lounge. I didn't have to catch the elevator to get to my room, so I was pretty clueless as to the number of floors. I asked the bartender. He obviously knew why I had asked, because he told me the Picassos were in the penthouse and it took up the entire top floor.

At around a quarter after one in the morning my room door opened. Where did Sandi think he was at this time of morning? I turned the television off and stood up from the couch wearing lingerie with heels. He looked me up and down, sort of as if he was attracted to the sight of me, but then again he looked agitated.

"What's up?" I asked.

"That was some bullshit you pulled at the bar."

"Rick, she started talking to me."

"And that was your cue to get up and leave then."

"I'm sorry. I didn't want to give her the impression that I was uncomfortable around her."

"Yeah, whatever. Why were you even over there?"

"Was I supposed to stay in the room?"

"Nah, but you don't need to be anywhere you can get up close and personal with my wife. Got that?"

I nodded. He pulled me to him. "Now come here and take care of me."

He took off my bra and panties and we had an hour of rough sex. It didn't feel like it had earlier. I was chafed again after he finished. He handed me some money before leaving. "A'ight, shorty, I'm out of here in the AM."

"I thought you requested me for two nights."

He looked into my eyes. "I changed my mind."

It was fine with me, because aside from the financial gain, I'd only agreed to see him again because I thought he was a sweet guy. I certainly wouldn't lose any rest over not feeling him inside me again.

He had been careless in booking me at the same hotel with his family and now he was mad that his wife and I had happened to run into each other. He was more than a piece of work and I was emotionless as I closed the door behind him.

15

When I got back to DC Thorne kept his promise and we hooked up. He came over shortly after I got in. Bruno was staying at the kennel an extra day so we had privacy. He picked up food from a restaurant a few blocks from my house. When he knocked on the door I felt warm and fuzzy inside. I don't know why, but I felt excited to see him. Dressed in his usual Ralph Lauren button-down and jeans, he stood there posed for a second when I opened the front door.

"London Bridge."

"C'mon in."

He handed the bag of food to me and I walked over and put it on the counter. I returned to give him a hug. He held me tightly. When he finally let go he held on to my hands and looked me up and down.

"So how'd it go this weekend?"

I explained to him how Rick had acted after catching me talking to his wife. Thorne told me that typically clients don't want any interaction with the wives even if they are careless enough to book the same hotel.

He said, "This is where I would normally tell you that will probably be your last encounter with him."

"I know. He seemed pretty angry."

"I said normally. Rick called today and he wants to see you again next week."

"Are you serious? After he just walked out like that?"

"He probably was pissed, but between me and you, I have never had another girl agree to see him twice."

I shook my head. "I know why."

"Yes, I've heard. So you're a rarity and he knows it. A man like that is not going to pass up a chick that can handle him."

"I don't know if I handle him or I'm the only one stupid enough to just deal with it."

"You're not stupid at all. You got that extra something. I can't put my finger on it yet, though."

As happy as I had been at the thought of not having to have sex with Rick again, I was even happier that he still wanted to. That made me feel special, because I'd thought for certain he would be on to the next one. Even Thorne looked impressed.

Just as we sat down to eat, my cell phone rang. I hopped up to grab it.

"Hey, Kari."

"Hey, stranger. Where you been?"

Why was she certain that I had been missing in action? It's not as if she had called and I hadn't answered.

"I've been chilling."

"I stopped by earlier yesterday because I had something to show you. When you didn't answer, I figured I would use my key to check up on Bruno."

"Why didn't you just call me?"

"Because it was a surprise."

"What was the surprise and why was it so urgent?"

She explained that she had decided to cut and dye her hair

and halfway through getting it done she had looked in the mirror and felt like Boy George. So she rushed to my house with her hair half done, hoping I could help her. She waited for close to an hour because she didn't want to go back out on the street. As she talked I was trying to figure out where I could say I'd been. My eyes were stretched wide and Thorne looked at me inquisitively. Kari was on the other end waiting for an explanation.

"I'm sure it's not as bad as you think. I was in New Jersey. My mom's brother is sick."

"The one you don't like?"

"Yeah, but she wanted me to go in her place and I just took Bruno with me."

"I was like, 'Where is London when I need her most?'"

I wrapped up the call. "I'm never too far away. Next time just call me. I just got back and I have to unpack so let me go."

When I hung up, Thorne said, "That's the hardest part, huh?"

"What's that?"

"Coming up with lies about where you been and what you're doing."

"Yeah, how do you manage?"

"Well, it's not hard for me because I just field calls. Make connections. You know? I don't have to go anywhere unless I want to."

"So why are you here?"

"London, you're something else."

"No, I'm just curious. Do you have to spend so much upfront time with everyone you recruit?"

"Some people don't have to be convinced to do this. Some people are just open."

"Do you think I'm open?"

"It's not up to me to determine if you're open. You are as open as you want to be. My job is to present an opportunity. If you're interested, cool. If you're not, cool. If you wake up tomorrow and decide you're done, that's cool too. For every woman that decides she won't, there are two that will."

Thorne's job was to make being a call girl a desirable profession. I wasn't sure I believed that it was so easy convincing women to sell sex. Then again, maybe it was, because never in a million years would I have thought I'd do this.

Thorne and I chatted a little while longer. He didn't make any advances toward me and I wondered if the connection I'd assumed we had was just a part of the game. I kissed him at my front door. He held me close and whispered in my ear, "Good night, London Bridge."

When he walked out, I longed for him to caress me like he had on the first night.

16

It seemed like I had lain down with the devil one day and when I woke up an entire year had passed. I had gone from one or two dates a week to as many as four. Before long I felt like the expert on men. I spent most nights with a new man learning what made him tick. Whatever there was to know, I quickly learned. It didn't take long before I could look at a man and know why he was there and what he needed from me.

I thought for certain that TC would want to book me frequently, but I didn't hear from him again until exactly one year later. Thorne sent me the information for my engagement. While he didn't recall that I'd had the same client, in the same hotel room, a year earlier, I did. Despite how many men I had entertained, there were the few cases where I grew to care about what happened to them long after I closed the door to their hotel rooms. TC was definitely one of them.

I purchased a large bottle of Rémy and put it into a gift bag before heading to the hotel. When I arrived TC opened the door looking a bit more confident than before. He almost looked like he wanted to sweep me up and spin me away. I said, "I'm so happy you kept your promise."

"I had to. You really made a difference in my life."

"Good. How's your marriage?"

"Things are a lot better."

"So did you put your foot down?"

"I did."

"And how'd you do that?"

"I never felt the need to list the things I did, but I had to start letting her know what I brought to the table too. These were not just her things, these were our things."

"See?"

"Yeah, and it seemed like the more I acted like a jerk the more she respected me."

"Listen, it may seem like you're being a jerk, but women respect strength. How strong are you if everything I tell you to do, you do it? Certainly you don't want to do everything I tell you to do. You just have to stand up for your manhood from time to time. A lot of women will say that's being a jerk, but it's really not."

"Why did it take me until I was over fifty to figure that out?"

"I don't know. How's everything with the people you owe?"

"Well, I'm in the process of getting that in order. It seems like when I took control of my house, I was able to take control of my business. I was scared of how people would view me if I messed up, but I kept hearing your voice in my head telling me that people mess up and that didn't make me a loser. So I was honest and I told my partners how I'd messed up the money." He laughed. "And you'd never believe this: They invested more money for me to fix the situation."

"You're the leader of the pack now."

He laughed and hugged me. "I owe it to you."

He kissed me and slowly pulled me back to lie on the

bed. I thought it was interesting that now he'd taken control of his life, he felt confident enough to push up. He touched my breast and I wrapped my arm around his slim torso. He climbed on top of me and landed pecks on my neck and face. I ran my hand down the back of his head. I was laughing inside, thinking about how different this time was from the last. He'd gone from a wounded puppy to an alpha dog and it was entirely my doing. This was a bit more attractive. Though I wasn't sexually attracted to him in any shape or form, I liked the new him and I planned to turn him out so that he could get even stronger.

I pulled his shirt out and reached my hand down his pants, grabbing hold of his penis. It was shockingly medium in size. I'd expected he would be extra-small based on his character when we'd first met, but this was a pleasant surprise. He seemed to be very anxious as he began sloppily kissing me and touching here, there, and everywhere on my body. I said, "Slow down."

I started giving him instructions. "Kiss me there. Stay there for a while."

He seemed to appreciate the lesson. Finally I instructed him to slowly remove my clothes and told him to remove his. I told him that I would bend over and let him enter from behind. There is nothing like that position to make a man feel like a leader. After he put on a condom, he inserted himself into me. I told him to spank me. He tapped softly on me. I told him to do it harder. It took him a minute, but TC eventually got all into it. I was yelling, "Thank you, daddy."

TC didn't last long, but I knew my effect on him would last longer. He fell onto my back and kissed my shoulders. "Thank you. Thank you so much for everything."

He repeated expressions of gratitude to me when he paid

me for the evening. I knew that was probably the last time we'd see each other, because he'd gotten what he came for. He was empowered and the sex was just the topping. My job was done as I left the hotel feeling like I had cured another sick dog. On days like that, I felt like I was living my dream.

17

Kari was so busy on the dating treadmill that she didn't have much time to hang out. I didn't complain, either, because after almost eighteen months in the business I was consumed. I was over making up stories. I had told the umbrella lie and everything else fell underneath it. As far as Kari knew, I was Thorne's mistress. She was completely against adultery, and for weeks she tried to convince me that I should leave this man alone. I claimed to love him and that I thought he was really leaving his wife. It was easy to pretend that I wanted to be with Thorne, because partially I did.

When Kari called early in the morning on my twenty-fifth birthday, I had been up all night with a client. I answered groggily, "Hey you."

"Happy birthday, chick."

"Thank you."

"What you doing today?"

"I don't have anything planned."

She paused. "So I guess he took you out before your birthday."

"Yes, Kari."

"Cool. So we can hook up later when I get off work."

"Okay."

I sat up and my head was pounding. My birthday had completely slipped my mind. After washing my face I threw on some sweats and grabbed Bruno to take him for a walk. We headed in the direction of the café. I needed a double shot of espresso. When I got my coffee I sat outside at one of the tables. The spring air helped to wake me.

I was normally scheduled for a massage and bikini wax every Thursday, but I figured I would treat myself a few days earlier. I texted Kari and asked if she wanted to meet me at the spa after she got off work. She agreed. I scheduled us both for the works and light fare. Afterward we could do whatever Kari had planned.

Kari met me at the spa, not far from the DC waterfront. As she walked down the street, carrying her oversized backpack filled with books and papers, I was glad that I had decided we would have a relaxation day. Women who work every day don't do this enough and they are more likely to need it than me.

She had chopped her hair off so much, trying to make it right, that now she was just short and curly. It fit her, though, and actually gave her a more mature, attractive look. She smiled as she approached. I hugged her.

"Thanks for reminding me about my birthday."

"No problem."

"It was just completely off my radar."

"That's crazy. I never forget my birthday."

"Mine is probably not that important to me."

"Don't say that, Lon. So, did *he* wish you happy birthday?"

"Of course he did," I said, as we entered the spa.

It was calm and quiet. Tuesday was probably the ideal day to be at the spa. They had Kari fill out a questionnaire since it was her first visit. Then we went with two separate massage therapists. After our massages we went to a small room for a light fare before getting manicures.

As we sat in the private room, Kari said, "London, don't you want to be with someone that will remember your birthday?"

"Kari, I am with someone who remembered my birthday."

"Not me, silly. I'm talking about your boyfriend. London, it's been almost two years."

I smiled. "And I'm having a wonderful time."

"Don't waste your life away being a mistress."

"I won't."

We ate quietly for a few more minutes. "Oh yeah, Kari. I wanted to bring you down here anyway so that you can see these condos I'm thinking about buying."

She nearly spit her food out laughing. "On what salary?"

"I have a dog-walking service."

"The only dog I see you walk is Bruno."

"Shut up."

"For real, London. Ever since you hooked up with Thorne, you haven't done anything but chase him around the world."

I rolled my eyes. "I don't chase him around the world. I accompany him."

"Whatever, so how do you plan to pay for this condo, or is it going to be in his name?"

"It'll be in my name."

"London, I know he's been wining and dining you and giving you a lot of money, but that could stop tomorrow when he hires the next temp."

"I wasn't a temp."

Laughing, she said, "But you know what I'm trying to say."

"I know what you're saying."

After we ate we went to have our manicures and pedicures. We sat side by side. Kari reached out and touched my arm while our feet soaked. "I hope I didn't offend you, but you need to have a stable income before buying something. My dad says rent until you can afford all that comes along with buying. You have plenty of time to purchase something."

"But it seems like renting is just throwing away money."

"Daddy says it's paying for a place to stay. If you fall on hard times renting, you move. If you fall on hard times with something you own, you foreclose. So until you have a relatively dependable income, you need to rent."

"Well, no income is guaranteed."

"No, but some are more stable than others."

What Kari didn't realize was that I did have a stable income and I could probably depend on it. However, the things she said made sense.

My phone rang and it was my mother. I contemplated momentarily before picking up. "Hey, Mom."

"Happy birthday, young lady."

"Thank you."

"So what are you doing today?"

"Kari and I are just hanging out."

"That's good. Well, you girls have fun. Just wanted to give you a call."

I was glad that she didn't pry any further. She hung up before she had the chance to irritate me. That must have been my birthday present.

Kari and I headed back up to our neck of the woods so that she could drop off her stuff. We decided to change our clothes before going out. We stopped at my place first and I grabbed some clothes for Kari and me. I decided I would dress her for the evening. She was way overdue for a make-over. Since I could spare the time for a change, I did. I spiked her short do with hair gel. I made her face and put a sexy dress on her. Even she stared in the mirror like she couldn't believe the way she looked.

We hadn't been out together in an eternity. We headed over to a club on Wisconsin Avenue that had a jumping Tuesday night happy hour. I could feel confidence radiating from her as we headed out of the apartment building.

When we hopped in a taxi, she said, "I feel like this was my birthday. Thank you, London."

"You're welcome. I'm glad you feel good."

"I do."

Feeling good is half the battle. It summons people to you. When we walked in the club we turned heads. More guys approached Kari that night than I had ever seen. That was my birthday present, watching her. I tried to fall back as much as possible.

Kari smiled from ear to ear as she soaked up the attention. It's funny how a little makeup, eyebrow wax, and a hairdo can change prospects. We closed the club down. As we headed back, Kari was so happy.

"How many numbers did you get?"

"Just two."

"That's good."

"London, I had so much fun."

"Good, me too."

"Do you even talk to other men anymore?"

I wanted to say that average guys were not even on my radar, but I decided not to. I said, "Yes."

"No, you seem very standoffish now."

She didn't even realize that I had been that way so as not to interfere with her game, but that was fine. "No, I just don't care."

"You're married to a married man."

I laughed. "Not really."

"Yes, really."

When we got out of the taxi, Kari hugged me. "London, happy birthday."

"Thank you."

I headed into my building, wishing that I didn't have to live a lie.

18

Whenever I traveled I put Bruno in a kennel and it was extremely expensive. So it was always funny to me how my mother acted like there was no money in dog care. I attributed that to complete ignorance. From time to time I really contemplated opening a kennel, but never took enough time off to really plan it out. The idea and the frustration with my lack of motivation always resurfaced when I dropped Bruno off.

Whenever we entered the kennel Bruno would be jumping up and down, overexcited. It felt good leaving him somewhere he wanted to be and it made it easier for me to enjoy myself and do my job.

I was on my way to Vegas to spend some time with the now-retired Rick. It had been close to nine months since his career-ending injury. He wasn't doing well emotionally. He had completely lost his identity. I watched the man I'd met two years earlier disappear right before my eyes in a matter of months.

He was insecure and bitter. You would think that after eleven years in the league he would feel like he'd had the chance to live a good life and would just be thankful. Instead, he felt there was more for him to prove. He was empty and lost without his uniform.

He still loved to hook up as often as possible and whenever he was hanging out with the guys he would ask me to meet him. Most clients like having the middleman because they don't want a call girl having easy access to them, but once they get to know you they often like to make direct arrangements. We had been on the direct system for a while. To keep the peace, I never told Thorne about offline hookups. I'd often tell him that I was going out of town for leisure.

Although Rick may still have had money, I no longer expected the ten-thousand-dollar all-nighters we used to have. He'd usually offer a nominal rate for the weekend, usually a couple thousand dollars. I had a soft spot for Rick.

When I arrived in Vegas it was around noon, and I caught a taxi to his hotel and got the key from the front desk because he was on the Strip with his friends. After getting settled I went to the mall at Caesar's Palace to grab a few candles and massage oil. When I got back to the room I set the mood. I placed candles around the room and ran his bathwater. I knew exactly what he needed. Finally I called to let him know that I was there waiting for him. I was wearing a black thong and a black strapless sequined bra and a pair of platform heels.

I heard his key in the door and began to dance seductively for him. I'd choreographed a pretty basic erotic dance. He was smiling from ear to ear. He liked that I still treated him the same as if he were still paying top dollar. With him it wasn't about the money. Maybe, beneath the surface, I was still his groupie.

"See, that's what I like."

I batted my eyes. "What? You like me?"

"I like the way you make a nigga feel like a man."

He may not have been able to play football anymore, but that sure hadn't affected his sexual stamina. He was still as long and strong as before, so I always used stalling tactics. Anything, a massage, a bath, a dance, hell, there had been times I'd even sung him a song. Whatever I needed to do to decrease the number of rounds, I did it, especially when he downgraded to the budget plan.

I told him to take off his clothes and lie facedown on the bed. I climbed on top of him and massaged his shoulders. He said, "Man, sometimes I feel like I love you."

"Maybe you do."

"I don't know. You treat me so good."

"That's 'cause this is what you deserve."

"And you ain't asking for nothing in return."

He always told me that he could love me, but I knew that he never would. We had an arrangement and it worked for both of us. Although we'd grown closer, I still treated our hookups like business. He never had to worry about me wanting more from him. I gave him what he needed and afterward I stepped off. There was nothing more enticing for a man.

After I gave him a full body massage, I told him we should get in the tub. He said he wanted to make love first. So I obliged. And by the time we were about to get in the tub, the water was cold and I had to run it again.

We made love in the tub and several times after we got out. It was around one in the morning, but Rick was still in the mood to hang out. I wanted to lie in the room and relax. He begged me to tag along. I reluctantly agreed.

When he got in the shower I checked my cell phone and Thorne had called about four times. I figured I would call him back in the morning. I wasn't sure if he was trying to put me on the spot or what. By hooking up with Rick at a lower rate, I could interfere with Thorne's business. I wasn't sure if he'd gotten wind of me being here with Rick.

We went to a party in the Palms hotel. When we arrived, it appeared that an entire professional football team was there as well. Rick and I sat at the bar, watching the crowd and analyzing everyone. Usually Rick kept pretty cool and standoffish. No one was ever sure if we had come together or not, but he was more clingy than normal. I didn't mind because it made me feel good. I liked when he was that way. We dipped out a little early and headed back to the hotel.

The next morning, when Rick went to work out, I called Thorne. He picked up, saying, "London, you're in Vegas, right?"

Nervously, I said, "Yeah, what's up?"

"Well, I had a girl who was supposed to be there. She thinks she has the flu. I know you're on your personal time and all, but can you step in for her?"

"What are the arrangements?"

"Tonight around eight, and then Monday evening. I can text you all the specifics."

"Same client both days?"

"Nah. Two separate clients."

"Tonight may be shaky, but I can probably do Monday. I'll have to change my flight because I'm supposed to leave Monday morning."

"I appreciate you. I'll send you the specifics, and how soon can you let me know about tonight?"

I sighed. "Okay, Thorne. For you, I'll do tonight also."

Going on those other engagements would make up for Rick's subsidized payment. Later that evening I told Rick that I had something to do and I'd be back later. I wasn't sure if he knew in his heart that I was going to see another client or not. I'd always given Rick my undivided attention whenever we were together for a weekend. I felt the need to give him an excuse. "One of my girlfriends is also out here, and I'm going hang out with her for a while."

Since I never asked questions, I figured he thought he would provide me with the same respect. "That's cool, I'm going out too. I gotta get my gamble on."

"I understand."

I showered and put on a nice dress and headed out of our hotel en route to another client's place. The client had a stocky build and it appeared that he could have easily been a ballplayer. I smiled as I entered and he smiled back. He reached out to shake my hand. "Zach."

"Nice to meet you, Zach."

"And you are?"

"Kyra."

He wore a wife beater and a pair of boxers. There was nothing sensual about the mood in the room. I wanted to get it over with and get back to Caesar's Palace. I said, "So, whatchu need?"

He sat on the bed and rested his head back. "Whatchu gonna give me?"

I pulled my dress over my head and said, "I can give you this."

He didn't really have much of a personality so I wasn't interested in seeing why he needed me. With his type I like to get in, do my job, and leave. These gigs were usually uneventful.

I took off my clothes, grabbed a condom from my bag, and climbed on him. I began kissing his neck. He cupped my butt and once he got an erection, I slipped the condom on him and slid down on him. He was what I considered a gymnast. We were from this position to that position. The constant position-changing prolonged the climax and I hated that. Anyway, it was finally over. He gave me a thousand dollars, and I showered and headed back to Rick's room.

When I got there he was nowhere to be found. I popped a couple of sleeping pills so that I would be so zapped when Rick came in that he wouldn't be able to wake me if he tried. I sent him a text: "Felt like I was coming down w sumthin. Took some medicine. I'll b knocked out when u get in."

My bases were covered and I lay down, praying that he wouldn't even try to wake me. I was wrong. It seemed like a few minutes after I put my head on the pillow when Rick started shaking me. I tried to talk but words wouldn't come out. I was in between a deep sleep and a light consciousness. I heard him yelling at me. "Bitch, when I hire you for a fucking weekend, you belong to me!"

"Rick," I slurred.

"Don't Rick me, bitch!"

I could see him tossing my things from the room but I was too sleepy to reason with him. I tried to lie down, hoping Rick would just relax. But he pulled me by my leg from the room. My body was limp and too weak to resist. I was still a bit dreary as I tried to sit up outside his door. Shortly after he slammed the door security guards came and flashed lights in my eyes.

"Ma'am, can you hear me?"

"Yes, I can hear you," I said.

"Have you been drinking tonight?"

Another guard knocked on Rick's hotel room door. When he opened it, the guard asked if he knew me. He said, "No. Never seen her before."

"Ma'am, are you staying in this hotel?"

I looked up at Rick and said, "This is my room."

"The gentleman says he doesn't know you."

I was too tired to fight and too embarrassed to dispute what Rick was saying. But I called out for him one last time. "Rick," I said, almost as if I couldn't believe he was acting this way.

Rick looked sternly at the security guards. "Get this bitch away from my room."

The guards began to gather my things. "No problem, sir."

They spoke to him with the utmost respect, and I'm sure they knew he was bullshitting, but it didn't matter. As they helped me to my feet I felt like a hooker, and it didn't feel good.

The guards asked if I wanted to go to guest services to see if I could get a room. There were rooms available and the security staff escorted me to one. They didn't want me harassing Rick, but at least I didn't have to go out on the Strip partially drugged up. I lay in the bed and almost immediately fell back to sleep.

I didn't feel the effects of everything until the next morning. I woke up feeling like I'd run five miles. My muscles were hurting. There were rug burns on my arms and legs. I was in so much pain, both physically and emotionally. When I had knocked on Zach's room door, I should have turned around instead. A piece of me knew that he knew Rick, but I figured they both knew what business I was in and it wouldn't be a big deal. Rick's reaction seemed as if he had been taunted by the guys and forced into a senseless rage. Then again, Rick had been extremely sensitive lately. I wanted to apologize for offending him, because it hurt me that he was offended and I wanted to make it right. I just wasn't sure that I'd ever have the opportunity.

19

I stayed in Vegas for the additional day to hook up with the second client that Thorne had booked. During the two days between the fallout with Rick and the next client, I had a lot of time for self-reflection. I began to wonder if it was time to call it quits. Maybe I should do something different. I'd saved up a substantial amount of money in the hopes of purchasing a condo, but I'd begun to think maybe I'd live off that money for a while until I could figure this all out.

I wasn't feeling as confident as usual as I knocked on the door of the new client. I was dressed in a semiformal black dress because the client wanted me to attend a banquet with him. A short, light-skinned, nerdy guy opened the door to a fabulous room at Bellagio. He reached his hand out to shake mine.

"Hello. Very nice to meet you. I'm Clyde."

"I'm London."

It was pretty easy for me to determine whether I would tell a guy my real name or not. This guy seemed like he was on the up-and-up. He invited me in and offered me a drink. I said, "I'm fine."

His skin looked a little patchy and his hairline was receding horribly. When he smiled it seemed to camouflage all his imperfections. His teeth were light, bright, almost neon white. It appeared as if they were perfectly chiseled porcelain. I wasn't surprised to discover that he was a world-renowned orthodontist and dental surgeon. He had perfected the smiles of many celebrities and obviously his own as well.

Clyde almost immediately proclaimed to me that he was a lifelong bachelor as we headed out to the event. That was rather odd. Most of my clients were married men and it was pretty much a rarity to have an engagement with a single man.

He seemed to be pretty open about everything. I asked if there were any dos or don'ts to follow when we met up with his colleagues.

"Not at all. They know that I'm pretty strange."

"And what does that mean?"

"I mean, like if you told them that I hired you through an escort service, I don't think anyone would be surprised."

"I think I'd rather just keep that between us. That would probably spark too many questions of me."

He laughed. "Yeah, probably."

Clyde seemed like a geek, but he was actually cool and adventurous. The evening slightly pushed those uncomfortable thoughts about Rick out of my mind. I was unexpectedly enjoying myself. We mingled with his colleagues, danced, and had pretty good conversation.

When we returned from the event Clyde asked me to come in. He was quite an interesting person, so I was curious to know more about him.

"So why did you deem yourself a lifelong bachelor?"

"Well, I've never been married. Never lived with anyone. Never really even been committed to anyone."

"And why is that?"

"I guess I'm too selfish."

"That would make sense."

"I like my freedom. I work hard. I play harder."

"And you don't feel that you could do that while in a relationship?"

"Now what woman do you think could handle a spontaneous man?"

"I'm sure there are some."

"I doubt it. I'll never be tied down."

"I understand."

When we returned to his hotel room he wasted no time getting down to business. He unbuttoned his shirt and had a really nice chest, to my surprise. After he took the shirt off there were more goodies in store. His arms were nice and muscular. He wasn't a bad catch. The entire time he was proclaiming how he'd be single forever, I was thinking, *Clyde, please, you are not all that.*

He asked if I would get in the shower with him and I agreed. I took off my dress, grabbed a condom from my purse, and followed him into the bathroom. He closed the door and steam began to fill the room as he kissed me in the middle of the bathroom. We clung to each other and I could feel him rising. He pushed me up to the door and lifted my legs.

As he slowly entered me, I moaned. Clyde was gentle and passionate. He took pride in his lovemaking. Usually I fake orgasms but I didn't have to with him. That was a first. Everything in this business was an act, but it just happened. I kissed his shoulders and rubbed the back of his head. I could tell he knew he was genuinely satisfying me. Being with Clyde made me long for real affection.

We showered together and shared a glass of champagne

afterward. Lying in bed, Clyde and I just talked about nothing. He was telling me about all his adventures. I just listened and I think he appreciated that. When he said he loved to deep-sea dive, I perked up. "I've always wanted to dive."

"You know, I've never once had a black woman say that to me."

"Really."

"Really. You should come to Mexico with me tomorrow."

Talk about spontaneity. I wasn't sure I was in the mood to up and go to Mexico the next day. "What part?"

"Puerto Vallarta. C'mon. It'll be fun."

Why not? I thought. All I really needed to be concerned about was Bruno, but that would just be a matter of calling the kennel and extending his stay. So I agreed.

The next morning Clyde got me a last-minute flight to Puerto Vallarta. We weren't on the same plane, but I arrived within thirty minutes of his. When we got there I had to immediately go shopping for some beach clothes because I didn't have any in my suitcase. Clyde went with me. He helped me pick out clothes. He was an all-out active participant in the shopping spree. I enjoyed that. He was extremely funny and people seemed to gravitate to him.

One girl asked, "Is he always so funny?"

I was thinking, *Girl, I know as much about him as you do.* Instead I smiled and nodded. I had to purchase a wet suit for my diving lessons. Clyde was a seasoned diver. I wasn't quite sure why he'd asked me to join him in Mexico because we would be spending our days apart, as he'd be out in the sea. I, on the other hand, would be learning how to dive in the resort pool with a bunch of other amateurs.

When we got back to our room both Clyde and I were tired so we jumped in the sack and drifted off to sleep. It was around a quarter to eight when we woke up. We were starving and headed out to find something to eat at the resort.

Over dinner Clyde said, "I'm glad you could join me. Sometimes vacationing alone gets boring."

"I would think it wouldn't be a problem to find someone to join you."

"Well, I like too much weird stuff and I don't want to deal with a bunch of eewing."

I laughed. "What's eewing?"

"You know how women do, 'Eew, that's nasty' or 'Eew, you want to do that?' That's eewing. I can't stand it."

"So are you saying women mess up your flow?"

"No, I'm just saying women live by a bunch of damn rules and I like to break the rules. If I feel like pissing in the pool, leave me the hell alone."

Eew. I decided to keep my thoughts to myself and smiled.

"All women aren't like that."

He nodded toward me. "Obviously. That's why you're here with me."

I hadn't totally figured Clyde out, but I got a feeling that being single was his defense mechanism. It protected him from himself, because it was clear that he was lonely. Somewhere in his past someone had done something to hurt him and he had subsequently become a rebel. I wasn't certain I'd figure it out this week, but if he became a regular I was sure I'd be able to read him a little better.

The first couple of days there I explored Puerto Vallarta after my two-hour diving lesson. Finally, around the fourth day, I was brave enough to take the plunge. It was breathtaking as I submerged. All I could hear were the peaceful sounds of the ocean. Fish swimming by, tropical-colored fish in schools. It was beauty in its rarest form. The sounds of the Earth were so far away. I could hear nothing but my own breathing. The compression tank on my back felt lighter under the water, just like all my issues—they floated to the top of the ocean as I sank deeper. At twenty feet below, I was convinced that I belonged here. No noise. No weight. No worries. I loved it.

When my compression tank began to signal that it was time for me to ascend, I was thinking *Damn, not now.* It was either now or that would be my last dive. I swam up to the surface and Clyde was climbing onto the boat. He slapped me a high five as I followed. Once we were both on board, he took off his goggles. Clyde seemed so sexy in his wet suit. It clung to his short, stocky body. Maybe it was the dive, but I wanted to lie close to Clyde and make continuous love to him. Or maybe I was trying to solidify my position in his life. I wanted to be his ride-or-dive chick.

20

Kari loved the attention she got wearing a sexy short dress, but she still didn't know how to shop for herself. So whenever I was in town I tried to make time to be her personal shopper. I gave her a call to see what time she wanted to step out. She answered, sounding frustrated.

"You would never believe this."

"What?"

"My AC is broken. I'm going to have to come over there until it gets fixed."

"When did they say it would be fixed?"

"It could be days. Several units in my building are broken and I just don't know."

How could I say no? But I wasn't sure I wanted her in my space, especially considering I was scheduled to see someone at midnight. Reluctantly, I said, "You know you're welcome to stay here."

"When Ian leaves, I'll come over."

I kidded, "Ooh, Ian. So he spends the night."

"Quite frequently."

"Why didn't you tell me?"

"I just wanted to make sure first."

"I can't blame you."

"Yeah, you know how it is."

"He can come too if you want."

"Nah, he's going out of town."

I wondered if that was true or if she was uncomfortable with me around her man. I had yet to meet him but I'd thought it was because of my schedule. It could have been intentional.

Around noon Kari came over, looking as blissful as I'd ever seen her. This Ian guy was panning out to be everything she wanted. She sat on the couch and began to tell me how she really wasn't interested at first, but that he was such a nice guy she gave him a chance.

"I mean, he's not tall, dark, and handsome, but we are so compatible."

"That's all that matters."

"Yeah, man. You're going to be shocked when you see him. He's not cute at all but he makes me so happy."

She had no clue how many unattractive men I had been with over the past couple of years. "Everybody wants somebody fine, but in the big scheme of things looks don't make you happy. Temporarily maybe, but not forever. That's why there are so many divorces."

"You're right."

It was hot and muggy outside so Kari and I decided to stay in and just have girl talk. I missed having someone around. Being with a different man every night was lonely. There was no substance to any of my relationships.

Later that evening Kari cooked dinner and I opened a bottle of wine. We laughed about old times and talked about our futures. She suggested that I do something more with my life. She couldn't understand how I was wasting all my qualities being the other woman. I insisted that I walked dogs for a living.

Kari looked at me with such concern that I couldn't be defensive. "London, the only dog you walk is Bruno. What happened to you? You were so smart. Now you're just chilling waiting for a married man to take you shopping. I miss my girl. When we were in school, you seemed so focused."

"Kari, I'm still focused. Trust me."

As I dressed to go out I thought about the things Kari was saying. From the outside looking in, I was wasting my life away. I hated being perceived that way, but I wasn't motivated to get up every day and work a nine-to-five for pennies. Then again, there were days when I'd rather sacrifice the money for normalcy. There were conflicting emotions raging in me as I headed out of the house.

Kari said, "You sure look pretty. Where you guys going?"

"Just out."

"It's late for dinner and you ain't dressed for a booty call."

"I still like to impress him."

"That's cool."

I arrived at the hotel in Arlington a few minutes after twelve. When I knocked on the door a tall white man dressed in a suit opened it. I entered and looked around. His iPod was connected to the clock radio and it sounded like elevator music.

"How are you this evening?" I asked, before sitting on the bed.

He reached out to shake my hand. "Timothy, and you are?"

"I'm London."

"Nice to meet you, London."

I pulled my dress up so he could see that I wasn't wearing

panties. He loosened his tie and began to unbutton his shirt. I kicked off my heels and scooted back on the bed and began to masturbate, hoping to arouse him quickly. His suit was on the floor in a matter of seconds. He got a condom and turned the lights out before diving into me. After a few strokes he flipped over so I could be on top. I pulled my dress over my head as I ground on him.

He grabbed my arms and placed them around his neck. "Choke me."

Ugh! I hated men with the choking fetish. I placed one hand around his neck and softly pushed my thumb into his throat. He said, "Harder."

I pressed a little harder, but it still wasn't good enough. He demanded I do it until he stopped breathing. I hated that game and that night was no different. I stopped moving and said, "I'm not going to do this."

"Just a little bit harder," he said, as he raised his butt to push deeper.

I decided to apply enough pressure to excite him, but not too much. Suddenly he stopped moving. It felt like he'd gone limp inside me. *Oh shit.* I jumped off him and began to shake him. He almost appeared to be sleeping. I turned the light on, rushed to the bathroom, and got a cup of cold water. I splashed it in his face and began to smack him. My heart raced. I'd begun to gasp for breath as I wondered what the hell I was going to do. I smacked harder and harder with all my might. *Wake up. You bastard. Wake up.*

He slowly opened his eyes. I panted as I covered my face. All my organs had stopped functioning too. He smiled at me and I wanted to spit on him. "What is wrong with you? This shit is not funny."

"Calm down. It happens all the time."

I grabbed my dress and slipped it over my head. "Not with me."

"We're not done."

"I am."

I grabbed my bag and stormed out of his room. I wanted no part of that. I had done the choking thing before but no one had actually passed out on me. He could keep his money for all I cared as the door slammed behind me. When I got to my car my heart was still beating fast. What if he had died? How would I have ever explained myself? Who would have believed it was a sex act gone wrong? What if I had gotten arrested for murder? My life flashed before my eyes. I was going nowhere fast.

When I walked into my apartment I leaned my back against the door as if I were being chased. It was quiet and calm. I checked on Kari and she was sound asleep. I sat down in the living room and all I could think of was being in jail. I felt like it was time to get it together.

21

When I woke up the next day Kari was making breakfast. She said, "Good morning."

"Morning, Kari."

"You got back early last night. I wasn't expecting you until this morning."

"Why?" I paused. "You know he's married, right?"

She turned from the stove. "Is that why you were crying last night?"

"Why didn't you check on me if you heard me?"

"London, through all that you and your college beau went through and the things you've gone through with your mother, I've never seen you cry. Ever. You're the hardest girl I know and I was just stunned. I didn't know what to say but I slept on it and figured I'd bring it up this morning and see if you wanted to talk."

I took several long, deep breaths. The past two and a half years of bottling up my feelings came pouring out. I told her what I'd been doing, why I'd been missing. I gave no names. I didn't tell her that Thorne was the organizer, but I told her my role and how I thought I was coming to the end of my rope. Kari was stunned. She couldn't believe that

I had stooped so low for no real reason except money. She reminded me that it was the root of all evil.

"London, you deserve so much better. Don't settle for that. Leave that to women without a brain."

After spending the morning explaining my complicated life, I called Thorne. He agreed to do lunch. We met at a bar and grill downtown. When I entered, Thorne was already seated. He waved me over to the table. I leaned in for a kiss on the cheek. I hadn't told him anything when I called, but he'd immediately picked up on me. He said, "Talk to me. What's going on?"

"I'm tired. I'm not sure I want to do this anymore."

"That's valid."

I'd thought he would try to talk me out of it, so I waited before continuing. "I don't really know how other people manage two lives and I've been doing this for too long. I don't even have a personal life anymore. I don't even have feelings anymore."

"So you feel like you're missing something, huh?"

"Not really missing something, but—"

"No, no. I understand because you do miss a lot."

"I guess. I don't know what I'm feeling."

"Are a lot of your friends beginning to settle down and get married?"

"Not those really close to me, but people indirectly related to me."

"It's typical that around twenty-six or so, women start envying their friends who are married and having babies. So they begin to resent the lifestyle, feeling like it has somehow prevented them from significant relationships."

"Yeah, I don't know what I feel right now. I think I just need a break."

He swallowed some water and shook his head, staring into my eyes. "London, I feel like I tried to teach you things, but then again I feel like I failed you."

"What do you mean?"

"I mean, what's your backup plan?"

I shrugged. "I don't know."

"Are you still walking dogs?"

"Not really. I create false receipts so that I can claim for taxes, but for the most part I haven't walked dogs in a long time and that's slow, slow money. I really don't know what I'm going to do."

"A part of this is my fault. You were always available and I let you be my go-to girl and I think it prevented you from pursuing all your other dreams. Now what are we going to do?"

"It's not the end of the world, Thorne. I have enough money saved to figure out my next step. Maybe I'll go back to school."

"I can use an administrator."

"At Quinn Forrester?"

"No, at William Thorne."

"What would be my role?"

"Making arrangements."

"You wouldn't let me do that. Would you?"

"London, you've done more than enough for me. You've taken the jobs nobody wanted to take. This is the least I can do for you in the meantime. Until we figure out what you're going to do."

"I've always wanted to open a kennel."

He explained the importance of taking an average idea and placing your own spin on it. He told me that he believed I was a good businesswoman and he would help me get my business plan together. He asked, "So what would you say you've been reporting as business earnings?"

"A little more than half. Whatever I deposit in the account is what I claim."

"Good, that's a start. If you're really serious about starting a kennel or dog motel, we will have to start with your current business earnings. Investors like to see what your earning potential is without a budget and the more you earned on your own, the more they think the business will return a profit with investors."

While we sat at lunch, he made a series of phone calls to get the ball rolling with my kennel idea. He set up a meeting with a company that wrote business proposals and instructed me to begin writing my ideas down. In the meantime I would be relieving some of his load as far as booking was concerned.

22

I was officially out of the business and living on savings as I followed all of Thorne's advice to start up my company. When my business plan was done we sat down in front of a few investors and, like the old saying goes, I only needed one yes. When I got it, it was a matter of getting things into motion. I found two brownstones side by side that were being auctioned off by the city. They were in northwest DC, right off of New York Avenue and just about a mile from the White House. The community was up and coming. There were many new condominium complexes being renovated and built. It was prime real estate. I had an architect design the blueprint for the facility. I wanted it to look like an upscale hotel. I used inspiration from all the rooms I'd been in as I tried to convey what I envisioned. We went with the name Unleashed. The investors liked it and so did I. My logo was designed by a graphics company and Thorne suggested I hire it as a brand manager.

Everything was in motion, and just as the contractors began working I realized we were drying up funds at an exponential rate. Thorne suggested I go back to the investors to see if I could get more, but they turned me down. If I got a loan and invested more of a percentage, I would earn more of a percentage on the back end. So I did just that. I went back to the bank for more money. It gave me pretty much a few more pennies, but I resorted to credit cards as a backup.

We were back in action, and in about twelve months Unleashed opened its doors. The business started out slower than I expected. I was practically robbing one person to pay the other. I hated living like that. I wasn't cut from the struggling cloth but I knew that all business owners had to do it at one point or another. Some of my ex-dog-walking clients stopped by for the open house, but no one booked a dog to stay. I opened the doors in the middle of October and maybe that had something to do with it. I couldn't imagine it would be summer before I reaped anything from this. I could hear my mother's voice telling me there was no money in dog care. As I struggled to make ends meet, I agreed.

It had been a year and a half since the incident and I had sworn that I would never go back, but as I stood waist-deep in debt, there was only one way for me to make the type of money I needed. I called Thorne and simply said, "Put me back in the portfolio."

"London, I think you should keep doing what you're doing. Things will turn around."

"Look, you've given me enough money and I've borrowed money from anyone who would give it to me. I'm back in. That ten percent you've been giving me for being your admin is not enough. In order for my business to survive, I have to make some money other ways."

Thorne was hesitant, but he knew as well as I did that there was only one way out. "Okay, London."

23

While the first year of running Unleashed was a struggle, after five years as a call girl business, it was my best one yet. Thorne would only hook me up with longtime clients and many of them were charming and respectable. Several were out of town. They were always the easy ones, just men who were away from their wives looking for a little something different while on vacation.

Clyde was glad that I'd gotten back into the business. Thorne told me he'd been asking about me since the Mexico trip. Once I was back in the game, Clyde and I went on three different diving vacations together. I don't know what it was about Clyde but each time I was with him, I returned home feeling like I wanted a relationship. And it was weird because although we vacationed together like long-lost lovers, once it was over I didn't hear from him until he either wanted to hook up or go away to dive.

Thorne called just as I was packing for my Australian vacation with Clyde. Maybe it was because Clyde was single, but I sensed a bit of jealousy whenever I went on vacation with him. Thorne asked, "Do you need a ride to the airport?"

"Thorne, you know I always get a car service."

He laughed. "Yeah, but I'm sitting here in my office, thinking about you and—"

"And you want to come see me before I leave."

I never knew if he did this with everyone, but after I became his assistant it seemed like our relationship went from warm to hot. When we were together I felt like it was just the two of us. It seemed like we had so much in common and that if I hadn't accepted his proposal, we might have found ourselves in a relationship from the start. I went back and forth in my mind with those thoughts each time he knocked at my door. Shortly after I hung up he rang the bell.

I'd barely stepped out of my clothes from walking the dogs. Bruno barked and looked at the door like, *Who the hell is it?* I laughed as I softly kicked him away from the door. Thorne walked in and Bruno jumped on him. He always pushed Bruno off like he was a damn nuisance. I didn't like how he did that, but I guess Bruno was a bit overbearing.

"Move, Bruno," I said as I kissed Thorne.

He held me tightly. "My favorite girl."

"Don't make me blush."

Men love to believe that we don't know when they're bullshitting us. He hugged me again. "You're definitely my favorite girl."

"And you're my favorite."

He tilted his head to the side and smirked.

"You are," I said, laughing.

"And it's snowing in California."

"Is it really?"

"London, you're funny."

He walked over to my couch and sat down. I sat beside him, tucking my right foot under me as I faced him. I placed my hands on his thigh. Referring to the small Saks bag he was carrying, I asked, "Is that for me?"

He shook his head no. I assumed he thought I would be disappointed. Instead I grabbed the remote and turned the television on. I continued to massage his thigh with one hand. He looked at me and said, "You're special. You know that?"

"No, tell me why."

He leaned over for a kiss. "You're just one of a kind." He reached for the bag. "Of course this is for you."

"Thank you. What did I do to deserve this?"

"You make me a lot of money."

I rolled my eyes and grabbed the bag. "So this is like a bonus, huh?"

"No, it's a gift from me to you."

I pulled the box from the bag. He'd bought me a pair of Gucci sunglasses.

"I know how much you like your sunshades. I certainly couldn't send my favorite girl to Australia without new shades."

Certainly he knew me well enough to know that I'd purchased multiple pairs of shades for my trip. He continued, "That would make me look bad."

"Why would you say that?"

"I want you looking like a million bucks when you're out with clients. That gets me more clients."

It was times when he talked like that that I felt like a piece of meat, but deep down I knew that Thorne had purchased those glasses because he wanted to get me a gift. Whenever he bought something for me he rationalized his purchase. I used to get offended when he explained his purchases; now

I just accepted them. It was clear that he thought about me more often than not.

I straddled him and wrapped my arms around his neck. "Are you sure that's the only reason?"

He smiled, but didn't respond. I gyrated on him. "I was on your mind, right?"

He nodded.

"I never leave your mind, do I?"

"No, London." He spoke in a slightly stern manner.

"It's okay," I said, as I leaned my forehead on his. We began to kiss passionately for what seemed like forever. He held me tightly and for a moment it felt like we were both caught up, as if he never wanted to let me go. A part of me didn't want him to. He was the one constant in my life and despite everything I knew he was there. As we clung to each other in the heat of passion, I wondered what he was thinking. I hoped that we'd always be this close. Suddenly, like he'd been struck by lightning, he stopped. His arms relaxed and his lips retreated. He'd never done this before. I looked at him and touched his face. "Are you okay, Thorne?"

"You know it's against the rules to fall for one of your clients."

"But you're not a client."

He looked into my eyes. "Don't fall for me, either."

I climbed off him and sat back on the couch. "What are you talking about? I never said I was falling for you."

"You wouldn't say it if you were. But I'm not talking about me. I'm talking about Clyde."

I laughed. "Thorne, c'mon now. What makes you think I'm falling for Clyde?"

"It just seems like every time you're about to go away with him, you get this look of euphoria. I just can't explain it."

"Did you ever think that I love the places he takes me?"

"But other men have taken you on trips."

"Most men take me to regular commercial places. Clyde, he picks eclectic vacations. And I just love it."

"If you fall for a client, you know I'll fire you."

I didn't speak immediately. I couldn't believe the one man, if any, I loved was sitting there threatening to fire me for no reason. If I did fall for Clyde and the feeling was mutual, damn if I'd need to work for him again. It was like he heard my thoughts.

"It never works out. He'll never see you as a serious prospect because of the way you met. That's why I have to constantly warn y'all not to lose focus. If you're going to have a relationship, he can't know you from this profession."

As often as I'd heard that and as much as I knew it to be true, it hurt hearing it like this. Why had he even come over to ruin my high? I wanted him to leave. I stood up. I was livid. "Thorne, I don't need you to keep reminding me of this. I know. I know they will always see me as a call girl. I know you can't turn a ho into a housewife. I know all of these things, so why in the hell do you feel the need to keep reminding me? You recruited me into this profession. You told me how wonderful it was. Now all I hear is that I'll never be with anyone seriously."

I stormed into my bedroom. He followed. "Just leave. Leave my house."

Bruno ran into the room and began to bark. He could tell that I was very upset. Thorne grabbed me and put his arms around me. "I'm sorry, London. Maybe I do that to protect myself. Maybe it's me that never wants you to fall for anybody."

I asked him what I'd wanted to ask for nearly a year. "Would you ever see me differently?"

He hung his head as he pulled me to him. "I don't know."

It stung me deep but I knew he was being honest. He had feelings for me that he couldn't understand. He knew better than to be spending time with me the way he had been. I was supposed to just make money. I was never supposed to become his mistress.

24

By the time I arrived in Australia I'd gone over a million different scenarios in my mind. What if Thorne left his wife and we lived happily ever after? Or what if Clyde fell deeply in love with me? Though I tried to live my life without feeling too much, those suppressed emotions slowly began to creep up and tap me on my shoulder. I wanted to feel special to someone too.

When I arrived in Sydney it was the crack of dawn. I saw the sun rise over the plane as we landed. I was completely exhausted from twenty-three hours in the air. By the time I made it through customs it was just a little after seven, but you couldn't tell by the refreshed and rested look on Clyde's face. He was waiting for me and showing every single one of his sparkling whites. *Wouldn't it be nice to have someone greet me this way every day?* But this was only a temporary fling that I would be compensated for. I had been doing this for so long, I didn't know what it felt like to go out with a man without calculating how much I'd earn, without knowing this man wanted nothing more from me than a couple of hours or days of my time.

Clyde wrapped his short arms around me and kissed my cheek. "London, I'm so glad you're here. This place is beautiful."

"I bet. I can't wait to see it."

"I can't wait for you to see it. Where we're going, from what I hear, is unbelievable."

We headed to check in with Jetstar Airways to get our flight to Hamilton Island. Once we finally boarded the plane I was done with the small talk. I wanted to go to sleep. Every muscle was achy, and before we took off I was out. A few hours later we arrived at Hamilton Island. There we boarded a helicopter to take us to our final destination. The Coral Sea looked like it was dyed the most perfect aqua blue. I wanted to jump off the helicopter and just dive in. I joked with Clyde about the thought and he suggested we try sky-diving. I'll pretty much try anything once, but that wasn't something I was interested in.

When we flew over the Great Barrier Reef, the largest coral reef system in the world, I was anxious to put on my wet suit and let the diving begin. All the beauty below made me forget how tired I was when I arrived in Sydney. Finally we landed on Hayman Island. The resort was breathtaking. I looked at Clyde and he smiled. "Nice, huh?"

"This is beyond fabulous."

The Hayman staff greeted us at the helicopter and we stepped into paradise. Our bags were carried away and would meet us in our suite. After we'd checked in we headed to the first-level suite. The private balcony hovered over the resort's pool. The architecture was futuristic. White tailored bedding and geometrically designed honey oak furniture accented the sleek and contemporary décor. I stepped onto the balcony as Clyde tipped the bellboy, who arrived almost immediately after we did. I stood there alone, soaking up the beautiful scenery. It was something from a dream. I had visited many places and very few had taken my breath away. I was at a loss for words. I looked out into the sea and reflected on what I had been thinking about earlier. I still wasn't sure if this life was worth it, but damn, how else or when else would I be able to see the world in this fashion? *I may as well do it while I'm young.* I lifted my shades to fully absorb my surroundings. I sat down on the patio chair and Clyde came out with a chilled bottle of champagne and two flute glasses.

"This is the way to get the party started," I said, laughing.

He popped the bottle and the bubbles poured out into my glass. I slurped the edge of the glass so it wouldn't spill over. Clyde sat down beside me.

"Do you love this place or what?"

"I think I do."

"My only gripe is that you don't see any of us walking around here."

I laughed, because I'd had the same thought when we flew into Sydney. I felt like a zebra walking through the airport and people were looking at me like a damn exhibit. I said, "This is quite a homogenous society."

His eyebrows wrinkled and then he said, "Oh yeah, I forgot you told me you were a biology major."

"Uh, and what does that have to do with anything?"

"Regular people just don't use the word *homogenous* like that."

"Maybe most people are in diverse surroundings and they don't have to use the word, but when you come to a place like Australia and everyone has blond hair and blue eyes, you can't help but say it."

"I guess, London." He lifted his glass as if to signal a truce. "I'm glad you could meet me here. I've been planning to dive here for some years now. My schedule never permitted, though."

I touched his hand. "Well, I'm certainly glad we were able to coordinate our schedules."

Looking into his eyes, I leaned over and pecked him on the cheek. Though money for him was no issue, I wanted to thank him for bringing me here.

"So is there anything particular you'd like to do today?" he asked.

"Sleep."

"I'll let you rest and I'll meet you for dinner. What do you think about that?"

It was a wonderful idea. Although I'd been reinvigorated by the sights, my body was tired and I needed to rest comfortably for a minute. I went into the bathroom to turn the shower on and came back into the room to grab my toiletries out of my suitcase. Standing in front of a long mirror, I pulled my hair into a ponytail. Clyde walked up behind me and put his arm around my waist. He kissed softly around my neck and shoulders. I reached up to wrap my hands around the back of his head.

"Can I take a shower with you?"

"Of course."

I came out of my clothes and Clyde miraculously was out of his in a matter of seconds. He said, "I forgot, you like your water super hot."

"There's a double-headed shower in here so you can have your water however you like."

"Perfect."

Adjusting his showerhead, I asked, "Is this good?"

He stuck his fingers under the water and nodded affirmatively. I stepped in and he followed. We kissed slowly and he held me as the water poured down our backs. We stood there clinging to each other for almost five minutes. Finally, he

began to wash my back and I did his. We both lathered up
and washed off a few times. His penis was poking straight
out at me. He'd placed condoms right outside the shower and
he reached out to grab one. After sliding it on, he asked me
to bend over. He entered me from behind and slowly began
to grind. I sighed pleasurably. As the water continued to rain
down on us, we made slow love until he climaxed. We both
did another rinse-down and by this time I was totally ready
to pass out for the rest of the day.

I dried off and lay in the bed naked. Clyde came over to
kiss my forehead. "I'm going out to see what other excursions are available and make reservations for dinner. Then
I'm just going to lounge around the resort. I'll wake you up
around six."

"Sounds good to me."

My head hit the pillow and I can't recall anything in
between that and Clyde tapping my shoulder. "London, were
you able to rest?"

Yawning, I asked, "Is it already six?"

"Actually, it's seven."

"Oh my goodness. I must have been really sleepy."

"You were."

"Good thing we'll be here for seven days. I don't feel so
bad about losing an entire day."

I sat up in the bed. Clyde said, "We have reservations at
eight."

"Okay, let me get myself together."

Clyde and I went to dinner at Azure, a restaurant on the
resort. We had a candlelight dinner on the water. Though
we'd been away several times before, maybe it was Thorne
planting the seed in my mind, but I began to wonder how it
would be to be with Clyde seriously. It was obvious we had a

lot in common. He loved adventure just as much as I did. He loved to travel and eat different foods. We were compatible. I wondered if he'd ever see me differently. He certainly treated me like a lady whenever we were together. I'd never had the desire to do this, but I asked, "Clyde, do you still think you'll be single forever?"

He nearly choked on the roll he was eating. "I don't know."

"You've never had the desire for something more real?"

"Sometimes, but then I just give you a call."

"So do you feel like what we're doing is real?"

"For the time that we do it, yeah."

"So why don't we talk in between times?"

"London, that's why I pay you."

My neck snapped back. "Huh?"

"I pay not to be questioned."

I'd definitely slipped momentarily. He was right. It was inappropriate for me to be asking these types of questions. Clearly I'd gotten too comfortable with our relationship. I began to understand why Thorne didn't recommend having regular clients for too long. Unconsciously, women slip into relationship mode when they see too much of one guy.

Clyde had drawn the line and I was back in working girl mode when we woke up at six in the morning to board the boat for our diving adventure. We both reluctantly rose to slide into our wet suits. Grabbing our equipment, we rushed out the door. I wasn't even sure I'd gotten all the sleep out of my eyes.

We hopped in the boat with almost ten other couples and we were headed to the Great Barrier Reef. As always, inquiring minds wanted to know if we were honeymooning or dating and how long we'd been together. Clyde and

I had a script that we followed. We'd been dating less than six months, we'd met in Vegas and discovered that we both enjoyed diving. It always seemed to generate a bunch of oohs and aahs. We had become good at smiling the adoration off and turning the attention to something else. This morning was no different. The diving coach gave us basic instructions like always. I was just anxious to get twenty feet below sea level so I could clear my head.

Finally it was our turn to climb into the small boat and sink into the water. I went first and Clyde followed. Watching the fish in the deep blue sea usually took all my pain away. As I sank deep alongside Clyde, the weight of my lifestyle was still heavy. I regretted it. The peace that I usually felt underwater was gone.

When we got back to the room Clyde walked out onto the patio and I sat in the room. He hadn't said much to me since the interrogation. I wanted to rewind my actions but it was too late. I walked onto the patio and stood behind Clyde.

"I'm sorry if I made you uncomfortable yesterday."

"Oh no, it's not heavy."

"I know you and I could never have anything serious and I should have never questioned why we don't talk in between times."

"I know you didn't mean it, London. I ask myself all the time why we don't talk in between times, but it just would never work. I'm a bachelor and you're a prostitute."

I gasped. I couldn't believe he'd said it so bluntly.

Raising his hands in a defenseless manner, he continued, "No offense, but as compatible as we are, what we are makes us incompatible."

"What are we outside of these self-imposed labels?"

"These aren't labels. They are traits. I like a variety of

women. You obviously like a variety of men. So why should we waste our time trying to pursue something deeper?"

"I don't like a variety of men."

"Look, London. Maybe you don't, but clearly you are not a monogamous person."

"I could be."

"And you could not be too. So, like I said, why would we even waste our time?"

It hurt to hear how he viewed me. I was completely capable of being monogamous but I figured trying to convince Clyde of it was a losing battle. So I simply agreed. I remained in business mode for the rest of our trip. If I was going to be with someone, it definitely wouldn't be with someone I had met this way.

25

I decided to stay overnight with my mother during my lay-over in San Francisco on my return from Australia. When I called to let her know that I'd be there, she sounded almost like she wanted to see me. It was close to midnight when I came in from flying all day. My mother pulled up to pick me up in her brand-new Lexus. Her hair was pulled back in a bun and she wore khaki pants and a peach short-sleeved sweater. She had accessorized with gold costume jewelry, a necklace and clip-on earrings.

We hugged when she stepped out of the car. It had been a long time since we'd spent any quality time together. That was by design on my part. Not sure exactly what she felt. She always told me how much she missed me, but I had mixed emotions about her. While I was grateful that she had raised me and given me a quality education, I didn't know if that gratitude translated into love.

When I sat in the car, it felt like she was a stranger. And I sensed that she felt the same about me. She looked at me strangely and said, "London, you look so gorgeous."

"Thanks, Mom."

She touched my arm and stroked it as we drove off. "London, you look so good."

While I appreciated her compliments, it made me wonder what she'd imagined I'd look like. I repeated, "Thanks, Mom."

"So tell me all the exciting things you're up to. What were you doing in Australia?"

"Well, I'm doing what I love to do. Taking care of dogs."

"So that's working out well, I see."

"Yes, extremely well."

I spoke with arrogance because she had tried her best to change my mind. She hadn't wanted me to be a vet or even work with dogs. She'd made it clear that she'd paid too much for me to go to school for me not to get a return. She would shoot herself if she found out what I really did for a living, which is why I kept my distance.

My mother lived in a high-rise condominium. We pulled into the building's garage and we headed up to her condo on the sixth floor. I said, "Wow, I never imagined you to live in a condo."

My mother had loved her house in Arlington. It was a large four-bedroom Colonial and she'd kept it meticulous. I would never have thought she'd leave, but I assumed she loved her job a little more. We entered her place and it appeared she'd settled in well. The place was contemporary and inviting. The smell of candles lingered. She walked me to the room where I would be staying. It was decorated almost like my room in our home in Arlington. It startled me and made me wonder if this was her way of feeling close to me.

"I'll let you get settled in. If you want, I'll make some tea."

"That's cool."

I was really in no mood for tea. Really, all I wanted to do was sleep. But it would be unfair to say that. So I changed into my pajamas, washed my face, and headed into the kitchen. The kettle began to whistle just as I walked in. She smiled at me, still seemingly cautious and distant. As she poured the water into the mugs, she placed her hand on my shoulder. "Do you still like a ton of sugar in your tea?"

She had always tried to restrict my sugar intake, but I still found ways to get it. My metabolism was like a damn race car. Everything I ate was burned up in a matter of minutes. I don't know why, but I always felt like my mother envied that. She stayed on a diet, always watching her weight, and I ate whatever I wanted and never gained an ounce.

"Yep, I'm still a sugar junkie."

She grabbed the sugar canister and sat down beside me. "You know, London, I'm glad you called."

"Oh, Ma."

"You get the stubbornness from me."

"What do you mean? I wasn't trying to be stubborn."

"No, I was. So many days I think about how torn our relationship is and I think about calling you to help you but I just don't do it."

"Help me?"

"I know it's hard out here, being young and trying to make your way. And I've just left you out there."

"I'm fine, Mother."

"Walking people's dogs? Is that really what you want to do for the rest of your life?"

It was interesting that even in her attempt to make peace, she couldn't resist being condescending. I shook my head, thinking, *This is exactly why I cut her ass off in the first place.* But I was glad that I had come here, so that I could finally get over the guilt I felt from time to time for wanting to disown her.

"Yes. I only have upper-class clientele. They pay me a lot of money to look after their dogs."

"So you're kinda like a dog nanny. These people take you on trips with them, in somewhat the same way."

Usually when I travel I tell her that I'm going with one of my clients. I just shook my head. I began to believe that I shouldn't even have made this stop. When I didn't respond, she continued, "Is this what you want to do forever? You're so smart. You could run a real business."

Little did she know I was running a business—a very lucrative one. I said, "Listen, I am very happy. I can afford to take care of myself and I don't understand why you can't understand that I'm doing something that I love."

She raised one eyebrow. "Do you really? Or are you afraid of real work?"

"Actually, I do. I'm content making six figures walking dogs and running a kennel."

"You earn that kind of money walking dogs?"

"Yes."

"Well, maybe it's not a bad deal, it just sounds so degrading. A dog walker," she said as she cringed.

I sat quietly as she tried to make small talk. I gave curt responses to everything, thinking I should have just gone to sleep. Obliviously she asked, "Did I offend you?"

"No, I'm not offended. I'm just irritated."

"Well, let me rephrase. Did I irritate you?"

"Yes, you did."

"Why does any- and everything I say to you irritate you?"

"Because you're a nag. Did anyone ever tell you that you nag?"

It was as those words exited my mouth that I understood

why men would rather pay for sex than listen to a nagging woman. It was easier to just get it in and keep it moving than to be bothered with this.

She covered her chest like she was offended. "Yes, Mother. You nag and it's irritating. We haven't spent much time together in six years and the first thing you want to talk to me about is what I do for a living. Let me give you a tip: That's superficial conversation and I refuse to participate in it."

Her eyes watered. I'd seen her cry before, but never over something that I'd said. She said, "London, can I ask you something?"

At this point I was still fired up, so I snapped, "What?"

"Do you love me?"

"Do you love me?"

"I asked you first."

"You verbalized it first, but I've questioned it my whole life. So, technically, I asked first. Do you love me?"

She hung her head. "You were six months old when I adopted you. It was through an agency and I was told that you were in foster care for those months. I don't know what happened to you, but we never bonded. I tried. I tried so hard to love you and I had committed to doing so. When you were a little girl, you wouldn't let me hug you. You'd turn your face when I tried to kiss you. I finally got to the point where you were just a little girl in my house that I had to provide for."

"Did you ever love me?"

"I tried."

She pretended like she wanted to cry but no tears fell. I smirked. She hadn't tried hard enough as far as I was concerned. I stood up and my eyes seared at her, wondering if she had the nerve to ask me again if I loved her. My response wouldn't be as complicated as hers. I loved her. I loved her for trying her best. I loved her for giving me her all in spite of herself.

I walked into the bedroom and sat on the bed. Something inside me said that I owed her an apology. I felt like she wanted to do better but just didn't know how, especially considering she hadn't carried me for nine months. As I stood to walk back into the kitchen, I bumped into her heading into my room.

"London, there are a lot of things that I would redo if I could, but . . ."

I put my arms around her. "Look, I'm sure I was hard to deal with. I'm sure I was cold. I don't know why, but I'm sorry and I just wanted to say thank you."

"You don't have to thank me. I did what I was supposed to do."

"I know, but I want to thank you anyway."

She came into the room and sat on the bed. "I always thought that it was smart for me to tell you that you were adopted at an early age, but now I don't know."

"Why would you say that?"

"I always felt like you knew that you didn't have to bond with me because I wasn't your real mother."

"I didn't understand any of that at the time. It was as I got older that I realized the difference."

"Can we start over?"

"We can try."

I didn't want to give her any false hope. We definitely had our share of differences and I wasn't sure I needed her meddling in my life. She could be overbearing when she wanted to be and I didn't really need that, especially not with my profession.

"Have you ever considered looking for your birth mother?"

"Nope. Never."

"I thought for sure you would have. I was always afraid of that."

"Honestly, I always felt like if she could give me up, then she doesn't deserve to know me."

"But everyone wants to know where they came from."

"Okay, so here's the question, does knowing your birth mother give you any more insight into who you are? I don't think so."

"I do. Because you had some strong ways as a little girl that I never understood and I always felt like some of those things were just in your DNA."

"I guess."

We talked awhile longer and she ended up falling asleep in my bed. It felt like this was the closest we'd ever been. I woke up early the next morning and she was in her room doing an exercise DVD. I inquired about her social circle here. Did she have a boyfriend? Friends? I discovered she didn't have either. She was reaching out to me because she didn't have any real relationships. She'd given her entire world to being the vice president of her company, and as she approached retirement she probably began to realize that the job couldn't love her back. When it dawned on me what she was feeling, I began to question how long my job would love me back. Though I'd convinced myself that I had time to spare, did I really? If so, how much longer would I be a hot commodity in this profession? My job might divorce me a lot sooner than I was prepared for. I didn't want to grow old lonely. A piece of me knew it was really time to start searching for real relationships. I didn't even know where to begin.

26

When I came back from Australia, Thorne called, almost sounding like he was in a panic. He asked if he could come over to talk. Of course, my hero is always welcome to come over for personal time.

He used his key to get in and I was in the shower waiting for him. He called out for me and I yelled back that I was in the shower. He came in and wasn't his regular clean-shaven self. He looked like he'd been through a war. I quickly stepped out of the shower. Spot-drying myself, I asked if he was okay.

He hung his head. "My wife has cancer."

I touched his face and pulled him to my chest. There was nothing I could really say. He was distraught and it was frightening to see someone who always had it all together look so scared. He controlled everything and this was one thing he had no control over.

"What happened?"

"She found a lump. She has stage four cancer."

I didn't know much about the stages, but I knew that stage four was pretty advanced. I wondered if she had just found the lump or if she had known for some time. It scared me to think that a woman could find a lump one day and be faced with dying the next. I had so many questions, but I decided to do my own research. Now was not the time to ask Thorne a million questions. I simply held him tightly and hoped there was some way I could make it better.

I grabbed a robe and invited him to sit on the side of the bed with me. I said, "Thorne, I'm so sorry."

"I mean, it's hard to hear that the person you love has something hurting them and you can't make it better."

Thorne had never once denied his wife or denied his love for her, but I hadn't known how much he loved her until that very moment. He was in as much pain as she was in. And it hurt me to see him like that. I rubbed his back and he just shook his head.

"We saw the oncologist yesterday and it has spread to her bones. She was in a lot of pain, but she kept making excuses and never went to the doctor's."

His voice trembled and my eyes watered. He looked at me like there was something I could do. "London, I have three boys."

"She's going to be okay."

He took a deep breath. "Chances are that she won't and I have to accept it."

"I hope you're wrong."

"I wish I was wrong. I just don't know. I'm going to cut back on everything that I'm doing. I'm going to be there for her."

"You should. She deserves that."

"London, she takes care of everything. If it wasn't for her, there is no way I could do what I do."

"I understand."

"I'm just trying to pay everyone a visit to let them know that business is going to slow down until I can take care of this."

"That's fine, Thorne. Don't worry about business. That should not even be your concern right now."

He looked me in the eye. "Trust me, it's not. I just wanted to be a man and come tell you face-to-face that I don't plan on making any arrangements until I know my wife is okay. That's going to put a financial strain on a lot of people, but I'm sorry."

"Thorne, go home and take care of your wife. Okay?"

I walked him to the door. I thought it was honorable of him to come tell me. After I closed the door, the effects of his announcement finally sank in. While Unleashed had begun to turn a profit, it still was trickling in and I was in way too much debt. I'd become too dependent on escorting. As I sat there sympathizing with him, I hadn't even thought to ask if I could assist him in any way. I didn't want to call him back. I was in a good enough position not to work for some months, but I was certain my savings would be gone quickly if I stopped escorting cold turkey. Something had to be done.

I let some days pass before I called him. Initially I asked about his wife. She'd had surgery and had already begun chemotherapy. Along with her mother, he'd pretty much been doing all the things she usually did, like picking up and dropping off the kids. I suggested he hire a driver. He humbly said, "My boys need me right now. I'm not going to send them off with some stranger at a time like this."

"You're right. I completely understand and it makes sense. Is there anything I can do to help you?"

He sighed. "I'll talk to you a little later, but probably, yes."

When Thorne came to my house I was prepared to tell him that I would perform the coordinating activities for him until things settled down. I just wasn't sure how I planned to say it. I asked if he wanted some wine and he declined. I asked if he wanted a cigar and surprisingly he didn't want that either.

So I took the direct approach. I said, "I really hate to see what you're going through. It's very unfair."

"It's life, I guess."

"Thorne, I hate what's going on with your wife and I really pray that everything gets better." I paused for a long time. "Have any of your girls called you yet?"

"Everyone is trying to be understanding, but I know it's killing a lot of people. Hell, it's killing me. I just don't have the time, though."

"I have a lot of your clients on that spreadsheet you gave me. You can forward your calls through me like you were doing before and I can do the booking until you're free again."

"I'm afraid I don't know when that will be."

"I mean, just to avoid destroying everyone's livelihood. You know?"

"London, I know I've taught you the whole booking-and-travel component, but more goes into this business and at the end of the day, it's a man's job. I'm not sure you're ready to deal with that."

"Look, you have a strong network of regulars and I'll just deal with them and their referrals. I won't accept new clients."

"Here's the thing about this business; you never know when one of your faithful regulars' wives will find out she has breast cancer and he's no longer a client. You have to always recruit new clientele. And not only that, you have to always recruit new girls. They fall off regularly too. Some of them fall in love with clients. Some of them can't handle it emotionally. I've gotten good at profiling women who will and those who won't."

"So you could teach me."

"I'll say this, maybe you can manage what I've already got going on and then if you choose to keep it going, you can."

"I can do that."

"It's not as easy as it looks."

"How do you want to work the financials?"

"London, right now I'm taking it day by day. I won't be able to help you in any way. So for now you can keep one hundred percent."

After merely two weeks of being the coordinator, I had to admit it was not an easy job at all. I'd thought I was making money as a call girl, but in two weeks I made about thirty hookups and close to twenty thousand dollars. That solved a bunch of money issues. It enabled me to hire additional help at Unleashed, and I was convinced that as long as I managed booking right I wouldn't have to go out myself.

I decided to only entertain my favorites; everyone else would have to be turned down. Most of Thorne's girls willingly followed me. Others questioned his passing the business down to me. When I asked him why, he told me that it was simply because I had asked. He also said he trusted me as a businesswoman, and I partially believe it had to do with the fact that he had taught me everything I knew about the business and figured I'd run it the way he would have. And he was right . . . only I planned to run it better.

27

Some of Thorne's girls branched off into managing their own careers with the contacts they had, but others had no choice but to follow me because I had the master list. Still, the ones who branched off left major holes in the business unit. The profiling part of my job came sooner than expected. How could I identify a chick who would be down just by looking at her? Thorne's approach was easy. He presented it to you by offering it straight, but being a woman, I didn't know exactly how to ask another woman if she wanted to work for me.

Suddenly I found myself sharing small talk with attractive women in the grocery store or at the gym or in the bookstore. Still, I didn't know where to take the conversation next. How could I propose it and how would I know what to say without being offensive? Then I decided to post an ad on Craigslist: "Looking for attractive female dog walker. Must love dogs, be friendly and in need of extra money."

I interviewed like crazy and finally hired a few girls to work at Unleashed, and I hoped that once I got close enough to them I could *expose* the real job. Thorne told me to pay attention to their backgrounds. Women who love to purchase purses and shoes that are beyond their means are usually good candidates. And the one that shocked me: housewives on a tight budget.

My first subject was a new girl I'd hired. She was pretty and friendly and she carried herself well. She was in graduate school, studying chemistry. I thought she'd be a good candidate. So I had to figure out my approach. I started out suggesting we go out for drinks on the days she worked, pretending I wanted to take her under my wing.

About a month passed and finally I asked her what kind of money she wanted to make. She explained that she wanted to make as much money as she could. She understood that dog walking wouldn't pay any bills but she liked dogs and it helped a little.

"What if I offered you a job that paid about five hundred to a thousand an hour? You could work when you feel like it and there are no standard work hours. How would you feel about that?"

"I would ask you where do I sign."

"You don't want to know what it is?"

"I don't care what it is, I'm down."

I smiled because she had no clue what she was signing up for. The money was enough of an attraction. "Don't jump too quickly."

"Listen, if I can make that kind of money, I'm jumping."

"How do you feel about being an escort?"

She paused and all her excitement ceased. "What kind of escort are you talking about?"

"An escort. It could be a date or quality time. Really whatever the gentleman wanted."

"If that's all I have to do, I'm with it."

"I have to tell you, sex is involved."

She seemed to be a little disappointed but I could tell she

was calculating how much she could make, the same way I had when it was brought to me. Finally she asked, "So how do you know these men? I mean, does any random guy come searching for an escort?"

"No, honey. No average Joe could afford to pay you that kind of money."

"I guess you got a point."

"Please don't tell anyone that I offered this to you, but I'm putting it on the table. I'll wait for you to let me know if you're interested."

It was about two days later that she came to me and said she was willing to try. I gave her the specifics of the business and she was on her first date about a week later.

My strategy seemed to work and I decided to continue running that ad in Craigslist. And that's how I got my girls. I built a team of dog walkers who were open and free-spirited. Once I had my team, I had to hire a glam squad to prepare them for my portfolio.

Keeping the girls was another matter. Every day I had to manage a different emotion. I didn't have the patience to deal with these emotions. Certainly there were times when I first started working that I had acted bratty or selfish, but damn. Women seemed so petty and unstable. Thorne swore this became addictive. I couldn't understand why. If the money hadn't been so good, there was no way I would have done it. There was nothing addictive about it. I couldn't understand how he was able to run a business, manage these girls, have a family, and never look stressed out.

I felt like between running Unleashed and coordinating these hookups, I was going to lose my mind. I didn't see where on Earth I could fit in a man. I had sworn when I stopped escorting that I would try to find a real relationship. But here I was in something a lot more challenging than merely hooking up with someone. At least as a call girl you can just quit. As the leader of the pack you have a bunch of people's livelihoods and happiness in your hands.

28

When Thorne's wife passed, I thought he would be eager to jump back into business. Instead he came to me to negotiate his percentage. He felt that he deserved it since he had handed the business over to me in a state of stress. I was open to him having a percentage, but he wanted a fifty-fifty split. Those numbers sounded ludicrous to me. It had been almost eighteen months since he had called it quits and I had recruited more clientele. It just wasn't fair. I was a seven-year veteran, and I was busting my ass to keep things afloat. I wasn't giving him half for doing nothing. He claimed that, with the responsibility of being Mr. Mom, he hadn't had time.

Not only that, in order for the transaction to be legal, I would have to contractually give him a percentage in Unleashed. All my blood, sweat, and tears had gone into Unleashed and it was finally becoming lucrative; I wasn't about to give him half. I offered him a percentage on all future bookings, but he was adamant about the percentage in the company. I wasn't going to let that happen. He was the one who had taught me to be careful with how you dish out percentages of your company.

I loved Thorne and I respected him, but this was baffling.

He'd never seemed shady to me, but I felt like he was trying to bully me. He implied that without him I would be nothing but a dog walker. His attorney called me daily to work the situation out, but I was not interested. If Thorne wanted to present something sensible to me, we could talk. A part of me thought that he would try to take me down, and maybe he did try, but from what I discovered, clients are loyal as long as you offer a quality product.

His demands began right after I purchased a new home in Cheverly. When I called him to share the news, he suggested that he hadn't thought I could manage recruiting, booking, and retaining this long. I think he knew I was surviving, but the thought that I was thriving obviously bothered him. Suddenly he deserved so much when he hadn't cared for over a year. I'd carried the load when he bailed out. I was the one dealing with all the stress. My phone was always ringing and my inbox was always full. And that wasn't a result of Thorne's transitioning the business responsibly; it was because I was determined not to sink.

Although we'd been in conflict, I still loved Thorne and felt like I owed him a lot, but I couldn't just let him rape me financially. The situation with him was probably the only thing that brought me to tears frequently. As I sat in my office at Unleashed, I stared at my phone, thinking that I should call Thorne and squash this and hash out the right numbers that would make everyone happy. My phone buzzed. It was a text message request for a biracial German chick I had recruited about a year before. It had been weeks since she'd called me or accepted a job. Thorne was always good about stopping by if he hadn't talked to you in a while. I was losing track. But after several requests for Taina, I decided to hunt her down. She was a twenty-two-year-old model who had come to the States at the age of eighteen to strike it rich. She had everything to make it in the modeling business. She was almost six feet, rail-thin, with a unique-looking face and long curly brown hair, but still she wasn't getting enough gigs to pay the bills. She did a lot of pro bono work so she didn't want to commit to a full-time job, so she had been the perfect candidate to respond to the Craigslist ad.

When I met Taina I knew it would only be a matter of days before she'd be willing to sign up. There was just something free-spirited about her. As usual, I took her out to dinner and proposed escorting, and without any convincing she asked how soon she could have her first hookup.

Taina was a dream call girl. She didn't require a bunch of glam work; she was sexually free and willing to take on the kinkier clients. She had been making me a lot of money in her short time. I would definitely have given her the most valuable player award. So not hearing from her slightly concerned me. I tried calling her again. The phone kept jumping to voice mail. Finally I decided to pop up at her home.

I stood outside her apartment for nearly fifteen minutes, hoping she would show. Just as I walked out of her building I saw her strolling down the street looking like she'd lost her best friend. I had to jump into therapist mode. I could honestly say that every girl who worked for me had some type of issue. I guess that's what made them prime candidates for the job. I always joked with myself, thinking, *I wonder what my issue was.* We can't see ourselves from the outside, so I would probably never know the answer.

I stood there waiting for her to cross the street. When she noticed me she looked the other way and began walking fast. I darted out into traffic, practically chasing after her. "Taina. I just want to talk to you."

When I caught up to her I was out of breath. "Girl, why are you running from me?"

"London, I'm sorry."

"If you don't want to do this anymore it's fine, but I just came by to make sure you were okay."

She sighed. "I'm not okay."

I hadn't been ready for that. I had assumed she had just quit, but the thought that there was actually something wrong scared me.

"What's wrong?"

"I'm pregnant."

"By a boyfriend, I hope," I said, praying that was the situation.

"No, a client."

My heart beat rapidly as I stood there thinking. Most girls I'd known who had inadvertently gotten pregnant on the job had never thought twice about it. They always got abortions, but the fact that she was standing there in front of me looking bewildered confirmed that wasn't in her plan.

"And you want to have the baby?"

"Yes."

"Who is the client?"

"Ervin Calhoun."

My stomach sank and left a bubble trapped in my throat. He was a Washington move maker, an assistant director of the Federal Finance Commission. This wasn't a good look.

"Taina, I know that you probably think this is the best idea, but you don't want a baby by a married man. And you're not even his mistress. He's been paying you for sex."

It had begun to drizzle, and before she could answer I asked her if we could walk over to her place. She agreed. As we walked, she said, "We are in love."

I rolled my eyes, because so often in this profession women get confused. Just because a man requests you multiple times a week doesn't mean he's in love. It just means that he likes sleeping with you and because he's paying he doesn't owe you an explanation. He pays for the convenience. Certainly it's not love. Understanding that she was dealing with some hormones and emotions, I decided not to go hard. Instead I said, "So, you both are in love or are you the only one in love?"

"He's told me that he loves me too."

"Have you told him you're pregnant?"

"No, I'm scared. I don't know what he'll say."

As we entered her apartment, I felt I had to be honest with her. "Taina, these men are just clients. You can't fall in love with them. Most of them are married men and they aren't going to leave their wives and family for a call girl."

"But he told me he would."

"Taina." I gave her an exasperated look. "Trust me, he won't. He's up to be the next director of the Federal Finance Commission. If they dig up that he's left his wife for a call girl, he won't get the job. And what I've found after nearly seven years in the business, men want power. He's not giving up his power for a call girl. He can find another."

She began to cry from my harsh words. I stood up to hug her. There was no way I could be easy on her. She had to understand that abortion was the only option. It was just that simple: *Call girl* and *love* should never be in the same sentence. While a client may like you a lot, he could never love you.

"But he told me he loved me."

"Well, tell him about the baby and let's see what he says then."

She pulled away from me. "I tried to call him at work but he told me he'd have to call me later."

"You know you're not allowed to contact your clients directly. That's my job."

"We were in a relationship."

Basically she was letting me know that they had already been violating the rules. She had been seeing him for free and confusing work with romance. This was an ugly mess and I could see that there was nothing I could say to convince this dumb girl that this was a bad move.

"Well, listen, Taina, really think about this before you contact him again. And trust me when I tell you that you don't want this. You don't want to bring a child into the world under these circumstances. Have you thought about adoption?"

"No, I want my baby."

Ugh. She had a hard head. I was trying to save her from rejection, but she was convinced. Some people have to figure things out on their own. I said, "Listen, I don't know how you plan to make this work, but I don't want my name involved in this. You and Ervin will need to figure out how you're going to keep this private."

I stood up. See, here's why this is a man's job. Thorne would have been able to tell her from his perspective and maybe she would have listened, but from me she wasn't hearing it.

The situation was the perfect reason to call Thorne and segue into resolving our issue. I still needed him. I sent a text message asking if he could meet for lunch and he agreed. When we sat down for lunch, Thorne could tell by the look on my face that something wasn't right.

He grabbed my hand. "You ready to discuss my proposal?"

"Thorne, we are definitely going to work something out.

You deserve a percentage. I'm just not sure you should get it from Unleashed. Maybe I will create a subsidiary company and we can work it out that way."

He smiled. "Wow, you were soaking it all up."

"I guess, but that's not why I'm here."

"So what is it that you want to talk about?"

"One of the girls is pregnant by Ervin Calhoun."

He wiped the sweat from under his glasses. He looked at me and shook his head. "That's not good."

"Who are you telling? And she's talking about having the baby."

"Are you serious?"

"I told her to keep my name out of this mess."

"It's not that simple, London. You can't just walk away from this. You have to make sure she keeps her head on straight."

"What else can I do? She claims they're in love."

He nodded. "That's typical."

"So what can I do?"

"Whatever you can to keep it from spilling out into the media."

Thorne suggested that I appease Taina and convince her that maybe Ervin did love her, but that if she loved him like she claimed she did, she wouldn't want to ruin him by demanding he leave his wife. I decided to tell her that he would eventually leave, but that now was not the time. Thorne didn't want her to retaliate because of rejection. He also suggested I hire a personal security guard.

"Why?"

"London, you don't want to play around with this one. Trust me."

"Is there someone that you trust to protect me?"

He promised he'd give the guy my information. He continued, "Now go back over there and make sure you get this girl's mind right."

I took a deep breath. I didn't want to deal with the drama, but I headed back over there. When I got there I knocked and knocked to no avail. Finally I left and headed back to Unleashed. I figured I'd stop by on my way home.

29

When I turned the key to my house, it dawned on me that I forgot to go back and check on Taina. I quickly pulled my cell phone out as I opened the door and walked in, turning on the light in the living room. I grabbed the television remote from the coffee table. I noticed that things were rearranged on the table. I wondered for a minute if I'd switched things around and I slowly backed away.

Usually Bruno was at the door before I could even open it. It was quite strange that I didn't hear his paws pitter-patting anxiously through the house. I yelled, "Bruno. Mommy's home."

Suddenly I felt a huge arm wrap around my neck and I was lifted off my feet. I tried kicking and fighting. My cell phone was still in my hand so in the hysteria I tried to dial. My assailant grabbed the phone from my hand and threw it. I saw the phone hit the wall and break into pieces. I tried scratching and biting, but I felt myself losing oxygen. So I just stopped. If this intruder wanted to kill me, he was big and strong enough to do so. He carried me into the basement and threw me on the hard ceramic floor. I looked up, and Ervin Calhoun was seated in front of me with two other big, muscular men standing beside him. While I was certainly scared, it now made sense why these men were in my house.

Ervin spoke first. "I got a call from my wife today and she told me a young lady was at our door and she wanted to speak to me.

"I couldn't imagine that. So I asked her name and she tells me it's Taina. She claims she is irate and demanding to speak to me. I tell my wife to call the cops and have this young lady removed. And she does. But now I have to explain to my wife why she was there." He shook his head. "Not cool. Not cool at all.

"So I decide to call Ms. Taina after she's removed from my house and she tells me she's pregnant by me and having my baby."

Aside from my heavy breathing, the room was silent. Finally he spoke: "I booked this girl through you. It's your job to protect my privacy. So if you don't handle her and make her go away, I'm coming back. And if I have to come back, you may as well say that I'll be the only one walking out of here."

"I will handle her, I promise."

"I know you will. Just know that next time I'll handle more than just the dog."

"Where's my dog?"

"I took care of him," he said.

"Took care of him!" I screamed. "Where is Bruno?"

"Look, I need you to know that I'm not playing with you. Like I said, we took care of him, and if I have to come back, we'll be taking care of you."

He stood up and said to the man who'd carried me into the basement, "Keep her down here until we're gone."

"I got it."

After they closed the back door the man let me go, and on his way up the stairs, he said, "The dog died slow."

I screamed, "No! No!"

He continued up the stairs and I ran behind him. "Where is my dog? Where is he?"

He pushed me back down the stairs and I tried to control the fall. I heard him close the back door and then I ran out to the backyard. Bruno was lying at the bottom of the stairs stiff. I ran down and held him in my arms, crying uncontrollably. "Bruno! Bruno!" I cried.

I ran back into my house with my dead dog in my arms. I rushed to the phone and it was dead. They'd obviously cut the wires from outside. I went over to piece my cell phone together. It was impossible. I was running back and forth. I didn't know what to do or where to go. This girl's stupidity had my dog murdered and put my safety at risk. I was angry with her and I didn't know how to get rid of her, but all I knew was I had to. I thought about going to a neighbor's house, but decided against it. All I knew was that I needed to talk to Thorne. I wasn't equipped to handle this, but I knew he was. I wanted out. I was lonely and scared. I didn't know what to do with Bruno. Finally I decided to place him in a box and carry him back to the backyard until I could figure out what I was doing.

I rushed out of the house and drove down Wisconsin Avenue, searching for a cell phone store but afraid to get out of my car. Finally I saw an AT&T store and went in to purchase a phone. I was jittery and anxious as I stood there waiting for them to activate the phone. Finally I got back in my car to call Thorne and it must have been the grace of God that he was available.

"Thorne."

"I already know. He came here first."

"He says he's going to kill me if I don't get rid of this girl."

"I know. But don't worry. We'll get rid of her."

"How? I'm not down for hurting anybody."

"First you're going to have to try to make her go quietly. If that doesn't work, we'll have to use force."

"Force?"

"Just do what I tell you to do and we'll be fine. A man by the name of Ramon, a bodyguard, will be calling you momentarily. He's going to be with you every step of the way and I'll be guiding you."

My heart was still pounding. I said, "Yes."

"He'll meet you wherever you need him to, right now. He's not cheap. He'll be about three thousand a week."

"Okay. That's fine."

I needed to go to Taina's house. I wasn't sure if they'd been there or not. I asked Ramon to meet me in the city a block from there. When I pulled up he was standing on the corner looking like a Secret Service representative. I wasn't sure if he was supposed to be incognito or what, but clearly he looked like he was there for protection. He was a little over six feet tall, with a clean-shaven face and a short haircut.

When he got in the car, I introduced myself again. "Hi, I'm London. Thank you for meeting me."

"No problem. Just want to let you know up front, I've done private security for everyone ranging from celebrities to athletes to politicians. So I know what you're dealing with and you don't have to worry. I know how they play, but I play harder."

I liked his confidence and I needed that. I felt better with him in the car. We found parking close to Taina's apartment, and I was looking over my shoulder as we walked to her place.

I'd called ahead so that she'd be waiting for us. She was in tears as she opened up. I reached out to hug her when we walked in. She looked like she was scared of Ramon.

"He's okay. He's here to protect us."

Ramon found a seat and I ushered Taina over to her bar stools. "Taina, this is serious. There were men in my house when I got home. Ervin is not playing with us. He doesn't want this baby, nor does he want to see you again. And if you love him like you claim, you wouldn't want to ruin his life."

"But he's ruining mine."

"You don't have to have this baby."

"I love him, though. I want his baby."

"But you do understand that it's not in the best interest of anyone involved. You'll ruin his career. He'll lose everything. Are you prepared for that?"

She shrugged.

"I don't think you're prepared for the media frenzy that will occur if you go on with this."

"You told me this was easy."

I wrapped my arms around her, because I had told her this job was easy. Technically it is if you can subtract emotion from it. I thought I'd explained that to her, but obviously it didn't get through. I thought it would be best if she stayed with me and that way Ramon could be there to watch over the both of us. We went into her bedroom to pack her things. She started showing me all the gifts he'd purchased for her over the past six months. The cards he'd given her. It's no wonder she assumed they had something special. I felt sorry for her, while at the same time I understood him.

When we arrived at my house I figured I could convince

her to have an abortion. After I showed her where she'd be sleeping, I told her to come down to the kitchen and I would make her something to eat. I had some leftover turkey burgers and string beans. It was just enough to feed Taina, Ramon, and myself. We sat down at the dining room table and it felt good to actually have some people in my home. While I dealt with people all day, every day, I was still somewhat abstracted from personal interaction. We ate and just had superficial conversation, but I was actually enjoying myself. I hoped that after a good meal Taina would be ready to talk.

I asked her to come into my study with me. When we sat down I grabbed both of her hands. "So, Taina. Tell me this. Why do you want this baby so bad?"

"London, I'm twenty-six weeks' pregnant."

She was still as thin as ever. My mouth hung open. Abortion was practically out of the question so late in the game. I nodded. A part of me was frustrated. I felt like she had intentionally waited until it was too late to do anything about it.

"So why did you wait until now?"

"I don't know. I just couldn't believe it for a long time and I thought it was best to wait until I absolutely had to tell somebody."

That was just dumb. I didn't know how they expected me to get rid of her now. I wanted to smack some sense into her, but what good would it do at that moment? I just wanted to run away. I had no clue where I was going but this was a burden and I didn't think it was my fault. My only mistake was believing this girl was emotionally stable, but as she sat there telling me that Ervin would come around, I knew I was dealing with a complete basket case. I told her to just go to bed.

I didn't think my brain could deal with any more. Ramon

sat in the living room concentrating on the television. I went in to check on him and he told me he was fine and that I should go to bed. He had everything taken care of. It was a good thing that Thorne had known what was coming down the pipe and had already booked Ramon prior to Ervin's coming to my house. He had known what we were in for and I had been completely oblivious.

I went up to my room, and although Ramon was right downstairs I was scared. I didn't want to shower. I didn't even know if I wanted to lie in bed alone. My cell phone rang and startled me. I tossed it on the bed. I wasn't sure I even wanted to be fielding calls anymore. I just let it ring. When it stopped, I picked it up to check and the call was from an unknown number.

It rang again. Then, after maybe the tenth ring, I tiptoed downstairs. When I passed the room Taina was sleeping in, I peeped in on her. She was resting like she didn't have a damn care in the world. A part of me wanted to choke her. Here I was being harassed for her stupidity. When I got down into the living room, I told Ramon about the phone calls.

He told me to stay down there with him if that made me more comfortable. When the phone rang again he told me to answer. The caller had a raspy voice. "Get rid of that bitch."

Then the caller hung up. I wanted to cry but I didn't have the energy. I told Ramon and he admitted, "They're not playing. We're going to have to do something with her."

"Like what?" I asked, with my eyebrow raised.

"Maybe send her to another state."

"I can't make her move if she doesn't want to."

The darkness surrounding his deeply set eyes stunned me. He said, "What's not done by choice is done by force."

I didn't know what he was insinuating, but it was definitely not something I wanted to be a part of. But on the other hand I wanted the harassing calls to stop. I wanted my life back.

Ramon could see how petrified I was. He affirmed, "We're not going to hurt her. We're just going to convince her that leaving is in her best interest."

It seemed like a pretty good plan, but I wasn't sure it would work. Ervin had this dumb girl twisted, and I felt like she would hold on as long as she could. It didn't seem like I could reason with her. I planned to follow Ramon's lead, hoping it would get us somewhere.

30

Two more days of harassing calls and my employees called from Unleashed to let me know that they'd received a bunch too. This had consumed my life. Ramon told me that he could get someone in Immigration to pull Taina's visa, which would force her out of the country. That seemed like a wise plan.

Since she was technically an employee of Unleashed, I would act as if Immigration had contacted me. Ramon's contact drafted a letter claiming that there was an error in the initial application and since she wasn't in school and hadn't made a certain amount of money in the past year, Immigration was after her. It was a long document and I knew she wasn't emotionally stable enough to interpret it all. So Ramon and I went home to talk to her. I started first. I said, "Have you tried to contact Ervin?"

She claimed she hadn't but I knew she had. He was her lover in her mind, but in mine he was a dangerous man and I wasn't trying to play any games with him. This girl was a damn airhead and I had to get rid of her like he said. And I wasn't willing to lose my life for her.

I said, "The reason that I'm asking is because I received this package at work today. Basically, it's from Immigration and it seems crazy that it just came. I have a feeling this is Ervin's doing because he has a lot of connections."

"What?" she asked anxiously.

"Well, it's threatening to deport you. They contacted me because I'm your employer. Obviously they have already been to your house. We don't want to play with them. If you violate, it's harder to get back in again."

"No, I want my baby born here."

"Listen, Taina. The last thing you want to do is have your baby here and then be deported. How are you going to afford to have a baby? I can no longer employ you. You don't have a work visa anymore. I'll be in violation if I allow you to work."

"No. No. I don't believe you."

Her accent was strong and resentful. She stood up and proceeded to stomp up my stairs. I rushed behind her and Ramon followed me.

"Taina, you don't get it. You have to go. I can no longer protect you or I'll be in trouble. I don't plan on being investigated by Immigration."

"You are just trying to keep me and Ervin apart."

I looked at Ramon like *Is this girl crazy or what?* He smiled patiently at me like everything would be okay. I couldn't imagine. Taina was a huge obstacle and Ervin knew that she would be hard to reach so he had to threaten me to get her out of his hair. Damn, did he expect me to kill this girl? Because that was probably the only way she would stop. She paced the floor in her bedroom and I sat on the bed. Ramon stood in the doorway.

"Taina, I'm not trying to keep you guys apart. Ervin is crazy. I'm sure he had your file pulled in Immigration and *he's* trying to keep you guys apart."

After I made that statement, and I recognized the instability heightening, I reverted back to appealing to her love for him, like Thorne had initially suggested. I guess he'd seen enough in his time to know how to deal with every situation.

"Look, I'm sure Ervin loves you but he's up for a major promotion and he'll be scrutinized and he will be ruined if people find out about you. But I do believe he loves you. He probably wants to be with you, but right now it's just bad."

Her puppy-dog eyes batted and she looked at me like I had all the answers. "You think?"

"I know. He just doesn't want to ruin his reputation right now."

"But why didn't he just tell me that?"

"Aren't you scared?" She nodded. "And I'm sure he's scared too. He doesn't know how to handle this. He just wants it to settle down and I'm sure he'll come back to find you. True love always does."

She smiled. "So you think he'll come back."

Ramon cosigned. "Yeah, he'll come find you, but right now you don't want to deal with Immigration."

"I will have to do everything over." She looked at me. "But can't you sponsor me?"

"Taina, let this die down. Go home and have your baby in a healthy environment. You don't need all this stress. Then I will sponsor you to come back to the country."

"Really?"

"Yes, I will."

"When do I go? You think Ervin will see me before I leave?"

"I doubt it very seriously. The stakes are too high for him."

She dropped her head. This crazy chick was really in love with Ervin. I felt sorry for her, but not sorry enough to die. I wanted this girl out of the country by any means necessary.

"We'll go to your place and get you packed up tomorrow. We can book the flight tonight. Have you told your parents that you're pregnant?"

"My mum knows."

"Is she happy?"

"She wants me to come home."

"See, you need to be with someone that can help you. Once the baby is born and you're comfortable with motherhood we'll work on getting you back here."

I actually hoped she'd lose my number, but I tried to appease her as much as possible just to get her out of there. Walking toward the bedroom door I said, "Relax and I'll give you more information about when you have to leave."

She nodded, but she definitely didn't want to go. It was all over her face. I walked past Ramon and rolled my eyes. He smiled and followed me. I went downstairs into the study and quickly started looking for flights. Ramon said, "You need to go with her to make sure she gets out of the country. She could do anything after she gets past those gates. You want to be on the plane with her. Once she's out of the country she won't be able to get back in."

"I don't want to go to Germany just to make sure she's gone."

"Sometimes you have to do what you have to do in order to have your peace."

Ugh. I hated this job. The money was definitely not worth this headache. Even while dealing with Taina, I had still been arranging hookups. I really wanted to plan my exit strategy, but I'd become dependent on the income. The life I lived was no cheap ride. I dropped my face into my hands. I wanted this whole issue to just disappear. Now I had to fit into my schedule some time to fly to Germany.

I searched flights and several had a layover at Heathrow. Ramon said, "If you get her to England, she's out of the country. Why don't you take the first leg with her and let her continue on without you?"

"Will you go with me?"

"Sure, why not?"

"Well, if you go we can stay a few days and come back. I really don't want to fly over and fly back. That much flying close together zaps your energy. I'd be out of it for a week anyway. So I may as well enjoy the city and then come back."

"Hey, I work for you."

We scheduled our flights for two days later and I found a nice boutique hotel for me and Ramon to stay in. I booked two rooms. I didn't assume that he was interested in staying with me. Not to mention that he worked for me and so he couldn't afford to pay what I charged for a night of my time.

I took Taina home the next day and told her to get all her necessities, and I hired a storage company to come and get her furniture. I told her that I'd pay for storage while she was away. Of course, I was still trying to convince her that she would be coming back.

A car came to pick up the three of us the next morning. Taina's suitcase looked like it could carry the Rock of Gibraltar inside. Both Ramon and I had medium-sized bags. When we got to the airport I felt like I was one step closer to peace. I just hoped she didn't pull anything tricky. Every step of the way she was surprisingly calm. After we got on the plane, I was so anxious for the cabin door to close. We backed away and she still appeared calm.

It was about six in the morning when we arrived in England. I finally exhaled. Her connecting flight departed about two hours after we arrived. We sat at the gate with her and, when she boarded, I unthinkingly hugged Ramon. "Thank you."

"Why are you thanking me?"

I breathed heavily. "I wouldn't have been able to deal with this if you hadn't been there. Thorne didn't have time to deal with it and I probably would have cracked. The Immigration idea was so ingenious."

"It's nothing."

"Let's go."

We left the airport for our hotel. In the taxi I sat close to Ramon. He was tall and strong. His skin was the color of honey. His pecs were puffed up like he could bench-press a ton. His hair was dark and even. And his face was clean-shaven. Damn, as if I had been too stressed to recognize, it hit me. Ramon was super-fine. I got a tingle in my panties just thinking about him, but I knew it was better that we just maintain our business relationship.

So I tried to push the daydream I was having about him out of my mind. Instead I went back to discussing Taina. "You can't imagine how happy I am that this is over."

"She was definitely complicated."

"To say the least."

We laughed and the taxi pulled up to our hotel. It was grand and architecturally pleasing: large columns and flags protruding from them. It was like we were royalty as the staff hurried over to the taxi to help us out and take our bags.

31

I'd traveled many places, but never had I been to my name-sake and I loved it. Ramon and I had neighboring rooms. When we arrived at my hotel room, Ramon continued past and headed to his. He watched as I put my key in the door. I said, "If you have trouble opening your door, you can always come in my room."

He laughed. "Do you want me to come in your room?"

"Only if you want to." I shrugged. "I would feel safer."

He walked toward me and I began to smile. I don't even know why I was entertaining this notion. It wasn't like he would be interested in pursuing a relationship with me. And from the moment Thorne had told me that if a woman is not in a committed relationship, she should never have sex for free, it was a belief I lived by. I had been a call girl for so long I wasn't even sure how to pursue a nonbusiness relationship. What I did know was that I was very attracted to Ramon. He wasn't rich like my other clients and he probably couldn't afford my lifestyle, but there was something calming and peaceful about him. And since I'd been the boss I hadn't even had sex that often, so I was definitely ready to be touched.

I opened my door and he came inside. "There's only one bed in here. What are we going to do about that?" he said.

"Haven't you ever slept in bed with a platonic friend?"

He smiled. "Actually, I don't think so."

"You're kidding me."

"Actually, I'm not. I can sleep on this sofa if you want."

In an effort not to be too forward, I said, "That's fine."

I went into the bathroom to wash my face and to put on my short teal spaghetti-strap nightie. I pulled my hair into a ponytail and brushed my teeth. When I walked out, Ramon had on nothing but a pair of navy Polo boxer briefs. There is no way one man should be blessed with a body so tight. His skin looked like satin and every bulging muscle was just the perfect size. Now he could definitely have me for free. I stood there stunned. He lay on the sofa and I kept staring. He asked, "What's up?"

"Nothing."

"You look beautiful."

"Thank you."

I wanted to tell him how fine he looked too but I couldn't bring myself to, and I figured that if I responded at that moment we'd be in bed together. If it was going to happen I wanted it to be his idea, and I didn't want it to happen on the first morning there. Men have funny rules about whom they will or won't take seriously. If I was going to be giving it away, I wanted to be taken seriously. I already had one strike: He knew about my call girl activities. My plan had been never to disclose that to men I could potentially date.

I climbed into the bed and scooted to the middle, hoping he'd ask if he could get in, but he didn't. When my head hit the pillow, I thought I'd be knocked out. Instead I lay there thinking about Ramon's body and his personality. I attributed my tripping to my lack of exposure to men who weren't clients. After nearly an hour of tossing and turning, I finally went to sleep.

When I woke up several hours later I looked over at Ramon resting peacefully on the couch. I turned the television on and the volume blasted out. I quickly tried to turn it down, but Ramon's eyes popped open. I said, "I'm sorry."

He sat up. "What time is it?"

"It's three o'clock."

"Wow. I had a pretty good sleep, considering you made me sleep on the sofa."

"You could have slept in the bed."

"One thing you'll learn about me is that I only go where I'm wanted."

"So are you saying that you were waiting for me to ask you to get in the bed?"

"Absolutely."

I shrugged. "So do you want to do something today? Maybe go to dinner or schedule some sightseeing?"

"Yeah, I'm down with whatever. We're here. We may as well have a good time."

I got out of bed and walked past Ramon. He looked me up and down. I knew he wanted to know what I was working with, but I decided to be a tease for a little while longer.

He told me he was going to go into the other room to get ready. I began to dress. It was quite brisk in early April and I wasn't sure I would be able to stay out long. I'm a warm-weather girl.

I put on a pair of long johns under my jeans and wrapped up in my scarf and hat before leaving the hotel. I met Ramon in the lobby, because I wanted to get some sightseeing brochures. He came into the lobby and smiled. I smiled back at him.

"So what did you find for us to do?"

Showing him the brochure, I said, "We can purchase the London Pass, which includes a few museum tours."

"Does it include the Globe Theatre?"

"Actually it does. Let me know you're a fan of Shakespeare?"

"I am."

"I'm glad, because I wanted to get tickets to *Romeo and Juliet*. I have the concierge checking for me and she's waiting for a call back. They may have tickets for tomorrow."

"Cool."

We hung in the lobby for a while, waiting for the concierge to give us a heads-up. When we were finally confirmed we headed out onto the busy streets of London to tour the town. Ramon wrapped his strong arm around me to shield me from the cold as I was looking at the map and trying to figure out which train to catch and which direction to go in. I was definitely not feeling the weather and was slightly disappointed that we had come during the winter.

We visited Tower Bridge and the Tower of London, and toured the Globe Theatre. We enjoyed the theater most of all. It was a replica of the original.

After a day of sightseeing I was ready to rush back to the hotel for some warmth. Instead we ducked into a warm little café and Ramon hugged me. "You warm now?"

I felt so protected in his arms. Although the tables were turned—I was paying him—it felt right and I didn't feel lonely dealing with this situation. I felt like I sincerely had someone I could depend on.

The next afternoon, as we headed out for the *Romeo and Juliet* performance, we canceled the remainder of the nights for the separate room. The play was subpar to say the least. The actors weren't that great and it left Ramon and me longing to re-create our own rendition of the play. We kidded as we headed to Covent Garden. We were told that was the place where we could find a bunch of bars and restaurants.

We barhopped and shopped. By the time we headed back to the hotel we were both tired. Still, we thought it was a good idea to order a movie, and we ended up falling asleep on top of the comforter with our clothes on. Ramon and I were getting quite comfortable with each other while we were overseas and away from the drama at home.

I hated the thought of returning home. A part of me wanted to just stay in England and start a new life. I felt like I didn't have anything to lose. If Ramon had been down, I would have. As we were packing up the night before we were to leave, I asked, "What do you think about just starting over?"

I asked in that fashion because Ramon had expressed to me that he'd made some wrong decisions in the past and had messed up with some powerful clients, which had caused him to lose a lot of business. He looked at me like it was a possibility and said, "Nah. I'm pretty happy in the US. I'm down for moving to another state, but I'm not sure I'm sold on London."

My eyebrow rose. He clarified. "The city, not the person."

"How sweet of you."

"Would you really stay here?"

"After what happened to my dog and those people being in my house, I could definitely just run away."

"What about Unleashed?"

"I guess you're right. I do have a business to run." I sighed. "But sometimes I just want to run away. Don't you?"

"Maybe one day we will."

I looked at him, wondering if *we* meant the two of us together or if he was making a general statement. Though we'd had a wonderful time in London, I didn't know where we'd go from there. I didn't take anything for granted, because I'd spent much of my adult life having a great time with men, but when the sun rose it was over. I couldn't really decipher what was going on in Ramon's mind. And I didn't even want to try. If I knew men like I thought I knew them, they would tell you what was going on in their minds if you were patient enough to listen. Otherwise, for sanity's sake, it's best not to assume anything.

32

Ramon hadn't asked any questions while we were in England. It was as if we were both living in the moment. On the plane ride home he finally asked the burning question: "How did you get into the industry?"

"I guess I was young and dumb."

"I can't imagine you being dumb."

"Well, I guess I must have been at one time."

"I always thought prostitutes were dumb, but you're definitely not what I typically imagined one to be."

"It was always hard to consider myself a prostitute. I know that's what it was technically, but I felt that my line of work was a little more on the classier side."

"I can give you that. Thorne has a different type of business going on. I'm surprised he trusted you to take over."

"Well, he didn't technically hand it over to me. He told me that he was quitting and if I wanted to coordinate hookups I could. I think at that time he was focused on his family and he didn't care what happened with that part of his business."

"Yeah, I can imagine that. He loved his wife. But now those kids need him more than the business."

"You got a point," I said, as I reflected on how distraught

Thorne had been when he came to tell me what had happened.

I was quiet for a moment, thinking about Thorne and wondering if I would ever have someone dedicated to me. It hurt thinking that it might never be a reality, so I switched to a less sentimental topic. "So, have you done a lot of security work for Thorne?"

"No, only when there's a code red problem, like yours. I don't do the sitting-in-the-hotel kind of gigs. But the women he's paid me to guard have all been unbearable."

"Unbearable?"

"Yeah, kind of like your girl Taina. But you seem rather levelheaded."

"You think?"

"The women I've protected for Thorne were all crazy. They piss their clients off and then they need help. I hate those jobs, but I can honestly say this has been a pleasure."

"Thank you."

I wasn't sure if he was trying to say the job was over or not. I was prepared for either, because I wasn't sure I wanted to pursue something further with someone who knew about all my dirty laundry. If there is one thing I knew about men, it's that they want to believe their woman has never been touched.

When we arrived in the States it was about five in the evening and a car met us at Dulles Airport. As Ramon put our luggage in the trunk he leaned over and kissed me. "I really had a good time with you."

"Me too."

We sat in the car and I said, "So how am I supposed to let Ervin know she's gone?"

"Well, if you get another phone call, just let him know that you've handled it."

"Do you think I still need protection?"

"Yeah, because I want to still hang around. And no, because you handled your business."

"Well, I'm flattered that you still want to hang around."

"Absolutely."

"So are you going to hang around for free or am I still paying for protection?"

"You don't have to pay me. I want to protect you."

I wasn't sure where he was going with this. Was he really trying to let me know he wanted something serious with me? I didn't know how to respond or what I should say. I took the honest road.

"Ramon, I would love to have you around to protect me. But let me tell you, it's been a long time since I had someone around just because they wanted to be around. I've sacrificed so much being in this business. I'm sort of at a loss when it comes to loving for free."

"My business is different, but pretty much the same. When I'm doing twenty-four-hour protection it's hard to develop relationships, and it's been a long time for me too. Let's just take it one day at a time and see how it works out. You down for that?"

I couldn't resist, so I asked, "How do you feel about my past?"

"Everybody has one."

"But not like mine."

"At least I know what it is."

He came to my house that night and it wasn't hard. He understood me and I understood him. He would be my protector and I didn't have to hide any of myself from him.

33

The day after I got back to DC, I spoke with an attorney about creating a subsidiary company that sold dog apparel. Once we narrowed down the business structure I spoke with Thorne about partnering with that company, but he declined. After the Taina ordeal, I realized that Thorne was an invaluable asset to me, and though he still wanted to play hardball, I gave in to his wishes and offered him the fifty-fifty split of all bookings.

A few days later someone called for Ervin and said, "What'd you do with the girl?"

"I flew her back to Germany."

"Did you make her get rid of the baby?"

"Yes."

I knew that was a lie, but I wasn't ready to deal with the harassment again. Although Ramon was there to protect me, I just wasn't in the mood to deal with it.

He said, "Good job."

Then he hung up the phone. I was glad that the situation was pretty much over. Although I had gained Ramon, I still mourned the loss of Bruno. It was so unfair that he had to lose his life because of that dumbass Taina. Bruno had been through everything with me and there were nights when I dreamed his little feet were running into my room. He didn't deserve what had happened to him. I had him cremated and his ashes were in an urn over the fireplace. My baby would always be with me.

It seemed like Ramon spent one night and never left. It was three months into the relationship when I causally asked, "So are we monogamous?"

He laughed as we sat in bed watching a movie. "Do you think I'd be here every day if we weren't?"

Ramon couldn't take the financial liberties that most men I'd been with could, but he was a good man. He was dependable, the type of guy you could set your watch to. Every day that I woke up to him, I was surprised that he'd really taken a relationship with me seriously. Not that I didn't think he should, but Thorne had warned me no man who knew my past would. So it was hard to believe and I wasn't sure I'd ever be completely secure.

When I opened the front door one night, the lights were low. I could smell food cooking. "Honey," I said.

"I'm in here."

After taking off my shoes, I walked into the kitchen to find him pulling lasagna out of the oven. It looked and smelled great. I always let him know how much I appreciated his efforts.

He said, "Go sit down and relax yourself."

It was days like these that really amazed me I had ended up with this type of guy. I walked out of the kitchen and headed upstairs to the bedroom. He had sprinkled rose petals all over the bed. I stepped into the shower and put on a silk nightie. I walked back into the kitchen and grabbed Ramon's waist from behind and lay my head on his back.

He spun around. "What's up, babe?"

"I'm just curious what this is all for."

"It's for you. Now go ahead and sit down at the table. I got this."

His effort to please me outweighed the mess that he had made in the kitchen, plus I knew he'd take care of that after dinner. When he brought the plates into the dining room, I couldn't wait to eat. After lighting a candle in the middle of the table he sat down.

I smiled at him. "You done now?"

"Yes, I'm done."

"Thank you."

He started the conversation by saying, "When we met, I had no clue we'd be here. But I'm glad we are. The other day you asked me if we were monogamous and I just wanted to give more than a verbal confirmation. This is something like a ceremony."

Ramon was a romantic and he proved it more and more each day. It was weird that he was the strong bodyguard and at the same time he could be so sensitive.

34

Being with Ramon gave me a strong desire for a family. I had never thought I would have that opportunity. I rushed home daily to give him all the things I felt a man should have. He was my soul mate. It just worked. I'd cut down on the number of hookups I arranged per week and I was no longer aggressively recruiting girls.

Love is funny. It makes money so insignificant. The more money I'd made, the more money I'd convinced myself I needed to make. Maybe that was because money was my only relationship of significance. Having Ramon made me lose the desire to grind like I once had.

We spent a lot of time hanging out and traveling with Kari and Ian and that seemed like more than enough. It was as if I had finally grown up. I was living an acceptable life now and I loved it.

I planned to bring my booking activities to an end as soon as the latest roster of girls I had fell off. Unfortunately, there was not one of them I thought I could pass the business to and Thorne wasn't interested. Unleashed's profits had begun to do well and we could survive on that. Ramon got personal security contracts from time to time. But when it was all said and done, all we really needed was each other.

I pulled up to the house at around seven in the evening and all the lights were off. That was strange because I always gave Ramon the blues about every light in the house being on when I came in. I stepped into the house and called out for him. He said, "Up here, baby."

I walked up the steps and he sat on the edge of the bed. "You know Ervin got the job as director."

"Ervin Calhoun?"

"Yeah."

"Well, good. I heard from Taina and she's happy being a mother. I don't think she's tried to contact him. She told me she's engaged to some diplomat. Sounds like she's over Ervin."

He nodded, but didn't say very much. It seemed like something was bothering him. But I figured he'd tell me when he felt like it. I went downstairs to put dinner on.

My cell phone rang. "I will kill you if you say anything."

My heart dropped. I wasn't sure where that came from. I assumed it was Ervin again. I rushed upstairs to tell Ramon. He said, "Don't worry. You got free protection."

My head started spinning. I didn't want to deal with this anymore. This was the final straw. I was done with the business. My home phone rang and it was a lady. "Hi, is this London Reed?"

"Yes it is."

"Do you run an upscale prostitution ring?"

"No!" I said, slamming the phone down.

I yelled out for Ramon. He came running down the stairs. "What's up?"

I told him and he hugged me. My heart raced. I wasn't in the mood for this shit again. Ramon said, "London, the media found out about Taina and your name was leaked too."

"How do you know this?"

"The phone has been ringing all evening. Your picture is all over the Internet."

"Why didn't you tell me?"

"I didn't want you to have to deal with this."

I paced around my living room. I couldn't believe my ears. In seven years in the business I'd been able to maintain privacy. I wanted to run away. The phone rang again. The next thing I knew there was a knock on my door. I opened up. It was the FBI.

"Are you London Reed?"

"Yes."

"You're under arrest on charges of prostitution."

"Arrest?" I shouted.

"You're being charged with eleven counts of prostitution. Anything you say can be used against you in a court of law."

I nearly blacked out. Thorne had taught me how to run this operation in such a way that I'd never get caught. So why now? When I had downsized the operation to almost nothing? My knees buckled as they placed the cuffs on me. I couldn't imagine being hauled out of my house in my upscale community. What would my neighbors think of me? I was scared and helpless. I looked at Ramon. He looked at me like for the first time since we met he couldn't help me.

They took me to the local FBI headquarters and stuck me in a room for questioning. The first agent walked in and told me that they'd been watching me for years but never had any hard evidence. I said, "So what kind of evidence do you have now?"

"Phone conversations. Letters."

"I don't believe you."

"Someone close to you sold it all to a tabloid magazine and it's ours now."

"Really. Show me what you got."

"Here's the deal. If you give us your client list, maybe we can make a deal."

"I thought you already had evidence. Why do you need anything from me?"

"We have you trapped in the case against Ervin Calhoun, but we know there are others. Tons of others, but we just don't have the facts. If you help us, we'll help you."

"I would like to speak to my attorney."

"Sure, but we're going to offer your attorney the same plea that we just offered you. So you need to think about it."

"If the plea is for me to ruin people's lives, I won't do it."

"Fine. You'll just go down alone."

"I want an attorney. I'm done talking to you."

He walked out of the room. Anger wouldn't allow me to cry. I couldn't imagine who'd exposed me. Who would have taped conversations?

I didn't get a bail hearing until the next day and bail was set for five hundred thousand dollars. I called Ramon and authorized him to take fifty thousand out of the bank. When he came to pick me up I cried for the first time. I apologized to him. He was involved in a big mess now. I wondered if he still felt like my past didn't matter. Ironically, he said he was sorry too.

Why would he apologize? He said he hated that I had to go through this. When we got home we sat on the couch and he held me tightly. He said, "I changed the phone number."

"Thank you."

"Now you're starting to get death threats. But as long as I'm here, no one will hurt you."

"I'm so thankful for you."

I wanted to erase my past and just be with Ramon. What had seemed like an easy way to make a buck was now haunting me big-time. I wanted to call my mother, but it was too late. I felt lonely and sad and all the things she'd warned me of had come to pass. She'd said money rules the world. You have to figure out how to make some money. But why had I found this to be the best way to do it?

I hated Thorne for recruiting me into the business. I wished I could go back to my small apartment. When he proposed this to me I should have spit in his face. I never imagined I'd be in so deep that I couldn't see a way out. I was faced with prison time and/or the option to destroy my clients' lives. I just couldn't do it. They had just been looking for an outlet and now the authorities expected me to betray them and be the tell-all girl. It was not in my character. As I expressed my fears to Ramon, I guess he didn't want to lose me. He suggested I offer a few names and see what they'd be willing to do.

"I can't."

"London, sometimes you have to do things that you don't want to do to preserve yourself."

"I wouldn't be able to sleep at night if I did that."

"And you still won't be able to sleep if you're in jail."

"I guess you got a point."

We were cuddled up on the couch when a big rock was hurled through the window. Ramon pulled his gun from his waist and motioned for me to get on the floor. With his back against the wall he peeked out the window. We heard car wheels peel off. Ramon went out the front door and checked around the house. He came back and leaned over me. "We need to go to a hotel. It's not safe for us to be here."

We went upstairs and grabbed some necessities. I thought it would be best if we left the area altogether. We drove closer to BWI Airport. I wasn't sure if we were going to have to skip town or not.

When we got to the hotel Ramon continued to try to convince me that I should tell. I couldn't even believe he'd think that was a safe thing to do. My head was spinning. I didn't know what to do, I was just thankful to have my personal bodyguard lying beside me.

35

I woke up the next morning convinced that in order to save myself I would have to expose a few people. They would get a slap on the wrist, but I would take a big fall if I decided to accept the charges. I tried Thorne's cell phone and the number had been changed. I called him at work and he picked up.

"Thorne, I'm sure you know but I'm in big trouble."

"I'm not exactly sure who I'm speaking with."

"It's London."

"I'm sorry; I don't know anyone by that name."

Of all the events in the past twenty-four hours, that hurt the most. Thorne acted as if he didn't know me. He was the only person I had truly trusted. I didn't know if Ramon's advice was right, but I had known that Thorne would lead me in the right direction. Instead he pretended I was a stranger.

I was stunned, and the last seven years of my life flashed before my eyes. I couldn't believe he'd lured me into this and could just hang me out to dry. I knew he had to protect himself, but his voice was so cold and crushing that I felt like nothing. It felt like all I'd ever been to him was a dumbass hooker. My eyes filled with tears and I tried to fight back the emotion. I bit my lips to restrain the pain that was dying to spill out. When I could no longer resist, I yelled loudly and finally broke down into tears. I screamed, "I hate you!"

Ramon ran out of the bathroom. "What happened?"

"I just called Thorne and when I said 'This is London' he said, 'Sorry, I don't know anyone by that name.'"

Ramon tried to hug me and I pounded on his chest. I had to release my anguish on someone and he just let me. I'm sure that my punches didn't faze him, though. I yelled, "Why me?"

All my anger was directed at Thorne. I felt used, abused, and led astray.

"You're in the type of industry where no one can be trusted. No one is going to step up and claim to know you."

When he said that, a weird chill ran up my spine. I began to wonder if he could be trusted. I just wanted to run away. I looked at him. "Will you claim to know me?"

"Of course I will, but I can't confirm or deny anything about your business. I really don't know anything."

Who was I really protecting? Not one of those men would protect me. I didn't want to go to jail, especially for a group of people who didn't give a damn about me. I went into the bathroom and slammed the door. I called the agent and said, "I'm ready to talk."

I called my attorney, gave him the rundown, and asked him to meet me at the FBI office. When the investigator came into the interviewing room he had a smirk like he knew that I would eventually talk. I was fine with that but I wasn't talking unless I knew it was worth it to me.

I said, "I've gotten a lot of death threats."

"Understandably so."

My attorney spoke. "What's the deal if she talks?"

The agent said, "Five years' probation."

"What about protection?"

"We can offer witness protection."

"For how long?"

"A year or as long as she needs it."

"Are you telling me that I may have to live with an alias for the rest of my life?" I asked.

My attorney said, "It's possible."

I wasn't sure what was worse. Didn't know if it was wiser just to see what kind of sentence I would get or live in fear for the rest of my life. I wondered if Ramon planned to be by my side through all of this. There were so many what-ifs circulating through my mind.

My attorney said, "So is there anyone in particular you want?"

"No, we just want to know who her clients are."

"So you are asking me to admit that I even have clients."

"Look, Ms. Reed. We know you have clients."

"Because of Ervin Calhoun. That doesn't mean anything. I hooked him up with a friend."

He laughed. "Ms. Reed, the evidence from the Ervin Calhoun case is pretty incriminating."

My attorney said, "Tell us what you have."

The agent stood up. "I'll be right back."

He left the room and I couldn't imagine what he could have. I wondered if Taina had sent them some evidence, because she had gone a lot more quietly than I had expected. Here we were a year later dealing with this bullshit.

The agent came back in the room and popped a CD into his laptop. It was my voice talking to Taina. We were in her apartment and I was explaining to her that men who pay for sex aren't going to make you their woman. I explained that Ervin Calhoun had threatened me and it was my responsibility to protect the girls who worked for me. I took a phone call in the middle of the conversation with Taina. I arranged a hookup. My entire body was trembling. It had to be Taina. She was the only one there that night. I said, "Where did you get this?"

"An undisclosed source tried to sell this information to a tabloid last year, but Calhoun wasn't in the position he is in at that time. They tried again when Calhoun got the job, and there was a bidding war. They got off with a lot of money."

"And how did you get it?"

"The Internet, where we get most of our evidence nowadays."

"You can't believe everything on the Internet."

"Voice recognition. Are you telling me this isn't you?"

"No. It's not me."

He showed me pictures of me walking out of Taina's place carrying her bags. "So is this not you too?"

My chest caved in. Since all this had been leaked, a piece of me had assumed it was Taina, but if she was in the pictures, who had taken them? My head was pounding. Ramon had been around through that whole situation, but I couldn't bring myself to believe that he was a part of this. I tried to focus my attention on what the detective was talking about but still I couldn't help wondering who had sold this evidence. Thorne couldn't have done it because it could take him down too.

My attorney looked at me and whispered, "We should take the deal."

I didn't know what to do, but I wasn't ready to talk. At

least not yet. I wanted someone's advice and not just Ramon's. I wasn't sure about him either. The detective said the offer wouldn't be on the table long.

"How long do I have?"

"Maybe until the end of the week. That's if I'm in a good mood."

"I hope you are. And one more thing, how can I protect my business?"

"I don't know, that's something you'll have to figure out."

My attorney and I left the building. We spoke outside about the next steps and he inferred that it would be in my best interest to tell everything. My stomach was in knots because I really didn't want to do it. I stood there after my attorney pulled off, staring aimlessly, thinking no one understood. Finally, I got in the car with Ramon. He put his hand on my thigh and I pushed it away. He said, "What's wrong?"

"Nothing, I'm just not in the mood."

I called the manager on duty at Unleashed. "How are things there?"

She said, "Pretty hectic. We're getting a lot of calls. There are no dogs here today. We've been getting threats."

"Why don't you lock up and go home?"

"How are you?" She spoke with such empathy.

"I'm holding up."

"You're strong. You'll come out of this even stronger."

"Thank you, Bethany."

"Whatever you need, I'm here."

"I'm not sure what's going to happen with the hotel now that all of this is going on. Hopefully we can ride the wave."

"I hope so. I really like working for you."

She had been one of those to answer my ad on Craigslist. When I saw how frumpy she was I knew she could never work in the business. So I hired her to do what the job specified.

"And I really like you. I may have to sell the hotel. I'm not sure, but go ahead and close up. Let the other employees know that we're going to be closed for the next seven days. That should be enough time for the dust to settle."

"I hope so."

I prayed so, but I knew better. I knew this was much larger than that. Ramon looked at me. "Where to?"

"Back to the hotel."

"So what did you tell them?"

"I didn't tell them anything. I needed to see what they could offer me. They are asking for my entire phone book and I just don't know if it's worth it."

"It's not worth your freedom?"

"My freedom at what cost?" I snapped.

"Look, I'm just saying..."

I heard my mother's voice. *Women always have to sacrifice.* I didn't know if this sacrifice made sense. I wanted to be sure that I didn't hurt anyone else the way I'd been hurt. I called Kari because I knew she was concerned. I didn't want to involve her, but I needed to hear her voice. She was the only person I knew without a doubt I could trust.

"Hey, Kari."

"London...honey. What's going on?"

"I lied to you when I told you I was out of the business."

"London, I know. What's going on? How did all of this come out?"

"I don't know, Kari. I should have listened to you."

"Not now, Lon. Don't beat yourself up."

Kari always had a way of finding the words to make me want to cry. Water welled in my eyes and I sniffed.

"Remember, you're the strongest person I know, London."

"Thank you, Kari, I love you. I will have someone keep you posted."

"Where's Ramon?"

I took a deep breath. I couldn't utter the words that I no longer trusted him. Kari got my drift.

"Okay, London. I'll be waiting by the phone."

When we got back to the hotel I began looking up the biographies of my clients. I wanted to be sure that I gave only the names of men whose livelihoods wouldn't be very affected. I wanted to stay away from politicians.

I copied and pasted names into a text file of those that I would reveal. Ramon checked on me from time to time to see how many names I had. I would cover the list up when he came over. I wasn't sure I wanted anyone to know what I was doing.

I logged into Ramon's bank account and queried the account for the month I initially hired him. I pulled up another window to check my e-mail account for the itinerary to England so I could confirm the exact dates. He had deposited twenty thousand dollars on the day we returned. I looked over at him resting on the king-sized bed. I didn't want to accuse him. I wanted to give him the opportunity to tell me the truth. I said, "Ramon, is there anything you want to tell me?"

He sat up. "Like what, London?"

"Were you the one who sent those pictures and tapes to the magazine?"

He looked through me. I wanted to yell and scream and

choke him, but I was numb. "You deposited twenty thousand dollars into your account around that time."

He still didn't say anything. I looked at him. "Tell me you
didn't sell me out for twenty thousand dollars. I would have
given you forty thousand to keep your damn mouth closed."

"London, I didn't sell anything to a magazine." He took a
deep breath and hung his head. "Thorne . . ."

The moment he said Thorne's name I felt numb. He continued to speak, but I felt like his words were distorted. "He
told me to capture everything from the second I met you to
the time we got Taina on the plane. He said he needed all
the evidence in case someone tried to link you or him to the
situation. That way, he could edit it and make it look like
whatever he needed if something came up." Ramon shook
his head and wiped his face. Breathing deeply, he continued,
"We've done things like this before in other situations. That's
how Thorne has stayed in the business so long without getting caught."

I closed my eyes, trying to absorb what he was saying. I
couldn't imagine that all of this was coming from a person
who was supposed to love me. I was nauseous. I was too
shocked to respond. He stood in front of me and put his
hands on my shoulders. I pushed him away from me.

"You're telling me that you've given him pictures before?
Why didn't you think it was important to tell me if it was
that innocent?"

"Thorne and I had been doing business long before I met
you and he never gave me any reason to believe that he would
do something like this.

"I'm sorry, London. If I would have known, I would have
never given them to him."

I began to heave. I wanted to burst with anger, but I couldn't speak. Ramon was too smart not to have known what Thorne's plans were. I blamed him as much as I blamed Thorne. I couldn't imagine that he could know he'd done this and lie in bed with me every night. I couldn't believe that his conscience didn't bother him. I walked toward the bathroom. I stood there, thinking I would vomit, but I couldn't.

I imagined it would be easier for him if I were yelling and screaming and crying, but I couldn't. I couldn't give him the satisfaction of my tears. I walked out of the bathroom.

"Ramon, I want you to go. I don't care where you go. I just want you gone. I don't ever want to see you again."

"London, how was I supposed to know? I would have never done this to anyone. I trusted Thorne too. He told me that he needed those pictures to protect us."

"Ramon, I don't know what to think. Why wouldn't you tell me about this as soon as the story broke?"

"I was afraid you'd respond like you are now."

"Just go. You're in the same boat with Thorne."

He backed away from me. "London, I'm sorry."

"Please go. Leave my keys."

I walked back to the desk and got on the computer. He got his stuff and slowly took my keys from his ring. I didn't look up at him. I wanted him to leave because I didn't want him to see me break down. When the door closed, tears poured from my eyes. I didn't have anyone. I never thought I would say this, but I wanted my mother. I wanted someone to hold me and tell me it would be okay.

I called her. "Hello."

"London, are you okay?"

"Not really."

"Do you want to come see me?"

I began to cry. "I'm not sure if I can."

"Where are you? I'm coming to you."

"I'm in Baltimore." I paused. "I'm scared."

"I know you are, but I'll be on the next plane."

36

My mother arrived at BWI at around three in the morning and I told her to catch a taxi because I was afraid to leave the hotel. I hurt deep in my soul thinking about Thorne, thinking about how a person could be so deceitful. Considering he'd sold all the evidence, I knew he had covered his ass. He always outsmarted the next man. I hoped he would burn in hell.

I heard a tap on the door and I peeked out before opening it. My mother walked in and held me. She said, "I'm sorry, honey."

"It's okay."

"I should have been a better mother."

"That had nothing to do with it. Don't blame yourself."

"I mean, why would you ever think about being a prostitute? It must have been something I did."

"Ma, not now."

I sat on the couch and she sat beside me. "You're right, London. Let's talk about the next step. Going over and over what's happened already isn't going to help you."

"I just need you to hold me."

Her eyes blinked. This type of affection was too much for her. She leaned in for one of her standoff superficial hugs. I said, "Hold me, Mom. Hold me tightly."

She did the best she could and we sat up to discuss how we would make our relationship better going forward. It was weird because, in my moment of humility, I could see so much of myself in her. My mother was a boss and although she hated my career of choice, that's why I had never wanted to work for anyone. She was anal and organized and I had adopted those traits.

My cell phone rang at around eight o'clock, alarming both my mother and me. I checked the ID because I had stopped answering unknown calls, although it didn't stop people from leaving messages. It was Bethany, the manager at Unleashed. She was yelling. I couldn't make out what she was saying. All I could imagine was that they were now after her to get close to me.

"Bethany, honey, I can't hear you."

"The buildings are gone. Nothing but ashes."

"What?"

"Unleashed has been burned down. Someone set it on fire."

I closed my eyes and let my knees buckle as I fell back on the bed. Finally, I wailed. I couldn't believe my ears. It wasn't fair. I had done nothing to deserve this. These people were afraid that I would snitch, so they were making my life a living hell. I couldn't take it anymore. I wanted out. I wanted to run away.

"I'm the backup contact for the security alarm so they called me." She paused. "London, it's going to be okay."

"Bethany, will you be able to handle things there? I can't come there."

My mother rubbed my back. "London, you're going to have to go away. You may have to tell some names."

"I am."

I called the detective shortly after and told him that I would hand over all my contacts, but I needed to be out of there as soon as possible. He told me that wouldn't be a problem. I asked him to come to the hotel.

He was there within the hour with a tape recorder in hand. He started off speaking my name and case number into the recorder. Then he looked at me. "You ready?"

I nodded. I pulled out the list and began spewing off names. I could tell by the look on his face that he couldn't believe half the names I was saying. I tried to incriminate Thorne by telling the detective he was my partner, but he told me that from the evidence they had I was the head of the ring. Thorne had Ramon give him just enough to make me look like the mastermind and him like the innocent bystander.

When I was done the detective stood up and touched my shoulder. "You've done a great job."

"No I haven't, but thanks anyway. What's next?"

"We have to find a safe home for you. You can't tell anyone where you are. You'll have to change your name. We'll get you new passports and IDs. We can take care of that today and have you out of here within forty-eight hours."

"And those names won't leak before you get me out of here."

He agreed and told me not to worry. I looked at my mother when he was gone. "I'll need you to stay here and try to sell my house or list it with a property manager."

"Not a problem."

"And you're going to have to deal with the insurance company for the fire."

"Don't worry. I'm here for you. I should have been here a long time ago. I feel like somehow this is all my fault."

"Mother, stop."

She nodded, but I knew she blamed herself. She was a perfectionist and her world was black and white, no gray. You went to work every day, you worked hard to prove yourself, and you never, by any means, broke the law. I'd rebelled against that type of regimen and thus had landed in a big old mess.

37

My hair had been cut very short and dyed auburn. The stress of the situation put about twenty pounds on me. The FBI relocated me to New Mexico. I felt rather uncomfortable, like I didn't belong, but the people seemed to be in their own zone. They knew nothing about the Dog Trainer Madam, the name the media had given me. I was just some black girl who'd moved here from the East Coast and anyway I looked completely different. The FBI had given me a transcript and a degree in biology from UCLA. So, of all things, I was teaching high school biology. It lacked all the glitz and glamour of being a call girl, but it was rewarding. Every day I went to work I thought about how stupid and stubborn I'd been. I should have taught school when I first graduated.

I had nothing to show for my many years in the business. All I had was a bunch of drama, no friends, and burnt bridges, but I looked at this as an opportunity to start again. Yet there was another side of me that felt like if I started over and built new relationships that would be more betrayal, because I would have to be evasive with everyone. I didn't want to be exposed, so I stayed to myself. I was known as

Denise Thomas. I was lonely and lost. My entire past wiped away with a few clicks of a mouse.

After a year I felt the press had died down enough for me to contact my mother. I longed to hear her voice. I blocked the number and wasn't sure she'd answer. She did and it was almost as if she knew it would be me. "Hello," she said anxiously.

"Mom."

"London. I'm so happy to hear from you."

"It's good to hear your voice too."

"I know you can't tell me where you are, but how's everything?"

"You'll never believe this. I'm teaching."

"That's great, London. Do you like it?"

"Actually, I do."

"You know this is your second chance."

"I hope so," I said, as tears filled my eyes. "I'm so lonely. I'm so afraid to meet anyone or let anyone in."

"London, this isn't forever."

"I know, but they're telling me that I should at least stay here for another year."

"I know, London. I just hate what has happened to you." She paused. "But there is some good news. Your house finally sold, so you have some money in the bank. You have some insurance money from Unleashed too. So you can rebuild somewhere else."

"Yeah, maybe."

"This time I'll help you."

"I'd like that."

"And someone named Clyde calls frequently to see how you're doing."

"How'd he get your information?"

"He told me that you gave it to him when you came here from Australia. He's been calling about once a month to check on you."

I slightly recalled giving Clyde my mother's information, but I couldn't believe he'd held on to it for so long. I hadn't put my favorites in the list of names. And Clyde was probably thankful that I'd had enough decency not to out him.

"So what does he say?"

"He's very polite. He calls and asks how I'm doing and if there is anything that I need. Then he goes on to say that he's just checking in on you. I actually look forward to Clyde's calls."

"Aww. Clyde," I said, thinking about all the good times we'd shared.

"Where'd you meet him?"

"You really don't want to know."

She cleared her throat as if she definitely didn't care to know all the details if I'd met him in the business. "Well, it seems like he really cares about you. He wants to see you if he can. I've gotten several calls of that nature, but Clyde is probably the only person I trust."

"Do you think I should call him?"

"I do, but do you think he's trustworthy?"

"I think so, but I definitely don't want to have that death-threat frenzy like before."

"Maybe you can call him just to talk. You don't have to tell him where you are."

When she said that, it dawned on me that I hadn't even told her where I was. I said, "I guess you're right. There's no harm in that."

She gave me his number and shortly after I got off the phone I called Clyde. He answered and I said, "Hi, Clyde."

"London."

He said my name with such compassion.

"Yes."

"I'm so glad you're okay."

"I am."

"I needed to tell you that I'd never enjoyed myself with anyone the way I did with you. And I didn't realize how much of an influence you had on my life until I had to sit back and watch you go through everything by yourself. I was supposed to save you from that."

"Clyde. It was nobody's fault but mine. I was in a dangerous business and I just didn't realize it because of the type of clients we had. Prostitution is dangerous on every level, but I guess I just didn't know."

"Remember the last time we were together?"

"Of course I do. We were in Australia."

"You were trying to tell me something. Or better yet, you wanted me to tell you something. At the time, I just couldn't do it. I just couldn't bring myself to believe that I had feelings for you."

"Clyde. Don't do this. Don't say these things just to flatter me."

"London, I'm not trying to flatter you. I'm telling you what I realized just as you were being taken down. I didn't even care if you gave them my name. All I knew was when I heard your kennel had been burned and that you'd been arrested, I could have done something to save you from all of that."

"What makes you so sure?"

"You were trying to tell me you wanted out, but I shot you

down. It was my way of looking at you as a prostitute and not a real woman."

"Clyde, if I wanted to get out, I didn't need you to tell me it was a good idea, I would have done it on my own."

"If I had told you in Australia that I wanted something more from you, would you have continued doing it?"

"I don't know. I can't say."

"I should have been honest with you then."

"And what would you have said?"

"I would have told you that I wanted more from you."

"So what am I supposed to do with that information now?"

"I haven't met anyone yet that likes to do all the weird shit that I enjoy except you."

"And what are you saying?"

"Tell me where you are so I can come get you."

"Clyde, it's not that easy."

"It is that easy. I'll come get you."

"Listen, there may still be people after me and if I leave this place, that means the FBI is no longer responsible for my protection. I'm scared."

"Don't be scared, London. I'll protect you. My house is big enough that you'll never have to leave if you don't want to."

"Who's going to travel with you then?"

"When we leave the country is the only time you'll have to leave," he said, laughing. "Otherwise, my home is your castle."

I thought for a few seconds longer. What kind of life was this anyway? It wasn't long before my loneliness overpowered my logic. I had to trust someone. "I'm in New Mexico."

I gave Clyde all the details to rescue me and he flew in the next day. He rented a car and came to get me. He packed up my modest things in less than an hour and we drove to LA. I wasn't sure this was the right decision, but I knew I needed companionship and I didn't want to live a lie anymore. Clyde knew all my dirt and still cared about me. There were no secrets and I appreciated that.

READING GROUP GUIDE

1) Do you think the average unemployed college graduate would have taken Thorne up on his offer?

2) What where the pros and cons of London's job?

3) What did Thorne see in London that made her a prime candidate?

4) What is your opinion about Thorne's advice that if a woman is not in a committed relationship, she shouldn't offer her services for free?

5) Did London trust Thorne too much?

6) When would have been an optimal time for London to get out of the game?

7) Was London a wise businesswoman? What were her strengths and weaknesses?

8) Did London's relationship with her mother affect her choices in life?

9) Were there similarities between London and her mother?

10) What statement did London's calling her mother in her time of trouble make?

11) Is it likely that London could ever have a successful relationship after spending so many years in the profession?

12) Do you think she really cared for Clyde? Did he care for her?

Ayana Blue is the radio DJ with all the answers on affairs of the heart. Until one caller wants answers on Ayana's affairs...

Please turn this page for a preview of Candice Dow's next book.

Available in 2012

1

I pulled up to a development in Buckhead, not far from Lenox Square mall. My producer Quentin had referred me to his Realtor friend. I'd done some online home browsing but this was the first place I was physically seeing. A silver Audi A6 pulled up a few parking spaces away at exactly two-thirty. I assumed it was my Realtor. After he got out of the car, I stepped out and headed in his direction.

He shook my hand. "Hi, Ms. Blue. Pleasure to meet you."

"Garrett, the pleasure is all mine. Call me Ayana, please."

"Okay, Ayana. The spot is in the building here."

Quentin hadn't given me any details about his friend aside from his being the best Realtor in Atlanta. As I stood there feeling strongly attracted to this man, I wanted to know everything. Was he married? Did he have kids? Was he heterosexual?

Garrett was wearing jeans and a black T-shirt with black-and-white Puma sneakers. He carried a leather backpack. I estimated that he was about five foot eleven; he wasn't short, but I had the feeling that he wasn't quite six feet. He walked ahead of me as we climbed the stairs to a second-floor garden condo. I was already not feeling the place, but I was definitely feeling the swagger of the guy in front of me. I watched his strong mocha arms as he rolled the code on the lockbox. Finally the door to the condo opened and we entered.

He said, "First order of business, I'll need you to sign these forms."

He handed the forms to me as we stood next to the countertop in the empty unit. He hovered over me as he told me where to sign and why I was signing. His face was clean-shaven with a nice dark mustache. His hair was cut low. He looked and smelled crisp: a lightly scented cologne mixed with Irish Spring soap. I inhaled him; his vibe was smooth and jovial, almost familiar.

"A'ight. Cool. Now that the business is taken care of, we can get to the fun part. We're going to visit every condominium complex in Buckhead. Cool?"

I said, "I'm really not the type that needs to see everything. I want to see the three best condos in my price range, preferably two-bedrooms with a den, and I can make a decision."

He stopped in the middle of the living room and laughed. "So Ayana Blue is not picky."

"Is there something about me that makes you think that I'm picky?"

He shrugged. "I shouldn't say this, but most women are picky. Usually dudes come to me, they see one or two places and they are ready to put a contract down. Women, on the other hand, I can spend two, three, sometimes even six months showing them everything on the multiple listing and they just have something in their mind that they're looking for and they don't stop until they get it. Nature of the business, though."

"So are you as patient and friendly with these women after month three?"

He laughed. "Of course. I earn a living from referrals. I'm as eager to show the first place as I am to show the sixtieth place. If I'm showing, I'm still in the game, and that's all that matters to me. Can I put food on the table and clothes on my son's back?"

Why did my heart sink? Just because there was a son didn't mean there was a wife. He didn't have on a ring, but that didn't mean anything either.

"How old is your son?"

"He's seven."

I had been so wrapped up in work that my flirtation was rusty. I entered the master bedroom and looked at the bathroom before I decided to pry further.

"What's your son's name?"

"Amari."

"He lives with you?"

He took a deep breath. "We have joint custody."

"So what's that like? Do you do week by week or do you have certain days and she has certain days?"

"Week by week."

We had toured the condominium and were scheduled to see another. I wasn't sure I should ask any more questions, for fear of pressing too hard. Maybe I should have come out and asked if he was single and ready to date. Instead I said, "Not sold on this place. We can go to the next one."

"Cool, you wanna just hop in the car with me?"

I shrugged and we headed to his car. He opened the door for me. *That was quite gentlemanly.* I smiled and thanked him. As we drove to the next place, he seemed to open up a little.

"I'm glad you're decisive, Ayana."

"Why is that?"

"I usually schedule showings in late evening or early in the day; late afternoon is bad for me. I pick up my son."

"It's your week."

"I actually pick up most days because my schedule is more flexible than hers."

"Whose? His mom's or your wife's?" I jabbed that question in quickly so that I could get the info I needed to either stop or continue flirting.

He laughed and looked at me. I couldn't help laughing too. That was tacky, but I wanted to know.

"His mom's. My soon-to-be-ex-wife. We're in the middle of a divorce."

"Ooh," I said, with screeching brakes.

"It's a nasty one."

That was a double ooh. We pulled up to the next complex. As we hopped out I shifted into counselor mode. "Divorces are never fun. I think that two adults who realize they are going in opposite directions should agree to disagree and come to an understanding as to how they are going to handle the family business apart. But unfortunately, emotions get the best of us and it becomes a battle."

"Exactly."

We caught the elevator to the top floor. This unit was a penthouse condo with a loft and den. As soon as we entered it felt like home. He looked at me and knew that we had struck gold.

He said, "Don't get too excited. We have others to see."

This place had a concierge, a twenty-four-hour doorman, a fitness center, and a meeting room. It offered everything I needed and more. It had mahogany hardwood floors, granite countertops, stainless steel appliances. Both of the bedrooms were large and considered master suites. The loft overlooked the family room. There was a bump-out eat-in kitchen and a formal dining room, as well as a petite patio off the family room. I imagined having my girlfriends over for our Friday night chats. The floor plan was ideal for me and my needs.

"I told you that I was simple. Didn't I?"

"Now simple is one thing, but it's my job to make sure you've seen at least three to five options before you put a contract on anything."

"If that means I get to hang out with you for a little while longer, that's cool."

We both burst out laughing. *Why did I even let those words come out of my mouth?* I really wasn't interested in dealing with a man in the middle of a nasty divorce.

"Ayana, you are cooler than Quentin made you out to be."

"What did he say about me?"

"Honestly?"

"Yeah, honestly. Even if it does hurt my feelings."

He looked directly in my eyes. "He said that he's never met a woman quite like you. He said he didn't even know God created women like you."

He nearly brought tears to my eyes. I had known Quentin respected me but to hear it from someone else was flattering.

"Aw. He really said that?"

"He said you're amazing and the man that snags you would be a lucky son of a bitch."

I felt almost bashful hearing these things about myself. I was at a loss for words.

"But you're not settling down anytime soon. Things are going too good."

It was clear that he was prying. "Garrett, no one should ever be too busy for love."

"Can I take you to dinner later on this evening?"

I appreciated his direct approach. Though I had placed the bait out for him, I hadn't expected him to bite so quickly.

"I love to eat."

"And I love a woman that likes to eat. Is seven a good time for you?"

"That works."

Garrett took me back to my car and we agreed to meet at Copeland's on Piedmont.

Garrett had sleepy eyes and they were so sexy under the dim lights. Over dinner I discovered that he had simply married the wrong woman for the wrong reason, but that it wouldn't deter him from remarrying. He wanted to do it again with the right person. He loved to cook and travel. He gave me a rundown of his family structure. He respected his mother and more important he loved his father and his grandfather. His family was close and festive.

A part of me wanted to wait to like him until I got the full report from Quentin in the morning, but I already liked him. I liked how much he knew about life, how much he wanted to know about me, and how straightforward he was about what he was looking for. There was nothing pretentious about him and that seemed to be the issue with most men I met. He was real. He was open. He was different.

Good conversation made the hours pass rapidly. The staff began to clean the restaurant around us as we sat absorbed in each other. Ten o'clock arrived too soon and I didn't want the night to end, but it was time to go.

After we left the restaurant and headed to the parking garage I was tempted to ask him to come back to my place, but I felt like it was too late. My car was a little distance from his, so he offered to drive me to it.

When I sat in the passenger seat, he looked at me. "Ayana, it's been a really long time since I was on the dating scene. And from all the horror stories I hear, I haven't been real anxious either. But tonight I feel different."

"I do too, Garrett."

He leaned over and kissed me. His masculine hand touched the side of my face. His tongue twirled slowly in my mouth and my vagina began to throb. It seemed like we were connected. Our lips were locked and neither of us pulled back. He wanted more of me and I wanted more of him. Could this be right? In a dark parking lot on our first date? Or would we ruin the possibilities if we were to succumb to our nature?

I knew better, but my body knew something else. I wanted to be wise, but I needed to feel him right there, right then. His hand slipped under my shirt and he began to rub up and down my back. He put his finger on the hook of my bra.

"May I?"

I didn't want him to stop. Whatever was going to be that night was going to be. He struggled momentarily to unhook my bra, but finally it popped open. He lifted my shirt and looked delighted with my double Ds. He stared at me for a second.

"You're beautiful. Your body is perfect."

A woman can never hear those words enough, especially when by most standards she's considered overweight. I was five foot five and 185 pounds, and it wasn't every day that someone put my body and perfection in the same sentence. That aroused me more.

The armrest between us restricted our closeness. He kissed my breast awkwardly before asking me to sit on top of him. As I climbed over to his seat he moved the driver's seat back.

He lifted my shirt over my head and I wrapped my arms around his neck as he made oral love to my breast.

"Can I have you?"

I nodded yes. From the bulge I felt through his jeans, I wanted to have him too.

"You sure?"

I nodded yes again. He put his hands under my skirt to feel me. "Ooh, you feel so good."

We kissed more as I tried to come out of my panties in the confines of his car and he unbuckled his jeans and pulled them to his knees. He grabbed a box of condoms from the armrest storage compartment and tore it open, taking one out before placing the box back. I was wet and he was rock solid as we shared an inquisitive, passionate stare for a few seconds. Was this right? Was this lust just too strong for us to resist? He used his mouth to open the packet and quickly put the condom on. As he held on to my thighs and I slid down on him, we both exhaled. All of our preoccupations and inhibitions dissipated as we united. We ground slowly and sighed deeply as if this was what we both needed. He kissed me passionately like we were longtime lovers. He looked in my eyes with each stroke. The warm and misty air made our skin stick together, forcing us closer. It felt better and better the longer he was inside me. It felt like he belonged there. Finally he exploded in me. His love coated my walls and I felt brand-new.

We talked inside his car for several hours longer. Finally, at around two in the morning, he drove me to my car. I looked at him and I knew at that moment this hadn't been a mistake. He saw the same something in my eyes. We kissed. We had tried to part several times throughout the night, and I knew that if I didn't take the first step we would stay longer.

"Garrett, I had a wonderful night."

"I would ask you to come home with me, but..."

I didn't want to know what had caused the *but*, because I was certain it would taint the wonderful night. "Don't worry. We have to see those other condos tomorrow. I'll see you then."

"Ayana, you're cool," he said, still holding my left hand.

I reached for the handle and opened the door. "Tomorrow?"

"Definitely."

His grip was even tighter. I set one foot out of the car and slowly pried my hand away from his. Soon after, the second foot followed and I closed the door. When I got in my car I wanted to scream with excitement, disappointment, frustration, and anticipation all at once but I didn't. I took a deep breath and followed Garrett out of the garage.

2

M̲y state of ecstasy spilled over into the next day. Garrett texted me bright and early in the morning. "U R A BEAUTIFUL WOMAN. CAN'T WAIT TO SEE U THIS AFTERNOON."

I had planned to ask Quentin all about him since he was the one who had referred me to Garrett, but when I saw him I no longer had the desire to. I didn't want any secondhand information on Garrett, I wanted to explore him for myself and to see where that would lead. Garrett's approach might have been different, based on the suspicious look Quentin returned to me.

He said, "How'd the home search go?"

"It was cool. We looked at two places and I'm looking at two today."

"See anything you like?"

I wanted to laugh. *Hell yeah, I saw something I liked.* I only wished Quentin had forewarned me.

"Yeah, I saw one place that I really liked."

"Cool. Garrett is a real good dude."

"He seems like it."

When I started the show, it was the first time in twelve hours that I wasn't thinking about Garrett. I love my job. It's not exactly what I dreamed I'd be doing, but it is something I do naturally without any thought.

While pursuing my PhD in psychology I started out on a journey to discover why all six of my good girlfriends and I were still single. We were all in our late twenties, had good jobs, and were attractive. Certainly the selection of good black men couldn't be that bad. There had to be something wrong with us. Were we too dominant? Were we too picky? Or did we just have bad luck? Assuming this would be the perfect dissertation, I began my research. Naturally, I decided to start with the women who were where we claimed we wanted to be.

After nearly ten interviews I was shocked to learn that many of these women in the socially imposed ideal situation were unhappy, and seven of them claimed they would not remarry their husbands. While I had expected to get responses about how great it was to be committed to the *one*, I ended up disappointed with the reality that men are men.

Besides being single, my friends and I were happy. Most of all we were free. With freedom came options and we knew we weren't stuck. Maybe that was why we laughed, traveled, and absorbed life. Suddenly my research shifted to single women. Were they all as happy as we were? After interviewing a few single women, I found that a large percentage of them were unhappy too. They felt like life had dealt them a bad hand. Could it be that being a woman is an unhappy existence in and of itself? Why did it seem that women were never satisfied? Finally, it hit me. The one common denominator among the unhappy women was that none of them had real good girlfriends. The women, single or married, with thriving female friendships seemed to get the most out of life.

I went to my adviser to let him know that my dissertation would be called *Girlfriends: The Therapeutic Effect*. He found my topic laughable until I began to explain. Women forgo the chance for true commitment and intimacy with each other, assuming that it can only be found in a marriage. My adviser was still quite perplexed as I continued. Men are completely incapable of giving women the amount of emotional security they seek. Women in turn beg, plead, and worry men to be something that they can never be, leaving themselves eternally unfulfilled. Finally he began to let down his guard and smile.

"Ayana, you're right. I think this will be quite interesting, actually."

"When women get in relationships, they feel like their girlfriends are disposable. 'Finally, now I can stop hanging out and just chill with my man.'"

He laughed. "This is very true."

"That's crazy. What is the shift in our brain that makes us believe that we can do without our girls now that he's around?" I paused, hoping the concept would sink in. "Men don't want to go to the mall. They don't want to gossip. They don't want to watch romantic comedies. Men don't give up sports or beer when they get into relationships. So why do we give up our natural antidepressant? Real girlfriends?"

He chuckled. "Ms. Blue, I'd like you to keep me posted. If your research is strong, I'll approve it."

He approved it and offered to help me find a literary agent. I had never imagined myself as an author, but he encouraged me to turn my dissertation into a book. He found my research and recommendations profound. With the coaxing of my girl crew, I turned my research into a book titled *Where My Girls At?* I was offered a two-book deal from a major publishing house and had no clue what I could write as a second book.

Then one of my good friends suggested that I write about how to be a good friend, because that was a skill not all women had. My first book talked about the importance of friends but didn't give instructions. The sales for *Where My Girls At?* had been nominal at best. A year later *Girlfriend Confidential* hit the shelves. My friends vowed that this one would not go down like the first. We had learned our lesson: Getting the book on the shelves means absolutely nothing if no one knows anything about it. We all put our skills together and I had my own in-house publicity team. We sent press kits to every media outlet, every female organization, and every sorority, and attended every chick conference we could find. *Girlfriend Confidential* became the topic of discussion at hair salons, book clubs, and girl groups everywhere. Women began to deem me the relationship expert. I started to get e-mails from people asking for my advice on every aspect of their lives. I'd only had my PhD for a little over a year; how was I supposed to help all these people? I wasn't ready for all of this, but opportunity after opportunity came knocking at my door. As I took more speaking and workshop engagements, I grew more popular.

Within eighteen months I was approached with the option to host my own satellite radio show. I was offered a lunchtime slot, from ten to two. The time slot already had a listener base, primarily African-American women. The show would be named after my book: *Girlfriend Confidential with Ayana Blue*. I accepted the job.

Before my first day on the air I was introduced to Quentin so we could map out the format of the show. He was a senior producer and had already designed a plan for success. On the first day he decided to have my girls in the studio with me. He felt that would give me an initial dose of confidence and he was right. It was like a night out with my girls. With each phone call I became more relaxed. With each day I was more certain that this was where I was destined to be. My listeners needed me, my voice, and my advice.

"You really have to be thankful for the little things. Don't focus so much on what he doesn't do as opposed to what he does do. My dad's favorite saying is 'Accentuate the positives and eliminate the negatives.' If you try that for one week, I bet you'll feel differently about him and your relationship."

I said, "You hear what I'm saying?"

"I guess it's just hard for me to understand why he can go play golf all day and not even think about how I feel."

"When he's out playing golf, he is thinking about you. He's releasing stress, possibly making business deals. Despite what time he comes home, he's happy. Right?"

"No, 'cause he acts like I'm not supposed to say anything to him."

"You mean he acts like you're not supposed to nag him. Just imagine you're having a wonderful day and you come home to him asking you 'Where's dinner? Did you feed the kids? Did you wash the clothes?' Wouldn't that irritate you?"

"Probably."

"I'm sure it would. You don't want anybody blowing your high. It's really that simple."

She laughed. "I never looked at it like that."

"Before you start flipping out on the brother, put yourself in his shoes."

"Thanks, Ayana. I'll try that."

"You're very welcome, girlfriend. And thanks for your call."

Quentin gave me a thumbs-up as we neared the end of another successful show. He loved my insight into men, women, and relationships. As if it weren't enough that my words had the ability to talk a woman off the cliff or boost her self-esteem, Quentin's response was a daily reminder that I was called to do this.

I paused. "You've been listening to *Girlfriend Confidential.* I'm your host, Ayana Blue, and we have time for one more call."

Quentin signaled to me that there was a caller on the line. "*Girlfriend Confidential.* Tell me what you want to talk about."

The caller cleared her throat. "I wanna talk about you."

"Okay," I said hesitantly, because I sensed agitation in her voice.

This type of call came in at least once every few days: women who wanted to keep being victims and disagreed with my trying to empower them. She huffed, "So, you're everybody's good girlfriend. Right?"

"I'd like to think I am."

"If that's the case, why did you fuck my husband last night?"

The engineer quickly disconnected the call. He was able to bleep the curse word out, but her point came across loud and clear on air. Everyone thought it was a random angry woman, but I knew I had gotten myself into some shit.

Kate nodded. *Eight days.* She could do this. Now was not the time to dwell on the fact that the only living things that had ever been in her care were some exotic fish that had added color to her condo. Until she'd accidentally knocked the heater into the aquarium and electrocuted them all in mere minutes.

"I don't want them to visit me, Kate. I just can't imagine them in these surroundings." He ran his hands over his face. "Haven't they been through enough in their young lives without seeing their old man—"

Startled by the raw vulnerability in his tone, she rushed to reassure her husband. "I understand. Maybe writing you letters would be less traumatic than visiting you here."

Looking at the haunted eyes of the man she loved, Kate vowed to be the best stepmother possible. Realistically it was the only thing she could do to help Paul. For the next four to five months, she was all the parent those children had.

Thank God kids were more resilient than tropical fish.

Tanya Michaels

Tanya Michaels can't remember a time when she didn't want to be a writer. She finished her first illustrated "book" at the age of nine and is now the award-winning author of over a dozen romance and women's fiction novels. Tanya has been nominated for numerous honors, including Romance Writers of America's prestigious RITA® Award and several Readers' Choice and Reviewers' Choice Awards. She currently resides in Georgia, where she's living out her version of happily ever after with her husband and two children. Visit her home on the Web at www.tanyamichaels.com.

THE N^Xt™ NOVEL

motherhood

WITHOUT PAROLE

Tanya Michaels

MOTHERHOOD WITHOUT PAROLE

Copyright © 2006 by Tanya Michna

isbn-13:978-0-373-88115-4

isbn-10:   0-373-88115-0

This edition published by arrangement with Harlequin Books S.A.

TheNextNovel.com

 HARLEQUIN®

PRINTED IN U.S.A.

From the Author

Dear Reader,

I have two jobs—writer and mother. Reference books have been published on both subjects. Support groups exist for both. But there's really no substitute for hands-on experience! As difficult as parenting can sometimes be for any mom, no matter how prepared she is, I began to imagine a woman with zero prior experience who becomes a stepmother, joining a family "already in progress."

What would that be like? And what if, soon after her becoming a stepmom, the children's father was temporarily out of the picture, leaving her to learn the ropes on her own? (Suddenly the challenges I occasionally face in my own role as Mommy looked a lot simpler.)

Meet Kate St. James, the result of all my what-ifs. I hope you enjoy her story of becoming part of a family and her realization that there are all kinds of success in the world, some harder to measure than others but infinitely rewarding. Watch for her friend Delia's story, *Motherhood Without Warning*, in 2007! More details about that book, as well as my other releases and reader giveaways, are available at www.tanyamichaels.com.

Happy reading!

Tanya

Thanks to all the readers and reviewers who
have let me know how much they enjoy my work.
You truly make the tough days worth it! And special
thanks to Anna DeStefano, who's been there for every
career and motherhood challenge I've faced,
always willing to brainstorm, encourage and
discuss hilarious GFY and TWoP posts.

My *first Valentine's Day as a married woman.* Forty-two-year-old Kate St. James stood barefoot in the modern kitchen, theoretically tackling an impromptu romantic breakfast while her husband, Paul, showered. In reality, Kate had barely glanced at the cookbook lying open on the kitchen island. Having not partaken in her morning caffeine rituals—the dark roast was still brewing—she'd been staring contentedly into space.

Mooning, her friend Delia would scoff. Fast-talking businesswoman Delia Carlisle was not prone to romantic sentiment. Then again, Kate hadn't been either until a couple of years ago. Until Paul St. James.

A well-paid technical writer in Richmond, Virginia, Kate had always been analytical and goal-oriented: Escape the Dallas neighborhood on the wrong side of Harry Hines Boulevard and her cloying, opportunistic mother. *Check.* Get an MBA. *Check.* Climb the career ladder until she was comfortably secure and self-sufficient. *Check.* By forty, Kate had accomplished enough of her personal objectives to consider finally making more time for a personal life. Especially one that included Paul, a handsome widower and CEO.

When their paths had first crossed two years ago, she'd taken only passing notice of the soft-spoken man still mourning his late wife. He and Kate ran in similar circles with mutual acquaintances, though, and eventually formed an attraction neither could ignore. Paul told her once that he'd been drawn to her strength, a welcome change from those who first noticed Kate's looks. On her part, she'd been impressed with Paul's sense of balance. She'd always been something of a loner, whereas he seemed to have well-rounded relationships and a laudable ability to thrive in the business world without resorting to cutthroat tactics. They'd married a month and a half ago, ringing in the New Year with an elegant evening wedding before Paul's children returned to their prestigious New England boarding school.

Children. Kate caught herself anxiously twisting the wedding band on her finger. Dropping her hands to her sides, she took deep breaths and conjured confidence. It was going to be fine.

She had endured a pressure-filled childhood and a mother most charitably described as "less than nurturing."

She had persevered her third year of college after ugly rumors of her sleeping with a popular professor had led him to leave his position.

She was fluent in programming languages, dealt with

tight deadlines with poise and excelled in a field dominated by men.

She could *certainly* handle two polite, if withdrawn, children whom she saw only several times a year. Just because Kate hadn't had a stellar maternal role model didn't mean she was doomed to emotionally scar Neve and Paul Jr. Preteen Neve had asked to join one of her friend's families for their upcoming spring break, and eight-year-old PJ was surprisingly quiet and well-behaved for a little boy. How much trouble could he possibly be for a week?

This summer both kids would be home for almost two months, but Kate had time to prepare. She would ask her girlfriend Patti for advice. Then there was Lily, Paul's former sister-in-law, who dispensed parenting advice whether it was solicited or not. Between Kate's determination to overcome the challenges of motherhood and Paul's guidance on how to cope with his kids, they would navigate any family situations that arose. *Piece of cake*.

Not that she, personally, had ever baked one.

Domestic skills had never been high on Kate's list of driven priorities…which should make cooking for her new husband even more special. He deserved thoughtful gestures and extra effort. Granted, in the weeks before the wedding Paul had grown uncharacteristically distant, but she'd given him space to work through any unresolved guilt toward his late wife, Heather, who had survived barely a month after the nasty shock of her stage-four cancer diagnosis.

Kate had been right to trust her instincts when it came to letting Paul sort out his feelings. During the short time they'd been married Paul had been attentive and affectionate. Delia joked that the newlywed phase wouldn't last forever—just one of many reasons *she* planned never to marry—but Kate was blissfully happy. A decade ago, watching her colleagues divorce and remembering her mother's unstable relationships with men, she couldn't have imagined herself married and trying to plan a homemade Valentine's breakfast. Yet here she stood, chenille bathrobe belted over a turquoise nightie Paul said matched her eyes, humming under her breath.

Kate returned her attention to the book on the countertop; Delia had given her *Six-Course Seduction*, a cookbook for lovers, as a wedding gift. A feisty, independent woman who lived with a man six years her junior, Delia had expressed surprise that Kate or any bride would "give up" her surname. *Well, not even Delia knows everything.* Kate had been nearly giddy to say goodbye once and for all to Katherine Brewster of Dallas, Texas.

Pushing thoughts of the past away, Kate reminded herself that the future was bright. The coffee had just stopped percolating when she heard knocking. Several raps at the front door, almost louder than they needed to be, with a borderline impatient cadence.

Frowning, she glanced at the digital clock on the microwave. All the appliances and counters in Paul's kitchen were the same immaculate white, and Kate loved the bright, spacious feel, even though Patti joked the room would make her feel as if she lived in a bleach commercial. Nine o'clock. While not obscenely early for Saturday, few of their acquaintances would disturb a recently married couple on Valentine's morning. Could it be someone ignoring the cul-de-sac's no-soliciting policy?

"Honey? Do we know who that is?" Paul's voice came from a couple of yards behind her, in the hall that led from their bedroom through the den and into the kitchen. He was barefoot and bare-chested, wearing only expensive jeans and wire-rim glasses as he absently rubbed a towel over his thick salt-and-pepper hair. Patti's opinion of Paul was a lot more favorable than the one of Paul's kitchen—she thought he could pass for Richard Gere's more attractive younger brother. High praise, considering how many times Patti had watched *Shall We Dance?* and *Pretty Woman*.

Kate smiled at her husband. "I was planning to ignore them until they go away."

Another series of staccato raps filled the house.

"Maybe we should check." He turned toward the front of the house with a sigh. "I'll get it. Whatever you're doing in here smells delicious."

Since all she'd managed so far was their normal coffee and melting some margarine in a pan with vague omelet notions, she laughed. His not being hard to please boded well for their marriage.

Through the cutout in the kitchen wall she watched him cross the living room. Paul had such a gorgeous house there'd been no question of which one of them should move after the wedding. Because of the angle, she couldn't see the front door, but she heard it open, heard low voices. A swirl of cold air found her, along with the words *federal agents* and *economic crimes unit*.

Head-to-toe goose bumps broke out beneath the chenille. *Agents?*

She took a cleansing breath, unconsciously falling back on relaxation techniques taught by a series of drama coaches. Paul was an important man, the CEO of an up-and-coming communications company. He'd left a more established corporation shortly before learning Heather was sick because he'd believed in this one so strongly. His move had paid off in spades…and stock options. Maybe agents needed to question him about one of the businesses he dealt with regularly? Or they could even want someone of Paul's expertise to consult on some kind of investigation.

That would be an exciting topic for the next country club event, but the clipped voices she heard and the agitation in Paul's tone spoiled the fantasy.

With barely a thought to her bathrobe or disheveled dark hair, she rushed to his side, attempting a smile. "Sorry to interrupt, but—"

"Kate." Paul's green eyes were wide, glinting with

tension and alarm. Something in his trapped expression made her think of a hurt animal who might bite and claw anyone who tried to help. "Call my lawyer."

She glanced from her husband to the two granite-jawed men in the foyer. One wore sunglasses; the other stared back with an expression so contemptuous she wished he would put on a pair. "I don't understand. What—"

"Now." Paul looked briefly like himself again when he added, "Please."

Dozens of questions collided inside her, but one thing felt certain. The honeymoon was definitely over.

CHAPTER 1

Six months later

"Are you sure you don't want us to come get you?" Delia asked over the phone. "We're good listeners. Well, Patti is. But I can get you drunk."

In the background, Patti Jordan huffed that booze was not a long-term solution.

Delia, who enjoyed riling the housewife with outrageous statements, retorted in a stage whisper that two of the best short-term ways for a woman to forget her troubles were getting nailed or getting hammered.

Actually, the promise of premium Grey Goose *was* tempting right now, especially since Kate's financial situation had changed in the past few months. Any liquor purchases she made in the near future would be limited to the affordably generic. *Joe's Vodka?* Yikes. But tomorrow would be difficult enough without being hungover.

"I'm sure." Kate tucked her legs beneath her on the bed, wondering if she'd ever get used to sleeping alone on the king-size mattress. Her old queen was upstairs, but sleeping in the guest room would only make living in Paul's home without him more surreal. *Adjust already.* It had been five weeks since the sentencing. "Thanks for the offer, though."

"In some ways, Katie, I envy you having the place to yourself. There have been one or two occasions I wanted to smother Ringo with his own pillow." Delia's live-in lover, Alexander, had been dubbed Ringo to go with Kate's and Patti's husbands—Paul and George. No John. But, like Lennon, Paul now had his own FBI file.

Kate fought the mad impulse to get roaring drunk and belt out "I Am The Walrus."

On the other end of the phone there was a muttered "ouch." Patti had probably thumped Delia on the shoulder for insensitivity, much the same way that she did whenever Delia tried to light a cigarette in Patti's home.

"So. Tomorrow." Delia cleared her throat. "Conjugal visit? *Très* kinky."

Federal prisons didn't allow that kind of visitation, but Kate didn't comment since Patti was now demanding, "What is wrong with you? Her husband has been sent to prison, you idiot. It's not a joking matter."

"You think making everything deadly serious is going to cheer her up?" Delia rejoined.

While Kate's two incongruous best friends quibbled as if Kate weren't even on the other end, she stared at her reflection in the vanity against the bedroom wall. Long dark hair, seriously needing a trim and deep conditioning, hung around delicate features pinched with tension. *How did I become this woman?*

She'd busted her ass to get a degree, leave Texas and start fresh. She'd wanted to become a respected business-woman with all the trappings of success. Now she was someone who created hushed silences at the club, snickers in her own office and awkward arguments over how to "handle" her during phone calls from friends. *Dammit, Paul.*

Rage flared, followed immediately by guilt. Was it petty of her to resent a man already suffering the loss of basic rights and privacies?

Though she worked hard to present a composed demeanor to others, she fluctuated wildly between anger over her husband's screwup and renewed vows to be a more supportive wife. It had been two weeks since the end of his initial no-visitors-allowed period, and she'd yet to see him. The minimum security "camp" in West Virginia might not be Alcatraz, but it was enough to separate Kate from the man she loved. Enough to interrupt not only the life they'd shared but their very lifestyle.

She made a perfectly nice salary, but she wouldn't have attempted mortgage payments on a house in this neighbor-hood by herself. The cushion of their savings account had been deflated by a luxurious tropical honeymoon that seemed a lifetime ago and mounting legal fees. In addition to being forced to step down as CEO, Paul had forfeited his stock in the company. Their finances had been so altered that the expensive tuition for his children's prestigious boarding school was no longer feasible. Kate had a week before the kids returned from a visit with their grandparents in Florida. *It will be fine*, she assured herself, even though she didn't have the energy left to dwell on that tonight.

"Dee? Delia! Hey, remember me? The person you called?"

It took a moment to get the woman's attention. Patti, the homemaker, and Delia, self-described ball breaker, had met through Kate. She was the linchpin of the threesome, but not even her presence kept the other two from occasional spirited bickering. At times it was entertaining, but right now Kate just wanted to go to bed.

"Sorry." Delia's tone was sheepish, Patti echoing the apology in the background.

"I think I'm going to turn in, but thanks for checking on me."

"That's what we're here for." In that, Delia and Patti were united.

Even though Kate hadn't felt social enough to join them at Delia's town house tonight, she appreciated their loyalty. Since federal agents had visited on that fateful Valentine's Day, members of Kate's social circle had distanced themselves from her and Paul. Not completely, in case he was acquitted, but enough that none of his taint could spill over to them. The same taint Kate had been trying to escape when she'd left for college—the neighborhood she'd lived in, her mom's disreputable boyfriends, Lorna's shrill insistence that Kate could better both their lives if she would only try harder.

Finally Kate had earned a better life for herself through positive visualization and years of hard work. But she'd never envisioned a husband in the pokey. What was the current slang for that, anyway? *Big house? Joint? Hoosegow* seemed outdated.

"You sure you want to make the trip alone?" Delia asked. "I know neither of us is an approved visitor, but maybe Lily… Then again, maybe not."

Heavy on the *not*, Kate agreed silently.

More than once, Kate had wished Lily lived farther away. Kate understood that Heather's parents, who lived in Florida, and younger sister, much closer in Richmond, wanted to stay involved with Heather's children and that the family had been a big part of Paul's life. But it was awkward to step into the new wife role and feel as if the first wife's sister was constantly judging you. Unfavorably. Lily made attempts to be personable, especially if the children were around, but she couldn't quite mask the disdain in her brown eyes, the conviction that Kate was a sorry replacement for the mother Neve and PJ had lost.

"I'll be fine by myself."

"Well, call one of us tomorrow if you need to talk. I'll

be home with my laptop, getting some work done during Ringo's tennis tournament. Then he's off to New York on Sunday, so I'll be free all week if you want company. Patti says drive safe."

Kate smiled, suspecting Patti dispensed that advice on an hourly basis now that her sixteen-year-old only child had his license. "I will. Good night."

"'Night." Delia hesitated only for a moment before adding in an uncharacteristically emotional tone, "This whole thing sucks. Paul deserved better—damn witch hunt in a post-Enron climate, if you ask me."

Too bad the courts had taken a different view. As she hung up the phone, Kate wondered idly if persecution of a man should more appropriately be called a warlock hunt.

The most genuine, decent man she'd ever known…and a judge wearing a black robe and a sanctimonious expression had pronounced him a criminal. Ironic, considering how many of her mom's lovers Kate had suspected were prison-bound. Lorna had a penchant for codependent relationships with destructive men.

This is different. Paul was a good guy who'd made a dumb hiring mistake.

During the wedding planning, when Paul had been understandably distracted, he'd given someone who had previous dealings with the company a finance position. Some of the man's freelance work the year prior, thanks to a 2002 legislative act, made the employment a criminal conflict of interest. A simple oversight. Then again, CEOs were responsible for the financial welfare of a lot of people and couldn't afford stupid oversights. Though she wanted to be outraged on her husband's behalf, the businesswoman in her knew it *had* been Paul's responsibility to double-check issues like this one. It's why he was paid the big bucks. Unfortunately, in his preoccupation, he'd made one or two other minor errors that the prosecution had painted as signs of impending corruption.

It had all come to light because of a quiet federal investigation of the company Paul had left before Kate met him. Apparently his previous employer had been releasing exaggerated financial reports, inflating their worth and cheating stockholders. Reasoning that Paul likely knew about this fraud before quitting, investigators had widened the scope of their inquiry to Paul himself.

No one cared that he'd walked away from a high-paying job because he'd started to have unproven suspicions about executive ethics. No one cared that, after losing his first wife when he'd expected their marriage to last another thirty or forty years, remarrying had given him a lot to think about besides dotting every *i* according to increasingly complicated corporate regulations. When you were a chief executive officer, "oops" was not a satisfactory defense.

Kate sighed, and when the sound fell too heavily in the empty room, she reached for the silver remote in the top drawer of her nightstand. With a press of her finger, a black-and-white movie came to life on the television. How was it she so desperately needed background voices when she'd had her own place most of her adult life? It was as illogical as her constantly craving sleep, then being unable to rest once her head hit the pillow. Last night she'd tossed and turned until after two in the morning.

Whereas Paul probably couldn't wait for each day to end—bringing him closer to the completion of his six-month sentence and a normal life again—Kate was unsettled by the recent passage of days. *They'll be home soon.*

For the past couple of years PJ and Neve had stayed for a few weeks of the summer with their maternal grandparents in Tampa. This year's "few weeks" had stretched into two months. Kate and Paul felt the kids would have a better time at the beach and visiting Epcot than sticking around for their father's trial. Still, with the new school year starting the last week of August, Neve and PJ would be returning a week from Monday. Was she ready for them? For their questions? Their wariness?

Neither of the kids had ever been overtly hostile to Kate, but she didn't get hugs and Mother's Day cards from them, either. She'd always expected Paul to be the glue that held them together as a family unit. And she'd anticipated half of that unit would keep attending school up the coast.

What if they hate me? What if I suck at this?

No. Swinging her feet to the carpet, Kate gave herself

a mental pinch. She rarely allowed herself to suck at anything. And negativity was a self-fulfilling prophecy.

The kids weren't troublemakers and they'd be in school most of the time, leaving her free to do her job as long as she found reliable help for a few hours each afternoon. She didn't expect mothering to be *easy*, but millions of women worldwide managed it, and she'd always been very capable. Plus, she still had a week to prepare. Seeing Paul tomorrow should go a long way toward reassuring her—they already had one month of his sentence behind him. Less than five to go. She could definitely handle single-parenting for under five months.

She padded to the bathroom to brush her teeth, her confidence restored. Kate St. James was a survivor. Nothing life or SEC regulations threw at her could reduce her to being Katherine Brewster again.

Ash, beech and poplar trees wouldn't change colors and hit their peak foliage until mid-October, but beneath the eighty-degree sunshine in the parking lot blew an incongruent breeze that predicted fall's arrival next month. Kate smoothed her hair and held her head high, this short walk suddenly more daunting than the entire drive over state lines.

At the sentencing Paul had squeezed her hand and tried to joke there were worse things that could happen over the summer than being sent to camp. Thank God no one on the prosecuting side had heard the remark. Public opinion already held that big-business crooks showed a distinct lack of remorse—hence increasingly stiff penalties for comparatively small infractions. But Paul had never set out to be a crook. His flippant remark had been only an attempt to reassure his new wife.

He wouldn't quite make it home for their first anniversary, but he would be back by Valentine's Day. Frankly she'd be willing to skip *that* holiday for the rest of their lives. Her bigger concern was Christmas. As much as she'd disliked Lorna growing up, Kate would have been startled to lose her. And everyone had adored the much-missed Heather. Had Neve and PJ acclimated yet to holidays without their mother? This year they wouldn't have their father either.

Only me.

A cheery thought to take with her as she walked from her locked car to the interior gated perimeter. She'd already passed through one arm of security to drive onto the grounds. She'd also had to fill out legal paperwork weeks ago simply to apply for the chance to spend a few minutes with her husband. The list of rules and regulations, including clothing restrictions, had made her laugh drily. Did they think she *wanted* to come in here flashing midriff and extreme cleavage? Classy.

Khaki was also forbidden. Anything that looked too similar to what the prisoners themselves wore was forbidden. But if prison administrators were worried about her blending in, shouldn't her being *female* help them pick her out of a crowd?

The internal sarcasm threatened to erupt into actual dialogue when a guard patted her down before allowing her to enter. Adolescent modeling auditions that had bordered on exploitative and a few grope-happy dates in her twenties had left her with a distaste for strange men touching her. Even knowing that the young man with the carefully blank expression was just doing his job, Kate flinched, hating him a little for that.

Realizing Paul must suffer the same indignities and worse, she forced a smile for her husband's benefit. In a moment he would be joining her, and she didn't want him to see her discomfort. She stood in the lounge area where they would spend their visit and shifted her weight from one foot to the other. *Lounge* seemed a glorified term for the collection of tables and padded chairs. It somehow resembled a library with no books and a grim color scheme.

"Kate!" Escorted by a guard, Paul crossed through the security doorway, beaming and still handsome despite the circles under his familiar eyes.

Her own smile wobbled before blossoming into something more genuine. Lord, she'd missed him. The brutal realization of how *much* was actually a relief. Her emotions had been on mute since the trial, as if the feelings were there somewhere in closed-captioning, but she'd been too numb to truly experience them.

When Paul's arms went around her, she hugged him tightly, trying to ignore the unpleasant sensation of being watched. The guard sitting in the corner made no effort to downplay his scrutiny of the mostly empty room. Visible security cameras recorded every action.

Paul let go but held her gaze as he said a gruff hello.

They sat a few tables from another inmate and, judging by the two men's similar facial features, his brother. Both men sent Kate appreciative glances. Her stomach flipped queasily, but she squared her shoulders, lifting her chin a notch.

"I can't believe you're finally here." Paul's words drew both her attention and guilt.

Finally here. She should have come sooner. "I'm sorry. Things at work… I need to make sure that my job continues to—not that it's more important than you."

"Katie." Despite the lackluster uniform and worry lines that had deepened since she'd seen him last, his patient green eyes twinkled. "You don't owe me apologies. You aren't the one who did anything wrong."

Should she tell him he hadn't either? They both knew it wasn't true. He'd made mistakes, and sometimes carelessness *was* criminal. Pretending otherwise would be a lie. Their young marriage wasn't cut out for the strain of dishonesty on top of everything else.

"I've missed you," she told him.

"Same goes." He was quiet for a moment. "I've been

looking forward to this visit, but there's something I need to discuss with you." Despite the resigned declaration, he hesitated.

"Whatever it is, we'll deal with it." She hadn't run screaming for the hills thus far.

"The kids will be getting back next Monday."

She nodded. *Eight days.* She reminded herself that she could absolutely do this. Now was not the time to dwell on the fact that the only living things that had ever been in her care were some exotic fish that had added color to her condo. Until she'd accidentally knocked the heater into the aquarium and electrocuted them all in mere seconds.

"I don't want them to come here, Kate. I know they're on the approved list, but I just can't imagine them in these surroundings." He ran his hands over his face. "Haven't they been through enough in their young lives without seeing their old man…?"

Startled by the raw vulnerability in his tone, she rushed to reassure him. "That's completely understandable. It's not as if they haven't gone months without seeing you before. That's practically the norm."

His jaw tightened. "What do you mean by that?"

Exactly what she'd said. "I'm just agreeing with you, Paul. They don't see us much during school semesters. Maybe writing you letters from home would be less traumatic than visiting you here. Maybe it is best for the three of you to get reacquainted…afterward."

"Right. Sorry." He sighed. "Guess I'm a little defensive when it comes to my parenting choices."

She knew Lily had read him the riot act when he'd first sent the kids away, four months after Heather's death. His contention was that he traveled a lot and the school would give them a first-rate education in a place not rife with reminders of their mom. He'd hoped they could heal there, make new friends. Lily had been furious, first losing her sister, then "losing" her niece and nephew. He'd even let it slip that his sister-in-law had once obliquely threatened in the heat of the moment to pursue custody if he couldn't take care of his own kids, though she'd quickly and apologetically taken back the rash comment. Kate certainly couldn't envision Lily and her husband housing two more children when they had four of their own.

After that, the arguing had ceased. But some of the resulting strain had endured.

Now the question of where the kids were educated was moot; Neve and PJ would be returning to Richmond, just as Lily wanted. Withdrawing them from the coming academic year at their private school had devastated Paul. He'd been remorseful enough over the business colleagues he'd hurt or could have hurt with neglectful stewardship of the company, but to once again upset the stability of his children's lives...

Looking at the haunted eyes of the man she loved, Kate vowed to be the best stepmother possible. Realistically it was the only thing she could truly do to help Paul. For the next four to five months she was all the parent those children had.

Thank God kids were more resilient than tropical fish.

CHAPTER 2

Normally Lily Foster spent Saturday evenings folding the week's laundry while watching rented movies with her younger kids and waiting for her older ones to meet curfew. Tonight she was pacing the kitchen that was so much larger, so much tidier, than her own. She hoped Kate didn't mind her using her spare key, but under the circumstances, it had seemed the best idea.

Lily just wished she knew when the other woman would be home from her trip to the prison, but all she'd received when she'd tried Kate's cell phone was an automated voice-mail response. Deciding not to explain the latest turn of events in a message, Lily had come to Paul's house to wait. The kids needed to spend the night in their own beds, not Lily's living room. Now that she was here, though, she felt uncertain and invasive.

If her big sister had lived, this place would have been Lily's second home by now. It sucked that Heather hadn't had more time to enjoy the house they'd bought after Paul's last raise before leaving his former employer to hire on as CEO elsewhere. Heather should have had years, *decades*, to make this place her own, warm and inviting, to create memories. After the move, she'd complained about being tired, but it hadn't slowed down her supermom schedule. When they'd all started to realize she was sick, they'd still been optimistic, not expecting anything as terrifyingly final as a late-stage cancer diagnosis.

The kettle on the stove began working its way toward a full-bodied burble, bags of Earl Grey ready and waiting next to an empty china cup. Lily's mother-in-law was known to say that tea always helped in a crisis. Although Lily suspected tea leaves weren't even going to make a dent in her worries about her family tonight, at least puttering around the kitchen gave her a small outlet for nervous energy.

Sometimes she expected the stress to come erupting out of her like steam from a teapot. As of today, her father was back in the hospital because of ongoing heart problems. Lily's mother was a wreck, having never recovered truly from burying her child a few years ago. *Please, God, let Dad bounce back from this. For all our sakes.* Paul's father had passed away before Neve was even born, but in the past five years the kids had lost both their paternal grandmother and their mother. Now, in a way, the children had lost Paul, too.

But gained a stepmother.

Neve still wouldn't discuss that with her aunt, how she felt about Paul's second marriage. Lily wished she and the children were closer, but it hadn't been easy when she had four of her own to look after and Paul had sent Neve and PJ several states away. His own flesh and blood! When they were traumatized and no doubt needed him the most.

She shook her head, knowing that getting angry over what was past wouldn't help anyone. But the frustration was there, bubbling beneath the surface. After all, she had promised Heather she'd look after the kids, take care of them like they were her own.

Paul loves his family, Heather had said, looking both frail and wise in her hospital bed, *but he was so busy providing for us, working up to his success. He doesn't know which stuffed animal is PJ's favorite or how Neve loves brownies with macadamia nuts but not walnuts or peanuts. You're a mom, you understand about the important day-to-day details he's missed. He'll need your help, Lil. Promise me you'll be there for them.*

When she'd made the vow, Lily hadn't known her brother-in-law was going to bury his grief in work and ship his kids to the prestigious Newsome Academy, one of the best private schools in the country. Lily had taken the news that Paul was seeing someone again with mixed feelings. Obviously, as his first wife's sister, it was difficult for her to see him with someone who wasn't Heather. Then again, she'd known Heather wouldn't have wanted him to live out his years miserable and lonely. So Lily had wished him well and silently hoped that the new woman in his life would help him bridge the ever-growing gap between him and his children. Or at least make him admit that there *was* one, that parenting wasn't something that could be conveniently scheduled for holidays, summer and Spring Break.

Instead he'd picked Kate. Physically flawless übercareerwoman Kate who had no children of her own or previous marriages. Probably because she'd been working so hard on that career of hers. *Just what the kids needed—two workaholic parents.*

Lily didn't resent the other woman's beauty; Heather had been gorgeous in a personable, unaffected, I'm-not-afraid-of-laugh-lines way. It was more that Kate was so impeccable in attire, coiffure, mannerisms and composure that it was nearly impossible to relax around her. When they'd all gotten together for Paul's last birthday, one look at Kate had made Lily aware that her hair had started sliding out of its ponytail in the car and that her trousers were sporting evidence of the family cats. Not to mention that Kate had all but admitted that it mystified her why any woman would choose to marry young and immediately have children when she could have gone to college and pursued a career, leaving her and Lily with almost no common ground over which to bond.

Her husband Bob's voice played in her head. *Give her a chance, Lil.* But this wasn't about Lily and whether or not she wanted to be buddies with the other woman. It was about Neve and PJ and what was best for them.

Lily had no doubt that if you wanted to plan a corporate takeover, Kate St. James was a good person to have on your side. Ditto planning a swanky dinner party and knowing which shoe designer was currently "hot." But caring for two wounded children who'd already been hurt quite enough?

The teapot shrilled, causing her to jump.

She'd turned off the stove burner and was steeping tea when the automatic garage door raised, a mechanical shudder that vibrated through the kitchen. Kate was home.

Setting her cup on the kitchen island as the door swung open, Lily turned. "Hi. Hope my being in your kitchen unannounced didn't startle you."

"The car in the driveway tipped me off." Kate smiled, but it didn't warm her gaze. "I guess you came over to hear how Paul is doing?"

Lily would have called for that, not ambushed Kate in her own home after a long drive. "Not exactly. Mostly I'm here because of the kids."

"Your kids?" Sounding confused, Kate settled into the closest kitchen chair.

"*Paul's* kids. Neve and PJ."

"Oh. Is there any chance we could talk about this tomorrow? Right now I just want to—"

"Neve and PJ are upstairs."

The way the blood drained from Kate's face wasn't exactly endearing. If she was so freaked at the prospect of stepchildren, couldn't she have found a guy who *didn't* come with a ready-made family? But despite her telltale paleness, the woman's expression didn't alter by a single twitch or frown line. Either Kate redefined *cool composure* or there was BOTOX work in her past.

Feeling bitchy over the thought, Lily did penance by offering her sister-in-law a cup of tea.

Kate shook her head. "No, thank you. Just explain why the kids came back early. Are they okay?"

"They're fine." *Physically, at least.* Lily sat opposite Kate. "My father began experiencing bad chest pains early this morning. It might be nothing, but with two past heart attacks, no one wants to take chances. His doctor ordered some medical tests and temporary rest. With all that going on, Mom called me to ask if she could put Neve and PJ on an earlier flight. I picked them up this afternoon. I thought about letting them stay with my brood for the night, but Neve...well, it's been a tumultuous year for the kids. She just wanted to come home."

"It's been a tumultuous year for everyone," Kate agreed absently.

Yeah, but we have the luxury of being adults and not a confused preteen girl about to turn thirteen who won't have either of her parents there to witness it. Knowing that her husband Bob would patiently cite this as the kind of judgmental observation Lily should keep to herself, she sipped her tea. She understood this past year had been rotten for

Kate's marriage. But when you were responsible for kids, they had to be your first concern.

Pushing back her chair, Kate rose. "If the kids are here, I'd better go talk to them."

Well, she gets points for that. "PJ's asleep already. He was practically snoring before I even turned off his light. Neve, last I knew, was reading in bed. I think it's wonderful that you want to talk with her, but aside from popping in to tell her good-night, it might not be a bad idea to…give her some space."

Kate arched a brow. "I haven't seen her since before the trial. How much more space could I possibly give her?"

The edge of sarcasm in the woman's voice was grating. "I'm not saying she's logical, I'm saying she's nearly thirteen. Having barely survived Brittney at that age, I know how moody they can be."

For the past two years Neve had been polite when she came home, but another female could see the subdued resentment in her clear green eyes. Now, with the introduction of a stepmother and Paul's arrest, Neve had become so surly and withdrawn that even her grandparents were commenting on her behavior. She probably couldn't decide whether she was still angry about being sent to boarding school in the first place or pissed that she'd been yanked out of her familiar surroundings. She was likely mad about both, a seeming contradiction that was perfectly reasonable to a girl that age.

"I may not have daughters of my own," Kate said stiffly, "but I was once a thirteen-year-old girl and am not completely clueless, believe it or not. Look, I appreciate your advice—"

"No, you don't," Lily said without heat. She was standing, too, suddenly aware of her defensive stance. *Of course* Kate wouldn't appreciate people popping into her house uninvited and unexpected and telling her what to do. Lily wouldn't either. "My heart was in the right place, though. Those kids mean the world to me."

"They're...important to me, as well." The words came out so awkwardly that it was obvious Kate and the children were in for a bumpy ride. Had the forty-two-year-old career woman ever wanted to be a mother or had she merely made the concession because she'd fallen for a man who happened to be a father?

"I would be the worst stepmother on the planet," Kate said, "if I came home and followed my original plan—which was a long soak in the whirlpool tub and a cold glass of sauvignon blanc—now that I know the kids are home. I'm not going to insist she open up to me or that we stay up braiding each other's hair, but I have to say *something* to her. Why don't you come, too? I'm sure you want to tell her good-night before taking off, and maybe your presence will keep it from being too uncomfortable."

Lily appreciated the compromise, if not the subtle emphasis on *taking off*. "Happy to help in any way I can." It wasn't an empty offer but a vow she'd made and planned to keep.

People talked about running away to join the circus, but Neve St. James thought that was a stupid plan. She'd been to the zoo enough times to know elephants stunk royally. And even though she loved horseback riding, stables didn't exactly smell like roses, either. So the reek factor alone was enough to dissuade her from the circus. Unless it was one of those *du Soleil* things, she mused, staring up at the circle-patterned plaster on her ceiling. Those circuses didn't have animals. Then again, *she* didn't have any freaky talents like being able to put her feet behind her ears.

She was stuck here.

Her first semester at the Newsome Academy she'd missed home so much she'd wanted to be curled up in this very room. Now that she was, it just felt…odd. What was the point? It had been her mom and dad she'd wanted, not the furniture and carpeting. Even knowing it was impossible, she'd desperately wanted to be a whole family again. Her dad, however, had wanted a fresh start.

She remembered clearly the night he'd shown her the academy brochures, nervous beneath his fake enthusiasm. "Look, you'd get to ride horses a lot there, Neve."

Like she'd be fooled? There were places in Virginia to ride horses, too. He'd insisted that he'd miss them, that he wasn't sending them because he didn't want to spend time with them, but the man was a lousy liar. If he'd done something criminal at work, there was no wonder he'd been caught.

At least he put us in a coed school. All-girl would have been a nightmare.

Though she wouldn't have admitted to her little brother that she found his presence comforting, she'd been glad he was at Newsome, too. Besides, if they'd been separated, she would have worried about PJ.

Starting at the end of August—barely weeks away— they would be in separate schools for the first time since he'd entered kindergarten. She'd be an eighth grader at a public middle school, while Paul Jr. would go to third grade at an elementary school. Newsome had continued straight through high school, breaking age groups up into different class buildings on the same grounds.

During their weeks in Florida with the grandparents PJ had been uncharacteristically calm about Neve's no longer being around to look out for him at school. He'd been too busy being excited about being home, being closer to Aunt Lily, making new friends—Neve would miss hers like crazy—and spending time with their father. Ha! Hadn't her brother noticed that even when they'd visited at Christmas they'd had to wait around for Dad to wrap up "important work" before he took them on whatever promised outing was scheduled? Besides, their dad wasn't even home. He was in *prison*. The guy who'd lectured PJ about why playing a good, honest game was always more important than winning and had warned Neve that her active imagination was no excuse for lying…and he'd committed a federal crime! Well, if she had to write some stupid school paper this year on who her heroes were, Paul certainly wouldn't be mentioned.

Even when he got out of prison, they'd have to share him with his new wife. *My stepmother*. The word mostly conjured images of evil psycho women from fairy tales. The stories her mom had once read her at bedtime, when Neve had been young enough to think she'd always want her room painted pink. *Wonder if the step will let me paint it black?* Four black walls might actually be too much, but it would be fun to ask.

Neve had met Kate two Junes ago, when she and PJ had come home for the summer. Dad had thought he was being suave, hinting throughout dinner that Kate, their model-gorgeous guest, was someone special. Unable to take the little suggestions that the kids treat Kate like "one of the family," Neve had asked outright if her father was getting married. She'd known. She'd known as soon as he'd started talking up his girlfriend before they'd even left the airport. The only girlfriend he'd had since—

She swallowed the painful knot in her throat, redirecting her thoughts to the comparatively easier event of her dad's engagement. Sensing her father was trying to break the news of an impending second marriage hadn't entirely prepared Neve for confirmation of her question. Dad and

Kate had exchanged glances as he'd nodded, then he'd looked expectantly at Neve, who'd felt like she couldn't breathe. PJ had appeared equally wobbly. The kid was so small for his age he looked like a baby half the time even when he *wasn't* on the brink of tears. Trying to get it together for both their sakes, Neve had asked what they were supposed to call their impending stepparent. No freaking way Neve was calling her "Mom."

Kate had seemed as weirded out by the idea of being a stepmother as Neve was at having one and quickly assured them that just Kate would be fine. Paul had beamed, apparently thrilled they were already blending as a family or whatever.

What did he know? After all, wasn't he in jail for something stupid? She wondered if Kate would give her the details if she asked. Aunt Lily mostly just wrung her hands, called the whole thing unfortunate and tried to change the subject. Neve used to be able to talk to her aunt about stuff, but it seemed like Lily and Dad weren't getting along so well anymore. Neve wasn't particularly thrilled with some of his decisions, either, but things were bad enough without rocking the boat. She was old enough to know better, but sometimes she just wanted the illusion that things were still close to the way they'd been when Mom was alive.

Footsteps on the stairs and muffled voices told Neve she'd be dealing with her stepmother sooner rather than later. She cast a wary glance toward the closed window. If the situation got desperate, she always had the circus as a backup plan.

* * *

Kate sucked in a deep breath, gathering her thoughts. Did twelve-year-olds typically shut their doors? Probably. Kate respected the kid's right to privacy, but when she'd been this age, all she'd had was a dividing curtain. If Neve kept the thing closed, how would Kate know if the girl was doing drugs or downloading school papers off the Internet or anything else it was Kate's duty to prevent for the next five months?

On the other hand, it wasn't as if she'd been monitoring Neve's every move while the budding teen was in New England, either.

Knowing that PJ's room was far enough down the hall the noise probably wouldn't bother him, Kate knocked on the door. It opened to reveal a young woman, seemingly taller than she'd been mere weeks ago, with green eyes that were huge on her angular face and frizzy wheat-colored hair. Neve didn't speak, giving Kate a mild state-your-business glare.

"Hey," Kate said. "I wasn't expecting you guys yet or I would have been home earlier."

Neve shrugged. "How could you know Pa-pa would get sick?"

Behind Kate, Lily made a small sound, and Kate kicked herself for not telling the other woman she was sorry to hear her dad was in the hospital. Basic etiquette! Kate was known to be the best person in the office for coolly dealing with sudden crises, but anything involving the kids threw her off her game. *Well, it's your first night. You'll get better at this in no time.*

And there was no time like the present.

"Can we come in?" Kate prompted, feeling bizarrely like a vampire who couldn't enter without a specific formal invitation.

The girl moved aside in wordless grudging concession.

"We're not keeping you up, are we, dear?" Lily asked, hovering in the background like the world's largest butterfly. Nature similes seemed appropriate to the earthy, doe-eyed, dark-haired woman who didn't look much like pictures of her late sister. "You're probably exhausted."

Neve remained silent as she sat on the corner of her double bed, but her nostrils flared delicately. Kate bit back a grin, guessing Lily had fretted over the kids all evening.

Kate suspected Paul's sister-in-law considered her "aloof." *Then we're even.* Kate considered Paul's sister-in-law to be potentially smothering.

"If you are tired," Kate said, leaning against a small desk near the doorway, "we can talk in the morning. I just wanted to say hi, see if there was anything you needed."

"Like what?" Neve's tone was neutral, but there was an air of challenge in the way the teenager tilted her head, as if scenting ineptitude.

"Um...towels?"

"Thanks, but PJ and I know where everything is." Her eyes narrowed. "Unless you've changed something?"

"No, everything should be in the usual spot. Well. I guess I'll let you get back to, um, whatever." Taking a stab at congeniality, Kate smiled in Lily's direction. "Thanks for providing supper for them and tucking them—"

"It's not like she had to help us into our jammies," Neve muttered. On the contrary, the young woman was wearing silky mint-green pants with navy cuffs and a matching button-down nightshirt that made her look like a junior Victoria's Secret catalogue model, slumber-party edition.

Kate met the girl's sarcasm with a raised eyebrow and a quelling glance. At least she hoped it was quelling. "Why don't you tell your aunt thank you before I show her out?"

"I can show myself," Lily said crisply. "No need for drawn-out goodbyes when I'll probably see you all again tomorrow."

So soon? "We'll look forward to it."

"Good night, Neve. You know you can call me anytime you need anything."

Neve nodded, and Kate grimaced inwardly. Oh, sure, *Lily* didn't get any flippant retorts about towels.

Lily paused at Kate's side. "You should feel free to call me, too, you know. Whenever you need help."

The offer might have been more appreciated if Lily hadn't sounded so damn sure Kate would need help. Immediately and often.

Kate would show them. Single mothers juggled jobs and children all the time, and she'd conquered every goal she'd ever set for herself. Motherhood would be no different.

CHAPTER 3

Kate's first thought was that she was being watched—the kind of focused, silent stare that might come from a dog who needed to be let out for his morning constitutional. Slowly recalling that she didn't own a dog, she struggled to open her eyes.

Her gaze immediately collided with a small boy's. *PJ*. Reality clicked into place—the kids had returned and today would be her first full day alone with them. Her heart thudded in her ears. If she were awake enough to think rationally, she would tell herself she'd known this was coming. What difference did it make that it had happened earlier than expected? But *rational* had apparently hit the snooze button.

"Morning, PJ." Since she was lying on her side and he was leaning against the mattress, his face was mere inches from hers. Unaccustomed to waking under close scrutiny, at least she'd managed not to scream, curse or otherwise traumatize him.

He blinked at her, his face a miniature of his father's except for Heather's hazel eyes. "Do you know how to make waffles?"

"Good question." She yawned, trying to remember if they had any waffles in the freezer.

"Your breath is stinky."

That's what you get for standing so close, kid. Was she supposed to reprimand him for being rude or applaud his truthfulness? "Let me brush my teeth, then we'll talk about waffles."

"Okay." He waited until she stood, then fell in step with her. "Neve says you probably can't cook."

Kate was irritated by this assessment, but the girl wasn't entirely wrong. "I can cook some things." Including a shrimp pasta dish that was her single cooking-for-a-date meal and a layered dip that was her fallback dish for social events where she wanted to make a good impression by bringing something. Unfortunately that repertoire got old fast and would be of no help for breakfast. She paused in the doorway. "PJ, I have to go to the bathroom now."

"Okay," her new shadow responded.

"Alone, all right?"

"Sure. I'll wait here."

Since she'd never been one to carry on conversations from inside the stall of public restrooms, it was a little weird to have PJ calling questions through the door.

"Do you ever watch cartoons?" he asked conversationally. "That's what I was doing, but my show went off. Neve's taking a shower and couldn't play with me. She said when she's done, she'll find me some Pop-Tarts or something, but

I want waffles. And she takes too long in the bathroom. Always brushing her hair and stuff. Are *you* done yet?"

When she opened the door, PJ practically fell onto the tile floor. It didn't take a child psychologist to understand why he might be a little clingy right now. Kate would be patient with his being underfoot.

As long as she could avoid tripping over him, they would be fine. "So…waffles, huh? Let's see what I can do."

A search of the freezer revealed that there were no instant waffles to be found. Maybe she had a recipe? It dawned on Kate that she only owned one cookbook—a novelty gift on cooking for your lover. She gestured toward the family room, visible through the wall cutout above the kitchen sink.

"Do you want to watch television? Maybe you can find more cartoons. I can call you when the waf—when breakfast is ready," she amended, hedging her bets.

"Okay."

"Thanks, buddy." Appreciating his agreeable manner, she surprised herself by ruffling his hair. When he shot her a warm, approving smile, confidence filled her. She could definitely do this.

The mothering part anyway. The waffling part grew fuzzier as she pulled one foreign apparatus after another from the cabinets in search of the waffle iron. Her attempt to separate eggs was only partially successful, but how much damage could a little yolk do to the recipe? She'd begun pouring lumpy batter into the iron when her step-daughter suddenly made her presence known.

"What is *that*?"

Kate jumped, glancing at the book open on the kitchen island. "A cookbook." The waffle recipe was on the right-hand page, opposite a tasteful yet provocative breakfast-in-bed photo.

"But he's not wearing a shirt. And…" Neve took a closer look. "You're not supposed to let us see stuff like that."

"Then stop looking." Kate shut the book with a snap, then shoved it behind her back for good measure. "Speaking of clothes, what are you wearing?"

Neve glanced down, her expression genuinely quizzical. "Shirt and jeans."

Yes, but the sparkly blue shirt had the word *Juicy* emblazoned across the chest. What was that supposed to mean? Then again, Kate wasn't about to start making parental objections before their first breakfast. She knew enough from Patti to choose her battles, and that didn't include what Neve wore around the house. "All right. I—"

"Are your waffles burning?"

"Damn. Shoot…that's not what I meant. The first thing."

Grinning, Neve leaned against the kitchen island as if waiting to hear other things Kate shouldn't say in front of them.

"Why don't you go keep an eye on your brother?"

"He's just watching TV. I can see him from here." Neve peered around Kate. "You have batter left. If you want, maybe I could make the waffles. I used to help my..."

Heather? Well, that would explain why Paul owned a waffle iron in the first place. "Thank you. I still need a shower. Are you responsible enough to take over kitchen duty?"

"Of course." The nostalgic expression had been replaced by one of almost haughty adolescent confidence. "Not like I'm gonna burn down the house."

"Great." *Because I'm not sitting through an* arson *trial, too.*

Kate made it through the shampoo cycle before the water heater gave up the ghost. Rinsing conditioner from her hair with increasingly cold water, she decided PJ must not have been exaggerating about his sister's bathroom schedule. Just how long *had* Neve been in the shower? As Kate wrapped herself in a towel, a strange buzzing drew her attention to the bathroom counter. Her phone, in vibrate mode, was pulsing across the cultured-marble surface.

Bangs dripping into her eyes, she answered. "Hello?"

"Kate—wonderful." Delia's voice was strained. "Please get down here and tell these kids to let me in."

"You're at the house?" When Kate had retired to her room last night, she'd been unable to sleep. She'd called her friend, but Delia hadn't said anything about coming by today. "I can't even believe you're up this early."

Normally the other woman slept in on the weekends—called it powering up for her sixty-hour workweek.

"I've been awake since the crack of where-the-hell's-the-sun. I could come in and tell you about it or I could stand on your front porch all morning using my cell phone minutes."

Kate laughed, knowing perfectly well her friend had unlimited calling for keeping in touch with clients and property managers. "Give me just a second." Once she'd shimmied into a pair of slacks and a cardigan, she hurried down the stairs. "Neve? PJ? Open the front door."

"We're not supposed to let strangers in," Neve called from the kitchen.

PJ, engrossed in a cartoon where a sports car was talking to a bear, barely glanced in Kate's direction.

"It's not a stranger. She's my friend—I'm giving you permission." Since Kate was closer to the door than either of the kids, she opened it herself.

Delia raised her eyebrows. "New bouncers, huh? They're effective."

"Maybe you should have tried a cash bribe."

"Don't have much on me, but I did bring this." She held up a bottle of champagne. "How do you feel about mimosas?"

Kate loved Delia but occasionally thought Patti might have a point about their friend's fondness for alcohol. "Under the circumstances, that's probably inappropriate."

"Well, you know me."

Kate swung the door wide. "You can join us for waffles."

Or pools of batter, which were what Neve had managed to create.

"Oh, snap," the girl was muttering in exasperation, trying to sop up the worst of the mess. She shot a sheepish glance over her shoulder. "I think I poured too much. It overflowed and steam went everywhere, so I unplugged it before I set off the smoke alarm."

Who was Kate to criticize? She hadn't done much better. "You go talk PJ into cereal, and I'll clean this up."

"I'll try," the young woman promised.

"Nice shirt," Delia said as Neve left the room. "What? I liked it."

That figured.

Delia set the bottle of champagne on the island. "You should put this away for some other occasion. I actually brought it over as a…gift. I won't be drinking much for a while."

"Oh?" Had she and Alexander fought about alcohol?

Her friend chose not to elaborate. "So what are you doing with them tomorrow?"

"With who?" Duh. "Good Lord. It hadn't even crossed my mind." What would the kids do Monday while she was at work?

She'd been alternately looking into affordable afternoon help and wondering if Neve was old enough to babysit her brother a few hours a day after school. She'd even planned to take off the week before school, to smooth the transition, but now she needed a more immediate course of action. She couldn't take off *both* weeks and she was supposed to be finishing up an important project this week.

The ability to meet deadlines—even when they changed last-minute if production was moved up—was critical. The manuals that accompanied each technological product had to be carefully written and proofed. What kind of example was Kate setting for those she supervised if she couldn't meet her schedules?

Where could she find help, someone to watch the kids tomorrow while she set something up for the rest of the week? Patti didn't have an outside job, per se, but the woman was on so many community and charity boards she worked nearly the same number of hours as her corporate counterparts. *Maybe Lily…* She'd certainly made it clear she would be available to help. Kate just worried how it would look that she needed to be bailed out so soon.

Mulling over her options, she ran a washcloth across the batter-smeared countertop. She frowned at the open cookbook. Neve had obviously used Kate's absence to sneak a peek.

A sarcastic observation forming on her tongue, she turned toward Delia but was struck anew by the shadows under her friend's eyes. Kate had been too easily sidetracked by her own problems. It was time to find out what was wrong with Delia.

"You want to talk about it?"

"It's nothing major." The normally indomitable Delia fidgeted, glancing toward the other room where the kids were quietly watching television. "Actually, it is. But still not the end of the world, right?"

Somewhere beyond minor but shy of apocalyptic— that narrowed it down. "Whatever 'it' is has obviously been worrying you. Those bags you've got going on aren't exactly Fendi."

Delia bent her knees, peering at her blurred facial reflection in the microwave door. "Just a little exhaustion a decent eye cream should take care of. Like I said, I've been up for hours."

"Did Alexander wake you leaving for the airport?"

"Nah, his flight's not until noon. And—" Delia drew a deep breath "—I'm sort of avoiding him."

Kate pitched her washcloth into the sink. "What's going on, Dee?"

Delia had said on occasion that she couldn't see herself staying permanently with one man. Could she be trying to figure out the best way to end things with Alexander? Then again, Delia wasn't shy. If she wanted a man out, Kate imagined she would simply say so.

"Hell, Kate, I'm forty-three years old."

So? Delia had hit her professional stride as an executive

for a leasing company that oversaw commercial properties, she looked fabulous and, by all accounts, had an enviable sex life with a thirty-seven-year-old man who laughed at her jokes and danced with her at country club events. Unless…was Delia wanting to settle down, and *Alexander* refused to commit?

"Please don't tell me forty-three's a bad age," Kate joked. "I'm coming up on it fast."

"Forty-three is great for certain things. But pregnancy?"

"Pregnant!" Kate hadn't meant to shout. She never raised her voice. In a near whisper she asked, "When did this happen? I mean, when did you find out?"

"About five o'clock this morning."

Kate made her way to the two-person breakfast table in the corner and sank into one of the chairs, gesturing toward the other. "How sure are you?"

Delia sighed. "I don't know. The box was at the back of the cabinet—a two-test pack with one left over from God only knows when I bought the thing—and I didn't think to check for an expiration date. So maybe it was wrong?"

"Maybe? I've never used one."

Delia rolled her eyes. "You're probably one of those every-twenty-eight-days girls you could set a calendar by. You're organized even on a *biological* level. I didn't even notice when I missed the first period. I stay busy, and frankly it's not like I'm anxious to experience the cramps and accompanying joys. But then when I realized I'd missed a second one… I got up at five this morning, needing to pee for the third time since going to bed, and knew there was no way I could fall back asleep. But honestly I was expecting a negative. I figured that it would just confirm my suspicions that after forty things get less predictable. Well, this was certainly unpredicted! I haven't figured out how I'm going to tell Ringo, but the man's likely to keel over in shock at the news."

Which explained avoiding him and using the extra time of his New York trip to think it through. "You should get a second opinion," Kate said. Surely there was room for error in an expired grocery store pregnancy test.

"Oh, trust me. I play tennis sometimes with an OB and I called her on the way here. She told me to swing by her office first thing in the morning, but she went ahead and answered a few questions."

"About your age?"

"For starters." Delia stood, clearly restless, and ended up by the island, pivoting the champagne bottle on its base. "Risks, side effects, the drinks I've had lately. Even I know pregnant women shouldn't have alcohol, but the doc said I wouldn't be the first woman to imbibe before she knew she was expecting. After talking to her, I'm not as worried about what's past as what the hell happens next."

"Wow." It was a lot to take in. Kate could only imagine how her friend felt.

"Yeah. Pregnancy? Wow barely begins to cover it."

"Is someone pregnant?" Neve chirped.

Both women jumped, having been so intent on the conversation that they hadn't noticed the teenager at the carpeted edge of the kitchen. Or the woman who was arriving behind her.

"Lily!" Kate stood. "I didn't hear the doorbell."

"I opened the door when I saw her drive up," Neve offered.

Maybe Lily was just here for a friendly cup of coffee, but Kate couldn't help thinking of a woman in her office who'd adopted a baby and was periodically subjected to unannounced visits from social workers. "Well, good morning. You remember my friend Delia from the wedding and…everything?" The two women had seen each other in the courtroom, as well. "She came over to help me with breakfast for the kids."

Lily's laser-beam gaze shot from the bottle of champagne in Delia's hands to the cookbook open to a bare-chested hunk, then back to Kate. "Uh-huh. Well, is there anything I can do to add my assistance? PJ says he's really hungry."

"Starving," the little boy moaned from the next room with drama Kate wouldn't have thought the easygoing child capable of an hour ago.

"I, um, was just about to pour cereal." At least she'd cleaned up the mess caused by their waffle attempts. "You can grab some bowls, if you'd like. Or check the fridge for fresh fruit."

Delia volunteered to do the latter, burying her head in the refrigerator.

Lounging in the doorway, Neve watched the women retrieving milk and silverware. "So is someone having a baby?"

Lily actually dropped the bowl in her hands, her gaze flying toward Kate.

She thinks I might be pregnant, Kate realized. It was almost funny. But not.

The possibility was less laughable with Delia sitting there facing that very real prospect. Besides, Kate couldn't scoff at the thought of herself being a mother. Even if she never gave birth, Neve and PJ were here now, her responsibility. *Not just for the five months, either.*

Though she imagined the situation would become easier once Paul was home, her life had been changed for years to come. Unlike her husband's temporary confinement in West Virginia, motherhood was a life sentence.

If there was one thing Neve hated, it was the way grown-ups were allowed to change the topic when they didn't want to answer a question. Kate had conveniently declared breakfast ready without ever addressing the baby issue again. Like that would work if a kid tried it, Neve thought as she chased soggy cornflakes around the bowl with her spoon. She could just imagine her father demanding, *Would you like to explain the grade you got on this pop quiz?* and her trying to respond with, *Hey, Dad, did you know I could roll my tongue into this funny U shape?* It would never fly.

Then again, since when had her father taken a pressing interest in her day-to-day schoolwork? As long as her final grade on the report card was okay, he gave her plenty of space. States and states of it. One of Neve's science teachers had said that the ability to curl your tongue was genetic. Since Neve could, either her father or her mother should be able to, as well. *Wonder which one.*

She should ask her dad next time she saw him. At least then she'd have an opening line for her first visit to the jail. Her throat clogged as she tried to remember if she'd ever seen her mother do it. Mom made funny faces when no one was looking, just to make Neve and PJ laugh. And she always made macadamia brownies on days that sucked.

Lately it felt like most days sucked.

"Can I be 'scused?" PJ asked. He sat at the small table with Neve, while the three women in the room ate standing around the kitchen island. The cornflakes hadn't merited a sit-down meal in the carpeted dining room.

"It's *excused*," Neve corrected. "You're too old to talk like a baby."

"Neve." Aunt Lily's tone was sharp. "Yes, PJ, you may be excused. Put your dishes in the sink first, okay?"

"*Excellent* idea, Aunt Lily," PJ said, crossing his eyes in

Neve's direction. "After I rinse my bowl out, can I play the Xbox?"

Brat. "You'll need help hooking it up," Neve reminded him. Their father put it away in the closet when they weren't home. She wasn't sure why it bothered her so much. After all, she could hardly envision Dad and Kate sitting down to a challenge match of *Crazy Taxi*, but still... She didn't like to think of her things stuffed onto crowded shelves and forgotten while her father and Kate did whatever it was boring, married adults did.

Mom was never boring.

She glanced up to find Kate looking at her. "What?" It came out disrespectful, and she was surprised Aunt Lily didn't reprimand her again.

"Are you all finished?" her stepmother asked.

"Yeah, I guess I wasn't very hungry." Now that breakfast was over, would the women carry on the conversation they'd abruptly ended? "But I could stay and load the dishwasher for you if you want."

Kate raised an eyebrow, looking suspicious of the offer. Just because she couldn't make waffles didn't mean she was stupid. "That's all right. Why don't you and PJ go play? Maybe you could help him get his video games set up."

"Sure." *Go play? I'm not six.* She was beyond the stage where she dressed Barbies in her room while the grownups had their Very Important Talks.

As soon as PJ had all the cords plugged into the right

outlets, Neve grabbed the Harry Potter book she'd been reading and sat in the silvery-gray armchair closest to the kitchen. The chair wasn't nearly as comfortable as the couch or the recliner closer to the television set, but she wouldn't be able to hear anything from either of those seats.

Right now it sounded as if Kate's friend Delia was saying goodbye. Neve made a point of concentrating hard on her book when the tall blond woman walked through the living room to the front door.

"Well, I didn't mean to make her uncomfortable," Aunt Lily said. "How was I supposed to know she was pregnant?"

"I don't think she's ready for people to know—that's the point." Kate's tone was civil, but even a kid could hear the tension between the two women.

"Then, if I can give you a little advice, don't bring controversial subjects up with kids in the next room. They hear more than you think." As if realizing the truth in her own words, Lily suddenly lowered her voice.

The rest of the murmured conversation was a lost cause, so Neve gave up and tried to pay attention to what was going on at Hogwarts instead. But not even Hermione, her favorite character, could distract her. Controversial? That meant, like, scandalous. Was Delia's having a baby a scandal because she was so old…or because she didn't want to have one?

Adults should be more careful, in Neve's opinion. They should be responsible so that there didn't end up being kids all over the world who felt unloved. *If I ever have children, I'll love them all the time.* Even when they were annoying, like PJ. And she would sure as hell never kick them out of their own home because she didn't have time for them.

CHAPTER 4

Although she'd offered her help—numerous times—
Lily had to admit she was a little surprised her sister-in-law
was taking her up on it. Especially so soon.

"I understand if you can't do it." Kate was already back-
tracking, jamming spoons into the basket portion of the
dishwasher.

"No, no. We'll work something out. Brittney has drill
team rehearsal at the high school and Davis has football—
all the sports programs start meeting before school starts—
but maybe Bob can drop off one or both of them. I'll swing
by here with the two youngest to pick up Neve and PJ, and
we'll have time to make it back to the schools before practices finish."

Kate blinked. "I'm lucky you drive something big
enough to haul around all these kids."

"You and Paul might want to think about getting a
vehicle besides those tiny cars you drive. Even without four
kids, Neve will have girlfriends she'll want to take to the
mall, PJ will have teammates. You may want to carpool
with some of the other moms, but you'll need more room."

"I'll, um, think about it."

Yeah, you do that. Kate rarely objected to any suggestions outright, but she didn't exactly give off a flexible vibe. As far as Lily was concerned, flexibility and a sense of humor were two of the main weapons in a mother's arsenal. Lily could understand not wanting to trade the sleek model Kate drove for a minivan, but the car, in Lily's opinion, functioned as much as a status symbol as a mode of transportation. She wouldn't call Kate a snob, exactly—well, maybe she would.

Stop it. So she has more money than you do. It was your choice to have a big family and no outside job. Four kids required strict budgeting. But it was more than Kate being affluent or wearing nice clothes.

It was the way she never got caught in the same outfit twice or the way she dressed up even for Sunday cereal with the kids—what, she didn't own a pair of jeans? True, Kate was a natural beauty, but she also seemed to put a lot of effort into appearance. Her makeup, her well-tailored, wrinkle-free slacks, the manicured lawn she paid someone to keep perfect, the curtains that were carefully color-coordinated to the throw pillows.

Lily didn't know who, if anyone, the woman was trying to impress, but one thing Kate would learn soon enough: kids had a way of making life a little messier. Lily hoped for all their sakes that her sister-in-law was more adaptable than she seemed.

* * *

Not even noon yet, and Kate was ready to call it a day. All-nighters in graduate school had been less draining than this first morning with the kids. In their defense, however, they hadn't put her through the ringer as much as Delia's unexpected announcement and Lily's unexpected arrival. Considering the favor their aunt had agreed to do tomorrow, Kate tried not to seem happy to see the woman leave. *Good thing I have minor acting experience.*

"Well, looks like it's just the three of us," she announced, dropping onto the sofa after Lily's departure.

Neve glanced up from a thick novel just long enough to spare a dubious look. Clearly she didn't think "the three of us" had the same companionable feel as, say, musketeers or even amigos.

Good thing Kate wasn't a quitter. "Since your aunt is going to watch you while I'm at work tomorrow, we should do something together today. Any suggestions?"

If Neve didn't exactly brighten, at least she let her book fall closed. "Shop for school clothes?"

Without pausing in his complicated joystick maneuvers, PJ shook his head. "Shopping is boring!"

Actually, Kate enjoyed shopping. Or did when she had spare cash with which to make purchases. "A fun outfit for the first day may be in order, but you won't need much to supplement your wardrobes, right?"

"Wardrobes?" Neve's eye roll was perfectly timed with

her sigh of disgust. "You do know we wore uniforms at Newsome? I barely have enough regular clothes to get me through a week."

Even though Kate knew this was an exaggeration, she had forgotten their previous school clothes were provided by the Academy. As fast as she'd noticed kids grew, they probably *did* need substantial wardrobe supplies, especially for when the weather turned cool in another month or so.

"Too bad Aunt Lily left," Neve said wistfully. "She'd know from Brittney where the cool places to buy clothes are."

"Hey, I know plenty about clothes," Kate said. Not even the disdainful teen could argue Kate was a bad dresser.

When it came to shopping, though, Lily obviously wanted the crown for expert bargain hunter. It drove Kate a little nuts the way Paul's sister-in-law wore her thrift like a badge.

Oh, do you like Brittney's dress? She found one in a magazine and we improvised a pattern. Who can afford the price of a formal dress she'll wear to one homecoming dance and then relegate to the back of her closet?

Yeah, we'd talked about going a different color with the furniture in the den, but once I saw the love seats were fifty percent off, who could resist? I figure Bob can grow to love fuchsia.

Any woman was entitled to a great buy every once in a while, but Lily made Kate uncomfortable, remarking on a cute purse and asking if it was new, just a hint of disapproval in her tone or commenting wistfully on Kate and Paul's honeymoon, mentioning that it had been years since she and Bob had been able to splurge on a luxurious vacation. "Got those four college tuitions we plan on paying," she'd sometimes joke.

Even though the comments never seemed to bother Paul, Kate found them to be a little too reminiscent of her mother. Lorna Brewster had always had a "woe is me" air about her, a way of working comments into the conversation so that those who were better off felt obligated to either help her or feel guilty about their own successes. One of the many reasons Kate had informed Lorna that she didn't have to spend her money to travel to the wedding. *All we need are your best wishes, Mom.*

With both of Paul's parents deceased and Kate estranged from her one known relative, it had been natural to have a small, private wedding. The fact was, if Lorna got a look at how well-to-do Paul was, requests for family loans were sure to follow, even if they were cleverly disguised passive-aggressive requests.

But Lily hadn't asked for money as far as Kate knew, and it was beside the point now since they had none to lend. Kate didn't think she needed to start clipping coupons—yet—but once Paul came home, who knew how long it would take him to find a good replacement job and what sort of salary he'd be offered. She doubted another CEO position would fall into his lap, especially with his now murky record.

"Could we go to the pool?" PJ asked cheerfully. "It's better than Florida. No jellyfish."

Apparently Neve had been stung one year at the beach and PJ had spent the past couple of summers afraid to go back in the water. To PJ, jellyfish were the new *Jaws*.

The posh neighborhood included membership to a large pool and private clubhouse. They could spend the afternoon there without spending a dime, not counting the semiridiculous check she and Paul had written to the mandatory homeowners' association in January.

"Now that sounds like a good idea," Kate agreed. "What about you, Neve? Want to take advantage of the last couple of weeks of summer? It will be fall before you know it."

"I like fall," the girl said. "Everything's dead then."

Chipper sentiment.

Just as Kate began to worry that Neve was headed for teenage years filled with Goth clothing and suicidal poetry, Neve added, "It's easier on my allergies. Summer's not so bad, but spring is miserable."

"Ah." Come to think of it, Kate should probably make it a point to learn more about both children. As far as she knew, no one would go into anaphylactic shock at the sight of peanuts or shrimp, but there were dozens of potential missteps she would rather avoid. Especially those that might lead to emergency room visits. She had one dizzying moment where she realized how much she didn't know. Hell, Patti had left more explicit instructions when

Kate house-sat for her once than Paul had for turning over his children.

But that's just because he trusts you and knows you can do this. Whereas Lily's little pop-ins, unsolicited advice and frequent offers to assist seemed to stem from a suspicion that Kate wasn't cut out to be a mom. Well, by the end of the month Lily would just have to admit she was wrong.

"I guess going to the pool would be okay," Neve allowed, sounding a lot like royalty who'd just deigned to spend the afternoon with commoners.

"So why don't we all change into our bathing suits and meet downstairs when we're ready?" Kate had been working too many hours to loll around poolside this summer, but she assumed the suit she'd taken on her honeymoon still fit.

In the privacy of the master bathroom she tugged the supportive top into place and checked her butt in the mirror. Assured that the navy-blue one-piece with dark green detailing wouldn't send anyone running from the pool area, she tossed some sunscreen and a paperback novel into a shoulder bag, along with several oversize towels. Once she got downstairs, it struck her as comically ironic that she'd worried about *her* suit being indecent.

While PJ looked the way an eight-year-old boy should—scruffy but adorable in baggy SpongeBob trunks and an orange tank top with a frayed hem—his older sister looked as if she might be auditioning for the lead in *Lolita*.

"Where did you get that bikini?" Kate hadn't meant to sound shrill, but her stepdaughter didn't seem to notice the tone.

Neve stretched, showing off the suit. Not that there was enough material to make it a legitimate article of clothing. "I spent Spring Break with my friend Krista, remember? She and I got matching bikinis, only hers is green."

Kate had assumed Neve was developing curves, as young women normally do, but she'd never seen them showcased in scraps of hot-pink, with white plastic rings holding together the bra cups and connecting the front and back fabric on the bottom. Lord, seeing his granddaughter in this getup was probably what landed Lily's father in the hospital.

Kate took a deep breath. "I'm all for fashion, Neve, honestly. But until your dad gets back, I'm trying to do the best job I can to…to fill in for him. Do you think he'd want you to go to the pool dressed—" *undressed* "—like that?"

The adolescent shrugged, the casual gesture at odds with the intense expression in her eyes just before she ducked her head. "I don't think he'd care. He's never commented on my clothes. Or much else about me."

Oh, Paul. Kate had heard both his arguments for boarding school and Lily's criticisms against it and had sided with him. After all, Newsome was touted to be one of the best educational facilities in the country, with devoted staff and excellent programs. But she had a feeling that his daughter at least was less than thrilled about being shipped off while he carried on with his post-Heather life.

For the first time, she was concerned about how the kids would react when they were told their father didn't want them to visit. He planned on telling them himself on the phone—an announcement she wasn't in a hurry to preempt—but it would be some time before he was allowed a call.

"I don't suppose you have another suit?" Kate asked.

"No." Neve jutted her chin out, and Kate recognized the gesture for the stubborn challenge it was.

"All right." What the hell. In two weeks summer would end and the bathing suit would be a moot point. It didn't make financial sense to buy a new one the girl would outgrow by next year's beach season. "Should we walk to the pool or drive?"

"Seems silly to use the gas for such a short distance. There's an energy crisis, you know." Even now that the bikini objection had been withdrawn, Neve's tone made it clear she hadn't forgotten the censure and wouldn't be forgiving anytime soon.

"Walking it is, then." Kate glanced at PJ. "That okay with you, buddy?"

He nodded, volunteering no opinion on his sister's wardrobe or North American fuel limitations.

When they arrived at the pool, Kate had to admit

Neve's suit no longer seemed out of the bounds of decency. At least not in comparison to the others on display. The Hansons' summer au pair was sunbathing in an ice blue string bikini while the two Hanson boys, older than PJ and younger than Neve, tried to drown each other in the deep end. In another lounge chair a teen had removed her top and appeared to be sleeping on her stomach, wearing bikini bottoms that bordered on being a thong. Kate had the urge to cover PJ's eyes.

The boy, however, wasn't old enough to care about scantily clad young women. "Do you have any coins, Kate?"

"He likes to practice swimming at the bottom to pick them up." Neve pulled a book out of her shoulder bag and took up residence under the shade of a table umbrella.

With Neve off in her own fictional world and PJ diving for dimes, Kate half wished she'd brought her laptop. She had some writing she could be doing, but working seemed to defeat the "quality time" spirit of the outing. Besides, the computer screen was damn hard to read in direct sunlight. But maybe tonight she'd put together some kind of schedule, times when she could be with the kids but also stay ahead on her office work. With a little multitasking, there was no reason her office performance had to change at all with her newest circumstances.

"Kate! Why, Kate St. James, is that you?"

Oh, hell. Lowering her sunglasses slightly, Kate noticed

a trio of women entering the gated poolside area. Leading the pack was Celeste Parker, treasurer of the neighborhood association.

Kate managed a smile. "Yep, it's me all right. In the flesh." Although not quite so much of it as Celeste.

While the redhead wore a modest sarong-style skirt over the bottom half of her one-piece, she was spilling out of the low-cut top. No doubt to best showcase the breasts her husband had purchased for her fortieth birthday.

"We've barely seen you at all since…well, you know. It's just so *brave* of you to be out and about." Celeste glanced from Neve, at her table a few feet away, toward the pool. "Poor dears. I hate to think how many milestones their father is missing."

Though the comment was directed at Kate, it was easily overheard by those nearby. Neve shut her book with an audible thump and glared in Celeste's direction.

Kate felt like glaring herself but wouldn't give Celeste the satisfaction. "Well, it's been nice catching up with you ladies…." *Now go away.*

Celeste smiled. "We should do this more often. Of course, you've always had such a hectic schedule. And now that your circumstances have changed, we know how busy you must be."

When Kate had moved into the neighborhood, she'd quickly realized that she was in the minority of full-time working women. Some of the wives, Celeste included, were home most days and had formed tight cliques. Though they smiled at Kate and chatted with her at cocktail parties, she'd never truly felt as if she belonged. Now the feeling multiplied tenfold.

She shouldn't care; she didn't even *like* Celeste Parker. But she'd endured smugness in her youth, from the kids who could afford better clothes and, as she got older, from the boys in her class who'd heard rumors about how "easy" her mother was. It had been freely speculated at her high school that Kate had landed some of her local modeling jobs by bestowing sexual favors on casting directors.

She'd deflected snide remarks and knowing glances her whole life, but she was successful now. She'd worked hard, married well. Dammit, she should be at home catching up on work or watching an old movie with Paul, not baking beside an overchlorinated pool with no idea what to say to her stepchildren and letting Celeste frigging Parker make her feel as though she were in sixth grade again.

As Celeste offered a saccharine "toodles" more appropriate to a nineteen-year-old sorority pledge than a noted attorney's wife, Kate turned her attention to PJ.

The boy frowned. "Are you okay?"

"Just fine, buddy."

No sense ruining his outing by explaining that sometimes people stung more viciously and deliberately than jellyfish.

CHAPTER 5

You have four *new messages*. Kate sat on the edge of her bed and hit the answering machine's Play button.

"Kate, it's Patti. I should probably be giving you your space after your visit, but I had to check in. At least let me know you got back from West Virginia safe."

West Virginia and her trip to see Paul. Lord, had that only been yesterday? Between the kids' unscheduled arrival, Delia's bombshell this morning—

"Kate!" Patti again. "Oh. My. God. Delia just called me. I cannot *believe* this. Never in a million years would I have pictured her… I'm shocked. Stunned. Speechless."

All evidence to the contrary, Kate thought wryly. She hit the Skip button, fast-forwarding over the rest of Patti's words to see who the next caller was.

"It's me," Delia said by way of greeting. "Just wanted to say I'm sorry if my showing up for breakfast made things any more awkward for you. I know this is an adjustment period for you and the rugrats, not to mention I doubt I'm Lily's favorite person. But thanks for listening anyway."

"Do you and Aunt Lily get along?"

Kate started at the question, hitting Stop as she turned to face her stepdaughter in the doorway. "I thought you were in the shower, washing the chlorine out of your hair."

"I'm headed that way," Neve said with a shrug. "Is that another adult attempt at not answering a kid's question? Or should I say a *rugrat's?*"

"Don't mind Delia. She has her own way of talking. Our friend Patti is always telling her how outrageous or obnoxious she is, but it's more attitude than substance."

"They're your friends—Patti and Delia? I wondered...." Neve shifted her weight, fixing her gaze on the burnished-gold valance hanging above the bedroom window. "Those women at the pool today, from the neighborhood—are you friends with them?"

"Not exactly." Tactful but honest. "As you said, they're our neighbors. I'm cordial when I see them, but we're not close."

Some of the tension drained from Neve's posture. "Oh. Good. I wasn't sure if, like, she would be over here or anything. She bugs me. Who does she think she's fooling with those fake boobs?"

"I'll bet if you were one of your aunt Lily's kids, she'd ask you to show more respect for your elders." As soon as the halfhearted admonishment had left her mouth, Kate wanted to kick herself. Why had she reintroduced Lily into the conversation?

Neve was persistent enough not to have forgotten her

original question. "You think Lily is a good mom, but you don't like her?"

"I never said that. We both love your father, we both want what's best for you kids." Should she have said, "We both love you kids"? Would that sound forced? Would Neve even welcome a sentiment like that? "We're just very different."

"Yeah." Neve laughed. "Aunt Lily can cook."

"Maybe this would be a good time to remind you of that respect thing we just talked about."

"I kind of remember Patti and Delia from your wedding, but you didn't have any family there."

"I'm an only child. And my father split when I was just a baby."

"Your mom's not…gone, too, is she?"

Kate flinched at the unexpected question, the naked pain in Neve's eyes and empathy in her voice. "No. She's alive, she just lives pretty far away. She couldn't come to the wedding, but she sent a present." Would it be insensitive to admit she hadn't wanted her mother at the wedding when Neve would never even have that option?

"You're her only kid and she didn't bother to show up when you finally got married? Sounds like the two of you don't like each other much either."

She's not wrong. And yet Kate was squirming, feeling as if she was coming off as very antisocial in this conversation. "You know what, Neve, it's complicated. And if you don't shampoo soon, your hair's gonna turn green."

Neve rolled her eyes and turned toward the bathroom. But she paused in the hallway and looked back over her shoulder. "My mom didn't say a lot of bad stuff about people, but I don't think *she* liked Mrs. Parker either. And that was even before the fake boobs."

Kate blinked, surprised at both the indirect comparison to Heather and the faint note of approval in Neve's voice. Uncharacteristically dumbstruck, she cast about for the right response, but Neve was already gone.

Lily wasn't sure what to expect when she arrived at Paul's house Monday morning. So when her youngest, six-year-old Tad, rang the doorbell, she had yet to place a mental bet on whether she was about to walk in on chaos and the foul smell of burned oatmeal or Kate impeccably dressed and serving egg-white omelets.

I was right about the impeccably dressed part.

Not all women would have been as memorable in the silky, lightweight slate-blue pantsuit. Her dark hair was pulled back, and she was in the process of putting in pearl-and-sapphire earrings while PJ and Neve finished muffins and fruit salad. Lily was cheered to see the pineapple-strawberry-and-cantaloupe mixture had come out of a plastic grocery store container. If Kate had time to get up in the morning and dice fresh fruit and *still* look like that before eight o'clock....well, too many things in life were already unfair.

"Good morning," Lily said as her two sons plowed beyond her to see if there were any more muffins. Right, because she hadn't *just* fed both of them half an hour ago. Her soon-to-be-eighth grader, Davis, had been eating her out of house and home all summer, but Tad and eleven-year-old Nick were gaining on him. It was difficult to tell whether teenage Brittney ate so little because she was too preoccupied with her weight or because her brothers just didn't leave enough. "Tad, Nick, at least greet your cousins before you start stuffing your faces."

"Mornin'," Nick muttered around a mouth full of blueberry.

Tad, young enough that Lily still had hope for the way he'd turn out, looked shamefaced. He removed his hand from the muffin he'd been about to take and smiled at his cousins. "Hi, guys. Kate, you look real pretty today."

Kate grinned. "Thank you. Would you like a plate? We have plenty of food. Lily, anything for you? Coffee?"

"Thanks, but I'm more of a tea drinker." And she was never going to look like Kate if she ate double breakfasts. Then again, she'd given birth to four children—she was never going to look like Kate, period.

"Well, then…would you mind if I had a word with you in the other room?" Kate asked.

"All right." Lily followed the other woman, clueless as to what to expect but finding herself wary. She didn't even know *why*, and maybe that was it. Kate remained an unknown.

The two women had virtually nothing in common. Different musical tastes, different sense of humor, different worlds they moved in. Lily had never owned a business suit, and corporate Kate would be out of her depth sewing ear-of-corn costumes for the *Veggie Patch* first-grade play. In theory, maybe Paul and his children should bond them, but the reality was more awkward, especially given his absence and how much Lily still sometimes missed her big sister.

"What can I do for you?" Lily asked. She was not only eager to help, she'd be relieved if someone took her advice for once.

Kate bit her lip. "A couple of things, I guess. Yesterday you said something about PJ's *teammates*. Were you speaking hypothetically or was I supposed to have him enrolled in something already?"

"Oh, no. His school doesn't have organized teams the way they do at the middle school and high school level. There are just different community organizations he'll want to be involved with. Groups will have sign-ups when you go to the elementary open house next week."

"Oh, good. I was afraid I might have missed a deadline somewhere."

Lily smiled reassuringly. "No, you're doing fine."

"Terrific. Should I just let him pick out what he wants to sign up for, then?"

"Aside from soccer? It's probably best not to overload him when he already has so many changes to adjust to right now."

"But he likes soccer?"

Tell me you are kidding. "You know he was on the team at Newsome last year, right? Scored one of the goals in an important match."

Kate winced. "Maybe he mentioned that sometime? I just, you know, so many other things going on…"

Right. But all parents had stuff going on. Frustration filled Lily. Had Paul even mentioned his son's athletic activities? He shouldn't be treating Kate and the kids as if they were on two different planes of existence, he should be working to bring everyone closer to a family. If Lily were closer to his new wife, maybe she could talk about how worried she'd been after Heather's death, how Paul had become more withdrawn. But her input had not always been welcome, and Kate had to take some of the responsibility, too. If you married a man with two kids, you should make a concerted effort to get to know them. Learn about them, pay attention to them. Not just buy them ridiculously expensive Christmas presents, as Lily had diplomatically pointed out to her brother-in-law a few weeks before the wedding.

"Kate's just trying to make a good impression," he'd said, defending her overpriced and slightly age-inappropriate gifts.

"You can't buy children's affection!" Lily had protested. But she'd bitten back any hint of I-told-you-so when PJ broke his complicated robotics toy before they'd even thrown out the tree.

Sighing, she came back to the present. "I know you have to get to work. Was there anything else?"

"Maybe. Have you and your kids already finished all your back-to-school shopping? Neve reminded me yesterday that they needed more clothes. I think she'd like it if we went with you and Brittney, if you haven't already taken care of all that...."

Up until now, the two women had mostly been in each other's company because of family occasions and Lily's determination to look after the kids. This was the first time Kate had freely extended an invitation, and Lily took it as a sign of progress. "We'd love to have you join us! Why don't we meet at the mall next weekend?"

"Um, that would be super."

"Super," Lily repeated.

They might even have fun...but with six children, Lily was bringing plenty of aspirin.

Actually, she found herself thinking fifteen minutes later, as she maneuvered her crowded van away from a dry cleaner's pickup window, she could use some of that aspirin *now*. Nick had won the coin toss to sit up front and kept playing with the radio buttons, while Neve sulked directly behind him. PJ and Tad were companionably occupied in the backseat with a handheld video game that was surprisingly loud for such a small unit.

"Doesn't that have a volume control?" she asked her nephew.

"I think I broke it," PJ answered without meeting her gaze in the rearview mirror.

Thank God the boy liked soccer—the real kind, not cyber—or she'd worry about his lack of fresh air and human interaction.

"I don't understand why we couldn't stay at home," Neve said. "I'm plenty old enough to take care of myself and PJ for the day."

Lily tried not to be hurt at the very normal desire for independence. "Hey, it's not so bad spending the day with me, is it?" She'd missed the kids terribly after they left; it had been a little like losing Heather again.

When no answer was forthcoming, Lily went for the laugh. "I'll have you know, your aunt is very cool. I can bust a move and raise the roof with the best of them."

Next to her, Nick snorted. "That's just sad, Mom. Be glad Brittney isn't here so she doesn't have to worry about you 'embarrassing' her." He used air quotes with the fairly accurate imitation of his sister's high-pitched protest.

Lately Brittney's existence seemed to revolve around cute guys, not letting her parents or brothers embarrass her and the bathroom scale. *If I ever catch her skipping meals, I'm throwing the scale away.* Come to think of it, that sounded like fun regardless.

"Brittney's boy-crazy," Tad announced to no one in particular.

Another snort from Nick. "Like Davis is any better. You know that fancy underwear magazine that comes in the mail for you, Mom? I think he has it up in his room."

Lily sighed. *You order one racy undergarment off the Internet for an anniversary…* Maybe it was time Bob had certain talks with their son.

"He's obsessed with girls," Nick continued, making it clear by his tone that *he* would never succumb to his older brother's lack of mental faculties. "He even said Kate is hot for an old chick."

"You boys do not refer to women as 'chicks.' Ever!"

"How come she doesn't look like you, Mom?" Tad asked innocently from the back.

God love the boy for not asking, "How come *you* don't look like *her?*"

"Everybody looks different, that's part of what makes us special. Kate's pretty. Nothing wrong with that." Lily glanced in the mirror at Neve, who was staring through the window and was unnaturally quiet. "Aunt Heather was pretty, too."

"Very pretty," Neve agreed so softly Lily wouldn't have caught it if she hadn't seen the girl's mouth move.

Lily could see a lot of her sister in her niece. Except that Heather had been cheerful by nature, and Neve had been understandably moody lately. How did Lily empathize with everything the kids had been through without sounding critical of their father?

"I don't understand why we don't call her 'Aunt' Kate," Tad continued. "Neve and PJ call you Aunt Lily. And Kate's married to Uncle Paul."

Neve spun around in her seat. "That doesn't make her my mother. Or your aunt."

"Yes, it does." The frown was audible in Tad's puzzled tone. "Doesn't it?"

"You're both right," Lily said. "But Neve already had a wonderful mom. Kate doesn't replace anyone or change that."

There was a moment of glum silence, and Lily thought perhaps talking about Heather wasn't the best way to start off a fun-filled day together. "We still haven't decided what we're going to do today! What sounds good?"

"The zoo," Tad suggested.

"Too hot!" Nick complained. "Let's go see a movie."

"Maybe. Depends on what's showing," Lily said. "And if you want concessions, it comes out of your allowance."

"I'm not sure PJ and I get an allowance anymore," Neve said. "Kate hasn't mentioned it."

"Well, I can help you out today. But you know you can ask Kate about it. She's…family now, and you should take her your questions."

"Why? So she can blow me off?" Neve demanded. "Adults suck."

"Hey!" Lily ignored the impulse to pull the van over and settled for a stern look over her shoulder. "I don't want to hear you talk like that. And your statement isn't fair. I'm sure Kate is trying hard. And I'd like to know what *I* did as an adult to warrant that. I know a lot of bad things have happened, Neve, and you're entitled to be frustrated, but a good attitude can make a major difference."

"A good attitude wouldn't have saved my mom or kept my dad out of jail, would it?"

Lily sighed. "No. But do you think your mom would be happy about your current attitude?" From the back, she should could hear sniffles and realized that PJ had come far enough out of his video world to be upset by the tense conversation. "Neve, maybe we could table this discussion for a little later."

"See?" the girl whispered almost to herself as Nick turned up the music. "Blown off again."

CHAPTER 6

Kate was gathering her purse and keys when her boss knocked on the doorjamb outside her office.

"Do you have a second?" Bryce Connor asked, his deep voice as attractively masculine as his dark features. Bryce made a great manager—his demeanor naturally encouraged people to defer to his authority.

"Of course." She was meeting Delia and Patti for lunch at a nearby restaurant, but rule number one of a successful career was that you *always* had time for your boss. "What can I do for you?"

"For me, nothing. For one of our affiliates… They're undermanned right now and can't keep up with their production schedule. They've asked me, as a professional courtesy, if we have anyone on staff who might be willing to take on some extra work as an independent contractor for product manuals. I couldn't let you have company time to do it, but if you're interested in a little freelancing, it's nice money. No one meets deadlines better than you, Kate. I can always count on you."

She was thrilled by the praise—and the opportunity for

extra money! This would be perfect. Sure, she had the kids now, but they'd be in school by the end of the month. She'd have free time while they were doing homework and after they went to bed. All she had to do was stay organized.

"I'd love to do it. Thank you for thinking of me, Bryce."

He inclined his head. "You were headed out?"

"Lunch, but I could postpone…."

"No, no. You go on. Stop by my office when you get back, and I'll give you a contact name and the particulars."

She was whistling as she walked to her car, but her mood dipped when she reached the restaurant and saw Delia. Her friend had sounded shaken when she'd called midmorning, saying that she was officially nine weeks pregnant, but she looked positively awful. Seated in a horseshoe-shaped booth, Delia was pale against the navy-blue upholstery and slumped with her chin in her hands.

"Hey." Kate slid in next to the bleary-eyed woman. "How are you holding up?"

Delia laughed weakly. "That's the difference between you and me. Me, I would have announced that I looked like crap. I know I do. You're being tactful and socially correct."

"What you look is stressed. Is there any way I can help?"

"Oh, sure. Because you don't have your plate full with the incarcerated husband and the stepchildren who hate you."

"They don't hate me." *I hope*.

"You replaced their dead mom. Of course they hate you."

"I thought for a change we wouldn't be talking about my problems." Kate glanced around, trying to catch a waiter's eye so she could order a drink. "I take it Patti isn't here yet?"

"Stylist appointment. She's running late but just called me on the cell." Delia ran a hand over her short, nearly platinum hair. "Do you know I can't even get my hair colored for the next two trimesters? I went to a bookstore last night, you know, just in case. Got a copy of *What to Expect When You're Over the Freaking Hill*."

"You are no such thing." It was startling to hear Delia discuss herself as though she were past her prime. Her normal philosophy was to grab life by the balls and hang on for the ride—with her high-powered career and doting younger man, she'd seemed to be doing a great job of it. Kate then recalled her own smiling facade at the pool the other day and wondered if any woman was entirely what she seemed on the surface.

"Well, I feel old," Delia said. "Or maybe it's just how tired I am. And queasy."

"Morning sickness?" Kate made a mental note not to order anything with strong odors, like fish.

Delia was quiet for a long moment. "Nerves. I have until Friday afternoon to figure out how to tell Ringo.

Some guys I dated were actually so clueless they might not have noticed. But I figure with him living in the house, he'll catch on when I start eating pickles and ice cream and blow up to ten times my normal size."

Kate started to ask if Delia had any idea how Alexander would react but stopped herself. She suspected Delia hadn't even fully processed her own reactions. Other than shock that the hormone-based birth control she'd been using hadn't prevented this. Sure, the labels always said stuff like "88 percent effective," but you assumed the twelve percent failure would happen to someone else. Kate had the fleeting thought that once Paul was home and everything was normal between them again, they were going to be *doubly* careful about birth control. Then she felt guilty for being relieved that it was her friend in the predicament instead of her.

"Hi, girls. I hope you didn't wait for me to order!" Patti declared as she wiggled in next to them, her shoulder-length auburn hair gleaming with quality salon product. "It's been such a packed morning, what with getting my hair done and working on the fall fund-raiser to help fight heart disease. You two will be buying tickets to the dinner, right? Shoot, I really do have to get out of worthy-cause mode. Delia, I should have asked straightaway how you're doing."

"Does that transition mean you see me as a hopeless cause?" Delia's tone was mock indignant, but her ice-blue eyes twinkled.

"Oh, no," Patti chided. "You're not baiting me. I refuse to get exasperated with a pregnant woman when we could be focusing our energies on all the stuff to do. There's a nursery to decorate, showers to throw. It will be so much fun!"

"Chirps the woman who had her one and only child in her midtwenties," Delia grumbled. "Like a sane person."

The assumption of a nursery made Kate bite her lip. "Have you...? It's okay if you don't want to discuss it yet, but you'll be keeping the baby?"

Silence fell across the table, and Kate could see Patti hadn't even *considered* other possibilities. Finally Delia sighed, the small sound breaking some of the tension.

"Yeah. Call me crazy—and I don't know what, if any, part Ringo will want of all this—but yeah. If the kid turns out like me, who else could possibly love her but her mother?"

Kate chuckled obligingly, then turned to study her menu. Deep down, she wasn't sure the parental connection was all it was cracked up to be. Had she ever felt a bond between herself and Lorna Brewster?

Not unless you counted shame and resentment. Someone had once told Lorna that baby Kate was cute enough to be in infant commercials, hawking diapers or mashed plums or whatever. With dollar signs in her eyes and ambition in her heart, Lorna had dragged her daughter to open casting calls around Dallas, meeting with modest success.

There had never been any national ad campaigns, but Kate had done print modeling as a child and small jobs on and off into her adolescence. When she reached school age, her mother had pushed her toward plays, hoping Kate would have a flair for acting, would somehow make it big and get them both out of their dilapidated one-bedroom.

Lorna's own occupational ambitions had been less lofty. She'd slept during the day while Kate was at school, then left for a late night waitressing shift once she'd tucked her daughter into bed. Various neighbors had stayed in the living room or been on call next door as Kate got older. The biggest problem with Lorna's job had been her habit of falling for regular clientele, men who tipped her and told her she was beautiful. She'd have more after-hours drinks than she should, spend nights with men she barely knew, then rant and rave about them when they left her just as Kate's father had.

But you'll never leave me, will you? You're the best thing I've ever done. And my ticket out of here.

Before Kate was even Neve's age, she'd already resolved that she was damn sure getting out of there, and if her mom wouldn't sober up or start creating her own life plan, then she wasn't letting Lorna drag her down. Kate could succeed on her own. And she had.

When she got married at the beginning of the year, it had occurred to her she'd no longer be making it or breaking it alone. She had Paul. But everyone was alone, weren't they?

Whether Alexander helped Delia pick colors for the nursery or fled the country at the mention of impending fatherhood, he wouldn't be the one who waddled late into client conferences because he'd been overcome by nausea. Or the one who went through the turbulence of labor.

Lily was so critical of Paul because he'd sent his children off to get a good education instead of coddling them close after their mother passed away. Kate knew that losing Heather must have hurt like hell, for Paul and both kids, but maybe Newsome had been a good thing. Neve seemed like a smart, capable kid with an independent streak. If she was a little angry at times, well...Kate had made that edge work for her, and she was sure plenty of others had before her.

There were far worse things in this world than learning to be self-reliant.

Kate was twenty minutes later picking up the kids from Lily's house than she'd planned, but Bryce had waylaid her as she was leaving the office. And somehow those five lost minutes had multiplied in traffic and at red lights. She'd done the responsible thing to call and let them know but had only received an abrupt "Sure, whatever" from Brittney before the teenager had clicked back over to the other line.

"Did Brittney give you my message?" Kate asked when Lily opened the door.

The other woman nodded. "She said you'd stayed later

than expected at work. Were you able to get something in place for the rest of the week?"

"My friend Patti is helping me tomorrow and Wednesday, but she's swamped Thursday and Friday."

"Well, I'll round up the kids. And I have a casserole wrapped for you. I wasn't sure what your dinner plans were," Lily said, "so I made myself useful."

"Thanks." Mostly Kate was grateful. But there was a part of her, the part that had always succeeded at everything, that wondered if Lily's favor stemmed from her doubting Kate's culinary skills. Which were admittedly minimalist, but she'd planned a perfectly nutritious chef salad.

With the casserole in hand, she followed the kids to the car noting that neither seemed particularly perky. Were they unhappy about coming home with her? "How was your day?"

"Okay," PJ said unconvincingly.

Neve said nothing.

"Did you have fun with your cousins?" Kate asked, turning out of the subdivision. The houses on Lily's street were all at least fifteen years old, giving the neighborhood a weathered but distinctive feel.

"When Davis came home, Nick didn't want to play with me anymore," PJ said. Obviously he'd been left to keep six-year-old Tad company. PJ got along fine with his young cousin—as far as she could tell, PJ got along fine with most people—but he was at the age where it would have chafed him not to be invited to play with the older, cooler boys.

"What about you, Neve? How did you spend your day?"

"Reading."

"Good book?"

"I guess."

At least her responses aren't monosyllabic. Kate flexed her fingers on the steering wheel. Was she supposed to fish for responses or respect the girl's boundaries? "You don't have much to say tonight, hmm?"

"Earlier she said you suck," PJ provided helpfully.

His sister whirled on him. "You little—God, no wonder none of the boys wanted to play with you, brat."

"Am not!"

Kate cleared her throat. If her stepdaughter had been griping about her, that could explain Lily's suspicion that Kate couldn't even prepare a decent meal. "Neve, did you have a specific complaint about me?"

"I didn't say *you* suck. I said all adults do."

Terrific. But at least it wasn't personal. "Most kids probably feel that way at one time or another."

"What about you?" Neve asked, voluntarily engaged in the conversation for the first time. "*You* ever feel that way about the adults in your life?"

Hell, yes. "To some degree. But I ultimately realized that *I* was responsible for making changes in my life, that being mad at others was a waste of my energy when I could be working on taking control of my circumstances instead."

"Kids don't have any control," Neve argued.

"Of course you do. You make choices every day that will all lead somewhere—you're determining your own path." Did she sound like a bad radio shrink? "And you're the only one who controls your attitude."

Neve was quiet, pensive. "That's sort of what Aunt Lily said."

"You're *kidding*."

"So about this determining my own path thing? Why do PJ and I need a babysitter? Girls my age are babysitters."

Was she right or exaggerating? It wasn't as if Kate had ever had occasion to call a sitter. Neve would be thirteen soon. A teenager, albeit a young one. If it was Neve alone, Kate wouldn't hesitate to let her stay by herself. But with a little brother? Sibling rivalry was apt to break out even with a boy as comparatively easygoing as PJ. Kate had spent plenty of time alone as a girl, but she wasn't about to start using Lorna as a model mother.

"Well," Kate said slowly. "Next week I'll be home. This week I have help through Wednesday. If over the next few days you show me that you're capable of making good decisions and maintaining a mature attitude—and if PJ agrees—then the two of you can stay by yourself on Thursday and Friday." And if they didn't destroy the house on either of those days, she would be partially assured that they'd be okay during the school year, staying a few hours alone between when they got home and when she did.

"Really?" The single word held a wealth of both enthusiasm and skepticism.

Kate tilted her head. "You heard the ifs, right? We'll see how it goes. But, yes, I meant what I said. I try to be honest with you guys. So feel free to ask me things."

"I have a question," PJ said.

"Fire away, buddy."

"What's for dinner? I'm hungry."

She laughed—not exactly an earth-shattering inquiry. "Your aunt Lily made us a casserole of some sort. Anything else? Neve?"

"Well, I *was* going to ask about allowance, but after the babysitting thing, maybe I shouldn't press my luck. I'll wait for a better time to discuss it."

"Better" meaning after Kate had committed some heinous screwup and Neve thought she could negotiate more money? Even though Kate had no plans to be outwitted by someone a third her age, she couldn't help grinning. *I was right, she* is *a smart kid.*

Saturday morning, formerly a time for lolling in bed alongside Paul—maybe reading the paper together, maybe making love—Kate stared at the ceiling, trying to ignore any pang of longing.

"It's not fair that newlyweds have to give up sex," Delia had said weeks ago.

Kate had doubted she'd miss the sex much simply

because she'd gone large chunks of her adult life without having it, when she'd been prioritizing work over dating. She'd never been one for one-night stands, although there had been a lover who had found his way back to her bed several times after his transfer to the opposite coast ended their relationship. Before she'd met Paul, she and her ex-boyfriend had had a standing dinner date—which usually led to breakfast—when he came to Virginia on business.

Still, though the man had presented an occasional oasis during her dry spell, she was able to push sex out of her mind when it wasn't available. She'd spent enough of her early years feeling physically objectified that she'd been thirty before she learned to truly enjoy sex without being self-conscious about the whole act. Making love had been the last thing on her mind when Paul was sent away.

Unfortunately it was sometimes the first thing on her mind when she woke, half-asleep and reaching for someone who wasn't on his side of the bed. Her body missed him. She missed him. But the double-edged sword was that it would get easier each day, wouldn't it? Maybe there would come a time when she slept sprawled across the entire mattress and didn't notice his absence at all. Which could make for an awkward homecoming. Always adjusting.

Was that what families were? One experimental, transitional phase after another?

She *was* adjusting, getting used to the kids being here. She knew even before the doorknob turned that PJ was about to pad into the room. He was another reason lolling was unlikely to take place on Saturdays. The kid never slept past seven o'clock and frequently kept her company while she brewed coffee. Conversely Neve was not a morning person.

"I was just getting up," Kate called to her stepson as he came into view, a pillow-creased face and tousled hair above a Batman pajama shirt. "Meet you in the kitchen?"

"Okay. I could scoop the coffee into the filter if you want. I know how."

"No, that's all right, buddy. It's part of my routine, how I greet the day." Plus, she'd seen firsthand results of what happened when PJ scooped or poured anything. The kid was all thumbs—no wonder soccer was his game of choice. How could anyone who spent so much time mastering the eye-hand cyber challenges of PlayStation and Xbox be so woefully uncoordinated in real life?

Thank God his sister had convinced him earlier this week that a crystal bowl was not the proper container for chocolate-coated puffed-wheat cereal.

"Why don't you just go find us some cartoons?" Kate suggested. If she wanted a CNN update, she'd have to catch it in her room.

After PJ had gone, she brushed her teeth and slid on a pair of camel-colored trousers. Kate could fully appreciate that her stepdaughter didn't want to dress like a woman in her forties, but Kate's goal for the day was to avoid purchasing any garments with words like *sexy* or *tasty* on them. *Foxy* and *sassy* were negotiable.

She found PJ sitting at the kitchen table, eating a banana.

"I used to get the newspaper for Dad every morning," he said as he watched her prepare coffee.

"Oh. Well, maybe that's something you can do for him again after he gets home." She'd canceled the subscription. With the copies of the paper at the office and the various news programs she caught on television and radio, it had been a few bucks she could save. More, it was no longer a daily reminder hitting her front door at six in the morning that Paul wasn't where he should be.

That it was also petty vengeance for the local papers using her husband as a headline wasn't the point.

"I miss Daddy," PJ said.

At least he could say it. Neve rarely mentioned him, especially in a positive way, and Kate was leery of pushing the issue. "Me, too, kiddo. And I'm sure he misses you, but it'll be great when he comes home in a few months. You'll get to see him every day!"

"Will we see him soon?"

"Um…" The honest answer was no, and she'd told the kids they could ask her things and that she'd tell them the truth. But wasn't it best if they heard Paul's decision from him? He was scheduled to call next week. "You know, once school starts, time will be passing a lot faster. You'll have classes, all your new friends and soccer games! Fun fall things like Halloween and the school carnival," she added, glad she'd gotten the scoop from Patti on normal kid activities for September and October. "Before you know it, your dad will be back. Okay?"

When he nodded, she took the opportunity to find a less painful topic. "I'm feeling adventurous today. Want to try to make pancakes? You can stir." Patti had chuckled over the homemade waffles attempt and highly recommended the wide world of boxed mixes.

"All right!"

By the time Neve joined them, dressed in low-slung jeans and a bright red tank top but still sporting unkempt tangles of frizzy hair, they'd thrown out the first burned batch and had created a plateful of pancakes that could almost be called golden-brown.

"Hey!" Neve sniffed. "Something smells almost edible in here. You guys run to Denny's for takeout while I was sleeping?"

"You're hilarious," Kate said.

Neve just grinned. After her initial crankiness on Monday, the rest of the week had been easier. Tuesday and Wednesday, the kids had stayed at Patti's house.

"I like her," Neve had confided as they'd rinsed dishes after a glamorous grilled-cheese dinner. "She's sort of like

Aunt Lily, only…well, maybe a little cooler. But don't ever tell Lily I said that, okay? I love her."

"I can keep a secret," Kate had promised with a smile. She had it on good authority that part of what made Patti's house cool, besides the private pool and water slide in the backyard, was sixteen-year-old Leo and his dimples the size of craters.

But Neve's brief appreciation for the boy was nothing compared to her excitement when Kate stuck to her word about letting the kids stay home alone on Thursday and Friday.

"No using the oven. Microwave only," Kate had stipulated. "And no going to the neighborhood pool while I'm at work." The obligatory No Lifeguard on Duty posting had never seemed so critical as when Kate had backed out of her driveway Thursday morning.

Thursday evening, Neve had accepted an invitation to go to the movies with a girl who lived a few streets over. The two of them had gone to elementary school together, before Neve went to Newsome, and had kept in semiregular touch between e-mail and Neve's visits home. Rebecca would be attending Neve's middle school, so hopefully that was at least one friend already made.

PJ hadn't maintained any lasting bonds during his brief school years in Richmond, but he seemed unconcerned. The kid was a trouper, in Kate's opinion. They'd spent a companionable two hours playing Monopoly while his sister had been out having a social life. It had been PJ who'd reminded Kate of how soon Neve's birthday was.

"Since she's not here, maybe we should talk about what we're going to get her," he'd said as he'd rolled the dice across the kitchen table. "You do know Neve's birthday is coming up?"

"I know," Kate had assured him.

"Just checking. We heard Aunt Lily remind you about my soccer. I'm not mad that you forgot."

Had she forgotten or had she ever known? While Paul certainly discussed his children from time to time, he hadn't regaled her with anecdotes and tidbits of information as often as one might expect.

Then again, maybe she should have shown more interest, asked more open-ended questions about the two kids she'd known would become part of her life.

"Kate?" Neve nudged her stepmother back into the present. "Earth to Kate! You don't want to burn the last pancakes."

"Good point. So who's hungry?"

Neve thrust a plate toward the stove. "Load me up."

Kate nodded. "They say breakfast is the most important meal of the day."

"I don't care about *that*." Neve laughed. "I just want to make sure I have plenty of energy for the mall!"

Noting Neve's good mood this morning confirmed the suspicion that shopping was the way to the girl's heart. But school was about to start, and soon they'd hear from Paul that he didn't want them to visit. If Neve took it badly, Kate suspected it would take more than new jeans to help her stepdaughter cope.

CHAPTER 7

When Kate walked into the mall, she immediately spotted Lily and her middle two children, Davis and Nick—both of whom were bigger versions of Tad. All of the boys looked like their mother. There was something unrefined about her features that translated really well on the masculine faces, and her sons would undoubtedly grow to be handsome young men.

"Brittney's not coming?" Neve asked, her face falling.

"Let's find out," Kate said. "Hi, guys."

"Morning!" Lily waved to them. "You kids excited about school starting soon?"

Nick rolled his eyes. "None of us are kindergarteners, Mom. School's not that big a deal. Except homework, which is a drag."

"Well, I'll bet Neve and PJ are excited about going to school here and getting reacquainted with old friends. I still think it's a shame that Davis and Neve won't be at the same middle school. If you only lived a few minutes closer…"

Imagine. Kate managed not to grimace. "That's all right.

Neve's already seeing some of her classmates. On Thursday she went to the movies with Rebecca."

"Wonderful! So did the kids stay with Rebecca's family on Thursday and Friday, then?"

"No." Kate bit her lip. "I decided—"

"Kate let us stay by ourselves," Neve said on a near squeal. "Isn't that awesome?"

Lily's eyebrows couldn't have shot up any higher if they were jet-propelled. "Awesome."

"Uh-oh." Detecting her aunt's lack of enthusiasm, Neve turned to Kate, her voice a "whisper" they could probably hear in the food court. "Is it okay that I told her that or was that supposed to be a secret between us?"

"No, it's fine. I would never encourage you to lie to your aunt," Kate said hastily. "So. Won't Brittney be joining us today?"

There was a moment's hesitation—an unspoken "We'll talk about this later" hovering over Lily's head like a comic strip character's thought bubble. "She's here somewhere. She's saved up some money this summer and is off on a spree with some of her girlfriends. I'm supposed to call her cell phone before we have lunch so she can meet us."

Kate glanced at Neve to see if lunch was enough to placate the young woman or if she would be annoyed at being blown off for Brittney's high school buddies. If they'd only invited Neve to join them, she would have been delirious. Kate understood the feeling. She'd had one or two close friends in junior high and high school but certainly nothing like the gaggle that always seemed to accompany Lily's popular daughter. Kate hadn't had a lot of shopping sprees, either. There had been the two or three outfits she'd worn to make a good impression at auditions, but she hadn't been allowed to wear them to school except on picture day. What would happen if she stained one with marker or the state-provided cafeteria food?

As Kate grew older, her clothes had become important for work, being taken seriously as an upwardly mobile professional, but she could admit that she took a deeper pleasure in them, too. In buying things she *wanted*, not garments that just happened to be on the clearance rack and close enough to her size to overlook any flaws or ugly fabric choices. With that thought in mind, Kate vowed not to push Neve toward any unflattering outfits simply because they were on sale. Money was tight, not nonexistent.

She pressed her hands together, steepled beneath her chin. "Who's ready to shop?"

The boys weren't quite as excited as Neve, but they were happy to jostle along, pointing out sporting-goods stores and video-game displays. Tad, Kate learned, was absent because Bob's office had an annual Bring Your Child to Work day shortly before school started. Bob picked one kid each year, and this was the first time Tad had been deemed old enough.

"I'm sure Tad is really enjoying that," Kate murmured as all three boys tried on jeans in separate dressing rooms. Neve was a few yards away, looking through a rack of skirts Kate wished were longer.

Lily let the subject of Tad drop, taking advantage of their moment alone. "So you let the kids stay home by themselves?"

"Yes."

"I see."

Kate sighed. "Don't you think that, as their guardian, I'm entitled to make that decision?"

"Technically. But as a woman without a lot of parenting experience, you could have consulted with a mother who knows those kids almost as well as her own. In a way, it's irresponsible that you didn't at least inform me! My house is closer to your place than your office. In case of an emergency, they could have called me. If you'd given me a heads-up, I could have made myself available or phoned to check up on them."

Irresponsible? Kate ground her teeth. "I doubt Neve would appreciate the additional checking up…any more than I appreciate being second-guessed and practically challenged in front of the kids. It's not unreasonable for a girl her age to be left in charge, and not everyone has the benefit of a relative living close by. So thank you for your...helpful spirit, but we're doing just fine. There was no emergency. The kids didn't get into any trouble, which I think proves that I made the right decision."

"Or that you were lucky," Lily shot back. "Did you even run this by their father before you abandoned the search for child care?"

"I didn't make this decision because I was having trouble finding someone to watch them," Kate insisted. "I did this because I made a promise to Neve."

They both glanced in the girl's direction, making sure that their quiet but intense conversation wasn't being overheard.

"Yeah, the two of you seem a little chummier," Lily observed.

"You *want* the children to get along well with their step-mother, right, Lily?" Maybe Heather's sister was having difficulty with the kids accepting Kate as their mom.

"Of course I do! But because you're getting to know each other over time. Not because you let them get their way or—" Lily broke off as Nick threw open a door to strike a rapper pose in his baggy jeans and football shirt.

"Looks good, huh?" Nick asked.

"At least it actually fits and you're not wearing pants that fall down around your ankles," his mother replied. "Davis, what about you? You're taking forever."

Kate used the break to join Neve by a display of dresses in autumn colors. The important thing, she told herself, was that she and the kids were bonding. Maybe it would be nice if she and Lily could do the same eventually, but…one hurdle at a time.

Soon after leaving that store, the three boys banded together to demand food, proving once again that the male of the species lacked the shopping stamina of the female. As promised, Brittney joined them for lunch. Neve followed her cousin's example of ordering a small salad. PJ, on the other hand, ate not only his burger and onion rings but Kate's side of fries, as well. Amazing that someone so small could pack away so much food.

Kate sat in the middle of a long table, flanked by her stepchildren, nibbling disinterestedly at her chicken sandwich as the buzzing white noise of the mall droned in the background. They were seated between a children's carousel that ran every five minutes and Senor Kung Pao's, a place that served both Mexican and Chinese cuisine.

"Kate?" Neve's hopeful tone cut through the warbling calliope music and a man announcing that order number thirty-six was ready. "After lunch, can I go with Brittney and her friends? They're going to hit a few more stores, and I thought, if you didn't mind…"

Studying her stepdaughter, Kate saw how much the girl wanted to spend her summer afternoon with fashionable teenagers instead of two fortyish moms. *Dear Lord, did I just think of myself as a mom?* Weird but not entirely painful.

"I think we can work that out." She glanced to the girl on the other side of Neve. "Lily, do you let Brittney take one of your credit cards or put stuff on hold so you can buy it later?" Kate wasn't sure they'd let someone as young as Neve sign for anything.

"What's your budget for their fall clothes?" Lily asked from the end of the table, miraculously able to follow the conversation despite the cacophony and her constant reminders to the boys that if they didn't slow down and actually *chew* something, they were going to choke to death.

"I don't have a set budget, per se." She'd just resolved to let each of her stepkids pick out a few outfits that were durable or flattering, with plans to protest anything overpriced or inappropriate. It wasn't as if she'd never shopped before.

"Right." Lily turned to hand Nick a stack of napkins, but not before Kate got the impression the woman was rolling her eyes.

Kate pulled her checkbook out of her purse and ignored the pang the account balance gave her. It was a perfectly respectable sum but with a lot of demands on it. She set her ATM card and pocket calculator on the table.

"I'll work out a figure and get you some cash," she told Neve. Then it would be up to the girl to make some sound financial choices. "Just don't buy anything that can't be returned without me there. And nothing that shows too much skin!"

Neve was too excited about going shopping with her

own bevy of teen wardrobe consultants to be defensive. "I'll pick out clothes you love, I promise!"

Kate smiled. "It's more important to pick out clothes *you* love."

"And don't blow it all on one outfit," Lily added, her admonishment including both girls. "Keep in mind, there are five days in a school week."

"We know," Brittney insisted with an eye roll she'd no doubt inherited from her mother.

Twenty minutes later the boys were clearing the table and racing each other to the nearest trash can while Neve was counting out twenties and swearing on all that was trendy that she wouldn't lose any of the money. Kate suspected the only reason the girl didn't *skip* down the corridor, past a smoothie stand and a hut where you could get your ears pierced in the middle of the mall, was that Brittney would find such a display uncool.

After a quick stop at a shoe store, where Lily tutted that Davis had bigger feet than his father, Nick and Davis begged to stop for a video game.

"Just think of it this way, Mom," Davis cajoled with a mischievous smile, "if you let me blow my allowance at the arcade, it will be that much less sex and violence I get to see at the movie theater."

"Davis!" Lily swatted her oldest boy on the back of the head. "At least *try* to set a good example for the younger boys."

"Couldn't I be a cautionary tale instead?"

Kate couldn't help the laugh that escaped her. For all his smart-aleck attitude and adolescent preoccupation with cars, girls, sports and video games, Davis was a kid with above-average intelligence and a contagious smile. Eighth-grade girls beware.

His mother shot Kate an eyebrow-raised glare, making it clear she didn't appreciate the snickering.

Guiltily Kate cleared her throat. "PJ, do you want to play one game with them?"

When Neve had glibly mentioned allowance the other day, Kate had pushed the topic aside, but she'd have to give it serious consideration. She knew Paul had sent the kids monthly stipends, but now that they were living at home, Kate was absorbing some of the snack and entertainment costs they'd had to pay themselves at Newsome. Plus, finances had changed since then, anyway.

The boys took off to race vehicles and shoot at bad guys, and an awkward silence descended.

Lily's conversational opener came out of the blue. "I figured that after this we could go to Wal-Mart." She misread the surprise on Kate's face, possibly taking it for confusion. "You have heard of Wal-Mart? Large—"

"I *know* what Wal-Mart is," Kate snapped.

"The mall's great for clothes, but we'll want to go somewhere else for school supplies. Wal-Mart or something else close by that has lots of different items at a reasonable price."

Was it Kate's imagination or was there a contemptuous undercurrent in the way Lily drawled "reasonable price"? *She's a reverse snob.* Lily had often seemed vaguely envious of Kate's wardrobe or the luxuries she spent money on. But it wasn't as though Kate was financially irresponsible or that she thought she could win the kids over with expensive goodies. She simply worked hard to earn her salary, and if she occasionally pampered herself—or the kids, who'd had their fair share of hard knocks—she refused to apologize for that.

Wouldn't Lily be shocked to know that when Kate was younger she had aspired to new purchases at Wal-Mart? She remembered carefully picking out items for layaway that she and her mother could pay off a little at a time with her modeling money. Kate refused to win Lily over with self-pitying stories of her childhood. *We'll either learn to like each other or we won't, but who I used to be is irrelevant.*

Kate hadn't even given Paul a detailed description of her past. Why would she? It was only the woman he loved in the present who was relevant. And she'd worked too hard to leave that girl and the stigmas surrounding her behind.

If Kate had thought the food court was loud, it was nothing compared to the back-to-school chaos of the retail store one parking lot over from the mall. A sprawling, supersize warehouse filled with everything from car parts to crayons to jewelry, seemingly on sale, and the whole of Virginia had turned out for the bargains. Neve had already satisfied her wardrobe cravings, and PJ was getting tired.

All of the kids were growing increasingly cranky, and Kate didn't entirely blame them. While she acknowledged the possible conveniences of having fresh produce, a pharmacy, a gardening store and undergarments all under one roof, it made for a lot of hiking back and forth. Her feet were beginning to throb in time with her temples.

As Lily checked the fit of sneakers on Nick, Kate took the opportunity to sit on one of the nearby benches. They'd split up to get some supplies and had just regrouped. Neve wanted to try on shoes, and Brittney was giving her younger cousin tips for walking on high heels. Kate chuckled at her stepdaughter's wobbly attempts, then glanced back to where Nick, Davis and PJ—

Shooting to her feet, she double-checked the head count. Four kids. Two boys—both Lily's—and two girls. Well, PJ's feet were still a lot smaller than his cousins', so maybe he'd rounded the corner and was on the other aisle, looking at shoes in more appropriate sizes. Did an eight-year-old even know what size shoe he wore? She quickly headed to the next row, glancing up the empty aisle before checking the one on the other side.

No PJ. She raced back to ask Neve if she knew where her brother was.

The girl shrugged. "I was talking to Brittney and figured

he was with Nick or Davis. There's a bathroom back here—maybe he went in there?"

The bathroom. Right. After all, they'd been in this store for what felt like a week and he'd had that giant soft drink before leaving the mall.

"You stay here," Kate instructed. "I'll check the restroom."

"The guys' restroom?" Neve said incredulously. "Why don't we send Davis in looking for him?"

Kate glanced toward Lily and her sons. "I have this covered. Just *stay here* and keep your eyes open for him." She was already striding away before Neve could agree.

At the men's restroom, she swung the door open wide and hollered inside. "PJ! Paul St. James Jr., are you in there?"

A balding man in a bowling shirt came around the corner. "Can I help you with something, ma'am?"

"I needed to see if my stepson is in there," she said.

"I don't think so. Hold on a minute." A moment later he reappeared, shaking his head as he passed her. "Nope. No one in here but me."

"Thanks." *OhGodohGod.* But maybe Neve had already found her brother. Kate would go back there now. First, though, she couldn't stop herself from asking a uniformed store employee to check the restroom one last time instead of relying on the word of a total stranger who could be a criminal for all she knew. When the clerk confirmed what the other man had already said, Kate hurried back to the shoe section.

Lily met her with wide eyes. "PJ's missing? Since when?"

Wasn't that like asking a person where the last place they'd seen a lost item was? If they *knew*, the damn thing wouldn't be *lost*, would it? "I'm not sure. Kids, when was the last time any of you remember seeing him?"

No one could recall. Davis and Nick had been looking at backpacks together, and Brittney and Neve had been engrossed in girl talk.

Kate ran a hand through her hair, feeling as if she might unravel right here in front of the half-price-sandal display. "No one remembers seeing him? How is that even possible?" The hypocrisy of the question assailed her. Why couldn't *she* remember? It was her job to watch the kids.

"All right." Lily clapped her hands together briskly, taking charge. For once, Kate was glad. "We should split up. The boys and I can retrace our steps in one direction. You go in another. And Brittney and Neve head up front. You two can have him paged and wait for him there if neither of us finds him first."

Kate murmured her agreement, although given the constant stream of warbled announcements that had played on the intercom overhead since they'd come into the store, she wasn't sure PJ would even hear. Still, it gave the girls something constructive to do. And maybe PJ would be actively listening for an announcement like that, especially if he were scared.

She shuddered at the idea of him alone, feeling forgotten in the giant store. Next to Lily's kids, he was such a little boy....

Realizing her hands were shaking, Kate clenched her fingers into tight fists. They'd find him. "You girls stay together! And *wait* for us up front. Brittney, Lily, you both have your cell phones? Neve, you know my number? Whoever finds him first, call the other two."

Both girls nodded immediately, Neve looking a little pale beneath her summer tan.

Lily reached out to squeeze the girl's hand. "It will be all right, baby. We just got temporarily separated in the crowd."

On that note, they headed their agreed-upon ways. The crowd *was* thick today, making separation understandable, but all the more reason to keep a close eye on a child. That must be what Paul's sister-in-law was thinking. Honestly Kate didn't blame her in the least. She was disgusted with herself. An eight-year-old boy, for Christ's sake! This wasn't like misplacing car keys or a pricey pair of sunglasses.

She caught sight of a woman tugging a resistant tousle-haired little boy in the same color T-shirt PJ had been wearing, and her heart accelerated. Adrenaline kicking in, she hurried toward them in a burst of protective speed. As she got closer, however, she realized that this was not a case of kidnapping, merely a tired mother whose son was demanding some sort of toy and didn't want to leave yet.

The adrenaline didn't subside, roiling through her as she

sped past shoppers, her gaze constantly darting from one side to the next. Maybe PJ had wanted to look at toys? Lily and her sons were combing that section, so they'd see him if that were the case. Inside her purse she had one hand locked around her cell phone, willing it to ring, willing him to be found.

When she did finally see him, the scene was so normal it almost didn't register—just a boy unconcernedly playing at one of the video-game displays, moving the joystick and having no bloody clue how frantic others were to find him. Or that he was even lost.

Relief punched her so hard her knees almost buckled. In its wake followed fury.

"Paul Anthony St. James!" Wow, was that her voice that had just bellowed through the crowd? Amazing that the computer monitors on display hadn't shattered.

Her volume had certainly been effective. PJ turned immediately, his eyebrows raised in such a startled, quizzical expression that she might have laughed if she hadn't been such an emotional wreck. Rushing toward him, she almost pulled him into a hug but stopped herself at the last moment, aware she was still trembling, needing a moment to regain her composure.

"You can't just wander off! You scared me to death." Again, she couldn't believe it was herself she was hearing. Especially spouting maternal clichés, the way Lily always did. Was "Because I said so" looming in Kate's near future?

PJ's eyes were huge. "I figured I could play one of the games for a second while Nick and Davis looked at backpacks." He jerked his thumb toward the aisle in question, barely visible from within the electronics department.

"That was fifteen minutes ago! You didn't tell anyone where you were going, and we were all worried." Speaking of which, she had to phone Lily and Brittney and let them know the search had ended successfully. As she dialed, she noticed the way PJ's lower lip had begun to tremble. Her knee-jerk reaction was to feel guilty for scaring him, but wasn't it best if he understood the severity of disappearing in a crowded public place? "Brittney, he's with me, so tell Neve he's fine. He got sucked in by a new video game and didn't realize we'd walked off. We'll see you up front in just a sec. Why don't you go ahead and call your mom, too?"

It wasn't cowardice on Kate's part that she didn't want to talk to Lily. It was only that she wanted PJ's aunt to know he was safe as soon as possible and she couldn't do that while reassuring her stepson at the same time. She knelt closer to his height, wondering what to say. Telling him she wasn't mad would be a lie and dilute the impact she'd just made. "I know you didn't worry us on purpose. I'm very, very happy to see you."

He sniffed. "You're not angry at me?"

"I am. And I think you're grounded from playing video games for the rest of the weekend. But mostly I just want you to remember not to walk off again. Always let me or Lily know where you are, okay?"

"Okay." Then he surprised her by throwing his slim arms around her so suddenly she rocked back on her heels. "I'm sorry."

After the initial shock ebbed, she brought her hand up to the back of his head and simply hugged him back.

They walked together to the front of the store, where the other kids fussed over him like a hero returned from a battle. Lily looked caught between wanting to scoop him up and wanting to shake her finger at him, much the way Kate had felt moments ago.

Lily glanced up. "You let him know how important it was that he doesn't do this again?"

"She took away my video games until Monday," PJ said solemnly.

After a moment's consideration, Lily nodded. "That seems fitting. Now that we've got the drama behind us, what's say we get checked out so that we can all get home in time for dinner?"

This raised all sorts of questions and opinions from hungry children, but above the din Lily's eyes met Kate's. There was none of the censure that Kate expected and even felt she deserved. Instead there was a note of empathy.

Something in her sister-in-law's knowing expression seemed to say, *Welcome to the club.*

CHAPTER 8

Following the physical demands of marathon shopping and the emotional punch of losing her stepson, Kate was not up to cooking. She let the kids order a pizza, marveling that anyone would voluntarily ingest a pineapple-jalapeño-and-mushroom deep-dish. They ate their meal off paper plates in the living room while watching a DVD, one of those ubiquitous family films where kid befriends animal and after either kid or animal or both overcome danger, all ends tear-inducingly well.

PJ, who'd become her cheerful shadow over the past week, surprised her by sitting even closer than normal on the sofa. She would have expected her first "grounding" to lead to resentment, not affection. Ever since she'd found him by the video-game sampler, he'd stuck to her like glue. Maybe he was subconsciously making the point that he wouldn't wander off again.

Long before the end of the movie and the rolling credits, he slumped against her, slack-jawed and snoring. His weight wasn't unpleasant, and she tousled his hair, feeling remnants of her earlier relief. Thank God he'd been all right.

"He never makes it to the end," Neve commented, her tone making it clear that *she* was much older and sophisticated.

But not so world-weary that she wasn't sniffling and wiping her eyes in the last five minutes of the movie, Kate had noticed. "I'll carry him up to bed as soon as I clean up." Paper plates and individual bags of microwave popcorn littered the living room.

Funny. Despite its name, this room had rarely looked "lived" in until the kids had arrived. During their short marriage Kate and Paul had spent more evenings at the theater, the club, business dinners or even working at home than watching television on the couch. When they did watch TV together, it was often in bed. Having Neve and PJ around definitely changed things.

But Kate was almost getting used to being tailed from room to room, as Neve did now.

"So your friend Delia is coming over for lunch tomorrow, right?"

"And Patti, too." Was this a roundabout way of asking if Patti's *son* would be in attendance? Hardly. Teenagers with the freedom of a driver's license rarely opted to spend the afternoon with three middle-aged women.

Neve nodded absently, dismissing Patti and proving Kate still didn't have a clue how her stepdaughter's mind worked. "And Delia's pregnant."

"Right. Neve, is there something specific on your mind?"

The girl took a deep breath, clearly mustering courage. The way she fiddled with the ends of her hair, however, betrayed her nerves. "Does she *want* to have the baby?"

The question was unexpected but easy to answer. "Yes, she does." Delia had been shocked by the discovery of her pregnancy—as had Alexander, who'd first mistaken her "we need to talk" opener as her dumping him—but Kate's friend had already channeled her no-nonsense fierceness into protective feelings for the baby.

"What about you?" Neve asked suddenly.

"Do *I* want a baby?" Did Neve worry that once Paul came home, he and Kate would have a baby together that displaced her stepchildren? "Oh, honey. No, I don't think that's going to happen."

Neve rolled her eyes. "Duh. You're kind of old to be pregnant, aren't you?"

Hey! "I'm younger than Delia!"

"But she's like a…what's that word? Exception, but it starts with an A."

"Anomaly? If you think I'm too ancient to get pregnant, why did you ask about my having babies?"

"I just meant in general." Neve studied the floor. "Did you want to have kids? Before you married my dad?"

In other words, *Did you want us?*

She hadn't *not* wanted them. Kate doubted that would be very reassuring. Frankly she wasn't sure how she felt about it herself. How could she have been so ambivalent about something like two children when she'd always gone after other things in her life so passionately? This was proving a lot more awkward than anything else she'd ever undertaken. When you were married to your job, you weren't as worried about its first wife.

"Well...some women are naturally maternal, like your aunt Lily. She probably always knew she wanted to be a mother and she's good at it. Patti's like that. From what I know, your mom was, too."

At Neve's flinch, Kate decided perhaps *she* shouldn't be the one to bring Heather into any future conversations.

"The rest of us have to work harder," she continued. "I don't think Delia knew how much she wanted it until it happened to her. It's a little like that for me, the not knowing. But having stepchildren gives me all the benefits without the waddling and barfing I hear pregnancy brings."

Her circuitous answer was met with thoughtful silence, and Kate wondered if her response had been good enough. She couldn't gush about how much she'd always wanted to be a mom because it would be a lie, but she didn't want Neve to feel unwelcome in her own home, either.

Finally the girl nodded. "I guess I can understand that. It's not like *I* wanted a stepmom."

Touché. Kate smiled. "But we'll both do the best we can, right?"

"I can do that." After a pause she added shyly, "You did

a good job with PJ today. I mean, he got in trouble, but you didn't scream at him or anything."

"Honestly I was more scared than mad." Having children under her care made her feel far more vulnerable than she ever had as a single woman living alone. "When I think about what could have happened just because I took my eyes off him for a few minutes...."

Renewed guilt swamped her. What would Paul say about her misplacing one of his children? For a woman who tried so hard to be good at everything she did, that kind of failure was inexcusable. Hell, it bordered on criminal negligence!

Neve cleared her throat, then grinned impishly. "So would *now* be a good time to discuss allowance?"

Neve wasn't sure why the junior high school seemed so *huge* when she knew the Newsome campus was way bigger. It's what Mandy Malloy would have called a paradox—even though she was only a year older than Neve, Mandy always talked like she was practicing for the SATs 24-7. Some of the girls at Newsome had thought Mandy was a show-off, but Neve hadn't minded. Mandy was quick to share anything she had and helped Neve with her math homework.

I'll probably never see her again. E-mail wasn't the same thing as really being able to talk to a friend.

"You okay?" Kate asked, catching up to Neve in the center of the library. Today was the day when parents and students could tour the building and meet the teachers before school started next week.

"I'm fine," Neve lied. She liked Kate more than she would have expected, but that didn't mean she wanted to talk about every little thing. How big a loser would she be to stand here babbling about how she already missed her old classmates and wondered if her new ones would like her? She'd see Rebecca on the school bus, but the two girls had compared schedules and didn't have any courses together.

"Want to go try to find your locker?" Kate asked.

"All right." Neve was glad her stepmother wasn't pushing to make sure nothing was wrong.

She trailed Kate into a hallway that smelled like some industrial disinfectant. The janitor had probably been busy getting the entire school ready for parent day—spotless floors and gleaming rows of blue lockers were more likely to impress moms than the students themselves. Neve didn't worry about stuff like graffiti on the locker; she just hoped she'd remember her combination.

They'd yet to determine which locker was hers when a bell sounded overhead. It seemed ear-splitting. The principal had announced during the welcome assembly that after a few minutes of wandering to familiarize everyone with the layout of the school, they'd go through a "practice day" with the bells ringing every fifteen minutes so that students could report to their first-, second-, third-period classes and so on. It was a test run for next Monday, as well as a chance for the teachers to drone on about their curricula and goals for the year.

Kate had started at the gonging bell, too. "Wow. That's pretty loud, huh?"

"Guess I don't have to worry about not hearing it," Neve said flatly. She wished she were at Patti's with PJ, swimming in the backyard pool and talking to Patti's son, instead of here. Even though parts of her summer had been boring, she suddenly wished it were one or two months longer.

"Well, let's find your homeroom." Kate handed over the map. "Lead the way."

Neve had made one wrong turn by the time the two-minute warning bell sounded, and the milling crowd was daunting. Despite the overall campus at Newsome, class sizes were small and hallways were rarely so packed.

"Any chance I could talk you into homeschooling?" she joked weakly.

"Oh, that would be *great* for my career," Kate said with a wry smile and a quick shake of her head.

Based on the amount of time Kate had spent on her laptop and phone Monday and Tuesday, her career was pretty important. Neve wasn't entirely sure what she did, other than write out boring manuals that someone else dictated. Didn't sound like rocket science.

"Look," Kate said, "I think this is the room we want. D205."

"Terrific." They made it through the door as the final bell rang.

A tall man with bright blue eyes stood at the front of the classroom. He didn't seem old enough to be a teacher—he looked a little like Tom Welling, the actor on *Smallville*. She'd always thought he was cute.

"Good morning." The man smiled at the roomful of parents and kids.

Definitely cute. Neve felt herself sigh.

"I'm Mr. Grayson, eighth-grade honors English teacher. We'll wait for a few more minutes before we get started— there are always a few stragglers at the beginning of the year. Don't worry, I won't start counting tardies until the second week of school."

He was right. At least half a dozen more students piled into the room after he'd already introduced himself the first time. Eventually he got around to discussing what the class would cover, including poetry and an overview of different literary periods, from *Beowulf* to early American novels. Neve usually loved to read, but some of the books on the semester list didn't seem that interesting. Then again, maybe the young, enthusiastic teacher would find a way to make them fun.

As they headed for second period, Kate nudged Neve with her elbow. "So. That Mr. Grayson was kind of a hottie, huh?"

"Ew." She did not need her stepmother scoping out her teachers. Kate could practically be *his* stepmom! And was that even fair to Dad, rotting in jail?

"Sorry. Just trying to bond."

"Well, don't. Not over guys, anyway."

"Noted. Look, here we are."

Earth Sciences. Joy. This teacher was a woman—one who looked as old as the rocks they'd be discussing and didn't appear to smile. Ever.

Third period was Fine Arts, where they'd do mostly drama and a few choir exercises. Ms. Cameron—or Bianca, as she invited the students to call her—was a colorfully dressed young woman with supershort hair and great shoes. She'd just encouraged everyone to look around the room and "get comfortable in the space" when she approached Neve and Kate.

"You're Mrs. St. James, aren't you?"

Kate nodded. "And my stepdaughter, Neve."

"Nice to meet you both." The woman offered Neve a welcoming smile, then turned back to Kate, lowering her voice to a whisper. "I think you'll find that this sort of class, which encourages free expression, will be really good for Neve, helping her sort out her feelings about everything she's been through recently."

Neve's face was hot, and she knew it must be turning red. Her first opinion of "Bianca" had been a good one, but she hated the way the woman was talking about her as if she weren't standing right here! And she didn't like the way the teacher's voice sounded. *She doesn't even know me. She doesn't know what's "good" for me.*

"I just wanted to let you know that my door's always open," Bianca said, speaking directly to Neve this time. "If there's anything I can do for you, dear…"

"I'm fine," Neve snapped.

"Of course," the woman said, her voice that kind of soothing sympathy adults gave to little kids who got hurt.

I don't have a boo-boo. My mom's dead and my dad's gone and I can deal with it without people like you!

Anger welled up in Neve, mixed with humiliation, and all at once she was choking on it. God, was she actually going to *cry?* She hadn't let herself do that in a long time, but she suddenly felt overwhelmed. Afraid of making a fool of herself and becoming a laughingstock among her peers before school even started, she spun on her heel and stalked out of the auditorium-style classroom.

Kate would be pissed at the rudeness, but Neve didn't care. At least not enough to stop. She found her way to a deserted girls' restroom, where her stepmom caught up with her.

Neve had arrived only seconds before and had just turned on the faucet. She splashed some water on her face, not speaking first or turning to see if Kate looked mad.

Instead her stepmother's tone was gentle. "Are you all right?"

"*Stop asking me that!*" Neve's voice reverberated off the tile walls, and she cringed at the way it echoed back, making her sound hateful and childish. Even PJ had outgrown temper tantrums.

"I'm sorry," Kate said. "It was a stupid question."

"Really?" Neve peered up through her bangs, wanting to see the woman's expression but not ready to meet her eyes. "You're apologizing? I'm the one who yelled."

"Just don't make a habit of it."

Neve's lower lip trembled. Somehow the fact that Kate was being so nice about it made her feel even weepier. "Can we go? I swear I'll find all my classes on Monday or ask someone for help if I get lost, but I just... Can we go?"

Thinking it over, Kate sighed. "Yeah, I guess so. Let's head out before they ring the bell and the halls get crowded again."

Numb with relief and gratitude, Neve shuffled through the hallway feeling like a sleepwalker. *Trapped in a bad dream.* Did all kids think middle school was a nightmare?

Maybe it'll get better.

Well, it *had* to, didn't it? She still had no idea where her locker was, but so far, she'd already antagonized one teacher and hidden out in the girls' room to cry. And school didn't even start for another four days.

After telling Kate she didn't care what they listened to on the radio, Neve didn't have much to say. Instead she just stared out the window. But she saw that drama teacher's face, not the scenery they were passing.

"Kate? That woman knew about Dad, right? When she mentioned what I'd been through 'recently'?"

Another sigh. Did Kate always sigh this much or was that Neve's fault?

"Yeah, that's what she meant. Your aunt Lily feels that it's best for teachers to know what's going on in their students' lives so they can better understand each kid and—"

"She doesn't understand anything about me!"

"You may be right."

"Did Lily make you tell all my teachers about Dad?"

"No. I had to fill out parental information, stuff about my guardianship and your home life. She just helped me find the upside in it. The truth is, your dad made the news. He was in local headlines when he was a successful businessman, which made for juicy headlines after he was arrested." Kate cast Neve a quick sidelong glance. "I don't want to upset you, but you're a smart young woman and old enough to understand about gossip."

Neve nodded, thinking of some of the girls she'd gone to school with—ones who pretended to be everyone's friend and were so sorry whenever something bad happened but not sorry enough to keep from gossiping about other people's tragedies. "Does everyone know? They'll...be talking about me?"

"I doubt it. I just talked to the principals and guidance counselors at your school and PJ's. Presumably they've given some kind of file to your teachers, but there will be lots of people who are completely unaware. Some of the students *might* have heard about your dad from their parents or on the news, but I'm sure eighth graders are more concerned with other things."

This was just like it had been when her mom died.

All of Neve's teachers had known, treated her differently. They'd been trying to make it easier on her, but nothing anyone said or did was going to bring back her mother. Acting weird around Neve or telling her she looked pretty didn't help, and when the teachers had started treating her as if she were special, some of the kids had reacted. A few had resented it, others had taken the teachers' lead—letting Neve win games at recess, giving her part of their dessert at lunch. People had only been trying to be nice, but she'd hated it anyway.

She'd tried to talk to her dad about it…and the next thing she knew, he'd packed her off to Newsome. That wasn't what she'd wanted at all! She and her mom had been close, could talk about everything, but it was so much harder with her father. Maybe because he was a guy or because he hadn't spent as much time with her and PJ, always being so busy with work. But being sent out of state certainly didn't encourage her to make the same mistake of opening up to someone again. The angry part of her suspected her complaints about the awkwardness at school had been just the excuse he'd needed to get Neve and PJ away. After all, once they'd been gone, he'd had a fresh start. Top boss at a fairly new company, dating Kate not long after...

Could they have a *second* fresh start now that she and PJ were back? "Kate, when are we going to talk to Dad?"

"Tonight." She pursed her lips as if she were troubled about something but then smiled. "You'll both get to talk to him on the phone tonight. I know it's been frustrating that you weren't able to speak with him sooner, but you got here earlier than expected. For now, he only gets fifteen minutes every two weeks, so I won't talk long. I want you and PJ to have as much time as possible. You can tell him about your new school."

"And when will we actually see him?" Neve pressed. "How soon do we get to visit?" She felt so stupid at times like this, mad at her dad but wanting to be with him anyway. Sometimes she wanted to crawl into his lap like some kind of baby and have him hug her. He wasn't an extraordinarily tall guy or even that big, but he'd seemed so solid and strong when she was little. Like he could protect them from anything.

What utter BS.

"Um...visit?" Kate echoed. "Well, that's something you'll have to discuss with him this evening."

She's lying. Not in the sense that she wasn't telling the truth, but she was definitely being evasive and not saying everything she knew either. Neve shook her head, glaring out the window. So much for being a smart young woman who deserved the truth. Kate had been pretty cool today, not bitching about Neve's behavior and agreeing to skip the rest of orientation. That made her a halfway decent guardian.

It didn't make them friends.

CHAPTER 9

Kate flinched when, later that evening, the door to Neve's room slammed shut upstairs. PJ, happily telling his father that he was looking forward to tomorrow's elementary school orientation, didn't seem to notice the way the house shook on its foundation. Then again, he'd also managed to ignore the tension permeating the dining room during dinner.

Since Kate had actually cooked tonight, she hadn't wanted to eat in the living room or serve the kids at the two-seater kitchen table while she stood over the island. But the silence had seemed even bigger in the spacious, more formal room. Neve had been increasingly withdrawn since they'd left her school—not even picking PJ up from Patti's and saying hi to Leo had perked her up.

So dinner tonight had involved little conversation, only the ticking of the antique grandfather clock and PJ slurping his spaghetti noodles. *Which were overdone to the point of rubbery, and you put too much oregano in the sauce.* Too bad she'd let her pride stop her from buying a canned sauce. The food might have been more edible, but, dammit, she was trying here.

She'd even thought she'd gained some points today, hustling Neve out of that parent-teacher disaster and away from any peer scrutiny. In general, Kate didn't endorse hiding from one's problems, but she had vague recollections of junior high. Neve was going to have enough problems this year without breaking into angry tears in front of her soon-to-be classmates.

Unfortunately any ground Kate had gained had been lost, slashed and burned during the subsequent car ride.

I should have just told her the truth, Kate mused as she poured herself a glass of chardonnay. The bottle had been a gift from Delia after she'd purged all things alcoholic from her town house. Alexander, of course, could still imbibe, but if he and Delia didn't come to some kind of agreement soon about his future involvement with the baby, maybe he wouldn't be living there much longer.

"The extra privacy would suit me just fine," Delia had said with forced bravado. "Not like I need an audience for my throwing up every half hour!"

Kate empathized with the nausea. Her own stomach had been twisted in knots for hours, half dreading the collect call from the prison switchboard and knowing it would be bad when Neve learned she wouldn't be seeing her father anytime soon. But Kate had truly felt it was Paul's place to inform the children of his decision. If Kate *had* spilled the beans, would Neve have adopted a shoot-the-messenger attitude? That was human nature, so maybe there'd been no way for Kate to win this one no matter what she'd done.

"But don't you want to see us, Daddy?"

The sudden hurt in PJ's tone jarred her from her thoughts, and she stepped closer to the boy. Unlike his sister, who might resent the invasion of personal space and eavesdropping, she suspected PJ would find the nearness reassuring. She flashed him an encouraging smile as he spoke into the receiver.

"But we miss you. I...I guess so," he said in response to whatever explanation Paul had given. "Yes, she's right here. I l-love you, too."

Though he was taking the news with considerably less fury than his older sister, the boy's grip tightened momentarily on the phone and his lips quivered.

She was getting used to feeling protective, but the potent anger that welled up within her took Kate by surprise. No matter how much she wanted to be a supportive wife, right now she wanted to smack her husband upside the head.

PJ swallowed bravely, holding out the cordless phone. "H-he wants to talk to you. Can I play my Xbox now?"

"Absolutely, honey. Give me a minute and then you can show me how to play that game Davis let you borrow, okay?" *Thanks a frigging lot, Paul.* He'd upset both his children, leaving Kate to deal with them when she was rarely sure whether or not she was saying the right thing.

Uncertainty of any kind was foreign and unsettling enough to piss her off further.

She inhaled deeply, though, trying to keep the irritation out of her voice. Inmates earned privileges as time passed, and right now she got to speak to her husband so rarely that the last thing she wanted to do was turn their brief moment of conversation into a fight. *Plenty of time for that once he's home*, she thought with a flash of grim humor. "Hey."

"I'm sorry they showed up early," Paul said. "I know that must have thrown you for a loop."

"Don't be silly—you can't apologize for their grandfather's heart problems. Although Lily told the kids he's doing much better now." If Paul wanted to apologize for his own negligence and getting himself arrested in the first place, that would be different. But he'd already expressed plenty of guilt over his mistakes, and rehashing wouldn't change anything. "The kids and I are holding our own. You know, when I'm not losing them in public places."

"It was an honest mistake, Katie, one that could just as easily happen to a biological parent. None of us is perfect." His voice cracked a little and it took him a second before he could add, "Neve's pretty ticked off at me?"

"At both of us. She's mad about your decision and furious I didn't warn her about it. Are you sure you don't want me to call her back to the phone? Maybe you could—"

"No, my time's about up, but you know I'll call again when I can. You'll smooth things over with her before then."

"Well, I'll try to, of course. But, Paul, I—"

"I love you. Talk to you in two weeks!" And then he was gone.

She held the receiver away from her ear, staring at it. He'd *hung up* on her? The anger she'd been trying to push away flared again.

He did warn you he was out of time, she rationalized. Maybe there'd been a surly guard standing nearby with an egg timer. She knew nonattorney calls were either monitored or recorded. Or perhaps an inmate named Big Jack had been impatiently awaiting his turn with the phone.

But Kate couldn't quite shake the feeling that Paul had seized the chance to avoid her and his own kids. Worse, she was beginning to think this was a pattern for him. When Heather was alive, had she done all the emotional "heavy lifting" for the family? How uncomfortable *was* Paul when it came to dealing with his children's distress?

If I can learn to cope with it, their father sure as hell can.

Lily might have some answers, but Kate would feel a little like a traitor asking his first wife's sister about his potential failings. Or at least mistakes. For now, Kate would muddle on without a native guide. After all, she was an intelligent, competent woman who'd already won over at least one of the kids.

With that thought in mind, she joined PJ in the next room and struggled through half an hour of video game play. She kept hoping Neve would come downstairs, but there was no sign of her. Not even footsteps overhead.

Do I check on her or give her space? She didn't want to come off like that cloying drama teacher who'd been overbearing with her companionable concern. Then again, it would be hypocritical of her to be angry that Paul wasn't better at communicating with them if she were down here avoiding conversation, too.

"PJ, I think I'm going to sit this next round out, okay? I'd like to check on your sister."

He actually looked away from the screen long enough to meet her eyes. "You sure that's a good idea?"

Great. Even the oblivious eight-year-old thought she was nuts for bearding the lioness in its teenage den. "No, not entirely. But I'm going to give it a try."

With an oddly mature and philosophical nod, he returned to his game.

What, no prebattle salute?

She rehearsed several lame opening lines as she climbed the stairs, but they would all be pretty useless if Neve wouldn't even open the door. Knowing there was only one way to find out, Kate knocked.

The pulsing music on the other side of the door ended abruptly. "What?" Neve snarled.

"It's Kate. Can I come in?"

"It's your house."

Not the most generous of invitations, but Kate took it. Her stepdaughter was sprawled stomach down across the bed, a spiral notebook lying open in front of her and a stereo remote next to her on the comforter. Neve immediately snapped the notebook shut. Diary, Kate guessed, wondering if she should assure Neve she'd respect her privacy or just pretend not to have noticed.

"I thought we could talk," Kate said.

"About my father?" The last word dripped such tangible hostility Kate expected to see it forming a puddle at Neve's elbows.

"For starters."

"There's nothing to talk about." Neve glared, just daring her stepmother to argue.

Time for a strategic retreat? "All right. We don't have to discuss it now. I also wanted to talk about your birthday."

Neve sat, her eyebrows shooting up in a way that was reminiscent of her aunt. "Really?"

"Absolutely! It's coming up soon and we haven't talked about what we're going to do to celebrate."

"Well, let me think." She cocked her head to the side in exaggerated concentration. "My friends don't even live in Virginia, neither of my parents will be able to make it and I know we don't have the money for a major party or big gifts. Sounds like a celebration all right."

The girl's sarcasm was fast eroding Kate's patience. Everything Neve had said might be true, but none of it was Kate's fault. "Look, I know you're mad, and you have the right to be. But we've already talked about attitude. I'd appreciate it if you don't take everything out on *me*, okay? I'm trying."

Neve said nothing, staring at her bedspread.

"You could do the same," Kate nudged.

Their gazes locked in what became an unintentional stare down. Kate felt petty for not wanting to look away first, but it seemed somehow important that she not back down.

Finally Neve stood. "Are we done here? I want to take a shower before bed."

Kate refrained from pointing out that it was still hours away from when Neve normally turned in for the night. "Yeah, we're done here." Great. She'd told the kids she'd be honest with them, but today it felt as though she was prevaricating left and right. *Done?*

She suspected a new wave of problems had only just started.

PJ's orientation—thank God—was a lot simpler than Neve's had been. At his elementary school, students stayed in one room the entire day to learn their subjects except for brief excursions to the gym for physical education and a room at the front of the building for musical appreciation. His teacher, Mrs. Duncan, seemed genuinely caring about her students without being overbearing. Although Kate was tempted to amend that observation when Mrs. Duncan reminded the parents for the third time to get involved with the school.

"We're all a team," she reminded them in her bright, perky tone. "Working together for the well-being of your child. I hope you'll all sign up for PTA and the class roster of storytellers. For the past couple of years I've had a different parent come in each Friday to read to the kids. And, of course, there are all manner of school activities, such as our fall festival in October, our…"

Kate tried to imagine explaining to Bryce, her boss, that she needed *more* time off to read chapters of *From the Mixed-up Files of Mrs. Basil E. Frankweiler* to a bunch of third graders.

She didn't have a clue who Basil Frankweiler or his wife were, but the book was one of several listed on a sheet of bright pink paper. There were other lists and colorful papers, too, all part of the packet Mrs. Duncan had eagerly thrust at each arriving parent. One orange sheet read Show-and-Tell Schedule at the top. The woman explained that while show-and-tell would not be part of the regular curriculum this year, many students had enjoyed it in previous grades. So she divided the kids up into groups for the first week of school, assigning each a theme and a day.

"It helps them get to know each other and is something familiar most of them have done before," she'd said. "They'll take turns participating during our first week. After that, we'll only do it for special events, like around Thanksgiving, when they'll bring in something that represents their family's specific traditions."

At that, she'd shot Kate an understated but sympathetic glance.

As sweet as Mrs. Duncan seemed, by the end of the

teacher's presentation her cheerful voice was sounding just a bit too chirpy and loud. If Kate were a student who had to listen to that for six hours a day, she'd bolt for one of the windows and the chance to escape as soon as the teacher turned to write something on the blackboard. But she tried to seem more enthusiastic for her stepson's sake.

"Mrs. Duncan seems nice," PJ said as they walked toward the freshly painted cafeteria. There was a bright mural full of caterpillars and butterflies, and although Kate detected some symbolism there about the school's purpose, she found bugs an interesting choice for decorating the building's main eating area.

"Very nice," Kate agreed. "I bet you'll like it here. Don't you think?"

"Sure," PJ said.

It was so refreshing to have a stepchild speaking to her with some degree of civility. Neve had barely growled good morning before taking a bowl of cereal up to her room. Kate hadn't been sure how to react. Should they be allowed to eat upstairs? It had never been specifically prohibited, and doing so after their rocky evening last night seemed like a bad idea. They had bigger issues to deal with than cornflake location.

So Kate let it go, then spent her own breakfast wondering if she was letting the kid steamroller her. *Wimpy stepmoms and the teens who run roughshod over them…next on* Dr. Phil. She'd never actually seen the show, but if things kept up the way they were going, she might have to TiVo some self-help shows in the afternoons.

Nonsense. The kids are healthy, Paul's confident you can do this and even Lily hasn't called to check up in a couple of days. If Kate started judging herself by the mood swings of an adolescent girl, it would be a rocky four months. She just had to be patient and continue letting the kids know she was there for them. Next week, when they had school to concentrate on and were out of the house more, it would probably all get easier. Then Kate would have her days free to continue working as normal and bond with the kids in the evenings.

The cafeteria was a lot more crowded than the small classroom had been, and the din of dozens of overlapping conversations had her nostalgic for the dulcet tones of Mrs. Duncan's voice. Tables for community organizations, after-school day-care programs and parent-awareness causes were lined against the wall with banners proclaiming troop numbers and team logos. She was here to sign PJ up for soccer.

Kate St. James, soccer mom.

Talk about things she'd never expected! Of course, falling in love and getting married had only been on the periphery of her life plan. Aforementioned lover and husband then going to jail, nowhere on it at all. At least she'd had time to adjust to each development. What about sudden changes like Delia peeing on a stick and having to completely reimagine her future three minutes later? Or Paul and Heather getting the medical results that not only was she sick, she didn't have long to live?

Sometimes Kate wasn't sure he'd ever recovered from that shock. Maybe his being distant was a way of protecting himself. The funny thing was, she'd never seen him as distant during their courtship. As a lifelong loner, *she'd* been far more aloof than he had. He'd been willing to give her space when she needed it, but he'd been a generally loving man. During his trial, however, he'd pulled away from her in a lot of ways. And after he'd seemed almost relieved to get off the phone with his own children the other night, she had more empathy for Lily's occasional frustration with Paul.

I'm a soccer mom and I'm starting to see Lily's point over my husband's? She looked around surreptitiously to make sure none of the Four Horsemen was riding into the school.

Pushing thoughts of a potential apocalypse aside, she found the table she and PJ needed and stood in line with other parents and nervous kids. Most of the adults here were women, but a few fathers mixed into the crowd. In some families, both parents had come, and Kate experienced a twinge of anxiety. Would a lot of dads be making it to school events, reading to PJ's classmates? Would it underscore Paul's absence?

Whether Bryce thought reading chapter books was a good use of her workweek or not, Kate would adjust her schedule. She had to compensate. *I'll just bring more work home on the evenings and weekends. No problem.* She was flexible, and her boss would quickly see that even with her new family responsibilities, her job performance wouldn't suffer.

"Hi," the man seated on the other side of the table greeted them in a warm baritone, making her aware that it was her turn. "I see we have another future Jackrabbit."

"Jackrabbit?" She came out of her musings, studying the logo on the banner. "Ah, that's the mascot."

The sandy-haired man winked at her. "We made out pretty well. Two of the other teams in the league got stuck with pine vole and muskrat."

She laughed. "Jackrabbit works. They're fast, right, PJ? You guys will run circles around everyone else." With the community leagues, there was no trying out for teams. Any kid in the right age group who could pay the minimal dues for uniforms and other fees was allowed to play. When one team filled up, they looked for volunteers to start another. Apparently they'd run out of good names early on.

"PJ?" the man echoed. "Nice to meet you."

"You, too," the boy said shyly. He was soft-spoken, but there was no mistaking the excited gleam in his eyes when he took in the brochure pictures of happy children kicking a black-and-white soccer ball up the field.

"I'm David Harnett. The kids usually just call me Coach D." He cast a glance toward Kate's ring finger and the gold-and-diamond wedding set there. "Please tell your husband we're always on the lookout for assistant coaches."

"Oh. I—that is, he...he's away. He'll be home in a few months, after the first of the year. Don't expect to see him at any of the early games."

The man clucked his tongue. "I'm sorry. That must get difficult for you and PJ. Armed services?"

"Come again?" Since she was already flustered, it took a moment to process the question. "You mean is he in the military? No."

"He's in jail," PJ volunteered.

Both adults stared at him, then at each other. Kate might have gotten around to discreetly mentioning that to the coach eventually, but she'd planned to at least introduce herself first. And wait for a time when there wasn't a crowd of other parents standing over her shoulder.

"I see," said Coach David, quickly looking down. "Well. I think that's all the paperwork you'll need to take with you. Just make sure we get everything back, filled out with the required signatures, along with photocopies of his birth certificate and up-to-date immunization record."

"Thanks." Placing her hands on PJ's shoulders, she steered him through the throng of people.

"Kate? Why are we walking so fast?"

She slowed immediately. "Sorry. I guess it was just starting to feel a little claustrophobic in here."

Whether he knew what that meant or not, he didn't ask. "Was I not supposed to say that about Dad? Being in—"

"No, it's fine." Although if she really felt that way, why

was she so compelled to interrupt him before he said *jail?* "I mean, it's unfortunate. And I know he's sad not to see you guys. But you can be honest about it."

"Good. Because I don't really think he did anything wrong."

She bit her lip. Technically Paul had. Not with any malicious intent, though, and she didn't want the kids to blame their father. "Well, he did make a mistake, but it was an accident."

"So this is like time-out for grown-ups. I hit a kid last year because I wasn't looking where I was going. The teacher told me that even though it wasn't on purpose, what I did still hurt him. I had to apologize and sit on the sidelines in time-out for ten minutes during recess."

Kate smiled despite herself. "I hadn't looked at it that way, but you're right. PJ, does it bother you at all that your dad's in 'time-out'?"

"No. It makes sense. I didn't like not getting to play when I had to sit out, but I felt bad about hurting the other kid."

She was thinking how well-adjusted and wise this little boy was when he suddenly added, "Besides, it's not like Neve and I normally see Dad every day. We're used to him not being there."

He said it with such matter-of-fact sadness that her heart squeezed and she hated herself a little for being relieved, when she and Paul first got engaged, that the kids had been away at school.

That night, while the kids watched a movie downstairs and after Kate had indulged in a bubble bath, Patti hooted with laughter into the phone.

Kate had relayed PJ's announcement to the flabbergasted coach that Paul would be unavailable for team practices because he was a convicted criminal. "You might see the humor in the situation, but I didn't dissolve into giggles."

"That's because you never dissolve," Patti said drily. "You don't break down, you don't panic, you don't lose your temper."

If that seemed slightly less true than it had a month ago, who was Kate to argue her friend's high opinion of her? "Well, I certainly try not to. What would be the point?"

"Being human? Sorry, sweetie, but I worry about you. What if you suddenly snapped?"

Hmm, maybe Patti's praise hadn't been praise after all.

"Patti, the closest I've ever come to snapping was one time when I stayed up three days in a row to study for finals in college and was running on nothing but caffeine and sleep deprivation. Trust me, I'm feeling a lot more stable now than I did then. I have friends like you to vent to and the support of my husband, even if it is long-distance. And these are good kids, despite one of them being a little moody. I can do this. I just have to accept that sometimes eight-year-olds say things that…catch you off guard."

Her friend chuckled. "Kids will constantly matter-of-factly embarrass you in the most public of places. Then they hit puberty and have the gall to complain that *we're* embarrassing *them*."

Kate leaned against the pillows at the top of her bed, running a hand through her damp hair. "Are you sharing all this motherhood wisdom with Delia or do you plan to let her find out the hard way?"

"I hate to break it to you, but I think motherhood is more intuition than wisdom. No two kids are the same, which means different problems. Though it helps to commiserate, eventually each woman has to find her own solutions." She hesitated. "You don't talk about it much, but I gather you and your mother aren't…close?"

Close? They hadn't spoken since their annual cursory call on Christmas day, and Kate dutifully sent a present each year. She'd mastered the art of a tasteful gift that was neither expensive nor personal. Lorna certainly didn't know about Paul's incarceration—the scandal wasn't big enough for national coverage—or even that he had kids. Kate had merely said they were celebrating the holidays with "his family." What would be the point in getting into specifics about people Lorna would likely never meet? Besides, Lorna had tried to use her own child to her advantage. While Kate couldn't think of any way to do that with grandchildren all the way from Texas, why take the risk? As soon as she'd been of an age to legally take jobs without parental consent, she'd fallen into the habit of telling Lorna no more than absolutely necessary. It cut down on potential schemes or embarrassments.

Not that I'm bitter. "You gather right, Patti. My mother and I lead very separate lives."

"Sorry. I probably shouldn't have brought up a hot-button issue on top of everything else."

"No apology necessary. It's not like there was a tragic, dramatic goodbye scene. I just went my own way when I was old enough, and that was probably best for both of us. My mother clothed and sheltered me, but she wasn't the most…maternal person alive." Kate was learning that to care about kids, there were times when you had to put them ahead of what you wanted and had envisioned. Lorna wasn't necessarily evil. She was, however, boozy, malcontent and self-absorbed.

And I am nothing like her. She'd been able to talk to PJ about his dad today, and Neve would come around sooner or later. Meanwhile, she resumed work on Monday, and everything was set for the kids to start school.

It was all falling into place.

"You're late," Bryce Connor observed mildly, his expression not nearly as casual as his tone.

Kate shrugged out of her raincoat, less than thrilled

that the weather had conspired to make her morning even worse. Way to make an impression on the boss—take a week off, then don't get to work on time your first day back.

"I'm so sorry. Weather, traffic, the kids starting school. But I plan to grab a cup of coffee and put it all behind me. Give work my full attention."

"See that you do." Bryce handed her a thick binder. "The latest changes from the development team. We need to amend the manuals accordingly and compare them against each other to make sure no mistakes go out. I was just about to take these to Joseph."

Joseph was the unofficial second in command on her team. Exceptionally smart when it came to technical expertise, exceptionally thick-skulled when it came to social skills. Even though Kate didn't consider herself the people person that Patti was, she knew how to network and get along well with others in corporate situations. Which was one of the reasons she'd been promoted over Joseph, who'd been employed here about the same amount of time as Kate. Her willingness to always go the extra mile and his temper had tipped the scales. Her colleague justified his impatient outbursts by claiming he did not "suffer fools." Of course, with his IQ, he applied that designation to ninety percent of the people around him. Kate was sure he didn't consider *her* his intellectual equal.

He'd grown cockier in the past few months. She'd taken off some time to plan her wedding and enjoy her honeymoon, having no idea that she'd have to rely on Joseph's backup support once again for Paul's trial. After the conviction, she'd thrown herself into work and was trying to make up lost ground.

She tightened her hold on the binder. "No need to dump these on Joseph. I'll handle them."

Bryce nodded. "Good. And it's nice to have you back."

It was nice to *be* back—in a known, predictable environment where she excelled. Up until now it had been the morning from hell. While she'd known Neve wasn't a cheerful morning person, it hadn't occurred to Kate to try a dry run for the first day of school. Maybe she should have started waking her stepdaughter up early a week ago, getting her out of the habit of sleeping in. Kate had assumed that once the alarm went off, Neve would get out of bed.

Such had not been the case. And Kate was fairly certain the snooze button on Neve's clock had been permanently damaged this morning. Kate had been trying to get both herself and PJ ready while insisting every eight minutes that Neve get out of bed. That had all been manageable, but the rain had slowed traffic to a crawl.

Then she'd had to turn the car around and crawl *back* to the house fifteen minutes after they'd left. She'd completely forgotten PJ was part of Monday's show-and-tell group. Once he'd remembered, he'd become pitiful—as though he were doomed to be the first elementary child in history to flunk show-and-tell. Kate had tried to convince him to find something in the car he could use, but no dice. Unlike Lily's van—which spilled iPods, footballs and white paper bags from burger joints as soon you opened the back door—Kate's car remained spotless. Helpful when picking up a businessman from the airport, not so much when you were short one show-and-tell item.

Kate might not have figured out a way to reach her still-sullen stepdaughter, but, dammit, she would not be a show-and-tell failure! Still, telling Bryce that she'd been late because she'd had to retrieve a tacky tourist snow globe from Florida didn't seem wise.

No, now was the time to restake her territory at the office, impressing her boss and letting Joseph know she was on top of her game. Announcing that PJ had weekly soccer practices so she would need to leave half an hour early on Wednesdays and asking what would be the best morning for her to read to his class? That could wait until later.

CHAPTER 10

My *favorite day of the year*. Lily sipped her tea, closing her eyes and taking in the blissful silence of the house. The first day back to school. It was amazing housewives all across the state weren't out dancing on their lawns. This was her payoff for surviving the summer, the daylong declarations of "Mom, make him stop…." and the matinee pleas of "I know it's rated *R*, but all my friends are seeing it." Of course, the school year came with its own chaos, which would be multiplied this year now that she was room mother for Tad's class and a football mom, in addition to attending Nick's spring sports games and Brittney's drill-team events.

Thinking of the kids and their various schedules, she wondered if Kate had successfully signed PJ up for soccer. *I can't believe she hasn't called.* It had been radio silence since their shopping expedition over a week ago. Lily had considered phoning, of course, but she'd blundered offering her advice at the mall. All right, she'd been a little critical, but she had those kids' best interests at heart!

After seeing the panic in Kate's eyes when they couldn't find PJ, she firmly believed the other woman had those same interests. Kate's lack of parenting experience aside, she was doing the best she could in Paul's absence. That counted for a lot, in Lily's opinion. So she hadn't called, not wanting to be perceived as nosy or pushy. Maybe it was best to give the new family space.

Still, there was space and then there was *space!* Neve's thirteenth birthday was later this week, and both kids should have attended new school orientations. There was lots to talk about. Was Kate not calling because she had everything miraculously under control—in which case Lily might have to hate her—or because Lily had alienated her?

Bob's right. If I can't get along with their new stepmother, it could seriously hurt my relationship with those kids. Ironically the very opposite of what she'd promised her dying sister.

She swallowed past the sudden lump in her throat. What was she doing sitting here and getting all philosophical and mushy, anyway? Wasn't she supposed to be lazing about, watching soap operas and eating chocolates straight out of the box? *Yeah, right.* Standing, she snorted at the unlikely image. She'd grab the mail, get a quick breath of fresh air, then figure out how to best sequence today's errands.

Waving to some neighbors, she flipped through the day's assortment of bills and advertisements as she walked back toward the house. One envelope—sent from prison— almost stopped her in her tracks. She'd written to Paul three times since his incarceration, but this was the first response she'd received. Maybe she'd seen *Shawshank Re-*

demption too many times, but she had a sudden image of Paul, shoulders slumped as he sat on a bunk in a grungy cell, trying to finish a letter before lights-out.

"Get a grip, Lil."

Inside the house, she read through his letter, tears pricking her eyes when she saw the mention of Neve's thirteenth birthday.

I can't believe my baby girl will be a teenager! She's growing into a young woman as beautiful as her mom. Heather always knew the perfect ways to celebrate big occasions and holidays, didn't she?

Heather had possessed a casual, infectious joy that had made even silly things seem special. As a girl, she'd thrown birthday and tea parties for their stuffed animals and dolls. Was that one of the reasons Lily found it so difficult to warm up to capable, beautiful Kate? She seemed a good woman and a legitimately caring one, but there was little "casual" or "infectious" about her.

As you may have noticed—as you've correctly pointed out—I don't have Heather's innate knack for perfect parenting.

The self-deprecating comment sliced at Lily like a paper cut. Yes, she'd criticized Paul's decision about sending the kids to Newsome, but she believed he was a good father. He'd get even better with practice that didn't come from separating himself from his children.

> One thing I will say about this place—it gives you time to think. And I may actually have come up with a good idea. I remembered taking the kids to the botanical gardens. I was afraid Neve would be bored the first time, a spirited little girl with nothing more to do than look at flowers, but she was enchanted. She could stay still forever if it meant not scaring off a butterfly. Can you help me with a present? I could ask Kate, but I've already heaped so much on her. And it seems right asking you to help me recreate a memory that included Heather.

Through blurred vision Lily took in the details of the gift Paul had in mind. She caught herself actually nodding to his request. But then she hit a line at the end of the letter that she had to reread twice before she could believe it.

> Kate has probably already mentioned this, but I've decided it's best for the children not to visit me.

Lily skimmed his rationalization, furious. Did he not *learn?* One moment he'd been waxing poetic about how quickly kids grew up, the next he was once again finding reasons to miss more of their lives. Yes, she could understand why it would be awkward and difficult for them to see their father. But awkward and difficult came with parenting.

For the first time since his sentencing Lily had the thought that maybe it was best he was behind bars...where he was safe from her and her impulse to throttle him!

"Can I come in?" Kate called, her tone resigned but determined.

Like I'm allowed to say no? Neve wasn't quite brave enough to try it. She thought about ignoring her stepmother but had learned that Kate's request for an invitation was really a formality. If there was no answer, Kate just barged right in, saying with a bright smile, "I knocked first, but obviously you didn't hear me."

So Neve opened the door, meeting the woman with a scowl. "I'm doing homework."

"It's the first week of school. How much work could they have assigned already?"

Neve arched an eyebrow in challenge. "Have you *seen* my reading list?"

"Actually, yes. I'm the one who has to buy all those books, remember?" When Neve moved out of the doorway to resume her spot on the bed, Kate joined her there, too. "I'm pretty sure that list is for the semester, not the week. They don't mean for you to get so carried away with academia that you don't have a life…or a birthday. You keep avoiding discussions about it. Trust me, birthdays come whether you want them to or not. I've been trying to hide from mine since I turned thirty."

That was probably a lie meant to help them "bond." Why should Kate worry about her age? She was prettier than a lot of the moms, even those actually in their thirties. The thought gave her a pang, as if she were being disloyal to her mom. Heather St. James had been a different kind of beautiful. Softer. She hadn't owned any snazzy suits like Kate's, but there was no one else Neve would rather look like. Be like.

Deep down, though, she knew she was failing her mother. Heather wouldn't be so grouchy with everyone, snapping at PJ for no good reason and slouching in the back of class in the hope that teachers wouldn't call on her.

"Neve?" Kate asked, her tone just a little too gentle. The motherly note in her voice made Neve want to throw things. Slam doors and scream at no one in particular. It also made her want to lean into the woman for a hug, where she could stay until she'd cried it out and felt better.

You're not a baby. She wouldn't be sobbing all over anyone. Kate might wish she could skip her birthdays, but Neve wished she were older already, cooler, sophisticated. Tougher.

"Can I get my belly button pierced for my birthday?"

"*What?*" Kate's eyes were huge.

"We could go together." She barely remembered getting her ears pierced—how bad would it hurt? Couldn't be too awful, she reasoned. Lots of people did it.

"Not a chance in hell."

About the response Neve had expected. Truthfully she wasn't sure she wanted anyone poking holes into her there, but it had been a nice fantasy. It would have made her infinitely cooler than those girls at Maddison's table who had snickered when she'd tried to sit with them at lunch.

The memory made Neve want to lash out, although at the time she'd slunk away. She'd made one or two friends but mostly by process of elimination. "I don't think my father would want you talking like that in front of his children."

"You're right," Kate said easily. "But he'd be a lot more troubled by his daughter with a navel ring than my use of *hell.*"

He wouldn't even know unless someone specifically mentioned it. "I suppose a tattoo is out?"

"Unless you're talking about the temporary kind, you suppose correctly." Kate tilted her head to the side. "What about getting your ears double pierced? You only have single holes now."

Huh. That might not be a bad idea. "I'll think about it. But I really do have homework I need to concentrate on. And don't you have company anyway?" Neve knew Delia and Patti were stopping by tonight for coffee and chitchat.

"They're not here yet, but I'll let you get back to your work."

When her stepmother left, shutting the door behind her, Neve's body sagged with relief. She'd managed yet again to get out of a conversation about inviting friends over for her birthday. Kate had dropped hints the other day about some big girlie slumber party, saying she could order all manner of disgusting pizzas and borrow Patti's karaoke machine.

Dodging the discussion was easier than admitting her only real friends were Rebecca, who was busy with practices and teammates now that she'd joined cross-country/track, and Seth Baker, a guy from the Drama class who was even more of a misfit than Neve. There was another girl at lunch—Cherry—but the jury was still out on her. Neve glanced in disgust at the wall calendar hanging by her window. Her birthday. Big woo-hoo.

Then again, thirteen had to be better than twelve.

A belly-button ring? Kate snorted as she put fresh beans into the coffee grinder for her and Patti. Delia would bring her own favorite brand of bottled water.

"This late at night, I use decaf," Kate had told Delia. "You could have that, right?"

"Yeah, but why torture myself with something that smells like coffee and looks like coffee when I'm staying away from the real stuff? It's like that girl in the comic strip who's always pulling the football away when the bald-headed kid goes running to kick it."

That's probably what Neve would come up with next, Kate mused—shaving her head. Or dyeing it some un-natural color. Honestly was it even legal for a thirteen-year-old girl to get a tattoo? And this was just the *cusp* of the teenage years! Six more after thirteen.

Thinking of Brittney and her three younger siblings, Kate felt a whole new respect for Lily.

A tap at the kitchen door drew her attention, and Kate turned to greet her friends. She'd left the garage door up so they could come in the back way and not use the doorbell. Although Neve was still awake doing homework, PJ had sacked out pretty early, worn out from the first few days of school. She got the impression he was settling in a lot easier than his sister, which made sense. Third grade was probably easier than junior high even when your dad *wasn't* in prison.

"Good evening, ladies."

Delia came through the door first, almost waddling, which was strange because she hadn't had any evident weight gain yet.

"Are you walking funny?" Kate asked, too tired to be diplomatic.

"Bathroom," Delia called as she went past. "Talk later, pee now."

Patti laughed as their friend disappeared around the

corner. "She's had to go ever since we left her place. I hit one pothole on the way over and I thought she was gonna go for my throat."

"Why didn't she go before you picked her up?"

"Spoken like a woman who's never been pregnant," Patti said, shaking her head. "She did go then."

"Ah. Well, the coffee should be ready in a few minutes. I've got dessert, too, if you're interested. Cheesecake from a great deli nearby."

Kate reflected on the cheerful memo that had arrived in the mail today. The Jackrabbits would be holding their annual bake sale soon to help raise money for the soccer team. Traditionally Kate wasn't much of a baker, but how hard could it be to make brownies? No one was saying she had to put together a fudge-marble cheesecake from scratch.

There was one thing Kate knew how to put together—social events. Paul had been an important businessman, and they'd had their share of dinners, cocktail parties and community events.

"Patti, do you know what Leo's plans are this weekend? I know it's last-minute, but I was hoping the two of you could stop by for a party. Friday, maybe. Neve won't be expecting it then since Saturday's her actual birthday."

"A surprise party?" Patti frowned. "It's a nice thought, but I'm not sure ambushing her is the way to go."

"I've tried the direct approach. Thirteen's a big birthday. I can't just let the day go unnoticed." She felt almost desperate, as if this were an important test. Kate had never been a fan of failure.

Aware that Neve still missed her friends from Newsome, she understood why the girl wasn't eagerly putting together guest lists. But Neve liked Leo. If the teenager came by and Lily brought the cousins over and Rebecca, who lived nearby, attended—well, that would feel like a modest crowd, wouldn't it?

She's still going to notice her father is gone. Kate suspected that's who Neve most wanted to see, even if she wouldn't admit it. Every time Kate broached the subject of Paul, the girl stonewalled her.

"I don't know," Delia said, returning to the kitchen. "Don't underestimate a good ambush. Life surprising me with this baby is one of the best things that's happened to me." As she spoke, one hand fluttered protectively in front of her abdomen. Kate didn't even think her friend knew she was doing it.

Patti wasn't ready to concede the point. "Yet when Alexander ambushed you with a marriage proposal, you—"

"That was not a proposal. That was a legitimacy clause for his unborn child." Delia's tone grew more agitated, putting a lot of uncharacteristic emphasis on her rapid words. "In the *entire* time we've been together he's *never* mentioned wedding vows! You don't find it the tiniest bit coincidental that he *suddenly* wants to make an honest woman out of me *now?*"

"It's like you said," Patti rejoined, remarkably calm in contrast. "Sometimes surprises help you realize what you wanted all along."

Delia looked so irritated at the suggestion that she actually marry the father of her baby—since she was sure the baby was the only reason for that proposal—that Kate fell into her long-held role of mediator. "Maybe we could find a different topic before we raise the pregnant woman's blood pressure? And I think the coffee's ready."

The three women adjourned to the cushier seating arrangements of the living room.

"Well," Patti said as she settled at one end of the sofa and Kate took the other, "we can talk about the brilliant organizing and negotiating I've done for the club's fundraiser...what's wrong with that?"

Subtlety had never been Delia's strong point, and Kate couldn't very well miss the slicing motion her friend was making with one index finger across her throat.

"Oh." Comprehension dawned, and Patti glanced at Kate. "But that's just silly club stuff. I'd much rather hear about how things are going for you."

"Since when don't we talk about the club?" Kate was puzzled. This time last year, the country club had been the one thing all three women had in common. Now they also shared various forms of motherhood. Surreal.

"No, we can talk about the club," Patti backpedaled. "I mean, of course we can. But you know how pushy I get! If you're not careful, I'll be whipping out tickets for the fund-raiser and trying to get you to buy a roll for your office. Who needs that pressure? I completely understand if you can't make it this year. You have the kids to look after, for one...."

Kate narrowed her gaze. "Is this because you don't think it's a good idea for me to come or you don't think I can afford the price per plate?"

"We do inflate the cost something awful," Patti said, looking deeply into her coffee cup.

"Sure. To raise more money. Everyone who attends these things understands that.... You really don't want me there?" Kate couldn't believe she felt like an outsider with her two best friends.

Delia sighed. "It's just, this would be your first big club event without...a date."

"You mean since Paul got himself sent up the river?" Kate asked drily. She'd joined after she and Paul had started dating and playing tennis there. "I'm coming to this thing. It's for a good cause, and everyone will see that I am doing *just fine*."

What was it Celeste Parker had cooed that day at the pool? That Kate was brave for being out and about, as if a more discreet woman would hide her shame in the privacy of her own house? Screw that. Kate knew how to hold her head high. They'd all see that when she showed up gorgeous and unflappable the night of the charity dinner.

"You can sit with me," Delia offered with a wry grin. "That is, if you don't think hanging out with the unmarried, over-forty broad who's knocked up will hurt your reputation."

Kate laughed. "I'll risk it."

CHAPTER 11

Glancing at the time display in the bottom right corner of her computer monitor, Kate winced. Already after one! She'd planned to phone Lily this morning and see if they could meet for lunch today, but she'd been too caught up in work.

Well, it was too late for lunch, but she could still call about Neve and apologize for it being so last-minute. She'd just been working so hard to get manuals prepped for a new product release. Vowing to work half an hour late today and pick up dinner—a *cheap* dinner—on the way home, she reached for the phone on her desk. After all of the "secondary emergency contact" information she'd had to fill out on school paperwork, Kate had the number memorized.

Lily answered on the third ring. "Hello?"

"Hey. It's Kate. Did I catch you at a bad time?"

"This is fine. Everything all right?"

"Sure. I just thought we should talk about Neve's birthday."

"Which is the day after tomorrow."

"Yeah. I meant to call sooner," Kate said. "Honestly."

"It can't be easy to juggle kids with a full-time career," Lily said. "I was going to call you today if I didn't hear from you, but I take it you have birthday plans well in hand?"

"Not with any help from Neve," Kate admitted. "She's rather unenthusiastic. I tried talking to her about it, but I've decided it's time to bring the mountain to the party girl."

"What?"

"I thought we'd throw a surprise party. Mostly family with a few close friends. Is tomorrow evening possible? Really, I would have called earlier if she had made any suggestions for how she wanted to celebrate. Maybe I should have been more assertive and made plans myself before now."

"No." Lily's tone was thoughtful. "You were trusting your instincts by giving her time. But I think you're doing the right thing by not letting her duck away and hide from it."

Kate found herself sitting a little straighter in her office chair. Lily's praise was unexpectedly affirming after Patti had worried a surprise party could be a bad move.

But then Lily muttered, "There's already enough avoidance in this family," and Kate's shoulders slumped.

She's talking about Paul. That, however, was a mine-filled discussion for another day. Right now they had a party to plan. As quickly as possible.

Kate glanced out the window on her way to the kitchen, not seeing Neve's bus yet but hearing the gears as the giant orange vehicle chugged up the street. Most days, because of their different bus routes, Neve arrived home to an empty house about ten minutes before PJ. He had a key, though, and was supposed to call Kate or Lily if he ever got here first.

Today Kate had come home early. Lily had left ten minutes ago, smuggling the presents and decorations into her minivan so they could get to their destination. She'd also brought over Paul's gift so Kate could see what Neve was getting from her father. Kate had been deeply moved and hoped Neve was, as well. The small piece of jewelry, though not terribly expensive, was a sign that her dad loved her, that he recalled special times they'd shared and was thinking of her on her birthday.

As soon as Kate heard the front door open, she called out quickly so that Neve wouldn't be startled to find someone else in the house. "Hey! How was school?"

Though she didn't answer, Neve rounded the corner, her feet clad in socks. If Kate could only get *PJ* in the habit of kicking off his shoes when he walked inside, before tracking all manner of Virginia soil across the carpet.

"Kate. You left work awfully early." The observation was tinged with suspicion.

"Well, it's Friday. Isn't that supposed to be more fun than the rest of the week? I thought I'd take off sooner than usual and that maybe we could do something." The only official birthday plans, as far as Neve knew, were the trip to the mall to get her ears double pierced tomorrow and dinner at Lily's house Saturday night. Instead Lily's family, Patti and her son were meeting Kate and the kids tonight at a local arcade and putt-putt golf course. PJ was in on the plan, and Kate had to admit he'd done a better job than she'd expected keeping the secret for the past twenty-four hours. It probably helped that he spent most of the day in a building on the other side of town from his sister.

"Something like what?" Neve asked.

Kate shrugged. "We could wait for your brother to get home and see what everyone feels like." Then they'd talk Neve into PJ's putt-putt suggestion, which would seem less rehearsed if it didn't come from Kate. "You have any homework?"

"Of course." Neve opened the refrigerator door and pulled out a two-liter bottle of soda. "My earth sciences teacher is a hag. She gave us two chapters to read this weekend on top of the reports we've been working on to hand in next Wednesday."

"You know, I once had a teacher whose class I dreaded, but when I applied for my college scholarships, I was really grateful that she'd instilled such a strong work ethic in me."

Neve shot her a look that pretty well summed up her opinion about retrospective life lessons on sunny Friday afternoons.

Kate lifted her hands in surrender. "Hey, I get it. You don't want mini lectures from me, you just want to be left alone so you can get those two chapters out of the way."

Whatever response Neve had was cut off by the sound of yet another bus passing the house. Moments later PJ came barreling inside.

"Hey, Neve! Hi, Kate! Why aren't you at your office?"

Kate grinned at him for remembering to be "surprised" to see her. "Afternoon, buddy. I thought we could all do something fun together. I'll have time for more work this weekend on my laptop." Quite a bit of it, actually. But she had work every week, and Neve's birthday only rolled around once a year.

He scrunched up his face. "Will you still have time to help me with my project?"

"What project is that?"

"Mrs. Duncan assigned us a dia..." He frowned, then tried again. "Dia...this box thing."

"Diorama," his sister supplied as she rifled through the once again open refrigerator. "Kate, can I microwave a couple of hot dogs for a snack?"

Kate glanced at the package in her stepdaughter's hand. "*That's* what you normally eat for snack? I always assumed it was a piece of fruit or maybe an ice-cream sandwich."

Neve nodded. "I might have those afterward."

No wonder groceries were costing more than Kate had anticipated. "Actually, why don't we decide what we feel like doing? We can get a bite while we're out." She'd get more specifics on the diorama later.

"Could we do something outside?" PJ asked. "Like go to the park?"

Neve rolled her eyes, not noticing Kate's startled look that PJ hadn't remembered the script. "The park's lame."

"What about putt-putt?" PJ actually winked at his stepmother while Neve was putting the hot dogs away. "That's not lame, and we haven't been in ages. They've got all those cool video games and stuff, too."

Neve considered this, while Kate tried not to laugh. "Yeah, okay. Putt-putt sounds good."

Let's hope she still thinks so once we get there.

Unfortunately Neve's friend Rebecca had had other plans, but there should be enough people there to give it a party feel. Of course, since Neve had shown no signs of wanting a party, her reaction was hard to predict.

Kate suggested they all change their clothes, and then they piled into the car.

The large putt-putt parking lot wasn't even half-full. The place probably did more business on Saturdays and Sundays or later on Friday when high school boys brought their dates there. The thought of Neve dating made Kate's heart skip a beat. She was very glad Paul would be home before that became an issue. Even if Neve decided she liked a classmate between now and then, the worst that would happen would be Kate dropping them off at a school dance or the movies. No car dates for a couple of years to come.

Thank God.

Probably because Kate knew it would be there, Lily's vehicle stood out, painfully obvious. Would Neve say anything? But if the girl had seen it, she'd obviously written it off as just another minivan. As they walked inside, Kate felt almost anxious and realized this was the first surprise party she'd ever thrown. Her own childhood had included few birthday parties, although when she was around six or seven, Lorna had put together a party using the theme of Kate's favorite cartoon character at the time and invited practically everyone in their small, ramshackle building. They'd either been having a good month financially or Lorna had been feeling unusually sentimental.

The stray memory caught Kate off guard, but she allowed herself a brief smile. Today was about Neve.

PJ had rushed ahead, pulling open the door and disappearing to the left of the arcade games and air hockey table.

His sister followed after him. "Hey, we check out clubs *this* way, you spaz."

A second later she walked into the party room where everyone assembled yelled "Surprise!" and blew shiny noisemakers Patti had left over from a New Year's Eve party.

Neve froze, and Kate almost bumped into her from

behind. *I wish I could see her face.* Was she smiling, simply staring or scowling?

"Happy birthday." Lily came forward to claim a hug.

"Thank you," Neve mumbled into her aunt's shoulder.

"You're welcome. But if you're talking about the party, that was Kate's doing." Lily stepped aside so that her children and husband could also greet the birthday girl.

Neve hugged her uncle Bob, traded some giggly comments with Brittney and moved on to greet Patti and Leo. As she was talking to them, she craned her head back in Kate's direction, her gaze bright and excited.

Happy birthday, Kate mouthed.

"What should we do first?" Patti asked. "Mini golf? Food?"

"Presents!" PJ and his cousin Tad chorused. "We want to see what she got."

"Is that all right?" Neve asked uncertainly, glancing toward a folding table that had been spread with a festive cloth and stacked with bags and boxes. It wasn't a huge stack, but it was festive nonetheless.

"It's your soiree," Kate said. "But remember, my gift to you is the trip to the mall tomorrow. PJ's going to play at a neighbor's while you get your ears pierced and pick out one special outfit."

Neve bobbed her head. "Okay, so what do I open first?"

PJ had given her a video game he thought she might like; her cousins, various girlish accessories and Leo had purchased a CD by a group he'd apparently mentioned to her over the summer. Neve smiled shyly and told him she was sure she'd love it. When all the other boxes were unwrapped, Kate and Lily exchanged glances.

"There is one other present," Kate said softly, as Lily's brood argued about which game in the arcade was the coolest. "It's from your dad. You can either open it here or later. Completely your choice."

Neve's grin faded momentarily, and she swallowed. "Might as well open it now. With all the others."

Lily handed over the delicate gift bag, just a tiny gauze white square stuffed with colorful tissue-paper confetti. Neve pulled out the jewelry box inside and popped it open. The pendant was a lot like the manner in which it had been wrapped—delicate but bright and eye-catching. A small butterfly alighting on an only slightly larger flower.

"Your father wanted you to have this note," Lily added, passing over a folded rectangle of paper.

Neve read it, blinking the entire time, then swallowed again. She tucked the note in her pocket, surreptitiously wiping her eyes with her other hand. "Kate, will you help me put the necklace on?"

"Of course." Kate lifted her hair to clasp the chain, glad that Lily was organizing everyone to go start games, giving Neve a moment of privacy. "There."

Neve turned around, her expression expectant.

"Beautiful," Kate pronounced. "Now would you like

some money for games? Leo was offering to show you how to drive a go-cart."

The girl snorted. "Show me? I'll clean the track with him. My friend Krista and I used to go to this place near her parents' whenever I visited. I kick go-cart butt."

"I'll keep that in mind when I start placing side bets on the races." Kate pulled her wallet from her purse. "Here."

"Thanks." Neve took the money and pivoted toward the door, then spun back around suddenly, throwing her arms around Kate's middle in a wholly unexpected hug. "Really, Kate. Thank you. For the presents, the party, everything."

"You're welcome." Kate felt *she'd* just been given the best gift.

Cliché, perhaps. Corny, definitely. But true nonetheless.

"You look awfully happy today," Seth commented as he set down the orange tray.

Neve glanced at the tall, dark-haired boy with a smile. "So normally I look grim and bitchy?"

He flushed so quickly she felt bad about teasing him. "N-no, I just meant you look, you know, nice."

"Thanks." She liked the fellow eighth grader, she just wished he weren't so shy. As easily as he flustered, it was sometimes difficult to carry on a conversation with him.

But he was kindhearted and a great artist. He'd shown her his notebook of sketches when they were supposed to be doing some stupid drama exercise last week. Their teacher, "Bianca," had some bizarre ideas of how you were supposed to prepare for acting. Neve thought Seth was decent-looking. If he stood a little straighter and maybe cut his hair or at least brushed it out of his eyes, the girls around here might be quicker to talk to him. Of course, that would only send him stammering in the other direction. Poor guy.

"Whazzup?" a female voice asked as her tray hit the table with a plastic clang. Cherry. Short with blindingly platinum hair, she was the opposite of Seth. There was nothing shy about the angry girl who'd been sent to live with her mother and attend school in Virginia. Cherry was quick to share the details of her life with anyone in earshot and had informed Neve on the second day of school, "Dad got the stepmonster preggers, so they didn't need *me* anymore. Here I am, exiled from L.A. to this nowhere part of the world."

To an extent, Neve totally got the girl's attitude—especially about her father remarrying and her being sent away and having no vote in the matter. Divorce problems aside, it couldn't be easy to attend middle school with the name Cherry. But part of Neve envied that Cherry even had a mom.

"I was j-just saying Neve looks nice today," Seth admitted, taking her "what's up?" literally instead of as the generic greeting it was.

Neve changed the subject. "I got my ears double pierced this weekend." She pulled her hair aside.

Cherry nodded but, having three holes in each ear herself, wasn't that impressed. She quickly turned the conversation to her own favorite topic: Cherry.

Neve listened with half an ear. The blonde's stories were usually entertaining, but a little Cherry went a long way. Still, it would take something seriously offensive for Neve not to let someone sit with her at lunch—especially since that's what Maddison Brant and her friends had done to Neve on the first day.

Maddison had gone to elementary school with Neve, and Neve had been happy to see a familiar face in her lunch period—a face sporting artfully applied makeup and attached to a body that had filled out a lot since fourth grade. Maddison was the school's reigning beauty queen. And reigning snob.

She'd taken great delight in drawling, "Oh, *look* who's back to join us after going off to her elite academy. I guess you don't get to be quite so elite when your daddy's gone to jail."

Did I ever do anything to her or does getting beautiful just turn you into—

"Nevvie! Are you listening?" Cherry demanded. "They put those extra holes in your ears or your head, girl?"

"Sorry. Guess my mind wandered."

"So, um…" Clearing his throat, Seth chose to join the conversation. "What did you do this weekend? B-besides the ear-piercing, obviously."

"Actually, it was my birthday. So my stepmother and brother and I had a little celebration. No big deal, really, but—"

"Oh, Lord. Was it one of those things where she tried to become your best friend? It makes me crazy when they act like that," Cherry griped.

"Nah, it was all right," Neve said. "Kate's okay for a stepmom. I mean, it's not like she's ordering me to scrub the castle or sending me into the woods with the huntsman, so I can't complain."

After a moment, Cherry laughed. "Depending on what the huntsman looked like, maybe I wouldn't mind getting lost in a big, scary forest with him."

Seth flushed but pressed on. "S-so did you get anything good?"

Neve fingered the pendant she wore but didn't feel like explaining how she and her family used to go to the botanical gardens. "This guy I know—Leo—gave me a pretty cool CD. Great new band."

The bell jangled overhead, giving them five minutes to clear out and return to their classrooms before the next lunch group was herded into the cafeteria.

"Algebra." Neve sighed. "I so don't feel like going today. This weekend's homework gave me a splitting headache."

"I'm surprised so many of us actually make it to class here," Cherry commented. "With security this lax, the principal is practically begging kids to ditch. Back in L.A...."

The girls got separated in the swarming exodus, but Neve was surprised to find Seth next to her when she put her tray on the conveyor belt.

"Y-you like bands?" he asked. "You sounded excited about that new CD. My brother's in a band. They practice in our garage every Thursday. You c-could come over some time. To listen. If you wanted."

She smiled. "Thanks, Seth. That sounds cool."

His mouth dropped open. "Really? You'd come over?"

He must be even shier than she'd thought if this was his reaction to having a friend over. *I should really stop feeling sorry for myself.* Even though Rebecca was a lot busier now, she was still nice. And so was Leo—Neve had taken wicked delight in beating him at go-carts, although he might have let her win because it was her birthday. He was so much fun and had those dimples…too bad he looked at Neve as a kid. Like three years was such a huge difference? It would be *so* cool to have an older guy like her. Maddison Brant wouldn't be nearly so smug then.

Sighing, Neve waved to Seth, making an absentminded promise to ask her stepmother about coming over.

But when Kate arrived home that evening, she had her frazzled face on, and Neve decided it wasn't the right time to ask for favors. Friday and Saturday had been pretty cool, all devoted to Neve and her turning thirteen. By Sunday, however, Kate had dragged her laptop from room to room. Between helping PJ with his diorama and ruining two batches of practice brownies, though, she hadn't seemed to get much work done.

"Any chance I can talk you kids into sandwiches?" she asked now as she shut the garage door behind her. "I'm swamped tonight."

"Sandwiches are fine with me," PJ said from the living room. His class had had a field trip today and his only homework had been to write a paragraph about what they'd seen. He'd already finished it and stuck it to the refrigerator with a magnet so Kate could check the spelling. Neve would have looked it over for him, but she was bogged down with her own more difficult homework—algebra equations, currently spread across the kitchen table. She couldn't wait until she graduated from school and put solving for X, as well as problems like Maddison Brant and lunch-period seating arrangements, behind her permanently.

"That sounds good to me, too," Neve agreed. You couldn't burn sandwiches. Well, except for grilled cheese. "Do we still have peanut butter left?"

"I think so." Kate set her briefcase and laptop on the kitchen counter so she could shrug out of her jacket.

Neve glanced from her math book to the amount of work it looked as if her stepmother had brought home, then back to the algebra. *Snap.* Did this mean life *didn't* get easier and more relaxing once you were an adult?

CHAPTER 12

Kate was managing to ignore her growling stomach Wednesday afternoon, but the ringing phone was harder to dismiss. Since she was in enough trouble today without snatching up the receiver and snarling "Yes?" she stuck to the more professional script.

"Kate St. James speaking."

"Hey," Patti said, sounding hesitant. "Are you okay, sweetie?"

No. She was far from okay. *Miles* from okay, entire time zones...

This morning, just as she'd been about to turn in a finished manual, she realized she'd overlooked a whole section. While it was definitely for the best that she'd been the one to catch her mistake—since when did she make colossal mistakes?—it had resulted in several frantic hours of extra work when she had other projects that needed attention. She'd had to ask Joseph for help and nearly swallowed her tongue trying to voice the question. This time last year she'd never had to ask anyone for help professionally.

She was the go-to girl people came to with their crises. Wasn't she?

It hadn't helped that she'd been in a bleak mood even before she'd left the house. Neve hadn't been able to find her history book, and as Kate had helped her look, she'd realized for the first time how truly messy the place had become. When she'd married Paul, he'd had a woman who'd come in to clean once a week. That monthly bill had been the first and easiest budget cut after he'd lost his position. Kate was highly organized and capable of keeping up with a little dusting and laundry.

Except kids seemed to attract dust like that *Peanuts* character she'd always assumed was a comic exaggeration, and the laundry was out of control. Three people couldn't possibly wear so many clothes! And speaking of clothes, when had Kate's favorite skirt become too tight, no longer zipping to the top? Apparently she'd had too many fast-food dinners recently. She was at work today with a *safety pin* strategically located beneath her jacket.

"Kate?" The concern in Patti's tone had doubled during the brief silence.

"I'm fine! A little distracted with work right now, but you know me. I'll have it all back under control in no time." She'd just ignore her growling stomach; skipping lunch would give her more time to catch up and help her fit back into her clothes. And she'd tell the kids that the allowances she'd agreed to now came with certain chore stipulations. The three of them would work together to keep the house in better shape. No problem. None whatsoever. "What can I do for you?"

"Well, when you didn't show up for lunch, Delia and I got worried...."

"Lunch?" Dammit. How could she have forgotten her *friends?* A few pages in a work manual had been bad enough. "I am so sorry! A problem arose at work."

"Don't sweat it. Delia and I are thumbing through a baby-names book just for fun and mocking all the ridiculous choices. We'll finish lunch by ourselves and get together with you some day when things are calmer, okay?"

"Thanks, Patti. You guys are the best!"

Even though she knew her friends weren't going to hold the slip against her, Kate got off the phone feeling guilty and even more uneasy than she'd been before the call. Not long ago, her existence had been fairly limited: she'd worked. She'd worked hard, she'd worked long hours. There'd been no social life to speak of, but she'd done her job well. She'd been appreciated and admired in her office. Now her life was bursting at the seams with people and activities, but she didn't feel particularly successful in any area.

Especially baking. She stifled a groan. PJ's first soccer practice was tomorrow, and there was that goody sale out at the field to raise money. Kate knew how to follow simple instructions, but she couldn't be held accountable for the whole "stove temperatures and cooking times may vary" problem. Her first pan of brownies this weekend had burned. When she'd attempted to mix a second batch while also helping PJ with his homework and working on her laptop, she'd inadvertently doubled some measurements and ended up with goo that wouldn't set.

Forget the goo. After this manual screwup, she had bigger problems. She'd just buy cookies and have the kids shove them into plastic sandwich bags for the bake sale. *Show me the Virginia law where it says only homemade goods are acceptable.*

All right, she was back in charge with a plan. Step one, stop on the way home to buy a great cookie selection, then talk to the kids about a new housework schedule and catch up on her freelance project that had been sadly neglected for the past few days. She'd stumbled, but she would regain her ground.

Just as soon as I get something to eat. All this thinking about sweets had made her doubly aware of missing lunch. She dug in her purse, thinking that a candy bar from the vending machine would go a long way toward boosting her mood. Guiltily she recalled her resolve to diet off the few pounds she'd gained but discounted that part of the plan for now. It turned out Patti had been right a few weeks ago—a woman could only endure so much without snapping.

It was in the interest of public safety that Kate got her hands on some chocolate.

* * *

"Sorry I'm late!" Kate called as she rushed into the kitchen. "There was a department meeting at the end of the day and I couldn't get away." She didn't mind the kids being alone in the afternoon, but she tried to get home before it started getting dark. Which was going to be increasingly difficult over the next few months, she realized, with the days getting shorter. That hadn't really occurred to her before now.

"It's okay," PJ said. He'd dumped a pack of markers across the kitchen table and was drawing a picture. Kate guessed it must be homework since his recreational choices leaned more toward video games than art. "Neve told me you had to stop at the store and wouldn't be home at the usual time."

Cookies! "Sh—snap." Kate did a quick edit to her stepdaughter's expletive of choice. "You know what, buddy? Because of that meeting, I didn't get a chance to go to the store."

His eyes were wide and alarmed. "But what about the bake sale tomorrow? All the Jackrabbits are supposed to bring something."

All the Jackrabbits' parents, *you mean*. She hadn't realized when she signed him up for practices and games that there would be extra time drains like team picture day and baking. Just as she'd thought the kids returning to school would mean she had her days free to *work*. Now there were requests for her to volunteer for holiday parties, work on festival booths, chaperone field trips and read to class-rooms full of kids—wasn't that something teachers and librarians were already paid to do?

Honestly how did parents with school-age kids earn a living in this country?

"I'll take care of it," she assured her stepson. No reason to panic the kid just because she felt as if *she* were coming apart at the seams. "Your soccer team is not going to be short-funded this year because of us, I swear. You know, those markers are going to dry out if you leave all the lids off."

He sighed but dutifully capped the ones he wasn't currently using.

"So where's Neve, anyway?"

"Phone." PJ jerked his head toward the ceiling, indicating his sister was upstairs. "She had to call some guy about homework."

Some guy, huh? Kate wondered if homework was just an excuse. Then again, Neve had been struggling with math. Kate had taken a look at some of the problems Monday night—she could solve them herself but didn't have a lot of practice explaining *how*. The study session had frustrated both her and Neve, taking twice as long as expected and severely shortening Kate's work schedule.

Maybe a peer tutor wasn't such a bad idea, especially if the guy shared his knowledge for free.

"What's for dinner?" PJ asked.

"For you guys, hot dogs. For me, celery sticks."

The celery didn't quite hit the spot.

Later that night, as she worked in her bedroom, Kate resisted the urge to wash her unsatisfactory dinner down with a nice Cabernet. She'd been distracted enough lately without the wine. Still, distractions were unavoidable when you lived with two kids, and she looked up with a resigned sigh when someone knocked against her open door.

"Oh. Hey, Neve. I was expecting your brother. Thought you were back on the phone again."

The young woman shook her head. "Just with Cherry. She's nice, but sometimes she gets on these rants, so I got off the phone fast."

"Okay." Kate removed her reading glasses, rubbing her eyes with one hand. "Was there something you needed?"

"Do you know anything about poetry?"

At one time, she had. This week, however, it seemed as if she barely knew anything about her own field of expertise. "Um, haikus are short and Shakespeare wrote a lot of sonnets? I take it you have some kind of poetry assignment? I hope you didn't put your homework off until right before bed after you've been on the phone all evening."

"It's not due tomorrow," Neve snapped, her posture turning defensive. "And I wasn't on the phone that long, only for a few minutes with Seth to talk about math and just now. I didn't call Cherry, she called *me*."

What Kate wouldn't give for a Rewind button today. "I

didn't mean to imply you weren't taking your schoolwork seriously. It's just that I feel strongly that education is the most important tool you'll ever wield." Where would Kate be now without the scholarships that had allowed her to reach her goals?

"Well, I don't know about wielding or whatever, but I think I need help with this poem."

Further explanation was cut off by the ringing phone. Kate answered since she was the closest. "Hello?"

Nothing, just a drawn-out pause.

"Hello?" Kate didn't even try to hide her annoyance, and the person on the other end disconnected. "Either a wrong number or I wasn't the person they were hoping to talk to."

She hoped it was the former. If boys with crushes started calling the house and hanging up, she'd need to see about caller ID. Her life had enough interruptions already!

"Now what were you saying?" she asked Neve.

"Mr. Grayson assigned everyone all these different emotions, which we have to write poems about, then read in front of the class on Friday. Mine's 'loss,' but I'm having trouble putting together anything that doesn't sound dumb." Neve grimaced. "Maddison Brant got 'rage,' so she'll probably write about how she broke a nail once and got all pissed off."

Kate had no idea who Maddison Brant was. "You know better than to say *pissed off*."

"I could say ticked, but it would mean the same thing," Neve argued.

Too tired to debate semantics with a thirteen-year-old, Kate put her glasses back on. "If the assignment's not due until Friday, why don't you sleep on it and maybe something will come to you? Then we can talk about it tomorrow." *And I can try to get some work done before I fall asleep where I sit.*

"You'll be at PJ's soccer practice tomorrow. Just forget it. I'll brainstorm with Seth or something. In fact...he asked if I could go over to his house tomorrow evening. Could I?"

Kate bit her lip. "Will his parents be there?"

"Absolutely!"

"I won't be able to give you a ride—"

"His family's got that covered. I'll leave their phone number on the refrigerator," Neve volunteered. "You'd like Seth. He's really quiet and shy but a good student. And we both think Miss Bianca is off her nut."

A distinct possibility, as far as Kate could tell.

Since nobody would be home with Neve tomorrow evening anyway and Seth could help Neve with her homework, it sounded like a good deal all the way around. *Better to have her going to chaperoned homes than trying to sneak guys over when I'm not here.*

"All right. But you make sure to leave that number," she added in her most parental tone. *Lily would be so proud.*

* * *

Bryce had sighed when she'd left work early—joining the ranks of his other employees who had kids and all manner of strange commitments—but at least Kate had remembered the soccer practice and arrived on time. Of course, there was the small matter of not having any baked goods, but she had that under control, she assured herself, pointing the keyless remote at the car.

"You're sure no one will be mad?" PJ asked, boyishly adorable in the shiny blue-and-white uniform.

"They are trying to raise money for your team," she reasoned. "They'll be thrilled." Probably.

"Okay." With one last skeptical glance, he ran off to join his teammates on the public field.

There were actually three fields, two soccer and one softball, all of which were in use right now as various family members and caretakers sat on bleachers and benches or chased siblings around the nearby playground. Beyond the slide and swings was a cement building that housed a small concessions stand in the middle and, at either corner, restrooms. Since concessions were only sold during actual games, the tiny space was dark and empty now. There was, however, a thriving snack business at a folding card table with a bright poster board that read Jackrabbits Bake Sale in puffy paint taped to the front.

Kate was dutifully headed in that direction when a perky blonde waved at her.

"Hi, there! Could we interest you in some yummy snickerdoodles for a good cause? This is our first team fund-raiser of the year, and it means so much to the kids!"

Not sure what a snickerdoodle was—or why a woman over thirty would use the word *yummy*—Kate shook her head. "Actually, I'm one of the fund-raising parents. Kate St. James."

Seated next to the blonde, an efficient-looking brunette in a turtleneck began nodding immediately. "Of course! PJ's stepmother. I'm Deanne Gruber, team mom. We spoke on the phone." She stood and reached across the table to shake Kate's hand.

"And I'm assistant team mom, Claudia Jones. That's my husband over there, assistant coaching." The blonde blew a kiss in his general direction. "We're a very assistful family."

Kate couldn't quite chuckle along with the woman but managed a strained smile. "How nice to meet you both." *Would I be antisocial if I spent the rest of practice working on the laptop in my car?*

Once again sitting, Deanne flipped a folder to a modified version of the team roster and put a check next to Kate's name. "So what did you bring us?"

"A checkbook, actually." Drawing on Claudia for inspiration, Kate tried for a bright, chipper tone.

Both women frowned.

"I wasn't able to bring the brownies I made," Kate said.

It was fine by her if they assumed she'd forgotten them at home or that a family dog had ingested them, rather than explaining she'd created two inedible batches. "So I thought I'd just make a donation to the team."

"But that defeats the purpose of the bake sale," Deanne said. A little too self-righteously.

Kate's patience had been stretched already this week, and the woman's tone wasn't helping. "How could it possibly defeat the purpose of raising money for me to give you a check?"

"In addition to raising money, we want to teach the kids life lessons. Like responsibility and remembering to keep a commitment once it's made." Deanne's voice was as overly patient as a kindergarten teacher's but without the friendliness.

"I did not forget. I—did you just write something by my name?"

Deanne flipped the folder shut. "What?"

"You did, you wrote something about me!" Kate reached for the roster, but Deanne clutched it to her chest protectively as if Kate were a crazy woman trying to steal state secrets.

Claudia stood, looking outraged on behalf of their team mother. "Mrs. St. James, I have to ask you to take a step back from the goody table."

"Oh, for… This is ridiculous." Kate took a tiny step backward because she didn't want PJ blacklisted from the one sport he enjoyed. "I do teach the kids responsibility. Particularly by getting up every morning and going to my job. It's not easy balancing a career with taking care of two kids by myself, but I prioritize. So I'm sorry your brownies got prioritized beneath my helping PJ with his homework and my not getting fired! Now who do I make this check out to?"

Deanne looked as if she might refuse the money, but by now several other parents were approaching the table—most carrying cellophane-covered plates, damn them—and the team mom seemed eager to end the awkward scene.

After Kate had ripped out the check and put it in the woman's hand, she spun back toward the direction of her car, almost colliding with a smiling man about her height. He had sandy hair that was a little thin on top and a handsome face.

"I'm sorry. I didn't see you there," she said stiffly.

"No, it's my fault. I was coming over to say, well, go you!"

"Go me?" The comment was silly enough to make her smile without making him sound inane.

"Michael Seeger." He extended his hand, holding hers a beat longer than Deanne had. "My youngest is number ten on the field. I couldn't help but overhear your comments to Frau Gruber." He adopted an accent and clicked his heels together when referencing the team mother.

Kate's pang of embarrassment at having been heard

faded into laughter. "She does take this whole team-mom thing pretty seriously, huh?"

"You have no idea. Wait until December! When my oldest boy played, there was a Christmas ornament sale to raise money. But of course, not everyone celebrates Christmas, so we now have items from many theologies and cultures to push on our loved ones, with Deanne announcing everyone's totals at the holiday banquet. Guess who always has the highest number?"

She could almost imagine Deanne with a pie graph showing how well she'd outsold everyone else.

"You've inspired me," Michael said. "I think this year I'll just write a check and throw the ornaments in my closet."

"You don't think I've traumatized PJ by throwing cold cash at the organization instead of baking snickerdoodles?" Assuming a snickerdoodle was something that required baking.

Michael chuckled. "So he'll need a little therapy. It'll probably build character. At least that's what I tell myself whenever I psychologically scar *my* boys. I was just about to grab myself a soft drink from the vending machine and find a place to watch practice." He leaned toward her, lowering his voice conspiratorially. "Someplace far away from Deanne and Claudia. Want to join me?"

"Sure." Kate breathed a sigh of relief at having found a kindred soul. Now that she knew not *all* the soccer parents were superpeppy individuals with memorized cookie recipes at the ready, she suspected she'd enjoy the season a little more. And it sounded as if Michael was already pretty familiar with the organization. Maybe he could introduce her around.

Feeling some of the tension melting out of her body, Kate handed over a dollar for a caffeinated cola and hoped Neve's evening was turning out well, too.

Wow. It had been Neve's first reaction when she'd met Robbie Baker, Seth's older brother, and whenever she glanced toward the cute bass player, it remained her only coherent thought.

From the purple beanbag chair next to her, Seth whispered, "Didn't I tell you they were good?"

She nodded wordlessly. The band was tight. Solid beat and decent lyrics, as far as she could tell. Occasionally Robbie's smile distracted her from what the band was singing. She'd always suspected that beneath Seth's shaggy, shy exterior there might be a nice-looking guy—Robbie had more than realized the potential she'd glimpsed in his younger brother.

An inch or two taller than Seth, he carried the height with confidence and broader shoulders. His hair was about the same color but cut short, leaving a clear view of deep brown eyes that were soulful and amazing. Every time he looked her way and grinned, Neve's face warmed.

He must think I'm an idiot.

But the sixteen-year-old had been really nice to her when he'd driven to her house to pick her up. Seth had been in the car, too, doing the gentleman thing and letting Neve sit up front. As usual, Seth had been fairly quiet, so Neve and Robbie had fallen into conversation. He was funny and smart. Patti's son, Leo, was nice, too, but he had a way of making Neve feel young. Robbie treated her like an equal, asking her opinion on stuff and seeming to take it seriously even though she wouldn't be in high school until next year. By this time next year they'd *both* be students there. Together.

The thought drew a sigh, and she barely noticed when Seth stood.

"Be right back," he said softly. "I have to…you know…the b-bathroom."

"'Kay." Neve sat enraptured, clapping her hands when the song ended. The band was comprised of four high school juniors, including a female keyboardist, a male lead singer, a male drummer and Robbie on bass guitar. They were playing to an audience of Seth and Neve, the keyboardist's boyfriend and the drummer's ten-year-old sister, who was clearly a regular at these rehearsals. Whenever Neve glanced at the kid, she was singing along, her head bopping and her braids keeping rhythm with the music. The detached garage was crowded, but the raised door and evening breeze kept it from feeling stuffy.

"Why don't we take five?" the drummer asked his band-mates. "I could use something to drink."

Everyone else was in agreement, so Robbie offered to go into the house for beverages. He turned his big brown eyes in Neve's direction. "Want to come with me and help carry everything?"

"Me?" Standing, she wiped her hands on her jeans. Her palms felt clammy. "Okay."

The brick house was almost twenty feet away, which was probably why Mrs. Baker didn't object to the noise. Light emanated from all the windows, but the yard was dark. Clouds had blotted out the stars and the moon, and Neve shoved repeatedly at her hair as the wind whipped it around.

"So are you and Seth, like, together?" Robbie asked casually.

"What? No! Nothing like that. I mean, he's sweet, but we're not *interested* in each other. Just friends. He's been explaining some algebra stuff to me. He's really good at it."

Robbie nodded. "Yeah. He was flipping through my calculus book the other day and I think he could even do some of the problems in there."

"Wow, calculus." Robbie was so grown-up.

"Too bad for Seth," Robbie said, apparently not talking about math anymore. "I was thinking he was lucky to be with you."

Was he kidding? She didn't have guys drooling after her. Her hair was completely unmanageable, her complexion unpredictable and, while she didn't *hate* her body, she was no Maddison Brant.

Nonetheless, she managed a fairly normal-sounding, "Thank you... So I guess the artistic stuff runs in your family? Seth's drawings are great, and you have your music. That's really cool."

"Thanks." He stopped just shy of the back door, reaching toward the handle. He caught a strand of her hair right before it blew into her face, tucking it gently behind her ear. "You're pretty cool, too."

I could just die. It seemed the likely outcome since her heart had stopped beating. But at least she'd die happy.

CHAPTER 13

There had been periods in her life when Kate hadn't grasped the heartfelt mantra "Thank God it's Friday." After all, she *liked* the office, meeting the challenges, exceeding expectations. Most of her weekends just meant continuing work at home, where supervisors couldn't see all her efforts. Those days of not grasping, however, were behind her.

She still had to catch up on work this weekend, she acknowledged as she stretched in her office chair, but she was looking forward to doing so in casual clothes. She might get wild and crazy and sleep in until at least eight, since nobody had to get ready for school. When had she started feeling tired all the time?

Oh, yeah, when she'd started staying up after the kids went to bed, trying to juggle both the freelance assignment she'd arrogantly assumed would be a piece of cake on top of everything else. In the past, consultant work had been easy. Of course, in the past, there had been no kids asking her to do last-minute laundry because tomorrow was "plaid day" or asking for her help with a book report no one had bothered to tell her about until the night before it was due.

Not all parenting responsibilities were unpleasant, though. The kids made her laugh sometimes and tugged at her heartstrings in unexpected ways. She was even looking forward to PJ's first soccer game. It occurred to her that she should take pictures for Paul. Did they own a camcorder?

She could ask Neve. The girl must have had fun last night at her study buddy's—she'd practically been singing between bites of cereal that morning. Kate hadn't talked to her much about the evening, but if this Seth was half as inspiring as Kate suspected, it explained why Neve was no longer worried about her poetry assignment. Kate had double-checked with her before bed that it was done but hadn't had a chance to read the final product. Maybe this weekend.

"Kate?"

She glanced up at the sound of her boss's voice. "Come in. What can I do for you?"

"If you have just a second—"

"For you, always."

He smiled. "Then I—" This time he was interrupted by her phone ringing. "Go ahead. I'll wait."

"Kate St. James," she said into the receiver.

"Mrs. St. James? Vice Principal Dean," a stern-sounding woman introduced herself. "I'm calling about Neve, who's in my office right now. I realize this doesn't give you much notice, but could you come speak with me this afternoon? Ditching class is a rather serious offense and not how we like our students to start the year."

Neve, who had received exemplary grades at Newsome, was playing hooky? "You're *kidding*."

"Mrs. St. James, I rarely call parents in the middle of the workday to make jokes. Furthermore, I assure you that I find nothing about skipping classes humorous."

"Right. Of course." Kate shot her boss an apologetic look across the desk. "I'm on my way out and should be there in about twenty minutes."

As she hung up the phone, Bryce raised his eyebrows. "I assume there's been a slight amendment to the always-time-for-me clause?"

"One of the kids is in trouble," she said, grabbing her purse out of the bottom desk drawer.

"Is everything all right?"

"Oh, she's not hurt. Just…well, it's complicated. You understand."

"In theory," he said with a nod.

Bryce himself had no children, merely the three purebred dogs that his wife showed competitively. In the past, Kate and Bryce had bonded on days when his secretary was out because her daughter had chicken pox or a woman in tech development missed a meeting because she was taking her twins to the dentist. The only childless married people in the building were her, her boss and Joseph. Was this another professional advantage Joseph was gaining over her?

Racing to her car, she told herself it was wrong to think

of the kids in terms of how they could harm or benefit her career—it bordered on selfishly reminiscent of her own mother. Still, as long as the kids wanted groceries and video games, they all needed Kate to keep that career going strong. And stunts like today's weren't helping.

Shit, shit, shit. Neve wasn't stupid enough to say it out loud—she was in enough trouble already—but there were times when *snap* just didn't cover it.

She wanted to be mad at Cherry, who had suggested more than once that skipping was a breeze. Or maybe she could direct her anger toward Maddison Brant. It was the thought of Maddison's smirk that had kept Neve from English class today.

Last night when Kate had asked about the poem, Neve had lied. She'd known her stepmother would be furious if Neve admitted she'd been too busy listening to Robbie's band to finish her homework. Neve had honestly planned to write the poem, once she was in her room, but she'd been preoccupied. She'd sat down with a spiral notebook, prepared to write an excellent and thought-provoking verse on loss. Forty-five minutes later, she'd written only Robbie's name and, experimentally, *Neve Baker*. Besides, it was hard to feel loss when she was grinning ear to ear.

So Neve had gone to sleep, figuring she could write the thing this morning. After all, a poem only had to be a few lines long.

She'd awakened with a real idea—writing about her mother, how much she missed her. But by the time she'd reached school, the thought of presenting the poem was making her nauseous. There was no way she could stand up and read something so personal with Maddison and her snotty friends snickering at their desks.

Instead Neve had ducked into the girls' locker room, hoping she could stay there during first period and no one would be the wiser. Dumb plan, but then, this had been her first attempt at ditching. If she ever skipped again, she'd think it through better. Feeling the vice principal turn the evil eye on her, Neve fidgeted in her chair. *Not that I'll ever skip again.*

If Kate killed her, classes would be beside the point.

The thought of how her stepmother would react had been bouncing through Neve's mind ever since the vice principal had called Kate at work. When Vice Principal Dean had informed Neve it would take a while, Neve had been glad to postpone the confrontation. But the wait had strained her already frazzled nerves.

What could she say to Kate to explain what she'd done? The more she thought about it, the more anxious she became. The vice principal, busy with some sort of paperwork, had glanced up with a harrumph when Neve started drumming her fingers on the arms of the chair. By the time the office secretary knocked on the door to announce Kate's arrival, Neve still hadn't worked out her best defense.

Vice Principal Dean stood, straightening her ugly green blouse, which looked as rigid as the woman wearing it. "Mrs. St. James?"

"Yes." Although Kate was speaking to the school's disciplinarian, her gaze was locked on Neve's.

I am so dead.

"Please have a seat next to your daughter."

"Stepdaughter," Neve interrupted before she could stop herself. Stupid! Why draw attention to herself?

"Of course," the vice principal said smoothly. "I knew that. I apologize for misspeaking."

Kate didn't answer.

Vice Principal Dean seemed perfectly comfortable carrying on the conversation by herself. "As I mentioned on the phone, Neve is in my office this morning because she chose to take an unexcused absence in English."

Kate's gaze cut toward Neve again. "English? Is this because of the poetry assignment? You *told* me that was finished."

"It was! Well…" Neve bit her lip, already feeling too guilty to lie again. "All right, when I said that last night, it wasn't entirely true. I hadn't…worked out all the wording yet."

"I suppose you and Seth were busy with other things?"

Neve's face flamed. Her stepmother sounded so accusatory. *She might as well call me a skank in front of the vice principal.* "Seth and I are friends. We weren't doing anything. Just listening to his brother's band last night."

Kate's eyes narrowed. "I thought you were studying?"

"When Mr. Grayson gives us tips for creative writing, he says music helps some people."

"You're grasping at pretty weak straws, young lady."

"It doesn't matter. Band or not, I finished my poem before class." Neve lifted her chin. It had been a damn good poem, too. "I just...wussed out about reading it and made a mistake. What, like *you're* perfect? You can't even make chocolate-chip cookies for a bake sale!"

Kate sucked in her breath. "That's enough."

"But it's true!" Neve hadn't cried when she'd written that poem about Mom, but the tears were rushing to the surface now. That she couldn't stop them made her even more furious. "Did you know my mother made these incredible brownies? They were the best in the state."

"I'm sure they were good, but I've been a little busy trying to stay afloat at work to take cooking classes."

"It was better when I had a mom who could stay at home," Neve flung back.

"Yes, well, your father *wasn't in prison then*, so she had that option." Kate pressed a hand to her mouth, looking horrified.

Seeing her stepmother lose her composure didn't actually make Neve feel any better about losing her own. Drained of the majority of her anger, she just felt suddenly small and very tired.

Vice Principal Dean leaned forward in her chair.

"Maybe your stepmother and I should talk alone? You can wait outside my office while we discuss the situation."

"Situation?" Neve swallowed. "It was just one dumb stunt. A-a dare. One of the other girls dared me not to go to class. I know it was stupid to go along, but I'm trying to make friends in a new school."

Nobody looked convinced by the last-minute lie. So much for the drama teacher's theory that the best work came through improv.

"I see," said the vice principal. "And would you please tell me who this other girl is?"

Neve stared at her hands. "It's not cool to narc on other kids."

"And skipping class is 'cool'?" Even though Kate had lowered her voice from before, there was no mistaking her tone for calm. She was even angrier than when PJ had wandered off at the store.

Which isn't fair. He inconvenienced everyone and could have gotten himself kidnapped. All Neve had done was change her mind about reading something personal in front of kids who wouldn't get it anyway.

"You've had trouble making friends here," the vice principal prodded, "haven't you, Neve? I've spoken to your counselor. And Ms. Cameron, your dramatic arts teacher, is also quite concerned."

"Ms. Cameron is a flake." How did you rise to a position

like vice principal without even the ability to tell which of your faculty members were whacked?

"Neve! Wait. Outside." The way Kate bit off the words didn't bode well for Neve's immediate future.

"Fine." She stood, thinking that perhaps her long-ago plan of running away to the circus hadn't been such a bad idea.

The way she felt now, she'd even be willing to don some of those silly leotard costumes that looked like wedgies waiting to happen, just as long as she didn't have to recite poetry while wearing them.

Calling on the self-discipline she'd spent years cultivating, Kate didn't slam her door when she got in the car.

Damn, she wanted to, though. She was furious with Neve for skipping—hadn't the kid *listened* when Kate had tried to explain how important education was?—and even irritated with that steely-eyed vice principal. It had felt as if the way the woman had interceded had lessened Kate's authority.

Because you were doing so well on your own? Kate cringed inwardly. She could not blow up just because the kid missed her mother's brownies. Not that she was excusing Neve's behavior—the girl was in a world of trouble—but Kate had to remain the adult. Levelheaded despite her frustration. Once the two adults had been alone, Vice Principal Dean had started in on what a difficult transition Neve must be going through during the already confusing and tumultuous time of adolescence. Kate had wanted to scream. *You don't have to tell me it's a difficult transition. I'm living it, lady!*

But she hadn't screamed, she wasn't slamming doors and she would take care of this. Really, what choice did she have? This situation had been thrust on her and the children the minute Paul's verdict had been turned in. She threw a little of the anger she was feeling his way, too, just for good measure.

So now what? Did she ground Neve until senior prom so that boundaries were set and the kid knew to take her stepmother seriously? Or was Kate supposed to proceed with compassion so that the kid didn't feel misunderstood and unloved, turning to mistakes like early sex to replace the affection and belonging she didn't think she was getting at home? Good Lord. Parenting was enough to drive a person to drink. Which, of course, would be bad parenting.

Which would lead to an even greater sense of failure and desire to drink.

Obviously Kate needed to say something, but she wasn't sure where to start. She thought back to Neve's comments in the office and wondered if, despite her protestations to the contrary, the girl had simply skipped because she hadn't completed the assignment.

"Did you really write a poem for class?"

"Yes! I told you I did."

Kate counted to five silently before continuing. "I know that. And normally I would have taken you at your word. But you've abused my trust this morning."

Neve scowled, her silent glare boring holes in the windshield.

"Could I see the poem?"

"No."

A moment later Kate realized no further information would be forthcoming. At least not voluntarily. "Neve," she said warningly, not really sure where she went from here.

"It's a poem about my mother." The words came out with the same friendly warmth as bullets. Sprayed from a machine gun.

"I see." *Damn.* Why hadn't Kate seen that coming? Neve had told her it was supposed to be about loss, after all. Maybe Kate should have put aside her work when Neve first asked for her help the other night, paid more attention. But, hell, they needed her income. She shouldn't feel like a bad guy just because she cared about her job and was doing her best to support her husband's kids.

After a deep breath, Kate took what she hoped was a tactful approach. What were the chances Neve would meet her in the middle? "I'm sure it's very personal to you. The best poetry should be personal. I'll bet—"

Neve snorted. "The other night, all you knew about poetry was that 'Shakespeare wrote some sonnets.'"

Kate stopped at a red light, applying more force to the brake than she'd intended. "Do you really think now is the wisest time to get snippy with me? Or have you just decided that today's your day to act without thinking?"

The girl slunk down in her seat.

"Vice Principal Dean spoke to your English teacher between periods. Did they explain to you what was agreed? Mr. Grayson won't give you a zero for this assignment because you're normally a good student for him. But the minute the final bell rings on Monday morning, you'd better be standing at the front of his class, prepared to read a poem aloud. If you're uncomfortable sharing what you wrote about your mother, I suggest you use this weekend to write something new. You'll have plenty of time because, aside from going to PJ's game with me, you're grounded."

Though she clenched her jaw mutinously, Neve didn't protest the punishment. A few minutes later, though, she asked, "For how long?"

"I'm not sure yet, so don't push me." Kate took a left, glad they were almost home. She wanted to lie in a dark room with a cold cloth across her forehead.

"It won't matter what I write," Neve muttered. "Maddison will still laugh."

"Maddison? Who is she and why does her reaction even matter?" She didn't wait for an answer. "You're a young adult. It's time to grow up. You can't throw away your grades because of some kid in your class. Running from adversity only hurts you, Neve. Don't you think Maddison is going to laugh when she hears about how you were sent to the vice principal's office and taken home?"

"Like you remember anything about being my age? You're gorgeous." It didn't come out as a compliment. "What do you know about being ugly and unpopular?"

"You are not ugly."

"You weren't either, were you?" Neve was almost pleading, as if she wanted to be told her stepmother had once been an ugly duckling until the beauty fairy magically appeared one day to fix all her problems.

Kate had been one of the best-looking, if never better dressed, girls in the school—and being so noticeably attractive had created a whole different set of difficulties. In her current mood, Neve wouldn't relate to those, Kate decided as she hit the garage door opener. Her past wasn't relevant, anyway.

"This isn't about me. *I* faced down people who gave me grief. I'm not the one who ditched class. I'm the one who very responsibly went to work and had to leave early yet again because of you and your brother."

Her stepdaughter flinched.

Kate had been trying to demonstrate her own ethic and instill some of it into the girl, shame Neve into taking more responsibility for what she'd done today instead of blaming it on this Maddison person. But the words had come out too harsh, as if she resented the kids' presence. She replayed the comments in her head, trying to hear them with an insecure thirteen-year-old's ears.

"Neve—"

The girl had yanked off her seat belt and flung open the door. "I'm going to my room. That's where I should stay anyway, since I'm grounded."

"You deserve to be grounded. But I am sorry if—"

"Forget it. You were right. This isn't about you."

Kate watched her go. *Maybe if I put the car in Neutral and just go lie in the driveway behind it....* Nah, they weren't on enough of an incline.

She took her time entering the house. With over forty-eight hours to enjoy the sullen vibes of an angry adolescent underfoot this weekend, Kate should pace herself. She knew she was justified in the grounding and thought allowing Neve to go to the soccer match was a kind exception on her part. A chance for the girl to get a little fresh air, be around people who *weren't* her wicked stepmother.

Thinking about Neve's last social outing—to Seth's house—annoyed Kate all over again. The teen had played her, making it sound more academic than it had been. Then Neve had glibly lied to Kate's face about being done with her homework *and* ducked out of class to top it all off.

Were there other small dishonesties Kate hadn't even caught yet? How much trust did the girl still deserve? If Neve looked tired, did Kate start rifling her things looking for drugs? Should she write to Paul to ask his advice or was that just adding to his emotional burden and making him worry about situations at home he was in no position to control?

By the time she'd reached her room to change clothes, questions were swirling around her skull in the beginnings of a killer migraine. The blinking light on her answering machine fed into her pessimistic mood. Maybe it was PJ's principal and the kid was beating up first graders for their lunch money. Admittedly Kate couldn't imagine him doing such a thing, but she hadn't imagined Neve playing hooky from class. Especially not the one with the hunky teacher.

Sitting on the edge of the bed, she hit Play thinking, God, *what now?*

A completely unexpected voice from the past filled the room. "Hello, Katherine. It's your mother."

CHAPTER 14

"**I** don't get why I have to go to this stupid game," Neve complained as she sat at the kitchen table, pointedly not eating her breakfast.

Part of Kate wanted to let the girl stay home—her sunny mood certainly wasn't going to add to the day—but the rest of her vetoed that idea. "Are you kidding? You're going to support your brother. Not to mention that I don't think you've earned the right to stay home by yourself. I'm not convinced I can trust you."

"You know why I didn't want to go to class, and it was a one-time thing. It's not like I was in the girls' room smoking."

"This isn't just about Mr. Grayson's class, although that alone is sufficient for me to ground you. What about Thursday night? You let me think you and Seth would be working on homework and instead it turned out to be…"

"His brother has a band. We listened to some music for a little while. What's the big deal?"

"You get to ask that question after you're getting all A's and I turn into one of those overprotective-to-the-point-of-being-neurotic sitcom moms. *Not* when several of your teachers are worried about you being distant and you've been caught lying."

"So you're saying I should try harder not to get caught next time?" Neve tossed out, challenge radiating from every pore of her body.

Were all teenagers possessed by evil? *There is no way I gave my mother this much trouble when I was thirteen.*

The thought led back to yesterday's unexpected phone message. Kate had replayed it twice after the children had gone to bed. Lorna had simply said she'd been thinking of Kate and that they should talk. She didn't mention a reason why, which was suspicious considering how long they normally went between phone calls. Kate couldn't remember the last time her mother had called out of the blue. Eventually Kate would call her back, but she had enough on her plate today.

She was busy with PJ's first game and fending off her stepdaughter's verbal attacks. If Neve's moodiness didn't clear up on its own, Kate would have to call Lily. She'd considered doing so last night but hadn't quite been able to do it. In part, she wanted to give Neve the benefit of the doubt, let her overcome her own mistakes without tattling to the girl's aunt every time something happened. But also, asking others for help didn't come easily to Kate. She'd worked too hard, too long not to need others.

Today should be about PJ, though. Kate took the opportunity to point that out. "Your brother will be down in a minute, and you had better be cheerful about this game. It means a lot to him. It's not his fault you're grounded. Or even mine. So you can keep looking at me like that, but it won't change a thing. If you can't shape up, I'm going to have to rethink this Seth boy's influence on you. Maybe you shouldn't be talking to him on the phone or going to his house again."

Neve rolled her eyes. "Seth doesn't have any influence on me. Just because he's a boy doesn't mean I like him the way you think. And if you won't let me talk to him on the phone, *you'll* have to go back to helping me with my algebra."

One point to the teenager. Kate shuddered at the memory of their last tutorial math session.

"I found my shoes," PJ called happily, "so we can go now."

"All right," Kate replied, trying to echo his tone. *Cheerful* is the watchword. They were all going to have lots and lots of fun today. Whether they damn well wanted to or not.

"Kate!" A man's friendly voice hailed her over the modest noise of the soccer crowd. "There are some seats here if you need one."

She climbed the bleachers, feeling desperately grateful for an adult ally this morning. "Michael, it's nice to see you again. This is Neve, PJ's sister."

Neve mumbled something that might have passed as a hello.

"A pleasure to meet you," Michael told the girl, graciously overlooking her disposition. "Is your brother excited about playing?"

"I guess." Neve turned to Kate. "I have a couple of dollars in my pocket. Can I get a drink at the concessions booth?"

"Sure." Honestly Kate wouldn't mind a few minutes of respite. The girl's mood had a way of clinging to everything around her like suffocating ash.

Once they were alone, Michael smiled teasingly. "This is the kind of comment that always got me in trouble with my ex-wife, but you don't look so good this morning."

"Gee, and she didn't appreciate observations like that?"

"Yeah, go figure. Seriously you look like you could use a friend. Everything all right with Neve?"

"That obvious, huh? I guess the fact that she was trying to get me to spontaneously combust with her eyes was a giveaway."

"Not uncommon teen behavior, though. What is she, fourteen?"

"Just turned thirteen."

"My oldest is fifteen now, and I've heard girls are even more difficult than boys. Um, that probably didn't reassure you. But what I meant was, knowing how moody mine can be and how often we butt heads, I can imagine what you're going through. The good news is, after Neve, PJ will probably be a walk in the park."

"Thanks." By the time PJ was this age, Paul would be back. But that wasn't terribly helpful in the here and now. "It's nice to know I'm not alone. When I had to pick her up at school the other day, I was feeling like the worst parent ever. I didn't know if I should go soft on her and hug her or set an example or…" She sighed. "Nothing felt right. Oddly enough, even if I *had* hugged her instead of grounding her, I doubt she'd be behaving any warmer toward me."

"So what caused this grounding?"

There was no sense that he might criticize her choices, which made talking about it easier. Still, she didn't want to dive into the whole you're-not-my-mother complex the kid was giving her. *So I can't bake brownies. I have other attributes, if she'd give me a damn chance.* "It's complicated, but I think it started with a guy—"

"Uh-oh. You really can't trust us guys."

Kate smirked. "She had a homework date that turned out to be more of a date date—even though she's denying that—and when the homework didn't get done, she skipped class rather than face the music. Actually, there's…more, but you get the gist."

"So you grounded her for the homework part and the skipping, but the 'more' is why you wanted to hug her."

"You're good," she said, impressed by his astuteness.

"No, it sounds like *you* are. You recognize whatever

emotional pain she's feeling even though she brought trouble on herself. You're a good mother, Kate."

She laughed uncomfortably. "Me? I can't even do bake-sale cookies, remember?"

"The trick is Rice Krispies Treats. All you need is a box of cereal, a stick of margarine and some minimarshmallows. Easy to learn, tough to screw up. You can even come over tomorrow afternoon, if you'd like, and we'll make a practice batch for the kids."

Kate blinked, feeling as if the conversation had suddenly taken an unexpected roller-coaster turn and she'd spilled out onto the tracks. "Tomorrow?"

"Sure." His easygoing manner was different now. Not so much nonchalant as *trying* for nonchalance.

This was not good.

"If you and your kids aren't busy," he was saying, "you could come over for a cookout with me and mine. The boys and I love any chance to fire up the grill, but pretty soon it will be the wrong season for outdoor dinners. Or is that out of bounds since Neve's grounded right now?"

Kate chose her words carefully, wondering if she were overreacting to a harmless invitation. "Michael, it's sweet of you to offer, but—"

"Well, we single parents have to stick together," he interrupted, more visibly nervous.

"Single?" Just what sort of slutty available vibes had she been putting out?

Great. She was *definitely* sending mixed signals if she was even thinking terms like *putting out*.

"Michael, I'm married."

"What?" It was a toss-up whether the poor man looked more stunned or appalled. "When I heard you arguing with the team moms the other night, you said something about working and raising kids alone! You haven't said one word about a husband. Who isn't here today. Are you separated?"

"Not exactly. *No.* He's just away. Which is why I'm taking care of the kids by myself. Incompetently." Cheering drew her attention to the field, where the Jackrabbits had been awarded a goal. "My stepdaughter hates me and I just missed my stepson's team score because I was trying to explain myself to a nice man to whom I obviously gave the wrong impression. I am so sorry."

"Don't be." He rallied quickly. "My fault. You're wearing a ring. I hadn't thought to check before, I'd just assumed... And, hey, you could still come over for Rice Krispies lessons. Sometime."

She forced a smile at the vague invitation he'd felt obligated to extend. "Sure, we'll get the kids together. Sometime. For now, I should probably go get a rundown of the team's last play. I've got to make sure I congratulate PJ on anything he did! And Neve's certainly taking her sweet time getting back, so I should check on her, too."

Michael nodded, doing a decent job of masking his

relief that she was leaving, taking the sudden awkwardness with her. "See you around, Kate."

Not if I see you first. It was something she'd heard Brittney say once and seemed entirely appropriate now. Of course, what did Kate know from appropriate? She'd apparently been flirting with a soccer dad while her husband sat in prison.

You never flirted. You just enjoyed the conversation the other night.

Why wouldn't she enjoy it? Michael was funny, a good listener and, as far as she could tell, a decent father. There'd been nothing untoward in any of their conversations. Even his asking her out had been pretty G-rated. But a small echo of guilt wouldn't leave her alone. She had discerned from Michael's smile that he'd thought her attractive. While that wasn't a crime, part of her had liked being seen that way again. There'd been a time when she hadn't welcomed male appreciation and other times when she'd simply taken it for granted. But with her love life on hold for a mandatory six month sentence...well, it had been nice to know she still had it.

Even if there was nothing she could do *with* it.

Her guilt was magnified by Michael's observation that she'd never once mentioned her husband. Not a single casual reference? Hell, even Michael's wife had made it into discussion, and they weren't even married anymore! It wasn't that Kate had a cheating heart, it was that Paul's situation was delicate.

Or maybe this was about her situation as the spouse on the outside. The shame she felt. The awkwardness of explaining, *Oh, yes, I'm happily married to a wonderful man. We'll have you over for dinner once he gets out of federal prison.*

She was embarrassed. At forty-two she wasn't able to maintain the positive attitude that her stepson had, knowing this was just the temporary consequence for an unintentional offense. Kate was *embarrassed* by the man she loved.

Did treating Paul like a disgraceful secret make her an even worse wife than one who actually did flirt with other men?

"You guys must be getting tired of having to meet at my house," Kate said apologetically.

"At least by showing up here we know you can't forget again and stand us up." Delia rolled her eyes at Patti's scowl. "What? She knows I'm kidding! Besides, pregnant women are allowed to say outrageous things. Hormones, you know."

Kate grinned. "So what was your excuse before?"

With a laugh, Patti tucked her feet beneath her on the sofa. "Honestly I don't mind coming over. It's quieter than going out and gets me away from *my* house, where Leo and his friends were shooting hoops all evening. They ordered pizzas for dinner, and the feeding frenzy was terrifying. Piranhas don't pick bones clean as fast as those boys cleared out three cardboard boxes. I'm happy to let George monitor the situation and escape to more civilized surroundings."

Civilized? Good thing Neve was upstairs.

PJ was at an impromptu sleepover at a teammate's house, invited after they'd won their first game of the season. But the fresh air and soccer victory had done little to improve his sister's disposition. She'd been surly with Kate, then seemed on the brink of tears when she'd dropped something in the kitchen earlier. Adolescence. *Fasten your seat belts, emotional turbulence dead ahead.*

Delia was patting her expanded stomach. "I don't mind coming over either, but once this kiddo is born, we'll have to do girls' nights at my place. Looks like way too much work to schlep along the Diaper Genie, porta-crib, bottles and nine thousand other things I'll apparently need to take care of a single ten-pound being. But Paul will be home by then anyway, so he can watch over Neve and PJ. Everything will be back to normal for you."

Normal? Something that bore an unfortunate resemblance to hysterical laughter burbled from Kate's throat.

Her two friends exchanged pointed glances across the living room.

"Sweetie?" Patti asked hesitantly. "Anything you want to tell us?"

"Well, I haven't mentioned my impending nervous breakdown but only because I figured it was self-evident."

Kate ran a hand through her hair, absently registering the ragged ends.

She couldn't remember the last time she'd had a trim. Or a manicure. Hell, she could barely remember the last time she'd made it through an entire workday without arriving late or leaving early or being otherwise interrupted by her new child-rearing commitments. She truly hadn't expected motherhood to be *this* hard.

And her obstacles raising Paul's children didn't even touch on her mixed feelings about Paul himself, wanting to be a supportive and forgiving wife one minute and wanting to bitch him out the next for putting them in this position, for not taking a more direct approach with his own kids, for not at least writing them more freaking letters. Not that she was allowed to call and give him a piece of her mind. She still wasn't sure if he was he *hiding* behind the prison's outside-communication rules.

"Sorry. Don't mind me," Kate said. But she'd no sooner waved off their concern than she decided it might be best to get a second opinion on her day. "Do you guys think it's normal for me to be checking out other parents? A single father asked me out this morning."

"Hell, yes, that's normal," Delia said. "By checking out, you mean noticing he was attractive, right?"

"Well, yeah. We kind of hit it off."

"But you didn't say yes when he asked you out…did you?"

"Of course not!"

Patti exhaled audibly at this, apparently relieved by Kate's continuing fidelity. "Then I'm with Delia. Nothing wrong with chatting up some guy or thinking he has a nice smile—"

"Or nice ass." Delia waggled her eyebrows.

Kate laughed despite herself. "I didn't think to check."

"If you weren't even ogling, don't beat yourself up. No one expects you to be a saint." Delia jerked her thumb toward Patti. "She's close enough to be annoying. Don't you go sprouting a halo and wings on me, too."

Patti just chuckled, not even dredging up a comeback or an offended "Hey!" at the mention of her occasional self-righteousness. The two women seemed to have grown closer over the past few weeks.

"I'm definitely not a candidate for sainthood," Kate said wryly. The other night she'd wanted to take a swing at a woman running a bake sale. *Forget saint, I'm not even an overachiever anymore.* If she didn't regain her balance soon, underachiever was a possibility.

What kind of example would that set for the kids? She was their daily role model, although that pressure combined with the already high standards she tried to hold for herself just made her chest feel tight.

"Do not sell yourself short," Delia said, her sincerity bordering on intense before she flashed another grin. "Me, I'd have been climbing the walls before now just from the lack of sex!"

Kate turned the spotlight away from herself. "I guess you're going through something of a dry spell now yourself. Between being pregnant and arguing with Alexander about your collective future?"

"Well…it seems pregnancy hormones ramp up other appetites than just hunger for food," Delia shared. "Ringo and I are still negotiating the commitment issue, but we've agreed to check our differences at the bedroom door. He's trying to seduce me into seeing things his way, and for now, I've been letting him. The sex has never been better."

Kate blinked. Her worldly friend, who'd regaled them over margaritas with wild stories of her thirties, was having the best sex of her life *now?* At forty-three and in her second trimester?

"Delia, show some compassion," Patti chided. "Kate's having the world's worst first year of marriage. She doesn't need to hear the salacious details of your love life."

"Don't be so sure," Kate said. "It's the closest I'm getting to action." She truly hadn't expected to miss sex so much. Intimacy hadn't seemed that important to her before Paul. Now that he was away, she was getting a clearer look at how much their relationship had changed her. Unfortunately she was also getting a clearer look at some problems, such as the gap between him and his children. And her own inabilities to handle as much as she'd confidently assumed she could.

Patti clucked her tongue sympathetically. "I always did say a vibrator was a girl's best friend."

"Hmm, does poor George know about this opinion?" Delia teased. "Honestly I'll try anything once, but the battery-operated substitutes just don't do it for me. What are you supposed to cry out at the crucial moment? Oh...*Duracell?*"

The ridiculous commentary made Kate grin. When the phone rang, all three women jumped guiltily, as if they were high school freshmen on the verge of being caught with a copy of *Playgirl*. After a brief silence, Patti giggled, making the comparison even more accurate.

They heard footsteps clomping on the landing upstairs and Neve hollered down, "Am I allowed to answer that? Or should I let you get it since *I'm* grounded?"

"No, you can talk," Kate called back. Perhaps because she was feeling so grateful for her girlfriends and their ability to cheer her up, she was in a generous mood when it came to allowing Neve to talk to her own friends. "But if it's for me, tell them I'm with company and will have to call back some other time."

Saying it made her realize that she hadn't given any more thought to returning Lorna's call. Should she ignore the message? For all she knew, Lorna had experienced a sentimental tipsy moment and wouldn't even remember dialing Kate when she was sober again. Meanwhile, Kate was lost enough trying to figure out how to be a good mother. The last thing she wanted was to get sucked into second-guessing herself as a daughter, too.

Neve ran toward the cordless phone. She hadn't expected permission to talk and was going to be seriously depressed if it was a wrong number or some soccer parent wanting to enlist Kate in some fund-raising car wash or whatever.

Thoughts of soccer parents made Neve scowl as she reached for the receiver. She hadn't liked the look of that Michael guy today. Or, more accurately, the way he'd looked at Kate. She'd wanted to yell, *Hey, that's my step-mother, you sleaze!*

"Hello?" she answered.

"Hi." A guy—not old enough to be Michael or some other man Kate might know—cleared his throat. "Neve?"

"Yeah. Seth, is that you?" Maybe he had a cold.

"No, actually, it's Robbie, his brother. I got your number from him. Hope that's cool."

She fell back across her bed, grinning like an idiot. "Completely cool." A *boy* was calling her. She owed Seth big-time for this.

"So the band just finished practice and Donald—our drummer?—announced he got us a gig. It doesn't actually pay, but it's a start. There's this sweet-sixteen party the first Saturday in October, and I thought you might like to hear us play somewhere other than my garage." He paused. "If you're not doing anything that night."

A high school guy was inviting her to a party? *Eat your heart out, Maddison Brant!* Of course, that would require Maddison actually having one.

"I would love to hear you guys." Neve didn't know if this counted as a date, so she didn't want to jump to conclusions and embarrass herself. But she didn't want to play it too cool and discourage any interest, either.

Then there was the bigger problem: Kate. Would she agree to let Neve go? Even if Neve weren't still grounded then, Kate was annoyed that Neve had gone to Seth's for the band and not the homework. And would she overreact to Neve's getting an invitation from a slightly older guy? *I'll deal with that later.* For now, she was basking.

"Great." Robbie sounded sincere but casual. Very guy. "Tell your stepmother I can pick you up if you need a lift. Depending on your curfew, I could drop you off, too, but I have to stay until we're finished with our set...."

"Of course." The thought of Robbie bringing her back was so much more enchanting than Kate coming to get her as if Neve were some kid at a playdate.

"Seth will come with us, too," Robbie said. "And the keyboardist's boyfriend will be there. So at least a couple of people you know."

Seth? Well, not so enchanting, but his presence might make it an easier sell to Kate. When Neve said *party*, she didn't have to mention it was a high school one—which could lead to an automatic no. There would be at least two eighth graders.

"Let me check my schedule and I'll call you this week," Neve suggested, proud of how mature she sounded. But once they'd ended the call, she couldn't resist a muffled squeal and a full-body wiggle of happiness.

After she'd turned off the lights and tried to go to sleep, however, her happiness morphed into anxiety. She'd been a pill to her stepmother the last couple of days. What were the chances that Kate would be in an understanding frame of mind when Neve asked about this? This was important. But even if she said yes, Neve had to get through her stepmother meeting Robbie and Seth. *Please, God, don't let her embarrass me.* Although even that seemed a small price to pay for admission to a social event that would enable her to spend more time with Robbie, that would make her feel like part of the in crowd and not an outcast even her own father avoided.

Neve tossed and turned. Her mother had joked, "A glass of milk always soothes away my problems…especially when I'm using it to wash down half a dozen cookies."

I miss you, Mom.

Knowing homemade cookies no longer awaited her in the kitchen, Neve nonetheless opened the door to her room. Lights and laughter from downstairs meant Kate's friends were still here. How lame was Neve that even her over-forty stepmother had a better social life?

Being invited to a party by a sixteen-year-old boy wasn't lame, though. She just had to figure out a way to go.

"Hi," Patti called as Neve came down the stairs. "Did you come to tell Delia she's being too loud and bawdy?"

"No." Neve flashed a halfhearted smile. "Just wanted a glass of milk and maybe some munchies."

"Munchies get my vote," Delia agreed. "Kate, lead us to the junk food!"

"You might have cleaned me out already." Kate nodded toward a serving plate on the coffee table, empty except for some crumbs.

"I should have brought over the mini quiches I have at home," Patti said. "And the éclairs. They're tiny but delicious. You guys should really get on one of the planning committees for a club event. We all got sent home with some complimentary samples. Everyone's going to love the menu! Not like that year where the girls spent half the budget on overrated crab puffs and caviar and skimped on the desserts."

Neve scrunched up her nose. "I just don't get what the big deal about caviar is. Éclairs rock, though."

"Patti's part of the team that put together the country club fund-raiser I'm going to in a few weeks," Kate said to Neve.

"The first Saturday in October," Patti said, looking proud of whatever work she'd done on the event.

Neve's pulse kicked into overdrive. The first Saturday? As in, the night Robbie's band would be playing? It was practically a sign. Her heart racing, she retreated to the solitude of the kitchen and poured that glass of milk she'd craved.

Maybe she could go to that party without Kate meeting Robbie after all. Neve didn't feel good about lying, but if omitting a detail or two improved her chances of going...

This must be what adults called a moral dilemma.

Cherry was doing a school report on a racy movie, using the R-rated film to make her point in the paper. Seth had asked if she was sure her examples would be all right with the teacher. Cherry had merely smiled and said it was better to do and apologize later than to ask first and get shut down. Maybe she had a point.

But Neve's conscience must have been directly linked to her abdomen, because when she got out of bed Sunday morning, her stomach was cramped into knots. She spent most of the day doing as little as possible and vegging in front of the TV, although Kate made her practice her newly written poem for English class twice.

"It doesn't rhyme," PJ had remarked.

Stupid. What did he know about meter and stanzas, anyway?

"Mr. Grayson will love it," Kate had declared. "Of course, he would have loved it even more if you'd actually shown up to deliver it on Friday when it was due."

Neve had rolled her eyes but refrained from comment.

Now, curled up in front of a Sunday-night cable movie,

feeling restless and uncomfortable in her own skin, she wondered if what she was feeling was performance anxiety. The combination of feverish excitement over Robbie's call and prickly irritability over having to read poetry in front of Maddison and her friends wasn't a good combination.

She woke Monday morning with a raging headache and the desire to pull the blankets back over her head. Well, to be honest, she had that desire *every* time her alarm clock gonged at her. But the headache and cramped stomach were new.

"What's the matter?" Kate asked as she pushed down the frozen waffles in the toaster. "You look even less chipper than usual."

"I don't feel good," Neve muttered. "I think I should stay home today."

Kate's eyebrows rose. "Nice try. Look, I get you're probably embarrassed about last Friday, but the best way to get past that is to get right back on the horse."

Neve could insist that this wasn't about embarrassment, but explaining that it was stress over potentially lying about an upcoming party wouldn't help. Who knows? Maybe it was an honest case of the stomach flu. If she hurled at school, Kate would feel really, really guilty for making her go.

"Is this going to be a weekly occurrence?" Thank heavens Bryce looked more bemused than aggravated.

"I'm really sorry about having to duck out early," Kate said, frantically gathering her things.

Neve must hate me. It seemed a given, although the school nurse hadn't specifically mentioned loathing resentment in her phone call. She'd been too busy tossing around the words *menstrual cycle.*

"It's a...woman thing," Kate told her boss, sparing the details.

He shook his head. "Last week it was a kid thing. Tell me you don't own a cat. If you have to leave tomorrow because of a Siamese thing—"

"Tomorrow—I'll stay all night if that's what I need to do to complete any outstanding projects. You have my word."

"No, don't stay all night. Honestly you look a little tired lately." Bryce peered at her. "You know, Joseph—"

"How about we finish this conversation tomorrow?" she interrupted, not wanting to hear the rest of his words. "Right now I have to go." She rushed by before he could protest. Her annual employee review was the first week of November. She was going to have to brainstorm some major ways to suck up before then.

For now, she was trying to decide what to say to Neve. Had her stepdaughter talked about womanly stuff with her mom? Or had Heather assumed they'd discuss it when Neve was older? It was a sure bet *Paul* had never mentioned the monthly rituals of cramps and tampons. This situation called for female backup.

Simultaneously driving and dialing, Kate hoped like crazy that Lily was home.

"Hello?"

"Lily! It's Kate."

"Hi, it's good to hear from you. Everything okay?"

"Mostly. But I could use some advice. You must have been through this with Brittney."

There was a wry sigh. "Honey, you wouldn't *believe* the things I went through with that girl. I take it this is about Neve?"

"Yeah. She's officially a woman today. The nurse called me at work." That school must have Kate's office on speed dial by now. "I guess this is about the normal age for girls to start their periods? Honestly I hadn't given it much thought." She'd been juggling plenty of other things and was starting to feel like she was dropping the balls. Which had rolled away, tripped bystanders and led to angry lawsuits.

When had she lost control of everything? More importantly, how was she going to regain it?

"Do yourself a favor," Lily was saying, "and never suggest to Neve that you'd assumed she was already having them. Or are surprised that she's starting this early. Teenage girls are hypersensitive to feeling like freaks, so whatever age they start at, *that* is officially the normal age."

"You think she's going to have a lot of questions? Or want to talk about sex?"

"With you? Don't be ridiculous. She probably just wants to curl up with a heating pad. Did any of the kids see that her period had started? If that's the case, she probably also wants to transfer schools."

Yikes, that adolescent nightmare hadn't even occurred to Kate. "I'm not sure. I'm on my way to get her now."

"Want me to meet you at your house?"

Yes, please! "That would be fantastic. Thank you, Lily." Kate wasn't sure why she was so discombobulated over something completely natural and inevitable, but this felt like a mother-daughter kind of moment. And as Neve had made clear in the vice principal's office, Kate was not her mother. Better to call in someone who had actual experience.

Maybe someone with more on-the-job training would have known to believe Neve when she'd said she didn't feel well over breakfast. Unfortunately the kid was now due not to feel well once a month for many, many years to come.

If she'd been suspicious that the girl was faking that morning, Neve's sincere misery was hard to miss now.

Kate walked into the nurse's office, empathizing with the girl's pale face and low groan. "Hey, there." Since no one else but the sturdy-looking nurse was in earshot, she offered a wry, "Welcome to womanhood."

Neve grimaced. "Sucks so far."

"It'll get better." Sort of. Decades later, the wondering about when exactly menopause would hit and how noticeable the symptoms would be would come. Probably better not to mention that now.

Kate signed the release form the nurse had handed to her on a clipboard and grabbed her stepdaughter's backpack.

"I was in gym," Neve said when they were in the car. "I've been feeling awful since this weekend. Then in English class, my head hurt so bad I could barely concentrate on Mr. Grayson after my poem—and we were actually talking about literature I *liked* today. My vision got weird and spotty."

"Sounds like the beginnings of a migraine," Kate said. Ah, the many joys of hormones.

"I got a soda and some aspirin from Cherry, but I just kept getting crankier. Then when it was time to change for gym, I saw the blood. Nobody else noticed. The nurse gave me a pad." She cast a curious glance at Kate. "Do you have those at home, pads and stuff? Or are you done with all that?"

"No, I still have a few years."

"My friend Krista that I vacation with, her mom is younger than you but doesn't have them. I think she had 'all the plumbing removed.'"

Kate laughed. There were days when that was tempting.

They pulled into the driveway about the same time as Lily.

"What's Aunt Lily doing here?" Neve asked.

"You don't mind that I told her, do you? I thought…you might need someone to talk to."

Neve's eyebrows shot up. "About what? I read *Are You There God? It's Me, Margaret* like three years ago. We have HBO. Plus, I do take health classes. I know all about sex and reproduction stuff."

"Oh? Then remind me not to leave you alone with a guy until you're thirty. Except that Seth boy. You've finally drummed it into my head that you're not interested in him."

Neve laughed, but it was a strangled sound.

"What? You've changed your mind about Seth?"

"No, no."

"So is there someone else? Spill, girlfriend!" Kate did her best imitation of Neve on the phone with Rebecca.

"It's so sad when old people try to sound cool." Neve was out of the car before Kate could respond but still moving slower than usual, holding her abdomen.

Lily had arrived with the best kind of medicine—pints of ice cream in many flavors. She also carried pink boxes of feminine supplies so Neve could decide for herself what she preferred to use without the embarrassment of debating them in the middle of the grocery store. In another bag she had a stack of "chick flick" DVDs.

Once Neve was sprawled on the couch, waiting for Kate to plug in an extension cord for the heating pad, she showed more interest in the movie marathon. "What did you bring, Aunt Lily?"

"An Amanda Bynes comedy, that one where Reese Witherspoon is sort of a ghost but not and, in case you're feeling retro, *Ten Things I Hate About You*. You pick what to start with while we go put the extra ice cream in the freezer and get spoons and bowls."

Neve nodded toward one of the small cartons. "Who needs bowls?"

In the kitchen, Kate reiterated her gratitude. "Thank you, thank you for coming over. I really appreciate this." Originally, back when things were more tense between her and Lily, Kate had been determined to handle life's little surprises by herself. Of course, she hadn't realized how many surprises two children could create in such a short time.

"Happy to help. None of mine are home yet. And the older kids can take care of Tad once school's out. I left a note, glossing over specifics." Lily propped one hip against the kitchen counter. "Honestly, though, all I did was save you a shopping trip with a grouchy thirteen-year-old. You would've handled it fine. You've been...doing a surprisingly good job. Shoot, that came out too condescending."

Kate laughed. "Nah, it was just the right amount."

Lily might not be so quick to praise if she knew about Neve skipping class last week. Was that the kind of thing a kid did when she was being raised right? *Maybe I'm being conceited.* The act of teen rebellion didn't necessarily have anything to do with Kate. Or her mothering skills.

"So," Lily began, "are you going to mention this to Paul? That his firstborn baby girl is an adult? Or is going to think she is."

"Ouch, don't put it that way. The thought of her driving and dating and God knows what else…"

"Tell me about it. Seems like yesterday Brittney was playing princess dress-up and wanted to be my best friend forever. It goes fast."

"And Paul's missing it," Kate said, the words slipping out unintentionally.

"Yeah, but not just since this prison sentence," Lily said softly. She'd tried to make this point before, but Kate hadn't been ready to discuss it.

"I know. You were right about the kids going to Newsome."

Lily's mouth fell open. "Really? You agree with me?"

"It wasn't that difficult." Kate grinned. "After all, *you* said *I* was doing a good job."

Lily smiled back but turned serious quickly. "Will you talk to him, then? You know I've tried, Kate."

It was disorienting to go from years of not even interacting with a single family member to being caught in the middle of a family squabble. Disorienting and uncomfortable, but maybe she could come at it indirectly, without putting him on the defensive. "Since they won't be going back to the boarding school, that part's not an issue anymore."

"But what about him not letting them visit?"

Kate couldn't help stating the obvious. "He's in prison. I don't think he wants them to see him there." Even though she'd recently written him to suggest he send the kids more letters, she still understood his initial reticence about bringing them to a jail.

"And after he gets home? It's only a few months away. I hate like hell that he's gone, but the truth is, with all the kids' fall activities, he'll be back before you know it. Will he still distance himself from them? Losing Heather was hard on all of us." Lily's voice broke and she took a moment, no doubt thinking of her sister. "We don't stop living because she did. I know you and I haven't always been close, but his marrying you was a step in the right direction, being part of life again. You have to make sure he keeps taking those steps with the kids. It would be so easy to make finding a new job a top priority, then fall back into working long hours to reprove himself professionally."

True. Kate now had firsthand experience at how difficult it could be balancing work and family—and she wasn't trying to live down a federal crime. Having a spouse to pick up the slack would only make it easier to work those long hours. Which fit the picture she'd gotten of Heather. She didn't doubt the woman had been lovely, a devoted wife and mother, but had she given Paul the swift kick in the buttocks husbands sometimes needed?

Granted, Kate hadn't been a wife or mother long, but she was learning.

"Kate?" Neve called from the living room. "It's been a few hours since I had those aspirin. How much longer do I have to wait before I take something else?"

Lily grabbed some Chunky Monkey. "I have something to take your mind off the cramps in the meantime." She shot Kate one last look of beseeching approval before leaving the room.

I think the torch has officially been passed to me.

Later, as the three of them sat giggling at a much younger Heath Ledger serenading from football bleachers, cartons of ice cream and frozen yogurt sitting empty on the coffee table, Kate smiled over the unexpected turn of the afternoon. If only *all* life transitions came with frozen desserts and funny outtakes.

CHAPTER 15

Wednesday afternoon at work, Kate scowled at the phone, wondering if it would be unprofessional to yank the cord out of the jack. Yesterday she'd allowed Neve to stay home from school one extra day, and the girl had called four separate times with various questions or random observations.

At least we're bonding.

This morning Delia had called with way more details about an OB checkup than Kate had ever wanted to know. But she'd needed to share with someone, and apparently Alexander had moved out. He was no longer content to sleep with Delia and let her shrug out of more commitment. Kate wondered if her friend was making a huge mistake but refrained from passing judgment.

Was there some cosmic law that stated interruptions at your desk mounted in direct proportion to how much you needed to accomplish? Honestly if Kate weren't behind schedule, she could probably sit here for six hours without the damn phone ringing once. Letting it roll to voice mail was a risky proposition—if it was someone calling with a change to one of the manuals or, worse, something wrong with one of the kids, she needed to know immediately.

"Kate St. James speaking."

"Kate, it's Chastity! How are you, darling? We haven't seen you at all for weekend tennis."

That's because my doubles partner is in prison, which you know perfectly well. Chastity Dillinger was one of the country club women who'd worked with Patti on the fundraiser. Chastity was also the most ironically named woman in the zip code, having "test-driven" numerous men before landing her second rich husband, Gavin.

"I hope everything's all right with you?" Chastity asked, her tone just begging for details that could be shared with others. *You should have heard her. I called her at work the other day, and the poor thing was a wreck.*

"Everything's fabulous," Kate volleyed back with faux enthusiasm. "In fact, I'll be seeing you all next weekend for the fund-raiser."

"Really? Well, Patti told me you'd bought a ticket to be supportive, but I wasn't sure we'd be seeing you."

Kate could still hear the woman reporting back to her friends: *Yep, the convict's wife is actually showing up stag. Can you imagine?*

"Hey, since you are going," Chastity said, "what if we get together this weekend for some shopping? With all the planning I put into it, I haven't had time to buy a gown!"

"Sorry, I'm awfully busy," Kate answered, not sorry at all.

She and Chastity had never been retail buddies before, and Kate wasn't about to start now, spending hundreds on a dress she didn't need when there were more pressing budgetary matters.

"Of course. I keep forgetting you're getting your first taste of stepmotherhood now! That probably leaves you no time for a life *at all*. I don't know what I would do if Gavin's son actually lived with us instead of just staying every other weekend."

Yeah, life must be tough trying to balance four days of partial custody a month when you had a live-in housekeeper and a full-time career as a trophy wife.

"If you need anything, you call me," Chastity ordered. "Smooches!"

Kate rolled her eyes as she hung up the phone. Chastity would fit right in with soccer Claudia, she of the *yummy* and *assistful*.

Having appeased the work-interruption gods, she was protected from further distraction until about four. By then she was feeling more chipper about her day's output and didn't have to force a smile into her voice when she answered the phone.

"This is Kate St. James. How may I help you?"

There was a long pause, followed by what sounded like a...gulp? Maybe Neve was calling to report accidentally blowing up the microwave or some other household tragedy.

"Katherine?"

"Lor—Mom?"

"Yes. I'm sorry to resort to calling you at work, but didn't you get my message?"

Kate pinched the bridge of her nose, trying to get her bearings. It had been juvenile to just ignore Lorna. Kate hadn't called back when she could control the circumstances, and now here she was, caught off guard. She was surprised Lorna even had the number. *Oh, my God, what if something's really wrong?* Like her mother needed half a liver and Kate was the only possible donor.

"I should have returned your call," Kate said cautiously. "Obviously you have something important to discuss."

"Yes. I've been working up the courage to talk to you." But the confirmation sounded absent, distracted.

"Wait—have you been calling the house and hanging up?" She'd assumed it had been kids playing pranks.

"A few times. This really isn't easy. Katherine, do I have *grandchildren?* I called the house just now, and... How could you not mention that?"

Dammit. Kate didn't feel like opening this particular can of worms at her desk. "I'm barely processing being a stepmother myself. I guess it's nearly impossible to register you as a *step*grandmother."

"You don't register me as a *grand*mother because I was such a lousy mother. To you."

Kate blinked, shocked at the directness of the words, although the apologetic undertone was familiar. Lorna had mastered the art of saying she was sorry. Usually her apologies to lovers, friends and family ended with, "I swear I'll do better. If you could just help me get back on my feet temporarily, then I can…"

Unsure what to say about her mother's parenting skills, especially since Kate was in some doubt as to her own, she said instead, "I'm sorry you found out like that. What did you say to her?" Now that the surprise was receding, protectiveness had kicked in.

"It was all I could do not to quiz her, but that didn't seem right. I just asked for your office number. I-I thought I heard another child in the background?"

"Her little brother. Until recently, they were away at boarding school. Why were you trying to get in touch with me? Before you knew about the kids?"

"Because you're my daughter."

"Uh-huh." Not to be a cynical bitch or anything, but she'd been Lorna's daughter for over forty years. Once it had become clear to Lorna that Kate wasn't going to pursue her "God-given modeling talent" or otherwise support her mother, she hadn't seemed all that interested in keeping touch.

Her mom exhaled wearily into the phone. "You probably aren't all that excited about claiming the title of my kid, are you? I got that message loud and clear last fall. When you informed me that you were getting married and that my presence wasn't required."

Kate refused to let her mother guilt her. *It was my wedding day. I deserved to be happy with no manipulation or shame over her behavior.*

"I'm not complaining, if that's what it sounded like," Lorna said hastily. "My own daughter not wanting me to be there was a wake-up call. When I got off the phone with you, I was upset and washed down some orange juice with a bottle of vodka. I was crying and feeling sorry for myself and went over to a neighbor's for sympathy. And to see if she had any orange juice."

Same old Lorna, Kate thought with disgust.

"But she wasn't sympathetic. She told me it was no surprise I'd lost my daughter. At the time I'd recently lost my job and my latest boyfriend, and she told me that if I didn't get sober and find a new income, I'd probably lose my apartment. I got scared. I didn't want to be old and homeless and alone. So I quit drinking."

"Good for you," Kate said, wondering how many times her mother had pledged to do that. Pledged to get more education, stop falling into bed with men she didn't know well enough, stop looking to her daughter to rescue them both.

"You don't believe me." There was no question or accusation in Lorna's tone, Kate would give her that much. "It's all right. I know I'll need to prove it to you."

"You have nothing to prove to me." *I wasn't part of your life until five minutes ago!* Lorna had eloped to Vegas during

Kate's freshman year of college, and Kate hadn't even met the stepfather who'd filed for divorce months later.

"I do if we're going to be a family," her mother insisted, an unfamiliar steel in her voice. Kate remembered her as being more petulant than determined. "When I started going to meetings last fall, I wanted to be sober one year before I contacted you. No booze, no men. Technically I still have two months to go, but I cracked because...well, the holidays are coming. And it's been too long since I spent them with my daughter."

"No," Kate said before she had time to process it. Frankly this was more shocking news than if Lorna had called needing a liver. The holidays were going to be difficult enough for the kids this year. She wasn't adding her unstable mother to the mix. "I wish you well, Mom, I really do, and I hope this cleaning-up-your-act thing sticks. But you have no idea what's going on in my life right now—"

"I want to, though. I want to see you again, meet your husband. See my grandchildren."

They're not your anything, Kate wanted to snap.

"I don't blame you for being opposed," Lorna said, "but people do change."

That gave Kate pause. After all, her life had certainly changed. Not just the circumstances, the external stuff such as where Paul was currently residing, but her. Internally. She found herself not as good at balancing stuff she'd always assumed she was a natural at, like her career, yet was caring about the kids in a maternal, possessive way she'd assumed *wasn't* in her nature. People did change.

"Will you at least think about it?" Lorna asked, pressing her advantage when Kate hadn't argued.

"Maybe." Kate needed extra stress right now about as much as she wanted to go shopping with Chastity Dillinger.

"Well, that's something. Kate, I want you to know I didn't get sober for you. When you try to do it for someone else, it doesn't stick. I did that for me, so I could have healthy relationships in my life. Starting a new one with you is my top priority."

That doesn't make it mine. "I have to get back to work now."

"You always did have a strong ethic, even in elementary school, when you took those print-ad jobs."

Kate clenched her jaw at the memory of being dragged to auditions, at the feeling that she was supposed to be the float that kept their family adrift instead of letting it sink. If Lorna had truly believed her kid would be the only-child precursor to Mary Kate and Ashley moguldom, she must have been sorely disappointed. But Lorna's goodbye sounded sincerely proud. Even affectionate, reminiscent of the smiling woman who had thrown one great birthday party.

One in eighteen years.

Kate was so flummoxed by the call that she headed home at a quarter to five.

Neve practically met her in the driveway. "Kate? Was

that really your mom on the phone? After I hung up, I thought you might be mad that I gave out your office number, but why wouldn't your own mother have it?"

"Don't worry about it." Kate closed the car door behind her. "It's fine that you gave it to her."

"She probably had it before but just lost it, right?" Neve asked as they went into the kitchen. PJ, playing video games in the next room, was just visible through the window.

"I doubt it. I told you before, my mom and I aren't close."

"But that's stupid," Neve said with all the indignation of someone who didn't have the full story. "She's your mother. You're lucky you still have her. I think it's sad that you don't talk to her."

Kate turned to Neve, considering. "Just because she's a parent doesn't mean she hasn't made mistakes."

"Everyone makes those," Neve argued, still in righteous, I-have-all-the-answers teen mode. "But if they're family, you forgive them."

"I'm so glad you feel that way! I take it that when your dad calls tomorrow night, you're going to have a real conversation with him? Not sulk and pass the phone off to PJ as soon as humanly possible?"

Neve's eyes flickered with betrayal as she saw how Kate had trapped her. "What makes you think he even *wants* to talk to me? At least your mother made the attempt."

"For the first time in over twenty years," Kate pointed

out. "Your dad has never ignored your existence, he just doesn't always know what to say. Perhaps you're unaware of this, but sometimes you're not the easiest person to talk to."

On one of Neve's moodier days, that might have angered her, but after a moment she allowed a small smile, proving teens were unpredictable. "Well, maybe I can be a little difficult. Sometimes."

Kate pressed a hand to her chest. "Wow, the world's most reasonable thirteen-year-old! You're not trying to get a favor, are you?"

"No, I was just being reasonable." The girl's green eyes turned calculating. "Although... If I get an A on my history exam, can I go to Rebecca's the Saturday of your fund-raiser? I know PJ and I were going to stay at Lily's, but Rebecca has a run that day, and a bunch of the track girls are going to her house afterward for pizza and DVDs. She said her mom could pick me up on the way home from the meet and bring me back here. Or I can get a ride when one of the other girls is leaving.

"Please?" All that was missing from Neve's pleading pose were her hands clasped in front of her. "PJ will get to play with the boys, and Brittney probably won't even be home on a Saturday night anyway. I'd have so much more fun at Rebecca's. I might get home a little earlier than you but not by much. I'll be fine alone for twenty minutes!"

"The dark house at night won't creep you out?" Kate

asked, thinking of how empty and big it had seemed to *her* once Paul was sent away.

Neve shook her head. "I don't think we're renting any scary movies. Probably just comedies and *Pirates of the Caribbean*. Rebecca's still crushing on Orlando Bloom. I think her mom likes Johnny Depp."

"I'll think about it," Kate promised. "If you get an A on this exam and if you keep up with your part of the housework and if I don't get any disturbing calls from your school in the meantime."

"Talk about your fine print." But Neve was still more or less grinning. "Any other conditions?"

"Yeah. Try to give your dad a chance. I won't say he hasn't made mistakes, because if that were true, he wouldn't be in jail. But when he reaches out to you, will you try to meet him halfway?"

The happy exression was gone, leaving Neve looking more world-weary than any young girl should. "It sounds easy when you say it like that, but it's not."

Kate thought of her mom. "I know. But think about it? And if you want to talk about it in the meantime, my door's always open." *Always*, she told herself firmly. She worked a lot from home, but she had to be ready to push that aside for a few minutes when it was in the best interests of this family.

"I'll think about it," Neve promised. As she walked away, she fidgeted with the butterfly pendant. The one she'd worn every day since her birthday.

Kate chose to take that as a good sign and hoped events were starting to turn in their favor. *About damn time*.

As she traded small talk with a Richmond computer whiz over canapés, Kate was wishing that *she* were in jeans watching *Pirates of the Caribbean* with friends. Her conversational partner was nice but dull. She missed Paul keenly, especially since she'd rationed herself to just a minute the last time he'd called. The good news was, while Neve hadn't been very animated, she'd held to her end of the bargain and chatted for a few minutes. PJ had crowed about his soccer successes.

Kate wondered how Paul had done on his end of the conversation, but she didn't want to pry with the kids. Well, Neve anyway. The girl was trying, and any further pushing on Kate's part might be counterproductive. In nonparental settings, Paul was a great conversationalist, amusing but never snide—the specialty of some of the more predatory club members she'd avoided in the forty minutes since she'd been at the fund-raiser.

At least the dimmed chandeliers and decorative candlelight made slipping unnoticed into the shadows easier. Still, she'd be happy when they adjourned to the seated dinner in the ballroom, where she would be sitting next to Patti and Delia—her unofficial date. Kate was currently trapped in the hors-d'oeuvres-and-mingling portion of the evening, and her feet were beginning to throb inside her high heels.

Everyone she'd spoken to commented on how infrequently they'd seen her at the club lately. The funny thing was, she hadn't missed being here. Oh, she'd been in better shape when she was playing regular golf and tennis and regretted not getting more exercise, but her recent schedule was jam-packed. The only thing she truly missed about the social events she and Paul had so regularly attended was...Paul.

The first time she'd set foot into an upscale place like this, she'd felt as if she'd *arrived.* Succeeded in banishing her somewhat tawdry childhood and emerged a polished businesswoman in charge of her destiny. It had never occurred to her then that for all the outward trappings of success she'd finally achieved, her life had been, in some ways, empty. Despite the troubles she and Paul had encountered, falling in love with him had helped rescue her from a bland existence.

Darting her gaze to the side, she looked for Delia, a one-woman antidote to blandness. Earlier they'd exchanged brief waves, but then Kate had lost her friend in the well-heeled crowd. *Patti must be thrilled with the turnout.* Chastity Dillinger certainly was. Every time Kate had caught sight of the brunette, she'd been lapping up praise like a cat with cream. Her words of false modesty were practically audible over the string quartet. Kate could almost hear Patti's admonishments in her head: *So let her enjoy the moment. You know all her gossiping is just her way of trying to make herself feel better about being miserable in her own life.*

Thinking of Patti, Kate smiled. The other woman was definitely the conscience in their group of friends. And Delia was the "bad girl," albeit an affluent, socially acceptable one. That made Kate the…?

Unfortunately the man who'd been speaking to her took her sudden smile as encouragement to launch into a fresh topic. The second Kate could get a word in edgewise, she excused herself to the ladies' room, where she promptly encountered her pregnant friend.

"Delia!" Kate laughed. "I should have known you'd be in here."

"I should just stay put," Delia said, keeping her gaze on the vanity mirror as she touched up her lipstick. "By the time I finish washing my hands and fluffing my hair, I have to pee again."

"Well, don't leave without me." Kate opened a stall door, checking for expensive shoes beneath the other booths to make sure she and Delia were alone. "I'd forgotten how dull some of those people are."

"And annoying! You're lucky. At least you can drink. I have to tolerate them sober. And if *one more* person tries to touch my stomach, they will pull back a stump!"

The thought of anyone gutsy or clueless enough to pat Delia's baby bump made Kate grin. Good thing Delia couldn't see it outside the stall.

When Kate joined her friend at the sink, she said, "At least you make pregnant gorgeous. That 'glowing' thing is true."

Delia tossed her hair. "That glowing thing is the special effect of letting myself get talked into an overpriced dress in this great silk that I probably won't even be able to wear next month."

"It was worth it," Kate said.

"You don't think I look fat?"

"Not a bit." It was hard to miss the vulnerability in Delia's gaze, as out of place as it was. But the woman wasn't worried about her weight. If she was upset about something, it was that Alexander had used his ticket and come alone. Not approaching her once all night, as far as Kate knew.

"Well, thanks. You look nice, too."

Wryly, Kate considered her dress in the reflection. She'd worn it many times, but it was comfortable. Not a headturner, but there wasn't anyone here whose head she wanted to turn. A strangely liberating thought not to be trying to make a good impression on anyone.

"You won't believe who called me to go dress shopping this week," Kate began, wondering if she could segue from Chastity's transparent invitation for gossip to the call that had come after, from Lorna. Patti would automatically tell her to give the woman a chance; Patti was a traditionalist when it came to family ties. Delia was less sentimental, as her breaking up with Alexander instead of accepting his proposal had proven.

"If you dare tell me that you made time to shop with one of these rich housewives when you weren't available for the agony of hitting ten different maternity st—*oh*."

"Delia?" Kate wasn't as worried about the breathy exclamation that had ended her friend's threat as the shocked look on the woman's face. "You okay?"

"Yeah. There was a pain, but it's gone now."

"A pain? Why don't we get you somewhere you can sit down?"

"It's all right. The doctor said that what I described is normal stretching, and Patti concurred. I never would have guessed there'd be a time I called her on a daily basis, but she's been great answering questions. Even if she does give me shit about Ringo."

"Well, she—"

"Don't you start, too," Delia cautioned. "I think we've hid out here as long as we can without being offensive. Maybe we should go mingle."

Kate followed her friend, knowing that Delia was not concerned about what people thought. She'd simply wanted to avoid the Alexander discussion. Unfortunately he was the first person they saw when they were back out in the party. And Celeste Parker was standing entirely too close, hanging on his every word.

"You know, I see someone over there," Delia said, gesturing toward the opposite side of the room, "that I simply *must* say hello to." She stalked off, making it clear that despite her unwillingness to marry him right now, she still loved Alexander.

He'd noticed her and was watching her departure. Celeste, on the other hand, had noticed Kate and made her way over as Alexander slipped away. Would he try to talk to Delia?

"Don't you look darling tonight, Kate?" Celeste asked, her cheeks flushed from a couple of glasses of champagne. "I've always loved that gown on you. Must be nice to have a tried-and-true, go-to dress. Mine's new, but I haven't decided what I think yet." She did a tiny shoulder shimmy, her expensive fake boobs not moving much as she dropped her voice to a confidential whisper. "I'm afraid it's a trifle more low-cut than I realized in the store...but Mr. Parker certainly hasn't complained."

"There you two are," a woman chirped from behind them.

Kate turned, wondering when she'd become a "you two" with Celeste. "Oh. Hi, Chastity." The hits just kept on coming.

"Good to see you!" Chastity smiled brightly before adopting a pout she probably practiced in a mirror. "I hated that we couldn't get together for dress shopping."

"I decided just to wear something I already had in the closet. The more money I save, the more I can donate to worthy causes like tonight's, right?" Hearing the words aloud reminded Kate of Lily, always espousing the value of cutting costs. *Guess she's rubbing off on me.* Well, why not?

Lily had a lot of great qualities—she was forthright, helpful in a pinch, loving and a damn good mother.

Chastity was still bubbling her delight that Kate had joined them. "Even though Patti assured us you would be here, I had my doubts. You're practically one of those reclusive celebrities lately! Celeste did tell me she actually saw you out with the children about a month ago."

"Notorious, that's what she is," Celeste said, sounding more titillated than disapproving. "The scandal of having a husband in prison? It's like having our own neighborhood...Heidi Fleiss!"

Kate didn't like talking to Celeste much on a good day. Being compared to the tabloids' "Hollywood Madame" was the proverbial straw. Honestly wasn't that scandal a decade ago? Poor Celeste really did need a life.

Even Chastity winced at her friend's slurred pronouncement. "Don't mind her, Kate. Not everyone leads your tantalizing, unpredictable existence. Of course, we're all terribly sorry about Paul, but he'll be home soon. You have that red-hot reunion to look forward to. Oh, someone should throw you a party!"

The two women launched into plans for another social event that Kate ignored since she had no intention of letting her family be used as an excuse for more gossip over cocktails. A tantalizing existence? Yeah, the soccer bake sales and calls from the school nurse were a thrill a minute.

Then again, there *was* a certain nerve-racking excitement in feeling—for the first time in her entire adult life—out of her depth.

College had been challenging, but she'd known she could graduate with honors. Even work was more a deliberate journey forward than a real source of surprise or inspiration. But lately? Not knowing for sure what each new day would bring, what Neve might confide in her or what PJ might say to crack her up…

A waiter passed and Kate gratefully accepted a drink. "Ladies, if you'll excuse me, I'm going to get some fresh air."

The relative peace of the wide balcony beckoned her. Leaving the party behind, Kate headed for the open French doors, passing between two matching topiaries and resisting the urge to kick off her shoes for a few minutes. *Why am I here?* The charity they were raising money for really was a worthy cause, and she was happy to support Patti, who'd put so much effort into the social event. But this evening aside, why had Kate ever networked with some of these people? Because they were successful, good contacts to have? Because they represented the economic status she'd pretended to have on photo shoots, modeling junior clothes she couldn't actually afford to wear in her real life?

The truth was, she liked Paul's sister-in-law more than Celeste or Chastity. Maybe those two were bad examples—not all the women who belonged to the country club were odious snobs who worshipped at the altar of cosmetic surgery.

Still, they weren't necessarily Kate's friends, either. Aside from Delia and Patti, who among the guests had bothered to check on her after Paul fell from corporate grace?

I am such a hypocrite. I told Neve to grow up, that Maddison's opinion was irrelevant. Yet here Kate was, wanting to show her peers she was ultracapable and unfazed by what had happened with Paul. But why should she have to *show* them anything? It had been her mantra for too long. When girls in school hadn't liked her because she was pretty and boys had assumed she might be easy because she'd developed early or they'd heard rumors about her mom, Kate had marched into class, head high, her aloof manner meant to show them their snubs didn't hurt. Maybe if she hadn't been so aloof she would have made a few friends. True friends.

College had been about her GPA and competition in her classes, which had caused jealousy and rumors about her and a young professor. She'd never wanted to be like Lorna, who seemed to care more about her creature comforts than her own daughter. But honestly, until she'd met Paul, hadn't Kate prioritized financial success and trying to finally build an impeccable image over people?

"Kate!"

At the sound of Patti's voice, she turned to assure her friend she'd been just about to rejoin the group, but she quickly realized that Patti was upset. "Is it Delia? She said those pains were—"

"It's Leo. I mean, I just called him on his cell, doing the mom thing since I allowed him to drive to a party tonight by himself and I wanted to make sure he got there safe. He mentioned that Neve was there, and when I wigged out and pressed him for details, he said she just left with a high school senior."

CHAPTER 16

"Thanks for the ride," Neve said lamely as Shane, the boyfriend of Robbie's keyboard player, steered the car into the St. James' driveway. Tonight hadn't been what she'd expected right from the start, so why should its conclusion be any different? To begin with, she'd been racked with guilt over lying to Kate. When her stepmother had said good-night and told Neve to have fun before leaving earlier, Neve had felt like a heel. Everything had been pretty cool at home lately, even if Kate wasn't the world's best cook, and going behind her back tonight had been a shitty way to repay the woman for her efforts.

The really strange moment for Neve had been sitting and watching movies with Kate and her aunt Lily. The two women had laughed together, her aunt clearly approving of her stepmother. It struck Neve unexpectedly, a lightning bolt of revelation—*Mom would have liked her*. Somehow that had changed things with her stepmom. Neve could talk to Kate about stuff without feeling like it was a betrayal or something.

And now I've betrayed Kate. The irony was, sneaking out had been so not worth it. Robbie hadn't wanted her at the party as a girl, just as a groupie. He and the other members had been nervous before their first public performance and wanted the support of people who already liked their music. But by the second tune-up on the makeshift stage in some girl's ginormous backyard, it was clear the band had lots of new fans. Female high school fans whose presence had rendered Neve invisible.

Robbie had barely acknowledged her except to say his friend had to give her a ride home because the band had decided to play a few more numbers. "You don't mind, do you?"

"Of course not," she'd lied, deciding to leave with at least a shred of dignity since she was also leaving with one fewer friend. If she'd been annoyed at Robbie ogling all the girls his own age, Seth had been equally annoyed at her ogling his brother. *How was I supposed to know he liked me?* But now that she'd had an hour to think it over, she had to admit she'd been deliberately obtuse. Because she hadn't been interested in him that way, it had been easier to assume his friendship was merely platonic, too.

"Want me to walk you to the door?" her driver asked. "I can't just ditch you in the driveway of a dark house. That would be uncool."

"Suit yourself," she said. Kate shouldn't be home for another hour or two, so Neve wasn't worried about getting caught.

At least she wasn't until the front door flew open just

as Neve and Shane reached the first porch step. Kate billowed out of the house, still in her country club dress, glaring down at them like the Avenging Angel of Death.

"Where the hell have you been?"

Neve froze, sure that neighbors would be popping out of their houses any moment to see what the screaming was about. Her stepmother had never yelled like that before.

But Kate didn't give Neve a chance to answer before whirling on Shane. "And you! About to come into an unchaperoned house with a girl her age? Do you even realize how young she is? Does the word *statutory*—"

"Dude." Shane held up his hands, appalled. "I just gave her a ride home because Robbie and Seth weren't ready to leave yet. I have a girlfriend. In high school. I don't date kids."

Neve wanted to puke right there on the steps.

A kid? Lord, that's probably how Robbie saw her. She was so stupid. And mortified. Shane would probably tell everyone about this encounter. But she couldn't let him take the heat when she was the one who'd instigated this.

"It's true, Kate. He—"

"You. Be. Quiet. I don't know why you would expect me to believe a word you said right now anyway."

Tears clogged Neve's throat. "But—"

"Just get inside." Kate opened the door and ushered her in.

Shane was already beating a retreat to his car, clearly

wanting to distance himself from trouble. And possible bodily harm.

Very gallant, Neve thought sarcastically, wincing when the front door slammed shut. She and Kate had become friends lately. Maybe if she just reasoned with her…. "I know I should have told you the truth, but it really wasn't a big deal. Honestly you're kind of overreacting."

"Don't you dare criticize *my* behavior right now. Not if you plan to live to see fourteen." Kate had never felt so enraged in her life. It had been one thing to be terrified for PJ when he'd wandered off in Wal-Mart, but that had been unintentional. And he was eight.

Her thirteen-year-old, on the other hand, had known better. Kate had raced home in a turbulent hell of emotions, thinking about the sweet-faced kid who'd looked her right in the eye and made an ass out of her step-mother. Beneath Kate's fury, there had been bone-deep fear. Who had Neve left the party with? Was he a responsible driver? Would he try to take advantage of the girl who'd been so emotional lately?

Neve huddled miserably on the sofa in the living room. "There was nothing going on with me and that boy. I hardly even know him!"

"Which makes taking him back to an empty house a brilliant move on your part."

"I'm trying to explain. It was just a party, and there wasn't any drinking or anything."

"A party of high school kids? You had no business being there."

"I knew you wouldn't understand! If I thought you would have been enlightened enough to say yes, I would have just asked you."

Kate spoke through clenched teeth. "You're not blaming me for this." Paul had gone to jail for his screwup, and even Lorna was attempting to make up for hers. Neve needed to take responsibility.

Too on edge to sit, Kate paced. "No one held a gun to your head to get you to lie, but you might find my foot planted in your fanny if you ever try anything like this again."

"I won't. I only went because of Robbie and I learned my lesson. He doesn't even like me."

And if he did, would Kate have a teenager hell-bent on sneaking out again on her hands? "Who exactly is Robbie?"

"Seth's older brother, the one with the band. I *wanted* to tell you about him."

"Funny, I must have missed that in your little rehearsed spiel about Rebecca and her affection for Orlando Bloom."

"That wasn't rehearsed!" Neve had the sheer unmitigated gall to look wounded by this accusation. "I'd been trying to figure out how to ask about the party, but I was so afraid you'd say no. Then that stuff about Rebecca just popped out, and I knew you wouldn't check up on it—"

"Because I'm a sucker? Trust me, I'll be checking up on everything you do from now until your twenty-first birthday. Possibly longer. And you and PJ won't be staying by yourselves after school anymore."

"What? That sucks!"

"I don't even think you understand the gravity of what you've done, how much you've shaken my faith in you. If your father were here to see this…" Paul would be heart-broken to think of his baby girl as a duplicitous young woman willing to lie, scheme and sacrifice parental trust over some sixteen-year-old musician.

Tears welled in Neve's eyes. "I suppose next you're going to tell me it's a good thing my mother died instead of living to see me turn into such a screwup?"

"I would *never* say anything like that." Kate was mad, but she'd never been deliberately cruel to the kids. "And I'm sorry your mom died young, but that doesn't give you a free pass for making bad decisions. Everyone has problems. My mother was an alcoholic, but you don't see me using that as my excuse when I mess up. And I'll bet your mom, if she were here now, would be just as mad as I am now."

"You didn't even know her! You just married her husband."

"Which is why I'm currently the one responsible for you, whether you like it or not. And right now my decision is that you should go to your room before either of us says anything we regret. And if I hear your stereo blaring out of your room, I'll unplug it and remove it for the rest of the weekend." Rock music turned up loud—the classic F.U. from adolescents.

The minute Neve had stomped upstairs, Kate sank to the couch, hoping never to go through anything like that again. Patti and Lily deserved a freaking medal. The phone rang, interrupting her half second of peace. No doubt Patti was calling to find out if Neve was accounted for and safe.

Kate picked up the kitchen phone on the third ring. "Hello?"

"Hi—"

"*Mom?*"

"You don't have to sound so shocked. I explained how much it would mean to me if we could get reacquainted. I guess I still have a lot of ground to cover before I earn your trust."

Trust between mothers and daughters seemed to be the cosmic theme of the night. "Tonight is a bad—"

"I'm not sure you plan on finding a good time. Not that I blame you, but you never returned my initial message. You tell me you'll think over my request, but then two and half weeks go by with no word. I've been working to become a proactive person, and I'm willing to take bold steps to show you I'm serious. Which is why I've come to Virginia."

PJ preceded Lily into the house Sunday morning, hollering good morning and looking for Kate to show her the cool hand-me-down T-shirt Nick had given him. Lily smiled to herself, thinking that boys were much happier with yesterday's fashions than girls. Brittney and Neve were far more likely to open a full closet and complain they had "nothing to wear."

"I'm in here," Kate called from the kitchen.

Lily headed that direction, then froze in the doorway. "You look like he—not so good," she amended with a glance at PJ. She hadn't even known Kate *could* look this awful. "Must have been some party last night, huh?"

Kate laughed drily. "No." She was tucked into a kitchen chair, huddled in a terry-cloth robe. Her hair was skimmed back into a lackluster ponytail, which had the unfortunate effect of accentuating the dark circles under her eyes and her lack of makeup.

"Are you sick?" PJ asked, his head cocked to the side in concern.

"No, buddy. Just tired."

"Okay. Where's Neve?"

"Still in her room. Why don't you go play some video games while I talk to Lily, okay?"

Never one to turn down an Xbox opportunity, he departed immediately.

Kate nodded toward the coffeemaker. "Want a cup? That's a fresh pot."

"How long have you been up?" Lily asked, pulling down a mug for herself.

"You ask that as if I actually went to bed."

"What's going on, Kate?"

"Puberty. How much trouble did you have with Brittney her middle school and freshman years?"

Lily bit back a smile. "You don't want to know. The nightmares will keep you awake, and you really look like a woman who needs sleep."

"You know how Neve asked if she could go to Rebecca's last night while I had my country club event?"

Stirring sugar into her coffee, Lily nodded.

"Well, she had no intention of seeing Rebecca. This was about a boy named Robbie. Who's sixteen!"

Lily blanched. "She had a guy over here while the house was empty?"

"No." Kate shared the events of the night before, concluding with the emotional fallout. "I was furious. And terrified. And humiliated."

"That sounds like parenting," Lily agreed, leaning back in her seat. "Don't be too hard on yourself, Kate. Even the best kids with the best mothers screw up. We just have to discourage it from happening again. I hope you grounded her for the rest of her natural life?"

"*And* any unnatural ones."

"Good for you. This may have been an isolated incident."

"A few weeks ago she got caught skipping school."

"Oh." Lily was shocked and a little hurt her new friend hadn't mentioned it before now. *She could have talked to me if she was having trouble with Neve.*

Kate sighed. "I thought *that* was an isolated incident. I considered telling you about it, but...who likes admitting that they aren't doing a good job? Which is how I felt at the time. Multiply that by a thousand and you'll have an idea of how I'm feeling now. Was I cocky not to question her story about going to see Rebecca, not to even suspect she was capable of such a bold-faced lie?"

"Of course not. We can't automatically expect the worst all the time or we'd have to be sedated." God, the trouble kids could get into. It was a scary world out there if you were determined to dwell on the negative.

"Answer this," Kate pressed. "If one of your kids had asked to go somewhere, would you have checked with the parent first, at least confirmed the alleged plans?"

"I don't all the time, not with the kids' really good friends whose families I know well."

"But someone you'd never met? A while back she asked if a friend's parents could pick her up for a study session while I was at PJ's soccer game. I didn't even call them to introduce myself. Now I doubt the boy's parents were driving. I think it was this Robbie kid."

Lily winced. No, she wouldn't have let her kids go to a strange family's house without at least a quick phone call to the parents. But then, that was her. She had her own foibles and failings. "Is he encouraging her bad behavior?"

"I don't think so. He seems to be an indifferent crush clouding Neve's judgment."

"Hormones are the devil."

Kate didn't respond.

"Is there something else that's bothering you?" Lily asked. Granted, this was all difficult to take, but Kate seemed unusually defeatist.

"Try *everything*." Kate rubbed her temples. "I'm supposed to be catching up on a freelance project today and all I really want to do is sleep. Then there's my estranged mother wanting to have lunch with me."

"Your mom's in town?" The woman hadn't even come to Kate and Paul's wedding. Then again, *estranged* probably covered that.

"She blindsided me! She wants to repair our relationship and meet her grandchildren. Since I wasn't returning her calls, she flew to Richmond, if you can believe that. Who shows up from out of state with no warning? Although, given our past, that's really one of the least objectionable things she's ever done."

"How long has she been calling?" Lily asked, feeling bad that Kate was dealing with even more than she'd realized.

"A few weeks. She drank a lot when I was growing up but claims to be coming on her one-year anniversary of sobriety."

"Are you going to see her?"

"Not a chance! Give in to her manipulative behavior? I needed time to think, and she wasn't pleased with the results, so here she is."

"Maybe." Lily thought it over. "But will you regret

missing the opportunity if she goes home and you didn't take the chance?"

Kate stood, the purposeful tilt of her chin at odds with the bleak uncertainty in her gaze. "Lily, I'm hell at family relationships. Aside from a rote Merry Christmas, I've barely spoken to my mother in over twenty years. And I don't seem to be any better at the mothering end of the parent-child relationship. Neve has been lying to me, and I'm probably going to get PJ blacklisted from soccer. I don't get along with the other moms, but I did unintentionally encourage a single dad to ask me out. I'm failing here."

"At least Neve didn't get away with lying to you, and I assume you didn't tell this dad yes. If it makes you feel better, I certainly didn't get along with *every* mother affiliated with Brittney's ballet lessons or scouting troops."

"Damn." Kate sighed, the ghost of a smile not quite materializing on her lips. "If you would just get on the bandwagon and agree that I'm doing a lousy job, it would make asking this favor a lot easier."

"What favor?"

"You hinted once that the kids might be better off with you and Bob—"

"That was a long time ago," Lily interrupted. "And I said it without thinking. Kate, I know Paul loves the kids, and you're doing a hell of a job with them. I'm sorry that I jumped to conclusions about you just because you hadn't had children of your own. The kids are in school now, they have a routine."

"I don't mean you should take them forever. Good Lord, you have four of your own. I just thought maybe for a week or two while I try to make a dent in this mounting pile of work. Just temporarily, Lily. Please."

If anyone had told Lily six months ago that her poised—what *was* Kate? A sister-in-law once removed?—would make such an impassioned plea for assistance, Lily never would have believed it. Nor would she have believed herself capable of not interfering, letting Kate sort out her difficulties alone. *Because I have faith that she can.*

"Kate, I can't help you here. Between now and college, Neve is going to screw up plenty more times. As will you. I do on a near daily basis, trust me. You guys work this out now, as a family, and you'll be stronger for the next crisis. If it sounds like I'm abandoning you in your hour of need, this is the best thing I can do for you."

Changing emotions rippled over Kate's face like dappled sunlight on the surface of the water. Surprise, irritation, a kind of desperate hope. And finally weary satisfaction that someone believed in her. "Thank you, Lily."

However, a second later Kate added with a wry smile, "But when she drops out of high school and runs off to be a roadie for some metal band, expect this conversation to come back and bite you on the ass."

CHAPTER 17

Kate fluttered from room to room, still not quite able to believe she'd agreed to this, glad there was no audience for her jitters.

"I may not be willing to take them into my home, but I can take them off your hands for a couple of hours," Lily had said. "Long enough for you to talk to your mom."

"I'm not sure I want to," Kate had responded.

She still wasn't. But Lily had been persuasive. Besides, Kate knew that Neve was still angry with Paul—over boarding school, over the prison sentence and not wanting to see them, over not doing a better job comforting her and PJ when they'd lost their mother. Could Kate push her stepdaughter to try harder with Paul when Kate herself wasn't at least willing to give her own mother a second chance? Maybe Kate was just being stubborn like Delia.

Of course, I have good reasons. But Delia no doubt considered her breakup with Alexander well-motivated, too. Kate wasn't willing to expose the kids to Lorna, but she was at least willing to see her mother. If their relationship never got any better from here on out, at least she would know it wasn't because she'd been too scared to make the attempt.

Family *was* scary. But she got up and tried every day with the kids, and after what she'd been through last night with Neve, how bad could a few minutes with Lorna be?

Now that she was feeling less desperate—talking to Lily had helped immeasurably—Kate couldn't believe she'd actually asked the kids' aunt to temporarily take them. *Not one of my prouder moments.* In Kate's defense, she'd made the request in an emotional moment of sleep deprivation. She was considerably more fortified with coffee now.

And by the acknowledgment that Lily thought she could handle whatever came.

Including my mother, she thought when the doorbell rang. She headed for the front door, rehearsing her greeting with as much focus as a college thespian memorizing a Shakespearean monologue.

"Hello. Welcome to my home." Good thing she'd practiced that or the shock of her mother's appearance might have left her speechless.

It had been twenty years, after all. So it was no wonder Lorna looked so much older.

"Thank you for having me," the white-haired lady answered.

Lorna had been many incarnations of blond over the years, most of them store-bought, but her hair was now a natural and dignified silvery white. It was also cut very short, the kind of 'do you expected from First Ladies, not serial-dating, hard-drinking diner waitresses. Her face was weathered with wrinkles, but her gaze seemed more alert and perceptive now than it had back in her thirties.

"Can I take your coat?" Kate asked.

Her mother handed over a pale blue Windbreaker. "Such good manners. I'd love to take credit for raising you well, but we both know you basically did the job yourself."

"I…" There had been times in her life when Kate would have liked nothing more than to confront her mom. But before Kate was even twenty she'd become a person who suppressed volatile emotions. Unlike Lorna, who'd expressed every thought and feeling to anyone in her path, Kate had closed up.

Although the neighbors who'd heard her yell at Neve and poor Shane last night might feel differently. Nothing like having kids to get you in touch with your emotions. Now she, PJ and Neve had to work together to make sure Paul did the same. Kate knew from her brief newlywed period that he was perfectly capable of expressing his affection. If guilt over sending the kids away was stilting his relationship with them, well, dammit, he'd just have to get past it. *We're all human*.

Including Lorna Brewster. "It's good to see you. I wasn't sure it would be," Kate admitted. "And I don't particularly appreciate that you tried to corner me into it, but…I'm glad you're here."

Relief poured out of the woman's eyes, which were bright with tears for just a moment. But apparently she no longer cried at the drop of a hat. "Thank you for agreeing to see me, even without the rest of the family. If everything goes well, there will be time to meet them later."

"Maybe," Kate said, not committing to anything. The events of the past few months had left her more flexible and open to change than she may have once been, but she wasn't an impulsive fool, either. "Lunch isn't anything special, just sandwiches."

"Fine by me." Her mother followed her toward the kitchen. "This is a beautiful home. I always knew you'd do well. You've been strong, special, since you were born. You were trying to lift your head in the bassinet before we even checked out of the hospital. Those modeling casting calls? You stood out in the crowd every single time. You busted your butt in shoots, then in school on top of it. I haven't done a lot in my own life that I'm proud of, but I'm proud of you, Katherine. From your scholarships to a decent living and a wonderful house with a new husband. You're an inspiration."

"Thank you." The words were nice, but they were still just words. Kate was playing it by ear before she got too invested. Or explained where the "new husband" currently was. If all went well, maybe Lorna *could* see them for the holidays.

But if not, that would be okay, too. Kate knew Lily would help make the occasions festive for the kids, and seeing their father around Thanksgiving and Christmas would perk the kids up, as well. Just as soon as she convinced Paul that the visits were a good idea. She wasn't worried about being able to talk him into it.

If she could sit here and eat a civil lunch with her own mother after twenty years, anything was possible.

"PJ, are you almost ready?" Kate called up the stairs Friday morning.

"Just packing my overnight bag," he answered. "I'll be there in a minute."

Lily would pick them up from school today, having agreed to keep the kids overnight so that Kate could get an early start to see Paul tomorrow. It was the last visit she planned to make by herself, although she hadn't said as much to the children—just in case. She wasn't raising their hopes until everything was definite.

It was that same protective instinct that had kept her from introducing them to Lorna, although their lunch last weekend had gone better than Kate could have possibly expected. Her mother had flown home Tuesday after some sightseeing and sent Kate an e-mail letting her know she'd arrived. They planned to keep in touch, and if her mom continued on the path she'd set for herself, they could talk about all of them getting together next year sometime, once Paul was home and the family dust had settled.

Maybe by then Neve will even be speaking to me.

The girl was ready for school and sitting on the couch

looking over some pages. Was she really reading or just avoiding conversation? At the beginning of the week Kate had assumed the silent treatment was a grudge for being grounded. But Neve didn't seem so much sullen as she did…jittery. Maybe she was shaken by how much she'd messed up and how much she'd upset the adults in her life. Apparently Lily had given her quite the lecture Sunday, adding her own disapproval and letting it be known Lily had Kate's back.

Kate sat next to Neve, trying not to invade her personal space. "What you got there, something for school?"

"Drama exercise. Seth and I are supposed to do it for class today, and I'm making sure I know my lines."

"Want some help with it? You know your brother, he's going to be a few more minutes."

"No, it would sound dumb, you reading the guy's part. Besides, I think I have it memorized."

"All right. But you don't have to do everything alone." At least that's what Kate had decided this week when she'd finally bitten the bullet, gone into Joseph's office and asked him to handle some things. As much as she'd dreaded it, it had been a huge relief. Bryce had even congratulated her on delegating well, the mark of a good leader.

It was only the delusional control freaks who thought they could do it all.

Neve swallowed. "I feel alone. People don't stay. Or

they stay and I go. I...heard you the other morning. Talking to Aunt Lily."

"Which morning? Sunday?"

The girl's eyes went jewel-bright with tears. "Yeah. When you asked her to take us."

Oh, shit. "It's not the way you think, Neve."

"Sure it is. I was a royal pain in your butt and you wanted me gone." She squared her slim shoulders. "Who could blame you? I brought it on myself. Do you know I told my dad once that the schools here were too hard after mom died, that it was weird having everyone know? And then he sent me away."

"No, I didn't know that. But I'm sure he thought he was doing the right thing. I, however, am not sending you anywhere."

"Because Lily didn't want us either?"

"It's not like that at all! Lily loves you. And..." Kate thought it over and decided to go with her gut, even if the admission wasn't appreciated. "I do, too."

Neve drew back, her gaze skeptical. "But I've been a pain in the ass, getting into trouble and giving you attitude. I'm not even your kid."

"In the ways that count, you pretty much are. Being an occasional pain in my butt isn't going to change that."

"Really?" Neve looked wary, afraid to believe what she was being told.

Kate regretted not making all this clear sooner. "Really. I was only tired the other day. And afraid, scared that I wasn't doing the best for you and your brother."

"Are you kidding? You were totally cool when I got my period. And when you let me get my ears double pierced. You make sure we always get our homework done. And that we're healthy and have stuff we like to eat, even though you can't cook so great—"

"Hey!" Kate laughed. "You were on such a nice roll until that last part."

Neve's expression was impish. "Well, families *should* be honest, don't you think?"

"Actually, yes. If what you overheard was bothering you, I wish you'd talked to me about it on Sunday instead of just letting it worry you."

"I wish I had." She nibbled her bottom lip. "I was so nervous. I've finally gotten used to my bedroom again. And *you* wouldn't want to share a bathroom with Davis, Nick and Tad, either."

"Very true."

"Kate? I'm sorry I said you completely sucked as a stepmother. You don't. And I'll try not to be such a pain."

"I'll hold you to that. But don't think if you make a mistake that you're not welcome here anymore. You can't get rid of me that easily, okay?"

The girl hugged her, relief coming off her thin body in waves. "Deal."

* * *

"Was it as bad as I heard?" Cherry asked, jerking her head toward the lunch line, where Seth was still waiting for his sloppy joes.

It was so unfair that not only were they supposed to eat this stuff, they had to stand around awaiting the dubious privilege.

"Our drama exercise? Yeah, it was harsh." Probably Neve's fault. There hadn't been any kissing or anything in the short scene they'd performed today, but it had been a romantic exchange. Bianca had no doubt thought she was playing Cupid by assigning it to them, but Seth's natural shyness coupled with the tension between him and Neve ever since that ill-fated party…he'd frozen. It had been so bad that for a second Neve thought he might bolt from the room the way she had during orientation back in August. That seemed a lifetime ago.

The teacher had told them they'd try again tomorrow and quickly called on the next group.

"Do you think it's because he likes you?" Cherry asked. Neve blinked. "You knew about that?"

"I'm obnoxious, girlfriend, not stupid." Although Cherry had mellowed as the semester progressed, she would always be outspoken. "It was obvious."

"Not to me. I didn't know until…" She broke off, seeing that Seth was headed their way. Getting caught talking about him certainly wouldn't dispel the tension between them.

On Monday she'd been surprised that he still sat with her and Cherry after he'd been so annoyed Saturday night. Then again, where else was he going to go? More than a month into school, groups were pretty much drawn. She, Cherry and Seth were stuck with each other. The thought made her grin. Sure, Cherry could be a little loud sometimes, and Seth a little quiet, but...*it beats being alone*.

He'd just passed Maddison's table when one of her friends leaned over to say something that made all the girls snicker nastily. Seth paused, glancing toward them.

"What, you have something to say?" Cramped as the cafeteria was, Maddison's challenge was clear to anyone in a two-table radius. Then again, she liked the sound of her voice enough that she could probably project to the back row of the Carpenter Center without any formal training. "Because the way *I* hear it, you can't string two words together."

The unprovoked assault surprised Seth so much that he couldn't respond, which only evoked more giggles from Maddison's vicious circle of friends.

Without even realizing what she planned to do, Neve swung her leg over the bench seat and stood, ready for a fight. She strode toward the other table but didn't wait until she got there to address her foe. "It's true, Maddison, acting isn't Seth's calling. He's more of an artist. Really talented, too. I'll bet *you* are a terrific actress, though. You're loud and two-faced enough to fake sincerity."

Maddison's jaw dropped and a little squeak came out. She recovered more quickly than Seth had. "Why, you—"

"You know what, Maddison? Feel free to finish that sentence for the benefit of your friends, but I don't really care what you think of me." Neve spun on her heel, and Seth fell into step with her.

That felt *good*.

No doubt Maddison and her gang would think up little ways to torture Neve for the duration of the year, but what the hell. They pretty much did that anyway. Besides, Maddison might actually back down if she thought there was a chance Neve could embarrass her in public.

"That *rocked!*" Cherry said the minute Neve and Seth sat down. "You are my new hero."

Seth was nodding, putting to rest Neve's belated concern that he might not have appreciated the interference. "Yeah, thanks for, um, sticking up for me."

Neve grinned, feeling liberated and invincible. An emotion that probably wouldn't even last until sixth period—all the more reason to enjoy it now. "Hey, what are friends for?"

Kate took a deep breath, knowing that just because something was right didn't make it easy. *Baby steps*. Which was exactly what she planned to tell her husband.

He looked much the same as he had during their last visit, although maybe more haggard around the eyes. Still handsome, though, and her heart clutched in her chest when he smiled at her.

"God, it's good to see you," he told her.

"Likewise. I miss you so much," she admitted. *We all do.* "But your absence has helped me realize a lot of things, too."

His eyebrows went up. "What kinds of things?"

"That you have had a very profound effect on my life, Paul St. James. You were the first crack in the foundation."

"That doesn't sound like a good thing." He leaned back in the chair, frowning quizzically.

"No, it was. Without falling in love with you, I never would have been in a position to open up to other people, too. Like my mother. Your kids."

"Your mom? You've been talking to her?"

"She came to see me."

He clasped her hand across the round tabletop. "Honey, that's great." Then his face fell. "I hate like hell that I couldn't meet her."

"Don't feel bad about that. The kids didn't either. She and I have some stuff to work out before we decide whether she's part of the bigger picture. But we're trying. Which is what I need you to do. What your *kids* need you to do, Paul."

"You're not still talking about your mother, are you?"

"No. I'm talking about you. You are a wonderful man—"

"Perhaps not the world's best CEO," he tried to joke with a self-deprecating grin.

"And apparently you've held on to your sense of humor. But you're also—" she tightened her grip on his hand, either to dilute the sting of what she was about to say or to make it more difficult for him to pull away "—something of a coward."

"*I beg your pardon?*"

His raised voice got a warning glare and a cleared throat from the nearby guard, and Kate spoke hastily before Paul could get himself in trouble.

"For a long time I lived in fear and didn't even realize it. But I was scared of ending up in a life like my mother's, scared of failing, scared of what other people thought. Or at least giving their opinions too much sway over me. I only truly started letting people get close to me since meeting you. My friendships have deepened beyond the superficial, and—"

"This all sounds terrific," he said sarcastically. "So why are you calling me names?"

"Because as your daughter wisely pointed out earlier this week, families should be honest with each other." She watched his face soften at the mention of Neve. This man loved his children so much—*how* did he not realize that distancing himself from them was bad? "You're nonconfrontational. When you realized that you were working for a crooked company, you quit. Left."

"I stood up for my principles. You make it sound like I ran away."

"I applaud your integrity, but you have to admit that

leaving was the easier route than whistle-blowing. And then after Heather passed away you sent the kids to Newsome."

"Did Lily send you here?"

"Nobody sent me, not even the kids, who miss you like crazy."

"It was a very good school." His face flushed with anger. "And it was a *very* difficult decision. You don't know what I went through!"

She had an inkling. "If it makes you feel better, I came close to making a similar decision about a week ago. Things haven't been quite as rosy as I might have led you to believe. So I came to the conclusion that maybe I wasn't really what was best for the kids. I thought maybe Lily could take them."

"You were going to hand off my children?" He paled. "You didn't even talk to me about this!"

"How could I? When I tried to tell you on the phone how upset Neve was about your not seeing them, you brushed me off with assurances that I could handle it."

His anger had drained, perhaps when he'd realized how hypocritical he'd sounded about her trying to pass on responsibility. "You can handle anything, Kate. When you put your mind to something, you're amazing."

"I'm glad you feel that way. Because I've made up my mind about this—the kids are coming to see you."

"What? I know you have good intentions, but I'm in prison."

"I'm aware. And so are the kids. They love you anyway. Seeing you here isn't going to change how they feel about you. But it might give them some reassurance as to *your* feelings for *them*."

"I love my children." His voice was a broken whisper. "I've always loved them. But Heather... God, she was so good at everything. After she died, I was a disaster. I felt like I was doing it all wrong, like they'd be better off in a stable environment without an emotional wreck of a father who was working too many hours and second-guessing everything he did."

"Want an opinion from someone new to this parenting gig?" she offered. "Half the job is just showing up. That's what they need from you right now, Paul. And if it makes you feel better, we have Neve's vote of confidence. Her exact words were that I don't 'completely suck' as a stepmother."

He gave a bark of startled laughter, then sighed, digesting everything she'd said. "What about me? Any verdict on my degree of suckiness?"

"Well, you were smart enough to marry me." Kate smiled. "So we figure there's hope for you yet!"

Running a hand through his hair, he thought over her proposition. "It won't be easy for them to see me here."

"It will be harder on *you*," she said. "But frankly I think, in the scheme of things, that first visit won't be nearly as scary as the fights we're going to have with them about curfews, surviving driving lessons—"

"I see your point. If they're willing to come, then, yes. I want to see them. I want… I want to be a family again, to rebuild it. With you."

She wanted that, too, so much more than she could have anticipated when she'd first accepted his proposal. "A fresh start for all of us."

They hadn't even been married a full year, so God only knew what the coming years had in store. But she wasn't worried anymore. Kate knew she—no, *they*—could deal with it. Together.

Maggie Skerritt can't get away from weddings…

The P.I. is dodging her mother's plans to turn her upcoming wedding into an 800-guest circus and is investigating the murder of a runaway bride. With her own wedding jitters, and a sudden crisis of confidence about her profession, Maggie thinks staying single—and becoming a bartender—might be better choices after all….

Wedding Bell Blues

by Charlotte Douglas

HN69

Available December 2006
TheNextNovel.com

HARLEQUIN®

Next™

Who said widowhood meant growing old gracefully?

Confessions of a Not-so-Dead Libido

by Peggy Webb

See, see! There is life after fifty . . .

Longtime best friends Patsy Leslie and Louise Jernigan decide to jump-start their not-so-dead libidos and prove that there is life after 50! But when life puts their friendship to the test, Patsy and Louise learn that maybe what they need is to grow wings and learn to fly again. . . .

Available November 2006
TheNextNovel.com

HN66

You can't give to others…
until you give to yourself!

Supermom Abby Blake is going on strike. Having
made her stand, Abby's not about to let anyone
stop her—until her sworn enemy Cole whisks her
away to Paris for some R & R. When the sparks
start flying Abby thinks that maybe this "strike"
should grow into a year-round holiday....

The Christmas Strike

by Nikki Rivers

Available December 2006
TheNextNovel.com

HN71

If only Harvey the Wonder Dog could dig up the dirt on her ex!

The last person she expected to see at her husband's funeral was his other wife! Penny can't bring herself to hate his "wife" or toss his amazing piano-playing dog out on his rump. But thanks to her ex's legacy and Harvey's "amazing" trainer, Penny's ready to run with whatever curveball life throws at her!

The Other Wife

by Shirley Jump

Available November 2006
TheNextNovel.com

HN68

HARLEQUIN®
Next

Nora's life was changing at a pace faster than the Indy 500...

Her birthday a whisper away, she had her first hot flash and was prematurely becoming a grandmother. But going from primo designer to a prime suspect in one day is a bit too much—leading her to discover that older doesn't mean wiser. It just means feeling more free to be yourself.

Change of Life

by Leigh Riker

Available December 2006
TheNextNovel.com

HN72

HE LIVES INSIDE AND
OUTSIDE—THE LAW . . .

**Burt Hammond—brilliant, dynamic,
fiercely independent—rises to the top
of the California business world,
gaining power, money, women, and
glamour, propelled by a thirst for
revenge . . .**

THE MIDDLE MAN

a novel by

DAVID CHANDLER

BALLANTINE BOOKS • NEW YORK

For Rita,
Always my love.

Library of Congress Catalog Card Number: 80-66504

ISBN 0-345-30024-6

This edition published by arrangement with
Arbor House Publishing Co.

Manufactured in the United States of America

First Ballantine Books Edition: February 1982

Prologue Is Epilogue

WASHINGTON, D.C.: MAY 22, 1970

GORDON EBERHARDT, serving his first term in the Senate of the United States, listened as his college classmate, sometime friend and generous contributor to the realization of his political hopes was being assessed for destruction.

- The chairman of the subcommittee, a formidably constructed southerner with a head carved out of pink granite topped by a fringe of white hair, pushed back the sleeves of a jacket become somewhat too large for his frame after a recent illness. His mouth moved hardly at all as he spoke. His authority was unquestioned.

"We have a clear duty here," the chairman said. "But, of course, we must be fair." Another senator had taught them all a long time ago that enemies must be approached in a sporting fashion, else the engine of undoing could be turned dangerously around. Eberhardt studied the renowned senator. Not too long ago the old man was considered by many in his party a possible candidate for President. Somewhere, suddenly, a circuit had been broken; the dream died quickly, secretly, after years of work and nurturing. Eberhardt had heard whispers about an embarrassing connection which could be used against the candidacy. He had no doubt that this was behind the decision to go after his former classmate. He also knew the veteran politician was aware of his own tenuous connection to Burton Z Hammond. Knowing things like this, after all, was what made the senator the power he was.

"We'll be fair," the chairman went on. "I propose to give the man his first opportunity to speak publicly and on the record. No longer can he hide behind his clients' skirts." The senator chuckled, he thought ironically. "Or their pants." Gordon Eberhardt responded with a wan smile just in case the older man had him in focus. He relied on the gentleman's support in many matters and did not want to appear impolite or unappreciative.

2

"Is there any comment?" the old man said. Gordon Eberhardt was startled—the question was addressed directly to him and he had not realized he had been so closely observed.

"Where do we propose to hold the hearings? Here?" Eberhardt's voice was grim and judicial.

"It comes to me that for full media coverage there's no place better for our purposes than here in Washington," the chairman said. "Let's face it, this guy has lived and operated too long in dark corners. Who he is, who he works for, what his connections are, what he's trying to do, they're big news out there. Let's flush him out."

The subcommittee chairman could sense he had them all where he wanted them. "We have been given a priceless opportunity," he went on quickly. "I speak as an American troubled by what he sees happening in our country. Government is losing control. Sinister forces we know nothing about are moving into positions of power with a strength so far unknown to any but themselves. We need one man to embody this wicked tendency I'm talkin' about, someone who aptly symbolizes everything dangerous we want to prove, and we have him now."

At Yale, Gordon Eberhardt had known Burton Z Hammond, an amiable fellow with no social credentials but with the poise, charm and grace of an assured winner that won all the friends any man could need. Hammond never spoke of his family, but he was always free at holiday time, which told them something. He was tall; striking pale good looks, wirey like most guys on the track team. He was supposed to have set some important schoolboy record out there in the California boondocks for the mile, his specialty. Before the end of his freshman year, and for all his four years, he made his mark against Cornell, Brown, Harvard and Princeton. He never had problems with girls, any of them, anywhere. Nor with women. Unlike the others, he never spoke about any of that.

He was always ready to give anybody in his entry at Saybrook College a hand with the books too, and Eberhardt, who tried out for the track team and could only make the cross-country squad, was surprised to find him an excellent and serious student as well as an athletic-scholarship guy.

They lost touch after graduation, but the first time Gordon Eberhardt ran for elective office a check came. After that, it was always a pleasant surprise to find among

3

contributions to his campaigns one from California in the name of Burton Z Hammond, Esq. So he had become a lawyer! California? Odd. Eberhardt would have thought New York would have been more to the man's style. The donations got bigger as time went on; they also came from West Coast unions and companies Gordon Eberhardt had never had to deal with, but they came as cash and with no strings and never—and this was the odd thing—never a subsequent request for special consideration. Once Eberhardt wrote and in return was answered: "Dear Gordie, Why shouldn't I? I choose my friends carefully and never let go unless I have to. You always were a good and straight-talking man. There's a need for guys like you out there."

Later came word of Burt Hammond's intimate association with Jerry Haggerty, the California labor boss who began his career by being charged a Communist in the thirties and who was now said to be a front for organized crime. Gordon Eberhardt watched Burton Hammond move onward and upward with his notorious client. The Golden State Labor Council grew stronger than ever, and its vast pension fund, the Golden State Workingman's Fund, kept growing wealthier and more potent, despite thickets of new laws and regulations.

Why? How? Even here, in a committee which consisted mostly of law graduates, the blame was put on Burton Hammond, a lawyer operating without an office or a listed telephone in the city he now called home. Eberhardt hesitated as a hand vote was called for. He had never known Burt Hammond to ask, even by indirection or at third or fourth remove, any favor or special consideration. And, realistically, what could one senator do? He raised his hand with the other ayes.

PALM SPRINGS, CALIFORNIA: MAY 25, 1970

Eddie Gorman woke after nine, something he was never able to do when he was at work managing the Hotel Sierra Nevada in Las Vegas. There was always a critical problem that only the general director could solve.

He emerged into warm sun and paused on the terrace to look at Mount San Jacinto rising nine thousand feet over the backyard of his home in Palm Springs. The

4

grass around the swimming pool was a green carpeting; the water glistened and danced. The desert air was hushed.

Eddie Gorman dove into the crystal pool, made one turn and swam back to where he had dropped the terry robe. He loved Palm Springs for its quiet and its calm at this time of year.

He got into a pair of walking shorts and shirt in his dressing room, carefully hung up his robe to dry, brushed and—as usual—admired his hair. He was patting it with the palm of his hand to finish its grooming when he heard behind him a voice like cast iron say his name.

Eddie Gorman turned and saw two men he had never seen before and a nickel-plated revolver fitted with a silencer inches from his forehead. "Sit down," the iron voice said.

Eddie's hand shook; he sat down. He saw one of the men take out a length of rope and a small cassette tape recorder. "Putcha hands in back, Eddie," the man said.

"You don't have to do that," Eddie protested mildly, trying to regain the air of authority years of managing great hotels had given him.

"Don't tell us what we gotta do, Eddie," the man said amiably. He found Eddie's hands and began expertly to tie them. "This too tight, Eddie?" he asked.

"I don't talk to machines," Eddie Gorman said. "Who sent you guys?"

A hand slapped his face from the blind side so hard a million little lights exploded behind his eyeballs. "You don't ask questions, Eddie, when we tell you, you talk."

They froze when they heard a car pull into the driveway. One of them went to a window and saw the garage door open to a white El Dorado and a radio signal. "That the wife, Eddie?"

"Send her away," Eddie pleaded. "She doesn't know a thing about my business."

After a moment, a wailing Margaret Gorman was brought in, one arm held behind her back, a blue-gray-coiffed lady running to fat, jewels on her fingers. She was pushed to the sofa beside her husband.

Eddie looked up to the men. "Don't harm her, that's all I ask." He pressed his body against hers. "It's going to be all right, Mag, it's only a misunderstanding."

The room hummed strangely as the men set up the little tape recorder. Only the buzz of the countless motors

5

near and far that sustain life in the desert, the air conditioner, the refrigerator, the freezer, even the swimming-pool filters and heater outside could be heard in the quiet.

"Eddie," one of the men said, "what you're supposed to do is tell us who you been seeing and just what you been saying to them about business. You talked, right, Eddie?"

Margaret Gorman began weeping again, silently. Her husband sighed and pressed a cheek against hers. "Yes, I went to them," he began softly. "Can I tell you why?"

"No one wants to know why, Eddie," one of the men broke in. "They said to tell you they got to know who and what you said when you went. And what kind of deal you made for yourself."

"I told them nothing they don't know. I swear," Eddie Gorman said, his body heaving like a man trying to throw up something vile that had found its way to his stomach.

Margaret Gorman clung to her husband's arm as he talked on, her cheeks glistening with tears she did not attempt to dry. Close as they were, she did not know of these trips and meetings he spoke of, in Los Angeles, in Seattle, in New York, Chicago and Detroit, in the Bahamas, in Acapulco, in Zurich, Phoenix and even in Washington, D.C. She did not know the names. She did not know of the plans for acquiring and building a string of vacation resorts around the world. She did not know of the proposal to move into the international air-carrier business. When Eddie was finished, silence and the hum of the machines filled the room again. She clung closer than ever to his arm, as if to tell him she understood and forgave the small lies and deceptions he had used to cover his absences.

"Thanks a lot, Eddie." One of the men leaned over and carefully removed the small microphone he had hung around Eddie Gorman's neck. For a moment Eddie thought that the statement was all they wanted, that they were going to let him go after all. He became aware of the hands tied behind his back. He saw the big weapon rise before his eyes and then all the lights in the world went out. He never knew about Maggie's scream and the bullet that ended it for her too.

Courtney Hammond found her grandmother in the carriage house, working with the old wheelwright who came up from Los Gatos whenever his arthritis permitted. They were both flat on their backs under the ladies' black brougham. "Damnit, Mr. Gildea," Flora Levering was saying, "there's got to be a way. Whatever it takes, just do it, sir."

The old lady caught sight of Courtney's feet and scrambled out from under the beautifully restored carriage. Her age was uncertain; only she knew for sure. Some books said she was into her eighties; she insisted she was seventy-four. It didn't add up; the daughter of the founder of the line and the fortune had to be well past her seventies. But she was above simple, obvious facts. She stood erect and proud and made her own history, now in stained jodhpurs and battered shoes, her hair a mess.

It was how Flora Levering usually looked at work at Wildoaks, the vast estate not far from San Francisco which her father had built shortly after the 1906 earthquake and which had been her home all her life. There—whether in any of the sixteen gardens, its innumerable stables, the museum-like carriage house or on the line in the reforesting at the ridge above the five-thousand-acre estate—Flora liked to be with the men who did the work, and to use her hands as they used theirs.

She bade the ancient wheelwright keep working under the carriage and walked outside with her granddaughter. Courtney Levering Kendall Hammond was of a height with her; she reminded the old lady of the days of her own youth and beauty—a long neck, a proud chest, bold, blue eyes and a chin that could not be resisted. She stopped dead in her tracks when she saw that her granddaughter, again, had brought another one of those suited-up government agents to see her.

Courtney began by turning to the visitor. "Sorry, sir, I'm not sure I remember your name." She went on: "He seems to think we know where Burt is, grandmama."

"Let's not play games," the visitor broke in impatiently. "I remind you ladies the law carries very severe penalties for—"

7

"How dare you come to my home and talk threateningly to us?" Flora Levering snapped.

"The government is looking for your son-in-law, ma'am—" He turned to Courtney. "—your husband. You have no idea where he is?"

"If we did know, be assured we wouldn't tell you," Courtney said.

"And Burt Hammond is wise enough to spare us that obligation." The old lady brushed a strand of hair which had fallen from the loose gray crown knotted on her head. "Now, sir, would you be good enough to let me get back to work?"

The visitor turned to Courtney for assistance. "What did I tell you?" she said.

"As long as I'm here, may I speak to your brother, Mr. Kenneth Levering Kendall, Mrs. Hammond?"

Flora Levering broke in before her granddaughter could answer. "No one here has heard from Ken for some time. He's done this before."

"Has he been receiving income from the estate?"

"You probably know he drew a very substantial amount of cash from his inheritance. For what purpose, we don't and we did not and we do not now want to know."

The visitor looked from Flora Levering to Courtney. "If you should talk to your husband," he said quietly, "tell him that he can run, he can hide, he can play games with us, he can delay, he can stall, but sooner or later the government is going to have him."

"I'll bet he's aware of that," Courtney Hammond replied crisply. "Let me take you to your car."

PEARBLOSSOM, CALIFORNIA: JUNE 1, 1970

"Hi," said the man in the blue Mustang at the gasoline pump of the Chevron station. It was in the high desert, a hundred or so miles from Los Angeles.

"How are ya?" the man in the white de Ville said.

They did not shake hands, nor regard each other more than casually. They waited for the boy to fill the gas tanks, the man in the Mustang passing the time until the Cadillac was ready to go by pretending to search for something in the trunk. They left together, each having paid cash, offering no word of farewell to the other. Some miles down the road, a sign said DEVIL'S PANHANDLE. The cars turned off there and pulled up one behind the other. The men got out and squatted on the burned grass on the offroad side.

"You got a handle on this one, Jack?"

"Gonna be tough after what happened in Palm Springs."

"Assholes."

"Somebody strings two together and you know what they got to figure," Jack said bitterly.

"So it costs them more, what the hell? This one just got to be handled more special," Muttie said.

"And made to look clean."

"But how?"

"That's why they're payin' what they're payin', pal."

"You got it with you?"

A pat on the coat that hung loosely from his shoulders. "Who you think you dealin' with? Sure, I got it."

"I need time."

"How much?"

"You been tailin' him before you come here. You tell me."

"He moves too smart. That's why we come to you."

"There's all his women. You try to nail him that way?"

"Fucks around pretty good, huh?"

"I don't know for sure, do you?"

"The wife. Got more money and better looks than should be legal. What about that palace she lives in?"

"You got his moves figured?"

"No one has, not even John Edgar Hoover and all his boys. That's why I need time."

"You ain't got it. And it's got to be made to look natural. Did you ever meet a guy who didn't have a hole in his defenses somewhere?"

Down the road a white car was throwing a plume of dust behind it as it raced toward the Devil's Panhandle. The two men at the roadside turned their heads to hide their faces from the passing car. A fat envelope was passed from one of them to the other.

"It'll go bad if you fuck up," Jack said.

"Don'tcha think I know that?" Muttie said. He burned rubber and spit gravel as he spun his car around and headed back to the main road. Jack stood there thinking, and after a while he got into his own car.

The tide was pulled back as far as it ever went. The man walking at the water's edge was bundled in an old Air Force bomber's jacket and a wool stocking cap. The wind, even in summer, blew in hard, wet and cold up here in Mendocino County. The sun was hidden by banks of low, rain-heavy clouds.

Burt Hammond needed time to think. He came to Janet Morgan's hideaway on this remote shoreline because he knew that all the people looking for him would not get to consider it as a possibility for a few days. Janet Morgan was a film star, one of the greatest, a strongly opinionated lady whose career was marked by dizzying highs and sickening lows. Though her work was the most important thing in her life, she did not flinch when he told her why he had come to her house. Some years before he had not hesitated to commit millions of dollars to finance a film project of her own when she found herself frozen out of pictures. They had become lovers. There had even been a proposal of marriage just before he married Courtney Levering Kendall.

He saw Janet now on the narrow path from the windswept house atop the knoll above the barren beach. She was wearing a heavy white-turtleneck sweater, and her hair was flying behind her as she ran toward him. "You ordered a car," she chided him. "And didn't tell me."

"Time to go, Jan," he said. "Can't have all those people wasting taxpayers' money looking for me."

She pressed her head against his chest. "I love you, Burt, always have."

"And I love you. Always will."

"You say that to all your women," she teased.

"Damned right. I never loved a woman I don't still love."

"I've got the career to keep me warm, so I don't mess up the head with jealous notions. But what does your wife say to that?"

"Courtney's a stand-up lady, Jan. Just because there's all that money, don't think she's soft. She's proved it more than once or twice. Thanks for the use of the hideout."

"I'm always glad to get back at the FBI and the government after what they did to me. Don't go back——" she broke off suddenly. "They'll ruin you."

"They didn't ruin you."

"You were there to help me start the career again. But who's to help you after they finish with you?"

"It isn't the government I have to think about."

"You mean you've got other enemies out to get you?" she asked, as carelessly as she could manage.

"I grew up learning to live like a moving target. I know how to survive." He paused to look back at the long bleak beach, the angry surf surging forward as the tide turned. "I guess I'm pretty good at it by now."

"You a crooked lawyer?" she said with a little grin, as they started to walk again. "I was always afraid to ask. You know me, the knee-jerk liberal, the anti-Vietnam War protestor, hate-the-establishment kid; I always put the crime stuff out of my mind. But all your deals. That enormous pension fund. Those labor fatcats. Those racket-guy types. Haggerty, that gone-crazy-with-power labor boss you've always been working for. Are you a part of the dirty stuff?"

"Why didn't you ask me that when you needed the money for your picture?" he said without rancor.

"I didn't care then."

"No one does, when it means getting what you need. That includes me, I'm sure." He started up the hill.

"Don't let them destroy you, Burt," Janet Morgan called to him.

BOOK ONE:

The Imperial Valley

(1955-1958)

1

GLEAMING, so fresh off the showroom floor the relentless desert sun had not yet begun to weather its bright red paint, the 1955 Corvette streaked down the landscape of Burton Hammond's boyhood. Dead ahead to the left was the old storage tower with the marker SEA LEVEL near the top, fifty feet above the ground. To his right the sun danced on water brought a hundred miles from the Colorado to the All-American Canal that had been his father's life, and his death.

He was back. In New Haven and Morningside Heights they laughed when he told them quite earnestly he wanted to go back to the valley after college and law school. They brought out that old chestnut about not going home again. When he broke his reticence about what had brought him to Yale and Columbia Law, the rape of his father's farmlands, the murder, his words had been spoken to the deaf. "He's dead, Burt, it's your life now. A guy with your promise doesn't bury himself in some desert farming community. You could own the world."

"I begin there," he said flatly.

The town had not changed much in the ten years he had left it. The road was wider and better. Shopping centers had sprung up. He did not see as many green-carder Mexicans from across the border as peopled the remembered fields and streets.

At Fifth Street an impulse made him turn the wheel and take the car past the big Victorian-style house where he had met Mrs. Wilson. He had heard about this war widow from up north who had come down to sell a house she had inherited. He had taken one look at her and seen every woman he had wanted since the first day the sexual thrust within him sprang to life. Girls he had had by the score. It had never been a problem. They left notes for him in his locker in school, they came up to him at dances or when he was warming up for a race on the track, they maneuvered to encounter him when he walked or when he had to drive his father's pickup. He was a tall and engaging youth, bold and handsome. He first heard the words, "I love you," when he was twelve. He had tall girls, short girls, timid and bold ones, rich, poor, blonde and Mexican; he made love in cars, in stables, barns, silos, on the floor, in water, or bathed in the desert's 110-degree heat. But he had never made love to a woman until that day in this house. . . .

She was *old,* he had to keep reminding himself, probably the same age as the mother he had lost when he was ten; his mother would be thirty-four now. But, old or not, the lady was electric. He had not felt this way since he and Tom Merrick had peeked through the back window of the American Legion Hall when there'd been a smoker and they'd seen the strippers from L.A. dance without a stitch or a pasty.

Mrs. Wilson had intimidated him, but he was also sensible enough to know she was not only unattainable; she was rich and he needed a job. "I heard you bought this house, ma'am, and are putting it up for sale. You're sure to want to do some cleaning up first before you start showing it."

She had eyed him narrowly and smiled. "Who told you that?" she said behind a cigarette she was putting flame to.

"Just figured, ma'am."

"You're a bright young man. But I'm very demanding."

"I'm good, ma'am. I can do yard work and paint, inside and outside, even fix the plumbing and electricity if it's not too complicated."

"What's your name?"

"Burton Z Hammond, ma'am."

"What's the Z for?"

"Zilch. Or a zillion. My father doesn't believe in junior. He's also Burton Hammond."

"Close your eyes," she said without warning. Confused, he did as he was ordered. "Pity," she said, walking away. "Wasting lashes like that on a boy."

"Mrs. Wilson," he called to her departing figure. She was wearing white shorts cut above her thigh and a halter with a single strand across her back, pretty daring even for a backyard in the Imperial Valley. "Have I got the job?"

15

She turned at the door. "I like a boy with gumption," she said. "Start tomorrow."

She was going into the house. "Mrs. Wilson." He stopped her again.

"Yes?"

"I'm not a boy."

She had him painting bathrooms and stripping wallpaper and turning over long-neglected flowerbeds and going under the eaves to clean out hornets' nests. Sometimes she talked to him when the summer sun was too hot or there was lunch or a pause for a soda pop. She knew about his father and his struggle against the Amalgamated Valley Farmers. His father believed in small farms and was the head of a movement to keep the limitations legally set for the irrigation water the farmers were entitled to from the All-American Canal. For years, all over the valley, everybody was conniving to break the old law, adding 160-acre lots through absentee relatives and other devices. Hammond was almost alone in the fight to hold to the purpose for which the canal had been authorized in 1902; he was universally detested for it. Mrs. Wilson knew about Burt's mother's untimely death. She even knew about his straight A grades in high school and that he had set a Southwest Desert Conference record for the mile.

"Half of me wants to be a farmer like my father," he told her once. "The other half wants to be a modern Alexander the Great."

"And which half will you listen to?"

"My father's in trouble. They're trying to take his farm from him."

"So you'll stay?"

"He wants me to go but I wouldn't leave him. He needs me here. He's got enemies all over the place."

"If you left, where would you go, what would you do?"

"Yale," he said without hesitation. "I read about it. Then the Columbia Law School in New York City, ma'am. I like the idea of a great law school in a big city."

The day before Mrs. Wilson was to leave to go home, he heard her voice call to him from her bedroom. He was sweeping leaves behind the house. "Come here at once, Burton."

He found himself in a shade-drawn room, the air conditioner rattling noisily in the window and chilling the air

16

with a steady icy breeze. "Here, Burton," Mrs. Wilson said. He was blind in the dark after the bright noonday sun. "Haven't you ever seen a woman's body when it's ready for love?"

He began to make out the naked figure spread sinuously across the sheeted bed. He hesitated.

She laughed, a silvery laugh that rang out like a small bell. "Dear boy—forgive me, dear, dear Burton, I know you well enough now to know what's going on in that financial-wizard head of yours. Of course I'll still pay you for your work. I've decided to be foolish now that we won't ever see each other again after tomorrow. Don't be afraid of me."

"I'm not afraid," he told her. "It's only that I've been working in the hot sun."

"I've passed you dozens of times with that hot, clean man-smell on you. I adore it." She lifted herself from the bed, and he saw the cropped pubis, the petals of her rose and the secret bud they encased. He did not move until he felt her hands and heard, "Here, let me help you get out of these jeans.

"Slowly, my darling, slowly," she whispered, as strong and knowing hands took hold of her body and lifted it into position at the head of the bed.

A few days later he was sitting with his father and his father's ladyfriend, Maria Luisa, who came over from Mexicali to do the heavy housework for the local ladies for five bucks a day. The night air outside was still, soft as a goose's belly. Pop laughed so hard at something Maria Luisa said they heard the canvas under him tear. That made them all laugh again and Pop fell to the ground, spilling what was left in his bottle of Acme beer.

Burt liked Maria Luisa. She was fat maybe, but she had a fine chest that was always trying to break out of her blouses and shirts. She was good for Pop. Had two kids down in Tuxtla Gutiérrez, near the Guatemalan border, which her husband got to keep when they divorced. That was the law in Mexico. "I'm a broken jug," she used to tell Burt. They talked Spanish, border Spanish, *pocho*, it was called. "Your father, he put the pieces together."

What got them laughing was a story of Maria Luisa's, about a lady who had taken a dollar from her pay for a bologna sandwich she had made for herself in the middle of the day. "Four dollars I get from eight in the morning until six, and I got to make a chile *colorado* yet for their supper. So I make one so hot when they eat it tonight I bet they explode!"

They sat quietly after Pop found another camp chair. Burt knew it was harvest time for the alfalfa, and he knew Pop's credit was not very good and the contractors wouldn't bring in the big machines unless there was cash on the line. Burt said he had enough money for the job; Pop could always pay him back after the crop was sold.

Maria Luisa was surprised Burt had that kind of money. "He's probably got a lot more stashed," his father said jovially. "Tell her how you made it this time."

"I bought a wrecked two-door Chevy. I know a mechanic and a body shop across the border where they do the kind of work our guys won't or can't."

"He takes a hundred dollars and makes five."

"Six, Pop," Burt amended. "The guy I sold it to didn't have all the money so I get an extra hundred for carrying him for three months."

"A genius with money," Pop said. "With a kid like that I may wind up a rich farmer."

They laughed again and grew even more quiet; Maria Luisa knew that father and son had had some shouting matches about the boy's future. The son wanted to stay and help the father. Down the road they saw headlights coming toward them. A big white Cadillac convertible drew up and Mrs. Wilson got out in a flurry of garter belt and stocking. Burt brought her over to meet his father and Maria Luisa. Pop was sullen. He knew by now that she was in business with Ellis Griswold and the Amalgamated Valley Farmers. There were few secrets along the All-American Canal.

"I wish you'd reconsider your position and come in with us, Mr. Hammond," she told him when Burt introduced them.

"Never," he said and he took Maria Luisa's arm. "You'll excuse us, ma'am."

She and Burt watched them go into the little frame house. "He's wrong, you know," Mrs. Wilson said.

"He loves this farm," Burt said to no one in particular. "To him it's not a factory."

"Griswold says small farms like this are finished. In ten years the new machines will work thousands of acres. Harvests will be tripled, prices doubled and doubled again."

He turned irritably toward her. "That what you came to tell me?"

"I'm not leaving tomorrow," she said. "Thanks to you. Came to tell you that, and to apologize."

"For what?"

"For thinking you a boy. You're more of a man than anyone I've ever known." She turned suddenly and headed for the car. "Will you come by tomorrow?" she called from behind the wheel.

He walked slowly to her. "No. Tonight."

Her eyes went to the little house. "Your father?"

He got into the car beside her. "Knows. Don't have to tell him, any more'n he has to tell me what's in his head."

"You're lucky to have a father like that."

"I know."

On the highway, the car roaring at seventy with the top down, her hair flying behind her, she turned to him. "I adore you," she said. "It's mad, but I do adore you. You're better than anyone I've met in years—and not only as a lover. Maybe I could even love you. Could you love me?"

"How can I love someone who's spoiled everything for me? What'll I do when you go away?"

"You're going to conquer the world, remember?" she said, and her silvery laugh rang out as the hot night rushed past them.

2

"You any relation to the Hammond who—" the voice on the phone began.

Scandals and unsolved murders by persons unknown, even a decade old, have a long life in communities where not much happens in any given year. "His son," Burt broke in.

"And you're a lawyer and you want to help us?" The voice could not resist a bitter laugh. "We got no money."

"I didn't ask that. I said, 'Do you need a lawyer?'"

"You better come and see for yourself, *hombre*."

He remembered Pop saying, back in 1945, "You want to help me? I don't need you in the fields. I don't even need all that money you earn. You make a lawyer of yourself, a good lawyer. Power is what counts, getting it, using it, and that's where courts and governments come in and why we need lawyers. These sonsabitches and dirty crooks down here take the existing law and turn it around to do what the language plainly says can't be done, and there's not one lawyer got the balls to help me."

His father was fanatic on the subject of water; it embittered everything he did. The farm was fighting for its life. The banks were refusing credit, and without their help his father was always refinancing the original mortgage and paying prepayment penalties and higher interest, or taking out second trust deeds on the land to buy seed. Burt, with his instinct for money, knew that was bad. But Pop wouldn't touch his son's money, even at the risk of going under. "That's cased money, kid, your lifeline and mine."

"I'm not going to be a lawyer, Pop, it's as simple as that," Burt said. "I'm going to stay here with you."

Mrs. Wilson had been the cause of another fight. "She's enemy, son," his father had told him, when he had come back after spending the night with the lady after her call.

"She wants to be your friend," Burt had replied. "She says Griswold is getting a lot of capital together and forming a big farmers' cooperative. You could come in. And keep our three hundred and twenty acres. They'd lease it back to you and you could still be part of the land company."

"Her pussy must be pretty good, makin' you think I'd ever sell out. It's you she's fuckin', kid, not me."

"Don't talk like that, Pop."

"Let me tell you somethin'." He came up to him and put a finger at his face. "I may be a stubborn former Okie who don't have sense enough to get out of the way of the steamroller of the future, but I've always been my own man, son. That's a mighty fine-looking lady that latched on to you. She'll honey you with soft talk and love-stuff you never knew existed except in dreams, but if all it comes to is you forgetting who you are and what you got to do, you are nothin', just a rich lady's stud. These here

20

two one-hundred-sixty acres, they're *me*, making it by myself, do you understand? Me. Beholden to no man." He sighed deeply. "Even with the banks and guys who own the second trust deeds and a few local shylocks, not to mention the tax people. It's still mine. I got to fight but I'm still my own man." He stared at his son for a time. "Get out of here," he said.

Later Mrs. Wilson told him, "Yes, he's anathema to Ellis Griswold but also to a lot of other people in the valley. They blame him for all the money they could be making and aren't. He's really beginning to make some headway. They're afraid of him. That's always dangerous."

"That's why I'm not going to college," Burt said. "I'm standing with him and that's that."

"How beautiful the body of a young man is," she said to change the subject, her finger tracing a long line from his navel to where his member stirred to her touch.

"My father says you're the enemy," he said, moving his body slightly away from her.

"I'm also the lover." She had lost all interest in anything but the man beside her. "Why should I want you to go out in the world? I'd lose you there. Here you'd always be mine." The liquid fire of her mouth seized his root.

"I love you," he said.

"What we do, that's what you love," she mumbled. Suddenly he found himself without her. "You are a man but young, let me bring you to full manhood, my love." She lay beside him, holding his head between her hands. She moved it past the fullness of her breasts and the roundness of her stomach. He broke from her grasp. "I don't do that," he said.

"I divined that the first time, my darling. So I'll show you how."

"No," he said pushing her hands from his head. "No."

"*I* did it," she teased. "Don't *all* your girls do it?"

"The dirty ones no one wants. And the *putas* across the border."

"I'm not a whore. Do you like it when I do it?"

"I've never made love to a woman—just girls."

His mouth touched hers; she widened it for him. She could feel the full hardness of his member search inside her thighs to find fulfillment again, but she turned them from it. She smiled as his lips caressed her nose, her eyes, her ears. "Yes, darling," she murmured. "You will love many women." She pressed both hands against each side of his head, fingers clamped to his ears. "Now, my love, my man, you must not be afraid of what a man can do with *his* mouth." She shifted her hips again so his thrusting would not penetrate her. He was hers now, his mouth all over her mouth and throat. She pushed his head down until it touched a breast, then a nipple. "Yes," she said as his lips found an unexpected joy. Her hands kept his head clamped tight. "Yes," she kept saying, "yes." She pushed his head, down, down, past the hardness between her breasts, to the gentle roundness of her belly. " 'My beloved is mine,' " she said, but he heard no words, Biblical or otherwise; to him it was all murmurs and assents as he struggled against her for a moment and found himself lost in a sea of new, delicious sensations. " 'And I am his,' " she said. He still heard no words, only what he thought were cries of ecstasy. She pulled his head hard toward her when she felt timidity, disdain, uncertain reluctance. ". . . 'feed among the lilies . . .' " she moaned, as she held his head tighter than ever. . . .

3

WHAT was the Kingdom of God, and why had they once built a church all the way out here, a weatherbeaten wooden box on concrete piles over blowing sand? Where had the Kingdom gone to? The new occupants had nailed a sign over the door: FIELD WORKERS INTERNTL. Two of them had come out when the red car pulled up, more interested in the automobile than the driver.

"This here an American car?"

"General Motors is going after the sports car business . . . Comes two ways . . . Stick and automatic . . . This is a four-speed stick . . . Had it up to eighty . . . Probably could do better without a muffler and headers . . . Sure, you want to drive it? . . ."

They took it for a spin. They returned exhilarated, but

when the three of them went inside, the elation of the ride turned flat, like stale beer. There was one wooden table and a number of bridge tables, upended boxes for chairs. Disorder everywhere. Piles of mimeographed material next to trash bins.

"What makes you want to help us?" Jaime Rodriguez asked after a time.

"I told you my name."

"We got no time here for squaring bad deals," Raul Portillo said. These two seemed to run the organization. They were not very well disposed to him even after the ride in the new car. "We got money problems, no unemployment insurance, them growers bringing in *braceros* across the border to work for a dollar. Besides, we got no money to pay a lawyer."

"I didn't say anything about money," Burt said in Spanish.

"You speak Spanish pretty good. Where'd you learn?"

"Just learned, same as you. Studied it in college."

"How you gonna support yourself? That car, them Ivy League threads. Them shoes, I bet they alone cost more'n twenty dollars. We don't have twenty dollars in the treasury."

"Look at this place of yours. No wonder you guys have got no money."

Portillo laughed bitterly. "One thing we don't need, some *rubio gringo* telling us what we got to do. What do you know, you're not one of us?"

"That's right. And I'm not going to insult you by pretending to be. I could wear dirty jeans or chinos and a torn plaid shirt too. I'm me. You guys are you, I'm your lawyer." Burt got to his feet. "Still, maybe the growers are right. You guys haven't got the sense to organize a basketball team."

"Wait a minute." Rodriguez stood before him, a beefy man of about his age, the skin on his face down to his shirt burned from being too much in the sun. "You come to us figuring you could get law customers?"

"Only to support my lavish lifestyle," Burt replied with a grin. "It's about time someone reminded the courts the liability laws extend to all, Anglos or not. I figured that could support me all I need for now, but your organization will be my main job."

After a moment Rodriguez said in English, "We sure could use a lawyer," and he put out his hand.

Four days later, four deputy sheriffs with batons emerged from two cars to chase off nine men and two women in front of the gate of the Castroville Ranch where some sixty Mexican nationals had been imported to bring in the lettuce crop. The uniformed officers were approached by a man in a torn straw sombrero waving a sheet of paper. "This here is an injunction from the federal court," he said. After reading a few minutes, the deputies got in their cars and drove off.

It was the first of a series of counter-moves that brought a spirit of hopefulness to the men and women trying to organize themselves in the fields. The *Imperial Valley Press* and other newspapers from as far away as San Diego and Los Angeles began to run stories about unrest in the fields and workers putting down their implements. Handbills began to be distributed in town blaming the labor strife on outside agitators and calling for people to protect their way of life.

When a truck turned over carrying a crew of fieldworkers on the Bishop ranch—which was not one the fledgling union had chosen to move against, being stronger than most and offering somewhat better working conditions for the men and women in the fields—Burt asked Jaime Rodriguez:

"You know anything about that accident on the Bishop place?"

"Sure. The *contratista* checked it out. He told the guys it was really their fault because too many of them climbed in. The sheriff's office agreed. Too many guys made it illegal."

"How many were seriously hurt?" Burt asked easily.

"Fourteen. One guy real bad. Eight still in the hospital. But like I say, they got no case. The *contratista* said he can't even get paid for the damage to his truck."

"Fourteen," Burt murmured. "Too bad the ethics of my profession doesn't allow me to contact them. But if any of those guys happen to be friends of a friend of yours, Jaime, I'd tell them to see a good lawyer."

Within a week, eleven of the injured field workers, or their wives or children, called on Burton Z Hammond.

Not long after that, Burt was stopped at the front door of the county courthouse by a gentleman he did not know.

"I'm going to bring charges against you to the bar association, counselor," he was told. "Or didn't you know it's unethical for an officer of the court to go about hustling business?"

An editorial in the *Press* attacked self-serving exploiters of the Mexican-American farmhands who were mere tools in the hands of promoters and hustlers of the worst kind. It called for some kind of community action "before it is too late."

Burt Hammond heard that the Federal Bureau of Investigation was making inquiries up and down the valley about him.

He settled his first claim against the insurance company in the Bishop matter when the most gravely injured of the fieldworkers died in the hospital.

He did it by persuading the insurance-company adjustor to think of his dead client and his family in the same terms as any American who had been deprived of life. It was a considerable victory because up until then fieldworkers, especially those who were Mexican nationals or Americans of Mexican origin, received token payments of a few hundred dollars. It meant his other clients could look forward to better settlements. "Since we've got nothing to lose and I've got nothing but time, tell your people I'll go to court to get what they deserve." In any event, the tactic worked.

Handbills began to be circulated in El Centro and Brawley. Mimeographed on low-quality paper, the typescript was uneven, the grammar shaky, but the message certain:

STAMP OUT COMES FROM OUR VALLEY

In hysterical language, full of exclamation points and protestations about its belief in what it called legitimate union activities, something called Defenders of American Rights called for citizens to write or wire their congressmen to insist that the House Un-American Activities Committee visit the valley to extirpate alien influences and subversive communist forces. It went on in this fashion on both sides of the paper, single-spaced, taking in the Yalta Agreement, the war in Korea and the continuing truce meetings at Panmunjom, the State Department, Alger Hiss, Klaus Fuchs, the recently executed Rosenbergs, Guatemala, health insurance in Britain, the CIO, the United Nations, income taxes, mothers on welfare, and a proposal to fluoridate drinking water.

When Raul Portillo brought the sheet to Burt Hammond, he glanced at it briefly.

"I thought they'd get into this kind of shit against us a long time ago," he said.

He kept no office. People reached him at the fieldworkers headquarters, or at the county hall of records, or at the courthouse. One such was a large young lady in sandals; she was short but graced with a face of utmost loveliness.

"My name's Helen Mendoza," she said. "I've got experience as a legal secretary in L.A. I came down here when my father died and my mother didn't want to come up there. I've been following what you're doing, and anyway I'm bored hanging around the house. Can I work for you?"

"Someone put you up to this, Miss Mendoza?" The direct approach was not in the Mexican style; he had become wary of tricks Griswold's Amalgamated people or the local police or the American Legion Commiehaters were trying to pull.

"I like what you're doing," she went on. "I've seen others come down for a couple of months and run away when it got to them."

"I was raised down here."

"*Sal si puedes*—get out if you can. All of us who were born here know that. How come you came back? How come you work so hard for us? How come you don't make believe you're one of us? I tell myself, a guy like that, he hasn't got a secretary, I got the experience and I'm good. I've got to work for him. Still, I don't blame you for being suspicious."

"Why don't you level with me and tell me who put you up to this," he persisted. "If I can't pay you, who does, the Amalgamated, Griswold? Maybe the FBI?"

"My father worked the Bishop place for fourteen years. A tractor pushed the life out of him against a wall in a shed. I don't have to tell you how little we got. It's why I made up my mind to be a legal secretary."

"When do you want to start, Helen?" he said.

She was heaven-sent. She could handle most of the routine work.

His own time was being taken by a wave of dissent and opposition wherever he went in the fields.

"This big money you been makin' offa us . . ."

"That rich joint you live in. Lookit the car . . ."

He thought he could handle that kind of thing. He patiently explained the fees he got as a lawyer in the Bishop case were contingent on winning. If he lost, he was paid nothing, not even his expenses, which were considerable. Investigators, photographers. And he charged no more than was usual. As for the Desert Sun Motel where he lived, it might look great to them but it was just okay, he'd lived in better places. Anyway, he didn't believe people should apologize for their dwelling places.

"There's something else, *abogado*," a bandage-wearing member said, wiping his face with the flat of his hand. He looked across the table where Jaime Rodriguez sat. "You tell him, *amigo*. This story we heard, supposed to be absolutely true, it's been comin' back at us, all the way from Yuma. It could hurt the union we're tryin' to start."

"What's the story, Jaime?" Burt pressed him gently.

"You're a Red agent," Jaime came at him quickly, as if to be rid of the words. "That's what brought you here in the first place."

Anger first, then a sense of absurdity made him explode with laughter. But he quickly realized how grave a matter it was to Jaime Rodriguez, a good and earnest union man, perhaps even to his friend, who had once taken a terrible beating in its behalf.

But there were some things that growing up in the times he did a man was prepared for. In law school the fever was confronted, but only academically. Army cadets studying Lee's tactics at Gettysburg could not be more dispassionate. His classmates, he himself, kept apart from the agony that was wracking the nation, whether out of timidity, as some said, or naked fear, as others insisted, or a desire to have a blameless record so it would not diminish the job possibilities, as everyone wished. For his part, Burt Hammond felt no one really knew lies from truth; all the facts were never laid on the table. *Was* Harry Dexter White . . . ? Did Hiss really . . . ? Why didn't the Rosenbergs . . . ? Fuchs, May, McCarthy, Judy Coplon, Bill Remington, the names of the confessed and the unrepentant alike, none had won credibility—Burt Hammond had dealt with them only

27

when a court proceeding was worth a note in the *Law Review*. It was a battle fought a million miles away, on another planet.

He heard Jaime speak: "Is it true? Are you a Red?"

"I'd never reply under pressure to a question like that," Burt said carefully but without hesitation.

"All you have to say is if it's true or not true," Raul went on. "What's so tough about that? For the good of the union."

"The good of the union we can talk about. Have I helped it or haven't I? But my politics I have a right to keep private, whatever they are. It's basic, can you understand that? The pressure to answer can be made to ruin a man's life. I find that detestable."

"You're duckin' the question, *abogado*," Jaime said.

"It's a union-busting dodge," Burt went on. "The people pressing the point now don't give a damn about theoretical politics. They want to wipe out the union. Someone's after you guys through me."

"But ain't you still duckin'?" Jaime said.

"An improper question," Burt responded. "Have you known me to do anything illegal in all the time we've worked together?"

Jaime Rodriguez seemed embarrassed. "Some people are saying trying to form one big farm union is straight Commie tactics," Raul interceded softly.

"Then truck drivers are Communists, and the mine workers are Communists, and the auto workers."

"It's different with us, they say," Raul protested, "because—"

"Save your breath," Burt broke in coldly. "It's not different, no matter who says it. Farm workers are entitled to the same benefits as factory workers. Decent wages. Portable toilets in the fields where men and women can relieve themselves without shame. Work breaks like other people get, even if it only comes down to a drink of water in the hot sun. Yes, and the benefits of the social security system, which everybody else in the country has except the agricultural workers. That's what I've fought for. I left a pretty good future in New York for this. Why? It's sort of complicated. I'm trying to get paid back for what some people owe me. Now you guys can fire me."

He rose, but they would not let him go.

4

"HEY, man, I hear you're some kind of lawyer."

Burt Hammond turned. He saw a garishly painted face, pale, brown skin highly rouged, red lips glistening with gloss, sweeping, frankly fake lashes, blue eyelids dusted with silver spangles. An ebony, shining wig with a flower in it flowed around shoulders bare to below the cleavage. She was wearing far too little dress for this part of the world, at least when the sun was up.

"Yes, ma'am, I'm a lawyer all right." He was polite, but he looked down the courthouse corridor for an excuse to separate himself from this lady.

"I need you. I've managed to find a way to get into trouble even in a shithouse town like this."

If the makeup was shamelessly outland, the voice and the words surprised him, soft and gently cadenced and wholly intelligible. Nevertheless, he continued to look past her for escape. A lawyer knew instinctively to be chary in dealing with strangers like this.

"You're the only lawyer in this town who'd help me. I work the If Club."

The guys kidded about the If Club, a striptease and jazz joint below Main Street. Her name was Stormy Ball. Said she had been busted with two customers driving her to the fleabag where she had her room, when the cops found grass in the glove compartment. The two creeps laid it all on her, and the fuzz bought it. She held out two hundred-dollar bills.

"Can't help you, miss. I'm not into that line of work."

"Hey, this is my career they're tearing apart, Mr. Lawyer. I never yelp when I've got to pay for what I've done, but all I did here was take a ride home after work in a town I don't know very well. They'll give me a record. I can't afford that. I'm going to be a star. How would that look when they write me up?"

He could not resist a smile. Naivete under the boldly

29

inviting sexuality, get-up like a battleflag, take me, mister. Even her clothes, the neckline falling away as she reached to touch his forearm, flaunted whoredom. He suspected she could be a clumsy plant to entrap him with some phony morals charge. Not only a Red, but a threat to the community morality. Silly, of course, but his problems were big enough not to add strippers fighting drug charges. "I'm sorry." He freed himself from her grip.

"You're stranding me, man," she said without rancor. "Can't do a thing like that to an important artist."

Crazy, he thought. He hurried away down the corridor like a man remembering he is late for an appointment. He stopped where an exit gave him an excuse. Maybe not, he thought. Behind that nightmare makeup, behind the flaunted body were the carefully articulated words of an entrapped lady crying out for help. "An important artist."

That night he went to the If Club. The place was filled with faces that had been working too long in the sun. Like everybody else, he called for a beer and watched the bartender push the two-drink minimum at him. For five bucks Burt Hammond got back three, one in silver. The bartender was taking no chances. Around ten o'clock the place began to fill up.

The owner got up on the makeshift stage. "Okay, guys," he announced, sticking out his tongue lasciviously. "What you came for. Or I should say, what you'd like to come for. Beat your meat, I mean your palms, for the one and only, Stormy Ball!" He held his hands up to still raucous applause and hooting. "But first, you got to remember this here is a class act. The little lady does a little singing until she gets in the nude—I mean, the mood. So bring her on!"

She came out in a clinging dress, red and sinuously cut around the shoulders; an even more remarkable figure than he remembered. There was a piano on the stage; she remained good-humored despite the catcalls, assured the audience that there'd be stuff more to its liking later. "I'm working these joints because I need the experience. You see, guys, one day I'm going to be a big star."

"Your pretty ass is a big star right now, Stormy!" someone shouted.

Her voice was not large but it had a golden elegance as out of place in the If Club as crown jewels. The first song was upbeat, meant to get her audience to think about music for a time and it worked. Then she said she would do a number she herself wrote. Burt listened with astonishment to a song marked with knowing, dissonant chords and a high-flying lyricism that seemed counter to its purpose but which she somehow managed to bring together. Her music had blackness but was also creamy white. The lyrics seemed more fitting for the places he'd brought dates to when he went to law school in New York than some sweaty joint where the eternal grit from the windblown fields dusted the stage she worked from.

But the audience grew restive. "When do we get to see the tits, Stormy?" someone shouted. She stopped in the middle of her song, fixed her audience with a stare. "Time to earn the salary, guys," she conceded without self-pity and was on her feet.

Burt Hammond remembered strippers all the way back to the Legion Hall when he and Tom Merrick set up ladders and peeked in from the high window; he'd seen them at the Crazy Horse in Paris after graduating from law school. Little goes a little way, and who cares, was his response. But this lady worked with humor and style. And had a body that turned the raucous hooting mob to suppliant kittens. When she was finished, she was down to a tiny v and nothing else, her hands held so high above her they touched the ceiling. She already is a star, Burt Hammond thought. She owns the world.

She came out in a cotton shift, her forehead still bedewed from her exertions. Apparently her job called for her to pass among the tables and listen to what the men had to say. She saw Burt Hammond as she pulled her arm from one of the customers. When she reached him, she was as poised as a duchess gracious enough to accept a liege's apology.

"You changed your mind," she offered flatly.

He waved a hand at her. "When do you have to appear in court?"

"Tomorrow. Or should I say nine o'clock today?"

"I'll need to talk to you for an hour or so."

"You can drive me home to the dump. Wait by your car. I'll sneak out early."

In the moonless, hot night, vague, paranoid fears again assailed him. If she was a plant, it had certainly been elaborately contrived. A way to get at the men through him. Set him up with a flaunting bitch and knock him over. Perhaps he ought to be more discreet. *"Don't give us that. What lawyer confers in the middle of the night . . . ?"*

She came out holding onto the wig, five-inch stiletto heels clicking on the macadam. "There's always a couple of cats who think they get something extra because they bought two drinks."

He declined her suggestion to confer in his place, which made her smile. "You're something," she said. She directed him to the old, battered hotel built during the real-estate boom when President Theodore Roosevelt's and his father's favorite irrigation canal had been built, many years before. "All right," he said in the dark lot beside the building. "Now tell me everything from the time those two fellows offered you the ride home."

He made her go over the story three times, and it never varied. She was offered a ride home; she did not know there was dope in the car. She used grass, of course, she popped pills, reds, yellows, you name it, but not down here. Not with dudes like this. In her world she was turned on to dope by twelve. She was a music student. She wasn't kidding when she said she was going to be a big star. Nothing was going to stop her. She had a white mother and a black father who was a sideman with Mr. Edward Kennedy Ellington, did he know who he was, the Duke himself? Her mother couldn't take the mixed-marriage life and left her with her father's mother. Father got killed in a car crash, so she hardly knew either of them, or even who she was. She was a black girl with a white mother, except her father's people had so much white in them she didn't know if she was a white girl with black skin or a black girl with too much white blood.

She wasn't always going to be a stripper. She was a musician and she was working joints because an artist has to learn to work in front of people and the only way she could do that was in toilets like this. Even when the guys didn't want the music. She was learning how to own an ambience. Okay, so they wanted the bare ass. But she got what she wanted out of it, didn't she? And she got paid. She was buying the best coaching, she studied with a pupil of Darius Milhaud, did he know who that was? She had done a little light hustling for the bread at one time; that's no good, she went on easily. "It doesn't have the reality of working to an audience. A star has to learn that."

After a pause, he said: "Why do you keep saying you're going to be a star?"

"Because nothing can stop it," she said without resentment. "I've got my very special music. It's only a matter of time till the world discovers it."

He could not resist a smile. "What's your name?"

"Stormy Ball."

"Your real name. I know about these made-up names strippers use, like Tempest and Blaze. I mean the name on your birth certificate."

"It's Stormy Ball now." She was drawing a line before which he had to stop. "Is there anything illegal in that? My checks from this joint, my social security, my driver's license, everything's under that name."

"Not if there's a legitimate purpose. But we're going to have to face a judge in a small town."

"So?"

"So he'll look at that name and think . . . well, what all people who don't go to the If Club think."

"You mean when they see me in person? This person here is Stormy Ball, you want her to look like 'My Little Margie'?" She opened the car door. "And she's going to stay Stormy Ball. If you don't like that, you can back out of the case right now. Thanks for the trouble." She got out of the Corvette.

He followed her. "We'll do what we can, Miss Ball. I'll pick you up here at nine."

"You can stay here all night." She saw the smile. "What's funny about that? Most guys try to get into me the first night. Wouldn't you like to fuck me?"

"Why should I be different? But I have to say, No, thank you, just the same."

"Don't lawyers ball their clients?"

He conceded that with a nod. "It isn't always a good idea." He had decided a while ago that she was too real to be a plant.

"Nothing wrong about it here. I'm the one doing the pushing."

"It'd be too easy, Miss Ball. For me. For you. You see, all I'm trying to keep in mind right now is seeing you don't have a record."

"You know something?" she said dreamily. "In my whole life no one ever turned me down before."

"How many men who didn't turn you down got to know you, Stormy?"

She lifted the hand that held hers and put it to a moist, painted mouth. "I'll probably never forget this." She rushed from the car.

Some hours later, they appeared before Judge Morton Scira. The defendant had chosen for the court appearance a very short, backless sundress; of course there was no bra; the legs were bare. When she sat, her careless skirt visibly drew the court's attention. The reporter, the marshal and the bailiff caught this, so the judge fixed the lady with a second look, this one stern and disapproving. He began by questioning the use of the name Stormy Ball and was reluctant to accept counsel's explanation of the law on the subject with which, Burton Hammond said, he had just refreshed himself. Judge Scira shot a number of thunderbolts at him about it, and about the defendant's refusal while being booked and arraigned to give any other. He was, however, finally convinced that he had no alternative but to accept counsel's reading of the law on the use of pseudonyms. Nevertheless, he eyed Burt Hammond's client severely. Burt was glad he had prepared himself for these proceedings as carefully as he had. He did not give his client an opportunity to testify. On various technical matters having to do with the manner of the arrest and what had transpired at the police station as shown by the record there, he persuaded a reluctant court that it had no alternative to dismissal.

Outside in the blazing late-morning sun, Stormy Ball said, "Is the two hundred going to be enough?"

"I've got a deal for you. Let's find a piano, you make some music for me and we're even."

"Where you going to find a piano this time of day?" Under the happy grin and the garish makeup he saw a very little, vulnerable girl.

"Get in the car, Miss Ball," he said.

"Wait here." He parked the car in the shade of the sign that said SIERRA MOTEL, Swimming Pool and Bar. Stormy Ball sank lower in the car seat and grinned knowingly. He came back on the run, opening the door for her and gesturing for her to follow him. "Bar's closed, but they'll let us use it."

The room stank of years of last night's spilled beer and clean-up chlorine. They were briefly blind when they came in from the glaring sunlight. He found the bandstand, shoved aside somebody's guitar case and pulled out the piano bench.

She looked at the bench only long enough to adjust it, and sat, eyeing him. He found a chair and brought it to the piano. "I'm not even very musical, but I've got a feeling about you, isn't that strange?" He turned the chair around and straddled it. "Who and what are you about anyway, Miss Stormy Ball?"

She grinned. "When I find out, I'll write a song about it." She played a few chords to test the instrument. "What do you know? It's almost in tune."

The touch to the piano transformed her—that and the dim light. There was still too much skin, too much gloss on the mouth, the wig was a mile too high and the lashes long enough to dust off the keys when she bent over them, but she was making her own music, and the intensity covered the garish phoniness nicely. At one point she turned to him and said, "I sure hope you're not one of those people who's got to have his vanilla chords." The lyrics were clearly her own, simple and autobiographical. She sang of a girl growing up on the streets, a girl yearning for a mother who abandoned her, a lost father, her first love, her first disappointment. One song even celebrated her deflowering by a kind stranger, clearly an older man who told her all the things she wanted to hear. Dreams and the terrible cost to make them come real. In most of the songs she sang of flight, and the ones about the dreams told Burt Hammond the young lady was into drugs in a big way; he wondered if she mainlined. He had doubts suddenly about her stardom; in college and law school he'd seen genius burn out. Mediocrity rose by sheer staying power while the brilliant ones zoomed erratically and fell to earth.

He became aware she had not played a note for some time. "What're you thinking?" he heard her say.

"I'm glad I was able to help you." He sighed as he got to his feet.

She rose from the piano. "Why don't you want to ball me?" she asked earnestly.

A little smile creased his face. "I still don't know."

"I scare you?"

"Not really."

"Then kiss me."

He took her face between two hands and brought his lips to hers. Her mouth was soft, surprisingly innocent.

35

"More," she whispered, and she parted her lips to him, then drew away. "Hold me, touch me, it's been held and touched, you don't have to be afraid." Her body was wholly naked within its little shift. She clung to him. "You *are* afraid," she teased.

"No."

"Got lotsa ladies?"

"No."

"Know why I want you? You're my prince, the man who saved me when no one else in the world cared." She found his mouth again.

"Any hundred-buck lawyer could've done what I did." His lips were pressed so close against hers she may not have understood what he said.

"My prince," she whispered, "who wouldn't take advantage of a lady in distress."

He pushed her from him brusquely. "You read too many books."

"I don't read books. I live." She sought his mouth again. "Why don't you want to make love to me?"

"I'm stupid."

"Take me to my place, will you?" she said crisply.

All the way back, she said nothing. When she got out of the car, she glanced only briefly at him. "I'd like you to take those two bills, Mr. Lawyer," she said.

"I've been paid, Miss Ball," he countered. The last he saw of her, her skirt was flying above her thighs as she ran into the old hotel.

He had a meeting in the fields outside of Heber later that day. Word had already got around about him and the stripper. His politics, his living at the Desert Sun Motel, his fees in the Bishop case, and now this. . . .

Later, when the meeting broke up, one of the men said the sensational broad from the If Club had split on the San Diego bus with all her bags that morning.

36

5

HE was back before Judge Scira two weeks later. Three men working for the Madero Farm Corporation were charged with arson in the midnight burning of a packing shed. Police claimed they had confessions from two of them, both of whom had attended organizing meetings.

A big fight at the entrance of a Coachella ranch was blamed on field-worker organizing guys refusing to move when ordered by sheriff's deputies. One of the men was shot in the arm from a weapon which did not, it was said, belong to the police. Judge Scira glowered at the wounded man's attorney, and ordered the man held in a prison ward.

The area papers, even the music-station disc jockeys, blamed it all on outside agitators and troublemakers. "We know our Mexican people," one editorial said. "They are decent, law-abiding people . . . Communist and anarchist tactics, brought into our valley by outside elements seeking only to create chaos . . ." the editorial continued until the bottom of the page. "ACTION NOW," it concluded. "SAVE OUR VALLEY AND OUR WAY OF LIFE."

Rodriguez and some of the others blamed it on hoodlum elements. Burt Hammond saw a larger pattern. The papers were right in one way. There were many more fights in town and out on the farms.

He felt the violence himself. A rock was pitched into his quarters at the Desert Sun Motel. One night, stopping for gas at Emmons' Shell station in Brawley where he had his car serviced, he came out of the rest room to find two men with stockings over their faces waiting for him. He saw the flash of a blade and a hand covered either with metal rings like a set of brass knuckles or a pipe of some kind; he could not tell. They came after him when he retreated, ran past where he hid and found him when he backtracked and was able to get hold of a tire iron.

He was ready for them. "Come on," he said, waving the iron, but they trotted off into the dark. When the police came, Matt Emmons insisted he hadn't seen anything, no masked men, he was busy under the hood of a stalled car, he said, and from the noise he figured some of the local kids were fooling around. The police did not seem eager to pursue the matter.

"You got to get yourself a bodyguard," Helen Mendoza had warned him a few days before.

"Just because I can afford one? What about the other guys around here being threatened?"

"They're not laying for them all the time."

It was like when he was growing up. When he did his practice running, people who didn't like what his father stood for tried more than once to run him off the road. Once he had opened his locker and found a small rattlesnake coiled among his gym socks and running shoes.

His father had grinned saturninely. "Anybody tries to shake your hand, make sure he hasn't got a knife or a gun in it." He thought a good deal about his father; if he had not come back he would never have really known how it was for him. They were fighting a lot at the end. "I don't want you to go to no cow college," his father had said. "We need some power out here, and you got to go first-class to find that."

"I'm going to stay here and fight them with you, Pop," he said.

"It's no kid game!" Pop hollered. "The little guys against the big guys, white hats, black hats, David and Goliath. We need power, or a handle on it. Get out of here and make something of yourself!"

When he got to Saybrook College and in John Jay Hall it all seemed a million miles away and ages ago. Yale men did not have fathers who were murdered in cold blood by men whose names you knew. "Sir, I know who ordered the murder of my father and I can prove it was you."

Pop and Maria Luisa had been listening to the radio in the little living room when "parties unknown," as the police report called them, came to the window and filled the room with four blasts from two 10-gauge shotguns, killing them both. The police were satisfied that a jealous ex-husband of Hammond's Mexican woman, as she was called, had traced her across the border, found her and murdered them both. Arrested by the Mexicali police the following day, the ex-husband committed suicide in his cell—with a .45 in his mouth. . . .

The place had not changed. The velvety desert night trembled ceaselessly with forebodings of violent days certain to come, like an earthquake fault. "Here," Burt said, handing the tire iron to a local policeman. "You'd better take this in case you decide to charge me with assault with a deadly weapon." He got into the Corvette and spun his tires as he sped away.

One thing he had learned from Pop. Run ready. Always ready. For anything.

He remembered how it had been when he confronted Ellis Griswold.

"There was an inquest, a full investigation by all the proper police authorities—even the FBI," Griswold said in a calm and measured voice. "Your father and I had our differences, but that sort of thing is not in my line."

"Yes, sir, I understand that's what you've said several times. I've read all the reports. Those reports are all wrong, and you know it for a fact."

"There are some matters not settled yet, I'll grant that. But, if the Mexican who killed them had lived we would've got a full confession."

"Yes, sir, that's the conclusion of the report. But it fails to account for one thing."

"And what is that?"

"The guy who killed my father was not Maria Luisa's husband."

He never forgot the unmistakable gasp Griswold made at the disclosure.

"The FBI checked the man's identity with the Baja California authorities," Griswold offered.

"Maria Luisa lived with this guy for a while, a year before she met Pop, but he wasn't her husband. Maria Luisa's only husband lives down near the Guatemalan border, and he hasn't been north of Tuxtla Gutiérrez in four years. But your people were looking for someone who could make the story work, and those two Baja policemen they got came up with the guy who said he was her husband and set him up to do the killing. He wanted the money so he must have told them he was the husband. Only they didn't tell him the jealous husband was going to have to get his too. Maybe you don't even know some of this. But you're still an accessory. The order to get rid of my father came from your office. No one was dumb enough to put it down on paper, with ten carbon copies to everybody involved, but I've got the names of the Baja police, even the amounts they were paid."

"It has nothing to do with me," Griswold protested stiffly.

"You couldn't have Burt Hammond around, financing himself for another year, not when you were setting up this Southern Border Land Development Company of yours and moving into the financial big time. Do you want me to go on?"

"So you could make trouble for us," Griswold grumbled. "It'd be a nuisance suit. If you want to go to court, go ahead. We've got nothing to be afraid of."

"It wouldn't be a nuisance suit, take my word for it. Not when a son is after retribution for the murder of his father and the loss of his family land. What would your underwriters on Wall Street think of it? A lousy nuisance action? Or an ugly scandal they would prefer not to become involved with?"

"Yes," Griswold conceded, "you could hurt us."

"Ruin you, sir. I tell you I've got enough even now for a good trial man to prove you an accessory beyond a reasonable doubt. I know the names of the Baja police officers and can produce them and evidence of ten-thousand-peso payoffs. Do you want more?" He paused for a long time. "Since you know I've got it right, what I suggest is a fair allowance while I'm at Yale and law school."

After another very long moment, Ellis Griswold said, "I'll do it out of compassion and because you seem to be an earnest and serious young man. It certainly does not imply that I agree with anything you've said."

"I don't care what you have to tell yourself, sir. You and I may have to settle accounts in full later, but right now, the deal is this: you give me an education and I give you a land company."

"What kind of man are you? Your father's dead and you're making deals!"

"Pop taught me, sir. Always look a fact dead on in the face. Not what could have been, what should be. What is. You can't win, Mr. Griswold, I can't win, not here, not now, but we can trade off my father's life for my education. You still get your company. And you buy ten years without me for my education."

"Get out of here," Ellis Griswold said.

40

"I'll send you the name of my bank in New Haven and the payment schedule. I've got money of my own, so I can manage until you make whatever arrangements you have to make. I want it the week before every Labor Day. Is there anything else you want to know now, sir? Is it a deal?"

Griswold's head nodded. "Yes," he said in a whisper.

6

WHEN he opened the door to the two adjoining rooms of his "suite" at the Desert Sun, a voice he knew at once said: "Burton." His eyes tried to pierce the impenetrable dark; since the rock-throwing, the drapes were always fully drawn. The air conditioner brought in air but otherwise the place was kept sealed day and night. "Don't turn on the lights, please," the voice said.

"How'd you get in, Mrs. Wilson?" Burt Hammond asked. "I thought I'd made enough special arrangements to protect myself here."

"The night maid wanted to know if I was your mother," Mrs. Wilson chuckled. "There was a time when I would've died. 'He'll be so thrilled,' I told her. Come closer, Burton. I want to feel your touch again."

"Let me light a cigarette for you," he teased her.

"I've heard about you clever Eastern lawyers," she parried. "Know how to strip away all pretense. You might be shocked, Burton, even at what's visible by a match-flame. It's been ten years."

"Nine," he said, and sat beside her. "Nine years, six months. I've never forgotten you, Mrs. Wilson."

"It's Hilary. Always been."

"Do you know I never think of you as anything but Mrs. Wilson?" His hand found her body. She seized it and brought it slowly to a breast. She appeared to be wearing a loose silk frock with nothing under it. "I missed you a lot, you know that, don't you? Even at Yale, with all the girls I found at Watch Hill and the

41

Hamptons and Grosse Point, the roommates' mothers I got to ball at the Atlantic Bay Beach Club, the Westchester-Biltmore and even the Bermuda race. Always kept comparing them with Mrs. Wilson."

"And I never lost touch with you, my darling," she whispered to his mouth as her lips found his.

"You were something," he said, finding the zipper in the back of her dress.

"Ten years older now. To a man of your age, a wrinkled and weathered hag."

"You still feel like a real, live woman. One of the few such creatures I ever found, and I looked everywhere."

The zipper went down to her waist. "Take me, my darling," she whispered. "All of me, let me take all of you, let me swallow you, let me fill myself with you."

He freed her from her dress as easily as he might lift and toss away a kerchief.

"I've wanted you so much, I've needed you so much." She melted when he found the secret bud. "Burton, Burton," she moaned softly. "It's been so long, I've needed you so very much."

Without warning, a lamp above her exploded with light. She suppressed a cry of surprise and turned from him as if in shame. Gentle fingers turned her toward him and brought her hands from the face she tried to hide. He looked at her, naked and terrified. Her hair was like soft flax, the flawless skin over the nose and chin, firm and strong, the eyes as luminous and large as he remembered, and her body as slim and elegantly proportioned as it had been in memory, more finely honed, perhaps, slimmer, but hard and golden to his touch. "I've missed all of you, Mrs. Wilson. Hilary. I want all of you again, the touch, the taste, the smell, and the look," he told her. "Let's hold nothing back, what do you say?"

Her mouth reached for his loins. "Yes," she cried, "anything, anything, as long as you're mine."

Later, he said: "Of course, you want a cigarette, Hilary."

"You're an angel. In my purse."

He found the box of English Ovals and took out one for her.

"You still don't smoke?" she said, taking a deep drag.

"I avoid the minor sins. I've smoked a little gange with musicians. Snorted coke and played bondage games with those fun-loving Roman decadents. What else?

42

Played trio games with the wives of a couple of old men who were nice to me. The only thing I haven't gone in for is local stuff, murder and stealing."

Mrs. Wilson coughed nervously and emitted a small and strangled laugh at an unexpected stab. "What's that supposed to mean?"

"That I'm not this fine, upstanding noble youth who doesn't even smoke cigarettes."

She tried to laugh again but found she still could not. "Yet, here you are. With those . . . those Mexicans of yours. That's noble. Charitable, anyway."

"You don't know them. They're too proud to want do-gooders or charity around."

"Then what are you doing here with them?" she blurted out. "I've followed you this far, Burton. *Law Review* at Columbia. A fine job with a big firm in New York. Then you quit, a year in Europe. And now you bury yourself here, among these migrant workers, these poor people who can't do anything but stoop in the fields. What for?"

"Been doing it for a year. Why has it taken you so long to come to ask me?"

"Frankly, I was afraid you'd throw me out."

"You see what I mean? You keep regarding me as this fine, upstanding youth. You're one of the great fucks of history, why would I throw you out?"

"I know you well enough to assume you know all about me and Ellis Griswold."

"Not quite everything. Did you ever put out for him, let him have a shot at the body? That used to agitate me when I first left. Otherwise, you can be sure I know everything that's on the record. You're a big stockholder, on the board of directors. What do you know about me and him?"

"He helped you through college."

"And law school," he added. "You ask him why?"

"He felt terribly sorry for the awful thing that happened to your father."

"Did he though? And so he helped the poor boy get an education—"

"Burton." Her hand touched his mouth. "Don't be a prisoner of your father's dreams. What's past is past. I've found out a good deal about your father. An absolutely marvelous man, your true, hard-bitten American maverick. I love his kind. He was crazy about his land and

43

wanted to protect it. Tough as he was, he would have faced the inevitable." She kneeled before Burt Hammond and sought his eyes until they fixed on her. "That dream, the small family farm, it's gone. You've got to live *now*. Your career mustn't be like your father's land. Lost, fighting for what can't be. You can't go on beating a dead horse. It'll never get to its feet again."

"I *am* living now. You think what I'm learning here is that the cards are stacked against the little man? That, given rich or poor, the law and the courts always wind up with the rich? I always knew that."

"Come in with us then. Let bygones be bygones. Ten years ago I saw a boy who knew how to look a fact in the face without flinching. Hard-working. Marvelous with money. And when that terrible thing happened, how remarkable you were. Your father's son without his obsession. All right, we could use you, someone who knows and worked the land. Who knows this part of the world. With what you've made of yourself."

"How would you use me, Hilary?"

"Sobordco's going to be big. Ellis Griswold may be whatever you think he is, but he's got vision. Growth! The new world coming. He sees this state doubling its population. It'll be the most populous in the country. We're building communities and whole new cities. The state will locate a new university branch around homes we build, businesses by the hundreds will come in, industries and factories—a whole world. And Sobordco will sit on top of it all. It's the future, it should be your future. Come in with us."

He grinned a little. "You're really a damned handsome lady, you know that, Hilary?" he said, taking a shoulder in his hand and moving her toward him.

"Don't patronize me," she protested. "I'm quite serious."

"I am too," he continued. "In some ways even more handsome than I remembered you. I never really appreciated you until I saw the rest of the world. What gorgeous breasts you have, the texture of your skin, even the flesh tones—"

"You're playing a game with me, Burton. I'm glad you adore my body, I adore yours, but I'm being patronized and I don't really like it."

"Then don't hustle me in behalf of Sobordco and Ellis Griswold," he said bluntly. "I can understand why you think he's marvelous. He's made you very rich and you're nowhere near the end of the road. To me he's a murderer or an accessory to murder."

"Burton, you're a lawyer. You know those charges could not be proved then. Certainly not now. You're looking for scapegoats."

"Not for scapegoats. Not for revenge against my father's killers. All I know for sure is it begins here, even if I can't tell you what the hell it is. But I'm sure of this. Griswold may have made it possible for me to be the man my father wanted me to be. But it doesn't square his account with me."

"Your father had many enemies out there, Burton. You have them too. Don't you think I know? Don't you think I hear things when I come down here? And it's not that ridiculous union that can't get off the ground and never will. It's a flea-bite, to us, to all the big land companies. You have enemies everywhere, even among those people as well as among the nice, church-going people in the towns, among the farmers themselves, even those who haven't put in with us but have formed their own big farms. You live here in this guarded fortress, behind drawn drapes. They tell me you can hardly be reached by phone. There are a lot of people out there who want you removed. Don't blame it all on one man."

"Are you warning me?"

"I'm telling you what I know. You know the desert better than I, Burton. It's always life or death."

"It's why I'm here, Hilary. *Viva la vida.*"

"It all points to death. Organizing the unorganizable, people whose work doesn't allow them roots, who have to follow crops and whom you've got to lose every harvest time. Fighting against the plain old self-interest of the locals. Sowing fear and hate wherever you go, even among the lawyers. I hear they wanted to throw you out of the bar association only you weren't a member. It's all negative. It's all deathwish."

"I'm going to tell you a story, Hilary," he said, unperturbed; "and that will end it. After I quit the law factory I went to Europe for a year. Lots of lovely ladies. My kind. I had to beat them off with a stick. There was one who didn't seem to tumble and of course when you're playing the game that makes it more fun. She was fantastic, beautiful and insolent about it, with good cause. I wanted her because though she had a title, she was gorgeously common, born to fuck, good for nothing but to fuck and you knew she was good at it and liked to prove it. But with me she played hard to get. In a way that made it even more fun. I worked to break her down. It was only a matter of time when I could have her, when she began to talk to me of her dreams and her politics. She turned out to have a narrow, squalid mind, full of hate for the poor, a proto-Nazi with the garbage of anti-Semitic sentiments, hating blacks and wogs, which meant all non-European non-blonds. My problem was: I loathe what the lady is saying and represents. Do I drop her or do I first get the ass I've been working so hard for?"

Hilary Wilson found the packet of cigarettes, opened the box and took out a cigarette. She had to lift herself to find a match and she seemed not at all surprised that Burt Hammond made no effort to help her. When she lit the cigarette, she took a deep drag and said, the smoke covering her words: "What did you do?"

"This," he said, and took the cigarette from her hands and put it out. Then he seized her hips and brought her body where he wanted it.

7

At Matt Emmons' service station, the lights were out, the pumps were locked for the night and Matt and Johnny Franco were finishing what was left in the bottle of VO. "I can't take the chance," Matt said, swinging the paper cup to his lips.

"What chance? All you got to do is leave me alone for a half-hour."

"Yeah, but what if—?"

"There ain't gonna be a *what-if*," Johnny Franco said, pushing his own half-filled cup to Matt. When Johnny Franco promised something he always came through. People always said, Johnny Franco was a Mexican but he didn't behave like a Mexican. Or think like one. He was like us, they said. Johnny said that too. He would speak of "them," meaning Mexicans, and "us," meaning everybody else and Johnny Franco. Johnny started as a foreman in the fields but he was too smart for that, got into contracting labor from both sides of the border and then got into bigger stuff. People said he had connections to the important people, like Ellis Griswold and the agents for the conglomerates who were buying into the valley. Johnny never affirmed or denied.

"You're gonna get that improvement loan, Matt." Matt Emmons knew most of his problems were over, but Johnny Franco could still see the doubt in Matt's eyes. "Now whadaya say?"

"I need it bad, John, you know that, but I'm scared."

"Accidents like that happen, you yourself told me."

"Once in a million."

"That's all the percentage I need."

"They could find out where the saw cut the rod half-way through."

"They'd have to look, wouldn't they?" Johnny Franco put what was left in the VO bottle into Matt's cup. "No one's going to look at anything. I'll see to that. Would I let you down?"

"The car's wheels in front buckle like they turned to mush, I tell you, it's scary. Every car I seen it happen to turned over like a crazy top, even at forty. And he goes a lot faster. Top down and no roll bar."

"You awready told me, Matt," Johnny Franco said impatiently. "The next time he brings it in for service."

"Why involve me?" Matt pleaded hopelessly.

"You're *not* involved. It's got to look like an accident, so I need a hoist, and yours is the one this car gets to see. I'm gonna owe you the fattest favor in your life and it won't cost you nothing."

Two weeks later, someone called Johnny to a phone. "It's here for an oil change and lube job," Matt said, without identifying himself.

"When's it have to go back?"

"Don't need it till tomorrow morning."

"See how easy it is? Leave it up in the air and close up soon's it's dark."

"Johnny," Matt Emmons said, "I got a chance to buy this corner. I need forty-two hundred to what I've got."

"So the lot's yours, Matt," Johnny Franco said. "Congratulations."

* * *

The red Corvette was rifling up 111 the next morning, the long stretch of the Salton Sea glistening to its left as it headed north. The front left wheel began to shake at eighty. Burt Hammond brought it down to seventy but the shaking persisted. Something new, he thought, taking his foot from the accelerator. He was coasting when the whole front end collapsed and the car flew apart in his hands. The fiberglass body splintered like a crystal ball around him. Fire and hot metal and stone engorged him in an open furnace. It was ten minutes before another car came upon the wreck. When the ambulance finally got there, attendants saw Burt Hammond and took him for dead.

BOOK TWO:

The Sonora Desert

(1958-1959)

1

HELEN Mendoza's meeting with Jerry Haggerty in San
Francisco had been planned for months, but she had
known nothing about it until today. The Haggerty name
was known to her, as it was known up and down the
Pacific coast, as that of a controversial Bay Area labor
boss. Had Helen Mendoza been aware Jerry Haggerty
was looking for her, she would have spent sleepless
nights. His reputation was far more intimidating than the
man. Some said Haggerty was tied to mobster elements
in Las Vegas, Chicago, Detroit and New York; others
told stories of his ruthlessness in wiping out opposition
within the unions he controlled; everybody agreed that
his power in Sacramento, Washington and in the labor
world had not yet been exerted to its full extent. "Jerry
wants" or "Jerry thinks" was always enough. A discreet
and generous contributor to many campaign chests, he
asked few favors but received many.

Of course, he had enemies enough to drown a lesser
man. In the recent past, many senators, particularly the
McClellan committee charged with investigating corrupt
labor practices, more particularly its young, contentious
chief counsel, Robert Kennedy, had been after his jugu-
lar. Jerry Haggerty was now used to this. It had been part
of his life from the moment he surfaced as a significant
figure in West Coast labor some twenty years before.
Deportation proceedings to return him to his native Ire-
land had been directed against him no less than three
times. Two attorney-generals of the United States thought
the cases were futile and unconstitutional, but powerful
senators who hated Haggerty went ahead anyway. There
were even courts which upheld them. Twice the Supreme
Court of the United States refused to sustain such rul-
ings. Six times he had been interrogated by government
committees to prove him subversive so that his citizen-
ship could be canceled.

He was a marvelous witness. He was frank, he was colorful, he was articulate, he was honest, direct, witty, capable of charming even ardent adversaries. In the Bay Area, employer groups which had once charged him as a man resolved to destroy the city now regarded him as a civic leader. Still, many believed him to be a crook, even if the openness of his own enterprises deflated their charges. Once he was hectored in court by a hostile Robert Kennedy who demanded to know why he had formed a very profitable personal company which employed members of one of the unions under his control. Haggerty was astonished at the young counsel's naivete. "If I have money to invest, why shouldn't I put it to work in a business I know something about?" he asked. What made him a formidable foe was that he had the total loyalty of hundreds of thousands of union men. They knew Jerry Haggerty always came through for them where it counted—in the money they earned.

He was a small man, wiry and agile. He remained remarkably fit for a man who walked no farther than from chair to car. He drank Irish whiskey in hearty and endless quantities and managed on no more than four hours sleep. He truly loved the men in his unions, and they felt it because there was hardly a ripple of opposition to him. By now, Jerry Haggerty was a man who insisted on having his own way, every time and in every situation and in every detail.

Helen Mendoza had to wonder why so important a man sat with a mere secretary. She also wondered why he was so gentle with her. He took the time to tell her how Burt Hammond had come to his attention long before the unfortunate incident on 111. He told her he regarded Hammond's work in the Imperial Valley as impressive but misdirected. He was impressed by the way Hammond had handled himself when the employer groups began subverting the membership and the local political hacks and the power establishment tried to destroy him.

He leaned back in his chair and told Helen Mendoza that he had some of his people try to locate Hammond after he skipped the hospital. "Pretty foolhardy on the guy's part," he commented. He had been told the doctors thought Hammond would be lucky to walk unaided again. Crippled or not, he believed Burt Hammond belonged in the Bay Area. Was the guy nuts, interrupting therapy? Had all the violence affected his judgment? Was he a hopeless case?

Helen Mendoza, sitting before Jerry Haggerty in the offices of the Pacific States Labor Council on Market Street, was not talking, not to Haggerty, just as she had not spoken more than routing denials to the police, not to insurance investigators, not even to contrite friends and associates like Jaime Rodriguez, anxious to prove their regret. . . .

She had been in the hospital when Burt had finally come through the fog of pain-killing drugs. "How long've I been here?" he asked her thickly.

"About three weeks."

Burt Hammond looked up at the cross-webbing of ropes and pulleys supporting his legs. His free hand reached up slowly and touched the bandages, thick over what had been his unscarred face. "What's all this add up to, Helen?"

"You're going to be all right."

"Don't lie. It looks bad."

"It is bad. A lot depends on you, they say."

"My legs, they going to be okay?"

"Maybe."

"My face?"

"Burns. Also abrasions. You were thrown from the car, safety belt and all. You'll need plastic surgery."

"The legs, that's the big problem, huh? How extensive? Don't hold back."

"Muscle tissue's there, but it's torn up. Most people get discouraged trying to get everything working again. It's going to be a long pull."

"I've got to get out of this place right now," Burt Hammond said suddenly.

"You crazy?" she cried out.

"I want you to get my car, wherever it is, and haul it to a private garage and keep that garage locked. You got all that?"

"Yes, of course. But don't worry about your car now."

"They'll try to kill me again."

"You're paranoid—"

"Listen," he snapped, "save your opinions about me. Do what I say."

She was there also when Burt Hammond spoke to his doctor for the first time.

"What is your name?" Burt said.

"I'm Doctor Philip Corry."

"How come you took me as a patient?"

"I'm chief of orthopedics here."

"Is that how it's usually done? Anybody who comes through the door?"

"When it's a critical emergency injury case. This lady said you had no physician of your own."

"You know who I am?"

"Of course."

"I have to tell you, Doctor. I'm afraid for my life here."

He saw Helen Mendoza and the doctor exchange a hopeless and incredulous glance.

"You're going to be all right," the doctor assured him. "This is a hospital."

"I want my door locked at all times. I want no one to come in without permission."

"Can't be done, Mr. Hammond," the doctor said. "You need extensive treatment, massage at least four times a day, physical therapy. There's got to be a lot of people looking after you."

Burt stared at him with dark, searching eyes, a look Dr. Corry did not comprehend because he himself had never seen the face of death inches from his own. "Okay," Burt said softly but without resignation.

When they were alone, Burt said: "I don't trust any of them. You're going to have to find a place to take me. Where I can hide."

"You *are* crazy," Helen said. "First, pray you can walk again."

"I'll walk all right," Burt said. "Buy a used half-ton pickup truck. Get a tarp fitted across the back. Take out all the money from the personal account, a chunk at a time. Every few days so it won't be too obvious."

He planned his moves so when he was gone he would leave no trace. He told her to look across the border for a hiding place, somewhere remote, where they knew about massage and could be trusted not to talk about the stranger among them. She worked at it as the days went by and his routine of therapy and massage began. He watched carefully everything they did.

He made no controversy when the details of his accident were spelled out for him. The police officers first on the scene had reported a powerful stench of gin in the wreck. He knew it was a fake; the bottle had been planted by whoever did something to the car. They had made no examination for alcohol in his body when he was brought in. "You were too far gone for that," he was told. "Our first job was to save your life."

Helen told him what was left of the Corvette could not be found. It was explained to her there had been some unfortunate goof-up and the wreck had already been trucked to a disposal yard as scrap with a load of other totals. The insurance company had already agreed to pay off its full value so there was no need to have the car. Retail, not Blue Book wholesale, she was assured.

"Someone's got to be damned scared," Burt Hammond had said. . . .

None of this did Helen Mendoza tell Jerry Haggerty. She had her instructions from Burt. Haggerty had been clever enough to trick her into coming north to see an aunt she had not heard from in years, but she was not going to give him what he wanted.

"All right," Haggerty conceded, "you don't want to talk. At least, tell me, how's he feel? That's the important thing."

"He's all right."

"Does he know what really happened?"

"He's got a pretty good idea." Like a carefully prepared witness, her responses were parsimonious. She had got over feeling intimidated by Haggerty's powerful presence.

"Where is he?"

"Where he's all right."

"What do you mean, *all right?* I understand the doctors figured he'd be lucky to walk again and he disappears just like that. Can he move around now?"

Helen stirred uneasily. "I'm not supposed to talk about him."

"Does he know you're here?"

"No."

"I'm only looking to do him good," Haggerty said, secretly admiring the fat girl.

"He's doing okay. He doesn't need any help."

"Was he afraid when he skipped from the hospital?"

"He's never afraid."

"Afraid's the wrong word. I guess he figured whoever got at that car might go after him in his room, right?"

"I'm not supposed to talk about any of that either," Helen said stiffly.

54

"Okay," Haggerty said. "I want to be his friend, can you believe that?"

"Why should I?"

"Because I don't lie, lady," Haggerty said, hammering every word. "Jerry Haggerty doesn't extend the hand easily but when he does it's out there for good. I like what I hear about your boss. I could use him around here. Do you believe that at least?"

"Yes."

"Okay. Then I've got to know a few things and I'm not going to make a fink out of you. By the way, I like you too. I like standup people. Can he walk?"

"Now, yes."

"What does that mean?"

"He couldn't for a while."

"But now, yes? Good. By himself? He using crutches?"

"He's walking by himself," Helen said, her eyes misting.

"What else?"

"The face took a terrible beating. There were burns . . ."

"Bad as all that?"

"Skin's a little tighter on the forehead, some minor scarring, but he looks good. Got the best plastic surgeon in Mexico City to fix him up. I'm talking too much."

Haggerty waved his hand carelessly. "He need money?" She shook her head.

"How often you get to see him?"

She did not answer that one.

"He can work for me. Tell him that."

"He wouldn't."

"What makes you so sure?"

"I know him. He'd want to work for himself."

"Hah! Even better!" Haggerty burst out a roar of approval. "What the hell, I don't need another in-house wise-kid lawyer! You tell him, he opens an office here, he's got himself me for a client."

"He likes it where he is."

"I'm offering him one of the great cities of the world—"

"He's not going anywhere."

"—where a man can make it big."

"He's not interested in making it big."

"That's not the man I found out about. This town is

55

for him. Name your pleasure, it's here. More women than he could want."

"He gets women wherever he goes."

"Here it's all in one convenient package. Women, money, power."

"He has all he wants now."

"A man's got nothing hiding in a hole."

"He thinks he's got everything. He says he's found something you and I wouldn't begin to understand."

"We've probably even got some of that in this town," Jerry said sourly.

"Don't be too sure. Life's different where he is."

"It's the same everywhere. Here he's also got the chance to get even."

"He's lost interest in revenge."

"They always say that when they're recuperating. He'll start wanting to pay back what was done to him in time."

"He doesn't care about money, about women, about power, about revenge."

"Why?" Haggerty said irritably. "Why?"

"He's in love," Helen said after a moment.

2

PLACIDA was her name. Never did a name more perfectly clothe a woman. When Burt Hammond first saw her from his canvas-shaded cot in back of the half-ton pickup, the girl-woman stood serene as a sapling; when she moved it was with a queenly and unhurried grace. She came to where he lay and stared at him on the flat-bed. Her skin was the gold of dark honey; she had black eyes shaded by a sweep of dark lashes, still, mysterious, unknowable eyes. Long-flowing, gleaming Indian hair touched his face when she bent low over him after men had lifted him to the ground. Her fingers went tenderly over his cheek, where the still-raw skin had been burned. She spoke no English. "You are welcome here, *señor*," she said. "My father has arranged everything." She had the high cheekbones of the superb Mexican woman, the handsome line from them to the jaw, the delicately carved mouth, all the fine beauty of her people when touched with the blood of their conquerors. "You will be well here."

He and Helen Mendoza had crossed the border at San Luis Rio, Colorado, just ten minutes before the small station closed down for the night, Burt quiet within the canvas that hid him. They were in Sonora, crossing the vast Desierto de Altar. At La Joyita he met Placida's father, a tall, grizzled man who spoke well, though sparingly, in both English and Spanish. Helen called him Don Pedro. "He's some kind of a faith healer," she began, but quickly amended it. "Could be a quack, I don't know. But he was a masseur in the States for years, and he worked over at that health farm for rich American ladies in Tecate."

Don Pedro sat in front of the truck with Helen until they came to rest in a tiny house just past Los Vidrios. It was cold and there were no panes in the windows, but there was electricity and Don Pedro stood over his body for a long time, studying what had happened to it and filling the small, empty room with ritual mumbling.

When they were alone, Burt said in a hushed voice to Helen, "The guy gives me the creeps. You sure he knows what he's doing?" But Don Pedro came back with a bottle of oil, and the moment the fingers touched his legs, Burt knew that fate had found magic hands for him. It was like no massage he had ever experienced. Don Pedro never stopped intoning his curious, atonal melodies as he worked.

They stopped for some days at San Luisito. "You must not go too far with the strength you still have," Don Pedro explained. At San Luisito he began more than massage; he bent the legs back and forth at the knee, gently, easing the joint past pain a fraction of an inch at a time. With every movement, Don Pedro invested the damaged limbs with a secret energy.

"I want to walk, Don Pedro," Burt said one day.

"You will do whatever you find the strength in your heart to do. I have seen an eagle with a broken wing soar again, and I have seen a sparrow with only a tail feather plucked from it die miserably. Do you pray?"

"No."

"I will pray for you."

"Are you a Christian?"

Don Pedro shook his head gravely. "You do not have to believe in what I believe. The power I have comes from my people, a thousand, many thousands of years ago. I lost it once. It has come back to me."

"I have to tell you, Don Pedro, that sort of talk always makes me uncomfortable."

"Then we begin well. I ask only that you do what my daughter and I tell you, that you do not grow impatient with us." He resumed his chanting. But the massage felt good.

From the open back flap he could watch the endless Sonora desert spin away in a plume of yellow dust. They seemed to have run out of road; through the spiraling sand he could see a two-track trail with a high grassy crown between the tracks. Helen could drive the truck no more than five miles an hour. He felt safe at last. When the car came to a stop, Don Pedro took Helen away. It was then he met Placida.

Don Pedro massaged him every morning. Placida massaged at noon and at day's end. In time, she helped him take his first steps, supporting him with strong hands, strong shoulders and a strong back. Her hair smelled of wild lemon and verbena. She refused to let him use the aluminum crutches which had been part of his therapy across the border. He remembered tales of catastrophe on people who had not followed conventional medical wisdom. People who tried to walk too soon and had been left permanently impaired. He wished he could pray.

Nevertheless, he felt himself grow stronger by the day.

He felt reassured that Don Pedro was doing the heavenly honors for him. He had thought the old man spoke in some Spanish dialect, but he chanted in the dying language of his tribe. There was a wise man who came out of the desert now and then, and from him Don Pedro was granted strength. "The eternal strength of my people and the endless desert is everywhere. Through the fingers of my teacher, that power comes to me, and I have passed it to my daughter. From us you will find your own strength. You will be a link in a chain our people have forged for endless generations. Our power flows into you."

One day the old man said he had to go. A flood of fear overwhelmed Burt Hammond. "Go where? Now? When

I can hardly walk more than a few wretched steps?" The routine had been solidly established. The morning massage by Don Pedro. The therapy before noon and the walk after the siesta with Placida. The massage by Placida at nightfall. Placida's hands were good, but in all the time he had elicited hardly a hundred words from her. He begged Don Pedro to stay.

His teacher had emerged from his own desert fastness, Don Pedro explained. "I go to seek further strength, for I have given you all within me. I will find new strength for you, *señor*."

"If you delay a few weeks, Don Pedro, I will pay you more money."

Don Pedro laid an understanding hand on his. "In your world, *dinero* is the key to everything, not here. Have faith in me and the strength that flows into you. Look for a new power within yourself. That will not only make your legs strong again but give you a new life."

Mumbo-jumbo, Burt Hammond thought, the mystical mouthings that always made him itchy. But whatever it was, it was working for him and he bowed his head. *"Si, mi maestro,"* he said. Yes, my master.

And one day Burt did not turn back after he had walked from her as far as he had been going in the month her father had left. He found he could keep walking and there was no pain.

He kept walking and found he had no desire to stop. He knew his long ordeal was over. He kept walking across the endless desert floor, following a road that always ended on the far horizon. He heard the thud of a horse's hooves and when he turned his head without breaking stride, he saw Placida on the brown-speckled galloping pinto, her legs bare to the thighs, the skirt flying behind her unshod feet.

"You walk as far as the horse can go." She pulled the pinto to a stop and slipped to the ground beside him. "My man," she said proudly.

He put his hands around her. She looked at him with reverence. "How far did I walk?" he said.

"To the end of the world," she said. "And the beginning."

He gestured to the pony. "Can he carry us home?"

"Yes, my man," she said in a dark whisper.

He slid over the small horse, taking up the reins around her. They said nothing on the way back, but her body was so close to his on the unsaddled mount he could feel its throb. At the compound, he dropped her at his house and led the pinto to the corral, closed the gate to the golden sun low in the sky. He found Placida with an earthen cup of cool water for him in his tiny cottage. "The Great Spirit is in your body again."

"You are my life," he said. *Mi vida*, he thought ruefully; every Spanish song, every protestation of love by an anguished suitor always said *mi vida*, the worn coinage of Latin lovemaking.

"Su vida es mi vida," she said.

She knew his body; he had never even touched her throat, her face. Her body was ripe, full, hard and warm like a melon in the sun. When she lay before him nude it was nut-brown and silken to his fingertips. She was muscled at the throat as everywhere, hard and hot like the desert, at the breasts, the stomach and the strong thighs. Yet she seemed uncertain, almost fearful of his embrace, until the softness of his kisses opened her body to his.

After that, they made love every day at the siesta and when night fell over the desert. She did not sleep with him. They spoke little. They shared bodies and the joy of his finding the strength in his legs again. When Don Pedro returned, Placida said nothing about what they would have to tell her father now that they had become lovers. But Burt did not hesitate. "I am going to tell your father about us, Placida," he told her.

"Do not," she said, her voice a plea.

"Do you doubt my love?"

"I do not know what you call love is," Placida said.

"Love is what we do together. It is how a man and a woman feel after their bodies have become one."

"But my body has always been one with yours. The strength of my body flowed into you from the beginning."

"I don't understand that kind of talk. I know what happened after I took you to my bed."

"Where you come from, do they not know of the Great Spirit?" Placida said.

"What happened in bed with us had nothing to do with a Great Spirit."

"I do not think I would be happy in your world," she offered calmly.

"Then I'll stay here and learn to see things your way." He took her into his arms again. Her skin was cool and smooth as a pearl; his body grew heavily moist in the intense desert heat, but her violent and passionate exertions had no apparent effect on hers.

Afterward they lay silent and thoughtful; he had the feeling he was losing touch with her, but he waited for her to say the first word. Finally she spoke: "In the night sky during the long summer, a star comes from the great blue and burns out as it falls to the desert floor. That is us."

"I'm no shooting star," Burt said. "I am a man."

"Who comes from his own world as far as the great blue."

"It is all one world, Placida."

"How can it be when we do not understand? When things I know, you do not know? I cannot leave here and you could not flourish under this open sky."

When Don Pedro returned, Burt said nothing until the old man came to him on the scarred wooden massage table. He spoke of his love for Don Pedro's daughter and stated his honorable and willing intentions.

The old man appeared not even to hear. He kept studying Burt's legs, touching and articulating them. "The deer cannot live in the canyon," he said.

"You speak of animals, Don Pedro. We are men and women."

The old man patted the legs but offered no reply. Later, he said: "You are a man and Placida is a woman. You shared a glorious adventure. To us that is enough. I have lived in your world. You do not have to prove what you call love by tearing your own life apart."

"I love her. She has *given* me life, she won't tear it apart."

"Life has given you life, *señor*," Don Pedro said. "Show your gratitude to life, not to a woman."

"I will never leave her."

"That is for you and my daughter to decide," Don Pedro said.

Some weeks later the three of them stood at the station shed at Beniamin Hill, where the train from Nogales linked up with the section from Mexicali for the long run to Guadalajara and the Distrito Federal. At the last minute, Placida refused to board the train with Burt.

"This is her home. This is where she is happy," her father explained as she sought her voice. "She will wait here for you."

"It is only to see the doctor to repair the face," Burt pleaded with her. "A month or two at the most. Then we will come back, Placida."

"I want to stay here. I cannot go with you. I am afraid."

"You count time," Don Pedro said. "To my daughter a day away from our desert is a lifetime, a year here is as nothing. She says if you stay away forever it will be as one day to her here."

The Nogales train was coupled to the cars from the peninsula. Down the tracks the engineer was blowing the whistle in the thin morning air. One, two, three, four times. Five. Six. Placida looked at Burt, turned, and ran away without a word.

"What does that mean, Don Pedro?" Burt asked.

"She knows you care for her but is afraid, señor."

"Afraid? I love her, doesn't she understand?"

"You would take her from her ancestral world. That is what she fears."

"For a short time—"

"Forever. And she belongs here."

"I will come back."

"She knows what you do not know. You must go back to your world."

"I don't want my world." For a moment he almost believed it. Perhaps he could force himself to believe it. "Tell her I'll be back, Don Pedro."

When Helen saw him in Mexico City, the swelling had almost entirely gone down. The burn marks were only a trace, the deep gash that had been carved across the cheek to the hairline had somehow been melted away. "I can't believe it," she moaned. "It's you again."

"My mother always said I had the sweetest tush in the world," he said, touching his cheek. "Want to feel my ass, Helen?"

They went out to San Angel for lunch in a fine house. Their hostess was a Mexican film star of considerable renown. She and Burt Hammond had shared the expertise of Dr. Sanchez and passed waiting hours in the garden of the private, expensive clinica. She found she could not keep her hands off Burt Hammond. She came to his bed and thought his initial reluctance to share it with her derived from his sense of honor and gallantry to a lady.

He did not tell her he was in love with someone. She persisted and in the end regained the esteem she would have thought lost if any man rejected her. As for Burt, mere fidelity seemed capricious. The woman he loved was ten million miles away, in a universe that scarcely seemed to exist in this world of silent white-coated butlers, gleaming old mahogany, Taxco silver and shining crystal.

"Send her home," Elena said, pointing to Helen, with no attempt to offer a pretext. They had had soup, fish, a *lomo* of pork, three vegetables, four wines, and a dessert creamy enough to float to the skies. "I want to be alone with you, *querida*."

"She and I have much work to do," Burt said.

"Gringos," she muttered, trailing off to the flight of steps in the great hall of the old house. "You all have no style."

"Me, I would've stayed," Helen said when they were on the street trying to find a taxi. "She's gorgeous. What the hell are you doing heading to your room with a fat, unsexy secretary?"

He told her about Placida. She listened without visible enthusiasm. " 'Gringos,' " she echoed. " 'You all have no style.' "

"There's something marvelous out there in the desert."

"To me, when you've seen one grain of sand, you've seen them all."

"Funny thing is that Don Pedro doesn't want me to stay."

"What does he know? A dumb Indian, right?"

"I know what he's saying. It would make sense with almost anybody else. But I don't belong anywhere. Never have. I sure as hell didn't belong in the Imperial Valley. At Yale they accepted me but didn't know what to make of me. New York turns out to have a very secret hierarchy—I got to kiss the ring now and then but I was always an outsider. So when Don Pedro says I don't belong in the desert, I believe him but it doesn't mean too much to me."

There was the Jerry Haggerty offer. Helen had brought it up a couple of times. A labor leader of almost unparalleled power, tough, aggressive, with a loyal constituency. More resources than he knew what to do with. "Maybe that's where an outsider belongs," she urged. "You'd be your own man."

63

He could not answer that. Logic and reason said one thing; his heart wanted to believe something else.

"I'll miss you, boss," she said finally. "Too bad. You could have been one hell of a lawyer."

3

HE approached Burt Hammond as the train was threading its tedious way north. Tall, white-haired, slim, he wore a pepper-and-salt tweed suit and could have passed for a man twenty years younger if it were not for the hair.

"I heard you speak Spanish," he said, with the drawl that gave away his Texas origins. "Could I ask you to do some talkin' in my behalf? I'm prepared to pay."

"It'd be my pleasure, sir," Burt said. "I do that for free."

"You'd have to be gettin' off at Mazatlan," he said. He pronounced it Mazz-at-lan.

"Which I'm not. Sorry."

"Pay you real good. You see, the girl I'm fixin' to marry's there and I got to make certain arrangements. Name's Christy, Joseph Charles Christy. I'm in oil, workin' the southern fields in this country. Found me the girl I want. Got all the money I'll ever need. You name the price, whatever, it's okay . . ."

It was a slow train. Looking out the window, he saw automobiles catch up and pass the lumbering iron. On an impulse, and because he thought he would lose hardly more than a day, Burt said, "I'll do it for you."

Joe Christy could not understand Burt's refusal of his money. "I couldn't spend all I've got and I never been married. This girl of mine, I told her, 'José come September,' and I'm as good as my word. Gonna show her what a good life is really like. The little girl deserves it."

Later that evening José-come-September, in a blue suit, white shirt and tie, bright and shining, the swain, eager and anxious, arrived to claim his bride.

The taxi let them out at a waterfront place with a "Dos Equis" neon sign in one of the windows. Burt Hammond had no doubt what it was when they walked into the Club El Dorado. The tables along the floor were occupied by the available girls. In the border-town of his boyhood, these would go for fifty to a hundred pesos.

"You know what kind of place this is?" Burt said.

"Sure, I wasn't born yesterday," Joe said. "Ask them for Lupita."

When Lupita came over she was skinny, and her satin gown was royal purple over a brassiere, pushing her full breasts toward her neck. But she was sweet and innocent and she exclaimed in Spanish, "José, señor, you have come back as you said!"

"What's she sayin' to me?" Joe asked eagerly. "She surprised?"

They had to make the financial arrangement with the boss to get her to sit with them. She kept staring at Joe and saying, "You have come back."

"Tell her I am taking her away."

Burt told her what was said. Lupita started to weep.

"What'd you tell her, what'd you tell her?" Joe insisted.

"He asks why you cry," Burt said to Lupita.

"How long does he want me for?" she asked Burt.

"He wants to marry you."

"Marry me?" Her voice quavered a little.

Burt grinned. "He is very rich."

Joe understood *muy rico* and he took out his wallet and thrust it at Lupita. *"Muy rico!* We marry! Didn't I tell you José come September?"

"No es posible," she said. "How could I go? You know it could not be arranged."

"He has a car here," Burt said. "He could tell your boss he wants to buy you for three days, and you could make it to the border."

"A girl tried that two months ago. They were suspicious and followed her all the way. I would be afraid."

"What do you want me to tell him?"

"Tell her I love her," Joe kept saying impatiently. "I will leave everything to her. Are you telling her that?"

"What is he saying?" Lupita said.

"He loves you and you would have all his money when he dies."

65

"Why would he die?" Lupita said, her eyes flashing terror.

"He means later. Maybe you could tell them you are having your monthly period and they would give you a few days off and you could tell them you are going out of town to see your mother. We'd walk out tonight like it's nothing special. That would give you a two-day start," Burt said.

"You know what they did with this girl?" Lupita said. "They tied her hands with auto chains to the back of the car and dragged her until there was nothing but torn flesh and bones."

"What are you guys talking about?" Joe said festively. "If I got to pay off, I'll pay off, there's no problem."

"The problem is," Burt said in English, "whom do you pay off? The guys who took your money would tell other guys, and they'd stop you and say you hadn't paid off the right guys and they'd tap you. Then there'd be another and another. Or the first guys would say you hadn't paid enough. That's how things are managed down here."

"They'd never catch me. I've got a new car."

"They'd catch you, count on it."

"Then what do we do?"

"Nothing you can do, Joe," Burt said, taking control in earnest now.

"Why, she's nothing but a slave."

"That's right. They bought her and raised her and trained her for his. They've got an investment."

"Well, I'll pay off all of them."

"But the more you want to pay off, the more valuable it makes her."

"We'll go to the police."

"That won't do you any good. The police are friends of theirs."

"The American ambassador. You know the weight my company pulls in this country?"

"Not in the El Dorado whorehouse, Joe."

"I want her." The tough old wildcatter was crying. "Poor little thing, never had a break. I know that. I'd enjoy making life good for her. Know what she did for me?" He brushed tears from his eyes. "I was dead, Burt. Gave me life! I mean, I screwed ladies from San Angelo to Dharan and Brunei, I had 'em in I-ran and Indonesia, wherever there was oil there were ladies and

Joe Christy had his. Then I died. I figured I'm gettin' old so what the hell, it's gone. Left me sad, but I just figured I'd took my share and more. Then I met her. Here! I'm alive with her, man. Hard as a rock! Make it two, three times just like that! I'm alive again."

A knot formed in Burt Hammond's throat and made it difficult to breathe. He thought of Placida, probably at this moment asleep in the infinite blue night that encased the desert. She'd given him life just as the little whore had bestowed it on Joe Christy. It was clear to him that Lupita and Joe could not marry, and it came to him that he and Placida—

"She tell you about the kid?" Joe was saying. "I'd take care of him too. Send him to school. To college. Give him my name."

"Yeah," Burt said wearily.

"Tell them I want to talk to the boss," Joe announced impulsively.

"I wouldn't, Joe. They'd rob you. That way you'd never get to see her again."

"What do I do?" he pleaded.

"I'd move to Mazatlan and come here a lot," Burt said.

"You're a cynical son of a bitch, ain't you?"

"Not really."

"Let 'em screw me, I've been taken before. She'll take the chance with me. I'm a pretty cute schemer myself."

"She won't go, Joe."

"Ask her," Joe begged Burt.

Burt Hammond told the girl what Joe proposed. He saw her face darken. She leaned over and spoke to Burt's ear as if someone other than the two Americans might be listening.

Burt nodded. He kept nodding as Lupita kept talking. On the floor, a dancer was doing a strip number where half of her was a gorilla undressing the other half, running a hand up and down the bare tit. Lupita ran out a door beside the stage.

"Where's she going?"

"Let's order a bottle of tequilla," Burt said. He ordered Herradura and it came with the limes and salt.

"Lupita's coming with me?"

"She said to tell you thanks but she is afraid for herself and her son. She doesn't want to see you again. You must go back alone. Let's celebrate."

"What kind of celebration are you talking about?" Joe Christy snarled.

"I celebrate people who can speak a terrible truth without flinching or self-pity. It's why I love and fear them. My friend—" Burt filled a shot glass and went through the lime-sucking, belt and salt routine. "She told me to tell you she has some bad moments here, but there are bad moments everywhere in life. She told me to tell you she would not be happy in a strange place even with all the money in the world. She told me to tell you she does love you, and believes you love her, but this is her world and God put her here for a purpose. She said she is glad you come-back-September, maybe you'll come back next September."

"Lemme have that there bottle," Joe said at length. He took two healthy belts, put the bottle down with a thud and looked at Burt as if he had never taken notice of him before. "What the hell you celebrating?" he demanded.

"Life. *La vida.* 'Life, life, eternal life.' "

"I could have given her the world," Joe said, beginning to weep.

Burt Hammond poured another tequilla. . . .

When they staggered back to the hotel, the man at the desk told Joe Christy his car had arrived. Joe took Burt's arm and brought him outside again to a Silver Cloud gleaming in the moonlight. "Had it drove here from the fields down south." The driver was a sullen-looking Mexican boy who wore a chauffeur's patent-leather billed cap with his jeans and cowboy shirt. "One of my e-meers gave it to me. What I did for that feller, he could buy himself fifty of these every day." Burt sought to untangle himself from the old man's fingers but they were like steel. He would not let Burt go to his own room. "I really like my Lupita. What I coulda done for that little girl!" he moaned.

"You're not going to cry again, are you?" Hoping against hope, Burt fell into a chair in Joe's sitting room, as far away as the wall allowed. He hadn't been feeling too well himself, even without having to hear the lover's lament. He put his head down on the table and thought of Placida, the peace he had known in the desert, and the illusion he had come to accept there, that any life is possible. Placida had proved wiser, perhaps more mature, than himself.

When Burt looked up, he was blinded by a silent burst of light like a contained explosion. He saw a diamond as large as the sun dangling in front of his eyes. It kept exploding inches from his nose, swinging like a magician's gimmick but bursting with burning colors as it passed—yellow, blue, green, gold.

Joe *was* trying to get himself crying again, but when they came they had turned to tequilla tears, not the real ones. "Got it for the wedding from Car-teer in Paris." The diamond was a pendant as big as the last joint on a man's thumb; it dangled from a chaste platinum chain designed to take nothing away from a fascinating gem. "This thing's got a pedigree, Burt. It's all wrote down in the bill of sale, it's even got a name but I can't say it." He dropped the stone and chain to the table.

Burt sat erect and reached out carefully for it. The coldness surprised him. "How much did a little thing like this cost you, Joe?"

There was a boozy laugh. "Want to buy it?"

"Yes," Burt said thoughtfully but without hesitation. "I could use this. Give you the last penny I've got in the world, how's that?" he went on eagerly. "Might have to borrow a couple of hundred from you for hamburger to tide me over till I start working again."

"You'd wipe yourself out for a thing like this?" Joe asked incredulously.

If he could not share a life with Placida he could give her everything else he had. Everything. "My secretary told me I've got six thousand three hundred and twelve dollars and forty-six cents in her custody. It's all yours, Joe. Is it a deal?"

Joe laughed again. "That'd pay the in-surance for maybe a coupla years."

"But how often have you made a deal where the guy gives you *everything?*" Burt looked up at him. "Doesn't hold back dime one. I'll make it ten thousand."

"Holding back on me, huh?" Joe teased. "You said you only had six and change."

"I'm charging you thirty-six eighty-seven and fifty-four cents for my services here," Burt said. "That brings it to ten thousand even."

"You not only got nerve, son, you got one hell of a head for arithmetic," Joe Christy offered cheerfully. "Ain't that charging a lot of money for one meeting that didn't turn

69

out so good for me anyway?" he continued in a teasing voice.

"You didn't say it had to come out your way, Joe. You said you wanted someone to talk for you and you promised to pay real good."

Joe Christy looked at him for a long astonished moment before he spoke again. "Ten thousand don't begin to make what this rock costs. How's about you do some lawyer work for me? Retainer for five years, say."

"I'm not a member of the bar in Texas, but you want work done in California, you're on."

"What would a guy like you want with a non-commerical gem like that from Car-teer?" Joe said after a moment.

"I'm going to give it to a lady who gave me back my life and refused to take what was left of it from here on out. I figure that's worth everything I've got."

"I'd like to go there with you. Take you in my car."

"Why not?" Burt said.

Three days later, the big white Rolls sat in soft sand up to its hubcaps. Burt and Joe emerged from the air-conditioned vehicle to study what the driver had done. "I had this machine built with a strong-ass low for desert driving, but the boy never could understand what I said. It's way over to the left, and back." Burt took the wheel, found the position in the gear box; the tires, moving scarcely an inch a second, took hold on the talcum surface. The car pulled itself out of the sand like an imperturbable gentleman briefly embarrassed by an unfamiliar environment.

Joe came up beside him in the chauffeur's section while his driver sat in back. "What's going to happen next, son?" Joe Christy said. "After you pay off here, I mean."

"Got a letter from my secretary. Going to open an office in San Francisco."

"You come to Houston with me you'll wind up rich."

"I'll wind up rich wherever I go," Burt said colorlessly.

The old man grinned knowingly. "That gonna be enough?"

"Don't know. I've never been rich."

"It's a kick for a while. Then you keep saying, what else?"

At the village, a couple of sleepy curs came out of the

70

shade to bark at them. Don Pedro emerged in *peon* dress, loose white cotton pants and a big shirt flopping to the knees. Burt asked the old man to put his magic hands on his friend.

He found Placida in the dark cottage. Slivers of sun through the shuttered windows caught her cascade of shining hair and dancing eyes. Her hair and her whole body teemed with the floral scents of the desert. Burt took out the platinum chain and its diamond and put it over her head. "If you would not take my life, I offer you everything it has achieved so far."

He might as well have encircled her throat with a turquoise and a coarse silver chain because she gave it no notice.

"I have known you, *mi hombre,*" she whispered. *"You* are everything."

They made love on the earthen floor, on two serapes spread side by side. "Not yet," she kept pleading. "No! No! I want every part of my body open to your coming. Not yet!" She climbed on him, rolled over on her back again without letting his body disunite from hers; she spread her legs as wide and straight as an eagle spreads his wings; for the first time he saw beadlets of perspiration across her forehead, but always she kept crying, "Not yet, *mi hombre,* not yet! Wait . . . wait . . ." Her hands were spread across his buttocks, pulling them to her on the downstroke as if she sought to take in his whole body, her cries becoming louder and more insistent, "No, *mi hombre,* no!" until in a burst of passion like the diamond he saw now glittering around her neck she shouted, "Now! now! now! I am wholly open to you! Give me your life forever!" and the little death the French speak of overwhelmed him; he was melted in her arms, and lost. He came back when the loving, familiar hands were felt again on his limbs, stroking them with a cool, water-moistened cloth. She was the silent girl-woman once more, returning him to life, grave, dressed in her cotton frock, the stone of fire lost in the bodice.

She held out his shirt to him as he dressed. When he turned to face her, she said, *"Vaya con Dios, mi hombre."* A little smile flickered briefly in the corners of her mouth and her dark eyes seemed to dance.

"Goodbye, Placida," he said.

"Goodbye, Burt," she said in English, the first she had ever uttered before him.

71

He grinned. "You've been holding back on me."

"When my father massaged the rich ladies in Tecate, I was the child who ran among the flowers."

"Still, you misled me," he teased her.

"Blame Don Pedro. He insisted. Otherwise each of us would lose a world. Your coming, your going, our meeting, our parting—he says it is all the drifting of sand, nothing is lost. You've heard him say that." She took his hand and put it to her lips. She did not come out with him.

He found Joe Christy sharing an earthen cup of herb tea with the old man. "He's a miracle man and he won't take money. I've never felt so good in years! I can see why you wouldn't want to leave this place."

Burt saw Placida in the doorframe of the cottage. She gazed steadily at the departing car but did not raise her hand in a gesture of farewell.

BOOK THREE:

Cities by the Bay

(1960-1963)

1

DEBORAH PACKARD was a born beauty, hair unalloyed gold, soft as the airiest silk, eyes blue and shining, skin pink and glowing. She had a face lit with smiling and joy. A creature made to love and to be loved, free of bodily restraint or social inhibition.

San Francisco was not yet accustomed to the free souls who were just beginning to invade their city with flowers and expressions of universal love, so the owner of L'Esperance, a small, expensive boutique, watched with astonishment as Deborah stepped barefoot from a beat-up Volkswagen van at the curb, walked to the window, lifted her granny dress above her waist and squatted.

Traffic on Union Street was brought to an immediate and noisy halt by the screams and protestations of the proprietor of L'Esperance, who ran from her shop, wailing distress and hollering outrage.

Deborah herself looked up without concern. A crowd quickly turned partisan, only a few more amused than shocked. Among them was Burt Hammond, still new enough to the city so he explored its streets every free moment, no longer surprised by whatever he saw. He leaned against the car from which Deborah had emerged, charmed by the sweet innocence of a flower child only four years old.

Burt Hammond watched Deborah being collared and lifted off her feet without resistance. Someone in the crowd called for the police. Someone else demanded the immediate presence of a parent. Civic order, Burt observed, seemed to be winning the day; things looked bad indeed for the little beauty. He felt something stir inside the van behind him; he turned to study the old Volkswagen for some clue, but it offered none except for the usual Mexican *turista* stamps, several years outdated, and faded chintz curtains. A door opened and someone whose sleep had been disturbed came out, hair a tangle to his shoulders, and muttered, "Hey, man, that's my kid."

74

"I think there is need here for a lawyer," Burt offered. "You one?"

Burton Hammond, Esquire, was not exactly soliciting business, but in the month he had been in San Francisco he learned again something he first came to know during his year of legal practice in New York. All new young lawyers are nonentities. It takes a miracle to bring a fledgling to that level of attention at which he becomes an individual. Battalions of starting-out lawyers are lost in faceless anonymity; to compound matters, every year fresh battalions join the ranks. Most remain ciphers all their careers, no matter how financially successful or how well known to their peers. The single great celebrated case—the arresting event that can skyrocket the young advocate to public eminence—eludes all but the few who dare to seek it out.

Burt Hammond had not yet approached Jerry Haggerty. "You're crazy, y'know," Helen Mendoza said. "He's a client waiting to throw a ton of money in your direction. He's got the clout you need. Why don't you go to see him?"

Burt Hammond knew his would-be client better than his secretary did. He had spent the month since his arrival reading everything available about Jerry Haggerty: transcripts of investigations and court proceedings from the thirties on, books, newspaper clippings, even minutes of union meetings made public for one reason or another. One thing Burt was now sure of: Haggerty had reached out for him because Haggerty was a man who prized independence above everything else. But how could a Burton Hammond continue to be independent if he had no stature except that conferred on him by the great and moody Haggerty?

That was his dilemma when he heard Miss Deborah Packard's father say, "Take over, man, I'm still stoned."

Burt Hammond pushed his way to the door of L'Esperance. There he freed his client, lifted her into his arms and pressed reassuring cheek with her. "Beat it," someone whispered to him. "They've called the cops."

Burt had a better plan than to run.

"Who are you people, is this a lynching here, what is your name, how dare you molest this child?" he demanded forcefully, among other things. In response, of course, matters of nuisance and public health were shouted to his attention, amid cries of protest at what was happening to a city being invaded by hordes of disrespectful hippies, as they were being called.

Not one but two police cars responded to the emergency. The evidence was plain enough. The police were properly outraged. Burt pointed out that what his client had done was after all no more than uncurbed dogs often were guilty of on the streets and the police did not descend on *them*. He declared that if the owner of the establishment wished to insist on a citizen's arrest (he was urging a course of action here the lady had not thought of until that moment) he would not file for false arrest if her action failed. This had the desired effect of fortifying the outraged lady. The police, confronted by a crowd, seemed anxious to clear the street and forget the whole matter. Burt pointed out that if the lady wanted a citizen's arrest it was their duty to take in his client. And if they wished to bring in the father, he could help them there as well.

Among the cars blocked by the traffic tie-up on Union Street was that of a photographer. When Burt saw the camera flashes he urged the police to get the matter over with, making sure he and his client were full-face to camera. "I love you," Deborah Packard said, planting soft, sweet lips on his nose. Flash.

"I love you even more," Burt said.

In court some days later, the attorney for the city seemed dismayed, when he did not feel ridiculous. "Aw, come on, you know better," he pleaded privately to counsel for the defendants. "We can't have people shitting all over the streets. I don't care about cats and dogs. People-shitting is specifically dealt with in the municipal code."

"Then the code is unconstitutional, too broadly drawn, insensitive to the needs of the very young and God knows who else," Burt said sternly.

"He's brought God in," said a reporter from the *Chronicle,* which had already run the picture of the principals in Union Street. "This guy is ready to go to the Supreme Court of the United States to define the constitutional limits of a citizen's right to shit."

"Precisely," Burt Hammond said.

The matter was page one for several days. One lawyer had lifted himself from the crowd.

Jerry Haggerty saw the stories in the *Chronicle* but amusement gave way to annoyance. He gave orders and Burton Hammond was brought to his office in Market

Street. Haggerty circled him like a tiger deciding when to pounce. "This where you got chewed up in that accident?" He put a finger on Dr. Sanchez's beautiful stitchery. "I've been waiting to talk to you. You got your nerve taking so long to get to me. Why didn't you call me?"

"I wanted to start a practice of my own."

Haggerty peered at him intently. "Gonna be your own man, huh?"

"I haven't been idle in your behalf, Mr. Haggerty. I know everything about you, short of what you've never spoken of to anyone, anywhere."

"Then you know it all, except one thing. I got some pretty big people looking to throw my ass in prison. That's not to happen. I'm too old, I'm too wise and I just don't like the life in any joint. So whatever it takes, I stay out. Can you handle that?"

"Robert Kennedy says you're in cahoots with organized crime and mobsters."

"Robert Kennedy is a spoiled brat, a rich shitheel who's had everything his way all his life. He talks too much."

"He says you're a connection to organized crime and that he can get you on racketeering charges."

"There isn't a labor leader living who hasn't had to deal with racket guys. When I started out they were loansharking and bookmaking. I stopped all that where I could. Some took over locals. I lived with them because I had to, like everybody else. Including the employers."

"Kennedy makes it sound like you've got them all working for you. Or you for them."

"Kennedy and his old man have been working to put the older brother in the White House," Haggerty said crisply. "That's why the runt has been after me. I'm a high-visibility target and it makes Jack look good in the papers."

"What happens if the convention nominates Senator Kennedy?"

"I've got a ton of money to give the Humphrey or Johnson people to stop it, any way they want it, under the table or on top."

"The Kennedys have all the money they need, and West Virginia proves they know how to use it effectively. I've got to figure we're going to have to face Kennedys at 1600 Pennsylvania Avenue for the next eight years. They'll own the Department of Justice, and that means a hundred lawyers preparing a vendetta against one man.

77

A team like that could find something to convict St. Francis of Assisi."

"I know that! Why the hell do you think I plucked you out of the goddamn alfalfa fields? Smart lawyers grow on trees around here. I saw one man taking on the whole shebang, the Amalgamated Farmers, the big corporations, the politicians and their police, the labor-baiters who yell bloody murder when someone wants a penny more an hour—even the FBI. You know they got you on their get-even list, don't you? And all this time I see one man pulling together them poor Mexicans no one in organized labor wants to bother with. I said to myself, that guy is the guy I want. All right, then, what do I do?"

"You may not like what I tell you about yourself."

"Try me."

"You've been in power so long you're in danger of becoming fossilized." No need to cover things with carefully turned phrases, Burt thought. From all he'd read, he knew where the problem and the solution lay. Haggerty was going to have to buy it sooner or later. He was as old-fashioned as one of his longshoremen with a hook. Even his strategy in fighting for survival. He could see the old man's pink face grow pinker, but Haggerty put aside the provocation without comment. "The fight begins in the unions you command," Burt Hammond went on. "Strengthen yourself there."

"I'm up to my ass in big trouble and you talk local labor politics?"

"Strengthen your base to strengthen the unions, one of your power sources. You've been opposed to mechanization, from the docks to the trucks to the factories. I've read all the reports, the minutes of all the meetings, all your statements. You've fired guys, you've chased them out of locals all over the state. You've got to make an about-face."

"Been fighting mechanization for ten years to protect our people," Haggerty murmured.

"You've been wrong. You're fighting the inevitable future. There's no standing still. Mechanization is here, more is coming." His voice died suddenly; Burt Hammond thought of his father. "It isn't a question of right and wrong," he began again. "Time and history make their own demands. I can't have my client cut down from the rear while he's fighting a new war up front."

A faint smile flickered mischievously on the Haggerty

78

face. "It means a total reversal of everything I've been saying to the members and the executive board."

"Tell them it's your new personal counselor."

"What else?" Jerry Haggerty asked moodily.

"There's got to be more than thirties militancy. I see us setting up a consolidated pension fund, taking in every big union in the state, to be run and administered by our own trustees and experts. I figure we'll be soon talking in the tens, the hundreds of millions. A billion in assets. The Golden West Trust and Pension Fund will pay higher pensions to its members than any existing plans. We'll be in charge of our own funds going into the money market. We'll keep the profit the banks have been taking for what we'll learn to do ourselves."

"Did you ever try to get two labor leaders to agree on anything involving money?" Haggerty snapped bitterly. "They'll think Jerry Haggerty's out to screw them."

"That figures. So we'll put them on the board. I set up an Oversight Committee to look after every dollar. They can sit there too. And that's where I'll sit. I'll advise you in everything, but that's the only official position I want."

"No, I need someone beside me all the time."

"Not beside you, Mr. Haggerty. With you. Keeping just enough distance so he sees everything and isn't overpowered. It's why I'm going to have clients other than Jerry Haggerty."

The old man grumbled but Burt Hammond could see the concession. He went into detail about the pension fund and its potential. In time he foresaw a new phase in the development not only of labor but of the whole American economy. There would be not millions but billions of dollars for capital investment when other big unions followed their lead. It would constitute a treasury beyond measure in history coming into the market. The power potential was endless, politically as well as economically. For once labor would have a handle on its own power.

"I figured you were a pistol," Haggerty said at last.

"Something else you ought to know about me, Jerry." It was the first time he had ever called the old man by the name everybody used; the old man grinned. "I spent a year in the desert learning how to walk and to live again. What you get down there isn't something you can boil down to a few words, but I was put in touch with forces I still don't understand. Maybe you lose that touch in places like this town. Maybe it was nothing but learning to walk and to look at yourself without revulsion, a lot of desert heat, moonlight and sweet people. But I'm sure of one thing. I can't belong to you, or to any man."

Jerry Haggerty frowned and grumbled unintelligible obscenities deep within his throat. He pulled open the drawer to his right in his desk and lifted the top of a steel box. Burt Hammond could not see the hands until they came up with packets of bills which the old man threw on top of the desk one at a time until there were five. "Twenty-five thousand," he said quietly. "That's to help you get started. Clean, good money. Weren't you the guy who was just telling me about the power of money?" Burt Hammond hesitated. "Take it. Here's a down-payment on the power you need." Jerry Haggerty made one bundle of it, stroking it as one might a kitten. "I love the feel of cash."

"So do I, Jerry," Burt Hammond said, reaching to take up the packets. "For what it's worth."

2

Across the bay, along Telegraph Avenue and behind the Sather Gate of the University of California, wherever any of the vast student body gathered, they knew of the intrepid lawyer in the Packard case. A counter-culture newspaper, the Berkeley *Barb*, treated Burt Hammond with a respect it reserved only for unfrocked Harvard psychologists and drug-sodden rock musicians. Hammond had fought for the ultimate freedom, it asserted.

They came to the office Burt Hammond had set up in a two-story brick residence in Pacific Heights. The downstairs became reception room, library conference room and his private *bureau;* upstairs consisted of a big living room leading to a terrace with a striking view of the bay, a bedroom, and a kitchen adequate for instant coffee and ice cubes. The living quarters were spectacular, furnished with militant taste: gleaming hardwood floor, Barcelona chairs, here a Mies, there an Eames, a Saarinen, the big slashes of a Franz Klein oil on the wall. It was Burt's first home completely his own; he had yet to learn how to protect himself from the professional decorator. Yet he was pleased that one of them had accomplished what he wanted: a prodigious setting visitors could not soon forget.

Burt Hammond learned again the first lesson of the one-man urban law office. There are twenty-four hours in every day, no more. Hence, he was forced to choose sternly among potential clients. He took on cases involving the rights of students to set up tables on university property, illegal search, police harassment, marijuana, suspended driving licenses, and, of course, that richest of lodes for the independent attorney, personal injury. He could afford to pick and choose, thanks to Jerry Haggerty, and he did so according to strict principles: merit, profitability and newsworthiness, not necessarily in that order.

He admitted this freely to Sue-Ann Martin. She was a graduate student in architectural planning who had come to him with a drug arrest. Susie was a young woman of surpassing loveliness, physically and spiritually. The Susie one saw seemed to float rather than walk, a visage clean of makeup, with full lips, wide eyes and a high forehead under a flowing crown of ripe-wheat hair. But there was another, even more compelling Sue-Ann Martin. This one told Burt Hammond she preferred not to have much to do with men—except to have their bodies now and then for her own comfort—because men thought they owned her just because they made love to her. "They try to destroy my independence."

"I love you, Miss Martin," Burt Hammond said from behind his desk when she told him this.

"Does that mean you'll take my case?" the young lady asked.

"I'm afraid so."

"I don't like you," Miss Martin said, and rose to go. He stopped her before she reached the door. "If I were ugly and hated sex, would you take the case?" she demanded.

"Probably not," he replied, adding, "to my shame."

"So you understand. Goodbye."

He took her hand. "I promise to change."

Sue-Ann Martin studied him. Finally she sighed and returned to his desk. "Do you mind if I light up?"

"Yes. Not here, please."

"Stuffy, huh?"

He shook his head. "Careful."

Neither of them wanted a permanent connection but it happened anyway. In time, each tried dating others, even going to bed with others, but it didn't work. "It's not that I love you," Susie said. "I like you, that's the problem."

Love, meaning romance, did not matter much to either of them. Susie had her project to complete for her master's, and Burt Hammond had Jerry Haggerty and the gentlemen of the labor movement up and down the Pacific Coast.

They were hard-nosed, realistic men, hides as tough as rhino, men of little speech and suspicious turns of mind, everything Jerry Haggerty had warned him. Many of them had set up pension plans of their own and saw nothing to their advantage in "going into the pension business," as one of them put it. They respected and feared Jerry Haggerty. He did not tell any of this to Sue-Ann Martin that night. He simply said they were like sailors on shore leave, looking for booze and broads; Burt Hammond was damned if he was going to curry favor with that kind of thing.

He heard Susie hiss a noisy drag and a moment later a plume of smoke drifted toward the ceiling above the bed. "I know a lot of friends who'd love to meet men like that, I mean all that power, all that—well, vulgarity. It's different. They might go to bed if they were intrigued but they'd never sell themselves."

Burt Hammond's parties, in his flat above what he called the peso engraving press, became a must whenever a labor baron and his retinue visited San Francisco. The girls around Burt Hammond were said to be the best-looking in town. As for the men, Susie commented, "They act like they want to go to bed but what they really like is someone to listen, make approving sounds and ask the right questions."

Where reason and fiscal projections failed to convince, Burton Hammond's parties succeeded. The Golden West Pension Fund was being brought into the world, with some wailing and crying, but with the same sensible and loving attention others at the university had devoted to the hydrogen bomb.

The key figure, without whom there would be no pension fund, was Matt Kusic. Jerry Haggerty and the big, bald labor boss from Seattle both respected and loathed each other. Kusic held the Pacific Northwest as solidly as

Jerry owned his turf; both had gone through periods when they were tar-brushed as radicals, leftists and pinkos. The words changed as the years rolled on, but what it meant was that both were once not considered reliable by their respective establishments. Now both held sway over a million workers with a combination of guile, compassion and toughness. They were, in fact, so much alike that it seemed almost impossible to Burt Hammond to bring them together.

Finally Matt Kusic consented to a visit. "His guys won't like those intellectual beatniks of yours, kid," Jerry said. "I'd suggest a dozen Vegas showgirls with false eyelashes long as cowcatchers on a railroad engine."

Burt Hammond knew better. Expensive call girls and hookers were always paraded before these men. As usual, he had done a lot of research into his man, retaining a reserved but highly competent private detective for this purpose as well. "He's something of a crook," Burt had been told.

"You know for sure?" he had asked Elmer Wright.

"He'd have to be . . ."

"You don't *know*. I never want anything from you you can't document. I don't want to hear from you what you think the client prefers to know. I need absolute fact only."

It was to be the beginning of a long relationship. Elmer Wright did turn up some interesting facts, in particular a mimeographed copy of a speech the young Kusic had made when he left his shop-steward job at the Bremerton shipyards to enlist as a Marine in World War II. "All my life I was brought up to hate war," Kusic had said. "All my life I heard all war is bad. I believe that, like I believe in my mother and father. But this is a good war; these maniacs want to destroy people, and since I love people I think I won't be sorry later for changing my mind." Good, Burt had thought. He is not an implacably rigid man. . . .

Before the party, Burt Hammond had had two sessions in his office downstairs with the Kusic lawyers. He gave in to every demand, even though they were as yet unauthorized to join the pension fund. He had met with Kusic in Jerry's office, just the three of them. "My lawyer's crazy, Matt," Jerry Haggerty said. "He's ready to give you the whole store if you just say the word."

But Matt Kusic did not affirm. "I don't think so," he said when he left.

"I know those Hunkies," Jerry Haggerty said. "Get him loaded and a blow-job and he'll concede. It's our last chance."

Jerry Haggerty was a prehistoric creature, of that Burt Hammond was now sure.

Burt met his hostesses an hour before the party, girls in long cotton dresses from thrift shops, grave, earnest young women who said they loved Burt's parties because it was all so dreamlike. How else could they meet Neanderthal men like this? All of them were named Candy, Cindy, Susie, Amy, Debbie or Chris. No one was Evelyn, Florence, Edith, Kitty, Lillian or Pauline. They liked the same music and the same books. They looked alike too. They were all really one girl, Burt often thought, earnest, gifted, sincere, and slightly adenoidal. They would not take money, even when he assured them respectable businesses frequently employed young ladies to hostess business meetings. When the Kusic party arrived, they took off the Jimi Hendrix records and put on the original cast recording of *Camelot*. Kusic seemed charmed by what he saw.

Burt watched him. Kusic did not drink. He liked the young ladies and he was as proper with them as a bishop. Burt Hammond realized how wrong Haggerty had been about the Seattle labor boss.

"Anywhere we can talk alone?" Kusic finally said to him. He picked up the hand of a girl named Cindy and kissed her fingers gallantly. "It's been a real pleasure talking to you, young lady." He turned to Burt almost without hesitation. "You're smart, counselor."

Burt Hammond took him to the terrace. It was softly lit, ghostly under the striped sailcloth canopy which covered it from the cold damp rolling in from the sea. "I want to tell you, I'd come in but for one thing."

"Name it, it's yours," Burt said.

"You couldn't deliver it. The name's Jerry Haggerty."

"He's the linchpin, Mr. Kusic, he's the dynamic that makes the pension fund possible."

"He's going to prison, you know that."

"They'll try," Burt said.

"They'd like to knock me off too. I may have to take a rap for what people who work for me have done under my authority, but I never laid down in bed with gangster types."

"I've been with him for over a year. I'd know if that was true. It's bullshit as far as I can see."

"He pays you well. I find the more you pay a lawyer the blinder he gets."

"This is my third start, Mr. Kusic, and I'm not afraid of starting all over again. And I wouldn't hesitate, if that were true."

"This is nicer, counselor. This place. These girls. This town. You've got it all."

"Yes, I have, I'll give you that, but I have to tell you Jerry has always been absolutely straight with me. I have his word he wants to be straight with the pension fund. I'll concede your people any concession they want, to assure the fund remains straight and absolutely devoted to the best interests of the working man. What more can you ask?"

He was appealing to the old idealist who'd left his welding torch to fight with the First Marine Division all the way from Guadalcanal to Palau; the young Czech refugee whose father, Elmer Wright had told him, was a socialist official back in the old country. "We run our pension fund through Wells Fargo. We got no complaints," Kusic offered.

"Yes, Jerry's looking for public support because the Department of Justice is after him, I'll concede that," Burt said before Kusic was ready to. "But sometimes the best things are done out of the narrowest of motives. At least he's doing it. Judge what he wants to do. He now sees our own pension fund as an opportunity to use the thrust of labor's money to influence corporate America— and the world. Don't you agree it's time for us to do that?"

"I draw a blank when it comes to finance," Kusic said wearily. "I just don't understand money."

"It always came naturally to me, Matt," Burt said. "You don't need to understand money, any more than you need to understand love. You just have to have it. The pension fund gives us money. *We* have it, not Crocker, not Wells Fargo, not Goldman, Sachs; we, us."

During a long silence Burt Hammond watched his visitor walk to the edge of the terrace and lose himself in thought. Inside they were playing twist music and the scholars were trying to show the labor barons how the dance went. The giggling could have come from the gym at a Y dance.

Matt Kusic came back from his meditation. "It could be a lot of trouble."

"Anything this big has trouble built into it," Burt said. "What happens when Justice moves against us?"

"We're ready. This makes us extra careful, Matt."

"At first I thought it was a scheme for Jerry to make himself a bigger man than ever," he said, almost to himself.

"Which he will be. And so will you, Matt."

Kusic hesitated. "It could work," he murmured.

"We're not kidding when we say we want to make this absolutely satisfactory to every union man in California."

Matt Kusic studied Burt Hammond as if he had never seen the man. "When I was a kid I came to America with old-world socialist ideals," Matt said dreamily. "I found heroes in guys like Gene Debs and Daniel de Leon, with people like John L. Lewis and Walter and Victor Reuther. I became more union than socialist. I forgot all that Marx-shit about workers owning the means of production. I saw what we had here and when I went abroad to those international labor meetings I'd look at those European guys now in their governments and still talking about nationalizing their sick railroads or their obsolete steel industry and I'd thank God for the Atlantic Ocean. But look what's going to happen to us now. While they're still fighting to control dead industries no self-respecting capitalist wants any more, we'll damn near own the country." Matt Kusic threw his hands high toward the fog-bound skies. "You got to give me one thing. This will be between you and me."

"You've got it, Matt."

"Look, I'm no saint. I've tilted the board my way more than once, who hasn't? I've skimmed cash where it couldn't be traced, padded an expense here, trimmed an obligation there. I never met a man who could swear on his mother's grave he didn't. But I live in a sixteen-thousand-dollar house and I bought the furniture at Sears Roebuck. I live good because wherever I go it's union work, but that's the extent of it. If Robert Kennedy's boys want to subpoena my records they won't find a hell of a lot.

"But your guy. Anybody he touches turns rich. All his friends are into big deals. Money leaks from every joint and seam, like a bad job of steamfitting. He's always asking for trouble. And the guys around him. Like you."

"What about me?" Burt Hammond asked.

"Lookit this place. Like I said, not bad for a young lawyer. I've got a right to wonder."

Burt Hammond remembered one of the guys in the Valley commenting on his lifestyle. "I've seen better," he said now, as he remembered saying something like that then. "I'm charmed by your modest home, Matt, but it's not a compelling argument. What matters is results, clout, power."

"And integrity? Doesn't that count?"

His father had integrity. "What about survival, Matt? Where do you rate that? We're into a go-go phase of economic growth. The big corporations are going multi-national, diversifying, moving into everything. That's the kind of power we'll have to confront any day now. No one's screaming bloody murder because their people do well, but let a labor man drive a Cadillac and everybody gets suspicious.

"Jerry throws money around, and I get my share. I work for it. So does everybody I know. I don't believe that cardboard suits and budget furniture spell integrity. Commitment to our people, getting them their share, that's what matters. Do you know anybody in the world who does that better than Jerry Haggerty?"

Matt Kusic looked out to the white fog blowing across the obscured nightscape. At length he thrust his hand out to Burton Hammond. "Count me in, Burt." The Golden West Trust and Pension Fund was born.

3

As if from a great distance, a hundred amplifiers and speakers boomed out her name, and the roar that greeted it was like a thunderclap directly over her. She came out of the dark slowly, the lights blinding, there were steps to be mounted, a hand to help her. She remembered to murmur, "Thank you," a star must always be gracious, and she heard the roaring speakers rise over the surge of applause. "Here she comes now—Roseanna Lee!"

Madison Square Garden? Shea Stadium? Soldier Field? The Coliseum? The Cow Palace? Roseanna Lee hesitated when through the battery of lights she began to make out the faces of her audience; she wavered unsteadily on the five-inch heels she worked in. Roseanna Lee? Shee-it, she was a stripper named Stormy Ball and she peered at the audience and saw it was composed of about ten men, widely dispersed from one another around the smoky room. She heard someone call out, "The bitch is drunk!" A star was always poised; she had to expect hostility; it was the price envy paid. A hand took hers and led her forward, the M.C. who had that day bought her fifty of the yellows and fifty of the reds. *"Here she is, guys, Stormy Ball!"*

Suddenly, alone, on the stage! Please, God, let the yellow take hold. The piano helped, a tiny recreation-room job she began to remember from the earlier shows. A few riffs and chords helped her even more. She could begin to place where she was. This was a joint about ten miles north of Santa Maria.

The toilets. "You're gonna have to play the toilets, the lowest, boom, zap, flush, gurgle—goodbye, Rosie. Whyinhell should *you* be different?" Lenny said. Hello, Stormy.

She worshipped Lenny. They all did. He saw everything through a magnifying glass of torturing clarity. He had lost the common universal human trait—the ability to lie. Somewhere he had heard the record she'd made for the Lynx label and he had managed to find her. Lynx Records was Jack Beach, a mean and crazy cat.

Jack wanted her to have it all. He was not a p-i at heart, but if a man had to pimp to get the bread to make all of Roseanna's charts happen, what the hell? Jack Beach turned her out. Railed at her. "What the fuck are you, a cheap stripper waving her ass in shit-joints, don't tell me you're above turning hundred-dollar tricks! And what are you puttin' ass out for, your music!" He turned her on to uppers so the johns would think the chick was cool and downers so the bitch could get through the rest of the night. Vodka-rocks to steady the nerves.

Through it all, Roseanna sensed a musical genius, off-center, maniacal but a guiding talent like none she had ever known. "Stronger, baby, stronger!" Jack Beach always hammered at her. "You ain't Doris Day, you're a black and white chick, sing black and sing white." He'd send her out on a trick, wait in the car outside, grab her money from her purse when she came out, but he was not jiving about the recording session. When that day came, he had the best sidemen in the business for her and all the instruments she had written for.

Then Jack got in trouble and was gone forever, offed, some said, in a big drug deal. Some independent company bought the master tapes, put on an album cover showing New Orleans at night. The record was in the remainder bins of the discount stores two weeks after its release date.

But Lenny found it, crazy Lenny, beautiful Lenny, truthful Lenny. "You are the greatest thing since Lady, you are the new America singing, you have the most fabulous tits and the curviest *tochis* I ever saw, you are as beautiful as Honey but you've got talent, which makes it a sin. But you can be a star if you want to be one." Lenny had his own kind of friends. "Singers nobody wants, but you've still got one hell of a body." It was back to Stormy Ball and the toilets. "Who knows, maybe Darryl Zanuck will be out in the audience and you'll be the next Jeanette McDonald," the booking agent said. In Lenny's world everybody felt obliged to make jokes.

She was into the reds to sleep and the yellows to wake up and the yellows to feel better and the reds to calm her and the yellows to lift her because it was tough to stay awake . . . and then you felt good, real good, and sometimes there was speed and you could stay awake forever. One owner said, "You sing too much, baby, fachrissake, they don't come to hear no singing, they come to see tits shake and a bare ass." But she held her ground; she was a singer; she was a star; she had made an album—"great," some knowledgeable people began to call it. Little clippings found their way to her sometimes, and she saw words that caused her eyes to cloud, words she could not stand to read because they were wonderful, even if futile, and she did not want to feel sorry for herself.

She was working a toilet in Victorville when she heard about them finding Lenny o.d.'d in the apartment on Hilldale. In the toilet, where else? She was into reds and yellows pretty good by then so there were no tears, just more pills. "Now you got to do completes, sweetheart, which means get out of the G-string and let 'em see what you got and lay off the music," another boss said. "Awright, sing if you gotta, but look, it's worth fifty more if you mingle, we'll make sure the law isn't around." They knew she didn't trick, but they wanted her there in front between the six shows every night, leading the jerk-offs on from nine to two. Everywhere she worked they said she stunk up the stage, she didn't know what to do with her fine ass. Who cared for her singing, she never did songs like "Mean to Me" or "Melancholy Baby," just the shit kids liked these days with hardly no melody . . . but when they saw the body, it didn't matter.

She did not drink. She did not take money from the customers. She was funny. If she got high enough she let them screw her, some of them said she *made* them screw her; she was a nympho, others said, and she would not take money, she was a nutty broad.

The trouble was she didn't know up from down, whether she was coming or going, and it was getting worse. When they'd give her her notice they'd tell the booking agent never to send her back, she was a doper and the Alcohol Control Board would get after them if they found out and who needed it? And the lousy music!

In Paso Robles—or was it Santa Maria?—she had already been given her notice and she had no money but she was proud, she was a star, somewhere she still had the reviews in the fly-by-night rock papers. One of them said, "The best thing since the Beatles. If the lunkheads who run the record business knew anything about music and where it's going . . ." This would be Shea Stadium and it would be the Rolling Stones there in the front row and Mick himself worshipping, the works, and she'd show the world . . .

"Throw her out!" "She's drunk!" she heard two voices call out.

She did a number from the album, "Men Are Kind," the lyrics lost, of course, because her speech was slurry and mushy anyway and the piano was out of tune, also of course. She always played the out-of-tune pianos very loud, but she was hitting a lot of clinkers. It was a street rebellion out there. Guys got up and booed and put their tongues between their lips and blew Bronx cheers. A voice cried out, "She stinks!" The boss of the place ran on the stage, tripping, but grabbing and shoving her off.

The M.C. took her to the airless closet where the strippers dressed and waited for her. Outside, he said, "You need any bread?" She shook her head.

"Can I take you to the bus station?" She shook her head again.

It was cold but she knew what would happen and it was not long happening. The car was a station wagon and one of the guys in front said, "Going somewhere, sweetie?"

"Why not?"

Two of them exchanged a smile and made room for her to sit between them. "How far you wanna go?" one of them said, the witty, daring one, turning to the other two behind them.

An hour later they all stopped at a cheap motel. Roseanna was dead asleep but they dragged her into the cabin. They tossed to see who would have her first and giggled at how things turned out. "You guys get the wet deck," said the winner. "Yeah, but you break her in for us," the witty one said.

She lay there, dimly aware, yet more asleep than awake, because she had taken four yellows. She did not move during the rapes, but the four were rapturous— never had so glorious a body wreathed the sordid sheets of their existence. She slept so hard that when they were done with her body they thought she was dead. "We can't leave the bitch here," one of them said, "they'd know it was us if anything was wrong with her." They got her clothed as best they could, pushed her into the car and let her off at a crossroad not far away, telling her to wait there, they'd be right back.

What always happened happened again and this time it was a Chevrolet and through the mists in her head she heard him say he was a salesman. "Aren't you afraid, getting into a strange car this time of night? Lucky for you I'm a nice man."

She popped a red and smiled wanly. He said, "What's that?" She said it was medicine. "Are you sure you're all right?" he said. "I'm a respectable man. I wouldn't want trouble. Where you going?"

"Wherever you're going."

"Oakland," he said, "but I have to make some stops."

"Can I ride there with you?"

"You're sure it's all right?"

He kept glancing over at her as she rested fitfully, her bare shoulders, her breasts very evident under the thin dress, her clothes like a rocket of shame that could light up the world. "I'm tired," he said some hours later. "Maybe I better pull over."

She was asleep, so he fingered her for a time, fondling her breasts and working his hand up her legs until he found it, and he clumsily explored her until he exploded in his trousers. He looked around and was grateful no one had seen them parked. He composed himself and tried to awaken her, like a man with sensible second thoughts. Roseanna slept the deep repose of the utterly weary and discouraged. He got out of the car, opened the door on her side and helped his passenger to the shoulder of the road. There he thoughtfully and gently also helped her to lie down under a shrub, the better to continue her rest.

The heat of day woke Roseanna. When she got to her feet, she staggered along the roadside. A car screeched to a stop beside her and the ballet was played out again, with one difference. This man tied her to a bed and beat her in a room in Cupertino and found the pleasure so unendurably delicious that he soothed the welts and stripes he had given her with hot towels and pain-killing unguents he always had the foresight to bring along. He also found Roseanna's pills and urged her to take them. Not knowing uppers from downers, he gave her six of each as well as three codeines of his own. When she slept, he put her into the car and stopped again in a shabby motel in South San Francisco. There he once again enjoyed Roseanna's body. This time his ecstasy, he felt, may have taken him too far. She was so out he was afraid she might be trouble, so he fled, leaving her sleeping in the room.

In time the police were called and since there was no identification, fingerprints were taken in the Emergency Room to find out who she was before they stomach-pumped her and threw her into the cold shower to bring her back to life.

4

FLYING north in the company jet, a stewardess gave Ellis Griswold the Los Angeles *Times* with his coffee and his eye fell on a story in the financial section:

A troublesome future lies ahead for a land conglomerate whose record so far has been one of repeated successes.

Southern Border Land Development (Sobordco), one of the Big Board's hot stocks during the recent market uprising, now finds itself land-rich and cash-poor. In the past decade, the huge San Diego-based land-conglomerate has burgeoned from a local building company to a major factor in the ever-expanding California real-estate market. It has had to pay a severely high price to achieve its position.

In a business where up-front outlays are mandatory and returns for primary investment are years in coming back to company coffers, Sobordco finds itself in the same plight as a little old lady who has given a handsome stranger a ton of her money because he's told her of a gold mine. A lot can happen, one way or another, but no one knows just what for sure.

The development of prime real estate as envisioned by the company looks to prove out a bigger bonanza than ten gold mines, but the prize may yet elude the management team organized by Ellis Griswold, who began as an Imperial Valley land developer a short decade ago.

Immediate cash is not the only problem. The Kennedy administration does not seem well disposed to speculation in land. Prices of materials and wages in the building trades have gone out of reach of potential buyers. Real-estate values have been dropping steadily. But even with these negative factors, Sobordco has to grow in order to stand still. It constantly needs new capital to complete projects already on the drawing board.

It is even now short of money for its newest and most daring project. And its troubles there are more than financial. Up to now the growth-oriented company has found little opposition to its high-powered plans. It is secretly studying a project on Thunder Mountain, on 100,000 acres of forested mountain land which looks to ignite an inferno of protest from environmentalists who would be sure to contend that another Disneyland . . .

Ellis Griswold threw down the paper. *Where the hell do those guys get their stuff?* He certainly had not spoken to anyone about Thunder Mountain. It was a closely guarded project. Had any of the dozen or so people involved with it already talked to the press? How stupid, how disloyal! Sure, there were objections on the board and with the planning staff; there were also bound to be shortsighted, self-interested politicians; and there were kooks springing up all over the country who objected to anything new and different. Another Disneyland indeed. What was wrong with that? Look at the pleasure the Disney operation gave millions of people! Look at the profits. There was nothing but endless mountain tract where the proposed Thunder Mountain development would be. Did anybody care about it until they saw what could be done to bring it to the world? The few hikers and Sierra Clubbers who used it now, how do you stack them against millions of families and their kids getting a chance to see Nature and the great redwoods? He had studied the Disney people's work, and he knew how to do better by a factor of ten. Disney's mistake was in not tying up *all* the land around the sun he created . . . Satellites, that was going to be the answer. There'd be Thunder Mountain but also Sobordco-planned villages, planned recreation centers, tourist hotels of the finest category. The choicest parcels were to remain company property, leased to prime tenants.

But it had to be kept secret. . . .

He was staying at the Fairmont. He was getting ready to leave for Hong Kong where there were money people. American money people were holding back just now. But in Hong Kong, they still sold their money—at a high rate of interest, true—but these were times when he didn't care what financing cost because he could make more than enough to cover such expense. And his contracts always carried a no-penalty clause for early payoff. He always insisted on that. But he kept all this secret, too, even the reason for going to Hong Kong.

Hilary Wilson came over for lunch. Bright, golden sunshine lit the suite; when she came in, he was, as always, taken by her. Age never seemed to touch her. She wore blue jeans and a leather flight jacket. She stood tall in high heels barely seen under the pants and her hair was knotted with a silk bandanna behind her neck.

He laid a hand briefly on her rump, a little humiliation Mrs. Wilson accepted like an ancient token of a regal conquest that had become ritual, and meaningless. "They're out to destroy us, Hil," he grumbled.

"You're talking about the story in the L.A. *Times*, I suppose."

His head swiveled to her accusingly. "How do you know about it?" he shot at her.

"Someone called me from L.A. and read it to me. The point you have to consider is not that plans for the project leaked out, but whether it can work."

"It's got to work. This one thing can set us up with a cash flow that could be fantastic!"

"I know, Ellis. But it's a new world. A young president, the post-World War II crop of kids just entering college. They're beginning to make their presence felt. If you lived up here, you'd see that."

"That's got nothing to do with Sobordco."

"I wonder. Thunder Mountain is just the kind of issue the kids might jump on. They'd never let you get away with it."

"Which is why I kept it secret."

"But can you keep them out of it now?"

"Why not? Rich snobs, wet behind the ears, supported by their parents. They don't even know what hard work is. They're not going to have any influence."

"They're not all rich, or snobs, and most of their parents are broke, and they usually have to work as well as go to school. All I'm saying, Ellis, is that they've got to be taken into consideration."

"How?" he said, almost desperately. He went into detail again about what could become the largest tourist at-

95

traction in the world, catering to the desire within all men, women and children to touch the world that was. He himself saw no conflict that his very accomplishment would alter one of the last wildernesses on the continent. In making it accessible, in the taming of it with plastic exhibits, tours, paths, hotels, rides, carefully structured views and surprises, he foresaw a capital growth enterprise of such vastness that it took even Hilary Wilson's breath away. "The government will build the roads, the tax structure makes it a cheap investment for us—the future is endless!" he announced.

"Forgive me, Ellis," Hilary Wilson said at length. "I didn't mean to be negative. It's certainly worth fighting for. But we've got to take into consideration the opposition."

He eyed her appreciatively. Down in San Diego women of her age and station did not dress in jeans and leather. This was a lady who kept in touch, one who had proved her merit to the company time and again, from the very beginning. "I'm going ahead with Thunder Mountain, no matter what. Can I count on you, Hil?"

"I'm there with you, Ellis. You ought to know that. You're a true visionary. I think this may be your greatest idea."

"And most profitable," he beamed. "Where you taking me to lunch?"

"Who do you think is practicing law in San Francisco?" she said over coffee in the court of the old Palace. "Burton Hammond."

"Do I care?" Ellis Griswold said dryly.

"He's doing very well. Name in the right columns all the time. Seems to move in two worlds—labor circles and some of the more interesting people at Cal."

"I still say, why the hell do you think I care?" Griswold demanded irritably.

"You made is possible for him to be a lawyer, didn't you?"

"I'm human. I make mistakes like everybody else."

"You know he's fully recovered from that accident."

"I don't know and I'm not interested." He stirred restlessly. It came to Hilary Wilson that Griswold had managed to put everything having to do with Burton Hammond out of his mind.

"He's sure not to think what happened was an accident," she offered after a moment.

"Probably wasn't. He had a lot of enemies among his own Mexicans."

"My hunch is he'd say he knows why they wouldn't have done it."

"So?" He looked down at his wristwatch. "It's late. I'd better be going."

"You had nothing to do with it, Ellis? I mean indirectly—"

"We talked about this once a long time ago," he said.

"I'm going to see him again, Ellis. He's too smart to play devious games with. I have to know what to say if he brings certain things up."

"Why bother seeing him?"

"Two reasons. He's somebody I can't get out of my system. Also, I'm afraid of him."

"Then for Chrissake stay away for the second reason."

"He's becoming a very powerful man, Ellis. That pension fund Jerry Haggerty has started—"

"He's in that?" Ellis Griswold looked up, surprised.

"He keeps far back, but I'll bet he's in control."

"My God," Ellis Griswold murmured. "Golden West Trust and Pension is moving into the big-time mortgage market."

"They're drowning in cash," Hilary Wilson went on. "The money comes in week after week, automatically, taken from the paychecks of a million union members up and down the Pacific coast. You wouldn't have to go to Hong Kong for slippery money."

"This is why you're afraid of him, and why you want to see him anyway?"

"I'm not sure. He always was a very realistic man. I can deal with him, but I have to know what happened."

"I hated what he did to me personally," Griswold said softly. "But I'd never condone getting rid of him that way. It was an accident."

"All right," Mrs. Wilson said colorlessly. "I believe you."

They both paused, looked about and seemed surprised to find themselves with nothing more to say. "Well, I guess I'd better get started."

"Good luck in Hong Kong."

97

He could not bring himself to go. "You think he *wants* to see you?"

"It's a small town socially, and he knows I get around," she said, getting up. "He'll face the inevitable. He always has."

5

Two marshals appeared early one morning at the offices of Jerry Haggerty, pushed their way past a clutch of secretaries and took a stand in front of the filing cabinets. "We have the subpoenas right here. Anybody trying to stop us is in defiance of the court!" they announced.

Jerry Haggerty stormed out from his own office, red-faced, furious. "Who the hell are you? How dare you break in!"

"We're taking your papers. Here is the judge's order."

"You're not doing a damned thing until I talk to my lawyer!" Over the years he had come to know his rights, but as he grew older he found himself unable to contain his temper and his poise. "You sons of bitches still have to obey the Constitution!"

The office staff struggled to restrain Haggerty. They brought him back to his private domain, closed the door and stood over him as he drained a glass of water and two fingers from the Old Bushmill bottle.

"Shall I call Mr. Hammond?" one of the women said.

"I have the right to confer with my attorney and I don't have to do it over the telephone!" he proclaimed by way of an answer.

"I'd better tell him you're on the way."

There was no answer at the law offices of Burton Z Hammond, Esq. "What the hell does that mean?" Jerry Haggerty demanded of no one in particular. "Try again."

There was still no answer. "Gimme that," Jerry Haggerty demanded. He dialed a private number that only he knew. A phone buried inside Burt Hammond's desk rang, as did an extension in his bedroom on the top floor. No one answered that number either . . .

* * *

Burt Hammond heard the bedroom phone call him. He let it make its soft, private buzzing: it could only be Jerry Haggerty. "I think someone knows you're here," Sue-Ann Martin offered after the sixth ring. He pretended not to care.

Just before the phone began to ring, Sue-Ann Martin had found she had lost one of her hoop earrings, so she got on her knees and began patting the bedroom floor in search of it. She had discovered the golden hoop but found she could not use it because the tiny silver post that went through the pierced ear was still missing. She resumed her quest on the floor, puttering behind the silken draperies and around the tables. Burt had vaguely heard her stir under the bed through a restless sleeping. Suddenly her voice broke out in a joyous yet ridiculing whoop under the bed. "What do you know!" Sue-Ann shouted. "A dirty-sound freak!"

He opened one eye to see Sue-Ann rise from her knees, smiling. "The great, cool good friend and lover turns out to tape the sounds of squeaking mattresses and his girlfriend's orgasms! Well, mother always said you could never trust any man."

"What are you talking about?" Burt said, opening his eyes sleepily.

"Dear man." Sue-Ann sat beside him and circled arms around updrawn knees. "I knew you couldn't be perfect, but I never thought you'd be into Dirty-Old-Man games." She seized his hand and dragged him from the bed. Far under it their eyes fixed on a tiny flat-black junction box. "I'd sure like to hear just what the hell we say during our lovemaking," she said without rancor.

Burt abruptly pulled Sue-Ann to the top of the bed and fell on her, his mouth covering hers. "It's a switch I had the housekeeper put in," he said against her lips.

"Some switch," Sue-Ann said, opening her mouth to his.

"Makes the lights go on automatically at dusk," he said, kissing her firmly. "Let's forget about the gadget, darling."

It was at that moment that the private phone began to ring. "I don't want to talk to anyone," Burt said, sounding as amorous as he could manage. "Did I remember to tell you lately you are one hell of a ball?"

"Why, kind suh, all mah men tell me that," Sue-Ann

teased, resisting, knowing some game was being played. "Hey, look, I'm going to be late for class." She tried to push him off.

"Be late," Burt whispered to her. She had uncovered something that had been planted by an enemy; his design was to make it appear to her and whoever was listening that he was free of any suspicion such a device was being used against him. And not to answer the certainly-tapped telephone.

The buzzing of the private line stopped. "I've got a class, lover-man."

"Come on, let me have you one last time."

The private phone began to buzz again. Even if he did not answer, he knew Jerry would be coming over in a high fury as soon as he could muster car and driver. Burt Hammond knew, however, that he had time enough to allay Sue-Ann's valid suspicions. Later, he would get to work figuring out who had bugged his home, probably his office, and how long the bug had been there, and what had been turned up that could be used against him other than the fact that when he went to bed it was almost always with a lady. . . .

They were on the street outside when Jerry Haggerty's black Continental drove up. Burt led a confused guest to the car. "Jerry, tell your man to take Miss Martin across the bridge to Berkeley," he said, winking broadly. "She's very late for school."

"What the hell goes on?" Jerry roared, ignoring Sue-Ann. "Why doesn't anybody answer your office phone?"

Burt Hammond made sure the car was on its way before he turned to Jerry Haggerty. "We start late. What's up, Jerry?" he said.

"I got a team of federal marshals in my office with papers saying they can remove my files, that's what's up! We've got to do something right now!"

"There's no rush," Burt responded coolly.

Standing on the sidewalk, Burt considered informing his client about his discovery that some agency was bugging his residence and probably his office. Agitated as Jerry Haggerty was, Burt decided quickly not to tell him. Knowledge of it could totally unravel his confidential relationship with his lawyer. Nor did he want to think what Jerry Haggerty would say about his lawyer's management of the security of his home and office. And quite properly.

He stopped the old man before he could go into the

100

building. "Let's talk out here. What'd you tell the marshals?"

"That I want to talk to my lawyer."

"Very smart. You have that right. They'll try to be absolutely correct about everything so all the evidence they collect will stand up in court." He linked his arm to Jerry's and started him walking down the street.

"Can they get away with a raid like that?" Haggerty asked.

Burt shrugged. "Did they rough you up or something?"

"Maybe I should've provoked them?"

"Probably wouldn't work."

"Do they have a license to go fishing in my files until they find something they want?"

"To answer that, I'd have to see what the judge gave them. My hunch is I can't stop them, but I can slow them down a lot."

"What the hell are we doing talking business on the goddamn sidewalk?" Haggerty blustered, and stopped walking suddenly.

"I wouldn't want any of my people to see how upset you are, Jerry," Burt covered.

"Maybe," the old man said, distracted, resuming the walk. "What are they trying to get on me, Burt?"

"I can't tell you just yet."

"Christ, there's all kinds of stuff in my files they could make mountains of. Guys I knew who could use a helping hand. So I send them a thousand. Maybe more. All right, so they've been in prison. So they know, maybe even worked for mob guys. I send them money because I knew them a long time ago and they maybe were nice to me when I was starting out and they need a hand now. Should I say when they call for a touch, Go fuck yourself, you worked for a mob guy, you did hard time, that rules you out forever? That's not my style." He looked over to Burt and thought he found his attorney's attention very far from him. "You hear what I said?" he demanded irritably.

"Jerry," Burt began slowly, "in all the time they've been after you, have you ever discovered listening devices, bugs, planted in your home or your office?"

"I have a guy. Best-in-the-West, like they say. Makes routine checks for me. They don't even try."

Which, Burt thought, was why someone thought the

way to get at Jerry was through his lawyer. A dangerous game. For them. He smiled bitterly. "I want you to compose yourself, Jerry."

"Gets tougher the older I get."

"It's important, Jerry. I know you've done it in the past. Be poised, be assured. I promise I'll let you know the bad news if I have to. Right now, it begins to look good."

"Look good?" he boomed. "They're waiting to put my whole life under a magnifying glass and that's good?"

"The more the better." He was not going to educate his client in the law of evidence and the inadmissibility of evidence illegally obtained. He turned his visitor around and headed him toward his building. "It's going to take some doing, however. You've got to trust me."

"Who's behind this? Robert Kennedy?" Jerry asked some moments later.

"No."

"Why not?"

"He hates you, but he's the attorney general and the chief law officer of the country." Burt was thinking of the bug when he answered Jerry. Who had planted it? He could not believe that Kennedy, a conscientious lawyer, judging from everything he knew about him, would be party to so illegal an act.

"You trying to tell me that arrogant runt couldn't get some judge to do that to me?"

"He's too clever for petty maneuvers, and this is clumsy," Burt Hammond said, still thinking of the listening devices in his own house.

"Does that mean you also rule out the FBI?" Jerry taunted him.

"Oh, they haven't always impressed me personally as being thoroughly conscientious about observing the letter of legality. Nor have I seen them operating with diabolical brilliance."

"I've been up against John Edgar Hoover too often to underestimate him."

"I don't. He's a rogue cop. A law unto himself. My feeling is he always hates his attorney general, and if Kennedy is what you think he is, he's got to distrust this one even more."

"Maybe it's the FBI trying to make time before Kennedy's people nail me, so they can take the bows in the papers."

"Very possible."

"What can we do about it?"

They were at the door. "Your Best-in-the-West guy who makes security checks for you," Burt said. "I ought to see him right away."

"You think they're onto you?"

"I think it's time for a careful check."

"He'll be here soon as he can."

Later that morning, Burt Hammond escorted his client back to the union offices on Market Street. He studied the papers presented him by the marshals. "One small problem," he said to them.

"There's no problem, counselor," the marshal pronounced with the calm assurance of a high court justice. "It's all there."

"We have to use some of those papers in the performance of our business. Besides, we have the right to know precisely what you're taking from the premises."

"What are you talking about?"

"An inventory. We'll need a Xerox copy of everything you remove. Of course, you're perfectly welcome to help yourself to everything."

"You can't make us do that," the marshal complained.

"Ask His Honor, marshal," Burt said pleasantly. "We'll be here when you get back."

The marshal looked about dubiously. "You'll try to go through those files and pull certain stuff while we see him."

"Why don't one of you stand watch while the other takes it up with the judge?" Burt suggested. "And by the way," he went on, "our copying machine is out of order, isn't it, Mr. Haggerty? You'd better make some arrangement on your own."

"You lousy creeps," the marshal said. "We'll see both of you in jail."

"Naughty-naughty," Burt teased. "Remember, you're an officer of the court here."

"Let me slug the son of a bitch," Jerry muttered between his teeth.

"Save it for when it counts." Burt led the old man to a chair inside his own office.

Jerry Haggerty regarded his lawyer sourly. "What in the hell are you grinning about?" he demanded.

6

His call was returned within a half-hour. "Someone here says you want to talk to us about your client, Mr. Jerry Haggerty." The voice was officious, careful, calculated.

"Are you yourself involved in bringing the Haggerty matter to the grand jury for indictment?" Burt asked.

"Yes."

"We ought to talk. But not on the phone. May I come to see you?"

"Say when."

"How's right now?"

His name was Oliver Hale Goodman, and Burt found out what he could about him in the half-hour before he presented himself at the monstrous Federal Building on Golden Gate Avenue. Goodman turned out to be a tall, courtly man, prematurely gray.

Burt Hammond came right to the point. "I would suggest the government save the time and expense of indicting my client."

"Why, we don't think it's any trouble at all," Goodman countered with heavy cheer. "As a matter of fact, it's going to be a pleasure for all of us. As for the expense, a mere bagatelle after what your client has been costing the economy."

"Have you had a chance to go through everything you need in the subpoenaed files?" Burt asked.

"A veritable treasure trove, counselor," Goodman said, grinning. "Your man is nothing if not forthcoming."

"Too bad you won't be able to distort a page of it, not even a sentence. Not now, not ever," Burt said grimly.

"What are you talking about?" Goodman asked, unsmiling now.

"Tainted evidence. Your whole case wouldn't get past the first appeal court, assuming you get a conviction."

"Thanks for your concern." Goodman turned openly

contemptuous. "I assure you, we're very much up on the law of evidence here and we know how to proceed."

"Are you quite sure you know what I'm talking about?" He had always suspected the Justice Department lawyers did not know what had been done.

"I certainly do. Those papers were properly received for review by this office," Goodman replied.

"I was talking about the bug."

There was a brief pause. "What bug?"

"Ah, you don't know?" Burt pursued. "A bug in my residence and another in my office." He snapped open his briefcase. "I have a report. Your experts will know the name of the man who made the investigation for us. He's done this kind of work for my client for years."

Goodman regarded the pages laid on his desk with distaste. "There's no bug in your office, Mr. Hammond," he said severely.

"No bug you appear to know about, Mr. Goodman," Burt corrected him. "I've got photos too, if you need them. I suggest you go to whomever you have to go to and find out about this clumsy and, may I say, illegal procedure. Then, if you decide to go forward to the grand jury, we'll be delighted to see you in court." He got to his feet.

"This is a trick, a maneuver," Goodman said, still sitting.

"I assure you it isn't, sir," Burt said. "We're talking about my client's life, not to mention his reputation, and you don't depend on tricks when that's at stake. I'd be pleased to hear from you when you satisfy your own doubts. You know my number."

"You won't hear from me, counselor, because the whole thing's inconceivable," Goodman said, rising, regaining a composure he had briefly lost command of.

"Let's talk lawyer to lawyer," Burt Hammond said. "The whole thing's obnoxious and destroys every bit of evidence you fellows so carefully and correctly gathered with your right hand. All that file stuff is tainted now. I believe you're as shocked as I see you. But you have a left hand that didn't tell the right what it was doing. We've both run into it before, haven't we, Mr. Goodman? The cop who's so absolutely certain his man is guilty that he gives his case a little illegal extra push. I'm glad to see you knew nothing about it."

Burt held out his hand. Oliver Hale Goodman looked

at it for a long time but in the end found he could not take it.

Burt Hammond came downstairs after a midday shower. Helen Mendoza looked up from the phone conversation she was engaged in and clapped her hand over the mouthpiece. "It's Special Agent Grizzard of the FBI."

Burt took the call. "We'd like to talk to you about an alleged illegal bug and any information you might have about it," the man said.

"I really don't have anything to add to what I've given the federal prosecutor," Burt told him.

Grizzard persisted. "Can't we just come over to talk? I assure you it won't take much of your time."

It only took a short time for two agents, Grizzard and a man named Blevin, to be sitting around Burt's desk. They both wore gray, single-breasted suits with hard-pressed lapels, characterless rep ties, black shoes and snap-brim felt hats.

"This listening device that you claim to have discovered in your residence and here in your office," Grizzard began.

Burt Hammond reached for a legal pad and pen and started to take notes.

"We have some questions about it." Grizzard paused, seeing Burt's pen fly across the page. "Are you always this defensive, counselor?"

"There are two of you and one of me to confirm what's said here," Burt said.

Grizzard's face darkened visibly. "You don't like the Bureau, do you, counselor?"

"It goes the other way, sir. The Bureau's got a special dislike for me."

"We find that people who fight us," Agent Blevin put in, "have usually got something to hide."

"I called you, remember?"

Blevin stiffened. He turned to his fellow agent. "Let's get to business, what do you say?"

"Sure," Burt said, smiling. "Fire away." His hand poised the pen over the pad. "What do you want to know?"

"A few things," Grizzard said coldly. "Your comment to the federal prosecutor's office indicates that you believe the device was installed by an agency of the government. What makes you think that? Also, we would like

106

to know whether your relationship with Mr. Jerome Haggerty is only that of a lawyer and client." Burt's pen came to a stop. He looked up at Grizzard briefly and resumed writing. "And, finally, if you did discover the device, why did it take you so long to report it to the federal prosecutor? And why to him and not to us?"

"Is that it?" Burt said. The men nodded. Burt took a deep breath, not so much of frustration but to let himself contain the anger that surged within him. He knew what he had; he had arranged a few fail-safe steps before he tipped his hand to Oliver Goodman and the Department of Justice. It fascinated him that people sworn to uphold the law could behave like the commonest lawbreakers: until the evidence was granite in front of them, act naive, play innocent. He didn't want to waste time with Grizzard and Blevin; on the other hand, anger, emotion, always got a lawyer in trouble unless it was deliberately employed for a judge or jury's benefit.

His voice was gentle and unruffled when he spoke. "I'll take your queries in my order. First, my relations with Mr. Haggerty. He has several lawyers working for him, in his own offices and elsewhere; for example, in our pension fund. But I'm his personal attorney. Next, why do I think the listening device was installed by an agency of the government, meaning, the Federal Bureau of Investigation? When I answer that I'll have answered your last question. After I discovered it, and because I was afraid of something happening just like this, I made sure to plant certain information in whatever record the device was making which I could later prove to disinterested parties was available only to the party using the machine. Am I clear, gentlemen? It's like when you people dust money with an invisible powder to show it really passed through a suspect's hands. Needless to say, I won't tell you what I planted, but it's there. And that's why I took so long reporting it. And why to him, and not, sir, to you. Is there anything else you want to know?"

The two men looked from one to the other. Blevin was the first to rise. "Your attitude about the Bureau," he began.

"Yes?" Burt said.

"Hostile," he went on. "You afraid of us?"

"I'm careful."

"Hostile," Blevin insisted. "Always have been. Down there in the Imperial Valley, also hostile. People who've

107

done nothing wrong have nothing to be afraid of from us."

"I'm never afraid, sir. I'm careful. I go out of my way to make sure everything I'm concerned with is done absolutely properly."

"That bug was not planted by any government agency," Grizzard insisted.

"Then go ahead and indict my client and make me prove it in open court."

"Let's go," Blevin said to his partner.

"Why do you always fight us?" Grizzard asked Burt Hammond, resisting his partner briefly. "We've got a job to do."

"So've I," Burt said. "But I do mine properly, which is to say, legally."

"Don't challenge us, mister," Special Agent Grizzard muttered through clenched teeth.

"I'll make a deal with you," Burt said, smiling. "I promise to do nothing to engage the interest of the Bureau if it leaves me alone from now on."

"Wiseguy," Grizzard hissed contemptuously.

"Let's go," Blevin said again.

Burt Hammond leaned against the door when he was alone. His whole body was sweaty.

Some weeks later word was carefully leaked to the papers that the government "at this time" had decided not to seek indictments against various labor officials known to have connections to known mob elements. It was said that although the Department of Justice had no doubt that what it had presented to the federal grand jury could be made to stand up in court, it preferred to go after a bigger score and prove how deeply committed certain labor officials were to convicted crime figures.

Asked for a comment, the press reported, veteran Bay Area labor boss Jerry Haggerty had said, "Now that the government has decided it has no case, let's hope it stops harassing us so we can get on with the business of making our members more secure in their jobs now and in the future that faces all American working men and women."

7

THERE was no other way out. He had to get rid of dear, lovely, enchanting Susie Martin.

Sex with her was still a splendid exertion, like tennis with a pro who returns everything, forehand, backhand, drop shot, top-spin, cross-court, slice, making his opponent stronger and better at his own skills. It was even more than a game to Susie, it was an enchanting ride among spaceless stars.

The problem was that all the magic had gone dead. It was going nowhere. Nothing that Susie said or did was that different. She made no demands on him, offered no complaint when he broke their dates, often at the last moment.

Finally, after four successive canceled meetings, he saw her on his terrace, plied her with unsweetened and unfiltered apple juice and told her flat out that was it, the end, they'd always be friends, there was nothing he would not do for her, she was beautiful and bright and a marvelous bedmate, but . . . He waited for the inevitable explosion of tears and the recrimination.

"Thank God," Sue-Ann said. "I thought you'd never get around to it."

"You mean you don't care?"

"Of course I care." She pressed a hand to his hot forehead. "I've seen it coming, my dear, but didn't know how to tell you. You're getting to be an older man now, Susie understands how it is when you're over thirty. You begin to think of that One Woman, offspring bearing your genes, even your name; it's biology, Burt, you can't help it. It's just not for me and I never pretended it was, did I, darling?"

He accepted a Mother Earth-ly buss on the cheek. "Is that what it is, Susie?" He inclined his head to her chest.

"You've balled your way through battalions of girls, in your case maybe divisions, and you've come to that great

109

truth of horny bachelordom. It's Not Enough. So it's mating time. Henry Higgins' consort battleship, you and her, ready for battle. And the dear little one, no doubt at three showing signs of genius. There'll be pictures in the wallet. I haven't known how to tell you I just have not got the inclination for all that shit."

He regarded her with freshly minted admiration and wonder. "Susie, you are marvelous."

She retired to the bedroom. He could see her with her cigarette papers and the little sack. When it came to leaving evidence, Susie was a rookie cop's delight, even to the burns from the loosely packed toque. He gave her her moment of release and found her at peace with herself when he joined her again.

"Let's make it together one more time," she said brightly.

"Do you think we should? After all, we've broken up, haven't we?"

"We're friends, Burt, what's a fuck between friends?"

As always, it was splendiferous, wild, skyrocketing, and dull as the fiftieth ride on the roller-coaster.

"What're you going to do, Susie? About a job. Anything you need, you let me know, political pull, money . . ."

"I wouldn't want any job that requires that. I want to do something in my own line—what, I don't know; but away from here, that I'm sure of. I really know about land use and such, Burt. Something'll turn up."

"Let me think about it."

"Isn't goodbye wonderful?" she said at the door.

"Was she right? he asked himself when he was alone again; was sex as fun-and-games simply losing its savor? Were the campus radicals right? Over thirty another world? He had never thought of marriage. Was it time to get started?

He had other, more immediate concerns at the moment. As personal counsel to the executive chairman of the Trust and Pension Fund as well as a member of its Oversight Committee, Burt Hammond did not involve himself with the details of how and where certain loan proposals were initiated. He kept his energies for final approval—and for making sure the federal rules regulating lending institutions had all been sternly followed.

A lot of the fund's money was going into gaming establishments in Las Vegas, and into resort hotels. Burt Hammond soon learned that almost everybody in that line of work had some kind of police record. If somebody knew how to run a casino, the chances were that he also carried a string of convictions going back to his youth. This had to be weighed against the man's more recent conduct, and how safely the fund's money could be entrusted to the former manager of a bust-out crap game in Englewood, N.J.

At first, he objected to all sorts of things and people. But in the course of putting the fund's money to work at the best rate of interest he could charge the people seeking it, he came to the conclusion that it was not a lender's business to go all the way back to year one. "If God can forgive, so can we," he said.

The pension fund had to be put to work, and with torrents of members' automatically-withheld contributions that flowed into it every week he had to find ways to do the job. Or they would drown in the flood.

Burt Hammond always saw to it that nothing in existing regulations was transgressed.

The important thing was, he said, that the fund was creating more money than it started with. Success tasted as sweet as it was said to be.

8

HELEN Mendoza came into his office so agitated that she fluttered, which was an accomplishment for a lady of her size; she found herself incapable of intelligible speech, also not her style. Burt Hammond finally made out that someone was in the reception room, had come in unannounced, and Helen did not know what to do about it. He had seen his secretary function under the pressure of unwelcome callers ranging from uniformed cops from the precinct to tight-lipped gentlemen heavy with the authority of the federal government, and Helen had always been composed, firm and unintimidated.

He finally settled her down and found out that his unannounced visitor was Mrs. Wilson. "What's she want with you? Why's she come here?" Helen burbled. Burt was too busy trying to restore his secretary to her usual self to reply. Helen raced on like a turntable out of whack; even the pitch of her voice was unfamiliar. Mrs. Wilson worked with Ellis Griswold . . . all that stuff was behind Helen's boss . . . better for him to forget than to open old wounds . . . Helen had eyes . . . she saw how it was back then with her . . . why didn't she just tell the lady he wasn't in?

When she escorted Mrs. Wilson in a few moments later, Helen abandoned her at the door. Burt prudently kept the desk between him and his visitor. He had thought of her often since that fiery day along the Salton Sea, thought of her down there in Sonora and in this city which he knew to be her home terrain. When he was new to it, he had walked its streets wondering what he would do if he saw her; often he came out on Geary Street during a theater intermission and looked at the back of some lady, sensing a certain high-style presence, the assurance in the broad shoulders, the slim line to the rump and the long straight legs he remembered. He would stroll past, but it was never Hilary Wilson.

She was more striking and beautiful than he recalled. Taken on a pound or two, her face full enough so he was sure she had not had to visit a counterpart of his own Dr. Sanchez. She dressed for the occasion in slim pants, casual blouse, a coat piped in leather; her hair was windblown, a pale lipstick highlighted her mouth.

"You're incredible, Hilary." He left his desk to bring her into the room.

"Lucky, I guess," echoing an old joke they once shared. "I smoke too much. Drink: Keep lousy hours. Let me look at *you*." Soft, remembered fingers traced the skin across his cheeks, the broken arch of his nose, and behind his ears where the scarring was more evident to the touch than the eyes. "I always said you'd be even more beautiful when life had eroded your looks. The doctors have done a remarkable job. Made you even more attractive."

"May I kiss you, Hilary?"

"Do you still want to?"

"Why don't I find out?"

As always, there was nothing beneath the top layer of her clothes. Long, serpentine fingers clutched his head and would not release.

"Yes," Burt said at length. "I'd like to, all right." He

moved her out of his embrace. "I have rooms upstairs over the store. Let me show you."

He brought her up to the apartment by way of the private stairway. She did not want coffee, wine, a soft drink or even a cigarette. "So," she said, smoothing her pants as she sat as if it was a skirt over her lap. "I read about you when you took on that case of the little girl on Union Street. See your name in the right columns. You've done very well, Burton."

"It's a living. How about you?"

"Half of the men in the world are neurotic, the rest are mostly gay and I have to make do with them, so there are obvious limitations."

"Sobordco? How's it coming there?"

"Better than ever. We're up to our ears in Orange County and the future looks great."

"I make it my business to keep up on Sobordco and all its problems, not to mention those of its president."

"You're not still carrying ancient grudges, are you, Burton? Ellis Griswold swears he had nothing to do with the terrible thing that happened to you. I've been with him a long time; when you're dealing in land you see a lot of ruthless and coldblooded things done. We've been into deals a lot bigger than we ever saw back there in the Imperial Valley. But I've never seen anything like that."

It took only a moment for Burt Hammond to reflect that this was a waste of his time. The lady had come to see him for her purposes. In the years that passed, he had not forgotten Ellis Griswold. He had learned patience, to trust the natural flow of the adversary's inborn character to betray him, as an Indian hunter does when he stalks his quarry.

He picked up her hands gently. "Let's not talk about the past, Hilary. You came to see me. What can I do for you?"

"I know the power you can exert with Golden West. I'm asking you not to let your feelings about Ellis Griswold make a difference."

"For your sake, I'll try." He hoped he sounded as if he meant it.

"We can't erase the past but we can put it aside," she went on. "I want to bring Sobordco and the Golden West fund together, without prejudice, and with profit to both."

"And you thought I'd stand in the way?" he said, as mildly as he could manage. "Let personal feelings interfere with my duties?" He paused. Then: "You're right," he conceded, he hoped convincingly. "I guess I might have done that. I'm glad you dropped in."

"Maybe I've been wrong about you all this time, Burton. You have changed."

He shrugged. "You're not having trouble raising capital on Montgomery Street or Wall Street?"

"The big underwriters feel overcommitted to us. We need to discover new sources for our developmental purposes, money that isn't looking for such a fast return."

"That would be that big project on Thunder Mountain?"

She looked surprised. "You know about it?"

"It was in the papers. A venture like that could involve a lot of risk capital, I can see that. What happens if it doesn't go through?"

"It will! It's a natural."

"I was thinking of environmentalists and lovers of your true unadulterated outdoors. They're a freaky breed when it comes to screwing up their wilderness."

"What always happens to those people, Burton?"

He knew. She knew. They both remembered a man who loved the small farm along the canal. They did not have to speak of it now.

"Could the company sustain a heavy loss like that if the venture flopped?" he pursued.

"It would be damned serious, I'll grant you that. But why should it go bad? We own the whole development on the mountain. Between Sacramento and Washington we get all the access roads and improvements built, at no expense to us. We keep an interest in the best real estate of the satellite towns and in the adjacent hotels and shopping centers. It can't miss. Those Sierra Clubbers and elitist kids who think the masses mustn't be allowed on their sacred terrain unless they're willing to backpack in for fifty miles—when push comes to shove, they lose. We know how to win the public support."

"Weight always wins, right, Hilary?"

"Doesn't it in the circles you move in, Burton?"

He sighed and got to his feet. "I'm not going to stand in your way."

She rose and came to him. "You're magnificent, my dear. Thank you."

He touched her cheek gently and left her for the phone.

"Helen," he said into it after a moment, "Mrs. Wilson and I won't be here for a while. Hold my calls, will you?"

"Where are we going?" Mrs. Wilson asked.

"To the bedroom, is that all right?" he said.

Later, he emerged wet and dripping from the shower, toweling himself and watching Hilary Wilson in the darkened room blow plumes of smoke to the ceiling. "I'm going to get married," he said.

Without turning her head toward him, she replied: "Anyone I'd know?"

"Haven't met her myself. Just feel I ought to start thinking about it."

"It wouldn't rule me out of your life?" She sat up, holding the sheet between her breasts. "I wouldn't like that. I'll always be available for assignations and rendezvous in motels, offices, couches and the back seats of cars with you, Burton."

"I think I've been looking in the wrong places. Maybe I ought to see what life's like over on your side of the barricades."

"Just as awful there for the men as it is for the women, darling." She fell back and sent another cloud of smoke ceilingward. "There are the emotional cripples, the mama's girls, the daddy's girls, there are the sickies, the uglies, the dulls. Of course some of them have money, I mean real money, old money, not like yours and mine."

"Mine buys as much as theirs, so I don't care about vintage."

"There are a couple of interesting girls, though. Do you mind that they wear shoes?"

"What'll they think of me?"

"Jerry Haggerty's Machiavellian adviser? Oh, they read the papers, the ones I'm thinking of. They know about the Teamsters, and they know about Jerry's Council, and they know about gangsters and all that pension-fund money going to Las Vegas, and how Robert Kennedy keeps saying what terrible persons all of you are. They'll be fascinated."

"Then do it for me, Hilary."

"They've got to be bummers in bed. My hunch is that they haven't yet been introduced to their clits."

"You'll be available, so what the hell?"

She rose to get into her clothes. He watched her move naked with assured grace, ageless, timeless. She caught his eyes on her and stood there for a moment before she pulled on the jeans. "You're serious? Why, Burton?"

"Curiosity, I guess. A new world."

"Ah, yes, I remember. You and Alexander the Great. White tie, three weeks from next Monday. That ought to give your tailor enough time. Right now I need a cab." She found a ribbon to tie her hair.

"I'll take you. You really know someone, Hilary?"

"Better see for yourself. It only comes out on very special occasions, like the opening of the opera season. I've missed the last few so it's been some time. You don't have to drive me. I'm going across the bridge to Oakland."

"I want to," he insisted. It wasn't the rich girls and the opera he wanted to talk about, although clearly Hilary Wilson thought so and he gave her enough reason on the way to confirm her suspicions. The business of the girls had been settled; it wasn't of prime importance anyway. Maybe that was part of what was wrong with his life these days. But he knew he had to know more about the depth of Sobordco's commitment to the Thunder Mountain project. And its vulnerability if, inconceivably, the whole thing blew up in their faces.

9

SOMEONE said he'd find Susie with everybody else on the campus. He left the car in front of her apartment house and found himself with a milling crowd on the steps of Sproul Hall. Pickets, signs, shouting, bullhorns, angry police, confused bystanders—none of this was new to him, but he had never seen anything like this. These signs did not carry pleas for more money or better working conditions or union recognition. FUCK, they said. When they did not say FUCK they proclaimed SHIT, PISS, CUNT or FSM. FSM? Had Yale failed him in not unveiling this Anglo-Saxon word that lacked a vowel?

"It's our world, not theirs!" a bullhorn proclaimed. Clubs waved over student heads. From Telegraph Avenue there came the wail of police sirens, screeching to a moaning stop. Television Station KGTV had a station-wagon at Sather Gate, and the demonstrators surged to it as bees to their hive. The operators of the big, bulky camera, working atop the wagon, struggled to keep their machines from toppling. The police began to use their clubs, grabbing girls and the smaller males. The crowd's protest crystalized. "Fuck!" it shouted again and again. "Fuck!"

Burt felt a hundred years old. He retreated in disgust and waited in his car for Sue-Ann Martin. When she returned, her face was streaked with perspiration and dirt and her silken hair was a rich tangle.

"I've got one quick question for you," Burt said. "What the hell is fism?"

"Free Speech Movement. We organized the demonstration."

His shoulders sagged. "So *fuck* is free speech? Well, you can't fight free speech. Like milk and mother love."

"If you can't say *fuck* in public there's no free speech," she announced. "Free speech begins with *fuck*."

"So all this demonstrating is just for the right to hold up a placard with a dirty word?"

"You older guys are out of it. Fuck is not a dirty word. Your mind is dirty. Fuck is just a word."

"I'll go farther than you. It *is* a dirty word and you've got a First Amendment right to say it, to write it, to read it—"

"They've taken in some of our people. You want to be our lawyer?" she asked eagerly.

"Whatever it started out to be, it's degenerated to dirty words."

"On the contrary, it hasn't gone down, it's going up and up," Sue-Ann broke in. "It began because we were told we couldn't solicit funds on a strip of land which belongs to the city after they'd stopped us from doing the same on the campus itself. Now some of us are saying to the world our right to speak out is absolute. The dirty words are to get attention. You think the media, the world, would care about polite protest?"

"I stand corrected."

"I adore you," Sue-Ann said. "I don't understand you, but I adore you." She tossed her hair joyously from side to side. "Did you come all the way across the bridge because you found out you can't live and not go to bed with me? Come on, we'll send the roommate out for pizza."

"I came to talk to you."

"Hey. I'm touched. You don't want my body, you want Sue-Ann Martin?"

"I want you to work for me. For pay. Maybe some of your friends too."

"Some more of your fascinating parties? Of course. That's not work, it's extracurricular social studies."

"I'm talking about initiating a movement to save a hundred thousand unspoiled acres from destruction."

"I thought it was only money and more money for your labor cats. I didn't know they cared about the land."

"It's a personal project."

"Something for you, the environment *and* money?" she said eagerly. "Beautiful! What do I have to do?"

"Did you ever hear of Thunder Mountain?"

"Of course."

"They want to carve it up, plasticize it and turn it into another Disneyland."

"Your people with all their money?"

"Never mind whose money. I want to know if you'd like to stop it."

"Things like that take a lot of money. Even shouting dirty words does, I've found out."

"Everything costs a lot of money. I'll handle that end. Can you get some of your people to set up an *ad hoc* organization?"

"What's *ad*—?"

"God, and you're in graduate school? It means a one-purpose outfit. A Save Our Mountain campaign is what I have in mind. I'd want my name kept out. You're the only one to know and to have any contact with me. Can you handle that?"

"I'm not as rattle-brained as I appear, Burton."

"It's why you're marvelous. Can you bring in some other people?"

"We could go into competition with the Sierra Club on this one."

"Sure, be as daring and bold as FSM."

"We'll camp there. They'll have to kick us off the mountain."

"Figure out what you need and let me know."

"I'll call you at the office."

"No," he said. "Never call me at the office."

"Why?"

"I always operate as if my phones are bugged. I prefer

you don't write me either. You'll get your money in cash. I have a man who works for me. He'll be getting in touch. Elmer Wright's his name. You'll call him to get to me."

"Hey, this is still the United States of America, isn't it?"

"Very much so. Therefore, be careful."

"I'm glad you thought of me for this, Burt." He knew she was serious. It wasn't just shouting dirty words for the sake of protest any longer.

10

IT was all pink and white, soft silken curtains fluttering in the breeze, a scent of jasmine and roses in the room when Roseanna Lee awoke. Her eyes remained fixed on the high ceiling and coursed down the walls, across a gilt mirror, a pretty picture in the Marie Laurencin style, a nightstand beside her and the flowered sheet around her own shoulders. She did not know if she was steady enough to sit up; dizziness made her fall back.

A face loomed over her. "You all right, Roseanna?"

In focus it became a man she had never seen before, a round, circular face with a heavy beard that had not been shaved that day.

"What's happening? Where am I?"

"You're in a suite in the Stanford Court Hotel, Roseanna," the face said with a gentle smile. "I'm Lou Birch and you've been here four days."

She forced a smile. "Funny," she said, "I don't remember checking in."

"You're here with a nurse. She had to go out for an hour so she asked me to take over."

"You my nurse too?"

"I'm head of IMC Records, Roseanna. You may have heard of us. We're a subsidiary of Brighton Industries. It's an English company in film, television and recordings."

"I've heard of IMC," Roseanna said, dizzy again and finding it difficult to force the smile. "I also heard of Co-

119

lumbia and RCA and Motown and Decca." She closed her eyes. Everything was blurred for a time, long or short, she did not remember when she came back again.

"You're under a doctor's care, Roseanna," Birch was saying. "You're going to be all right."

"Sure I am."

"We've been looking for you. Thank God we found you when we did. No one else knows what happened or where you've been."

"Neither do I. So what the hell?"

"IMC has great faith in your future, Roseanna. We think you have it in you to be a top artist, to be able to blast your way to the top of the popularity charts."

"Yeah," she said with no conviction. She tried to swallow but found her tongue stuck to the roof of her mouth. Lou Birch poured a glass of chilled water from a silver carafe. There was a bent-glass straw and he held it for her to drink from. She lay back on the pillow and tried to sleep but found she could not. "I don't feel so good."

"I'll call the doctor. He comes here to see you." Lou Birch chuckled. "See how important you are, Roseanna? You even get a doctor to make house calls."

"I hope he carries uppers with him," Roseanna said, smiling again. "I could sure use a handful."

"Honey, you're going to work again, that's the important thing."

"Not unless I get on my feet," Roseanna said. "And that means my little yeller dolls, Lou," she added. She started to weep, she did not know why, but she could not stop.

She was able to sit up. The nurse had a Cockney accent and was pretty enough for Roseanna to tell her she ought to be in pictures. "I'm trying, luv," Brenda Moore said. "Maybe I'll make it through you."

Dr. Jack Silverman fought her on the pills. "You've got to try to break your dependence on them."

"I can't work, I can't function, I can't even think music if I'm down," she pleaded. "I'm not really hooked, for God's sake, I'll stay off of speed, just give me enough to get me through the day."

Silverman and Lou Birch had a long, heated conversation in the sitting room. She could hear the loud voices. Lou Birch: "I'm not trying to save the world, Jack, I'm tryin' to run a business filled with crazy characters, all of whom have got handicaps my teacher in P.S. 19 would not approve of. We're already gambling a fortune in her. Give her what she wants."

"Find another doctor, Lou."

"Like *she'll* find someone else, Jack. They always do. This girl's got a future. A little nothing record of hers has built itself an underground rep that's amazing. We'll move her to a more pop area, give her promotion like she's never had—she could wind up selling like Elvis! And you hold back on a lousy handful of pills. I'll give you a tip. If she records for us, go out and buy all the Brighton stock you can afford."

A few days later she found herself in a house in the hills above Berkeley where there was a fine Steinway in a room with sound like a bell. Brenda stopped wearing the nurse's uniform and was there with her night and day. Larry and Lou decided the first album ought to be backed with San Francisco musicians. The San Francisco sound was very big, Jefferson Airplane and Led Zeppelin had reached gold. Roseanna had no objection. She was getting her pills and this Brenda could be handled okay.

The A & R man was named Larry Marshall, a young guy, blond, curly hair, handsome, whose only problem was that he kept proclaiming himself a lady-killer. "Your stuff's super, Rosey," he said, "but the world's not ready for it yet. We've decided the first album ought to be straight pop."

"Why in the hell did your boss spend all that money to find me if you want me to do 'Who's Sorry Now?' and 'Lipstick on Your Collar' like Connie Francis?"

"That little lady's Number One on all the charts! That's all I want you to be."

"Well, loverboy, if you think I'll play them vanilla chords and schmaltz it up with vibrato and a little-girl sob in the voice, you have got a surprise for yourself. I ain't Italian, I ain't even Jewish. Ah's a li'l ole black chick who's got to sing in her own way."

Later, Brenda said: "Hey, baby, *you're* the actress, not me. That was some bravura performance."

"I think Larry-Balls is right," Roseanna said. "But don't tell 'im yet."

"It's just a piece of paper, sweetheart," Lou Birch pleaded.

121

"It looks like a contract to me," Roseanna said, putting down the pen. "Why are we in such a hurry to sign?"

Lou looked around the room as if he had an audience. "'Why?' she asks. Because I run a business, Roseanna. I've got an executive committee to report to, I've got stockholders, and I've spent all this money and there's so much more yet to go, recording studios, arrangements, musicians. I'm gonna team you with the best conductor in the business. It all costs. And unless I get you on paper, they're after me."

She could see the logic in that. "But I don't know anything about contracts. The last time I signed I got nothing."

"You'll get, you'll get! My God, you'll be rich. Why do you fight me?"

"How *much* will I get?" she persisted in a small, little-girl voice.

"So it won't be the same as Elvis. Sinatra either. But you'll get what everybody else gets, is that bad? It's the standard contract, like everybody signs in the record business."

"What does that mean?" she said, still playing the little girl lost in the world of financial giants.

"That means if you sell five hundred thousand records you'll make five hundred thousand times more money than Franz Schubert made in his whole life!" Lou exploded.

"But this paragraph here," she said sweetly, opening the pages of the contract. "'Expenses Charged to the Artist.' What does that mean? Like, all the expenses you've laid out so far for me, I have to pay that back? Hospital, hotel, doctors, chartered planes, they're really all on my tab?"

"That's normal in the business, Roseanna, darling," Lou soothed her. "Otherwise there'd be no stop to what artists spend."

"Then how come the contract says nothing about how I know for sure I get whatever's coming to me if it tells me exactly what I've got to pay for?"

"You trying to infer a big company like IMC would screw an artist out of a few pennies royalty?" He laughed heartily. "You're in the big time, angel. We don't have to steal."

"So why don't you just put in something that says I can look in the books to find out for sure?"

He took her hands in his and kissed them. "Roseanna, darling, who in the world cares more for you? When you lay near death who found you? Who nursed you? Who believes in you, now and forever? I'll give you what everybody else gets in the business. I've got bosses too. You think I can go to them and tell them what I've done for an unknown artist, the money I've spent already, and expect a clap on the back? In the face, Roseanna! The woods're full of aspiring singers—the brass ring just happened to fall into your hand. Grab it, my girl, you won't be poor, you'll see!"

He held open his arms for her. She looked at them but instinct told her to beware of men who offered more than a woman had a right to expect. She turned her back and walked out to the terrace with its spectacular view of the haze-covered city. She did not see Lou Birch swing his head toward her with his eyes fixed on Brenda.

She felt Brenda's hand on her forearm. Both young women stared out at the view. "I'd sign," Brenda said.

"I feel bad, Brenda."

"I've got an upper." She reached into a shirt pocket. "Need water?"

"You kidding?" Roseanna popped one, swallowed it neatly with a gulp of air.

"Funny," Roseanna said after a moment, "a few weeks ago I'm stripping for a hundred a week and I pay my own expenses. Here I'm fighting a guy who says I'll be rich."

"Nothing's going to happen except good things, Roseanna."

"Yeah. Me and Connie Francis and Brenda Lee."

"Don't fight it. Get so big you make them do what you want, luv."

"I don't want to sign. I don't even understand that damned paper."

"At least these people are your friends," Brenda insisted.

"Look at all they're doing for me," she conceded. "Why can't I believe it?"

"You're nervous, luv. All you've gone through. It'll take a while. These are good people."

"Poor me." Roseanna forced a smile. "I'll sign so long as it's the same everyone gets."

"I'll call them and tell them."

"Why do I feel I'm being sold as a slave all over again?" Roseanna said.

123

Nights were the worst. In the dark, there swam visions of creaking, stinking stages, grinning faces floating in blackness, lips parted, eyes drilling the dark and not one gaze above her chin; long, ugly laser beams stabbing her naked breasts and mons Veneris. Men pinned her down in dreams, they raped her with dry, dirty fingers and penises like clubs, they slobbered on her face as they emptied themselves on her, in her and through her, they spat at her and pushed her from the stage, from the car, from the airplane, from the cliff, into fire, into water that swirled down the basin.

Brenda always knew. She found Roseanna in the bathroom searching for the sleeping pills. "You've already had four grain-and-a-half's tonight, baby."

"I can't sleep."

"You've got a lot of work to do tomorrow. The record session's not that far away."

"I'll never be able to do anything if I don't get some sleep."

"Try."

Brenda led her back to the bed and sat there with her, her presence reassuring and warm. "Why are you so good to me?" Roseanna said.

"Because you're beautiful."

"I need you so much." Roseanna flung her arms around her.

After a long moment, Brenda freed herself from Roseanna's embrace and went to the john. "Take two more, baby. We'll do something else tomorrow morning."

Dr. Silverman looked up from the reports.

"You've got to try to get off this amphetamine roller-coaster of yours, Roseanna," he said.

"You talk like I'm hooked, Doc," Roseanna said cheerfully.

"Maybe you are."

"Then millions of people are hooked, Doctor Jack, because what I'm doing everybody else is doing. Maybe not so much, but they haven't got as much riding on their crap-shoot as I have."

"I understand the tensions. In your business it's all or nothing. And all can mean instant fame and instant fortune."

"And nothing is waiting for me back in the toilets. You ever worked a toilet, Dr. Jack?"

"I'd like to suggest psychotherapy."

"What's that?"

"A psychiatrist. To help you lose your dependence on these barbiturates."

"Fine. And what kind of songs do I write then? Nice, clean white-bread and milk songs about ma, the kids and the PTA?"

"I want you to promise you'll think about psychotherapy. May I ask your companion to work with me to decrease your dependence? I don't want to do anything behind your back. I know she's trying to help you."

"Sure, doc." Roseanna said, smiling.

As the date for the recording session approached, Roseanna found sleep even more difficult to attain. She fell on the bed. Soon she became aware of Brenda's hand on her shoulder, the fingers cool and comforting. Brenda lay beside her, arms circling her. 'You're so alone, my darling, so very vulnerable. Brenda does love you so." Brenda kissed her, the lips parted slightly, the touch at the corner of Roseanna's mouth revealing a tiny, exquisite passion. Roseanna turned and sat up.

"Wow," she said. "How about that?"

They looked at each other and smiled with embarrassment. "I'm sorry," Brenda said.

"It's not the first time," Roseanna said. "Jack Beach used to fix me up with a few ladies in the better sections of L.A. for a C-note per. But it was always just the bod rented out and nothing happening inside."

"Something happened now?" Brenda said.

"I don't know." Roseanna looked around the room nervously. "I wonder if there would happen to be something called vodka in this here plush prison?"

"Lucky for you you've got the right connections." In a moment Brenda came back with a full bottle of Smirnoff and a handful of capsules.

"Thanks, Brenda. Now I'd like to be alone."

Brenda Moore was taken by surprise, and a little hurt. But she felt in the presence of an overwhelming force, a star, a real star, and she withdrew.

The chords came with the remembering, and then a melody and words, not in a fluid way, a song never happened that easily, but she knew where she wanted to go with it, and that was half the battle. A woman alone, vast spaces, a relentless, burning sun, thousands of hostile, leering faces and greasy hands, a stranded woman; then a man appears and lifts her and frees her, and suddenly he is gone. She rested her head in her arms over the keyboard.

Larry found her half asleep. He took her into his arms. "Take me seriously, baby." He spoke not so much of love as of a partnership, freeing her from everything but her creative work. "My whole life would be just to make you happy."

She was learning how to avoid answers. "Maybe I ought to marry the guy," she told Brenda later. "He'd be my personal A & R man, my manager, my stud. He'd protect me in areas I don't know anything about. After all, what's he want from me, only success? Gigs in Vegas, nightclubs, network TV, big concerts, gold records every time out. A million a year. What's wrong with that, except it makes me feel like a slave?"

Brenda saw it again, the fire of the star. She knew that Roseanna might well end up with Larry, and she wonderd where that would leave her. "I want you to do whatever you think would be best for Roseanna Lee."

"Why did I fight him? I've been kicked around so much, when somebody tries to help I bite, like a mad dog. I think I'm getting the shakes, Brenda."

"I've got some reds, darling. You won't say anything, will you?"

She swallowed the pills with vodka for a chaser. "You're sweet to me." It took a few moments for the drugs to catch hold but they made the world smooth as glass again. "I'm glad I found you."

Brenda's hand reached out and took Roseanna's, studying the long, delicately tapered fingers. "I don't want you to be hurt." She picked up the hand and touched it with her mouth.

Roseanna stared at her for a long moment.

"I'm sorry," Brenda said.

"Don't be. You're my only friend. You come through with the pills, don't you? The other ladies wore itchy tweed skirts, flat oxfords and talked down in the chest somewhere," she said without malice.

Brenda rose nervously. "You won't say anything, will you?"

"Sit down," Roseanna said. The authority in the voice

126

arrested Brenda. She sat rigidly at the edge of the sofa. "Am I going to be a star, Brenda?"

"Why else do you think Larry and Lou Birch are doing all this for you?"

"They pay you to make sure I do things their way?" Brenda Moore's head dropped. "Pills too? They know about that?" She took Brenda's hand in hers. "I'm glad. I couldn't live without 'em."

Brenda turned quickly. "I'm on your side." Her arms flung out and held Roseanna. "I love you. I want to help you. To be with you."

"Yes," Roseanna said, stroking Brenda's head. "Rosey understands. You're trapped too. We'll work it out." Her head was dizzying; pills and alcohol were doing what they always did in the second stage, blurred things, softening them, making the unreal real; memory and desire embraced in a whirling dance. She lay down. Her eyes fluttered to a close.

Brenda came to her knees on the floor beside her. "Here, let me cool you." She waved her hand over Roseanna's face and bent down to kiss the mouth. There was no resistance. "You're so beautiful," she whispered. When her hand found the round fullness of her breast, she leaned over and tenderly kissed it, until her questing tongue found the aureole and her lips closed over the tender bud of the nipple.

11

"No. No. Absolutely no. I recommend against it," Burt Hammond said.

"Look at him," Jerry urged cheerfully, "our lawyer's running scared."

Matt Kusic sat back in the big chair at Jerry's right hand and grinned broadly. "I never realized until now how easily money can make money just by being money. I'd hate to lose something like this."

"It's an ideal loan for us," Jerry Haggerty said. "Thirty

million to a successful, going business. Two points for the loan. The interest tied to the prime so if the Federal Reserve raises it, we get an increase too."

"When something that good's offered me, I always look twice," Burt agreed. "But . . ."

The Oversight Committee of the Golden West Trust and Pension Fund was in session for its November meeting. Composed of four members, it met on the morning of the third Friday of every month, Jerry Haggerty serving as chairman. Besides Matt Kusic, the committee consisted of Tom Humber, a power in Los Angeles labor politics, and the Fund's special financial advisor, Dean Heller, whom Jerry had brought in from Montgomery Street. Heller was a firmly conditioned boss' man; whatever Jerry was for, Dean Heller affirmed. He was colorless, pliant and fawning. So a dangerous adversary, as Burt judged him.

The committee met sometimes to approve or disapprove specific loans in special cases, but more usually on business which involved long-range or policy questions.

The Loan Committee had forwarded a touchy proposal. The Hotel Sierra Nevada in Las Vegas was planning a thirty-million-dollar expansion. Burt Hammond did not question that it was a good loan. The Sierra Nevada was already successful beyond any investor's fondest dreams; the new high-rise it projected would triple its earnings.

Jerry knew what the problem was. Although the Sierra Nevada had won some respectability during its existence, its connection to the notorious, still-powerful so-called Orange Gang out of the midwest was known by everybody still to exist. "Our lawyer's afraid of Washington," he snapped at Burt.

"Not afraid," Burt amended. "Just careful."

"If that little pecker you're scared of wanted to nail any of these people, he could've done so a hundred times. He's had special task forces and they've come up with nothing."

It isn't them he wants, Burt wanted to say, *it's you.* He paused for a long time before he spoke. "We can't anticipate what he's now planning."

"You did pretty good the last time Robert Kennedy went after me," Jerry said. "What makes you think he'll try again?"

"Someone else was stupid, not Robert Kennedy. You

can be sure he's damned angry, and it's not going to be like that the next time."

"You think I'm going to be afraid to move because of that little runt?" Jerry demanded.

"I look at it like this," Matt Kusic broke in to ease an evident impasse. "We make out good two ways in a deal like this. We not only bring in big money to the fund, but the thirty million dollars for new construction gives our building-trades people a lot of jobs."

Burt knew better than to try to counter *that* with a labor boss. "They're an unsavory group behind that hotel," he offered.

"Licensed by the Nevada Gaming Commission, a tough outfit," Jerry said bitterly.

"We're dealing with Crime Task Forces who have yet to make a move, kamikaze squadrons of young lawyers out to make a big reputation for themselves as crimebusters. *And* a determined attorney general whom we bested once and who's out to even the score."

"Well, I'll be damned if I'm going to shit in my pants every time his name is mentioned," Jerry barked.

"Maybe we can go into business with guys like the Sierra Nevada bunch at another time, later," Burt persisted. "But I'd recommend passing now."

"I says, let's put it to a vote," Jerry said suddenly.

Burt Hammond raised a surprised finger. "The Oversight Committee has always respected a veto by a single member. Are we going to change that now?"

"Yes, counselor." Jerry Haggerty grinned and looked around the table for disapproval. "Everybody knows all you lawyers are born deal-breakers."

Burt saw he had not only been overruled but that a new precedent had been set.

The next step came quickly. "I've got a proposal here that hasn't gone below us. A group of businessmen I know are ready to make a buy-out of Inter-Continent Airlines. The airline's up to their ass in cash-shorts and my people can take them over."

It seemed odd to Burt Hammond that the normal staff-study procedure had been bypassed, but he was willing to play along with what might prove to be the secrecy necessary for a corporate proxy fight. "How much cash do they need from us?" he asked.

"Nothing." Jerry Haggerty chuckled. "But they want us in anyway."

"Why?" Burt pursued.

"Maybe we look better than they do."

"Who are the people involved?"

Matt Kusic broke in quickly: "Same people from the Sierra Nevada deal." Burt Hammond realized that the matter had been taken up individually with the others and he had been excluded from these considerations. "Guy named Eddie Gorman will front, he's been running the hotel and other stuff for years. Very sound reputation. Seems like a Vegas hotel can use an airline bringing in people, they've been doing that anyway."

"But an airline as big as ICA?" Burt queried. "It's one of the biggest carriers in the world."

"Fourth biggest," Jerry Haggerty broke in. "It's why it's such a good deal for us."

"Hold it," Burt said. "You heard my rule. If a deal's too good, always look at it a long time."

"They have to move fast. I've already okayed it, counselor. Twenty million as a token, money they don't need, understand. Safer than safe."

"What you're saying, Jerry," Burt broke in, "is they're using the Fund as a cover."

"You might say that. If you wanted to make trouble."

Burt Hammond looked to Matt Kusic and the financial man from Montgomery Street for allies, but they evaded his gaze. "Well, well," he commented. "You won't need me to make that trouble, gentlemen. We might as well count on it."

"But you go along?" Jerry said.

"Have I a choice?" He accepted a murmurous approval from the others at the table.

The rest of the meeting ran routinely. Just before adjournment, Burt Hammond brought up the developmental loan to Sobordco for exploring the possibilities on Thunder Mountain. Jerry Haggerty was the only one at the table who offered a comment. "Isn't that the same outfit you had all that trouble with down there in the Imperial Valley?"

"Business is business," Burt said. "They'll be going through channels. I just want everybody here to know that I'd interpose no objection just because of my feelings about them. In fact I'll abstain on this one."

"After what you've done here today, Burt, anything you want's okay with us," Jerry Haggerty said.

Burt Hammond drifted toward the door more slowly

130

than the others. He found that Jerry Haggerty was hanging back too, clearly for a word with him alone. "What's with Matt Kusic?" Burt asked.

"You're surprised?"

"A little. There's a stink to that airlines deal, and he hasn't even got the excuse of it-makes-work-for-our-people."

"Now *I'm* surprised," Jerry said, and added, "at you. I always figured you for a guy who could look any fact in the face."

"Maybe I don't know it yet."

"His wife's brother has got a son. Runs a feeder airline out of Spokane."

"I get the picture," Burt said quickly. "But you know why Gorman and the Sierra Nevada people want into an airline as big as Inter-Continent, don't you?"

"I don't ask what I don't need to know. Or care about."

"Your lawyer had better, Jerry. I don't believe in the unexpected turning up later on."

"I'm really not interested."

"Try, Jerry. I'm not even sure they could get away with it. But what they're looking for is a communications network of incalculable value, and I don't mean assets and earnings. I'm talking about a shipping capability with a vast volume of airborne freight, to bury anything they'd be of a mind to move."

"It's an angle, I'm sure." Jerry had grown visibly impatient. He looked at a watch he pulled from a fob. "Hey, it's eleven. Time for a drop of the stuff. And, Burt, old kid—" He put away the watch and took a long time lifting his head again. "There's always an angle. Like, do I ask why you bring up that Sobordco matter? I don't ask questions there. You know what I'm trying to tell you? I figure it's an okay deal and you're into something. It's not a money-loser. Extend us the same courtesy. Or, like they say, one hand washes the other."

"My job's to protect you, Jerry."

A loud buzzing of voices outside the room caused them both to turn. A radio could be heard. During business hours? Jerry Haggerty sighed. "I appreciate that, counselor, but remember, I never ducked a fight."

The door flew open. Matt Kusic, his face gone bloodless, stood in the frame. "They've shot the President in Dallas!" he exclaimed and his voice broke apart. Burt Hammond ran to him, as if to confirm what he had just heard. The corridor was filled with office people milling from one cubbyhole to the next. A secretary fell against Burt Hammond. "Why? Why'd they do it?" she sobbed. He led her to a nearby chair. Transistor radios were a cacophony of different stations, going over the same words, Parkland, Texas Book Depository, Secret Service, assassin. Then the bulletin from the hospital. "President John F. Kennedy is dead."

Burt found himself back in the conference room. Jerry Haggerty had not stirred. "They've killed him, Jerry."

Haggerty looked up without expression. "Congratulations," he said.

"The President has been murdered, don't you understand?"

"I don't cry for enemies, and they were my enemies. Why shouldn't I be glad? With his big brother out of the picture, how long do you think the little shitheel will last? Johnson hates his guts after what the guy did to him at the convention. He'll make life miserable for the crud! Dallas is a break for us, don't you see?"

"I don't want to talk about all that now, Jerry." The old pier-brawler never quit, it was clear to Burt. When the opponent was down you gouged, you kicked, you won.

Jerry thrust a finger against Burt's shoulder. "It's my ass the brother was trying to put in prison with his support, remember! Whatever puts a stop to that is good. That's what I pay you to believe. Me, I don't give a damn about how you feel about anything else. You work for me! If I ever find you put your personal needs before mine, kid, I'll break you as fast as I made you."

Jerry Haggerty smiled beatifically and bent over to throw his arms around Burt Hammond. "Don't you see, I loveya, lunkhead! Take care." Jerry hurried out of the room. It grew quiet again. Down the corridor, through the open door, Burt Hammond heard the radios bearing the mourning voices from Texas.

BOOK FOUR:

The Golden Gateway

(1964-1967)

1

I'm not telling them anything they don't already know.

Edward Gorman was used to life in a pressure cooker. General manager of the Sierra Nevada Hotel in Las Vegas, he was its owners' chief advisor on other investments and acquisitions. He was in trouble now, cornered, frightened. All his life he had kept clear, except for the two busts when he was a kid, and now this: a formica and plastics hotel room with a parade of men from the Federal Crime Task Force.

I know they know more than they're letting on to me. I'm not really ratting, I'm saving the operation.

Edward Gorman looked at the Xeroxes that were passed to him. *My God,* he thought, *where in the hell did they get that?* He hoped that years of practiced imperturbability around gambling tables would stand him in good stead now. He felt the heat rise under the collar of his Sulka shirt.

"Just put a check beside the names you know for a certain fact are connected with Jerry Haggerty."

He put a check next to the name at the top of the page, although it was one he had not heard spoken in his presence in at least ten years. He put a check next to the one below it, a name held in contempt by everybody Gorman knew. He worked his way carefully down the page putting checks beside every name, sometimes pausing to give effectiveness to what he was doing. All he could do was hope to confuse them.

When he was finished, Oliver Hale Goodman looked briefly at the pages. "Every last one of them, Eddie?" Eddie Gorman nodded. "You're quite certain?"

Goodman went to the door of the hotel room he had booked for Gorman and came back with another young man in a suit two sizes too small. "This is the gentleman I told you about the last time, Eddie. He's here to tell you about your tax problem."

The introductions were scanty. If Gorman continued to show his cooperativeness, every break and consideration would be given him. While no one was making promises and offering deals, the government, the man was sure, would not press for anything more than financial settlement and would not insist on prison.

Edward Gorman asked for permission to go to the bathroom. Ever since the government nailed him, he was having the runs. It got worse every time they had him on a chair.

He came back, less feverish and refreshed. The tax man was gone. "When are we finished with these meetings, Mr. Goodman? They're very dangerous for me. You got to understand there are people out there who make it a business to be suspicious about everything."

"Tell me more about Jerry Haggerty, where does he come in?"

"The group is borrowing the money from him for the airline deal even though they don't need it. You already know all that, Mr. Goodman."

"His connection is deeper, isn't it, Gorman? Does he control everything? Why do you hold back on us? You see what I'm doing for you. Why don't you prove how grateful you are? Be more forthcoming."

"I'm trying."

"Do you know of any moneys Haggerty has received from people on the list? For whatever purpose."

"I personally never even heard of him getting a penny."

"You're being evasive again, Gorman," Goodman charged, bitter disappointment in his voice. "You ask me to believe there's no payoff? As far as I'm concerned you can rot in prison. We'll see to it you're left without a dime. That goes for your wife too, Eddie. *And* the house in Palm Springs. Your wife . . . think about what kind of existence she'll have with you behind bars. Have you no consideration for her?"

Gorman gave it a moment's consideration. "I suppose there might've been a payoff. On a higher level than mine."

"You suppose, or you're sure? *Suppose* doesn't mean a thing to me, Eddie."

"I'm sure." Visions swam before Gorman's eyes, dear, sweet Mag, his wife of thirty years whom he honored and worshipped despite affairs with other ladies going back to the first week of their made-in-heaven marriage; Mag, working for a living, a fate worse than his mind could cope with. "I'm absolutely sure," he amended.

"Good. Now tell me more about Jerry Haggerty's connections."

"I hardly know him, Mr. Goodman. I swear."

"I want you to confirm what we already have found out, Gorman. Don't play games with me."

What was the use? How could it hurt if I'm only telling what everybody knows from the papers and the TV?

Goodman wanted to know dates and places. Gorman was getting dizzy and now the whole shirt was sticking to his back, despite the air conditioning. His gut began twisting again. He wanted to be rid of this man.

"I won't need you for a while, Gorman. You've been helpful this time," Oliver Hale Goodman said at length.

After dark, an unmarked government car took him to the airport. No one saw him get off early the next morning in Las Vegas. Gorman was grateful for this good break.

2

"THERE is a rat loose."

Burt Hammond, in black trousers and white silk shirt, was struggling with a white bow tie when Jerry Haggerty found him. He took no notice of Burt's unusual dress.

"You know who it is?"

"Very high up." Jerry Haggerty found the tailcoat, picked it up, studied it, and let it fall to a chair without comment.

"That figures. You seem more nervous than usual, Jerry."

"Can they look at the Fund's books, Burt?"

"If they can't, Congress will damned well pretty soon see that they can. What's the rat saying, and what're they going to look for that I don't already know about, Jerry?"

"A few things."

Burt seemed satisfied with the tie. He picked up the white vest and put it on. Jerry Haggerty held up the coat for him.

"Why don't you tell me these things up front, Jerry?" The whole suit was vaguely embarrassing but not clumsy to move about in.

"You know me by now. I don't answer to any man. I do what's right according to my lights. So I put out some of our money."

"How much are we talking about?"

"A lot."

"How much is a lot?"

"More than the Sierra Nevada deal."

Burt Hammond whistled soundlessly. "But the Loan Committee okayed it all?"

"I okayed it. Heller sees that the committee rubber-stamps it. Why do you think I brought him in?"

"You've got more problems, Jerry."

"That's why I've bought myself a smart lawyer."

"I'm smart, all right, but not enough to undo what shouldn't be done in the first place."

"What's going to happen?"

Burt Hammond shrugged. "Can't tell. You don't really work with me, not the way a client should. So it's a roll of the dice."

"I help good guys, I don't care what and who they are, or were. I don't lose a dime for the fund."

"You've got a big heart, Jerry. I mean that." Burt put an arm around the old man's shoulder. "I'm going to the opera. You like opera, Jerry?"

The old man grumbled. "It better be out by midnight. You've got a date here then."

"I have?" Burt teased. "I haven't had a blind date since high school."

"Here. Tell your secretary to keep the lights low."

"One of your loan friends, Jerry?"

"The bakery workers are calling an industry-wide strike tomorrow. This guy would like to arbitrate."

"And I'm acceptable as the arbitrator?" Burt asked incredulously. "Me, your personal counselor, Jerry? How old is this guy, ten or eleven?"

"I told him you'd be fair," Haggerty went on unperturbed. "So be fair. His name's Sheldon. He may be kidding himself, but if you can bring him to a settlement it would be nice for him and good for us when we deal with all the other big baking factories."

Burt Hammond picked up the top hat the J. Press people had sent over from Post Street, but he decided against it. "I don't understand you," he said. "God knows I've tried. I admire you. The spunky individualist. The guy who's got his people more than any labor official in history. Why do you get involved in situations where rats can hurt you?"

"When I find out which rat we're talking about, I'll let you have the answer. Good night, counselor, sleep well at the opera."

3

THE trouble with us born survivors, Burt Hammond thought, is that we keep raising the odds against ourselves, taking always bigger risks, stretching luck to see just how far we have to go before it all breaks down. Jerry Haggerty had come through before. But now he faced worse than ever. In his old liberal-radical days he had never knuckled down, even though the whole country—every politician, every newspaper, every decent American—offered the litany of hate-the-Reds. Jerry remained a tough-minded labor leader and emerged bigger than ever. But now? He was finished. A spent force. The Justice people for a certainty had found someone close enough to nail Jerry Haggerty. And he was running scared.

And what about me?

On the stage they giggled when the little black boy entered the Marschallin's boudoir carrying a tray. Burt was thinking of his own future. The crazy, wonderful old man was a fraud, even to himself. He always had been sleeping with hoodlums. He still *likes* them. He genuinely does. He doesn't steal, I know that, I've seen everything, he's not as rich as he could be, maybe should be. That part of him isn't what's crooked. The man likes gangster-bravado, gangster-independence, gangster-antiauthoritarianism.

Where has it led me? Do I have principles? Principles are a lawyer's curse. You always gave them every-American-has-the-right-to-counsel and all that. But what should the lawyer do when he knows that, whether or not his client is crooked, crooked things are being done? What am I? Who am I?

Don Pedro used to say one's life is a grain of sand. Burt had come to see it not only meant you went wherever the wind blew you, it meant you were also a rock . . . in the infinite, as Don Pedro said, in the great blue sky beyond the great blue sky . . . a grain of sand was as enduring and as mighty as the oldest boulder on earth . . .

Enthusiastic applause and the fall of the curtain brought him back. Mrs. Wilson laid a jeweled and gloved hand on his. "Come, Burton, let's see to your future."

He followed her up the crowded aisle to the main lobby, festooned with banks of flowers and crowded with the formally dressed.

"We go to the north box bar, darling," she said. "Upstairs."

Small, but crowded, the corridor adjacent to the boxes had been hung with Gobelin tapestries and set with a dozen tables, all occupied. Burt came back with two gin and tonics.

"We're in luck, my darling," Mrs. Wilson said. "Right behind you, don't turn as if to look, make it casual."

Burt moved enough to glance at someone just turning too, but away from him. He saw long, stringy hair, a girl somewhat too thin and too tall who seemed to be wearing something which had fallen on her by accident.

"Spare me," he said.

"Her mother was a Levering, Burton, her grandmother is Flora Levering, the original Levering's only daughter, who married a cousin to keep daddy's name going. You know about the Leverings, don't you? Not only were they in gold mining, newspapers and railroads, they had the foresight to buy up half of San Francisco after the fire. Not to mention Oakland, Hawaii and Sacramento."

"What's that she's wearing? An ancestral flannel nightgown?"

"Mother's dead. Father was in the cabinet under Eisenhower. He was a suicide a few years ago."

Burt Hammond knew the name all right. "Sounds kinky enough to pass. And they have money."

"Not *have* money, darling. They *are* money. You'll find her bright, she's frightfully honest."

Before long Mrs. Wilson managed to bring her close enough to make the introductions. Courtney Kendall wasn't as bad-looking as he'd thought; his second impression was that she was rich enough to get away with being careless about what she had. Big, keen eyes and a smile that seemed to mock pretension. A strong chin. Not a bad figure under the rumpled tent.

"How do you like the opera, Mr. Hammond?" Courtney Kendall said.

"I'm learning."

"It's the first time?"

"Let him tell you about Callas and Tebaldi and Joan Sutherland," Mrs. Wilson offered. "He told me he used to go with a girl who dragged him to La Scala on every occasion." Mrs. Wilson waved to someone and was gone.

Alone, Courtney Kendall seemed embarrassed. "Forgive me. I was being condescending," she said. "Most of the people Hilary Wilson introduces me to don't know one Strauss from the other and come here to mingle with the swells."

"But that's why I'm here."

"At least you're frank. You're in real estate too?"

"I'm a lawyer."

"You're *that* Hammond? Of course. Defender of the rights of little girls and enemy of people like me."

The buzzer announcing the end of the intermission sounded. Courtney Kendall smiled wanly. "Good hunting."

He forced a smile. "No complaints so far." *Drop dead*, he thought.

At the next intermission he managed to lose Mrs. Wilson and head for the big bar downstairs. He decided he was wrong about her rich young ladies. As he'd learned back in his Yale days, they weren't worth the trouble. Who needed their damned money? Certainly not he. He turned to find Courtney Kendall and a somewhat tall man, drunk, sleepy, bored or stoned.

"Mr. Hammond, what a surprise to find you down here with the run-of-the-mill swells!" she announced cheerfully. "Mr. Hammond here is out scouting to destroy us, Ken. He's Jerry Haggerty's lawyer."

"Not destroy," Burt offered pleasantly, "out to save you from yourselves, Miss Kendall."

"Destroy makes better sense, Hammond," the man with Courtney Kendall said. "We're not worth saving."

"Sorry, my brother never could tell friend from foe. This is my brother Kenneth, Mr. Hammond."

Kenneth Kendall had skin like white paste that has been uncovered too long, deep-set eyes ringed with dark circles and pale, bloodless lips. "My sister's on your side too, Hammond. Don't let her fool you."

"He's notorious, Ken," Courtney Kendall went on. "God knows what we'll find on our streets when he's finished with them."

"*Our* streets?" Burt Hammond said. "Does that include me too?"

"See, Court, you're already partners with the man." Kenneth Kendall's speech was thick, not slurred; Burt Hammond decided the man was not drunk, after all, nor stoned. He had the bored elocution of the world-weary aristocrat. "You're okay, chum." He looked about. " 'Bye, Courtney." He drifted away, leaving two embarrassed people behind.

"You look like you don't want him to go away, Miss Kendall," Burt offered, when she turned back to him some time later.

"I'm worried about my brother," she said with sudden, and surprising, seriousness. "I haven't seen him for months and I don't like the way he looks."

Sisterly warmth, deep concern, unabashed affection for her brother made her seem real for the first time. She was not a cut-from-the-same-cookie-cutter young lady like the many girls he knew. In fact he knew more about the senior Leverings than he had let on to Hilary Wilson. The money there was not only old, it had to run into nine digits. He had left his own terrain to meet people like this, hadn't he? And he'd blown it. Stupid. With what Jerry was into, his own practice—his own world—could explode without warning. He had a client with a penchant for troublemaking and with enemies within his organization bitter enough to tell the Justice guys more than his lawyer himself knew about his activities. Yes, Burton Z Hammond was in deeper trouble than he knew, he'd bet.

The obvious thing to do was to make nice to this lady, turn on the charm, say the right things, make the right sexual moves, mild, strong, shadowy, whatever worked. He'd done that before; what successful cocksman hadn't?

He heard himself say: "I'd better find Mrs. Wilson. Excuse me, please." He left Courtney Kendall and all that old money standing alone in the crowd.

He thought about Courtney Kendall and Jerry Haggerty during the last act of *Der Rosenkavalier.* Had he been too abrupt? Did she know it was deliberate? He knew that girls like Courtney Levering Kendall get fawned over all the time; he'd taken the risk that she would remember him because he had not waited to be dismissed. He'd even told her he was here looking for clients. What the hell. What he had to do now was to appear to the world still to be Jerry Haggerty's man and yet somehow detach himself from him. One of his profs in New Haven used to tell how they built the Grand Central Station in New York. They constructed the new building over the existing one, which they tore down even as the new one was going up all around it, and kept all the trains running on time. There were places where even a whispered association with Jerry Haggerty could help him, as everywhere else it made him suspect and sinister.

He would not publicly denounce the old man. Where could he be independent yet somehow connected? Tear down, build and operate?

His mind kept going back to the Levering-Kendall girl. Had he been too brusque? The trick was to handle a super-rich like any girl. As with the more special a woman, the more routine the attention you offered and the less fuss you made, so the more ordinary the girl, the more special regard you paid her—the more fuss. Another of the great truths he'd gathered at Lux et Veritas. Still, a lawyer with a heavy overhead and a practice that was grinding to a halt ought, he thought, to have been a little more careful in dealing with an authentic Levering.

When the last bow had been taken, Mrs. Wilson led him through a sea of white ties and tiaras, introducing him right and left. He knew most of the surnames. "You're fabulous, Hilary," he said over her shoulder. "How do I repay you?"

"You already have, Burton." They were at the carriage entrance and there would be a wait for the car. "I talked to San Diego today. You could have vetoed that loan, yet you didn't let personal feelings stand in the way. Thank you."

"It's a good loan. No matter how I feel about Ellis Griswold." So they had bitten. If he left Jerry now, he would lose this hook that had been swallowed by Ellis Griswold.

"You always did know how to look a fact in the eye, Burton," he heard her say. "How do I repay *you?*"

"You have tonight."

"You liked Courtney Kendall? Top of the list, my boy. But probably impossible to net. God knows everybody's tried, if only for all that money."

"I'm afraid I struck out there. I was thinking of all the other rich and potent. Can we come here this weekend?"

"Only Tuesdays matter for you, darling. That's when your rich and potent come out of their golden cages. There's also Thursday afternoon, of course, but that's the old crowd who've passed control on."

"Make it Tuesdays. Maybe we can do something different so it's not as obvious next time. Give parties afterward."

"I always said this Alexander the Great would own the world." Mrs. Wilson hugged his arm. "Certainly. Tuesdays."

Waiting for a car too, Courtney Kendall, swathed in a chinchilla large enough to blanket an Oakland Raider tackle, saw them. Hilary Wilson followed her gaze to Burt Hammond. She turned and took his arm again. "As my grandfather used to say, Burton, 'Bonanza!' You haven't struck out, in fact you've probably struck a vein of gold." She turned and raised an arm to beckon Miss Kendall. "Courtney, my dear, do come and wait with us."

"I'm afraid someone's stolen grandma-ma," Miss Kendall said, coming over without hesitation.

"Lucky for us." Hilary Wilson suppressed a smile. "It's Courtney Kendall, Burton."

"I owe you an apology, Mr. Hammond," she began at once.

"Two apologies," Burt said. Why was he so damned hostile to this girl?

"You're right. I also took for granted you didn't like opera. Will you and Mrs. Wilson join grandma-ma and me at the club for coffee now? Please."

The lady was indeed begging. "Sorry," Burt Hammond said. He had that midnight meeting but he did not offer it as the excuse.

"You're quite sure? Grandma-ma has the car. I've really been looking for you."

"Oh, do let's go, Burton," Mrs. Wilson urged. "You'll adore Flora Levering."

"Another time, perhaps," Burt said.

"Then will you call me? Have you a pencil? I'll give you the number at Wildoaks."

"I'll find it."

"It's unlisted."

"I can get it."

"Do call me. Good night, Mrs. Wilson." Courtney Kendall departed, the embarrassment tighter around her than the chinchilla.

"What the devil was that all about?" Hilary Wilson said. "You turned *them* down?"

"Looks like, doesn't it, Hilary?"

"Why? You've got a date with some hippie girl who doesn't shave under the arms or use lipstick? For that you turned down Courtney Kendall *and* Mrs. Flora Levering? And you don't even want her telephone number?"

"Let's get our car, Hilary, I can't be late."

"Country boy," she murmured, like an accusal. "Forget Tuesdays in the War Memorial Opera House. The only world you're going to conquer is the Haight-Ashbury."

"Want to bet?" Burt Hammond said.

4

"He's waiting inside for you," Helen said, getting her things as she prepared to go home. "Haggerty said to call him on the private line as soon as you get a fix on the guy."

Ben Sheldon was so nervous he put down his cigarette, forgot it, pulled another from a pack and started to light it. He was about forty, taking on weight, a rumpled man who did not look at himself after he put on his coat. He was effusive with apologies and explained that he was anxious to come to terms before the strike because his business could not afford a day's delay.

He was Lady Tara bakery products; Burt knew the label from breakfast pastries Helen put in his freezer for Sunday brunch. Good stuff. Sold exclusively in the freezer cabinets of supermarkets. Sheldon perspired as he told how he had taken a concept and made it go. It was still going. He was the first guy to treat frozen pastries with respect, he said. Everything still made the old-fashioned way, only flour, sugar, butter, eggs, cream. In a year or two he would be national, orders were coming in from everywhere. There were even offers to buy the company from the big mass-producers, but Sheldon was saying no.

The strike would ruin him, Sheldon said. Maybe he was better off selling out. The union called itself a bakery union but it demanded things that worked okay if you were running an assembly line for automobiles, radios or mass-produced breads and cakes, but you just did not make Lady Tara products that way. Cheesecake and croissants and puff pastry had to be made the old-fashioned way, by hand. He was doing it, proving it could be profitable. Yet the union wanted him to put on so many assistants per baker. That kind of arbitrary rule might work for the big bread companies, but Lady Tara's bakers didn't need assistants, they needed more bakers. Such a union demand could drive him out of business by forcing him to change the formula that had built a successful going concern. Plainly and simply put it would ruin him, said Sheldon, out of breath.

It took Burt Hammond a moment to put things in place. He knew Alf Bengstrom who ran the bakers union, a tough autocrat who felt he ought to get more for his people every time the price of flour went up two cents a pound. But Burt knew that he saw in the rumpled man before him a character he had a special weakness for. And he had a job to do.

"Who suggested a sweetheart contract for you, Mr. Sheldon?" he snapped.

"A sweetheart contract? What do you mean?"

He *is* new, Burt thought. "It's where a union gives special breaks to one employer, for whatever reason. Is that what this is all about?"

Sheldon insisted he had come to Jerry Haggerty because he had met him once. He did not want to sink. He was that desperate. He was willing to make concessions. He swore that he had hidden nothing. He would open his books.

Burt picked up the tailcoat he had taken off earlier and

145

excused himself long enough to go upstairs and change. He pulled on a pair of old Levis and a pair of battered, comfortable Weejuns. He went to the refrigerator and found a can of grapefruit juice, then called Jerry Haggerty's private line.

"This guy's not going to be tough, Jerry." As always when they used the phones, discretion was the key. "How good a friend is he?"

"Met him once or twice, but then I've met everybody in the world once or twice."

"He says he could be driven out of business."

"So let him pay his people for the privilege of staying in business. His company's making money."

"He's a dying breed, Jerry. I've got a soft spot for guys like that, you know that. Can I work out something for the guy?"

"Bengstrom says it would be a big thing going in. The right pattern could bring the rest of the industry to settle quickly."

"I'll call you back when I've figured out something."

"You don't have to. I trust you with my life, so what the hell is this?"

The light was coming through the windows and the crew that came every morning to clean was letting itself in by the time an agreement was concluded with Lady Tara Bakeries that was acceptable to both parties. Sheldon looked like a tangle of slept-in linen, sweaty, smoking more cigarettes than ever but plainly content. Burt Hammond stood over him as certain pages of figures were initialed so there would be no misunderstanding at another time.

Finally Sheldon got to his feet. "I'm much obliged for your work. It'll cost my company, but at least this way I can stay in business." He offered his hand at the door. "By the way, what do I owe you for all this?"

Burt shot a glance at his wristwatch. "Twenty-five hundred."

Ben Sheldon muttered approval and made his way past one of the cleaning crew. Burt Hammond left a note on Helen Mendoza's desk. HOLD ALL CALLS. DON'T WAKE ME.

She found him at noon on the terrace, still in pajamas, trying to clear the cobwebs of sleep in the clear golden sunlight and the breeze that blew in from the bay. "This just came. What the hell did you do for the Lady Tara

Bakeries last night? Or does this go into a trust account for something?"

It was a check not for the two thousand five hundred he'd set as a fee but for twenty-five thousand dollars. He fell back in the lounging chair and put the check to his lips thoughtfully. A mistake? Businessmen don't make such mistakes. A payoff? He was well aware of the stringent rules under Taft-Hartley and he had done nothing that was not strictly proper. Then why? Lots of things came to his mind. In the end, he held out the check for Helen. "It's for legal services. Deposit it in the general account."

5

AT one in the morning, Lou Birch found the musicians conversing in quiet knots around the big recording studio. Larry Marshall knew there was trouble the minute he saw Lou's face.

"What goes on here? These guys are on triple-time!" he shouted. "What the hell have we got here, a superstar playing superstar games?"

Larry did his best to soothe him. "She took too many reds and just passed out. She'll be all right."

"Who let her have them?" Lou shouted. "What are we running here?"

"She's scared," Larry said.

"*I'm* scared! I've got a fortune tied up in an unknown bitch and I've got a lot of explaining to do if I'm going to keep my job, and she's scared! And I've still got twenty musicians making seventy-five dollars an hour each, or is it now a hundred and fifty? Are we running a business or is this a playtoy for incipient dopers?" He strode about the bare stage. Behind the glass of the control room he could see the engineers busy at a card game of some kind. "Let's get to work, everybody!" he called out. "Lemme hear what you've got so far."

"Yes, sir, Mr. Birch," he heard through the p.a. system on the floor. "What do you want us to give you?"

"What've you got that's in good shape?" Larry called out.

"Numbers one, three, four, seven. The others will need some recording with the four-girl chorus Rosey said would lift the middle part."

"Rosey said!" Lou Birch raged. "She's rewriting on the stage yet! No wonder the bitch needs downers. Who the hell does she think she is?"

"Play what's ready, Dick," Larry called out. He took Lou Birch's arm and did his best to soothe him. "What we've got is . . . well, interesting."

"I don't want to be interested," Birch said. "I want to be knocked off my feet. We're running a business, not a damned musical conservatory. Will it sell? That's what I want to know."

A cluster of violins began to trace a strange and slightly dissonant melody through the big amplifiers. And Rosey's voice came in a whisper and then began to sing in a casual way, a song of her own, a girl musing about a night and a man. Lou Birch sat down but the frown did not leave his face. When the song ended, he let out a long breath but gave no sign of being placated. Rosanna began again, a cheerful song this time, a sunny, bright melody which brought a brief smile until it turned into a series of dissonances and curious chords that left him astonished. He got to his feet. "Cut it! Cut it!" he called out. "I've heard enough."

He grabbed Larry Marshall by the hand and pulled him over to the wall. "You're out of a job as of right now. What did we agree to do, something commercial, right? You guys are all alike!" His face was red with anger.

"Take it easy, Lou, you'll have a heart attack," Larry said, gentling him.

"We're spending a fortune to do what some guy once did for a thousand dollars! And where'll it get us? Where it got him. I don't make records for avant-garde critics! I'm looking to sell a million records, not to appeal to the musical cognoscenti."

"This girl's music reminds me of the Beatles, Lou, it's personal, it's real, it's clever and when you hear it a few times, it doesn't go away. She could very well wind up bigger than we dreamed."

"You're still fired. Now get her ass out here and make her finish the session."

* * *

Convinced the company had a failure on its hands, Lou Birch cut the release back to a single, a small record with one song on each side, a product usually designed for very young people or to test the market. To everybody's surprise, the single sold out as quickly as it was sent to the distributors.

"So she's got a little underground public," Lou said. "I never denied that. But what the hell does it mean?" Nevertheless, he ordered a second, larger pressing.

"Oh, Who Am I?", Roseanna Lee's single, kept selling out. Five successive times. Lou Birch sent forests of flowers every time he ordered a new pressing. "How you feeling, angel?" he now said when he called. "Anything you need just ask Uncle Lou," he said. The complete album was hastily issued and went to the top of the charts within a week. Roseanna Lee was a hit.

Roseanna Lee was booked on the Ed Sullivan Show, which half the United States watched on Sunday night. She flew to New York and lip-synched her big hit (no one seemed to mind that the four-girl chorus on the record was nowhere to be seen on the stage of the Mark Hellinger Theatre) and won the heart of the nation; most of it that watched television proved their love by going out the next day to buy a record.

She was black and this was considered phenomenal. Immediately after she finished her promotional chores in New York, Roseanna put herself into a private sanatorium just outside of South Norwalk for psychiatric counselling and to be helped in breaking her dependence on drugs. Larry Marshall drove up with her to Connecticut. "Marry me, baby, we'll be a team. We'll conquer the world."

"Aren't you supposed to say something about how much you love me?"

"I'm crazy about you. Your career would be my whole life."

"What would your mother say?" she teased him. "Would she stick her head in the stove, you marrying a black chick?"

"This move would be good for your career. The public wouldn't think of you as black or white."

"That's true," she conceded, closing her eyes. "The problem is, what would I think I was?"

"You're one of a kind. Going to be bigger than ever!

149

Bigger than all of them! Let me take you there, Rosey."

"Who knows?" she said meditatively. "Maybe they'll teach me to be smart at this funny-farm you're taking me to."

"I'll wait," he said.

6

HILARY Wilson sat at midtable during the semiannual meeting of the Board of Directors of Sobordco in its San Diego headquarters. Ellis Griswold was in fine form when he announced the Golden West Pension loan and its concomitant benefits: other lenders would now come forward; takeover attempts by piratical companies could be thwarted; long-delayed projects could be put into operation.

"We are out of the woods, lady and gentlemen." His splendid, confident salesman-voice was resonant with success. "Our problems are over. Some of you may question the propriety of going to a labor organization for financing. My opposition to anti-American institutions is a matter of record. We have fought the closed shop and we have done everything in our power to give Americans the right to work, despite the opposition of labor unions, including the head of the organization with whose funds we are now doing business. But he is a realist, as I am. It's a new world, and your management is progressive enough to accommodate ourselves to existing conditions."

Hilary Wilson sat back in her chair and thought of Burton Hammond and wondered how *he* had accommodated himself, and why. There was a change, that much was clear to her. What caused it she did not know, but he had always been a man with a flair for making money, for expanding it, for playing with it. How else could she explain his using her in his new tack? "I don't want girls, I want money," he'd said. But he *had* money; everybody knew his practice was large and profitable. It was a mystery whose secret eluded her.

150

Ellis Griswold was again outlining the plans for the vast project called the Carlton Towns. His voice grew lyrical: the Carlton Towns would stretch from the ocean to the desert. Mountains would be leveled, canyons filled, new highways cut through fields of scrub and mesquite. He talked of parking lots as big as three football fields side by side, moving sidewalks (perhaps) which would hold shopping centers that could satisfy a family's needs from wombing to entombing.

Ellis spoke of a new concept, the Carlton Galleria, he called it. A vast, domed, all-glass canopy, as big as two aircraft carriers. With Ellis everything was always as big as a football field or an aircraft carrier. The Galleria would entice the customers in out of the blistering heat or the rain, and would once again show them how desperately they needed something they hadn't known they lacked until the deprivation was forcibly pointed out to them.

Hilary Wilson meditated: Had Burton Hammond been persuaded by her when she came to see him? Everyone knew his influence on Jerry Haggerty was tremendous. Surely, Burton could have stopped the loan and put the blame in a dozen places.

Or was he playing a game of some kind? She wondered if she would ever find out what moved Burton Hammond.

This made her think of him and the Kendall girl. What about *that?* Some kind of game there, too. Levering money was something off the scale all right, but Burton had all he needed. He did not have to go fortune hunting. Still, who knows? The son of a depression-battered Okie might never be satisfied with all the money he could make and would want more.

Curious, she thought, I don't know what makes Burton Hammond tick at all.

Ellis Griswold was at her side. The meeting over, he had broken away from a cluster of directors to put a troubled hand on her shoulder. A crook of his finger and she followed him to a corner of the conference room where they could not be overheard.

"Do you know anything about it?" he demanded severely.

"About what, Ellis?"

"Then you don't know," Griswold said. "It's crazy. We don't ever have that radical stuff down here. San

151

Diego's way too sensible, too conservative." She pressed him to find out what the devil he was talking about. "The PR Department alerted me just before the meeting. There's a group of radical hippies and beatniks and heaven knows who else outside right now, looking to embarrass us. How'd they know we were meeting today?"

"The kids are into that sort of thing. We know that up north."

"Exactly. But down here our kids don't go in for protest and demonstration. I don't want to be embarrassed in front of the board."

"Which is why they're doing it."

"I'm going down to see if I can't put a stop to it."

"You can't do that."

"It's my building, I can sure as hell chase them off."

"Don't do it that way," she said hopelessly.

"You stay here and keep the old boys happy," Ellis Griswold said.

A few moments later, she left the directors to their oyster bar, puff pastry and cocktails and took the elevator down to the street.

Through the big glass doors of the lobby she could see the commotion in the plaza outside. She pushed her way out past a timorous group watching from inside the building. The pickets were parading and shouting incomprehensibly. But their signs were well-made and legible. SAVE OUR MOUNTAIN. GRISWOLD KILLS. SOBORDCO MURDERS LAND. She saw Griswold in tense conversation with Bill Armstrong, the company's PR man. Armstrong was restraining his boss, holding him back by standing between him and the crowd.

She joined them. "Come on, Ellis," she urged.

"The cops. I want the police to arrest them," he growled. "How dare they slander me! Do you see what that sign says? Get their names! I want to sue them! The cops, where are they? What's happened to this country?"

"They've already been alerted."

"Let me get at them!" Griswold said again, trying to free himself.

"You've got to stop him, Mrs. Wilson," Armstrong said. "These people have already got the TV people here and they'd like nothing more than to provoke him in front of the cameras."

"Ellis." She stood before him too. "I won't let you go."

"Who are they?" he demanded furiously. "What's the country coming to when I can be called a killer?"

"It's their way of getting attention."

"I want their names, Armstrong!" Griswold shouted past her. "I'm going to sue every last one of them blind."

A pair of police cars arrived silently. They served to enliven the pickets and to bring the television men closer to where the marching was taking place.

"Please go in," the PR man begged Griswold. "If you let them get you involved—"

"I am involved," Griswold cut him off.

Two more police cars roared into the plaza, sirens wailing. Flashing long batons, the police started to move in against the demonstrators.

"They've got a special squad standing by," Armstrong said. "You've got to leave, Mr. Griswold, before it really gets hot."

"Come on," Mrs Wilson said firmly, this time not to be denied.

In the vast marble lobby, Ellis Griswold could not stop shaking. "Why did they do this to me?"

She soothed him: "You've fought and won worse battles, Ellis."

"Why?" he moaned. "All my work is for the future, it's *meant* for young people. Why are they doing this to me? What are they? Anarchists? Reds?"

She brought him to his office and put him into a chair. She made a drink for him, put it into his hands. "Thunder Mountain," she began, drawing a chair to be next to him. "I've never seen you so emotionally committed. Why's it so important, Ellis?"

He looked at her over his drink; he did not bring down the glass until all that remained in it were the ice cubes. "It could hurt us terribly."

"Not all our projects have been winners. Why is a setback on this one so dangerous to the company?"

"There's no way to recoup the money we put into that mountain if it doesn't work out. Urban land we could sell off if the deal went bust. Here it'd be a total loss. Who in God's name would want all that raw land if *we* couldn't do anything with it? Think what they could do to management, all the vultures out there!"

She took the empty glass and walked to the bar again. Burt Hammond must have thought of that. He knew—she knew—what Ellis Griswold and other below-the-

Tehachapi-Californians had not yet come to understand. Organized protest was now a way of life in the Bay Area. An anti-Thunder Mountain project would be sure to enlist the sympathies of all those environmentalist nuts who could not sleep nights for worry about the extinction of the snail darter. Burton Hammond would have thought of it. Did that explain—?

She held out the glass to Griswold. "Give *me* Thunder Mountain, Ellis."

"I wouldn't do that to you, Hil. It looks to be a long, ugly pull."

"There's no one can handle it better than I can."

"It's a vital deal for us, one we can't afford to lose out on."

"So give it to me," she said again. "I know how to make it happen. I won't let you down."

He emptied this glass as quickly as he had the first. That told her as much as any words he might have used. "It's yours. Get rid of those terrible people who want to kill us."

"Don't worry, dear," she soothed, in a voice like honey.

7

SCOFIELD his name was, high cheekbones under not enough flesh, pale blue eyes buried deep inside the skull and an ugly welt eight inches long from the neck to the back of the ear where a blade had left its mark. Scofield had got in trouble with one of Haggerty's building locals in San Raphael and had bought himself ten years in prison. Jerry said he hardly remembered him, but the local was one that was always in trouble, he recalled that, all right.

Scofield lay low until his parole expired. He came to Haggerty the day he was beyond the reach of the law. Jerry had brought him over at once. "Tell this man what you told me," he said with cold contempt.

"The only way I could get parole was if I'd help them

nail Jerry Haggerty," Scofield said. "It saved me four years."

"And you bought the deal?"

"Who wouldn't? The parole officer sets me up with a guy named Goodman. It's a con's game. Tell 'em what they wanna hear."

"Where? What's Goodman's whole name?"

"Down in the Federal Building on Golden Gate Avenue, there's three names, Oliver something. He thinks I've got to be sore at Jerry, maybe Jerry didn't do enough when I was on trial, maybe he shoulda done things for my family when I was on the inside. Do I want to get even."

"And you said?"

"What could I say? I said, What do I have to do? And they told me. Go back to Jerry. Get a job. Report to them whatever I can find out."

Jerry broke in: "The guy needed a break after serving his time. If I wasn't going to give those guys one, where the hell should they go to look?"

"Did the people on Golden Gate Avenue tell you why they wanted all this?"

"To get Jerry Haggerty. They said he was a crook who worked all the angles, they said he had a sharp young lawyer who knew all the tricks, that Jerry oughta be behind bars anyways and that the only way to get him was they hadda fight fire with fire."

"You were told all this by Mr. Oliver Hale Goodman?"

"Yes," Scofield said.

Later, after the ex-convict had been sent on his way, Burt Hammond said, "He could be lying."

"Sure, and angels could fly and clocks could run backwards, but they don't and he couldn't invent all that stuff."

"They'd impeach everything he says, you understand," Burt Hammond explained. "He's a convicted felon, he'd look like a bad guy to a bunch of jurors, they'd trip him up in other matters, make him look like a liar, even though all this may be true. To protect you, we've got to question how good this could be for us. Meanwhile, he's all we've got, but something else may turn up."

Four days later, the federal grand jury in Los Angeles, one of three around the country investigating Jerry Haggerty, returned an indictment against him. It charged that he had received illegal payments fifteen years ago from an employers' association to settle a strike. It was an old

155

charge which Burt Hammond knew all about. Did it happen? Was there a payoff? Long ago, Burt Hammond decided money did change hands, the strike was settled as a consequence but that none of this involved his client Jerry Haggerty.

"I want you in L.A. with me," Jerry said.

"You'd be a lot better off with a top trial man, Jerry."

"What's wrong with you?"

"No experience," Burt Hammond said. "Besides, you're better off with me behind you, not beside you."

"You're copping out? You don't want to be associated with me?"

"I'm associated with you where it can hurt me so I don't give a damn about everybody else. A good trial man doesn't need—wouldn't want—me to tell him what to do. He'd handle things his own way."

"I want *you*," Jerry said. "Period. You're the boss at the table."

"You're making a mistake, Jerry."

"It's my ass," Haggerty said. "I'm entitled."

There was a message from Courtney Levering Kendall. "She said to tell you she had to talk to you," Helen Mendoza said. "Is she one of *the* Leverings?"

"Why didn't you call me?" Courtney began, when Helen put her on.

"I've been working very hard."

"I read about it. I've decided you need a break from all that work. I know a marvelous stretch of beach where we can be alone. I'll send a car."

"I know how to drive, Courtney."

"Good. It's a little beyond Pacifica on Route One. I'll meet you in an hour outside of a fish place called Lee's."

"I don't think I can," he protested.

"I'm not interested in your excuses. I'm looking forward to seeing you."

"I'm very glad," Burt Hammond heard himself say.

Courtney Kendall was waiting for him outside the restaurant on Route 1, chauffeured in a jewel-polished Cadillac ten years old. She had done something to her hair. In jeans and a big sweater that fell below her hips, she seemed even prettier than he remembered. They said nothing and walked hand in hand to the beach and along it until they found the way blocked by a massive outcropping of rock a hundred feet high. The surf thundered into it and churned around the base furiously. A sudden surge sent them scrambling back to the very edge of the cliff that loomed above them. They laughed and found a dry place to sit.

"I've been finding out things about you," she said. "Some of it I can't avoid. Since I was a little girl, all I have to do is mention a boy's name and wheels in Montgomery Street start turning to find out who he is and why he's seeing me."

"The curse of being rich, Courtney," Burt said. "I've run into that before. Great for your ego, right? The only reason someone wants to see you is your money. How come with all that protection you girls always wind up with obviously pimpy types?"

"You'll notice I'm still free as the wind."

"You've never been in love?"

"Twice. Madly. Both turned out to be homosexual. My analyst said I attract fags because I frighten real men. Do I frighten you?"

"Nothing frightens me."

"I can tell you're not a fag."

"You were wrong about the two guys you fell in love with."

"I was, wasn't I? But not about you. Would you mind sharing some of your body heat, please? It's rather cold."

He put his arm around her. She pressed her head close to his chest. "About your money, Courtney. I make a lot. I spend a lot. Probably more than you do. It's never a problem. So you and your people can forget about it. I see you because you intrigue me."

"Good. Now how do I handle the stories I get about all your women? I understand you have thousands."

"Millions. I have them sent out by cargo plane after I'm through with them."

"Are you a hoodlum lawyer?" she said without pause.

"Yes. Does that ruin everything?" He turned to study her response.

"I love adventurous people, I love danger."

"Is that why you forced yourself on me?" he teased.

"I need you," she said gravely.

"Why?"

"I can't tell you—yet. But I do." She broke off quickly. "That has to wait. Let's talk about Mrs. Wilson. Do you go to bed with her? She's very beautiful, but isn't she kind of old for you?"

"I love ancient ladies."

"I'm a hundred years older than Mrs. Wilson, did you know that?"

"Of course. It's why I find you irresistible."

"I don't believe you're a hoodlum lawyer. I don't think Jerry Haggerty owns you. You're your own man. Just as I'm my own woman. You don't have to stay with Haggerty, just as I don't have to stay at Wildoaks. I *choose* to stay there, it's my world. Would you come there some weekend? I never ask anybody, but I'd love for you to come. Anytime. Say you will."

"I have some urgent business to attend down in Los Angeles, remember?"

"I've been reading about it. It's all over but the hanging, isn't it? I thought everybody loved the old man."

"Not everybody. A few still have old scores to settle with him."

"Will all this hurt you?"

"Could. Could also do me some good."

"I'll miss you." He was surprised to find her pressed against him again. His arms went around her to bring her body closer. "Come to Wildoaks when you can. It's a private, wonderful world, where you'll be free."

It had begun when he used Hilary Wilson to find the means to disentangle himself from Jerry Haggerty's world. But he was more entangled there than ever, even if he had been telling himself he did not feel an integral part of it. Bringing in Courtney Kendall now with his life and career in disarray made everything even worse, he saw that clearly. Wildoaks, indeed.

"Will you come to me when it's over?"

"Sure," he said, but he knew he was not saying the truth. Still, what did she mean to him, so far? Nothing, really. He owed her nothing. So the lie did not matter. "What about lunch?" he said.

8

IN Los Angeles the case of the United States against Joseph Jerome Haggerty was a theatrical event of spectacular proportions.

Local television reporters pursued him with unrelentingly fatuous questions. "How does it feel to be on trial?" "How do you like it in Hollywood, Jerry?" The old man met all the press with practiced grace. After all, as he told Burt Hammond, coming out alive after things like this had made him famous and powerful in the first place.

Jerry Haggerty gave no public indication of the fear Burt Hammond knew obsessed him. He showed up the first day in a vanilla-ice-cream worsted suit, sporting a boutonniere. The courtroom was crowded. Burt recognized a number of faces from the silver screen.

If the crowd behind the rail expected legal pyrotechnics and stagey confrontations, they were disappointed. Burt Hammond spoke in a whisper; he defused everything the government lawyers sought to explode. The sum of money involved was two thirds of one hundred thousand dollars. Burt Hammond never failed to mention the precise amount: sixty-six thousand, six hundred sixty-six dollars and sixty-six cents, so the sibilants became more important than the money and something of an absurd annoyance. Technicalities, procedure—this was what he concentrated on. He had done his homework carefully and nothing surprised him. He *wanted* the judge, jury, the press and all the celebrities in the courtroom to find the proceedings disappointingly dreary.

On the evening of the first day, Elmer Wright came to his room at the somewhat outlying Beverly Hills Hotel. (Jerry Haggerty and his inevitable retinue were staying at the Ambassador, much closer to the Federal Building, but Burt Hammond went his own way, as always.) The detective took him out in the garden for a walk, a precaution Burt Hammond knew meant something important had to be said privately.

"The government's got a guy named Stoker working for them. Haggerty will know the name. He's been a dissident for years. In and out of local offices. He's telling them Haggerty's been saying that Robert Kennedy is a son of a bitch and has to be got out of the way. He's also told them that Haggerty has asked him about plastic bombs that can't be detected."

"I don't believe him. Do they?"

"So they gave him a lie-detector test. You know what? He passed."

"Some people are good at passing tests. It's a gift, like being musical."

"Then this guy has got one hell of an ear. They believe it lock, stock and barrel."

"Anyway, he'll be of no use to them here."

He brought Elmer Wright into the Polo Lounge. They had a drink and talked about Sue-Ann Martin. She was camping on her mountain and kept in touch whenever she came down for supplies. She had a dozen other kids with her up there. The Save Our Mountain campaign was under way. "By the way, counselor," he leaned over to say, "all the people are looking at you like *you're* the movie star."

Two days into the trial, jury selection was completed. The government was into its case when the judge's clerk called the lawyers into chambers after the noon recess. A mousy juror named Mrs. Silvers had come to see the judge. Burt Hammond remembered the woman because he had sensed in her a sympathetic figure and he was glad when the government had accepted her. Mrs. Silvers had come to the judge and told him that a reporter for a local counter-culture paper with a big circulation had called her on the phone the night before. He asked her how she felt about the case so far.

Burt Hammond urged a mistrial but the judge and the government lawyers felt it could have been the work of a crank or a practical joker. No one had to tell any of them that any delay worked to Jerry Haggerty's benefit. The judge called the publisher and asked to have any planned stories held up. He was assured they would be. The publisher insisted the caller was not on his staff but had to be an impostor.

Mrs. Silvers was dismissed and an alternate put in her

place. The judge said it was possible also that the lady might have had fantasies of her own. But on the next day still another juror came to the judge with a story of a friend of a friend visiting him at home the evening before. It was worth ten thousand dollars, the stranger told this juror, if he would lean toward Jerry Haggerty. He would receive the money after a trip to Las Vegas where he would gamble at the tables for a day or two so that when he came back he could have a ready explanation for his newfound wealth.

Again Burt Hammond urged a mistrial. But the judge turned the matter over to the law-enforcement agencies and said he would dismiss this juror, seat another alternate, and proceed with the case.

Burt protested vigorously even as he knew it to be hopeless. Yet all was far from lost, he told Jerry over a stir-fried unshelled shrimp at the Yee Mee Low restaurant. It was the end of the first week in court. "That jury is bored to death, and that's okay with me." Tonight he sensed the trepidation in the old man under the public bluster. Jerry drank too much, certainly too fast, and he kept demanding new specialties of the chef. At length, he fell asleep at the table. Maybe he even passed out.

Burt Hammond did ten lengths in the pool, lifted himself to the deck and sat with his feet dangling in the water. Saturday afternoon poolside at the Beverly Hills was crowded with deck chairs and cabanas behind them, everybody startlingly tawny under the cloudless sky. When he recovered his breath, he made his way back to his own cabana where his brunch guest, Elmer Wright, sat uncomfortably in shirt and tie and dark three-button suit. "You are about to know the lady in the next cabana," he said, holding out a towel.

"Oh, my God," Burt commented.

"Obviously you haven't seen her. I've told her it's okay. Does the name Melba Adams mean anything to you? I understand she's the Number One draw in the film business. The waiter told me. In this town everybody knows everything."

"I can't stand her pictures. So squeaky-clean and decent and charming. All that sweetness makes me feel faint."

"Talks like a truck driver. Or like a truck driver's supposed to. I haven't heard language like it since I was in the army."

Burt Hammond looked up to see something descend from the sun, long, remarkable legs rising to a slender *cache,* square shoulders, full breasts barely encased in a narrow bandeau and a mass of hair piled carelessly atop a face clean of anything but oil. "Your friend here warned me you'd likely toss my ass out if I bothered you on your day off," she said.

"Even if I wanted to, I wouldn't be able to, Miss Adams." Elmer Wright got to his feet and muttered something about having to go, and it elicited no protest. Burt pushed his chair for Miss Adams to take.

"I've ordered a bottle of Pouilly Fuisse," Melba Adams said. "Hope you don't mind. I've got important business to talk to you about."

He looked at that face and that body and wondered why she thought she had to be so aggressive. He had no intention of subjecting it to deep analysis, however; he also knew better than to be too available. "I don't talk business for free, Miss Adams."

"I don't work for free either. Or so I once thought. My last three pictures grossed forty-two million. I'm being conned into another fucking lollipop-and-fudge masterpiece where 'bed' is the sexiest word allowed, and I don't let the hero jump into the pants until the vows are said—in church! And that fucking masterpiece will do twelve million domestic for sure. Know how much Melba Adams will wind up with after husband, agent and studio accountants get through with her? A fat zip. Zero. You tell me what you charge to get me out of the bear trap and I'll cut you in fair."

The waiter arrived with the cooler, wine and glasses. They waited until he left.

"However, I really am busy, Miss Adams."

"I read the papers, darling. Took a lot of pull to get the shmucks here to let me have the adjacent cabana. You don't think it was accidental, do you?"

"I didn't think about it. Just how lucky I was."

"More than you imagine, sweetie. This whole fucking thing can be settled with one goddamn phone call. It needs someone like you."

"And I could use someone like you, Miss Adams, but any problem requires a little preparation and time. That's what I don't have."

"Darling, I've been laying for you here, if you'll forgive the expression. I've talked the owners, my friends, to get me the suite next to yours, I've got it filled with enough evidence to prove my husband and agents and the studio have been stealing my ass blind for years."

"There are some good lawyers in this town," he offered.

"The best. But they already work for *them*. Come on up to the suite. The worst that can happen is you get to go to bed with me."

"I don't go to bed with clients. That is—as long as I can hold out."

"Lawyers don't turn me on all that much either, so we're even." She picked up her wine. "At least up to now."

"Where's your husband?" he said, emptying his glass.

"When the fucking hypocrite isn't stealing from me he's off doing religious charitable work. He's probably in Bakersfield in an onion field with his bleeding heart agonizing over the plight of some asshole old widow. We'd be safe anyway. He doesn't care what I do as long as he gets to take all the money."

"You're something," Burt Hammond commented.

"I'm a woman alone, Mr. Lawyer. Made it by working my pretty ass off since I was thirteen. All I know to do is look great, sing great, dance great and act okay. I've had to trust men. I'm thirty-eight years old. In two years they'll toss that butt on the scrapheap and people will say what a putz I was not to save my money. I need your help now."

Melba Adams had come well prepared. She had copies of her contracts, her income-tax returns, and a number of very interesting ledgers she had managed to take from her husband's locked files. The sun was hanging low on the western horizon when Burt was finished. Miss Adams had bathed, slipped into a shift, put on a touch of makeup, and was reading a film script when he found her in the adjacent bedroom.

"You're right, Melba, you're being stolen blind."

"So?"

"I'm going to make that one phone call. Then the genteel caper falls apart. You're going to need a good accountant when your money comes back to you."

"I'll find one. By the way, how much is that phone call going to cost me?"

"Nothing."

"Nothing?" she echoed.

"If I flop."

"Which you won't."

"Of course. How's a hundred thousand dollars strike you? Fair?"

"For one fucking phone call?"

"For one un-fucked-up career."

Melba Adams turned to a snifter of Armagnac he had not noticed before. When she came up for air, she put down the glass firmly. "You're practicing law in the wrong place, sweetheart. You ought to get your lawyer's ass down here. You could own this town. Who do you want me to call for you?"

"The guy who runs the studio. Say that Burton Z Hammond wants to talk to him about your contract. Give them this number. He'll be out somewhere, of course, have to do a lot of calling before he gets back to us."

"They'll circle the wagons from Malibu to Palm Springs."

"Won't do them any good. They'll find out, if they don't know already, that they've been into stuff the district attorney would give his eyeteeth to find out about. And, yes, you were right, they'll be scared to death of Jerry Haggerty's attorney."

She rose to get to the phone. "It'll take the assholes some time to get their act together. Why don't you wait here?"

"Can I use your shower?"

"I thought you'd never ask," Melba Adams said, taking up the telephone.

It seemed scarcely a moment before Mike Gilkey returned Melba Adams' call, but of course there are temporal as well as optical illusions. Melba handed him the phone and kissed his ear. "I'm going to jump into the tub, angel. I can't stand hearing myself discussed."

The two men spoke as if they were old friends. Burt said enough to show Mike Gilkey that the lawyer knew whereof he spoke; there were no threats, no recriminations, no expressions of shock. "I don't fight yesterday's wars all over again," Burt said, "but if I win today's I expect to get even." He laid down the terms for the new picture, a million dollars, total ownership of the negative, the studio to come out through its distribution, and a guarantee of two more films at terms to be agreed upon later, but no less favorable than these.

A silence deep enough to enclose a heart attack ensued. "It sounds tough, Mike," Burt Hammond said, "but you'll come out. If you don't, I promise to renegotiate. I'll be as fair with you as you are with us."

"I'll have to call you back," Gilkey finally said. He'd call his board chairman back east (and God knew who else).

"I'm free until Monday morning," Burt said. "About the lady's husband," he went on. "You understand that anything he's got coming goes to Miss Adams?"

Melba Adams stood beside him, a bath towel in folds shielding her nakedness. "I think I love you," she said with a laugh.

"Don't. That costs extra."

"Now I'm rich, who cares?"

They were not through with each other when the phone rang again. Gilkey said: "This is a conference call, Burt. Can I introduce you to the chairman of our board, Mr. Alfred Horn in Booth Bay, Maine?"

When Horn got down to business, he began by being combative, spoke of guns being held to his head in the middle of the night, refusing to be intimidated, pressured, or otherwise forced to do what he had no intention of doing.

"There's no pressure here, sir," Burt began, and went on to assure the gentleman that if his client did not achieve civil equity she'd have no alternative but to find satisfaction elsewhere. "I hope that doesn't sound like a threat, sir. You know how valuable a star Miss Adams is and I wouldn't be doing my duty to a client nor you to your stockholders if we wasted her talent and time in digging up a squalid history. Let's go forward . . ."

"Thank you, sir," Burt Hammond was able to say some moments later.

"You talk as pretty as you ball." Melba Adams took the phone from his hands and slid into bed beside him. "Now where were we when we were interrupted, pretty man?"

The government concluded its case Monday morning. The defense made routine motions for dismissal and such, all of which Burton Hammond knew the court would reject. After the noon recess, he began the long, tedious process of destroying the government's charges, one by one. The sibilants laced the air ceaselessly, sixty-six thousand . . . sixty-six cents . . . how did you know, where were you, are you sure of the amount, why, how, did you count it, did you see it, could it have been more, less, what did you do then that makes you certain now, or are you *less* certain now than you indicated earlier here? . . .

Two days later he was concluding to the jury. It had been the duty of the government to prove its charges, to establish its case, and this it had plainly failed to accomplish . . .

Behind him, as he faced the men and women in the box, Burt Hammond heard a shout, an incomprehensible stream of invective. He turned to see a short man in a pale blue sports shirt race down the short aisle from the back of the courtroom, take a handgun from inside the shirt and fire two shots at Jerry Haggerty. He could see that Jerry was unhurt. In the split second it also occurred to Burt Hammond that the marshals in the courtroom were remarkably unresponsive to the assailant. So he leaped across the defense table himself, coming at the gunman from above and falling on top of him with the railing at the intruder's back. The gunman was all hard muscle and stank powerfully, but Burt kept his hand on the wrist that held the weapon and was jackhammering the man's head against the stanchions of the railing. He felt his own head being slugged from behind and was wondering what the hell *that* was when the two of them were separated. The FBI men and the courtroom marshals had evidently decided both combatants were equally to be manhandled until the judge was able to restore order. He cleared the courtroom. He ordered the gunman sent away for observation. He turned to the jury and urged it to disregard what it had just seen, telling them it was not, after all, relevant to what they had learned after a long and tedious trial. He reminded them of their own sacrifices in performing their jury duty; he told them to what great expense the government had gone in order to bring this case to trial, not to mention the pain and expense to the defendant. The judge said he would consult with counsel in his chambers.

If he was controlled before the jury, he was plainly furious in his office. He seemed to suspect the whole attack was phoney and staged, by whom he did not have to say, even the government lawyers found themselves turning to Hammond. Burt Hammond lifted a bruised hand to the judge and let it drift to a torn shirt just below where his left ear had been battered by a marshal or an FBI man, but he offered no rebuttal. "The defense once again asks that a mistrial be declared here, Your Honor," he said softly, without expectation of success, as always. "It's denied, counselor," the judge said crisply.

The Los Angeles *Times* the next morning blazoned the shooting across page one. The *Herald-Examiner* reported talk that the whole thing had been stage-managed by labor sympathizers to get their beloved Jerry Haggerty off the hook. The assailant turned out to be a small-time hoodlum with a long record of petty theft and incarcerations in jails, prisons and mental institutions.

"They're crazy," Jerry exclaimed. "The guy almost blew my head off, didn't he?"

Burton Z Hammond moved the case to the jury as quickly as he could. By the end of the week, it had been sent out to do its duty. That evening it reported itself unable to reach a decision. They had been at it for less than four hours; the judge softly urged them to resume the next morning. That morning jurors asked to go over certain matters. The judge was patient with them. They came back an hour later for further elucidation. The judge asked them to reach a decision, going over the expense argument tediously, as if the money was coming out of their pockets, or his.

The next morning the jury declared itself hopelessly deadlocked, and it turned out it was hopeless indeed, six for, six against.

The judge declared a mistrial and called for a grand jury investigation of jury tampering.

Jerry Haggerty came to Burt Hammond's side and took his hand. "You did good, kid," he said. He had a chartered executive jet waiting to fly him back north. Burt preferred to go the next day.

There was a call from Melba Adams when he got back to the hotel but he did not return it. When Elmer Wright showed up, the two men walked on the grounds, where their words could not be easily copied, if at all.

"What do you think, Elmer, his people tampered with the jury?"

"He didn't tell them to."

"He doesn't have to say anything, does he?"

"In a way, he's their prisoner, Mr. Hammond."

"He knows what they do. He makes no effort to stop them," Burt Hammond said, almost to himself.

"I'm sure he could do it that way, all right."

The night air was heavy with the thick-sweet scent of jasmine. "It's a victory for you, Mr. Hammond," Elmer Wright said. "Now that Robert Kennedy is out of the government a lot of heavy artillery is gone. It remains to be seen what they'll do after this."

"I don't think they reached all six of the jurors, do you, Elmer? At least I won that, didn't I?"

"I do believe you would have hung the jury up anyway."

"What do you think will happen now?"

"They were very clumsy, I must say."

He always knew how to look a fact in the face. The time had come to look at a lot of ugly faces. But he had done that, hadn't he, here on the hotel grounds? When he was alone in his room, he called Melba Adams and told her he was leaving the next day.

"Where do we have the wrap party, sweetie? Your place or mine?" she said.

9

TURNING the corner, Burt Hammond saw the highly polished antique Cadillac in front of his building when he returned from a morning jog.

From the apartment upstairs he called Helen Mendoza. "How long has Miss Kendall been waiting?"

"Long enough to leave three cups of coffee untouched. Do you want to talk to her upstairs?"

He skipped the shower and came into the office with a towel around his neck and the sweat of his running gear still damp on his shirt.

"Why haven't you called me in all this time?" Courtney Kendall greeted him.

"I've been busy," he offered without conviction.

He did not tell her that life with Jerry Haggerty was turning out to be somewhat more sordid than he liked. It meant he had many second thoughts about involving her. He knew Justice's task force had him under surveillance, either in conjunction with or apart from the Bureau. He had also to consider a new Jerry, Jerry as adversary. Everybody—Jerry, his friends, known and unknown—they were all interested in whom Burt Hammond was seeing and what he might be saying. The lawyer in him did not think it wise to get too close to Miss Kendall.

But here she was.

"There've been some problems around here."

"You're playing games with me."

"I wouldn't do that to you."

"Are you my friend?" she asked gravely.

"I'd like to be."

"We had such a fine time. I didn't want it to die."

"I've thought a lot about you, Courtney."

"I need a friend," she said with desperation. She rushed into his arms and let him hold her for a long time. "I didn't know where to turn. Meeting you was providential. Then I lost you. You wouldn't even return my calls."

"I'm sorry. I'll do what I can for you, Courtney. What do you want?"

"It's my brother. Something terrible has happened to him."

He brought her to a chair and sat her down. "Why do you think that?"

"I know he's in trouble."

"I'm sure he can take care of himself if he is."

"He's a very foolish man."

"Aren't we all?" He looked down at his sweatshirt and the large fading stains. "Do you want to wait here or come to the rooms over the store while I shower and change?"

She rose quickly from the chair. "You don't believe me, do you? You think I'm just some hyper-nervous character? I'm not! Ken is in a real jam. He's probably locked up somewhere, otherwise I'd've heard from him."

"All right." He knew her well enough to be sure she wasn't hysterical just because the brother hadn't called for a few days. "Where might he be?"

"That's the point. I don't know."

"Could he have taken off, say, for New York or L.A. or Acapulco or Europe?"

"The estate offices on Montgomery Street tell me he's been pulling money out of various accounts."

"Can't they leave word at one of these places for him to call?"

"They have. He hasn't."

"Maybe he's angry at you."

"No. We've had our differences before and he's called."

"Or in love."

"No."

"Why not?"

"I just know. Take it from me."

"Okay, so he isn't in the mood to call the family."

"Rather large withdrawals," she said. "And then he disappears."

"Can't the people on Montgomery Street put a hold—"

"They have, where they can. But this is his own money. Look," she broke off, "all these things can be settled if I can see him and talk to him. That's where I need you. I'll pay you, of course."

"Of course."

"Whatever it costs. Before grandma-ma finds out."

"Why doesn't she know, isn't she in the same house?"

"She has her own quarters, you understand. Days go by when we don't see each other."

"And what matter if she knew?"

"She and Ken have had differences. She could change her will. She's threatened to do it."

"You have an address where he stays in town?"

"He has several places."

"I'll want them all," he said without comment. "And some of his best friends' numbers."

"He has all sorts of friends."

"I rather imagine. Do you have a phone book or an address book of his?"

"He kept all that kind of thing in his wallet. I'd see him pull this paper out, unfold it and make his calls."

"Hiding something," Burt said. "From whom?"

"Not from me. I can't imagine."

"Okay, I'll find him and tell him to call you," he said cheerfully. "Now if you'll wait, I'll change."

"I'd like to see where you live," Courtney said.

* * *

"It's beautiful," she said when she followed him into his apartment.

"A flash act is what they call it in show business," he said. "I tell you that because your opinion of me matters very much, Courtney."

"Nevertheless, I do like it," she said, smiling. "It's you."

"Then I'm glad." He had the impulse to kiss her cheek, but did not, for various good and sensible reasons. "I won't be long. Stay here."

The maid did not come in until noon; there were still a stale bottle of wine and two glasses on the nightstand and a lot of damp towels on the floor where his guest the night before had tossed them. He found someone's barrette and a couple of bobby-pins and pitched them into a wastebasket before going into the stall.

He sat on the marble bench and let all twelve shower heads hit him full force. He was not a little surprised to hear the shower door open behind him; he turned to find his visitor, jaw firmly set, stepping in.

"Why, Miss Kendall," he said, "imagine finding you here."

She moved into the storm created by the shower heads on all sides of the stall only to find no arms around her. The water stopped running.

"Don't throw me out," she said.

He had his hands on her shoulder and was turning her around. "I'll be very gentle as I do so."

"I've taken showers with men before."

"I've no doubt." He had her out of the shower and found a big red terry bathsheet and threw it over her.

"So why are you doing this to me? Don't you think I have a nice figure?" She parted the bathsheet so he could reach an honest decision.

"You have a splendid body, Miss Kendall," he conceded.

"And you don't like me?"

"I'm crazy about you, Miss Kendall." He came to her and brought the towel tight around her and took her into his arms. "You're beautiful. You're charming. You're bright. You're complicated. You're interesting. And you're very damned rich. Why shouldn't I like you?"

"Then why don't you treat me like any of your thousands of women?"

171

"One: because it turns out that I'm still an old-fashioned chauvinist pig at heart and I don't want to screw around with someone I may have other plans for. And two: I'm not just a man anymore. I'm now also your lawyer, remember?"

"All those activist girls with causes from Berkeley and San Francisco State? You don't go to bed with any of them?"

"They're not clients and they don't get sent bills."

"I'm not a virgin," she announced proudly.

"I should damned well hope so."

"And I think I love you."

He took her in his arms and held her very close, kissing her forehead now and then very gently. "I'm glad," he said. "I'm very glad."

"I know all about you. I've had Montgomery Street find out everything."

"My secret's out," he said, and touched her forehead with his lips again.

"Really kiss me," she demanded and arched her neck.

"Yes, madam." He put his mouth to hers. After a considerable moment, he said: "You're sure you're *not* a virgin?"

"Ever since my freshman year."

"Didn't anybody ever kiss you?"

"Of course."

"Didn't they tell you how it has to be done? You make the lips soft and you part them a little. I get the feeling you think it's a stamping process, something like certifying a side of beef."

She broke from his hold. "You goddamn fool! Don't you know what's happening?"

She found his mouth and pressed hers to it, hungrily, passionately, her hand seizing his root beneath the terry robe. "I'm scared to death out here, that's all. Scared of you! Help me! Don't handle me like I'll break! I'm just as easy a ball as those chicks of yours who leave their empty wine glasses and barrettes around the place, for God's sake. I'm not made of porcelain. Take me, fuck me, devastate me!"

"I'd be absolutely delighted, Miss Kendall," he said, letting his surprise shine through. He whipped the towel from her hands and took her into his arms.

* * *

Later, much later, he said: "About your brother. Does he always get into a lot of trouble?"

"It stays hidden."

"Is he homosexual?"

"Why do you ask that?"

"Makes no difference to me if he digs doing it with snakes, understand. I just have to know where to have my man look for him."

"Your man? You don't do this yourself?"

"Why, Miss Kendall," he said in mock surprise, "I thought your people on Montgomery Street told you about Burton Z Hammond, Esquire. Do you think I punch doorbells looking for lost people? I'm a very big lawyer, as you'll see when you get my bill. But we'll find Kenneth, I assure you."

"He's not entirely homosexual," Courtney said dully. "I know that for a fact."

"My man will do what he can."

"You'll let me know, no matter what?"

"Of course."

"All this other stuff that kept you from me—"

"No matter what."

"I trust you. I think I love you. Please don't let that scare you off, Burt. If it blows over, what the hell?"

"I like it, even if it scares me."

"It can't last, but it's nice while it does." She came closer into his arms.

10

It began in the Union League Press Club on Post Street. Burt Hammond had a midafternoon date with a reporter from the *Chronicle* who had done more than one favor in the past and who could not be refused. The bar was empty but for a trio of old friends celebrating a reunion. Burt turned to see Oliver Hale Goodman take a stool beside him.

"He won't be here," Goodman said.

"It must be important, going to all this trouble."

"To you, Hammond. Not to me. I'm leaving the government service."

"Sorry to hear that. You never were like some of the others, Goodman."

"Sure I was. Had to be."

"You didn't have your heart in it."

Goodman ordered Seagram VO and ginger ale, which told a good deal about him. After a sip he said: "Get your clients out of Inter-Continent."

"That's official?"

"As official as it can get without being official. The government won't let an international carrier be controlled by those people, it's as simple as that."

"Is there a deal for my client involved here?" Burt Hammond asked.

"Of course not, Hammond."

But he had to say that, of course.

Burt Hammond found Jerry Haggerty in his office later. A bottle of John Jameson and three glasses, all empty, stood at a corner of his desk. The old man, blowsy and unusually rubicund, growled a greeting. It had become like that between them ever since the trial; Burt Hammond had heard it before when people fell out of favor. He had also seen the old man reverse himself inexplicably.

"We're cornering the rats," he grumbled.

"Good. Anyone you suspected?"

"Is it ever?"

Burt Hammond told him about the obviously arranged meeting with Oliver Hale Goodman. A man departing the government was bringing a message of the greatest urgency, one it could not deliver itself without compromise.

"Screw'em. We're not backing down." Haggerty reached for the whiskey.

"There are at least two other government agencies involved, Jerry," Burt went on deliberately. "You have to ask yourself what you get out of it, whether the trouble you make for yourself is worth it."

"It's worth it, kid. I gave my word."

At the monthly meeting of the Oversight Committee, Matt Kusic took Burt Hammond aside. "About the airline deal," he began.

"Matt, it spells big trouble."

"I don't like it myself, Burt, but who knows anything about all the foreign international carriers? Why pick on this one?"

"This government has nothing to do with the foreign airlines, except to give them landing facilities and see they obey our regulations here. But this is a licensed American carrier."

"My son-in-law . . ." Matt began, and his voice drifted off.

"They won't let it happen," Burt said rigidly, "and I can't persuade Jerry. Maybe you can."

At the conference table, the airline deal left him outmaneuvered; because of his position on Inter-Continent he could not afford to raise objections to a variety of loans to organizations and people whose names and locations stank in his nostrils.

At the office, Helen Mendoza told him: "Miss Courtney Kendall called again. She says it's business. Shall I call her for you?"

"No."

She followed him into his office. "Why not?"

"Leave me alone."

"She wants to talk to you professionally. Why turn down her business? Come to think of it, why turn her down at all?"

"Get out, will you, Helen?" he said without malice.

"I know you pretty good, *abogado,* but this I don't understand."

Elmer Wright had been doing some special work for him ever since the trial. They met in Union Square and Elmer reported on it in his Plymouth two-door in the underground garage:

"All your bank accounts—trust, office, personal. They got a court order and they're going through all of them. Fishing. Hoping to find something on you. Is something there they could nail you for?"

"I've always been very careful. Who knows what can be tied to something they've found elsewhere? What else are they looking at, Elmer?"

"Credit cards. They've got a profile on you, they call it, that tells them everything. Where you eat, when and with whom, what you drink, when and how much and with whom, parties, gifts you give, how much and what kind and to whom, where you travel, when and with whom you spend time and for how long and where you stay and what you spend in hotels and for cars and for gifts and for whom and how much. Have I left out anything? The cards tell them everything the bank accounts don't."

"I get your drift. Anything else?"

"Two cars, one always parked across from your place. Ever notice them? One's a panel truck with 'Dependable Plumbing Company' across it. A 'sixty black Chevy."

"What're they looking for?"

"That's easy. What I can't figure out is, who puts them there? They're never together, the panel leaves and then this beatup van shows up, short job, busted fenders, got graffiti all over it. You've never noticed it?"

"Should I?"

"You're careful, Mr. Hammond, but you're going to have to be even more so, you understand? They're looking to see who comes and goes, probably got cameras working. I don't think it's the law."

"Haggerty?"

"You and him have a falling out?"

Burt did not reply; instead he asked, "Why do you think it wouldn't be the law in those two cars?"

"They're usually not that cute when they stake out a place. Government guys like to work with new equipment. It's just a sense I have. I could be wrong."

"You could be right too. Does that finish it for today?"

"Your friend Miss Martin."

"What about her?"

"Busted for grass."

"Serious?"

"It's a bum rap. She's too sharp to carry weed in her car. She knows how the police stake out for beatup VW vans like hers. She told me to tell you she wouldn't do anything to hurt the mountain. Somebody's given the word, probably planted the grass when they made the search."

"She's a good girl to work through you. Got enough money in the account to do what has to be done for her?"

"Don't worry. I'll get it down to misdemeanor possession. What I'd like to know is, who gave the word?"

After Elmer Wright told Burt Hammond about the extent of the effort being made to find out how he was spending his own money, as well as where and for what, Burt was more distressed at himself than at the nosey officialdom. He thought he should have been better prepared. After all, the Federal Bureau of Investigation and its agents were not unknown to him. He had no doubt they had a file on him going back to the days when he and his father were suspect because of Pop's agitation in behalf of the enforcement of the law embraced in the Water Conservation Act of 1902 that created the All-American Canal. His father had frequently called attention to the fact that elected and appointed officials alike were derelict in performing their constitutional duties to enforce that law, which surely must have been noted as subversive.

Burt Hammond thought he was wise enough to defend himself as well against private adversaries. To his father, the Amalgamated Farmers were an unofficial enemy he faced every day. It made life difficult at the bank, at the grain and feed store, at equipment dealers, and even at high school where his son liked to run the 880 and the mile and Coach Evans, saying they needed Burt for the hundred-yard dash, tried to wear him out running five heats before the sprint finals and the distance events.

Burt thought he had come to learn how delicate a shield is privacy. In the Imperial Valley everybody knew everything about the Hammonds. "Too bad your father didn't bring your ma to the doctor sooner," he heard frequently after his mother died of breast cancer. "What is the name of that Mexican lady your father is seeing?" If they did not know the name it was only because they didn't deem that detail worth acquiring.

When he returned to the valley, there were still growers—become richer and more powerful—and their organizations were swollen to near-sovereign status. At their urging, the police checked on him. The police—it meant paid adversaries out of four distinct jurisdictions, local cops, county sheriffs, state patrolmen and the awesome minions of mighty St. John Edgar the Hoover who knew all about everybody, including the sex life, which was something shameful everybody in the world wanted to keep most secret. Burt Hammond came to understand the consequences of living with so many policing agencies, and the thought that by the time he had gone into forced exile in Mexico he had become accomplished in outwitting the sons of bitches.

Had he turned careless? Was negligence the price that success exacted? Jerry Haggerty, after a lifetime in conflict with adversaries who made his own enemies seem like petty bureaucrats, was plainly headed on a collision course. Yet even Jerry was now placing himself beside all those faceless government agencies out to strip him bare of every vestige of privacy. Jerry had those two monitoring trucks working in tandem. The specialist who came to the office to make random sweeps for listening devices had come to him from Jerry. Long ago, Burt Hammond had learned how dangerous a tool the telephone can be, so there was not so much Jerry could get from that, but he must certainly have learned to whom his lawyer talked, even if he never knew much about the subject from those brief conversations. Of course, the specialist could also have wired the office, as the gentlemen of the FBI had once wired his bed.

Jerry he could handle. The government, *that* would take some doing. When Burt Hammond filed his next income-tax return, he carefully added up every penny he had received from the practice of law and his income from various profitable investments. He instructed his accountant to prepare a return which took no deductions whatsoever.

Harry Greenbaum, a quiet, pipe-smoking gentleman of the old school, was apoplectic at the suggestion. He called it absurd, ridiculous, childish, insane, and a few other things. "If you won't do it, I'll find an accountant who will," Burt Hammond told him.

Later, Harry Greenbaum pleaded: "But some of your legitimate expenses are a matter of record. Office salaries, for instance. What you paid for your office supplies. Your phone bills, subscriptions, various other services you needed to conduct your law practice. The government can find out that stuff, so why not tell them what they already know?"

"Let them find out for themselves. I don't want them coming to me."

"I'll grant you the items they usually jump on . . . entertainment, travel, gratuities, gifts, contributions. I'll give you—"

"You'll give me nothing, Harry, I want nothing. I want to be able to tell them what I do is none of their business."

Burt Hammond's banks were not prepared for such a customer as he proposed to be. He knew all about the disclosure regulations already in the books. Cash deposits or withdrawals in amounts over five thousand dollars were routinely reported to some authority, for example, but Burt Hammond had always taken that into account. He instructed his banks to reject all queries about him from whatever source, unless, of course, the existing law obliged them to do otherwise. In every case, again if the statute books permitted, he wanted the bank operating officer to notify him of all inquiries. "Who knows? I might accede to a request here and there."

Not very likely, but he could hope to pick up a clue that way. Burt Hammond made arrangements for the bank to pay his routine bills. He closed out three existing bank safe-deposit boxes and used his office safe exclusively. He was, he believed, the only man in the world who knew how to open that monster; he took care not to use the factory man when he changed the numbers to 34-0-18-04-43. Even then he did not feel wholly private.

But at least now he did not have to explain himself to any person or organization in the land.

11

THE Fillmore was jammed with two thousand wildly dancing, writhing bodies, the vast hall throbbing with amplified music that came off the walls like an endless avalanche, stroboscopic lights flashing like artillery at midnight, impossible to move around in except on the floor—but leave it to Elmer Wright to find him. In time light shows and bone-rattling music would engulf the globe but it was new to most San Franciscans still—certainly to a courtly, quiet man—but he found his quarry nevertheless.

He brought Burt Hammond far down the street entrance, past the line of hopefuls waiting to be shoehorned into the place. His face, Burt observed, was ashen with concern.

"Right away," he began. "It is most important that

179

you remove yourself for a time. My authority for this has never let me down yet."

"What're talking about?"

"Word is out, sir. Get Burt Hammond. I don't know if it's Jerry Haggerty. My hunch is, it isn't; he's got friends who make a career out of trying to anticipate what he may want done. We live in an age of these crazy loners doing history's job. Nuts and maniacs running loose with all the burdens of history on their shoulders."

"I don't propose to hide just because a few crazies are out there," Burt Hammond said.

"That used to be what brave people were supposed to say. It isn't just a few out there, sir. There are hundreds, maybe thousands. It's a new social disease. The nuts read the signals in the leader's face and run to do its bidding. There's a death sentence out there on Burton Hammond, waiting to be brought to execution."

"But no direct orders, that you're sure of?"

"Only as sure as one can be when he's seen nothing on paper or heard it with his own ears. If Haggerty embraced you publicly, said you were still his man, now and forever . . ."

Trouble erupted in front of the Fillmore and a police car, lights flashing, pulled up. "Will you do it, sir?" he heard Elmer Wright say. "Believe me."

He laid an arm on the detective's shoulder and started back to the hall.

"Don't underestimate them. Don't think the crazies don't know how to wait. The craziest make damned crafty killers."

"I promise."

"Thank you, sir. About the Kendall man, is now all right to take that up?"

"Why not?" he said listlessly. Who cared? The talk of a sentence of death was so sudden, even unexpected, it dissolved all emotion.

"They know him well in the Haight. Uses another name, of course. He throws his money around pretty well. No one knows he's a Levering, he's managed that very well. They all think the money comes from big wholesale dope dealing. The working girls know him as a look-freak. He's maybe double- or triple-gaited, a real sex-kook, him and her and him, her and her, her and her and him, S and M, leather and dildoes, and all the rest of those charming German imports. I don't think he

180

shoots shit, but he's surely into meth and LSD. A real charmer."

"But you can't find him for me?"

"I'm sorry to say, not at this time, sir. I'm positive he's not in the city. If I may say, that's not of such moment right now. I can't tell you how dangerous it is for you."

The police were taking away a couple of frustrated rock lovers when they got back to the front door. The music and the incessant drumbeat were flooding out the door.

"You're not going in again, sir?" Elmer Wright asked in a tone of shock.

"Don't worry, Elmer," Burt Hammond said. "It's too jammed in there for someone to take a gun out, let alone to lift it and to aim it."

And he had to think. Fast. Hard. Where better than here?

Clancy was fat, big-assed, a young kid with a carefully cultivated mean look. He manhandled people who got in Jerry Haggerty's way when he had to, and Jerry liked it. The old Jerry moved in the world without bodyguards or strongarms; it was part of his attraction. But the old Jerry was not this Jerry in anything except name; Burt Hammond knew that.

"It's late," Clancy said, blocking the door.

"Get out of the way, fattie," Burt said through clenched teeth. He saw the hesitation and the reluctant step aside but the burning eyes predicted a score that would remain to be settled in the imbecile mind.

Jerry looked up from a report he was reading. The hour was somewhere between three and four in the morning; men all over the world grew faint or weak from lack of sleep at this hour but Haggerty could work forever. It came to Burt Hammond he had never seen the old man so eager to work, sodden and stupid as he often seemed.

"I hear I'm a marked man," Burt Hammond began.

Jerry looked up from his pages. He let them drop to the desk top. "Aren't we all, God have mercy on us," he said, affecting a brogue.

"I don't mind being marked in God's hands, Jerry. I hear He's got an assistant this time."

"Why tell me all your problems, kid?"

"I don't know why for sure. I know this: I don't pro-

181

pose for them to get me. They're not from you, I'm sure of that, so I'm not asking any special favors of you."

"I'm glad you said that," Jerry said.

"But you're a client and I have certain obligations. I owe you a lot. I'm giving you up as a client, for starters. Not that we're even. We'll come to that. But I feel obliged to tell you what you've got to do to stay out of prison. Number one: Get out of the airline deal. They won't let whoever's using Matt Kusic's relative take over a big international carrier. It may sound possible to hoodlum operators who think cash can solve any problem, but the government of the United States will never permit it. Know *why* it's attractive to those operators, and why the government won't allow it? Can you picture what they can do with a private jet-speeded pipeline for money and dope that extends around the world?"

The old man reached for the Irish, but he had second thoughts. "Maybe you're right."

"I got the word, believe me."

"From one of your government friends?" Haggerty's voice rattled angrily. "They tell you this to help you stay on my good side, kid? What else they tell you? They tell you to give me up as a client?"

"You know me better. They've been trying to bust my ass since I came back to California."

"And you're tired of it."

"Not tired of that, tired of you." The pause was like that of a hangman waiting for his signal. "You don't want me anymore, Jerry. You don't trust me. The truth is, I don't trust you too much either. If some maniac out there has decided to put a bullet in Burton Z Hammond, the Jerry Haggerty I thought I knew would stop it with a word. This one puts me in God's care. I'll handle it myself and come out stronger than ever."

"Guns blazing back, like in the movies, huh?" The whiskey idea seemed like a good one now and the old man took a shot.

"No, Jerry. You and I remain in business together, whether we like it or not. We can't break openly. It'd be bad for you, maybe even worse for me. They'd go after us one at a time and they'd get us both. I'm not asking for your love, Jerry, God knows I don't love you anymore; I'm asking for your brains. Be smart. An adversary always likes to see disunity in the opposition. I'm your man, you're my man. That's the way it has to be. I'll

182

never do anything to hurt you. They can hassle me, push me around, disbar me, nothing can change that, no matter what I think of you, or you of me. Have you got that?"

"You miserable upstart, who you think you're talking to?" Haggerty snapped irritably.

"Save it, Jerry. I like being able to say that I never saw you do anything improper. I want to be able to go on saying that. I can, as of now. You did a lot of foolish, maybe stupid things, but a lawyer can't stop that."

"Get out of here," he rumbled.

"The government's out to nail us; they'd succeed, except that I'm going to outsmart them. You know I don't play ball with them; haven't your people who've been tailing me, bugging my phones and office, told you that? I'll always be your friend even if I'm no longer your lawyer."

"No one's my friend."

"I'm not fat Clancy, Jerry, you don't have to pay me to own me."

"You *have* gone crazy, kid, I see that now." Jerry got to his feet. "First, you tell me you're a marked man, then you fire me as a client and tell me how we're going to be pals forever. That puts you right up there with those crazies you're running from."

"Crazies are cool, Jerry. That's the best thing about them. They've got short attention spans, unless of course they've got someone like you keeping them on the ball. I don't. I never forget what I have to be doing. Think about it."

Burt Hammond looked at the bottle between them. He picked it up, studied what was left in it. "You drink too much, Jerry," he said. "It's getting to you, I think. You have to love a man a lot to tell him something no one else in the world would dare tell him. Goodbye, old friend, and thanks for everything so far."

It was all a little theatrical, he thought on the way out, too rich in emotion; maybe the old man could see what was real and what was not. Burt Hammond had the feeling that part of him was outside his body observing what was happening and not entirely persuaded by what it saw and heard. That outside part knew there were old scores to be settled, so Burt Hammond was going.

But he was not going. There was murder and near-murder to remember, and that never ended.

*　*　*

The day being Saturday, he had the office to himself. He sat at Helen's Selectric and typed a note:

Dear Helen Mendoza:
I instruct you to terminate the business of this office as quickly and as expeditiously as you can manage. I have gone over the outstanding business and see nothing in the clients' files which cannot be handled elsewhere. You may tell them what they will find out by themselves anyway, that Burton Z Hammond has decided to give up the practice of law here and has left San Francisco.

You are hereby and herewith empowered to sell this real property and all the furniture of the office and the residence. The art on the walls I want stored.

You already possess certain instruments giving you power of attorney over all my bank accounts. I now reaffirm their validity. I instruct you to go to Los Angeles and there to lease or buy, at your discretion and at whatever cost, the goddamnedest mansion/showplace you can find. You are to move into it with mamacita. Inform Elmer Wright to come down and make it as secure as possible from unwelcome intrusion.

You will, of course, be harassed by all sorts of people. You must inform them all it is none of their business. If news and police people are persistent about my whereabouts, assure them it's not only none of their business but that you don't know anyway, which you don't. I want a grand house, a lovely house, an impressive house. Also a cat, a black Persian, I think; a male would be better.

You are to do all this as quickly as you can.
                                    Burton Z Hammond

BOOK FIVE:

The Peninsula

(1967)

1

ON that same Saturday, 576 miles away, Roseanna Beth Lee became Mrs. Lawrence Marshall at the Clark County Courthouse in Las Vegas, Nevada. Afterward there was to be a small wedding breakfast in the Sutter's Mill Suite of the Sierra Nevada Hotel, where the bride was scheduled to make her nightclub debut that very evening.

The morning was hectic. Larry Marshall had brought the great Aristides Kupidon himself to choreograph and stage the act, Kupidon whose credits went back to Astaire and Rogers and forward to a succession of current Broadway musical theater hits. Backed by four boy dancers, Roseanna was going to show the world she not only was a great singer but was a total performer, dancer, monologuist—the works. "I'll have the Hollywood brass up there and there'll be picture offers, baby," Larry promised.

Roseanna was calm as the two of them, unaccompanied, stood before the clerk, muttered the necessary vocables and signed the papers. Although she promised herself she would not, she had swallowed a few reds and mixed a shot of vodka into her orange juice. When they came into the Sutter's Mill Suite everybody rose and greeted them with coups of champagne held high. Roseanna sat next to Lou and Julie Birch. She looked at a small box on her plate. It made Roseanna think of an Abba-Dabba candy bar because it was just as long and slim. When she took off the ribbon, she found a glistening bracelet of platinum and diamonds set in six clusters, each crowned by a coruscating gem.

Roseanna's eyes misted. "Lou and I know you'll be very happy," Julie Birch said.

Others came over with other splendid gifts appropriate to each donor's stature. For some reason, as she had told her doctors back in the private sanitarium in Connecticut, whenever things went well for her Roseanna began to fall apart. She felt sickish the more people put glorious tokens of their esteem before her.

Larry's was the last to be offered her. He helped her nervous fingers open a blood-red velvet box and take from it an enormous emerald necklace. Roseanna seized it with both hands as if to crush it. Everybody made suitable sounds of approval; Larry jested, "Don't break it, baby, it's not paid for yet." Everybody laughed.

He and Roseanna did not stay long. At noon there was to be a dress rehearsal with the full band and all the changes of costume which, Larry knew, were already in the star's dressing room ready for final fitting. She would make no less than four changes during her fifty-four minute act. Hairdressers and wigmakers were even now waiting for her, and of course the lighting and sound crews would be in the big room to make whatever final adjustments they required.

Larry paused before the door of the Governor's Suite. "Do I get to carry you in, Rosey?" he said. But he took her hand and led her into a flower-banked sitting room furnished with a heavy hand and nineteenth-century opulence. He did not let her go until they came to the bedroom where the bed had already been turned down. The management had thoughtfully put an uncorked bottle in a champagne bucket, and Roseanna's eyes found it without hesitation. Larry saw her walk to it. "Think you ought to, baby, you've got a long day," he said.

"I'd better," Roseanna said.

They were done with what had to be done in bed in a short time. She had not lain with her husband before but had always been intrigued by his boasts of sexual prowess, so she was surprised not only by the speed with which he attacked her and reached his own climax but by his timidity and his lack of ardor.

"I've got a lot on my mind, baby," Larry apologized. "I keep thinking where you've got to be and what I've got to do. I'm gunning for a picture deal. I've got a chartered plane down in L.A. and I'm still hoping the big guys from Paramount and Twentieth will be here. Joe Levine's promised me he would."

Roseanna shrugged. "I understand, Larry," she said.

When Larry Marshall left the Governor's Suite, he went to 1214–5 at the far end of the corridor. He rapped on the door and said his name when the voice inside inquired. He let himself into a sitting room awash with luggage and carelessly tossed clothes. "Where do you think you're going?" he asked Brenda Moore. "And why the hell weren't you down at the wedding breakfast?"

"I'm going home, wherever that it," Brenda said. "And I never eat breakfast. Any other questions?"

Larry took from his blazer a packet of hundred-dollar bills and put them on a table before her. "Count that."

"I'll take your word," Brenda said.

"Five big ones. All yours."

"Thanks," Brenda said and picked the packet up, regarded it briefly and dropped it into a half-packed bag. "Damned decent of you."

"There's another five thousand—"

"I was going anyway, Larry," Brenda said. "But a girl can always use another five thousand quid."

"It's yours"—Larry stepped to the bag and picked up the first packet of money—"only if you stay."

"You're kidding. I thought it was to promise to get out of her life."

"I don't kid when it's business. She needs you. I don't know whether you're good for her or bad. I know she's into uppers and downers again, all the good those phonies in South Norwalk did. I've got two million dollars in deals in Vegas and Miami right this minute and she's got to be handled, that's all I know." He put the money into her hands again.

"I didn't think she was going to go through with the marriage," Brenda said. "As late as last night, she said she was going to renege on it."

"Neither did I. But she did. And now I'm handling her. And it'll be good for her. I'm going to make her the biggest star in the world."

"You're shooting high. It's never happened with a black girl."

"She's a white girl, Brenda, with black blood. It's a new world out there, the old crap is falling apart. Even the racists look at her and dream of jumping on her. The blacks will be proud that one of them made the breakthrough. In Europe and Asia, where the big market for films is these days, her color is going to be a plus. I tell you we're going to own that new world!"

She looked dourly at him. "Maybe," she conceded.

"But she needs handling, Brenda, now more than ever. There'll be time to straighten her out later."

"In other words you want me to work for you?"

"Right. I've cleared it with Lou. He says yes."

"Something you ought to know," she began.

"Whatever, it's okay with me."

"Hold it." She took a long breath. "I love her."

He was slow in replying as well. "I know that."

"I mean, I love her, Larry. We've been making it."

"I know that too."

"And still it's okay with you?"

"Has to be. I've got no choice."

"Sure you have. Let me have that ten grand and I'll never see her again. That way she's all yours."

"And how does she get herself together to do two shows a night six times a week? Only Elvis is getting more money here and she hasn't even proved herself at the box office! How's that for a deal, how's that for selling? I can't afford to take any chances."

"She's a straight girl but she plays because she's scared. She could easily decide straight sex is a bore. Do you still want me to stay?"

"I'm not going to kid myself and say it won't happen again with you two. You have to stay. I need you."

"I don't know about you, chum," Brenda said, "but it's tough on me, her now being Mrs. Marshall and all. *I* don't like it, however Mr. Marshall feels."

"We'll work it out later." Larry grabbed her hands in steel fingers. "There's too much riding now to let personal considerations get in the way, don't you see?"

"You know something?" Brenda said. "Why is my stomach churning so? Do you think I'm getting sick? I love her, didn't you hear me?"

"I love her too, for Chrissake!"

"I believe it! She's gorgeous, she's talented and she has two million dollars in contracts right now, why not? And here I am, telling you I love her and fucking her life up like everybody else, for ten lousy thousand bucks!"

"There's a grand a week for you, Brenda, every week, under the table, aside from what you get officially."

"You know something?" Brenda went to a table where a lot of drinking things were kept. She lifted the vodka and took a belt, the way she and Roseanna had one time. She raised the bottle as if in salute to her absent friend. "My stomach has stopped churning."

Larry started for the door. "Don't forget, luv," Brenda called after him. "Every week. In cash."

189

2

A barbed-wire fence ran along the main road, interrupted only to let a two-lane hardtop get to the highway. He drove a good mile across the mountain cut-off. Rounding a curve transformed dry, untended fields into a golden sea of waving grain. Huge oaks blocked the view; when he passed them he saw Wildoaks, three sides of a huge brick quadrangle with sixteen chimneys dotting the red-tiled roof. The entry was paved, English style, with crushed pebbles; the walls and windows in front of the house were mostly hidden by coastal live oaks, Japanese maples and Irish yew trees. He was surprised to find no other cars. When the huge door swung open, a manservant in black pants and a checked vest smiled slightly when he said his name.

"You've been expected, sir. Would you be good enough to wait in the library?"

The library was shelved in dark walnut and had a floor done in the same wood. The books were old, fancy bindings, the works of Robert Southey and such. In one corner of the room his eye fell on an early Matisse and, as he walked over to it, he saw another. On another wall, hanging over a wood-framed fireplace big enough to roast a steer, he saw a Picasso of the classic period.

Courtney, in jeans and a plaid shirt, rushed into his arms. "Do you want a drink? Lunch? Are you going to stay?"

"No. No. Yes. Unless we get powerfully bored with each other. Then I reserve the right to remember something I completely forgot about."

"You'll have to walk. I'm having your car towed to a wrecking yard. Let's go to bed and talk later. See what a slut I am at heart? Why've you been so long coming to see me? Never mind, you're here, that's all that matters."

He kissed her, his hands remembering the long, hungry body, drawing it closer to his. "You're a marvelous slut," he whispered. "The best ever."

"You know just how to win the heart of a woman," she said through the kiss.

She brought him to her apartment. What was once a master suite had been turned into a sitting room large enough to accommodate a diplomatic reception; a balcony looked across the fields to the mountain in the distance; there was a small library and a pink bedroom. She clasped his hand at the canopied bed. "Your room's down the hall. Do you really want to see it?"

"More than anything in the world," he said, and fell with her on the bed.

Later, he said: "Do you want to know why I've come here?"

"To go to bed with me, of course."

"Also to hide out."

She kissed his chest. "You can hide here forever. Even the gardeners don't know who's in the house."

"These things have a way of going from boil to simmer to cool to cold—particularly after they find out what they're afraid of just isn't so."

"I hope it takes them a long time."

"I've been fighting you, Courtney. Keep you out of my life. Protect you from stuff like that."

"What do I have to do to prove myself?"

"Whatever it is, you're doing okay," he said.

Still later, he said: "Tell me about when you were a girl."

"My brother and I were born here. We have what you might call a hospital of our own, grandma-ma has always preferred it. They found my father in the carriage house. My mother died in France in a car accident. I had a wonderful childhood. I never got to know my parents, but grandma-ma was always with me and I had good nannies and governesses. I was brought up by my grandmother."

"Wildoaks is going to be a problem for us, Courtney, I see that," he said with a smile.

"I'm not as reclusive as it sounds. I went to Stanford, did the whole social bit. I was also cheerleader, played field hockey and carried picket signs for I forget what good causes. I was really your all-American girl-slob at heart."

"Is Stanford where you stopped being a virgin?"

"No," she said gravely. "That happened at Wildoaks too."

"Fitting for royalty," he commented. "Did you have lots of parties here?"

"My mother and father did. He was in politics. He had larger dreams than seemed to work out for him."

"Did his death hurt you?"

"I hardly knew him. Father seemed very coarse, barked at us rather than talked. Most of the pictures around here are things he bought, isn't that remarkable? He had such sensitive feelings for things on canvas but was dead inside for Ken and me."

"After the first lover, did you play around a lot?"

"No," she said. "Did you?"

"I grew up in farm country. Sex was the only nighttime diversion."

"Ken had lots of girls here," she said.

"By the way, I don't think he really ever liked girls," Burt said.

"But I know he did," she persisted.

"Numbers don't prove anything," he said. "What makes you so sure?"

"He was the boy who took away my virginity."

Burt looked at her for a long time. She said it evenly and without expression, as, a moment before, she had spoken of the dead father and mother. There was no self-pity, no offering him some token of the damage that had been done her for his further shock and dismay.

She smiled a little. "There. I didn't want to tell you that just yet, but it sneaked in."

He took her hand in his. "I'm glad it didn't embitter you."

"I love my brother," she offered simply. "I may be the only one. I'll always love him."

After a pause, he said: "My man's had no luck so far but we'll find him for you. My guy's the best skip-tracer in the business."

"Know why I love you?" Courtney said, her eyes down on their hands. "I can be me with you. I don't have to pretend. With everybody else in the world it's always lies. That's why I could tell you right off about me and Kenny. It wasn't just once, although he did rape me and for a long time I was terribly afraid of him. Grandma-ma knows and my mother knew but you're the only other one, and you're not revolted, I can feel that. My father was terribly disappointed in Kenny. He wanted a Born Leader, someone who would be a credit to the family. He got a boy who was bored with football, and color-blind. Father called him everything he could think of, fairy, sissy, nelly, nance, faggot, queer, pansy, Percy . . . Ken tried to prove himself by screwing the upstairs maids. My father hollered a lot at me because I sided with Kenny. He had no one but me. He said he loved only me in all the world. Still, Kenny took revenge on father by raping me. In time, well—he didn't have to. We were lovers." She looked down to find Burt's hand on hers. "If you never want to see me again, I'll under-stand."

"I love it when you're truthful and straightforward with me. I promise you I'll never let you down or give you cause to regret it."

"I feel strength and power in you."

"You're a strong lady, Courtney, never doubt it. You have to break from him."

"He's me, Kenny is, I'm him. We're twins, you know. He's fair, his skin burns in a minute. I'm dark. He's wild and impetuous. Crazy. I'm controlled, I always know what I'm doing. He gets into trouble. I've never even gotten a parking ticket. Yet we're one. Yin and yang. Opposites yet joined. Isn't that strange?"

"I don't like your brother, I have to tell you that."

"Sometimes I hate him. Loathe him. Detest him. He wrecks his life. He wants to wreck mine. But I love him too. It's deeper than love or hate, can you understand that?"

"No," he said.

"You want to get out of my life." She did not make a question of it.

"No."

"You can stay here as long as you like, until it's safe again for you. I shan't bother you."

He took her body into his arms again. "I know how it is when you exist beyond reason or good sense. I learned about that in the Mexican desert a hundred years ago. I don't care what once happened with your brother. But I'd want all of you now, I can't have him contesting for any part of you."

"Free me," she whispered against his cheek, "free me from him."

3

A few miles past the intersection of Topanga Canyon and the Pacific Coast Highway, where the road rises above the ocean floor past the Malibu Colony, the Holiday House sits on its own ridge. Never boomingly popular, knowing friends of the motel like it for its privacy as well as the splendid views it affords. In Suite 26, Hilary Wilson looked at her wristwatch again, walked impatiently to the window, parted the drapes to look again down the path she had carefully described and let them fall closed with a sigh.

It had been a bad day for the chief officer of the Thunder Mountain Improvement Company. A subcommittee of the congressional committee whose approval was essential for certain matters had met that morning in Fresno. That city had been carefully chosen. Hilary Wilson had spent a lot of time and effort in Washington convincing the committee's members and staff that the hearing was better held in Fresno than in Los Angeles. After all, she said, the area was closer to the smaller city in the San Joaquin Valley where its impact would be more immediate and its benefits to the economy better assessed. The subcommittee and the staff did not like the idea of Fresno. Press coverage there would be spotty at best. Los Angeles, about a hundred miles away, had two big newspapers, wire service bureaus, television stations. And there was nothing to do in Fresno anyway.

Hilary Wilson did not want Los Angeles. She did not want the big-city ecology- and environment-nuts with their talk of biological life chains and irreparable damage and endangered species. In the desert, a twenty-million-dollar dam was being held up because some miserable tadpoles no one but four biologists even knew existed ten years ago might be wiped off the face of the earth. The pesky, nagging kids and their long-haired professors

194

might put on their show in Los Angeles. She did not want that.

But leave it to them; they found out about the subcommittee hearing in Fresno, and they showed up. Hilary Wilson had anticipated no problems. The senator himself was from a southern state; there were those who said he would make a splendid president. Support among the leaders of the vast agribusiness in the valley could mean a great deal to an ambitious politician, Hilary Wilson had persuaded the honorable gentleman. She had even come up to his hotel suite in Washington at his invitation, watched without protest as he made his feeble pass, got himself drunk and satisfied.

In Fresno, the senator wore his best magisterial manner. He dominated the other two committee members and the staff. The parade of witnesses fawned before him as they told of what wealth the proposed development would bring not only to themselves but to all the residents of the great valley.

When the committee was about to close its hearing, voices of protest were raised from the room. The possible-candidate could not act as he would have liked, called them out of order, ordered marshals to clear the room, and adjourned *sine die*, claiming the press of other important official business.

The nuts and the longhairs, Hilary thought, were ridiculous, but the cameras clicked and whirred as if on signal; bored reporters began to write quickly again as the usual hysterical charges were made.

"A fine mess you've got me in," the senator muttered to her in the corridor, as he passed pressed by local reporters.

She got hold of his executive assistant and arranged the meeting at the Holiday House. "It's not that far out of his way," she assured him. "He'll appreciate the rest."

Maybe, she thought, *he's standing me up*. "I know the old goat," Ellis Griswold had said on the phone. "He'd sell his old grandmother for a vote or a campaign contribution." But he okayed her proposal.

Mrs. Wilson walked to the table where the whiskey, ice and water had been deployed. She turned down the radio a little and sat down for the tenth time in the hour. When the knock came she was as surprised as if she had not known she had been waiting for it. The senator walked in, his jowls and wrinkled forehead gray with dis-

195

approval. His executive assistant, Guren, knew what he had to do at once. His eyes fell on the Jack Daniel's and the ice and he marched to it.

"Helluva mess, helluva mess, girl," the senator said.

"Won't mean a thing, Senator," Mrs. Wilson said, standing aside for Guren to give the bourbon. They waited until he had taken enough to ease his nerves.

"They can make trouble. Don't want that. Look what they're doing to Johnson. Damn near got him a prisoner in the White House."

"That's the war, Senator," Hilary Wilson said. "This is an attempt to bring the beauty of unspoiled America—"

"I know, girl, spare me the pieties, please." The senator cut her off. He held up his glass for replenishment. "Tell me, Al," he said to the executive assistant, "what do you think? Maybe table this until the next session?"

Al Guren stared briefly at Hilary Wilson as he brought the new drink. "These are rich, spoiled, middle-class kids, Senator," he began, echoing a series of arguments he was enough obliged to Mrs. Wilson to offer now. "Whom does this riffraff represent, after all?"

"Would you be surprised if I told you we have reason to believe there is mob money behind them?" Hilary Wilson added.

"Oh, come on," the senator said wearily, "even the new junior senator from the state of New York has given up looking for mobsters under his bed. That won't buy ten votes, not in this day and age."

"We're working on it but we'll prove it," Mrs. Wilson insisted eagerly.

"Nice place," the old man said suddenly, getting to his feet. "When's our next appointment, Guren?"

"Tomorrow. Eleven. The federal building in L.A."

"Then?"

"You promised to be in Houston for that dinner."

The senator turned to Mrs. Wilson. "Got a place here for Al?"

"Yes." She found her Louis Vuitton. "And I've already set you up. Here's the key, Al." After she opened her bag, she turned as if quickly reminded. "Oh, I almost forgot. Some of us have got together and we've put together an expression of our regard." She held up an envelope. "It's for your campaign, Senator. With our best wishes."

"God love you, child," the senator said carelessly. He

did not even turn to see Al Guren take the envelope. "What you got in the way of vittles, girl?"

"No rubbery chicken and peas this time, Senator," she sang out. "I've got the kitchen alerted. Let me surprise you."

"I like it here," the senator said.

"One thing more." Mrs. Wilson spoke to the assistant but it was meant for her honored guest. "My president and I don't know how these things work, Al, but we'd like to do something more concrete than a cash campaign offering. He says for me to tell you Sobordco thinks this senator is the best friend California has, and we're ready to put a quarter of a million into bringing the convention to Miami where we know he's a powerhouse. All we need is to be told where, when and to whom to deliver our token of regard."

The senator's face was a mask. "Mrs. Wilson, your president's a smart man. We'd sure like to have the convention in Miami, wouldn't we, Al?"

"So the day hasn't been too bad at that, has it, Senator?" Hilary Wilson said, winking at Al Guren.

"See you guys later," Al Guren said.

"Not if I see you first," the senator said. It was always a good sign when the senator was in a humorous mood; Al Guren knew that, and so did Hilary Wilson.

"Come here, you pretty little thing," the senator said the moment they were alone.

She came closer and smiled easily when he put a hand to her breast. "My, my, what have we here?" He seemed pleased to find no opposition when he explored one and then the other. "Too bad I have to go to Houston."

"There's lots of time, my dear," Mrs. Wilson said.

"Yes, little lady, lots and lots of time for lots and lots of mischief." He withdrew his hand. "Fix me another bourbon and branch water."

She found him at the window looking out to the darkening Pacific. "You understand," he said, eyes still on the foam-specked surf far below them, "a politician can only do so much. He's got to have popular support."

"It's only a few loudmouths who oppose us, Senator," she offered. "The majority is for opening the mountain."

"It's the wheel that squeaks loudest that gets the most attention, girl. Popular support," he repeated.

"How?"

"You got to turn public opinion around. Hell, from

our point of view, what do we care about more wilderness? My pappy used to say wilderness ain't good for nothin' but to piss in unnoticed."

"How does one turn public opinion around, dear?" Mrs. Wilson persisted sweetly.

"Your opposition's got to do something that excites the wrath of decent folk everywhere. Saved my hide years ago when I stood for the legislature back home. Wrath on the other feller, that's the key. Nothin' like righteous indignation to get folks on your side. Come here and let me fondle them cute titties again, girl."

Her eyes glowed with a sudden awareness of something at once easy to accomplish and certain to give her what still lay just a fingertip away. "Yes, lover," she said, "but first *I'd* like a touch of something with branch over it."

4

FLORA Levering swept into the family dining room like a monarch delayed by affairs of state. She was almost as tall as her granddaughter, but age and riding injuries had bent her over somewhat. She wore a flounced silk-brocade skirt to her ankles and a heavy woolen sweater suitable for skiing; her bones were cold and she would damned well wear what she liked. Her handclasp was strong. Three weeks and two days Burt Hammond had been a guest at Wildoaks and he had not seen her before.

"I've heard much about you, Mr. Drummond," she said, before Courtney could offer an introduction.

"And I've heard much about you, ma'am."

"I know your Jerry Haggerty," the old lady went on. "Charming man. A scoundrel, of course. My son had several run-ins with him. Used to say Haggerty pushed the family out of the shipping business, but by then it wasn't anything we really wanted to be in."

"Someone wasn't being smart, ma'am," he offered.

"Shipping's bigger than ever now the world needs all that crude oil. It shouldn't be left to the Greeks."

She stared briefly at him. "Where's my sherry?" she demanded. "What does one have to do to get a drink around here?"

Burt took a glass from Courtney and put it before the old lady. "How do you like this place, Mr. Drummond?"

"I'm the wrong person to ask. Half of me always wants to run away from wherever I find myself."

"Stay here on our account. It feels better somehow with a male on the premises."

"Fact is, I'm considering moving my practice to Los Angeles." He had not told this to Courtney and he saw her head swivel toward him.

"Leaving that old rascal Haggerty?" Flora Levering lifted herself and went to replenish at the bottle of Bristol Cream. She returned to find Burt Hammond and her granddaughter staring at each other. "Haggerty's a blatant opportunist, I could have told you that. Once he wanted respectability. When he achieved it, he found it ashes in his mouth. So he's back to his old ways. Did he dismiss you or did you leave him? Or is he spreading his tentacles to our cousins in southern California?"

His eyes remained fixed on Courtney. "I think Hollywood can be a ball. A piece of cake. A lot of fun."

"Myself I don't much fancy cake, Mr. Thurmond." She drained the glass. "See if you can change the man's mind, Courtney." She got to her feet and started for the door. "I like what you said about the Greeks and shipping."

"Stay for dinner, grandma-ma," Courtney urged.

"Graham crackers and milk, that's all I'm to have. Depressing to eat and more so to watch. Good night, Mr. Gammon." She held out her hand to him.

"It's Hammond, Flora." He shook the hand, a strong, knowing hand, he found.

"Ah, yes." She glanced at Courtney and swept majestically from the room.

"She knew your name, of course," Courtney said.

"She doesn't trust me."

"Don't be foolish. She adores you."

"Does she know we're sleeping together?"

"In some ways she's very Victorian."

"I think she's never fooled."

"Funny," Courtney Kendall said thoughtfully. "Maybe I do underestimate her."

One evening Courtney said: "Who's Judge Crater?"

"Why do you ask?"

"Herb Caen says you disappeared just like him."

"Judge Crater walked out of his chambers one day and was never heard from again. About forty years ago."

She came over and sat on his lap. "That's that old man grandma-ma's got hidden in that house behind the old tropical garden. See how safe it is here?"

It was chilly outside but a full moon lit the big pool and the autumn trees behind it. "Did you mean what you told Flora about practicing down in Los Angeles?"

"Yes."

"I'd never go there, you know. Of course you haven't asked me, but I thought I ought to tell you just the same."

"You're a San Francisco snob, you know?"

"I'm snobby about the peninsula too, or haven't you noticed? I never want to leave Wildoaks."

"I understand." He took her hand and kissed it.

On the way back to the house she paused on a terrace. "Kenny," she began.

"What about him?"

"He's forged my signature and withdrawn rather a lot of money from a joint account intended for charitable purposes."

"And you're not going to do anything about it?"

"What can I do?"

"How are you asking me? As a friend, a lover, or a lawyer?"

"As a resident of Wildoaks."

"I understand your position," Burt Hammond said.

"I don't think you can."

"I try. You still come out looking foolish, you know. He steals and it makes no difference."

"It's only money."

"Correction. He's also stealing you from me."

She regarded him darkly, but offered no reply before she walked away.

He was jogging on the bridle path when a two-horse ladies phaeton, shining splendidly black, pulled up beside him. Flora Levering, in frayed and stained jodhpurs, put her head outside the rig. "Come on, I'll give you a lift." They said nothing all the way back to the stables. She was not through with him there. She took his arm as if she needed his help and brought him out of the groom's hearing to a hedgerow behind the carriage house.

"My granddaughter's much taken with you," she began.

"I'm much taken with your granddaughter, ma'am."

"It's her money, of course."

"Of course."

"You admit it?"

"How can I deny it? It's part of her, isn't it?" He watched her lips move nervously, as if she was saying words but could not make them heard. "She isn't the first girl I've gone to bed with."

"You have the temerity to admit you've taken the child to bed with you in my own house?"

"You knew that before this morning, Mrs. Levering."

"I know everything," she grumbled. "At least you're candid with me. Do you plan to marry her when she asks you?"

"Asks me? Where I come from—"

"It's a prerogative of royalty of money."

"Nothing regal to me about money, ma'am. I've never lacked for all I could use."

"I've known some very rich men in my time. I never heard one of them say he had enough."

"To me money's a tool, ma'am, nothing more—a commodity, a means. I treat it with great respect, but it's never an end in itself."

She looked at him quickly, as if for the first time. "Ah, so you've uncovered the great secret. Where's that leave my granddaughter?"

"I'm not sure. My practice is in disarray. My life's in danger. I don't want to involve her. I'll never be able to cut off wholly from Jerry Haggerty. I'm not even sure I want to or that I could even if I wanted to. Courtney's told me she'd never go to Los Angeles. She thinks a whole life is possible here at Wildoaks."

"And at our offices in Montgomery Street. The aged gentlemen who have been managing our affairs . . ."

"Are trust-bound and arthritic. Nobodies with a corner lot and some daring have made themselves millionaires while your old gentlemen make sure everything's absolutely safe. They wouldn't like me or my style. We'd be at each other's throats, and they'd win in the end. So you see I've even thought of that. Anyway, it would bore the pants off me. Down in L.A., I'm going to play around with otherwise taxable money. They wheel and deal down there but their eyes are necessarily on the films they make, so they can use a fellow like me. I'm bound to do very well. Life here or on Montgomery Street seems pretty dreary by comparison."

"If push came to shove, do you think Courtney would finally go away with you?" the old lady asked mildly.

"You know her better than I. You tell me."

"I think not."

"She must know the world of Wildoaks is dying."

"Of course. She stays for a deeper reason."

"Her brother is a deeper reason?" he said bitterly.

"How much has she told you?"

"Everything."

"Then you know. Why do *you* stay at Wildoaks?"

"To save my life."

"Maybe she does for the same reason."

"But here's where he knows he can find her. She sits here while he forges her name and steals her money. This is her prison. How does it protect her from him?"

"I'm afraid it's not that simple. You must understand this is their private world. They know every hill, every knoll, the caves, the running streams and the dry ones. They know the big house, all the houses on Wildoaks, they know where to hide, where to protect themselves, where to run to. They share all this as they share their common blood. She'd never leave it."

After a long pause, Burt Hammond said: "What would you do if you thought it could be love?"

The old lady's head turned toward him. She kicked her boot against a low retaining wall to free it of a clod. "Don't know. Never had any experience of love." Without another word she strode toward the carriage house as if she had just thought of something that had to be done at once.

5

BODY OF HOODLUM FOUND IN CAR

BURT Hammond saw the story somewhere in the back pages. Scofield, the dead man's name was. Burt Hammond recalled it well. Jerry had brought him in. Who had him shot, gangster-style? Back of the head. Stuffed in the trunk of a stolen car. The hired killer's ritual death package. In a few days the detectives assigned to the case would have no alternative but to wait for developments elsewhere, because the professionals knew how to kill one of their own without signature. Who could have hired these? Jerry's people? Prison people? Neither?

When he reached Elmer Wright at the safe number, the two men were talking from telephone booths. They could allow themselves certain liberties; names, for instance . . .

"Scofield," Burt Hammond said.

"I thought of that too. Very possible."

"If the contract was called off—"

"The hired guy wouldn't like it. Even if they decided to pay him off in full, he'd know he had something that could make someone feel very uncomfortable."

"And Jerry?"

"It was the people around him, sir. People think the guy on the throne makes all the decisions, but he's manipulated too. Haggerty wants you back. Been calling me every few days, Do I see you? Will I get word to you he's scared again?"

"What is it this time?"

"His old nemesis since the McClellan Committee. Robert Kennedy's campaigning for his party's nomination. Everybody needs to win big in California. All the contenders have to show the voters and the money people here how good they are. So Kennedy's subcommittee's subpoenaed the old man. It'll get a lot of time on TV and headlines on page one. Jerry says for me to tell you whatever you feel, you owe him this. The way I see it, he'll be yours for good if you come through now. You'll have everything you need to operate big down there in Hollywood."

"I've got that anyway, haven't I?"

"This way you've got it for sure. The people around him will know it's hands-off, now and forever."

"What's the word from the kids on the mountain?" Burt finessed.

"The usual harassment and petty obstructionism by the local policing agencies. They tried to toss them off on some trumped-up charges. Naturally the kids won. They're hanging in."

"And Helen Mendoza?"

"She's found a house the Shah's mother squandered a fortune on and decided was too pretentious after all. I've made it as secure as possible, which is not very. What do I tell the old man, sir?"

"What about the cat?"

"Black. Beautiful. Spoiled."

He grinned. "The garage at Union Square. I'm leaving right away."

He did not find Courtney in her apartment. No one knew where she could be. He rang Flora Levering on the house phone but she was not around either. They also did not know where she could be. He left a note:

Angel. Had to go. Be back for you soon as possible.
B.

He didn't say *love*. He wondered why. . . .

Jerry said: "You're like that little son of a bitch Bobby. Hot inside, cool as ice outside. You can handle him. You get me out of this without my spilling too much blood and I'm yours. You go south, you can tell those movie people you've got Jerry Haggerty in your back pocket."

"They're still gunning for you elsewhere, Jerry. Jury tampering down there, for example. What about that?"

"Their firearms always have got the safety off for Jerry Haggerty. I'm still here, ain't I? Now it's this little shitheel again. Outsmart him and you can write your own ticket."

204

"I don't have to, Jerry. You wrote it for me a minute ago." Jerry Haggerty came over and embraced him and Burt Hammond returned the bear hug. Both men were proud of victory.

6

FOR years one man—or his agents, his surrogates, his deputies and his assistants, his district prosecutors, his marshals, his Crime Task Force officers, his department's awesome police—had beset, harassed and fought him.

Robert Kennedy came into the committee room flanked by another subcommittee member and two aides, ten or fifteen feet from the table behind which Burt Hammond sat with his client, Jerry Haggerty. Their eyes never met. Burt Hammond kept studying the investigating senator. He was fascinated by the size of the man, even smaller than he had imagined; the nervous hands; the intensity with which he did everything; the shyness betrayed by quick, fretful movements; the glazed-over eyes which refused to return Burt Hammond's searching gaze.

Burt Hammond came into the hearing knowing his adversary well. The former chief of the Department of Justice, the boss of the FBI, the declared adversary of his client for almost two decades, the ambitious politician now become a senator from the great Empire State of New York and on the move to greater glory—he was an adversary to respect.

"How do I handle him?" Jerry Haggerty had asked during a briefing.

"Politely. Don't fence with him. Don't let him provoke you."

"That'll only make the little runt go after me harder."

"And be truthful. Always remember whatever was done with pension-fund money was entirely within existing rules and regulations. They may want to change those laws, but we're safe."

"So I don't even have to apologize?"

"If there's any doubt, don't answer. Turn to me."

"A strong and dangerous man," Burt Hammond had read in his preparations for the confrontation. "Torquemada," someone else called him. Jerry Haggerty had shown him a file of comments from powerful labor leaders across the country; with one or two exceptions he was disliked by all. "A phony," one called him. "A jitterbug," said the mighty George Meany, head of the AFL-CIO, the largest labor organization in the nation.

All through the questioning, Kennedy's eyes seemed unfocused. Was money lent to the Sierra Nevada? Didn't Jerry know who was behind the Sierra Nevada? Couldn't he tell mobsters from what Jerry had called "regular, good American citizens"? Why didn't Jerry come straight out and announce he had been mistaken? Or admit to his connection with mob elements looking for ways to launder their money?

Jerry, thanks to the lawyer beside him, remained composed. The Fund, he said, was a great responsibility. He was proud of what he had been able to accomplish for his people with it. As for the Sierra Nevada, why, that was an excellent deal for Golden West. A high return with a minimum risk. Las Vegas didn't scare him. Why should it? It didn't scare the hundreds of thousands of good Americans who visited it every year, did it? He did not know about mob people in Las Vegas. People bragged about "inside" stuff they knew nothing about, just to show they themselves were big men. These crooks, petty or otherwise, who squealed to the cops, *they* were liars.

The senator broke in and mentioned names which had come to him from a source he chose not to reveal. Did Mr. Haggerty know any of these? Mr. Edward Gorman? Jerry shook his head and turned to his counsel who put his hand over the microphone before them to guard the privacy of their consultation. "I heard the name, I never met the guy, far as I can remember," Jerry said. "The others he's gonna fire at me, some I'll know, some I may've heard of, what do I do?"

"Answer yes or no, but don't pick up on any of them," Burt Hammond said.

"I don't see why you have to consult with your lawyer over so simple a matter," the junior senator from New

York baited him. "Do you know these people or don't you?"

Burt Hammond put his hand over the mike again. "Don't be provoked." He noted that Kennedy still did not choose to have his gaze come to rest on him. "He wants you to get sore. Don't let him."

Jerry Haggerty smiled imperceptibly. He wiped his mouth with the back of his hand. "Sure, I know them. I know a lot of people, if you mean have I been introduced. Just as you have, Senator."

"You know what I'm talking about, Mr. Haggerty."

"The problem is I don't, that is a fact. You're trying to put some implication—"

"Don't tell me what I'm trying to do," Kennedy broke in.

Burt Hammond felt an urge to move forward toward his client, but held back. Jerry was doing all a lawyer could want, making his interrogator nervous and querulous; the manner of the questioning had become more important than its content.

"I wouldn't even attempt that, Senator," Jerry Haggerty said mildly.

Burt Hammond sank lower in his chair. "Relax, Jerry," he whispered.

Jerry Haggerty did as his lawyer advised. Yes, no, I may have. I'm not sure. Yes, yes. Yes. Burt Hammond had never known him to follow his advice so well. When the reading of the list was done with, Burt whispered in his client's ear and Jerry learned forward. "I want the record to show I have also met and sometimes had business to conduct with Franklin Roosevelt, Harry Truman, Dwight Eisenhower, Senator, as well as your father and your grandfather, with whom I spent a pleasant afternoon at a racetrack called Agawam, if memory serves. I also knew General MacArthur and Daniel Beard, the founder of the Boy Scouts of America, and someone once brought over to my table—"

"I get your drift," the senator broke in. "We're concerned here with your associations here and now. Why is it that today you deal almost exclusively with elements who exist beyond the law?"

Burt Hammond put his hand over the mike. "Don't answer that. Stall for time, Jerry. I think he's getting under your skin. Look at me and say something to me, anything, just to make it appear we're conferring. That's good," Burt went on. "When you get back to him, say you've forgotten what the question was, got that?"

Jerry did, and the laughter that ensued lost the moment for Senator Kennedy.

He turned to an aide beside him and engaged in a long conversation, both heads so close they overlapped to Burt Hammond's unwavering gaze. He watched Kennedy nod vigorously and turn to the table top, scribbling on a legal pad before him for some time as if alone in a room somewhere. At length the senator looked up, fixed his eyes on Haggerty and began to speak in what Burt regarded almost as a mumble.

"Among other investments the Golden West Trust and Pension Fund was interested in, I understand, Mr. Haggerty," he began, "was a proposal to help finance a corporate raid on Inter-Continent Airlines. Can you tell us about that?"

Not very adroit, Burt Hammond thought. Where was the crafty, cobralike attacker of his briefing papers? He put his hand over the microphone and conferred briefly with his client. "Answer very briefly and only what you know."

"What d'you want to know about it, Senator?" Jerry Haggerty responded.

"I'm asking you a simple question," his interrogator said irritably. "Why don't you tell me what you know?"

Burt Hammond put a quieting hand on his client's knee.

"Maybe I don't understand just what it is you're trying to find out, Senator," Haggerty replied. Burt Hammond patted the knee.

"Isn't it true Golden West was acting as a cover for mob elements seeking to take over an international carrier for their own purposes?"

"That's your interpretation," Jerry said.

"What's yours, Mr. Haggerty?" Kennedy pursued.

"A badly mismanaged company was up for grabs and some freewheeling guys who know how to make a buck figured they could take it over. I don't know who all the guys were. I knew a few who came to me, and I brought it up to the Loan Committee."

"Where it was approved."

Burt Hammond put his hand over the mike. He spoke to Jerry for some time, making sure Jerry Haggerty understood what he said. "The committees looking into the matter met in executive session, Senator. The plain fact is we finally withdrew from the proposition."

"But you considered it?"

"We consider a lot of things we don't get into. Don't you?" Jerry looked over to his lawyer. He saw a tiny nod of approval.

"Were you advised to back out of the deal, Mr. Haggerty?"

"I'm always advised, one way or the other, Senator."

Burt Hammond watched the senator turn to his aide. After a moment, he turned to face him and Jerry. For the first time the Kennedy eyes fixed themselves on him, studying him as if to fix him in consciousness forever. "Unfortunately, there isn't time here and now to pursue this matter," he said, eyes still steady on Burt Hammond.

"Ask if you're excused," Burt said to his client.

"This meeting's adjourned," the senator said, rising swiftly and walking from the room.

7

"BITCH! Who you think you're fooling with, one of your striptease-joint characters? I was born yesterday? Walk around with my cock in my hand? I don't know what's going on?"

"Nothing's going on, sweetheart." Roseanna came up to her husband and did her best to gentle him.

"Don't give me that!" He broke violently from her. "Every day! You leave this house, no one knows where to! What is it this time? A guy? A butch? Who you screwing now?"

What the poor guy always came to, Roseanna thought. "Larry, Larry." They were in the garden of the big house her husband had rented in back of the Beverly Hills Hotel. "It's nothing like that, baby."

"Brenda tells me you chased her out."

Nothing in her own life belonged to her, not even the right not to have certain people of Larry's choosing around her. It had been pathetically easy with Brenda. She'd given the would-be actress a diamond brooch and a call to an agent, promised not to forget a fat favor in return if the agent took on Brenda Moore as a client and got her work. It turned out a series pilot called *The Young Nurses* needed someone who could do Cockney. Larry had seen her hand in that, of course.

He was husband, manager, keeper. Nothing escaped him. He suspected an affair; he was wrong in that, but not in knowing that something new had come into her life.

It had begun a couple of months earlier. Larry was out for the afternoon. The doorbell awakened her from a drugged sleep. The housekeeper and her butler-husband were off somewhere. Roseanna arose unsteadily from the couch she had fallen on, walked to the front of the house and pulled back a curtain. She recognized the face and figure at once. In panic, she dropped the curtain and hugged the wall.

Everybody knew Janet Morgan. Her scandals matched her successes around the world. She had come to films from the theater and established herself as big box office from the start. After a successful film debut, she broke new ground by turning down the starring role in a much-vaunted big-studio epic to take a part in a de Sica film. The big picture was a flop; the Italian one, a worldwide hit. She found time to have affairs with half a dozen notable gentlemen and ended up, having settled in England, giving birth out of wedlock to a boy whose famous father was much married elsewhere. She returned to America, made two financially successful pictures and announced Hollywood was too boring a place to work in, so she was leaving again. She married the brilliant if slightly batty English director, Derek Frye, only to leave him to carry on a well-publicized extramarital union with a leading French film star. Then, like a puppy shedding its silken baby coat, she announced she was no longer interested in frivolous ventures and took a role in a small, independent film dealing with a political murder, a picture financed only because she would appear in it. It went on to become one of the largest of the year. With her share of the profits, Janet Morgan proved she was as prodigious an entrepreneur as she was a performer.

She could not get another job. A year had passed. There were no offers. One or two proposals had come her way and were quickly withdrawn. The reason was simple. With her left-wing French lover, Janet Morgan had visited Hanoi and issued statements from Vietcong Headquarters calling for an end to American intervention in Vietnam. She lent her name to Bertrand Russell's so-called trial of so-called war criminals in Stockholm. She used her fame to win invitations to college protest meetings where she expressed her views and her observations about what she had seen and heard. She called for an end to a war no one wanted and everyone hated. For this, no film distributor would handle anything linked to her name.

At the time of Janet Morgan's call, Roseanna peered through the window in a haze of downers and booze. Her first impulse was to hide, not to open the door. But she was certain Janet Morgan had seen her inside and she could not refuse to see such a caller. Roseanna found the door and opened it a little.

"I'm Janet Morgan," her visitor began, and could see at once she had come at a bad time. Roseanna's eyes were puffy, her speech thick and she leaned against the door for support.

"Are you really Janet Morgan? *The* Janet Morgan?"

"Yes, and you're *the* Roseanna Lee. I never gush but I have to tell you I think you're dynamite. Can we sit down? You sure it's all right for us to talk now? I'll come back later if you like."

"Please come in."

Somewhere in the haze she heard Janet Morgan say: "I'd like you to be in a picture I want to do. Co-starring. Name above title with mine."

"Think you came to the wrong place." Roseanna looked around for a wall to support herself.

"I don't think I have, Rosey," she heard Janet Morgan say firmly.

"Not like this all the time, unnerstan'? Can always get up for a gig." She was lucky to find a chair to fall into.

She looked up to see her visitor take both her hands in her own. "Listen, baby. I've been there too. If I can't help, I sure as hell can find someone else. Can I be your friend?"

"Even after you see me like this?"

"More than ever." Janet Morgan fell to her knees and pulled the hands toward her, relieved to see no telltale tracks. "What kind of shit are you into, Rosey?"

"Uppers and downers and vodka-rocks. Just enough to make the days pass, and to work my gigs."

"You'll be great in this film, Rosey," Janet Morgan said eagerly. "It's about two women. They behave the way ladies're supposed to. Mine, me, don't be nice to her, the bitch'll cut your throat. But life pushes them together. They become real, giving friends—and people. I'm going to be one of them, I want you to be the other."

Later, Janet Morgan said: "The people around you will try to talk you out of it."

Roseanna's hair was still wet from the ice water she had splashed on her face. A damp towel had left a stain on the cotton frock she'd gotten into. "Figures," she said.

"I had someone sound out your husband. He doesn't like me. Why should he be different?"

"I like you. You got guts."

"I like you, Rosey. You got guts too."

"Me? Look at me." She threw the towel to the floor.

"You had no friends. You've got a friend now."

"Gonna be tough," Roseanna said.

"Everything's tough. Even when it all works out, it's still tough. I want you to cold-turkey quit all the dope-shit. Can you handle that?"

"I don't know."

"You've got to make up your mind."

"I'm not strong like you."

"Hell you aren't. You made it to here, didn't you? No one gave you anything. Everybody used you. Yet here you are."

"I've tried to unhook before. They know me as a no-can-do in sanatoriums all the way back to Connecticut."

"Ever tried it with a sister?"

"Got no sister."

"Sure you have. Me. It doesn't take a genius to see you've always stood alone. Now you're going to find some real support."

After a moment, Roseanna drew a deep breath. "I'll try."

"Try's not good enough, Rosey. You've got to make it. It's not going to be easy, but then it's not easy for me putting this damned picture together, so what the hell. Can I count on you?"

Roseanna got to her feet. She did not waver and she

saw the room clearly for the first time since they had taken the house. "Well, here we go again."

Janet Morgan came up beside her. "Tell me what to do to help."

"Can't no one help Rosey 'cept Rosey, sister. You sure you want me for your picture? Never made one, you know."

But Janet Morgan had thought of that herself long before she had made this visit. "I hope that's our only problem."

Roseanna grinned. "I hope so too. They're pretty cute around here. What happens when they catch on I'm trying to get myself together? When I found my head and ain't going to unscrew it again for a while?"

"You'll handle that when it comes, Rosey."

And come it did. Here Larry stood over her, accusing her of sexual infidelity, as if she were incapable of any other faithlessness. In the time she and Janet Morgan began to walk and talk together, Roseanna Lee learned it was not going to be easy winning back her life and career. She would need, if not Larry's approval, his tacit understanding. Janet Morgan was having trouble getting her project moving; they required all the help they could muster.

"Trust me, Larry, baby," Roseanna circled her arms around him. "I'm not fuckin' around on you. I swear."

He at least *wanted* to believe her. She was grateful for that.

8

RAIN slashed at the brick walls and leaded windows, noisy on the ledges and terraces, as he waited for someone inside to respond. There was apparently no one around to answer the door. He pushed the signal again, hammered on the carved door, but still no one came. Water caromed off the slate roof like a waterfall, gushed from all the gutters and flooded around the house in large, dark pools. He found a French door off the big, formal dining room he could push open.

In the kitchen, the old lady they called the cook was already busy preparing to ruin the evening roast. She did not know where anybody was. He climbed the stairs to Courtney's apartment and found nothing there. He tried to reach Flora Levering on the house phone, but there was no answer.

He looked moodily out the window and decided it was storming too hard to go anywhere else. He was not even sure why he had come back. He felt drawn to Courtney Kendall by forces he did not understand. Maybe that was what pulled him to her. He was not even sure that she would be willing to link her life to his, on his terms.

When the rain let up, he would say the hell with it and start the long drive south.

The unceasing rain blurred time as it blurred the landscape. In the downpour, the big house seemed a prison, cold, stone, and hard, echoing floors. *This* was his competition. He went to the windows again to see how it was doing.

He had the feeling for some time that someone was watching him; when Flora Levering emerged from a dark room, he showed no surprise.

"They tell me our road's flooded near the highway since you came up," she said.

He walked away from her moodily and kept going until he found a small room with a fire and a bar bathed in warm light. He made his own drink and was pouring a sherry when Flora joined him. He pushed her glass to her across the bar.

"When'd she leave?"

"Just before sunrise."

"With Kenny?"

"With Kenny."

"Left no message for me?" Flora took the glass at last; he saw her head shake sadly. "Bad upbringing, grandma."

"Not sure she could have even if she'd wanted to."

"Was she in chains when she left?"

"Other forms of compulsion, Burt."

"Save it. She's not here. That's what counts."

"She loves you."

"She'll get over it." He put down his glass. "What the hell, so will I."

"Do you know what happens now?" Flora Levering said.

"Yes, indeed. I get in my car and get the hell out of here."

"And Courtney, what about her?"

"Seems to me she's got some problems."

"You have none?"

"None any more where she's concerned."

"I thought you loved her."

"I thought so too. I wanted to, anyway. But I've got to live now, meaning today, not yesterday."

"You're a hard man."

"I know what I want out of life and I work at it. Anything that keeps staying in the way has to be cut off like a dying branch."

"Kenny *forced* her. There don't have to be chains."

"I thought I found a strong lady. So I was wrong."

"He's evil. It isn't easy getting rid of such a person. I'm only his grandmother, but I know."

"Well, I won't let evil destroy my life too." He finished what was left in his glass. "Thanks for everything."

She followed him to the door. "What do I tell her when she comes back?"

"That once upon a time I loved a princess."

"I like you, Burt Hammond," Flora Levering called after him.

"And I'm crazy about you, Flora," he called back.

She watched the car speed across the flooded grounds.

BOOK SIX:

Pueblo of Our Lady

(1968)

1

Holmby Hills, the section is called, just west of Beverly Hills; more sedate, more exclusive, less well known. The big house had the fortress security he needed; it faced a corner so that the inevitable privacy invaders would have to cover two sides of the house at once. No sidewalks; surveillance would have to be conducted from parked cars, which could be identified. The house itself was perfect for his present needs, spectacularly vulgar. The previous occupant had done it in white and gold, carpeting deep enough to bury the ankles; marble, brass and crystal, and all the usual art posters. The garden was huge, wrapped around a swimming pool and a pool house. Helen Mendoza had chosen precisely what Burt Hammond had in mind.

He had a table held for him every day at the back of Le Printemps, the newest and most snob-approved restaurant in Beverly Hills, where fashions in eating places are as changeable as lapel widths and skirt lengths. He always had lunch alone; no wine, a bottle of Evian; quite often interrupted by the phone which Marco, the headwaiter, brought to him—Helen, of course, by prearrangement, in the first days when he knew nobody. The regulars called Marco over to find out who that man was. "He has asked me not to say his name," he said, as instructed. When pressed, Marco was permitted to say, "I understand he's Jerry Haggerty's lawyer here to look into some motion-picture deals." Instant, breathless recognition.

His first luncheon guest was Don Faversham, the best press agent in town, who chose his clients with care. His accent was New York aristocrat, his manner careless, self-assured. He did not think he was Burt Hammond's man.

"I took the liberty of looking you up in the morgue down at the *Times* after your secretary called. Hell, one story says outright that you're the secret connection between the mob and legitimate business."

Burt Hammond smiled without vexation. "What else did you learn?"

"That trial down here. Some people think there was jury tampering."

"What else?"

"You're Jerry Haggerty's hatchet man, the smooth-talking but tough fixer-upper. I'd say that's plenty."

"I'm a lawyer, Mr. Faversham, and take my responsibilities damned seriously. Officer of the court, sworn to uphold—the whole ethics business. I'll give you some background, but you're never to use it. My father wanted me to go into the law because he had this crazy idea that the law should be upheld—one in particular, the Reclamation Act of 1902, passed by the House and the Senate and signed by President Theodore Roosevelt. It's still on the books, Mr. Faversham. Ignored, openly subverted, flouted to make millions for the lawbreakers. Every administration since has ignored the law's stated intent. That includes Woodrow Wilson, Franklin Roosevelt, Harry Truman, General Eisenhower and John Kennedy. In the name of upholding law and preserving the American way, I myself have been beaten, assaulted with intent to kill. No one has ever been brought to trial for any felonies against me. But my phones are tapped. They will be tapped here. My bank accounts and tax returns are studied by crews of experts.

"The pension fund? They say it's crooked. Well, it could be better managed but so, I'll bet, could the Bank of America. I've never been charged with anything. My association with Jerry Haggerty is no one's business but his and mine, which is part of the ethics of the lawyer and client. It's all the other side's game but I've learned to be good at it. Although I have a few scores I'd like to settle, I don't break the law just to get even. I deal in big numbers and big clout so I can enjoy it."

"All this, here in our little old Tinseltown?" Faversham uttered with astonishment.

"Where better? From where I sit these people have everything: talent, looks, drive, charm, public acclaim. What they don't have is access to money that doesn't tell them what to do with their talent. That's where I come in. I propose to make funding available to the right people and the right films. I propose to show them how to shelter their money, how to save their taxable bucks and get to keep some of the dollars they bring in. I'll do all this with no fuss and paper, man to man, or man to woman; I much admire women, I find them less self-deceptive than men."

"You won't need a press agent, Mr. Hammond, you'll need a man with a baseball bat."

"Buy a baseball bat, Don."

He put forward his game plan and watched a smile slowly wreath the Faversham face. About one hundred big sharks in all of Hollywood mattered. Half of them were on the prowl in behalf of film projects they were having trouble financing for various reasons; the other half were never content with a conventional return on their risk capital. He had no wish to see his name in the papers. Faversham's job, he said, was to make him as obscure as possible while reaching out for the sharks.

Burt Hammond would have no office. An unlisted phone number at home was to be given out to no one. Here, at this table, he would conduct what business he had; here he would have his meetings. He was not interested in gossip, socializing, or Hollywood inside-stuff. In backing an enterprise the past did not interest him, except where it had become a dead weight on a talent. He had already learned that in the film business the creative side was paid not for current effort but for what had been done the time before. Everybody spoke of track record; two failures and you had better watch out. Three, the man was as good as dead. This was the opening wedge Burt Hammond was looking for. To real talent, he said, failure is the spur. He would look for a director and a star in trouble, driven to proving themselves again. He did not care about anything but the validity of the whole enterprise here and now.

"A party. In fact, a whole lot of parties," Faversham thought out loud. "Small. Exclusive. The kind they kill themselves for if they don't get asked."

"Hate 'em," Burt said.

"You won't make an appearance. I'll have all the people who never go to parties."

Faversham was as good as his word. Sunday afternoon, after a week of whispers about the flood of money available from sources that did not want to be identified, the usual crush of freeloaders and stargazers was not there. Don Faversham had seen to that. Some guests even wore neckties. Their talk was subdued and businesslike, most of them clearly proud at having been asked. No party champagne; Taittinger. No catered food; the buffet was flown in from Ernie's in San Francisco. Whispers over nervous laughter: "Mafia . . . pension fund . . . Jerry Haggerty . . ."

Scripts and proposals began to arrive. Burt Hammond had chosen well in retaining Don Faversham. The press agent's phone did not stop ringing . . . "You tell him for me, Don, anything he goes into I'll go into too, for all the money he wants . . ." They called from Houston and New York and West Berlin. It was important, Burt Hammond felt, to make a splash quickly. Money people had come to Hollywood before and had left without so much as a deal. He found a script and a package he liked. Don pointed out the producer had had three successive failures. Burt Hammond was as good as his word. "The flops didn't erase his talent." He liked this deal and he told the guy to go ahead and start to make his picture, the money was there. The guy had tears in his eyes and seized his hands to kiss them. "None of that," Burt Hammond said, and meant it.

2

THE explosion of the high transformer tower on the Bartlett road at the foot of the access road to Thunder Mountain flashed in the night sky briefly. Miles away, coyotes and dogs started to howl and bark. When farmers and fieldworkers in their houses and shacks got out of bed, they found all the lights out.

The California Highway Patrol was the first on the scene. By daylight the field around the downed tower was churned to mud by vehicles from the Pacific Gas and Electric Company, the sheriff's substation, two county supervisors, a sabotage expert on loan from the Los Angeles Police Department and an agent of the Federal Bureau of Investigation. Although finding tire tracks was now out of the question, a detail was set up to make a careful search of the area for clues.

Shortly after daylight, a young man with a black beard down to his chest came to Sue-Ann Martin's van near the creek four thousand feet up and twelve miles into the Thunder Mountain area. "They've blown up a main transformer down near the main road," he told her. Since none of the young people who camped out in what they called the Punch Bowl had electricity, the first anyone knew about it was when the battery-powered radios were turned on. "They're calling it sabotage. That means us."

"What you going to do?" Sue-Ann said.

"Get in my pickup and haul ass out. I'd suggest you do that too. I'll bet the *Polizei* are on the way here right now."

"I'd ditch the van," Sue-Ann Martin said coolly. "They'll be waiting to nail us."

It took her less than two minutes to throw her things into a backpack and start down a long deer trail that some of them had discovered a month before.

She had to hitch three rides to reach Los Angeles. At a market at the corner of Coldwater Canyon and Ventura Boulevard, she bought the *Times* for later news about the explosion.

The story said that police authorities had received a message they found under the windshield wiper of one of their vehicles. "This is just a beginning," the note read. "Get off our mountain, Amerika, it belongs to us." It was signed, "Friends of the Mountain."

"Even I don't have his phone number," Elmer Wright told Sue-Ann when she reached him.

"He's supposed to be such a big man and he doesn't even have a Dixie cup and a long string? What are you trying to give me, Elmer? I'm in big trouble. I've got to talk to the man. How do *you* get to talk to him?"

"I call and I leave a message and he calls me from a pay station. We have an arrangement."

"All right, call him and leave the message, and when he calls give him this number."

"I can't. It's Sunday. He doesn't go to where I can reach him on Sunday. Can you tell me what it's about?"

"Sure. Only why don't you go to a pay phone and call me from there too?"

The phone rang outside the market in minutes.

"Someone blew up a transformer tower outside the

222

mountain. They left a note incriminating the Friends," Sue-Ann told Elmer Wright. "It could eventually reach our man and hurt him bad, Elmer. I've got to see him."

"I'll give you the home address. Don't be surprised if you can't get in."

From one end of Mapleton Drive to the other, they lined the street, chrome to chrome, Mercedes, Rolls, Lincoln, Cadillac, Bentley, sleek Porsche and Jaguar. Boys in trim red vests were parking cars for the party at the big house on the corner. Sue-Ann surveyed the terrain, assessed the situation, picked up her backpack and scurried for cover on hands and knees behind a tall hedge. When she emerged again she was in something long, bare and suitable that she'd found in a thrift shop in Bolinas. She took off the hiking shoes she had been wearing, dug into the backpack until she found the gold sandals she'd had made for herself on Telegraph Avenue and a tiara of brass and semi-precious stones a sculptor-lover had once created for her. The thin Kashmiri shawl she often used as a blanket completed her ensemble. She left the backpack under a tree, went to the middle of the street and hailed a Silver Cloud descending on her. "Hi, we seem to need the Auto Club. You guys going to Burt's too, I take it?"

At the door a pair of burly men in suits they were growing out of checked names against a list. She stood chatting with excessive charm with one of the ladies from the Silver Cloud until they turned to go past the foyer. . . .

She surveyed all the faces in the big room but saw no sign of Burt Hammond. She went to a bar, to a library, all crowded with party people and their highpitched voices, but she did not see Burt. At the pool, at a tent set up beside the pool, no Burt.

Someone touched her arm and almost made her run; he turned out to be one of those overage cats dressed in weathered jeans and jackets his children would look good in. He had a graying beard and wore sandals without socks. "You looking for me?" he said.

"Why not?" Sue-Ann was glad to connect with someone, in case the tight suits in the front door decided to look around.

"I bet you're a friend from his San Francisco days." He brought her to the bar and seemed astonished she did not

223

drink. "Got some highpowered grass from Vietnam," he suggested.

"Later. Are you a friend of Hammond's too?" she asked.

"Hell, no, I never met the man."

She seemed surprised. "Then what're you doing at his party?"

"I'm always asked to his parties," he said. "My name's Joe Gould, I'm a producer, a *big* producer. His press agent always asks big producers. Don't mean *he* has to meet 'em."

"Where is he?" Sue-Ann said.

"Probably upstairs. Holding court for favored subjects sucking up for some of that pension-fund money like I'd like to. I bet he didn't operate in San Francisco this way."

"You're telling me he gives a big party like this and doesn't even come down?" She grinned, rather pleased. "He *is* something, huh?"

"Look, baby," Joe Gould said. "I've got a beautiful package to lay before him. You get me to Burt Hammond and I'll make it worthwhile for you."

"Just to *talk* to him?"

"Any American car you want, that a deal?" She took a card he held out.

"I'll do what I can," she said, her eyes fixed on the kitchen where she knew there had to be service steps in a house of this magnitude. She drifted as carelessly as she could manage past the kitchen's pantry.

On the second floor it was easy to spot what had to be the master suite. She walked to the door and took a deep breath. If he's in bed with someone, be real cool, she said to herself, say something like, *Mind if I join you?* Without knocking she pushed open the door.

She found Burt Hammond at work before a Louis Quinze table covered with books and legal pads.

"Hey, man." She offered her usual greeting, as if she had seen him the day before. "I really dig your pad."

He rose quickly to embrace her. She stood ramrod rigid in his arms. "Some guy downstairs says he'll buy me a car if I can get him to you. You don't show up at your own parties? You're upstairs in your room doing homework? I don't get it."

"It's an act, Susie, in a put-on town. Tell me the guy's name, you'll have a new car."

"It's too late for cars for me, Burt," she began darkly.

She told him about the dynamiting of the transformer tower and her escape from the mountain. He had heard nothing of it. He made her go over what she knew a second time.

"You had nothing to do with the sabotage?" he demanded firmly.

"Absolutely."

"Any of your people in the organization?"

"I know them, Burt. And they'd have clued me in."

"You never ran across some crazy up there, one nut—?"

"Crazies don't stay crazy long in the wilderness. They either leave or they become whole people again. I tell you we didn't do it, no matter who wrote that note."

He walked from her and went to the window and looked down to the pool carefully so nobody could see a figure upstairs.

"You know what you're saying, of course?" he said quietly when he came back to her.

"They did it to themselves."

Why had he resisted the thought? Torrents of memory assailed him. When would he take the lesson to heart? Right now, where he was, did he himself not prove it? People who did things did what they had to do to get what they wanted. The doers. The non-doers backed away. But those who wanted things accomplished could accommodate themselves to hard facts. Who should know better than a man between two worlds?

But such a man knows resistance is possible. Hadn't he learned that in the desert? "We'll fight them, Susie," he said at length.

"Burt," she began gravely, "where in the hell have you been living? Do you know what's happening outside of Beverly Hills? Who gives a good goddamn about a mountain? The kids want to get Lyndon Johnson out, they want to end this insane war in Vietnam."

"It's all one struggle."

"Know what they tell me? Who gives a damn if they pave over the whole mountain and line it end to end with Kentucky Fried, Taco Bell and McDonald's? What's an earthly paradise to a guy facing death in an ugly war he never wanted? What's it mean to a black dude still hustling for the rent in Watts? A Chicano kicking back to a labor contractor in Kern County for the right to weed a carrot field? They ask me why the hell

225

they should care about Thunder Mountain. Why *do* you care, Burt?"

"Maybe someday I'll tell you."

"Thunder Mountain is dead, man. They've got the bread to fill it with their plastic animals and bullshit exhibits and hot-dog concessions, and you might as well face it. They can outspend you a thousand times. You don't know what's been going on. Suitcases filled with cash. Money to Mexico, money back from Mexico. We're up against heavy operators."

"Wait a minute." She had almost persuaded him. Some vestige of what he had learned in the desert had sustained him: to preserve a corner of the world is a good in itself. And when it was linked to someone who had destroyed tiny parts of his own world more than once, the struggle was justified. "The scorpion has a right to life, but not to mine," Don Pedro had once said. He had been ready to give up for a moment. In the face of cataclysms abroad and at home, he had no right further to involve Sue-Ann Martin and her people. He was about to say that, but when she mentioned money, she was talking about something he knew about. How it was made, played with, worked—straight and otherwise. "Say that again about suitcases," he told her gently.

"Suitcases filled with cash," she repeated. "Going out of the account in Bartlett, California, man, Why would a big company take out large amounts of cash from a little old branch bank?"

"I'll ask the questions, Susie. First—you tell me how you know all this."

"I've got a friend. Works in the bank. He tells me things."

"Why?"

"I let him have the use of the bod now and then when it feels the need for something warm," she said unabashed. "He's sort of gorgeous, a little stupid, but very pretty and has a good heart. He worships me. Tells me stuff so I'll think he's hip even though the heart is set on being a bank manager."

"What does he tell you about the cash?"

"There's this new local company. Gets its funds from San Diego Main Branch. The money goes out for surveying, stuff like that. Office. Salaries. Sponsors Rotary and service-club tours to the proposed site. Talks by stooges to high-school assemblies in Reedley, Visalia and Dinuba on how they're going to improve on God on the mountain. A few thou here, a couple of thou there, usually paid in cash to some local guy—zoning, stuff like that, a permit when it's tough to get. Small-time stuff. Suddenly, bang, begins the big action. First, they send a draft to a Spanish name in Mexico City. Few days later, in comes a draft from the Banco Popular. Same amount. My friend thinks: *Funny*. But his is not to question why—you dig?—his is to get to manage a branch of his own. Next, in comes a lady, and out in a large suitcase goes all the money that came back in the wash from Mexico. My friend thinks: *Even funnier."*

"Your friend actually saw all this?"

"He handled it, man."

"Who was the lady, did he get the name?"

"Sure, she's the same H.L. Wilson who signs the checks on the account. She heads the development company."

He turned from her to stroke his cheek and to smile at the turns cupidity can demand. When he returned to her, he said: "Just how big was the Banco Popular draft? Did your friend tell you?"

"Don't do anything to hurt his job, Burt," she pleaded first. "The kid's trying to be with-it but he's stuck to a career in that bank."

"I won't be the one to blow the whistle on him, I promise you that. How much did he put in the suitcase?"

"Two hundred fifty thousand."

"He delivers it personally to this Wilson lady?"

"Manager gives him the day off to ride her to L.A. so she feels safe."

"She say anything on the way?"

"Only what blue eyes he has. I told you, he's gorgeous."

"Where does the airplane go?"

"Chicago. Washington. New York."

"So the money could have been going to any one of those places?"

"She's going to Washington."

"How do you know?"

"She teases my friend a little. Next time, maybe he'll come along. Has he ever been to Washington? He'd be a smash there, she says, all these dirty old men with roamin' hands. Charley-gorgeous thinks she's talking about Italians, of course."

"So she's bringing the bag to Washington. She say anything else?"

"Sexy she may be, stupid she's not. Why would the lady be carrying all that cash, Burt?"

"When I figure that out I'll let you know."

"Yeah, and I'll be sitting in the slammer knitting license plates."

He put a reassuring kiss on her forehead. "We won't let that happen to you."

"I'm a terrible claustrophobe, baby." Her arms circled him for comfort. "I'd die locked up in a cell."

He stroked her lovely flaxen hair, pledging his help. "Is there some place you can lay low for a while?"

"All the people I know are already hassled by the law," she declared ruefully.

He used the home telephone as little as possible, always with the greatest discretion. Faced with having to find a very private place, he knew of only one. He had to risk being overheard, recorded or both.

It was a call he had thought of making; but never had. He direct-dialed a number in northern California.

"Hello, Courtney." After a moment, he added: "It's good to talk to you."

"It's good to talk to you, too." He thought he caught a little quaver in her voice.

"How's your grandmother?" Thank God for fatuities.

"Would you believe that right now I can see her going hell for leather behind four matched bays in a spider phaeton?"

"Fabulous lady."

A pause and an audible sigh. "I tried to reach you last month," Courtney began and stopped suddenly. "You don't have a phone."

"I have one, but I have to be careful."

"It's like that again?"

"Nothing sinister, Court. Just got tired of party lines and people listening in." He made it sound as cheerful as he could. "Courtney," he began again, "I need a favor."

"Anything."

"Could involve you in some unpleasantness."

"Never bothered me before, did it? What do I have to do?"

"I've got a friend I want you to put up."

"Of course. Bring her up."

Burt smiled. "It's better she go by herself. She can get

on an airplane out of here right away. She'll wait in that restaurant just off the main concourse."

"I'll have on a fringed jacket over jeans."

"Don't look for her. She'll spot you. First, she'll want to make sure no one's tailing."

And that was it. What had happened that night she left Wildoaks with her brother? Had she expected him to wait? What had happened between her and Kenneth Kendall? It was as if nothing had ever come to separate them because nothing was there to begin with. "Thanks, Courtney," he said. When he put down the receiver he found himself staring at a dead phone until Sue-Ann took the instrument from his hand and cradled it. "What do you know?" she said. "The man's human."

"Huh?"

"He has a heart. He can be touched. He even bleeds. What happened? This lady wound my lovely knight? I'd made up my mind no matter what, we had to have one of our good old fucks, if only for auld lang syne, but look at you."

"Get going, Susie."

"No." She lifted his hand. "Let's go to bed. There's nothing like a good hearty ball to steady the nerves." She dropped the hand when he refused to move. "And I'm nervous, man. Got these chronic blues that there's no place left for people like me in this world, free, open, loving. Even up there in the wilderness they're out to off Susie Martin." She declared her premonitions cheerfully and dropped the dress from her shoulders. She stood naked and nut-brown.

He rose to take her in his arms. "Nothing bad's ever going to happen to my Susie."

"I *know* why they want to destroy me. Not that I'm going to let them get me. What have we here?" Her hand came to rest on a pant leg. "Why, it's the darling friend. Why are you keeping Hard-Boy from me?"

"Animal," he teased her, his head buried in her long hair.

"Thank you, isn't that lovely of me?" His mouth found her neck and savored the fresh, wheaty flesh. "I'm purged of all physical filth, darling. Been living on vegetables, nuts and fruits and haven't consumed any kind of carcass in months—doesn't the body smell pretty? Taste it, darling. It's absolutely Garden of Eden time."

He lifted her and carried her to a blue fox spread the

cousin of the Shah and installed over a Directoire couch.

But she did not recline passively, awaiting the stripped body. She sat up and watched with an almost detached air as the shirt and trousers came off. "I must say I hardly knew you when I came here. But there you are, my good friend Hard-Boy and his strong man." She softly pressed her lips to his source. "I don't want to die, you won't let them do that to Susie, will you, Hard-Boy, strong man . . . ?" He lifted her body to cover her mouth and he thought of a great wilderness bird wheeling and circling in the endless blue sky, so beautiful, so free, so vulnerable.

3

LARRY Marshall was troubled. Lou Birch began by trying to make light of his vexations, but Birch could read the telltale signs that spelled trouble. When a combination was successful—which is to say, when it was making money—Lou Birch did not believe in any kind of change. That is why he liked his artists to assume responsibilities even beyond their present means: marriage, heavy investments, big homes, expensive luxuries. Gave them something to work for, he said.

But Roseanna Lee was married. She was well managed, in every sense, not only as a performer and a songwriter but as a troubled lady. Now with what Larry was telling him, with Rosey quiet, without her usual highs and lows, Lou Birch knew there was stormy weather.

The English girl had been eased out of the picture. That showed them both the lady was up to something. Brenda was leaving a lot of money behind her. Why? Larry knew what the older man did not suspect. Brenda was in love with his wife, and beneath that rough-tough Bow Bell exterior beat the heart of a foolish romantic, ready to give it all up to prove something or other, probably her love.

But it was more than Brenda Moore. To Larry Marshall, Roseanna's whole life seemed changed. No longer were there phone calls to amenable doctors, to hangers-on in the entourage who knew such, or to still others who knew where to buy what had to be bought, and forget the prescriptions. He had always told himself that his wife's drug dependency (he did not like to call it addiction) was something he "had to live with." He had even tried in the first days of their marriage to free her but it had not worked. Dope, pills, dolls—call them anything, they enabled Roseanna Lee to work. They were part of her life.

He loved her. He really did. He knew he was not lying to himself. He needed her. He loved what they had accomplished, what Rosey had made of herself. She was a superstar. At the same time, he felt that he had made her success happen, that without him she would now be at the most just another singer. He liked that part. There was, also, the problem of why he could not get himself erect enough to make love to his wife. He himself did not understand that. He was able to perform with innumerable call girls and backstage hangers-on, but he found it impossible to unite Rosey's body to his and came to dread her occasional oral assaults on him.

He went to a doctor and, not liking what he heard, he found another, and ended going to none. Although he himself had many women, he seethed at the thought that his wife could make a fool of him with other men. Of course there was Brenda, but that had not bothered him so much. In fact it had assuaged him to feel that Rosey had gone lesbian. He comforted himself with thinking this change in her desires meant that nothing could ever separate them. He did not like it at all when Brenda put him straight when she walked out. Rosey played at it, experimented, Brenda said, but no artful tricks and fancy devices ever fulfilled her real needs.

He had only to read Roseanna's mail to see what she represented to thousands of men. Yet the rod that sent his paid mistresses to ecstasies they thanked him for remained flaccid for this universally adored person. He kept most of these letters from Rosey, as he would to conceal a failing, although she was able to laugh at the few indecent proposals that managed to leak through to her. "I'm still Miss Boobs and Ass, even if I think I'm someone else, huh?" she said. He began to be more jealous than ever of her, even though he never touched her anymore.

She gave him cause, he thought. Her parties with all those music types he had long since outgrown, mostly homosexual, interested only in laughs and getting high and balling. He was sure they were all covering for Rosey. All hours of the day and night; he never knew where she was.

Then it had stopped. All the dear boys, their friends, all her adoring gofers were gone. She did not sleep her days away. Her eyes grew clear. The phones weren't always ringing and the heavy whispers stopped. Once he'd known what it was all about, pills, pills, pills. Now she began to spend whole days by herself in her studio behind the house. When the accompanist and arrangers came by to work on new material, she was ready and eager to get started. She took up yoga, found a group that met every morning and joined the class.

Told of Roseanna's erratic behavior, Lou Birch suggested Larry make it his business to stay close to home for a time. "Treat her like a client, Larry," he urged.

The break was not long in coming.

"Think I'd like to do a picture," Rosey said one evening.

"We've been looking for the right property. Our problem is musicals aren't very hot these days."

"Not a musical. A dramatic story."

He regarded her closely. So that was it. "Well, we'll keep our eyes open."

Lou Birch warned him to find out more. "Do I have to tell you about performers? Ungrateful lot, all of them. Give them everything they ever wanted and they're still not happy." He was sure someone had gotten past Larry. "The wrong picture could ruin her."

Finally, some weeks later, Larry got Rosey to tell him about Janet Morgan's discreet visits. He masked his gut reaction and agreed the lady was a fine actress and that it would be a wonderful experience for Rosey. "Just don't lock me out of your life again, baby," he said temperately. "All I want for you is the best."

He knew a little about Janet Morgan but made it his business to develop more inside stuff. He knew better than to break his reaction to what he uncovered to his wife.

He waited for Rosey to be out of town for an engagement in Las Vegas. Unannounced, he presented himself at Janet Morgan's door. "Tell her it's Roseanna Lee's manager," he told the servant.

Janet Morgan eyed him warily. "Wouldn't it be better for us to talk with your client present?"

"She doesn't want to see you anymore, Miss Morgan."

"She never said anything like that to me the last time we talked."

"I'm her husband as well as her manager, so *I'm* telling you."

Janet Morgan decided not to take him on directly. "I'll have a script ready to be read in a couple of weeks. It's coming along beautifully. Why don't we decide then?"

"You got your financing set, Miss Morgan?" he asked with heavy sarcasm.

"I'm ready to finance it myself."

That told him, and she knew it told him, that the project had been turned down by the studios and the distributing companies. "That's something a manager has to take into consideration."

"Why don't we bring Roseanna in on these discussions?"

"Because *I* make the deals," Larry said. "How do you think she got this far?"

"I thought it had something to do with her talent. Look, mister, why fence? I know that Roseanna Lee wants to be in my film."

"Too bad she's got a bunch of dates from here to Tokyo and to London so she can't."

"You know you can get postponements."

"Sure, we could, but not your film."

"I don't want to fight with you, mister. I'm telling you this part will make a big dramatic star out of Roseanna."

"I don't care if it would make her the queen of England. She's not going to do any picture with you."

"So it's me," Janet Morgan grinned. "Do I offend you?"

"Roseanna Lee is not going to make her picture debut with you even if you get Ho Chi Minh himself to back it."

Janet Morgan held up her hand. "Save the rest of the speech, it's a little early in the day for righteous indignation from a pig-exploiter. Would you please leave my house?"

Larry found himself ready to slap the lady but managed to freeze the muscles in his arm. "You Vietcong bitch," he said. "Don't ever try to see my wife again."

Janet Morgan grinned bitterly and pretended to cower. "Yassuh, Massa Legree, Ah sho won't." She was laughing, though shaken, when he slammed the door.

Larry Marshall went to see his lawyer.

4

"It's all yours, Everett. The company wants you to have it."

Mrs. Wilson walked to the window and touched a switch. Forty feet of drapery hanging from ceiling to floor parted silently and opened to a broad balcony. Ten floors below, brown hills rolled to the ocean in endless waves. Everett Alan Pierce came up to her shyly. "But how could I afford an apartment like this, ma'am?" He was a tall young man, with big blond downy forearms and a face that might be difficult to take seriously for its upturned nose. His hair was fair, his eyes blue and an ineradicable dimple in his chin was like a badge of innocence.

"Dear boy, now you're with Sobordco, you'll be working out of here. Entertaining guests of the company, escorting them, showing them around. That's all part of your job. Has Mr. Armstrong shown you what's involved in public relations?"

"I still can't believe it, it's all happened so fast," Everett Alan Pierce said. . . .

It had all begun to happen right after the explosion when Susie and the other kids beat it from off the mountain.

Up until that day, Everett agreed with Susie that it was a rough deal. Down in Bartlett, everybody was all for Happy Land Park, as it was now being officially called, which was said to be its original Indian name and wouldn't scare off people, like Thunder Mountain. Happy Land was going to bring lots of business to town; it had already caused real estate to double, triple, and even quadruple in some places. The big hotel chains were buying or taking options on land where they planned to put up buildings. Fast food chains had bought on the corner of Fifth and Somerset, and the intersection down Main Street from the bank where he worked.

"It's a modern gold rush, Everett," his manager told him. "If things go on this way, we're going to run out of space and we'll have to put on more tellers. I'll bet they'll be giving me an assistant."

But that Susie was something. He could never really love someone like her, he knew that. Sure, she was beautiful, she was always on a high, cheerful, she never bumrapped anyone, she liked people, she liked her hippy life up there. And could she swing when she was of a mind! He'd had girls, more than his share, from junior high on, during his years at Reedley Community College when he was taking ten units a semester like everybody else to keep the hell out of the army and Vietnam. But there was never any lover like Susie Martin. She took sex like a guy. She laughed when he talked of love and thought it a joke. With other girls, a guy had to pretend making it was something more than it was. With Susie, she had this need like a man, and who cared if it wasn't love? "You keep it hard till I tell you to let go, baby," she said, and if he did that for her they were even, she told him.

If Happy Land happened, he would get a promotion, more money. He might even get to be manager if they moved Mr. Loomis up. Naturally he kept quiet about it. Sometimes he dreamed he would live like Susie and those other guys up on the mountain. He was confused. Then the explosion they'd set . . . an outright terrorist bombing . . .

When she split, his world collapsed. Without a word. No letter. Left her van behind, all her clothes, a litter of burned papers, and that was all. Then all the police and FBI people after her. Hard, intense men asking questions. He told them what he knew about Sue-Ann Martin. "The bank is glad you're forthcoming and totally honest, Pierce, but I'm surprised at the friends you kept," the manager said, and Everett saw his dreams fade.

He had been hoodwinked by physical passion the way he had been warned about a long time ago in Sunday School. The flesh. Behind all that sweetness they were building and assembling bombs up there in the wilderness. He didn't want to believe it, but with all the investigators around, didn't that prove it? Where there was smoke there was fire.

"I don't know how to tell you this, Mrs. Wilson." He paid a call at the suite the lady engaged permanently at the Mariposa Inn just outside of town for when she was there on business. "I didn't tell any of the people who questioned me because they didn't bring it up. But maybe you ought to know." He told her about how he had told Sue-Ann about the money in the suitcase. The draft to the Banco Popular and from them and how he had accompanied Mrs. Wilson to the Los Angeles airport. It was a big mistake, he saw that now.

"She's the only one you told about it?" It did not take Mrs. Wilson long to clear his conscience. "Can you be my friend, Everett? I see in you someone rare and special; am I wrong?"

They had dinner in her suite. Candlelight. A hi-fi spinning dreamy music behind them. He told her more about himself. She drank champagne with dinner. She was some kind of lady. Wanted to know in detail how Susie made love, all of it. You'd think he and Mrs. Wilson had been—well, why not, he thought. She was damned beautiful, old or not. He had never seen a beautiful lady like that. He wondered how old she really was? He'd guess damned near *forty*. His ma was forty-one but she looked *old*. Of course she never talked about sex; maybe talking about it made Mrs. Wilson seem younger . . . "Could you really hold yourself back for that girl just as long as she liked? I bet you're making that part up."

"She taught me how," he protested. "I can go on just as long as I want to." The champagne was pretty fine, none of that dollar-ninety-nine drugstore stuff. He forgot about Sunday School or the sins of the flesh.

Later, over brandy, Mrs. Wilson told him he was wasting himself in Bartlett with the bank. "Young men must set goals early, and be ruthless in achieving them, Everett. To own the world you've got to go out into it."

When he became aware of Mrs. Wilson's hand he thought he was in another place at another time. Everything became a blur. Talk about Susie!—the lady was a lioness. She did not let him release until they were both sobbing with exhaustion. She let him rest only briefly. When all their passion was utterly spent, Mrs. Wilson covered him and let him sleep. He had made love to girls before, never with a woman, he decided.

In the morning, when he opened his eyes, he heard: "Everett, do you want to own the world?"

He had his answer there on the penthouse terrace with that whole world she had spoken of spread before him.

He took her into his arms. "I want you. Would you marry me? I'm not as dumb as I look. You're beautiful, I love you, there's no one else like you in the whole world."

"Everett, my dear, you don't have to say that," she protested mildly.

"Guys my age have the same right as girls to marry older people. I don't think of you as old, I think of you as ageless. Say yes."

She let herself get lost in the surge of his youthful strength and innocent eagerness; she found it as heady as whiskey. "We'll see," she whispered and struggled free.

"Forgive me if I'm taking too many liberties, ma'am."

How sweet, how darling! He'd slept with her, he'd played his hold-it-back sex game with her until she climbed the walls, and now he bent the knee and still wasn't sure of her. "We'll see, darling boy," she said, and felt her eyes mist over. She drew in a deep breath. "First you must prove yourself. Be loyal, Everett, to the company as well as to me. The whole world can be yours, Everett."

"Just so you keep him out of the way until this thing blows over," Ellis Griswold muttered. They were in the president's executive suite of the Sobordco headquarters building. The sun was high above the broad bay, the new bridge to Coronado a free-flowing curve over sun-glinting water.

"The young man's going to be okay, Ellis. As for the senator—well, he's an old master at fooling around at the edges of the law."

"And Guren, his assistant? Sometimes the government nails them on something else and they talk to win immunity."

"I've promised him choice frontage across the main-access road entrance. He's got backing for a two-hundred-unit motel."

"You're wonderful, Hil."

"There's the girl, of course. But who'd believe a terrorist bomber? And she didn't actually *see* the money, did she? Everett *told* her about it, that's all. He could say he made it up to score with a revolution-minded chick."

"You're more than wonderful, you're a marvel." Ellis Griswold made a quick half-turn and seized her hands. "I bless the day we met."

"What I'm worried about is, who financed the girl and the rest of them?"

"Have you looked into that?"

"It wasn't the Sierra Club people or any of your usual environmental groups. This one formed just to stop us. Who could it be? Only someone after us, just us, right?"

He stared at her for a time. "Burton Hammond, Hil?"

"It fits. Berkeley. His kind of young lady. No wonder we could never find out where they got the funding. So we've got to assume that the girl has told him everything. He'll know she doesn't have much credibility. But he knows about the money we sent to Mexico and brought back clean. That could hurt us bad, Ellis. The new election laws—whatever, the manner of the contribution. *He knows.*"

After a moment Ellis Griswold said in a voice dry and cracked as crumpled parchment: "The man has got to be stopped."

"How?"

"There's always a way."

"As it turned out, there wasn't one before, was there, Ellis?" She had not wanted to believe when it would have made a difference. Now she realized she had been lied to, and it too made no difference.

"There're ways and ways. Take your friend the senator —seems to me for a quarter of a million he owes us some kind of favor."

"He won't like being involved."

"His subcommittee was in Central California, Hilary."

"What about the connection with Jerry Haggerty, Ellis? Why can't we exploit that? Haggerty's always in trouble with the government."

"We're into that fund of his for a lot of money."

"Yes, but Burton Hammond's no longer right beside Haggerty. What does that tell you? Would Jerry let him go if they were still buddy-buddy?"

"I'll look into it. Still, what about that boy? How do we keep him locked up?"

"He's working for TMD, my dear. Who better than a

young man who knows Thunder Mountain, lived there, and believes in it?"

"Yes, but—" Griswold began.

"There are no *yes buts,* Ellis. He's asked me to marry him. Says girls his age often marry men mine, so what the devil? Lovely, isn't he? Plus, it would give us someone who can't—not that he would—testify against me, which is to say us."

Griswold beamed. "We'll destroy Burton Hammond, Hilary."

"Yes." She nodded. "Too bad I still love him. Too bad about that."

5

HE looked up, fork poised in midair, and saw the familiar face, the body clothed in trim, well-cut trousers and a loose wool sweater. Don Faversham arranged these things and he had said nothing about Janet Morgan, but a star of her stature could not be denied. He waved the fork helplessly. "Forgive me, Miss Morgan."

"You've made your point," she countered sharply. "May I sit?"

"Please." Burt Hammond struggled to his feet and came down again when she sat. "I didn't know we had a date."

"We haven't, but here I am."

At first he wasn't sure he liked anything abut her, except the bravado. She was telling him she was in this dreadful restaurant only because she needed him and wasn't sure how else to go about it. He knew about her only superficially. It was surprising how little he knew about any of the people he had been dealing with. She talked a windstorm. Her pictures had always done well, she said. The last one made a fortune for her, although she had yet to see a red cent. She made no secret about her political opinions. Yes, she'd gone to Hanoi. Why not? Wouldn't he, if he had the chance to see certain things with his own eyes? And her statements: Were they wrong? Did people really want this crazy war to go on? Weren't actors people, didn't they have a right to their opinions? Couldn't she be judged for her work; did you ask your doctor how he felt about Cuba before you let him put a knife to you?

When Burt Hammond was finally able to get a word in, he smiled, somewhat amused, and said, "Is this why you've joined me here, Miss Morgan?"

"Obviously you're my last resort. I've been said No to, four thousand different ways. It's an art here in Hollywood. There's the blunt No, the maybe No, which amounts to the same thing. The unreturned-phone-call No. There's the it's-out-of-my-hands. The we-like-everything-about-it-but. The it's-not-our-kind-of-picture, the we-love-it-unfortunately-we-don't-think-it'll-make-money . . . and the we-love-you-Janet-but—. I've been given them all from one end of this town to the other."

"And you heard I can do the impossible?"

"I'm not sure I like everything I heard about you . . . this tough lawyer-type with connections no one's quite sure about. The mysterious wheeler-dealer. The go-go financial genius piling in the dollars while the whole world's going to hell. Maybe it's better for the career to go down the drain."

He leaned forward to study her. Without jewels, her hair pulled back simply, she emanated beauty, power and assurance. He could at once comprehend the source of her public appeal. A few people might find her directness and positiveness dispiriting, but her honesty and intense love of everything around her made her shine diamond-hard. As an actress she brought reality to whatever she touched.

"You believe everything you hear, Miss Morgan?"

"I know better. I need someone like you. The job offers aren't happening for Janet Morgan. I've decided to finance a picture of my own with that three million I haven't gotten yet. So I'm having the script written. Two hundred thousand on the line, up front, that's real cash from the piggy-bank. I'm back to worrying whether my checks will bounce, three million to the good or not. The writer I've got is good. Dear God, he'll stay as good as his first pages."

"And the three million you earned?"

"Tied up tighter than a dollar necktie."

"What about a release?"

"I thought you could help me there too."

"Tell me a little about the picture."

"Two women who are thrown together. A lot happens to them. They learn to need, to care, to be alive." She studied him carefully. "Don't tell me what the big boys tell me. The people don't want 'women's films,' whatever they are. Now's not a time for Joan Crawford and Bette Davis films, the four-hankie picture."

"That wouldn't bother me."

"This story says people are wonderful if they can somehow touch one another." She studied him again. "It's not too preachy. Two ladies on the road, one with a kid, that's all. You don't like it?" she concluded dubiously.

"It's a fine theme," he said.

"Thank God." She sank lower in her chair.

"What it says is decent, meaningful, wants saying."

"Yes."

"Real people in a real situation."

"Precisely."

"I hate it," he said bluntly. "It sounds like a bloody bore."

"It isn't."

"It's instructing us to be nice to one another. The great truth of life, Nice is better than not-nice."

"Why don't you wait until you read the script?"

"Because I hate being preached to, even if I agree with the preacher."

"That's my terrible failing." Her eyes were steady and self-revealing. "The writer says that's what we've got to avoid. We had a kind of fight about it. I want the picture to be good, not to be a sermon. You could help there too. See how cooperative I am?"

"I see something else. That you're not made of six-inch steel plate."

"Hell, I'm not even made of strong flesh and blood. I cry at weddings and pictures of babies. All I want is to make a good film that tries to do more than turn a buck. What's wrong with that?"

"I like that, Janet," he said gently.

"I'm just the kind who can't quit. I'll go down fighting, all the flags flying. Dumb, I guess. I've been busted for grass I was supposed to be holding, jailed in Buffalo because they found a dozen Dexys I used for keeping the weight down. Maybe I'm nuts, but half the time I keep thinking there's someone else on my phone. The gardener

241

turns up with an assistant with Brooks Brothers chinos and wing-tipped cordovans. I could lay down and let them throw the dirt over my face, I guess, but it's not my style, any more than it's yours. I don't know you, I know your boss or whatever he is, Jerry Haggerty. He used to be one of my heroes. So he's gone a little crazy. How could he help it? Paranoia's supposed to be when you think the whole world's against you. What happens if it's not an illusion? If all those FBI's and Special Task Forces really are out to nail you? What if you want to go on doing what you do best—in my case, make pictures that try to add one little jot that couldn't happen without me?"

"Madam," Burt Hammond said when she had finished and paused to find something she could arrest a tear with, "I'd be honored to be your lawyer."

She sniffed audibly. "I knew anybody on J. Edgar Hoover's shit list couldn't be all bad." She dabbed at her cheek. "I'm sorry I'm crying in public. Is everybody looking? It'll be all over town tomorrow that we're having an affair. Ladies cry at lunch tables in Hollywood only when their men break their hearts."

"Don't look now," Burt Hammond said. "I think I'm crying too."

She lifted her head. "My God," she said astonished.

"Let's keep it a secret."

"I think I'm falling in love with you, counselor."

"I beat you to it." He put his napkin away. "I'm already in love with you."

"I understand you say that to all your clients." She sighed. "Nevertheless, despite your reputation, I think you're fantastic."

"Hold on until you hear how I wouldn't let any of my people invest a dime in one of your socially conscious, public-spirited, or anti-Vietnam or give-women-a-break picture ideas."

"I could still love you. But I'd think you're spineless at the core."

"We can fight about that later. You give me the project I can care about and you've got your money. And your distribution. And we're also going to find out why you haven't been paid that three million."

"You can get that too, just like that?"

"Why not?"

"Why not?" she echoed sarcastically, and then she laughed, feeling better than she had in a very long time.

One day it came to him that the title of the picture she wanted to make was absolutely apt. Working with Janet Morgan was inhabiting a hurricane zone. *Eye of the Storm* indeed. What an interesting time, he thought, the FBI must be having monitoring her phones. Calls came from all over the world, usually crackpot projects and infantile leftist suggestions. The lady felt it undemocratic to have an unlisted phone, so some student who thought he could help the cause if she would give him the money to plant a peace flag atop Mt. Everest picked up the phone in Paris, Belgrade or Madison, Wisconsin, and asked information for the number.

And she'd talk to him! At first, he thought it was naivete. He came to see she was utterly sincere. No wonder so many people distrusted her. No wonder so many people found her irresistible. God knows, he told himself, he himself was ambivalent about her. He had become wise enough in the ways of actresses to see what she had in common with the others in her profession. Self-centered, driven, single-minded, egocentric—all the vital signs of stardom were there. Plus politics, and just plain intelligence. He found the bundle difficult to take. But she understood, and this made her even more attractive to him. "Is it any wonder women like me are hard to take? Why Miss Davis has had to call it 'a lonely life'? I'm glad you accept me as I am."

They were still fighting over various stories she thought she wanted to do. She did not go into detail about her favorite. *Eye of the Storm* was the picture she knew she had to make. She planned to bring in Derek Frye, her former husband, because, crazy as he was, he was marvelous with background and she wanted to shoot this picture totally on locations around the country. And of course there was the casting. But she told him nothing of her plans.

One evening, some weeks later, a quiet fell over them as she finished reading aloud the first draft of *Eye of the Storm* to the final fadeout. The writer had more than earned his pittance. She walked to the terrace of her house and looked out to the dark sea beyond the beach. She lived in a glorified shack some miles beyond the Malibu Colony with a nurse and her son; a simple house, a warm and pleasant one he liked to visit.

"It's good, Janet," he began when he joined her. "If it was Paul Newman and Robert Redford . . ."

"Yeah, I know." She turned to him in the dark. "Or Dusty Hoffman and Jonny Voigt. Tell me. Two men. A buddy picture."

"It's the market, Janet. It's not anybody's doing."

"It's my doing, it's your doing. It's conceding to the market's prejudices."

"Markets are. They don't have prejudices."

"Audiences are people. They're all of us. Someone has to point the way. Are you saying you won't back this picture?"

"I'm saying we may lose our collective asses, but isn't that what asses are for?"

She circled her arms around his waist. "I like you, counselor."

"I thought I heard you say once you loved me."

"Lunch-table talk. Like is harder to come by than love. You know about love, I take it."

"I think so."

"I'm glad you haven't made a pass. I mean, it gets so tiresome, so obligatory. Is that why you haven't tried here?"

"Haven't thought why. It was fun just seeing you and watching and being with you on this."

"It's ridiculous your driving all the way home every time you come here," she said firmly, like a judge coming down on an issue that had been in doubt. "Everybody in town thinks the affair is well under way. Would you like to sleep over?"

"I'll take the matter under advisement." He took her into his arms and kissed her for the first time. *Consort-battleship, hell,* he thought. *I'm going to have to fight for my life here.*

244

6

HE flashed FBI credentials as he sat down uninvited and dismissed Marco with a glare. Shockley, the name was. Gray suit, blue shirt, bluer tie. Looking for Miss Sue-Ann Martin and minced no words. He knew how the gentleman felt about the Bureau and would just remind him that what happened up there in Bartlett was a serious matter.

"Do you have a warrant for her arrest?"

"No."

Burt Hammond reminded Shockley that he had legally represented Miss Martin at one time. If the Bureau persisted in believing the preposterous story that those kids on the mountain were stupid enough to think they could get away with a bombing, he might have to play lawyer for her again.

Shockley was not there for any purpose just now but to be put in touch with the Martin woman. Would the gentleman be good enough to oblige? He was conversant with the statute books, so surely he knew what was involved.

"Are you threatening me, sir?" Burt Hammond casually threw down his napkin and left some bills beside his plate. Shockley took note that there were no credit cards and no signing of checks. He followed Burt Hammond to the carport and found that the boys had the white Rolls already waiting for him.

"How long did you send money to those people trespassing up there on that mountain?"

"I can't answer that, Mr. Shockley."

"Why not? If you won't tell us where the girl is, you can tell us about yourself."

"It's a loaded question, sir, and assumes a few things I'd never concede."

"Admit it. You supported those hippies."

245

"What I do with my money's my own business, Mr. Shockley. Ask the IRS."

"Think you're cute?" Shockley exploded without warning. "All that cash! So IRS knows!—we know even more about you!" Burt Hammond watched the gentleman grow loud, somewhat abusive, and running wild. "What're you hiding? What's your connection with Haggerty? You think we're finished looking into that jury business?"

"I thought you came to talk to me about Miss Martin." Burt Hammond got into his car and in his rear-view mirror saw his visitor stride angrily back to the parking boys.

This week they used a phone behind an Arco station in Westwood Village. As usual, Elmer Wright was precisely on time and Burt lifted the receiver at the first ring. Haggerty was anxious to talk to him. In person. Up there. No, he did not know what it was about. This morning Haggerty had sent his man Clancy to bring him to the office on Market Street and from the way the fat man confronted him, Elmer Wright did not think it wise to resist. All he could get out of the old man was that there was no time to waste.

Burt Hammond expected to find the old man in one of his bitterly angry moods, but was surprised to find him amiable and cold sober when he was ushered into the Spartan-plain office later that day. They sat next to each other on the ancient leather sofa, feet up on the battered table. They talked about Hollywood, and Haggerty made jokes about the availability of young women down there. Haggerty spoke of the California presidential primaries in June; he was of the opinion that his long-time adversary whose name he could not bring himself to say would lose this state as well as the Oregon party vote which preceded it. That brought him, by a kind of calculated misdirection, Burt Hammond was certain, to talk of the pension fund and how well it was going. *That,* in turn, brought a comment of surprise that Burt Hammond was calling on it far less than was expected. "Ain't they still makin' them flicks down there?" Haggerty teased, but listening for an answer. Burt had begun to explain the amazing availability of risk capital from private sources when Jerry Haggerty broke in with a soft and veiled comment:

"I know how you get a lot of your money. I looked into it." There was a long and significant pause. "That's why I called for you. We can use that situation. Got some money we'd like to put out with you."

Burt Hammond did not need warning flags to tell him what was coming; he played it naively. "You mean, pension-fund money, Jerry?"

"I mean two, maybe four million in cash, outside the fund."

"Is it a company or an individual looking for a tax shelter?" He tried to sound as if he did not already know the answer. He heard Jerry go through an old story without names or geography: friends, a favor, loyalty, a favor to be returned and no one to be hurt. There was this money and it had to be put to work, didn't matter so much about the return, let others look for a fat return, he was sure Burt would know how to handle this for him.

"Can you tell me more about the money?" Burt owed the old man the courtesy of going through the motions. The FBI was interested in more than Susie Martin, not to mention the tax people; he was not about to deal with sacks of cash from sources that did not want to be identified. Jerry's old trap: favors now for favors then, and God knows what else.

"Never mind where it comes from and whose it is. You'll do it for me, kid, right?"

"Don't see how I can, Jerry."

"Same way you put up with stuff you didn't like before."

"I never was involved with anything so blatant, Jerry. Certainly, nothing *I* knew about."

"The perennial Boy Scout," Jerry said bitterly. "You didn't know what was happening all the time?"

"Like what didn't I know?"

"Take the twenty-five thousand from Lady Tara."

"A legal fee."

"You usually collect such high fees?"

"I do now. Maybe more."

"Speak to Sheldon the baker. Ask him what he thought he was paying for. He called me that night and said there had to be some mistake or was it a signal, you asking for a measly twenty-five hundred? He expected to, and did, pay off. What about the trial down in L.A.? The lady who went to the judge with the story about that reporter calling her? You think she made that up? Or jurors Number four and ten? What do you know about that?"

Burt Hammond got to his feet. "This is where I get off, Jerry."

The old man did not stir from the couch. "Sit down, kid," he offered amiably. He patted the leather and grinned avuncularly until Burt Hammond sat again. "You don't really want to walk out, do you?"

"I don't need you anymore, Jerry."

"How you going to do your business without me?"

"That dirty money you want me to clean up for your dirty friends? I can raise ten times that from people with taxable money coming out of their ears."

"Know why, counselor? Those people think I'm in with you. If it's good enough for Haggerty, it's good enough for them. They're looking to make a big fast buck like everybody else. So it's not so kosher! Who cares, as long as they realize a twenty-five or fifty percent return? And if Haggerty is involved, that means it's possible. You're riding on my reputation, kid, like it or not. Without me, you're another lawyer-hustler, and there are a lot of them down there. Now, if you want to get up and get out of my life forever, go on."

"You think I wouldn't?"

"You left New York for that Valley, you left me up here, hell, I know you would, except for one thing." Haggerty rose to his feet with some difficulty and went to a closet that had been turned into a wet-bar a long time ago. He took a long time finding the John Jameson and a glass and pouring what he wanted down his throat. "What about that girl, Burt?" he began softly. "And what you going to do about your old friend Griswold?"

Burt Hammond stared at him darkly but offered no reply.

Haggerty put his feet up on the coffee table although he was doing it by himself this time. He himself went back a long time with that man, he went on. Anti-labor, union-busting, right-to-work, a prehistoric Californian who used to think organizers worked with a bomb in the back pocket. But a good deal's a good deal, and when Sobordco needed money, it worked out well for the fund too. The little shitheel couldn't say *they* were mob-connected. So he became a little friendly with the guy. So he found out more than Griswold would like for him to know, he'd bet. "Sit down, Burt," he said after a long pause.

He moved a little so Burt could join him again. "I don't

know what you're trying to work on that man, but why would you give it up now?"

"Jerry, you're a crook. I admire, even love, a lot of things about you, but you're a crook."

The old man grinned without resentment. "I operate. Everybody operates. You operate."

"Within the law."

"That so? You going to give the FBI this girl they're looking for?"

"What do you know about that?"

"I run a big store so I get to know a lot of things. Aren't you flirting with obstruction of justice? Think they couldn't make it stick in some jurisdiction? Come off it, counselor. Everybody's operating today. It's our new morality. Do a favor, get a favor. Not, *Is it proper?* Now it's, *Can I get away with it?* That son of a bitch Kennedy who's out to destroy me, you think favor doesn't get paid with favor? What about his giving half of that Nazi company the government took over during the war to the Swiss cover his father and all the family friends were involved in? Translate that into the terms of my life and ask yourself what the runt would make of that. Morals? Proper? Fair play? You didn't see him getting into the race until after Gene McCarthy proved in New Hampshire the sitting President could get knocked off. Tell me about guts and courage and the morality after the other man took all the risks and showed the spoiled brat he could get away with it. Meaning, not lose the Senate seat from New York that this Boston carpetbagger managed to buy with his old man's money. Take what you can get, Burton Z Hammond. Isn't that your game down there in Hollywood? Why blame me for playing it too?"

After a moment, Burt said: "The answer to your question is I won't give them the girl until I have to and I'm trying to work it so I won't have to."

"Good. If you can get away with it, it helps you with the lock you've got here on your old friend Griswold."

"You knew about that all the time?"

"He tried to do you in and you never said word one. I know you're not stupid. I figured no one's that high-principled."

"The obvious thing would have been to fight it. I saw a chance to stay close to him instead."

"Which you'll still have once you learn to go all the way."

Burt Hammond remained silent.

"Have a drink with me, counselor."

Still he said nothing.

Jerry rose. "Between us, the Teamsters and the AFL-CIO, we could raise one big stink for you about that quarter of a million contribution. Really clobber Griswold. You sure you won't have a drop?"

Jerry Haggerty looked up from behind the bar, a little surprised that Burt had not joined him, but he poured a drink for him anyway. He brought it to the table and put it down. After a moment, Burt took it into his hands, studying it as if he had never seen whiskey before. "It'll take some doing," he began in a soft voice. "I know a few guys down there hungry enough they'd do anything to get their picture off the ground." He sipped from the glass for a time. "Of course, they may be short but they're not dumb. And I don't believe in letting people know what I'm doing. But I'll figure out something for your friends, Jerry."

"They'll be much obliged to you, counselor," Jerry Haggerty said, lifting his own glass as if responding to a toast.

7

ELMER Wright had the Plymouth up to his speed, 50, at Daly City on the way to the airport. They sat in silence, comforted by the late-morning sun and the flow of life on all the wheels around them, coming and going in eight lanes. At the airport turnoff Burt Hammond said: "Keep going. I'll tell you when to turn off."

Elmer Wright coughed a little, as if embarrassed by what he should have known. "I wondered where you stashed that girl," he offered some minutes later. He kept his eyes steady on the road for a time before speaking again. "Your neck's out, isn't it, harboring and all, right, counselor?"

"I don't pay you for drawing legal conclusions. Drive."

At the cutoff to Wildoaks, Burt Hammond ordered the car stopped. "Thanks for the lift to the airport, Elmer. I can manage from here. Sorry I was a little curt back there."

"She'll need a new social-security number, and to keep away from anybody she ever knew. That's not infringing on the lawyer's territory, is it? Also tell her to kill off the girl she was and the whole lifestyle and to get far the hell away from the Bay Area," Elmer Wright said in parting.

Wildoaks sat in serene beauty, untouched, a million miles from freeways and the headquarters of the Federal Bureau of Investigation. It still looked wholly unpeopled. No cars were parked in front of the house, nor at the side of the house where Courtney might leave hers. He rang the doorbell. It was like waiting for a tomb to respond.

But, finally, one of the ancient retainers appeared. "Why, it's Mr. Hammond. Do come in, sir. Miss Courtney's been somewhat indisposed, sir, but I'll let her know you're here."

"Thanks, Lockhart, later. Where's Miss Martin?"

"She has quarters in the carriage house."

"You might tell Mrs. Levering I'm here too."

"Yes, sir, though she's not been at all well either." The old man looked ashen with fear and misgiving.

"Mr. Kenneth been here, Lockhart?"

"Yes, sir," he said, eyes opening in surprise—maybe relief—at the deduction, and turned to his duties.

"Hey, man," Susan-Ann Martin said when she caught sight of him. She rushed to him and remained in his embrace for a long moment. "What's happening?"

"You look good, Susie."

"All this sunshine, rest and fresh air, who wouldn't? And don't forget that I don't contaminate the bod ingesting animal flesh and other assorted poisons. When're you going to spring me out of this here *carcel?*"

"You don't like all the splendor?"

"Makes *Jane Eyre* and *Wuthering Heights* look like fairyland. That brother, he comes, he destroys, he flies off. And he's so charming the whole time. Aren't they supposed to have fangs and wear big black capes? He's fabulous at first meeting, though. I almost balled him. Then I got a whiff of the man behind the orthodontia and my virtue was saved once again. How come he descends on

251

this miserable place and they start vomiting, running fevers and going to bed? That tell you something? When do I get the hell out of this joint?"

"How about right now?"

"Goodbye, baby," she said, still clinging to him.

"Hold on. You're going to cut off all this lovely hair and get into a skirt, shoes with heels, and put on lipstick and mascara—"

"A living death," Sue-Ann moaned as much in earnest as in jest.

"Worse. Let's say, Indianapolis. You know anybody in Indianapolis?"

"What kind of creep do you take me for?"

"Or it could be Duluth. Yazoo City. Think of any place you'd ordinarily avoid like the plague where no one would look for you."

"It might as well be Indianapolis. How long do you think it'll be? Until the war is over?"

"I'll be working on it. Hang in. Can you?"

She looked around the carriage house. The larger part of it was set up like a museum, the old lady's prize possessions, tokens of an art as lost as the crafting of chariots. "What do you think I've been doing?"

"You don't like it here?"

"It's Alcatraz. Give me the cockroachy pad off Telegraph Avenue any day. Still, I like your lady. Can't you bust her out of these high gray walls?"

"Don't know."

"She doesn't gripe or complain. She endures. Very strong. She loves you."

"What about the brother? When'd he show up?"

"I think the man's a dealer. Wholesale. Wants me to go on some crazy cruise to Colombia. He dreams of bringing in white powder by the ton. What's with your girl and him?"

"You tell me."

"It's way past her feeling sorry. She loves him. I think he's a psycho, at least a dangerous freak. He's a fantastic manipulator. I can see how he manages to twist her around his little finger. He scares me too. He told me he has eight houses and never knows from one day to the other which one he'll use. That tells us something, huh? Also it beats Fidel Castro by two houses, I think. But Castro's only got Cuba and this guy's got all that Levering

252

money. Take care of the ladies, they've been pretty sick the last week, both of them. How do I get out?"

"I'll have someone drive you to the airport in San Jose. They won't be looking for you there." He took out his money and peeled off some bills. "All I've got are big ones. Be careful when you use them. American business-men have learned to be very suspicious about people who use currency. I won't be able to help you after this. I'd give my right arm, Susie, but I'll have to stay absolutely technically correct."

"I dig. They're laying for you too, huh?"

"Don't let anything scare you. Fear's part of their game, makes you run scared. You'll feel alone, but I'll be working for you."

"Don't let them do anything bad to Susie."

He took her again into his arms and kissed her fore-head. "I won't. That's a promise. Did I lay enough bread on you? I've got more than I need to reach home." He put other bills into her hands.

"You kidding? The minute I'm in San Jose I'm buy-ing me a mink-lined parka and a van to match."

"Get a new social-security card and a square job. That's so you won't attract attention to yourself. If you don't work, someone's liable to wonder about you. No head shops, no book stores, no second-hand clothes stores. Don't panic, no matter what you read in the papers." He pressed his lips against her hair, running his fingers down the long, golden flax. "It's so beautiful, Susie. I loved it when it fell on my face when we made love."

"So I've been told." She forced a grin through misted eyes. "Thousands and thousands of times."

"I love you."

"I love you, too," Sue-Ann Martin said. "So much I hope you find what you're looking for."

Flora Levering's lids seemed to flutter; they opened slowly. Her eyes were remarkably gray, the whites, cloudy. Her lips were chapped and flecked white at the corners. "How long've you been sitting here?" Her voice was dry as sand.

"Too long." Burt Hammond pointed to the nightstand. Ten or twelve little brown bottles were scattered on it, none from pharmacies or with labels he knew. "Who gave you these?"

"The doctor."

"Funny there's no proper labeling. When was he here?"

"Hasn't been," she said. "It's a kind of flu that's going around."

"He told you that?" Burt Hammond pointed to the phone on the stand.

"Kenneth spoke to him."

He laid a hand on her forehead. It was not as burning as it had been when she slept. "Don't touch any of these bottles."

"I thought I was hallucinating." Flora Levering's voice crackled like crushed underbrush. "Dreamed someone was poisoning me. I'd drink water and go sick. I'd recover and take nourishment and feel the clammy hand of death."

"Maybe you weren't only hallucinating. I'm going to see Courtney."

"Be kind to her, Burt."

"She's got to want to help herself. She's got to break with that brother."

"Easier said than done. Can I have a drink of water?"

He found a glass, sniffed it, did not like what it told him and brought it to the bathroom to wash it out and to fill it with his own hands. He watched her drink it in long, slaking draughts. He took the glass and put it down for her.

"What hold has this man got on his sister? Don't keep anything back. I know everything, Flora."

"They were two children inhabiting a world of their own. It's as simple, and frightening, as that. They made a pledge then. Never to separate, never to divide. It's possible when an imaginary kingdom really exists for fantasies to harden to reality too."

"I don't buy all that now, Flora."

"You don't have a fortress mentality from growing up in a world like theirs. Or should I say a prison mentality? You're better off rid of all of us for good."

He leaned over and kissed her forehead. "Get well."

She inhabited the other end of the house; as he crossed the long corridor to Courtney's apartment, he saw a Maserati with a crumpled front fender dig out in a cloud of dust and flying pebbles from the courtyard. He knew it was Ken Kendall's car; he wondered when it had come and why it was leaving so quickly.

He hurried to Courtney's apartment and found the

door locked. He pounded on it. "Courtney! It's me. Let me in, please." But it did not open. He went down the corridor to the door to her study. It too was locked. He returned to the sitting room door and pounded it repeatedly, calling her name. He thought she might be in a deep drugged sleep. He was now certain that Ken Kendall had been doping the women. With what, and how seriously, he could not know. Poison, heavy sedation, God knows what. Flu, hell! Ken moved around. So did Susie, who also did not share their food. He kept pounding on the door, hoping to rouse at the very least an upstairs maid with a key. But no one came.

At last he went downstairs for help. "But Mr. Kenneth and Miss Courtney drove away together some moments ago, sir," he was told. "Miss Courtney said to tell Mrs. Levering they'd be gone for at least a week."

BOOK SEVEN:

The Queen
of the Angels

(1968)

1

HE did not want to go back to Los Angeles. Everything ever said about the place was true, and worse. He had come to think it was like any other center of power in the world, only more gossip-plagued. What happened there also happened in Washington, New York or London, but it was all done with less discretion in the film world, calculated or not. Style and form paid off, not content, even though there had to be a semblance of substance to make the mockery work. They lived by and for images and shadows. He had been able to take the town because he had extracted the secret of how to subvert it. When he began, he could think of it as fun, a piece of cake, as he told Flora Levering. But it had gone stale on him.

Worse, now it was no longer a game.

He drifted among the towns in the great, fertile valley. He found people to talk to in the ham-and-egg lunchrooms and in the cantinas and bottle-beer joints in the Mexican neighborhoods. The familiar background of his boyhood had not changed much. The towns now seemed like paste-up jobs to someone away from them for a long time. Yet he found himself drawn to the prettified surface Americana, the green lawns and the bare-root roses along the driveway, the shiny late-models parked in the open garages, the paperboy throwing news of the latest disaster from southeast Asia from bike to door. He loved the vast fields bursting with crops waiting to be taken in. The great fertile plains, green with carrot tops and celery, with lettuce, sugar beets, onions and alfalfa, reminded him of his father's land. The richness of growing things returned a sense of life to him. He recalled the time when he seriously entertained thoughts of spending his life working land, and he dreamed of new starts. He knew it was impossible now; he'd been corrupted or changed by the city and all the things that had happened to him. Still, tacky towns or not, the fields were part of him forever.

He was the outsider, could not help it, even back on the terrain of his youth. He sat silent with a bunch of itinerant fieldhands in a fly-specked bar, Mexicans, Filipinos, a couple of craggy North Americans, even a black. He knew he had once been a part of their world but wasn't now. They toasted his generosity but the more rounds he bought, the more he made a stranger of himself.

He did not call the house on Mapleton Drive because he knew he was a stranger there too.

He thought about calling Wildoaks, if only to close a part of his life once and for all. He did not.

"Hey, Jan, about your picture—"

"Derek Frye is here and everything's all set. We're actually starting to shoot—"

"I'm backing out."

"You're what?"

"Can't go through with it."

"You're putting me on."

"The money's poisoned, tainted, Jan, it's crooked and if I touch it, I'm no good too and you wouldn't want that, would you?"

"What about my picture?"

He stared at the ceiling in the motel room in Modesto and laughed aloud at his day dreaming. Wonderful Jan, the driven and driving woman who'd risked it all. "You can't do this to me, darling. You're my last hope. These spineless accountants running the industry today want to make me a non-person . . ."

Hold on, Jan.

And what about Pop and his old friends in the Associated Farmers, now grown into the awesome Southern Border Land Development Company, Incorporated?

And Don Pedro?

"The Great Spirit is indifferent," the old Indian used to say. "Your pain is not his pain. You must go your own way to the end."

In the morning, he walked to the road and waited for a ride. Didn't thumb or ask, just stood there. "How far you goin'?" Wherever they went was okay with him.

Late one day he came out of a gas-station toilet. A hopped-up '56 Chevy two-door, the engine popping through mufflerless pipes, drew his attention. Two youths came out beside him as the attendant filled the tank.

"You like cars, sir?"

"How can I not? I'm a Californian. Got headers on this? Supercharger?"

One of the young men looked at him oddly. "You *do* know cars, don't ya? Can we give you a lift?"

"Sure, why not?"

"Don't you want to know where we're heading, sir?"

"Not really. Here, let me." Burt Hammond found a bill and insisted on paying for the fill-up.

"Sir—" one of the lads protested.

"It's my pleasure."

He rode between the two young men. Their heads were thick with too much hair and the driver wore a beard he did not trim, sparse in some places and too thick in others. They went to Fresno State. He asked what they were majoring in. "We're both majoring in Not-Being-Drafted." Laughter filled the car. It turned out they got academic deferments if they took at least ten units a term. The big problem was finding stuff that filled the bill. One of them had been in big trouble last year, flunked two courses. Went to the prof and begged. If he didn't get a pass, it meant getting shot at in the jungles of Vietnam. Lucky for him, the jerk felt sorry and gave him a D.

When Burt Hammond slept, one of the young men said to the other, "Dig the shoes. Pretty expensive-looking."

"What do you think?"

"Jesus, I don't know."

"You scared, man?"

Burt Hammond opened his eyes. Darkness had descended. "Just out of curiosity, where *are* we going?" he mumbled.

"Fresno."

"Do you always talk in your sleep?" one of the lads said amiably.

"Only when I go to Fresno."

At Madera they stopped for hamburgers and beer. He would not let them pay. "My treat, gentlemen," he insisted. The young men were puzzled. Apparently something like this had never been heard of. "Give you something to talk about one day."

In the car again, the young men grew silent. "Tell me about your girls," Burt Hammond said to make talk.

They giggled a lot and laughed about some escapade the year before at Pismo Beach, but without the details the story did not come off as hilariously to Burt Hammond as it did to them. They went from girls to various jobs they had worked at and this got them into what careers they were aiming at, which, it turned out, they were not sure of.

At Herndon they said they had better stop for gas. It was tomb-dark on the road. He tried to sleep again but he was not having any luck. The two young men limited their conversation to small, tense whispers. They finally saw an independent station. There were no lights on but Burt Hammond offered no comment when they pulled up.

"I'll go look for the guy." The driver seemed nervous when he took the key from the dashboard. "Gotta get something from the trunk," he told Burt Hammond without being asked.

"I gotta pee," the other said.

Burt Hammond got out of the car when he became aware that the young men had been away too long. No one was around to pump gas, as he had suspected from the moment they drove in.

He saw a tire-iron flash in the dark and the driver with a long and somewhat clumsy two-by-four held toward him as a weapon. "Well, well, gentlemen, what have we here?"

"Whatever you got in your pocket, throw it on the ground." The voice was harsh but nervous.

Burt Hammond's teeth flashed in the dark. "Gentlemen, I wouldn't. You're not the type."

From behind, lumber slammed into his back, just over the shoulders and below the back of his skull. He fell to the ground and lay there for a second or an infinity—he could not tell which. When he rose the two-by-four rammed him but he was able to deflect its full force, grabbing it as it swept past and pulling it from the hands that held it. He wheeled, seizing at something near him in the dark and found he had a shirt in his grasp. He held on as he was slammed across the shoulder with iron. Shouts filled the air. "I got him! . . . he's on me, hit him, fachrissake, hit him!" He was doing pretty well, Burt thought, when a stillness descended on him.

The noise of the roaring engine woke him, or maybe he wasn't out as much as he thought. He felt so bruised he was not sure he wanted to be awakened. He groaned when he made it to his feet because, he soon observed, they'd belted him pretty good, better than he had taken for a very long time. He rubbed his hand across the soreness at the back of his head. He sat down against the dark filling-station building and rested. When he was able to, he walked out to the road. He held out his thumb to a couple cars but he knew he wouldn't have success, not here, not in the dark, and certainly not looking as battered as he did when the headlights picked him out. He walked down the road for a time until he saw a packing shed that no one seemed to be looking after. He made his way through a wire fence and found a way to get inside. He was sore where he'd been hit, but he liked being inside a shed. It smelled of celery, fresh-cut sweet stalks. He flopped and slept better than he had in years.

The sun was rising high over the horizon before anything on the highway even bothered to slow down to look at him. He had pushed down his hair and done his best to clean up the pants that had got dirtied and tattered in the fighting the night before. A two-ton open truck slowed when the driver saw him alone.

About fourteen fieldhands were standing in the open cargo section. *"Que pasa, hombre?"* one of them called out. What's happening, man?

"I need a ride," Burt Hammond said in Spanish.

"Come on." A hand was held out for him.

The truck started down the road. "You're not Chicano, man." The usual surprise.

"Only by birth. Otherwise, I'm one."

They all laughed. "You speak pretty good for a gringo."

"It's been a long time."

"You going to the mitin?"

"What mitin?"

"Cesar. He's ending his hunger strike. The dead President's brother is going to be there."

To see him, on his own turf, not working the politician's ground carefully prepared by advance men and assistants —what an opportunity. *"Claro,"* Burt Hammond said.

"Viva la Causa," someone cried out.

A platform had been created by pulling up a flatbed truck in front of the screen behind home plate on the baseball diamond in the public park at Delano. The wire chain-link was decorated by rosettes made of bright-colored Kleenex tissues pulled between the openings. The union leader sat slouched in an upholstered chair, gaunt, clearly a sick and wasted man after the long hunger strike.

A priest was offering a benediction in Spanish. Kennedy sat just behond him, next to a lectern.

He looked smaller than ever. Out of place. Dark suit, tie, the points of his collar curled up. Burt Hammond hung back to keep out of the range of the man's gaze, though it seemed as glazed and unfocused as ever. He wondered whether the senator understood a word the priest was saying. "Our brother . . . a life of poverty and devotion . . . love . . . compassion . . . the poor."

Was this the same man he saw when he sat beside Jerry Haggerty? Burt Hammond looked around and was surprised at the absence of press or television people. Surely the ruthless Torquemada would know how to wrangle that? In the process that day in the Federal building, the avenging investigator had not turned out to be as formidable as his reputation. Was the scheming, go-for-the-throat politician as overrated as well?

Burt Hammond grinned, moved closer. Supposed to have the best political advice money could buy. No business here. The senator had been introduced in Spanish and approached the lectern shyly. He seemed a good deal less formidable than the ultimate vengeful animal. Burt did not have to be a professional in politics to see that damned few people at this *mitin* would make it to the polls in June when the primaries to select the party's candidates were to be held. Or in November when the presidential election would take place. What was the guy doing here? His speech, in English, which not everybody crowded around the platform understood, was halting and given in a weak and tentative voice. The crowd grew restless after a minute.

This isn't the same guy I know, Burt thought.

It has to be a cynical posturing. But why would a calculating and active vote-seeker come so far out of the way to a little town in the San Joaquin Valley where he couldn't buy a score of votes at best?

Burt Hammond watched him break a piece of the stale bread the priest had given Cesar, too weak to rise as he took the first solid nourishment in a month.

This man could be President and Jerry Haggerty will end up in jail. And so will I, Burt Hammond thought.

He's not so crafty. Where's the staff? Where for God's sake are the bodyguards? Didn't any of his highly paid people fill him in about what went on in these fields, what had been going on ever since man brought the water to the rich, parched soil? Burt Hammond knew about men who sat astride the land with fear in their hearts and guns in their closets. What kind of ruthless, relentless foe could this be up there?

It came to Burt Hammond: *The guy knows.* My father knew.

The man not only knew, he took the chances his destiny demanded, like one of Don Pedro's Indians, to go with it to the end, whatever and wherever that was. His own father too.

Me also.

What was a millionaire doing in front of a crowd of Mexican fieldworkers, most of whom didn't understand his talk of civil rights and promises of new and better days to come? *No votes here, man.*

Burt Hammond turned and talked to the street fronting the ball park. A local cab was parked at the curb. "You free?"

The cabbie eyed his soiled and bruised clothes suspiciously.

"Take me to L.A. You can run the meter all the way."

"You kidding, Charley?" His eyes moved from the clothes to study the face.

"If I don't come across, you can call the cops."

"Now I know you ain't kidding, you're crazy."

"I'll give you a hundred-buck tip too."

"Hop in," the driver finally said.

2

TWENTY-THREE. This was the number of times they had joined in an enterprise like this. Corcoran and Gildea knew how serious it was, and its implications. Both were graduate lawyers when they joined the Bureau. A phone tap was—or could be—different. Usually there was a court order. A judge was persuaded that the interests of justice or some high national purpose could be served by subverting existing laws and regulations governing the privacy of telephone conversation.

But breaking and entering—that was a different matter. At the beginning, say, the first six times, they had grave misgivings. But Len Corcoran and Hubert Gildea had learned that a cardinal rule of their developing careers was that whatever their superiors ordered was—*ipso facto,* as they used to say in law school—correct. They regarded themselves as surgeons performing a disagreeable but necessary operation. Or soldiers on a search-and-destroy mission they did not relish, or even see the purpose of. They followed orders. No to do so, they knew, was professional suicide.

So instead of brooding they went about their work with a certain bravado and good humor.

A van bearing the insignia of the Pacific Telephone Company came to a stop twenty feet from the driveway two minutes after the station wagon driven by Helen Mendoza with a Mexican-looking old lady sitting beside her turned away onto Mapleton Drive headed for Sunset Boulevard.

"We've got two shots, the best I can figure," Corcoran said, after it turned the corner.

"The service door, I'll bet." Gildea was the lock and key man, one of the best. It was said he could judge a man by the locks he kept on his house.

They walked around the house, equipment dangling from hips and shoulders.

Corcoran and Gildea knew where they had to go, as well as what they would have to do when they got there. They knew that the secretary and the Mexican lady went out every Wednesday afternoon to shop at the big Mercado on East First Street in distant downtown Los Angeles. The maid had a day off. There were no dogs. No mention of cats.

At the kitchen entrance, Gildea tried four of the keys on his big key ring without success. The two men stared darkly at each other at this unexpected turn. "Something's not right here," Gildea said.

"Take it easy." Corcoran smiled easily. "I bet it was the first one. Maybe needs a little graphite."

"I must be getting nervous after all these years," Gildea returned, trying to relax a little.

The next key he put into the door turned the deadbolt easily. A large black cat scampered out the door as they went in. They grinned as he raced toward the rose bushes.

"Entrez-vous, s'il vous plait," Gildea said, bowing and holding his arm in a courtly fashion.

"The Phantom strikes again," Corcoran responded with real admiration, and put a gloved hand on the latch.

They knew the floor plan and where to find the stairs that led to the room they were looking for. Shoulders back, heads high, they walked calmly but briskly, like two men a little late for an important meeting. At the top of the steps, Corcoran paused to catch his breath. "I must be getting old."

"Or fat. Over here." His companion jutted a finger toward the room they were looking for.

The French table with the leather top and the brass trim held a legal pad and a number of neatly stacked folders at one side. Corcoran sat at the desk, pulled a wire-ringed pad and a ballpoint pen from a kit-bag and began to make various notes about the material in front of him. Gildea went to a fireproof file cabinet in one corner of the large room. It was the first time he had seen this one but he knew all about its make and model. He had previously been able to learn it had been purchased from the Ideal Office Furniture Company, and through friends there and elsewhere had ascertained its serial number and hence the combination required to open the safe top-drawer.

Still, one could never be certain; there were always surprises. He put down his equipment, found a notebook in his back pocket and turned its pages until he came to what he wanted. He put the notebook on top of the cabinet, rubbed his palms briskly, interlocked the fingers as if to make them more supple, and went to work.

Corcoran, at the desk, could hear the file open. He turned to wink approval at his companion's skill, only briefly stopping his own work. Gildea, for his part, pulled out the safe drawer and searched among the headings until he came to what he was looking for. He pulled a file, spread it out on top and searched among its pages. When he found what he wanted, he brought it to the French table and put it down in front of Corcoran, who nodded without a word and took it aside for his own purposes.

Back at the file, Gildea closed the top drawer and pulled the second one. "Hey, look at this," he called urgently. When Corcoran joined him, he pointed to bound stacks of fifty- and hundred-dollar bills.

"Better count it."

"Means we've got to come back to check if it moves and where."

"So what? This place is a cinch."

Corcoran pointed to a file. "Wait'll you find out who's been getting helped by our friend." Corcoran's eyes danced merrily. "What'd this guy tell us in that other matter? It fits perfectly. Washington will love us."

"It's a veritable treasure trove." Gildea pronounced the word *ver-it-ahb*.

They worked for more than an hour in silence. The phone did not ring once, which they found interesting. When Corcoran was finished at the desk, he took out silicone-impregnated cloth he carried in a back pocket and went over the desk surfaces carefully. Gildea picked up a stack of hundreds, held them up for an admiring look, kissed them lightly as one might kiss a photo of a lady one had certain fantasies about, and returned it to its place before closing the file, locking it and spinning the wheel that secured it. He too took out his cloth and did some dusting. At the conclusion of their work, each changed places to inspect the other's work before departing. Both satisfied, they went down the stairs and to the kitchen and let themselves out the service entrance. The sun was high in the sky; the house was bathed in a hazy sunlight. There were rose bushes along the driveway; Corcoran liked roses and these were, he thought, admirable ones. They slipped off their gloves as they walked to the telephone truck. They swung into the seat and drove away. "Another day, another job," Gildea said. "Or as we used to say, *'Autre jour, autre fromage.'*" Gildea was proud of his knowledge of French slang. He always managed to let people know that he had been a French major before he decided to go to law school.

3

JANET Morgan did not inquire about Burt Hammond during his absence. Many others did, but of course they did not have their financing completed as she did.

Morgan had other things on her mind. Derek Frye insisted on some changes in the script; technical, he called them. The writer said her former husband was a pompous illiterate with no affection for words. The screenwriter was doing what had to be done.

Pre-production work had been completed. Location had found four splendid sites, outside of Tucson on the road to Tombstone; Bellingham, Washington; Placerville; and a town called Julian in the mountains around San Diego. She and Roseanna Lee were rehearsing their big scenes on a stage on the Samuel Goldwyn lot on Formosa Street. Morgan's instinct had been accurate: the lady was a natural and superb actress.

Trouble had been expected, but none burst open for a time. "I told my old man if he stood in the way, I'd lose him forever," Rosie told her producer and co-star.

When a man in the uniform of a marshal served her with a temporary restraining order of the Superior Court of Los Angeles, Janet Morgan had one thought only. She had to talk right away to Burt Hammond. Where in the devil had he been, come to think of it? Damned inconsiderate of him, all this time being out of touch; the least he could have done was order some flowers when rehearsals began.

She called the private number in the house. The phone number had been changed and there was no referral number. This angered more than distressed her, like a slight directed plainly at her.

She asked Derek to read Rosey with the kid actors who were up for the part, to find out which one would work out best. She got into her car and headed for the house in Holmby Hills.

Helen Mendoza's jaw went slack when she opened the front door and saw Janet Morgan. "All right. Where is he, Helen?" Janet demanded. "I've got to talk to him."

"Upstairs." Helen's voice was small with astonishment. "I think he's still in the shower."

She watched Janet Morgan take the steps of the huge circular staircase two at a time. *How could she have known?* He had not been home a half-hour.

Morgan found Burt Hammond toweling his wet hair. "What're we going to do about this?" She waved the legal document at him like a pennant.

"Hello, Jan. Where've you been keeping yourself?" he greeted her.

She did not understand the grin. "It's that pimp of a husband. Can they do this to me? I mean, actually stop production?"

He took the document from her hand. He let her talk without listening to her as he turned the pages of the court order.

Finally: "Who's this Roseanna Lee?"

"You mean, you never heard of Roseanna Lee? Where've you been living?"

"I've heard of her; I've also heard of Joan Baez, and Diana Ross and the Supremes. I don't know any of these new music people. What's she got to do with the picture?"

"She's playing the other woman. Isn't that a splendid idea?"

"According to this, the lady is under exclusive contract to IMC Records and Brighton Industries. They do not wish her to appear in your film. My hunch is that their lawyers know very well what they're doing. Has she signed such a contract as is described here? If so, you're dead, kid."

Janet Morgan had never thought to look at the contract and he would bet that Roseanna Lee hadn't either. Burt dutifully explained that exclusive-rights contracts were usually carefully drawn, for contingencies just like this. When Janet explained about the husband, their bitter words, he folded the paper and put it into her bag. "You'd better find someone else."

"It's a scam, Burt," Janet pleaded. "They've muscled, hustled and promoted this woman from the first day they found her. Uppers when she was low, downers when she was high, surrounded her with leeches just so she could grind out the dollars for them. She's cleaned herself of dope dependency. Talk to her. You can find an angle."

He tried to be sensible and lawyerlike. Janet Morgan's whole life was always in the project at hand, he knew that. But this was one time he could not help. And he was weary. The long ride down from Delano in a rattling Falcon had not exactly been a delight. They'd even had a flat on the Ridge Route. "I'm dead tired, Jan. Just come back from a long trip."

"You can do anything, Burt," she persisted. "Do it for my sake. She's a great artist and she'll be great in my film."

"What I'd like right now is about five hours sleep."

She took his forearm. "Later, my darling. She's wonderful, we've been rehearsing together, there's no one in the world as right for this part. See her at least. Do it for me."

He had never known her to plead so shamelessly. So he gave in.

Janet Morgan pulled up her car before the Stars Dressing Room building on the Goldwyn Lot. "I'll join you as soon as I can. Hers is the first one on the right as you come in."

The door was ajar so Burt Hammond let himself in when his knocking drew no response. A sitting room with makeup-soiled silk chairs and a mahogany table flecked with cigarette burns led to a smaller room with a hairdresser's chair and a big drier.

Roseanna Lee emerged from a bathroom, her hair turbanned, her body wrapped in a white bathsheet tied over her breasts. She was wiping her face with a handful of tissues.

"Miss Lee?" Burt Hammond said. "I'm Burton Hammond. I'm here to talk to you about your contract with Brighton."

He saw the stare, the rather mysterious smile as he told her why he had come, and he wondered what it was all about. "I used to know you," she said. She came closer, as if to reassure herself, he thought.

"I don't think so, Miss Lee. I wouldn't forget."

Inches from his face, she smiled broadly. "Nose used to be straighter. This—" Her fingers touched the skin at the hairline and felt the scarring Dr. Sanchez had had to leave. They followed the line behind the ear and to his cheek. "They moved the furniture around, huh?"

"Where do you know me from, Miss Lee?"

"Try Miss Ball, Stormy Ball."

He took a moment to put the name in place, a grin growing as he put on the face before him the sweep of the phony lashes and mascara and scarlet lip paint. "You said you were going to be a star!" He took her into his arms suddenly and happily.

"And I thought you liked it down there with those bean-pickers."

"You *made it*," he exclaimed. "You came through! Now I understand about the mask, and why you insisted your name was Stormy Ball."

"Couldn't have jerks come up to a big star one day and say, 'Di'nt I see you wiggle your tits in a strip-joint in El Centro?' could I?"

They kissed. "You're a son of a bitch, you know," she whispered. "I tumbled for you. Remember how you wouldn't take it out in trade? The only man I ever met who did that to me. And that dark bar you took me to where I played the piano?"

They turned to see Janet Morgan framed in the doorway.

"Hi, everybody," she said, unsmiling.

How long had she been standing there?

"I know this guy, Jan," Roseanna said.

"When I was working with the farm workers," Burt Hammond went on.

"I'm touched." Janet Morgan made a labored smile. "Shall I leave while you both recreate that lovely moment?"

Roseanna rushed to her side. "This is the guy you told me about." She turned to Burt Hammond. "Of course! The lady's crazy about you, man."

"I'm crazy about her." Burt Hammond came to Janet Morgan, took her chin firmly in his hand, turned her head and kissed her mouth. "She knows that."

"Yes." she conceded finally. "We're all crazy about each other. But what do you say, we get down to business? What about this damned paper?"

It turned out to be worse than Burt Hammond had anticipated. The record company and Brighton had handled every engagement from the very first, all the television appearances, the dates in Las Vegas, the concerts here and abroad. The relationship was so trusting that she never questioned anything. She had no reason to suspect chicanery of any kind, financial or otherwise. Compared to what she'd been through, Lou Birch, the head of the company, was like a father to her. As for Larry Marshall, she was his whole life, she knew that even when they were hustling her one way or the other, and he was also her husband. He helped her when she was sick, which she used to be a lot, as Jan could tell him. Yes, he hated Jan . . .

"No different from lots of people," Janet Morgan broke in. She was used to that kind of thing. The people who admired her integrity and guts as an actress hated her for the same reasons. She'd had a couple of unfortunate shouting matches with the gentleman, she told Burt. Sorry about that, but what could she do? He'd probably do anything to get back at her. Still, Burt Hammond knew what to do, she insisted, everybody in town said no one had more clout, he could do anything. He had, somehow, to keep Rosey in the film; she was tremendous in it.

"That won't work," Burt Hammond said thoughtfully. "From what you tell me, the guy's so angry at you he'd think that was just another reason to enforce his contract."

"There's always a way, isn't there?" Jan insisted wanly.

"Laymen think so, in any case. Renegotiate, they think. Try it some time when the other party is not interested."

"I see I need you bad again, Mr. Lawyer," Roseanna said. "Just like the last trip."

Suddenly he felt weary; he wondered how he had got to this room. He had committed her for four million. Two women with a lock on him were beautiful and importuning. He'd been away too long, allowed himself a luxury that seemed indefensible now. And what about Susie? Any minute now they'd go after her with a warrant for arrest. And a package would be coming from the old man, a laundry bag.

"I need you too," he heard Janet Morgan plead.

"We'll figure something out."

"Good," Janet said, taking Rosey's hand. "We've got work to do. Say goodbye to the s.o.b., Rosey, and tell him nicely if he tries to make a pass at you he's going to wake up and find your co-star has cut his throat."

"Goodbye, nice man," Roseanna Lee said.

4

THE girl named Lucinda Curtis took her break at three o'clock with the other waitresses. She had short, straight and blondish hair, parted on one side in a somewhat masculine way, but legs splendid in black hose and high heels under the red miniskirt uniform. She sat bent over, forearms on her knees, on a stool in front of her locker, considering various alternatives available to her in Indianapolis for spending her free time before she had to be back at her duties in the cocktail lounge of the Purple Onion.

"Hey, Lucy, wanna come downtown with me?" Cathy Acker called from her locker. "Lookit these here hotpants outfits they got on special at Rosenblatt's. Sixteen-fifty, used to be twenty-nine ninety-five. They're groovy."

Lucinda looked up. Something about Cathy Acker she did not trust. Acker was too spirited about being friendly, always pushing herself. That pose of hers, Lucinda thought, being a little stupid, how clever.

"I think I'll go home and sack out," Lucinda said.

"A movie," Cathy persisted. "They got *Paint Your Wagon* with Clint Eastwood down at the Paramount. How's about that?"

This is going to be the second time I've had to leave a job fast, Lucinda thought. This apple-faced chick is fuzz after me, there is no doubt. "Too much of a rush," she said.

"Then let's go get them hotpants, you'd look super in them," Cathy pressed. "I'll treat you, whadaya say? Lookit how cute they are."

Lucinda took the paper Cathy Acker thrust on her and studied the department store advertisement without much interest. Her eyes fell on a headline next to it:

FBI ISSUES NEW
10-MOST-WANTED LIST

The words blurred before her eyes; she turned quickly to her locker to hide her face. Of course, she thought, *of course!* This babe had to be one of them. She is carrying on about the goddamn ridiculous outfit because she wants to see how I'll handle this. "Not bad," Lucinda heard herself say without turning from the locker door. She felt dizzy as she read the story and pretended to care about "daringly-cut-satin-type shortie-pants with coordinated shirt and belt." Halfway down the story, she read: "Susan-Ann Elizabeth Martin is new to the list issued by authorities today. A graduate student with a fine academic record at the University of California, Martin is the known firebrand leader of a radical group responsible for bombings of public utility structures all over the Far West. The Bureau warns that the Martin woman is probably armed, knowledgeable about explosives and detonators and must be approached as an extremely dangerous individual. Martin faces twenty to forty years upon conviction . . ."

Lucinda Curtis closed her eyes in an attempt to steady herself on the stool. "Whadaya say, Lucy, come on, huh?" Cathy Acker persisted.

Lucinda filled her lungs and forced a smile. "I'm really beat, Cathy. You go. You find anything in my size, get me one too, okay?" she parried.

She watched Cathy leave the dressing room. Playing dumb, Lucinda thought, but doesn't fool me.

Or am I going nuts? Seeing shadows? This shnooky kid, she's one of them? Ridiculous. But you're running scared all the time now. That customer last night who tried to make time with you and kept saying you weren't the girl you pretended to be. "What's an over-achiever like you doing hustling drinks in a cocktail lounge?" he kept saying, "Who you running from, baby?" What about that?

A few minutes later she had Elmer Wright on the phone. "I've got to talk to him."

Elmer Wright knew a tensed, frightened voice when he heard one. "I can't do that. You're hot right now. It could be bad for both of you."

"I can't take it. I'm no good at these games. I jump at shadows. I'm scared."

"They've got to find you first."

"I see them everywhere. I'm cold out here. I want to come home. Let me talk to Burt, he'll understand."

"Hang in there, please," Elmer Wright said. "It won't be long."

"It's already forever, tell him that, will you?" Susie said. She shivered when she hung up the receiver.

5

"GRANDMA-MA is dead. *You* are dead, sister dear."

Courtney Kendall saw the drug-thin apertures burning with cold hatred in her brother's eyes. It had begun when, seeing Burt Hammond walk down the road to the house, Ken deduced a plot. Why was Hammond walking? Why no car?, he ranted. Why had there been no call from the man? Courtney had been deceiving him all this time, he snarled at her; he realized now there was no longer the sacred connection between them . . .

She had never seen him like this.

Courtney tried to persuade her brother she herself had no word of Burt Hammond's arrival. She did not know why he was coming on foot. He had sent Sue-Ann here; he probably wanted to talk to her.

"That girl has been here spying on me for him!" Ken Kendall exploded.

Ken had gone quite mad, Courtney knew, far beyond the wilder eccentricities with which he had once enlivened a dull existence. She did her best to allay his suspicions. The girl, she urged gently, wasn't capable of spying on anyone. He'd talked to Sue-Ann. Did he find anything devious about her? Was anyone more honest with herself and the world about her?

"Then he's coming to take you away!"

That would be even more surprising, she insisted. Still, Ken suspected a trick and he said she was not to talk to Burt Hammond. When she refused to go away with him, he broke into a sweat, his hand began to shake and he screamed at her that she was not to leave this room until he returned. Would she betray him now? Would she promise?

From the window in her apartment she saw Burt Hammond walk to the carriage house. Hopelessness overwhelmed her. Everything had changed in her life for the worse. She went to a mirror and saw herself, her face thinner than she had known it; even her body felt ravaged.

When Ken came back, the sweating on his forehead was gone. The pupils of his eyes were narrower.

"You shooting heroin these days, brother," she said mildly, making no question of it. "How long has it been? For heaven's sake, why?"

That was when he had said, quietly and without emotion: "Grandma-ma is dead. You are dead, sister dear."

"You need help, Kenny," she offered. "Let me help you."

"Yes, I need help, and right now! Those old farts on Montgomery Street have got me all tied up. I need money, Court. You're going to help me get it."

He began to fly on one of his highs again as the shoot spread out into all his blood vessels. He wanted never to see Flora again. He and some friends had a plan that would make millions, big millions, he could be free forever. And he would get it! Flora wouldn't give it to him, so he decided to get what he had coming from the estate in another way. The old lady would sicken and die, how about that? Courtney had had a taste of it, hadn't she? Did she like it? The old bag would die and no one would be the wiser.

"You're a monster."

"Little doses of pretty poison for you, sweetheart sister. Bigger for dear grandma-ma. Slowly. You might say undetectably."

She could not bring herself to hate him. Pity, yes, a terrible vision of what awaited him frightened her, but no loathing for her poor brother for what he had been doing. He read that in her compassion and kept sailing in private clouds ten thousand feet above the world. If Flora was dead, he'd get what was rightfully his. So let her die! She'd *had* her life. As for dear sister, Ken didn't really want her to die, but he was riven with this terrible feeling that they'd drifted apart, and he now realized she could be an enemy too.

She had to get him out of Wildoaks, Courtney saw. Make him think she was doing what he wanted. There was no reasoning with a madman. He spoke of attempted murder as if it were a game of chess. She would play it his way. Leave with him, do what he wanted where she could, raise the money he needed, but he must go from here.

That was when she left word for Flora that she would be gone for a week. She hoped Burt would stay away from the place she called home not for a week but forever. Even though she loved him, Wildoaks was noxious. Burt would kill if he found out what was going on. She would do what she had to do and come back. Ma-ma couldn't take it; father killed himself when it proved to be too much for him. Kenny lived under a death sentence, too. But Flora Levering had endured. And Courtney Kendall would endure, and so would the unborn child within her only she knew of.

6

CAPITOL had its circle; Transamerica, its pyramid needle; Universal, it's black tower; and Brighton, the parent of IMC Records, its pinkish not-quite-ellipse, twenty stories astride two domed edifices over a vast plaza, which is how it came to be called Lou Birch's erection.

Phallic or not, the executive offices were like executive offices all over the world. The floors were heavily carpeted, the walls richly paneled, the views spectacular, the desks burnished and the language tough.

"I don't see what we've got to talk about," Lou Birch said when Burt Hammond called. "I've got a lawyer for that stuff."

"I'm not coming as a lawyer, sir," Burt offered gently.

"Then you've got no reason to come over, Mr. Hammond." They had never met, but Birch had heard of his caller, knew of the money he could call on, and respect flowed from that.

"I'm a fair man and never ask for anything that isn't fair. I believe I can show you how this thing can be settled fairly."

Lou Birch finally acceded. He called Ted Ebenstein, head of the law firm that represented the corporation. "You made a mistake," Ebenstein declared primly. "I think you ought to call back and cancel. You don't deal with a man like that." But Lou Birch did not follow that advice. Instead he called Larry Marshall.

Burt Hammond was late. He wore suntans and a zippered jacket; his hair was tousled after a drive with the top down; he carried no case or papers.

"Let me tell you what I have," Burt Hammond began. He drew a narrative that caused Ted Ebenstein to stare first at Birch and then at Marshall. The company's chief counsel had obviously never been apprised of certain facts involved in the contract with Roseanna Lee. Burt reminded them of the state of affairs at the time the contract was drawn, the physical condition of Miss Lee, the assurances that were made, the pressures that had been applied when the young lady could be described as hardly capable of being in an equitable bargaining position.

Larry Marshall broke in heatedly. "That's a lot of crap! I sold her to Lou when she was nobody and going nowhere."

Lou Birch raised a hand to stop him and turned to their visitor. "You're ready to go to court to show the contract was based on fraud and deception, Mr. Hammond?"

"I have no wish to hurt your company in the slightest," Burt Hammond assured him. "You've got something I want, I've got something you want. I'd like to deal."

"You've got nothing we want, sir," Ted Ebenstein announced coldly. "That contract will stand up in court."

"Mr. Ebenstein, have you been told about Brenda Moore?" Burt asked amiably.

"Who is Brenda Moore?" Ebenstein asked.

"She's a stupid, erratic bitch," Larry Marshall exclaimed. "A liar, a would-be actress."

"Why waste time with what's done?" Burt Hammond turned to Lou Birch as if they were alone in the room. "I'm here to help some friends I like very much make a picture I've got four million in, and more to come, I'll bet. I'm not here to destroy or to hurt. What good purpose would be served to break a relationship that's been so profitable for you and Miss Lee? I want your help and I believe, Mr. Birch, I've got very special help to give you in return."

Lou Birch rose from behind his desk to lay a hand on Larry Marshall. "I'll talk alone to Mr. Hammond, Larry. Thank you, Ted, for coming."

The room was hushed when Lou Birch returned alone. "You smoke cigars? I've got some Upmann Havanas I bring back from England."

"Thanks, an Upmann would be wasted on me."

"Let me waste one on you," Birch went on. "I like you. I believe you. My kind of man. Doesn't want to fight, wants to trade, right?"

Burt took Birch's cigar, put it into his mouth and let the older gentleman place a big flame to it. The tobacco turned out to have a sweet and not entirely unfavorable taste.

"What've you got to give *me* that's so special, Burt?"

"Roseanna Lee, for starters."

He chuckled. "Whom I've already got."

"But could lose. Which we both don't want to happen."

"What else you got for me?"

"Burton Z Hammond."

"We've done all right here so far without Burton Z Hammond." A cloud of smoke wafted toward him. "By the way, what's the Z stand for?"

"Nothing. Everything. Zero or zillion. Whatever you want."

"Or zapped to the ass with mobsters and a corrupt pension fund?"

"You believe everything you hear, Lou?"

"What interests me is the clout. Crooked guys don't operate in the open, and everything's up front with you. How do you manage it?"

"Clout's what I want to talk to you about, Lou. Just like I know everything that happened with Roseanna Lee from the minute you people took her out of that drunk tank. I've learned that Brighton Industries, Limited, wants to expand its show-business operations. It has eyes to go into the American television market."

Lou Birch grinned. "We've been trying to keep it a secret."

"There are no secrets in this town. Only a few confidences shakily maintained."

"You talked to Ike Ash of Trans-Continent?"

"Never met the gentleman."

"Then how do you know?"

Burt Hammond shrugged noncommittally. "Let's just

279

say I always do my homework. I could help you there, Lou."

Lou Birch stared at him. Hammond knew the story, all right, though the negotiators on both sides had been sworn to secrecy. Premature word of the sale could damage trading in Trans-Continent Studio stock and cause worry among elements within Brighton. Yet this man had found out. Remarkable. The important thing that hit Lou Birch was that Burt Hammond might be just the man to break the logjam that had developed. Despite a substantial nine-digit offer, the negotiating lawyers had got themselves tangled in so much legal-detail haggling that the deal went dead. When Lou Birch himself got into it with the legendary Ike Ash, Trans-Continent's head, they'd both lost their tempers. Ugly things were said, bitter words snapped at each other, and Lou Birch was now of the opinion that Ike wouldn't throw him a bone if he were starving.

"Get me Ike Ash's signature and you've got Roseanna Lee for your picture," Lou Birch concluded. "That a deal?"

"Not quite, Lou."

Lou Birch's eyes widened with surprise. "You *can't* get it?"

"I didn't say that. In return I'll need a personal favor over and beyond Miss Lee's services, Lou."

Push had met shove. He realized Burt Hammond knew how badly he wanted those films. "What kind of favor?" he asked warily.

"One of your foreign accounts. A bank in the Isle of Man, better if you do business in Nassau or the Bahamas. Just you and me. No one on my side has to know."

Lou Birch stared at him glumly. "We're multinational, all right. Our money comes and goes through a dozen countries. But I don't like to do that on a personal basis and never have."

"And I'd never ask for myself. There are friends I can't turn down."

Lou Birch stared dead ahead for a long time. "I can see you're a good man to have on your side," he offered at length, "but what the hell's that got to do with me?"

"We all need friends."

"I've got all I need."

"But you didn't have Ike Ash until I got in there. One of these days I won't be able to turn you down, either."

Lou Birch looked at his cigar. It had gone dead. He searched for a match until he saw a flame held out to him. He found Burt Hammond's eyes as he puffed the tobacco to life again.

"Your friends are lucky, knowing a guy like you," he said.

7

"I want to take a long trip in it," declared the girl named Lucinda Curtis, looking at the battered little car. They were on a wind-driven used-car lot, and the salesman watched the lady, collar pulled to her chin, wool hat down to her eyebrows, circle the Volkswagen.

"The body needs work, but it's mechanically okay," the salesman said.

"I smelled gas when I drove it. What's that from?"

"Fuel line. These things always smell a little. Means nothing."

Lucinda pulled at the door on the driver's side. It failed to open. The salesman told her it had been "broadsided a little," which was why they could let her have it at the price. But it was in fine shape mechanically except for that fuel line, which he'd fix. He was surprised at all the cash she pulled out of her purse; for a moment Lucinda was afraid that he might do something, like call the police. But cash soon seemed to have overwhelmed doubt.

Still, Sue-Ann Martin did not leave Indianapolis at once. She read the *Star*, looking for her name as usual. When she did not see it, she grew more frightened as one is terrified by an unseen enemy whose presence is certain. The state was up for grabs by the Democratic presidential hopefuls, so they were hustling votes. Robert Kennedy was coming to town after an afternoon speech in Muncie that day, it said. Where was he talking? In the ghetto. She had the night off anyway. She felt comfortable among the blacks, more protected. She'd find a good rib place, maybe an understanding brother who'd know where to

281

connect with a lid, that would be nice, long time no toke, she smiled to herself. *This respectable life will be the death of me yet. . . .*

She was working on a second bottle of Schlitz, sharing a booth with two dudes and their ladies with naturals high enough to get lost in, when someone burst in the door, gasping:

"They killed the Reverend Martin Luther King in Memphis!"

Bantering and laughing inside the restaurant died instantly. "Turn on the radio!" someone called out. Someone else seized the forearm of the bearer of the news. *"Who* killed him? Who?"

The radio sprang to life and the news was there for all of them to hear in full detail. Men wept. Women wailed and embraced. Someone threw a beer bottle at the wall. The announcer said there were riots in some cities and urged the people in Indianapolis to stay in their homes. Police were alerted for trouble in the ghetto.

Trouble? She went out to the street. A chill, moaning April wind slammed across the decrepit buildings. From the next block she heard the shouts and happy cries of the festive political rally. A brassy group of musicians was playing "Happy Days Are Here Again." She realized the people in the meeting had not heard the news.

She pushed forward among them until she was close to the flatbed truck in a parking lot under a stand of dust- and smoke-blown oaks whose branches were being whipped by the wind. Spotlights were aimed on the truck and weren't doing what they should do. She saw Robert Kennedy in a black overcoat mount the truck gracefully, his face pale and drawn and she told herself, *he* knows, what's the damned fool doing up there in front of all these black faces?

"I have bad news for you," he said, and the amplifiers howled a little so he moved his mouth back from the microphone. "For all of our fellow citizens, and people who love peace all over the world . . ." he went on, and then told them of the murder that night of Martin Luther King.

A wail of woe such as she had never heard burst from the crowd around her. The sound of sobs and protests of disbelief filled the air; no one moved. The black-coated figure held up his hands. Some of his words were lost but she heard others: ". . . In this difficult day, in this difficult day for the United States, it is perhaps well to ask what kind of nation we are and what direction we want to move in . . ."

The police had warned of riots on the radio, but the crowd was quiet and listened and wept as the man in the spotlight told of the murder of a member of his family, and asked for compassion and love and spoke of pain falling on the heart until in despair and against one's will wisdom comes from God's grace. She found herself weeping. She wasn't Lucinda Curtis, she was Susan-Ann Elizabeth Martin and she was going home, California, maybe even to work again for the mountain, California, where she would no longer lie about anything, she would call Burt and tell him. If they were after her, so be it, she wasn't going to be afraid again, ever, not after tonight, not after she heard the man's plea to tame our savageness and to make gentle the life of this world. Maybe she was crazy thinking this could happen, maybe the guy up there on the buckboard truck was crazy for thinking the same thing, but who could be afraid if he was not afraid, and who cared what was waiting out there at the end of the road? She felt at peace with herself again, for she was Susie Martin once more, not a mole sentenced to live in the dark.

In the morning Burt reached her at the number she had left with Elmer Wright. She told him about how she had come to feel after hearing Robert Kennedy, after the murder of Martin Luther King.

Burt Hammond remembered not the public man but the gentle, uneasy one among the work- and sun-strained faces in Delano. "Nevertheless, you'd better watch out," he urged automatically.

"Someone's saying the same thing about you right now. He's you, Burt, divided, like you. All contradictions, yet straight as a redwood. Don't fight me, I'm coming home. I'll see you in about three days."

Outside, the gale winds of the previous night had not abated. It began to rain, a cold, driving rain. The battered VW's heater was in excellent condition and the car itself ran beautifully across the sunless plain, and she did not always smell the gas. The battered door sealed everything inside nice and tight. She felt good, as good as she had felt since she had left the beautiful, troubled mountain.

Susan-Ann Elizabeth Martin and her whereabouts were

the concern of other people not far from where she was headed. "That's all they keep asking Everett about," Hilary Wilson Pierce assured Ellis Griswold. "Where's that girl? Where'd she go?"

Marriage to a husband of notable puissance and staying powers agreed with Hilary Wilson Pierce. They were talking in the guest house in Bel-Air which Sobordco maintained for visiting top executives and for those important personages it wished to impress. Four master-bedroom suites on the twelfth fairway of the golf course and a small but competent staff. Griswold graciously gave it to the newlyweds for a few weeks. The possibility of a payoff scandal over the Miami convention quarter-million depressed him, especially with the temporary closing down of the Thunder Mountain project on which he had placed hopes for tax-advantage and not-too-distant profits. He had the usual gripes about Washington and the uncertain behavior of the money market, but seemed less able to accept them than he had in the past.

"They'll find the girl," she said. "You know of course who they're really hot to connect her to."

"He's too tricky for that, I'm afraid," Griswold said disconsolately.

"It's Burton's special gift. Could be his undoing."

"Did the girl blow up that tower, that's the question." Ellis Griswold filled the air with a groan as he shifted his position. "I mean, do you think the charge can be made to stick?"

"They'll get him, the way Washington wants him."

"God knows what he'll say to protect himself," Griswold muttered. "About the campaign money, about all our little slush funds—offense the best defense, you know how it works."

"We'd better prepare for that, Ellis." Hilary Wilson shuddered a little. They *had* gone a bit far. Had not checked with the lawyers; this wasn't anything they would recommend, she and Ellis knew that, or approve, or even countenance. It was a risk she had had to take.

She came up to where Ellis Griswold sat. "You know who'd know how to get rid of him. Our big investor in San Francisco."

Ellis Griswold stared at her glumly. "Who knows what goes on between those two?"

"Haggerty needs us," she broke in. "Whenever he's in

trouble he points to us to prove his respectability. Go see him, Ellis. He has the right connections."

"Think it might work?"

"Our trouble can be his trouble. He has to be shown the man's a danger to the fund and to him personally. He'll know what to do. Make our proposition irresistible."

They heard the front door open. Everett Alan Pierce came in beaming and happy after exertions on the fairways and greens. "Hi, Mr. Griswold." He rushed to his wife's side and planted a kiss on her upturned mouth. "Would you believe I birdied the seventh and shot three pars in a row?"

"You're a marvel, darling," his bride said.

"Everything okay, Mr. Griswold?" Everett asked cheerily.

"Hunky-dory," the old man grumbled.

"See you soon, sweetheart." He winked flirtatiously at Hilary and grinned a little shyly at Griswold's stare. "I'm going to take a sauna and a shower, honey. Don't keep me waiting."

"Yes, darling," she said.

Silence descended on the room when they were alone again. "Is all that for real?" Griswold muttered sourly.

There was no hesitancy or apology in Hilary Pierce's reply. "He loves me, he loves this life I give him, he loves Sobordco."

"He's so damned young." Griswold got to his feet to leave.

"Isn't that wonderful? Young enough to be thrilled with life."

"Don't you mind when people stare?"

"Lots of men prefer girls to women; what's wrong with a woman adoring boys? No over-thirty hangups, no too-late-to-cure neuroses. Anxious to learn to do things *your* way. Smooth-chested, and hard, Ellis, hard in every way. And they can even be tough because they know they've got a lot to lose." She wondered if the old man connected any of this to another young man in another world. "And, don't forget, he's my husband. We're safe."

"I'm scared of that other guy, Hilary." He made the connection, all right.

"Want to know the truth?" She opened the door for her guest. His driver sprang to life and hurried from the car to escort Griswold. "I am too. Go to San Francisco. It's worth whatever it'll cost, Ellis," she said.

8

HE saw that Don Faversham had a little bandage just below the left eyebrow when he sat down across from him at Le Printemps. "Your fault, my liege," he responded to Burt Hammond's question. "Some guy downtown asked about you and I didn't like his tone of voice." He declined to tell Burt Hammond what had provoked him. Burt regarded him with a new sympathy. *He must now know for certain what once he could not bring himself to believe. Same as with me. He'll stay. However, in the future we will both be quick to anger and violence.*

Faversham got down to business as if to be done with it. He reported that, despite all the leverage he had been able to apply, Ike Ash at Trans-Continent refused a meeting if it had anything to do with Lou Birch and Brighton. At first, Ash had offered no excuse but later begged off on account of the press of studio business: "The backlot unions and the drivers want a lot more money and my people are involved in some hard bargaining."

There was other news. The fellow from the FBI wanted him to call as soon as possible. Burt Hammond showed no interest. "See how this grabs you, milord," Faversham went on. "They're shooting around Roseanna Lee. The lady didn't show up yesterday. If she's not on the set tomorrow they have to close down production."

"Know where she is?"

"Of course."

"So what are we waiting for?"

"Not we. You. She wants to talk to you. How do you think I found out where she's staying?"

He found her in one of the top-floor suites in the new section of the Beverly Wilshire. A willowy brunette in skintight jeans opened the door. "Where is she?" he asked.

He found Roseanna Lee in panties and bra sitting on crossed legs atop an unmade bed. The nightstand held a half-filled bathroom glass; the ice-cube told him all he needed to know.

"I stink as an actress," she greeted him. "I'm no good. I know it. You should see what I look like up there on the screen. Back to the plush toilets, Rosey." She reached out for the glass, but he got there before her.

"Who's this?" He jutted a finger toward the glued-on pants.

"My chum Brenda. Say hello to Brenda."

"I've heard about Brenda, Rosey. Come with me, Brenda." He took Brenda's forearm in a steel grip and brought her out to the middle of the sitting room. "Tell me everything," he ordered.

"Called me. What could I do?" She had tried to talk Rosey out of walking off the picture. Couldn't. She'd also tried to talk Rosey out of roller-coasting with uppers and downers again. Couldn't there, either. The lady was upset, suicidal, scared of the future, she wanted something for the nerves, the old story. Wanted to talk to him, the only man who had ever really cared for her. She'd come through for her friend, hadn't she, through Don Faversham?

He looked past her to the bedroom. Rosey had fallen down in the tangle of sheets and blankets. He saw Brenda's jacket on a chair, took it and pushed it against her.

"I'm not bad," Brenda Moore pleaded. "I called you, didn't I?"

"You're not bad, Brenda." Gently he escorted her to the door. "You're just no good for her."

He had her out the door while she was still trying to frame an apologia.

He found Rosey in a drugged, restless sleep; he studied her for a moment. Her eyes opened; it was as if she had not seen him before. She closed them; she buried her head in a pillow. "I'm no good," she wailed softly.

He took her into his arms. "You're as good in that film as you can be, Rosey. Which is very damned good."

"I failed again."

"What the hell? We all keep failing. So you start all over again. Rosey, can I bring you back?"

"Please."

He carried her to the shower, pressed her body against the wall to keep it upright and turned on the cold, full force. She screamed protest, almost drowning in all the water pouring torrentially over her head. When he was through, she looked awakened and returned to a world she had drifted from.

He brought her gleaming pale-brown body to the bed. He stood over it; she was like a magnificent carving, the handsomely curved thighs, the faint hint of a rounded belly, the firm breasts. He found a towel and tamped her dampness with it, softly, tentatively. She shivered a little, from the cold, he thought. Her lips trembled, trying to form words which she could not utter. He thought about taking her into his arms but not like this, not at a disadvantaged moment. He satisfied himself with a kiss on her cheek and brought the towel to her head to dry her silken hair. He did what he could to smooth the damp sheets and pulled a blanket to her neck.

"He watched her eyes open. Know something? That lawyer in that shithouse town, I fell in love with him."

"And I've never forgotten that magic afternoon."

"You never even made a pass," she teased with a smile. "You turned me down cold."

"Oh, I'm a respecter of women, all right, a joy to the sex, a treasure, a stupid asshole."

"Was I that pathetic then?"

"I know this—I never forgot you."

"A busted stripper working a toilet who didn't even tell you her name?"

"An artist who sent shivers up my spine when she began to make her music, Miss Stormy Ball."

"You're the only dude *ever* turned me down. You and my old man, that is, but husbands don't count, right? With you I came to understand there was finding one man who listened to me, who heard, who cared and didn't want nothing in return. Know what it was like until you came into my life? Men in the dark with coats over their laps, never looking at my face. Guys passing a spaced-out bundle that happened to be my body from one to the other, slamming, sticking things or parts of them into it, smearing, biting, shoving, chewing, and sometimes hitting and throwing the garbage into the nearest can and running like hell to get away from it and themselves. Can you wonder that I came to hate guys? What you showed me didn't reach me all at once. There's no miracles in Rosey Lee's life, never were."

A silence loomed between them, so high they avoided eah other's eyes.

288

"Morgan kind of loves you," Roseanna Lee said, as if to acknowledge that the pause had become an embarrassment.

"And I kind of love her. We know it isn't a hell of a lot, but that's all right with both of us."

"You belong somewhere else?"

He nodded ruefully. "I run a very complicated love life."

"Not free?"

"Oh, yes, very free. That's what makes it so complicated."

She sat up, pushing the blanket away. She shook her head and pulled back her shoulders. "Hooray. We can ball and hurt nobody!"

He took her outstretched hands to him. "We could hurt *you*."

"Me?" She laughed uproariously. "Didn't you understand what I've been saying? You're the last man I remember wanting to make love to for the pure fucking pleasure of fucking, and that was five hundred thousand million years ago. How could you hurt me?"

"I'm afraid love can always find a way."

"I'm not afraid. I want the love you've got for me, I want to give you mine. As long as I'm not taking anything from Jan, I don't care about love eternal. I want you now. I want to erase all the lousy hate-fuckers in between. I want to prove that a dream comes true once in a while and things work out good." She was naked on top of the bed, on her knees and this time her arms encircled him as she fell over him. "I'm taking you, baby." He felt her lips on his and she was all over him and he did not fight her anymore.

It was dark when she opened her eyes. She saw him staring, gave him a small, deliberate smile and moved closer to him inside the sheet. "Tell me what you're thinking," she said.

"One hundred twelve thousand dollars a day. That's the overhead on the picture, hot or cold."

"Creep." She moved closer still and let her hand fall on his chest.

"That doesn't include a lot of other charges, Rosey. In pictures if you stop to sneeze the costs are astronomical."

"I saw myself in the dailies. I'm terrible."

"What's Derek Frye say? Janet?"

289

"That I'm nuts. They think I'm okay." She studied his face. "They think I'm good."

"I'll bet you are. That isn't you up there, it's another you. That's hard to take. You won't be the first one it's happened to." He took her hand. "Call Jan and tell her you'll come to work tomorrow."

"Is that why you came here, to get me back on the picture?"

"Of course." He turnèd and put his mouth next to hers. "That doesn't mean everything I told you wasn't true."

She lifted herself to get at the telephone. "What do I tell Jan?"

"The truth. But she won't even think about us until later. She wants to get her film made."

"You'll stay the night if I call her?"

"Wouldn't think of going. One hundred twelve thousand bucks. I don't leave until the studio car picks you up tomorrow morning."

In the darkened room he could see the light in her eyes dance. "And I thought it was love," she said.

9

HE was in his dressing room after a shower the next morning when Helen Mendoza came in, plainly irritated. "Next time I wish you'd be more careful."

He had not picked out his trousers; he turned to her naked but for briefs. "What're you talking about?"

She fled to wait more discreetly in his office-study, beside the Louis XV table. "I think it's outrageous. He could be killed dead. Mamacita's in tears. We don't know where he is."

"Helen, I still don't know what the hell this is all about." He pulled the chair and sat down to his work.

"Alejandro el Grande, mama's cat, *my* cat, *the* cat, he's gone, you let him out. He's a coward at heart, scared to death. We can't find him anywhere. He's probably lying dead somewhere on Sunset Boulevard this very minute."

"I didn't let any cat out," Burt said. "And certainly not Alejandro. I know his bad habits."

"But you did," she insisted. "When you came by yesterday afternoon, when we were at the market."

He looked up slowly from the pad he was writing on.

"We made sure he was in the house when we left," Helen went on. "When we came back he was gone. You must have let him out when you opened the door. No one else was here."

"I wasn't here yesterday afternoon."

"Then who could've let him out?"

Burt dropped his pen to the table. "Yes, indeed, who?" He got to his feet. "Go find el Gato. But first call that guy from the FBI and tell him I'm here. Any time he wants to stop by."

They had found the big, lovely cat high on a limb of a poplar near the garden wall by the time Shockley rang the bell. The FBI agent wasted no time. "I've got some questions for you," he announced.

Burt Hammond offered him a chair but the man was too agitated and impatient. There had been another bombing in Oregon and they were anxious to know if there might be any connection with what Shockley now called "the Bartlett gang." The agent made no effort to hide his irritation. Everything was coming to a boil; if the counselor chose to play things his way, it was going to be his problem, not theirs. They were plainly fed up, who did he think he was, did he know who he was up against, did he think they were born yesterday?

"I'm sure of one thing," Burt Hammond said, as quietly as he could. "You people sure as hell don't know cats. At least, not *my* cat. Come on over here, please, Mr. Shockley."

He brought the agent to his file.

"Naturally they'd wear gloves." He pulled a drawer lined with currency. "In dealing with a sophisticated adversary the rule is, be just as sophisticated. Believe me, sir, that's what I've done here."

"What're you talking about?" Shockley demanded with mounting irritability.

"Breaking and entering, sir. A very grave offense in any criminal code and one which isn't available to any-

291

one by court order, like, say, phone-tapping. Do I make myself clear? I don't say you had anything to do with it, Mr. Shockley, you may not even know it was ordered, but you might tell them to be more careful next time. While the gentlemen were letting themselves illegally into these premises yesterday afternoon they didn't see my cat. He's always trying to get out and he did just that when they broke in. You might tell the people in your office about their goof. If they've a mind to bring me to court, I'd welcome it."

All the muscles in Shockley's face went rigid. Suddenly he seemed human, real. His dull eyes revealed what bureaucratic manners could no longer hide: that he could easily be an unwitting part of so gross a crime. The awesome Federal Bureau of Investigation stooping to common criminality. Breaking and entering. Burglarizing.

"Tell your people I know what they did," Burt Hammond went on. "I've got proof positive. I really would welcome a court test. Is there anything else you wanted to tell me, sir?"

It took a moment for his visitor to compose himself and recover his poise. He kept shaking his head as if going over a number of things he had wanted to take up and was now, one by one, deciding against. He got to his feet. "I don't like you," Shockley said through unmoving lips.

"That makes us even, sir."

"No, Hammond. I can do something about it. You can't."

"You can but you won't, Mr. Shockley. Because I caught you guys playing dirty again."

"We'll see about that. Maybe Susan Martin will change matters for everybody. Goodbye."

Burt watched a smug grin grow more smug. "What about my client?"

"You mean to tell me you're not in touch with her, counselor? Tsk-tsk."

He did not tell Shockley she had said a week ago she was on her way and she had not yet shown up. "I have a right to ask and you are obliged to tell me: Do you have my client under arrest?"

"Tell you what, counselor. Why don't you take it up with the Supreme Court? If it's okay with them, we'll give you an answer." Shockley pulled open the door and raced down the steps as fast as he could.

* * *

Shockley knew more than he was telling.

TWO PERISH IN FIERY CRASH was the headline in the Socorro, New Mexico, *Daily News,* and even there it rated only a paragraph or two on page three.

VAUGHAN—An automobile fire on the road from here to Belen was said by state highway officials to have caused the deaths of two people and a pet dog today. A passing motorist told police he saw the car some fifty yards ahead of him burst into flames while cruising at seventy miles an hour. The passenger was able to open his door but was killed when he fell to the road. The woman driver, unable to open her door, died when the flaming car struck a bridge abutment at high speed. Names of the dead are being withheld until notification of families, the Highway Patrol said.

The man's name was Harold R. Schmidt, known as Curly, a University of Texas dropout with a minor police record. The driver was first identified by papers on her person as Lucinda Curtis. It turned out that there was no such address in Indianapolis as the dead woman's license said. Police officials followed their usual procedure and in good time a card was red-flagged at the new J. Edgar Hoover Building in Washington, D.C.

A phone call found local officials very obliging. For reasons of national security, nothing more was to be said; the matter was closed. Routinely, it was to be said, if there were any questions, the bodies had been shipped to the families.

The FBI checked out this Harold R. Schmidt. It was satisfied that the young man was but merely hitchhiking to Albuquerque with his dog, a Brittany spaniel named Sam. It was established that he had been seen in Amarillo the day before seeking to get a ride west. The driver, Susan-Ann Elizabeth Martin, alias Lucinda Curtis, had purchased the car for cash from Happy Jack Motors in Indianapolis. She had in her possession a small but significant amount of marijuana and the sum of four hundred and twenty-six dollars in cash. She had picked up the Schmidt man at a Texaco station in Vaughan, New Mexico, at eleven fifteen in the morning of the same day. The door on the driver's side was jammed from a previous accident. The salesman at Happy Jack Motors said the lady had been warned about it. The investigating agent was convinced that Schmidt had no connection with the political activities of the deceased and that the fire and the collision were in fact accidental and wholly unconnected to any previous activities of the Martin woman. It recommended a careful record be maintained because "activists of this stripe are always ready to impute sinister purposes to our activities and to look for far-fetched conspiratorial designs in what has been established as pure accident."

It was decided, on a higher level, not to reveal at once that full identification of the deceased had been positively confirmed, but to proceed as if this phase of the investigation had not yet been settled. This order was signed by the number-two man in Washington.

10

BURT Hammond sat down in the big car before Ike Ash's desk and waited for the man behind it to finish shouting into his telephone. It was an office somewhat smaller than a ballroom, furnished in a high style that had gone out of fashion at least ten years ago.

The name he had heard of, but he had never met the legendary studio chief until he was let into this office while Ike Ash was engaged on the telephone. It had to be worked this way because Ike Ash had left explicit word he did not wish to talk to Burton Hammond. However, a liberal application of cash by Don Faversham had opened doors to the inner sanctum.

Ike Ash stared at his unscheduled caller with a calm reserved for heavenly visitations. "If he doesn't come across, tell the son of a bitch he'll never work in this town again!" He slammed down the phone. "Who the hell are *you?*" he snapped at his visitor in a hoarse voice.

"My name's Burt Hammond. I'm here to give you something you want for something I need."

A scowl shadowed the Ash face. "I told your stooge, Faversham. I don't deal with Lou Birch or anyone connected with Lou Birch."

Burt Hammond forced a smile, determined to reject insult or provocation. He had prepared himself well. Ash was up to his ears in trouble; his pictures were losing money; Wall Street was predicting the end of his long reign at this studio. But the man and his family owned twenty-two percent of the company stock, and he was not of a mind to be dislodged, despite bad pictures, low grosses and a series of affairs with minor European so-called actresses without charm or beauty or, most sadly, talent.

Ike Ash, Burt Hammond had assessed, was one of those men determined to destroy what had taken them years to build. Thus, he did not care that the sale of the backlog could strengthen his personal position in his company and with its financial masters in New York. Lou Birch had personally insulted him and that was it. If Brighton offered him a billion dollars, he said, he would tell the creep to take his money and stick it.

"And as for you, young man," he concluded, "I've heard about you. I'm going to leave word at the gate if you ever show your face at my studio to throw your ass across the boulevard, you got that? I grew up in New York, I knew the strong-arms and *gumbahs* before you were born. Charley Lucky, Jimmy Blue Eyes, Frank Costello, Joe Adonis, I played poker with all those creeps, and I learned one lesson from them—hoods are no good, keep away from them, they never do one favor without wanting ten in return—and that goes for you, buster." He got to his feet. "Now I'll thank you to get the fuck out of my office."

Burt Hammond remained seated. "Sir, I am prepared to give you a blank check for those films."

"Not if you gave me Fort Knox."

"And to help you personally in any way you need."

Ike Ash's face turned crimson. He seemed unable to speak after this impertinence. *"You* help *me?* You shyster! You mouthpiece for crooks and hoodlums! I've chewed up and spit out shitpot lawyers like you by the dozen."

"Yes, sir, help you," Burt repeated calmly. "I can do that. What you've said here I don't take as anything personal, Mr. Ash. It's your style and, to tell you the truth, I like it. But you've got bad labor trouble on the backlot, and I could really help you there."

Ike Ash wheeled and walked to a wall to a fixture which contained a row of billiard cues. He had once fancied himself a world-class billiard player and the cues were a sign of his skill. He chose one and held it out threateningly. "You see this? I can brain you. And get away with it." He waved the fat end of the stick at an unflinching Burt Hammond.

Burt Hammond got slowly to his feet. "You really are the last of the red-hot moguls," he declared calmly. "I can't tell you how much I've enjoyed this meeting. It's been an experience I never thought I'd have. Too bad you're not interested in dealing with someone who loves your style and tried to copy it. You're a direct man, so I thought you and I could meet on a common ground. You've got something I need, I've got something that could save your ass on Wall Street, a strike settlement. But what do I get? Dialogue from your old gangster pictures. That dates you, this meeting dates you, your ego dates you, you're finished, Mr. Ash, gone with the wind that blew away Harry Cohn and Louie Mayer and Darryl Zanuck —too bad, because I have a soft spot for survivors and wanted to be on your side."

"I hate lawyers." Ike Ash fell into the huge chair behind his desk and swiveled it to face the wall and give the back of the throne to Burt Hammond. He wheeled around again. "I especially hate mealy-mouthed, double-talking, self-serving shysters."

"I've never encountered one, so I don't know what you're talking about, Mr. Ash. I know this. A good lawyer keeps his personal feelings from getting in the way of his better judgment. I have a hunch businessmen know how that works too."

Ash lifted himself from the chair. "Why, you bum! Who you think you're instructing?" He waved a finger at his visitor. "I took this company from nothing to—"

"Save it, Mr. Ash," Burt Hammond broke in. "I know you're a doer. In your time, among the greatest. But the world's changing fast, the music, the clothes, the language, the morality, and no one gives a shit what happened in the past, which is to say ten years ago. Which is to say, who and what you went when you built this company. I'm talking here and now. I'm talking big money for your company. Sure, I need what I've come for. So, goddamnit, do you. But I'm not going to suck after your favor, I won't bend the knee, snivel like some cheapie producer who needs your help. I'll manage, but you're headed for the dump. You want to go that route—goodbye, sir." He hesitated a moment, watched Ash fall back into his chair and close his eyes.

Burt Hammond felt the silence as he walked out the door of the oak-paneled office. He would not have been surprised to have been struck down from behind by the billiard cue. He made his way past a phalanx of unsmiling secretaries.

He walked down the hall to the main entrance to retrieve his car. A lot had depended on this move, and it had all come to naught. He had to think of the consequences with Jerry Haggerty, for one thing. Jerry would not accept what had happened. When Burt Hammond came to the main door he found a stiff-jawed studio cop barring his way.

"Excuse me." Burt Hammond moved to push past.

"Hold it a minute, mister." The cop laid a hard hand on his shoulder. Burt Hammond's eyes darted beyond him warily. The corridor was empty, the studio cop large. Various unpleasant alternatives presented themselves. "You Mr. Hammond?" Burt Hammond's nod was almost imperceptible. "You are to go upstairs, sir."

"You got balls, kid," Ike Ash said a few moments later. "Now tell me what you got for me if I give that louse a pass to get into business here in a big way."

"First, there's what *I* get," Burt Hammond offered, by way of testing the terrain.

"So let me hear."

"A fee, to be paid by Brighton and Trans-Continent."

"Fair enough. If you can bring off what no one else in the world could, why not?"

"And I'll want to talk to you about distribution for the new Janet Morgan picture I'm backing."

"That you don't get. Her name's shit and you know it."

"In some places so's mine, and so's yours. Just assure me your mind isn't closed."

"Okay. Now—what do I get for all this?"

"Let's start with a bonus you didn't think of. I'll arbitrate and settle that strike that's been going on here."

"Think you can?" Ike Ash grinned, displaying a row of ancient, cigar-stained teeth.

"I got *you*, didn't I, Ike?"

"You sure did." Ike Ash circled his desk to reach his cigar case. He grinned. "I'll be a son of a bitch. You sure did."

After that, it was more or less routine.

11

Burt Hammond had asked Elmer Wright to look into the strange lack of communication from Sue-Ann Martin. Weeks had passed since she had telephoned him from Indianapolis to expect her arrival in a matter of days.

Burt Hammond knew it had to be something very important to bring Elmer Wright to his house. The investigator had the San Franciscan's distaste for Los Angeles in a heightened degree. He avoided contact with that city as one might a leper colony, reason telling him that although the chance of infection was slight, contamination lay there nevertheless. Everything about California south distressed him, the smog, the traffic, the few parks, the dress of its inhabitants, the cloudless sky, even the sun, especially the sun. Having refused countless invitations to confer there, he came on his own only to find Burt Hammond hurrying to get dressed.

"I've been wondering," Elmer Wright offered dreamily. "Why did the lady marry the young guy? Was that significant?"

"What're you talking about, Elmer?" He had not known Hilary Wilson had married again.

Elmer Wright then gave voice to the threads of his investigations that had brought him south. Susie Martin had been carrying on what he called "a sexual affair" with a certain Everett Alan Pierce. This same Pierce had turned out, after the explosion, to be the police officers' delight, ready to relate every detail of his relationship with her that the law enforcers might find helpful. Pierce had met Mrs. Wilson in the course of his employment and now they had married. "Rather strange for a lady of her years and station to marry a small-town boy so suddenly."

Burt grinned bitterly. "He wouldn't happen to work for the Bank of America in Bartlett?"

Elmer Wright's head snapped toward him. "But I didn't tell you that. How did you know?"

So the witness who could affirm the illegal transfer of corporate funds had been buried. She *hoped*. Hilary Wilson had come a long way, he thought, recalling how she used to separate herself from any side of Ellis Griswold but the one that made all that money for her. Now, to still a dangerous witness . . . good God . . .

"You know what that tells me?" he heard Elmer Wright say. "Given the marriage, and given all the time that's passed, and given that the Bureau hasn't produced a defendant, and given that if they had one they wouldn't dare hold a suspect this long for fear an appeals court could later throw out the conviction—" Elmer Wright paused because he knew what he had to say would do to Burt Hammond. "Given all that," he resumed, "I think your girlfriend is dead."

Burt stared at him briefly and walked to the window. *It was true.* Susie would by now have got some word to him. Nothing could intimidate her for long. All the other explanations he had satisfied himself with simply were make-do theories to avoid the imperative—*why did she not get in touch with me?*

"Who, why, how, where, no one's telling us yet," Elmer Wright continued. "How do our friends get away with not notifying the next of kin and so on?—they'll say they simply took this long to identify her."

When the cab came to bring Elmer Wright back to Los Angeles International, the detective hesitated at the door. "I promised not to tell you, but . . ." He shook his head as if he had decided again to keep a confidence. Elmer Wright bent to get in but changed his mind once more. "Sir, I was briefly retained by Mrs. Flora Levering. It was a matter involving the same grandson you and I were concerned with some time back. I speak to you very unprofessionally now because you may have some personal interest here, sir."

Burt ordered the cab driver to turn off his engine and to wait. Kenneth Kendall, with his sister's knowing or unwitting help, had managed to extract no less than 'three million dollars from various holdings of the Levering estate. The three million was being put to some nefarious purpose the detective could not precisely pinpoint. Everything pointed to something sordid Elmer Wright wanted no part of. He declined the job. By then the doyenne of

Wildoaks had called him off the enterprise. She paid him off for his time and expenses, eliciting a promise not to bring any of this to Mr. Hammond's attention now or ever in the future. "Apparently the matter is closed," Elmer Wright said, "but since they were so explicit about ruling you out and since my first loyalty is to you . . ."

"That part of my life's over, Elmer. I'm past caring what the hell happens to any of them," Burt Hammond said.

Had he meant what he said? He watched the cab turn on Mapleton on its way to Sunset Boulevard and the freeway. *Forget it.* Things were moving fast; he was moving fast. A quarter of a million was the bill he sent for his services in getting Trans-Continent's film library for Brighton. IRS got wind of it—no secrets in Hollywood—and leaped on Ike Ash and Lou Birch. "Mr. Hammond deserves every penny," Brighton's attorney—the same highly respected Ebenstein who had laughed at him that first day—said in a formal statement to the press. "He succeeded in accomplishing what no one else in months of negotiations had been able to achieve."

Jerry Haggerty flew down without fanfare when his people learned that four million was back home, clean as a surgical gown. "I'm yours, kid, whatever you need." Haggerty was meeting with the truckers and the public employees' unions and he was riding high. He was drinking less but getting inebriated more quickly on an ounce or two. His hair was thinner, his complexion rosier, his tongue looser, his gut expanding. He had other friends with money problems, he said. Here was a chance for a fellow to get himself owed a big fat favor or two.

"How much?"

"Twenty-five, thirty million." Jerry Haggerty watched Burt Hammond's head nod knowingly. "They'll pay any price, counselor."

"How about you? What'll you pay, Jerry?"

"Name it."

"How much has Sobordco got in mortgages by now with the pension fund?"

"Almost a hundred million."

"You'd call those loans," Burt said evenly. "I wrote the master agreement. In very small print that even their lawyers thought highly improbable, you've got the right."

300

"I couldn't do that. Sobordco is one of the best outlets for our funds."

"I've got a producer wants to make a picture that'll take the company all over the world," Burt Hammond said almost dreamily. "London, Germany, Italy, Bangkok, Hong Kong, Taiwan. Lots of big-star names who get paid in funny money, lots of pre-production distribution deals all over the world, pounds, marks, lira, sterling, dollars. Your people get back their money sure, and a fat return if the picture's a hit." Burt Hammond saw the lights begin to dance in Haggerty's eyes. "You call all Sobordco's loans. You disapprove of Griswold's management of the company; the lady too, the one who got them into that mountain deal. That's the price, Jerry. The rest is easy."

"What else?"

"That illegal campaign contribution. Break that story out of Washington through some people in Meany's office. The press does the rest for us."

"Funny," Jerry Haggerty said, sighing like a man out of breath. "Griswold came to me not long ago and asked me what it would cost him to get rid of you with me."

"What'd you tell him?"

"I'd have to take it under consideration." Haggerty laughed at himself. "With me any offer is worth listening to." He got to his feet with effort. "But a good deal's better than any offer. You're on." At the door he asked: "You know a man named Eddie Gorman?"

Burt Hammond remembered the name from the committee hearings in L.A. "I never met him."

"They got him by the short hairs, and to save his ass, he's talkin'. The Crime Task Force has turned him around. He's now tellin' them whatever it is they want to hear."

"Can he make it stick, Jerry?"

"To tell you the truth, he's so well connected that for a time I thought maybe you and he could be in cahoots." He waved a hand helplessly. "I must be getting feeble-minded in my old age. I still can't quite figure you out."

He held out his hand. "So you're finally going to get even with that son of a bitch for what he did to your father and you?"

"No, *I'm* not," Burt Hammond said, *"he* is." He looked at his wristwatch. He was late for this damned thing he had promised to take Janet Morgan to. He urged Jerry Haggerty out the door.

He hadn't wanted to go, but she nailed him at the wrap party for *Eye of the Storm.*

The champagne had flowed that night on Stage Two of the Goldwyn lot. Janet Morgan came up to him. "I think you're a no-good, phoney-macho, two-timing, typically cheating male exploitive sexist asshole. Big-man took advantage of a very vunlerable lady. Hurrah."

"I got her back to work, didn't I?"

"That's even a worse exploitation. She thought—"

"So did I," he broke in. "But there's always hard reality. And I did save your picture."

"I hate love. The heart's problems are really a pain in the ass. Still, the fact remains you two-timed me, Mr. Hammond."

He took her hand and brought it to his mouth. "I'm glad to see you're not made of granite, Jan."

"In my special way, I love you, damn it all. I wish I didn't. I'm really perfectly happy to be your friend. On whatever terms. See how understanding I am?"

"We're fools, you know." He kissed the hand again. "We ought to make it permanent."

"I've done that, my dear, and I stink at marriage. I stink at parenthood, too, but that's another matter. Besides, I think you want the whole sentimental shtick that goes with marriage and that part of you belongs elsewhere, am I right?"

He thought of Courtney Kendall and remembered Susie Martin saying something like that. They were both right, of course. But he did not concede it.

"So I accept you as you are," Janet went on. "Will you promise me something in return, anything I want?"

"Of course."

"Take me to the Sports Arena tomorrow night. I've promised Jesse Unruh I'd meet his man Robert Kennedy, even though he knows I'm set for Eugene McCarthy."

"You've got to be kidding. Me and Bobby?"

"Let's beard the man in his own den. You afraid of him? Besides, you promised."

So he was stuck.

Up there on the brightly lit platform, facing more than twenty thousand cheering and applauding people crowded into the vast auditorium, Robert Kennedy seemed still more frail and small than in the ballpark up in Delano. The face had grown gaunt with the ordeal of travel, endless meetings and speeches. The eyes were bloodshot with sleeplessness or weariness, that was plain. Still glazed over as well.

Burt Hammond kept studying Robert Kennedy as one does a respected adversary. Nervous, plainly; not yet at ease before a crowd; at least, not as the center of its attention. As a speaker: not a rafter-shaker. He had a way of turning his head at what he had just said, in a kind of self-depreciative way, an attractive gesture which told Burt Hammond the speaker knew who he was and had not been inflated beyond measure by all the cheering and applause. His hands also trembled when he spoke. He could be witty, especially when he had to speak of himself; the sense of humor revealed a knowing and alert man. He shifted moods as he spoke, dead serious to jokey banter, but he was not playing the audience; it was the way he was.

Afterward, there were the usual autograph seekers and friends and fans anxious to be acknowledged by Janet Morgan. They pressed their way out of the vast hall.

"Pierre!" she called out, seeing a familiar head and a cigar. She took Burt's hand and led him to a reception room just the other side of the concession stand. It was already crowded with the usual familiar faces and those you thought you ought to know. He lost Janet Morgan again and found himself being pushed by knots of people, laughing or gravely conversant. Against one wall, the candidate was being introduced to people in an informal receiving line. Everybody got a word; even at his distance, Burt Hammond took note of the glazed and unseeing eyes.

He turned when he felt a tugging of his coat. "Come on, we get to go to an even more private group."

It was Janet Morgan they were ushering into a smaller and somewhat more privately furnished suite. About ten more people were waiting for the candidate. Ike Ash turned from a lady he had been chatting with; when their eyes met, Burt could see the astonishment.

"Hey, I didn't expect to see you here," he began. He looked up to see Janet Morgan. They had never met before.

"Mr. Ike Ash is going to release your picture, Janet." Burt exchanged their names.

"I never said that," Ash broke in.

"Nor did I say you did," Burt offered. "But you will, Ike. Say something nice to him, Jan, so he doesn't think you're a dragon lady in disguise."

She smiled wanly and moved away. "I thought she was big for Gene McCarthy," Ike Ash muttered. "What's she doing here? As a matter of fact, what're *you* doing here?"

"Same thing you are, Ike. Fishing." He saw Janet's hand signaling him.

Janet was the first to get ushered to the candidate's side. He knew her by sight and knew she was an early and devoted supporter of Senator Gene McCarthy.

"I'm glad to see you here, Miss Morgan." He held out his hand.

"I'm impressed with what I heard tonight, Senator," she said, and turned from him. "I'd like you to meet a very dear friend, Burton Z Hammond."

Kennedy's hand was outstretched; he stiffened with a shock of recognition when the name was said but did not withdraw it.

"The senator and I have met professionally, Janet. You must forgive her, sir, I did not tell her."

"I'm just a little surprised to find the counsel to Jerry Haggerty here."

"I believe in getting my facts straight, Senator, so I let Miss Morgan persuade me to come."

"Haven't changed my views on your client. I hear you're doing pretty well too."

Burt Hammond shrugged. "Your brother put it very well. Life isn't always fair."

"What do I do, console you or congratulate you?"

"I've wondered the same about you, Senator."

"You mean, as senator or candidate?"

"As a lawyer, sir. Who had a client by the name of Hoover, much like mine, one you could not always control but were held responsible for."

Kennedy looked over to Janet Morgan and smiled slightly. "Your friend's putting me on the spot, Miss Morgan."

"You're putting a lot of us on the spot these days, Senator," Janet said drily.

"Duty, Miss Morgan, duty. This gentleman represents a man I know to be an unprincipled scoundrel." He turned amiably enough to Burt Hammond. "Mind, as one lawyer to another, I don't blame you for what your client did or tried to do."

"I'm prepared to share any blame I'm responsible for, Senator," Burt said. "Are you, sir?"

"What blame should I acknowledge, Mr. Hammond?"

"The conduct of the Federal Bureau of Investigation, your responsibility when you were the chief law officer of this country." He felt Janet Morgan's hand come to rest on his forearm.

"You know as well as I, if you're talking about telephone taps and such, we always got court orders and moved correctly," Kennedy said.

"You blame me for Jerry Haggerty, sir; may I blame you for Mr. Hoover's illegalities?"

"Such as?"

"Common burglary, sir, breaking and entering, numerous blatant criminal acts and attempts to curtail basic constitutional rights."

"You actually know of such?"

"Sir, I was, and probably right now continue to be, the object of such illegal actions."

"You have proof positive?"

"I am ashamed as a citizen to say I have. It's not the first time in my life, not by a long shot. I have a client now who is missing, whose life is either in danger or already lost. I believe her whereabouts are known to your former subordinates, if I can call them that. All this bothers me, but worse, it makes me think of what you said that night when you asked what kind of nation we are becoming. My missing client was much moved when she heard you in Indianapolis. I myself heard you in Delano when Chavez broke his fast. I am impressed by you, even though I know when you become President you will do your best to throw my client Haggerty and me into prison. Can you assure me of all my rights? Will you, when you are President? What can you do now to help me find a client who's being held from her lawyer, and what are you going to do to stop my house being burglarized by the government?"

Kennedy stared at him, the eyes flickering and then going glazed. "Plenty," he said after a time, and held out

305

his hand for Janet Morgan. "Thanks for coming by." He turned to talk to someone else.

"What do we do now?" Janet Morgan asked after Kennedy left them.

"Pray," Burt Hammond said.

BOOK EIGHT:

Camino Real

(1970)

1

HE learned that Susie Martin was dead when he read it in the newspaper. No one at the Bureau did him the professional courtesy of informing him about his client, although they had sought him out fast enough when they were looking for her. It was too late for anger or remorse, too sad a moment to think of anything beyond her passing.

He went to a memorial service in Crescent City, near the northern border of the state. Her father ran the Chevron service station on the highway. Her mother worked in the office of a lumber company. "She made the world a more exhilarating place by her presence," Burt Hammond said to her parents. "She gave it light, and warmth, and laughter. She knew joy and she gave joy."

Her father would not take any money, even though Burt Hammond insisted she had been working for him and it was not an offer of charity or contrition.

Back at his table at Le Printemps, Marco said there had been an urgent message. He himself never took messages, of course. " 'You will take down exactly what I tell you and put it before Mr. Hammond.' The voice sounded like it belonged to a duchess who always got her own way. "What could I do, sir?" Marco apologized.

Burt Hammond took the note from the captain's hand. "I require your presence here as quickly as possible. Flora." He held it a moment, but finally crumpled it and dropped it on the table without comment. He ordered his lunch, and when Don Faversham came into the room, he asked him to sit. Faversham had his usual stock of high-level gossip after an absence of some days. Names varied; the stories did not. Burt Hammond was more interested to hear Morgan had assigned Rosey Lee to write a song for the main titles and to score *Eye of the Storm*. Terrific gimmick, Don Faversham said, he didn't know when a star had scored his own film since Charlie Chaplin. That meant a tie-in record deal, would he look into it? Faversham also had a script in his car for Burt Hammond to read. Richard Dodge, the current number-one male box-office draw in the world, had approached him for backing on a film he wanted to do independently. "Fifty million ladies dream of jumping on the guy, and the dolt wants to play an old coot in Alaska in a louse-ridden fur suit and a beard so thick you don't even get to see his wrinkle-the-nose bit. The major studios said no. absolutely no, even if it's Richard Dodge. We'd better pass too."

"Has any one of his pictures ever lost money?" Burt said.

"This is the one that's going to break the record. I just think you ought to read it before we turn him down.

"Tell him he's got his money. I don't need to read the script."

"This one'll *lose* it for you, Burt," Faversham insisted.

"The next one won't." He got to his feet. "We'll have to get that one too if he wants it for this one. Tell him that and bring him here."

"He doesn't come to places like this—ever."

"He wasn't looking for backing before, so he will this time." Burt Hammond went to the door.

He was sure of one thing. Wildoaks was in the past, just as the mud shack beyond Los Vidrios in the Desierto de Altar was gone from his life. It had been a tremendous effort to put Courtney Kendall out of his life, so he would not go there despite the gallant old lady's plea.

He drove down the incline at the end of Wilshire Boulevard and headed north to drop in on Janet Morgan. He was doing a comfortable 65 on the Pacific Coast Highway when a car driving to his left veered toward him without warning and cut him off. He swore, jammed on the lovely disc brakes and miraculously was able to bring the Rolls to a stop without a crash. A car behind him smacked his rear, not hard but definitely, like the kiss of a billiard ball. Before he knew what was happening, two men emerged from the second car and confronted him at each door. He saw a black, snub-nosed pistol aimed between his eyes. "It's all right, Mr. Hammond, don't move and nothing'll happen." When he turned his head something crashed into his skull. Up to that moment he had the feeling that he was a participant in a carefully rehearsed ballet. He would not have been surprised to learn that everything took place so efficiently that no passing motorist ever gave the cars a passing glance. He was still unconscious when they got to Oxnard; on a side street there, the cars rendezvoused. The man who took over his Rolls was dispatched to do what he had to do to hide it. Someone took Burt Hammond's pulse; satisfied with the reading, he pulled out a hypodermic syringe and busied himself fitting a needle to it with practiced fingers. Burt Hammond began slowly to come alive again, enough in any event to feel the pain that goes with being slugged with a woolen stocking half-filled with three pounds of quarter-inch steel bearings and the discomfort of discovering that breathing is difficult when there is a tight gag pulled between the lower and upper molars. Burt Hammond struggled briefly when he felt hands groping at his middle to get to his pants. He was not strong enough to cry out in pain when he felt the stab of the needle, then only the weight of hands holding him down. An image swirled in his mind: a truckload of gravel had crashed into him and that was why he was having trouble breathing. But then things began to get hazy and there was less weight on him, then none at all. He was grateful for the sleep that came in its place.

He could see the black and white cars in the fog that covered his house and the fields around it.

He came back from wherever he had been, struggling against the grasp of big men in khaki who refused to let him go into his own home. His father lay on the floor inside, a bloody hand beckoning him, but the police guys would not release him. . . .

When he awoke, a face he did not know grinned at him, loose-jowled, a four-day growth grizzling old yellow skin. The voice was too high for so big a man. "Your friend's on the way, Mr. Hammond. I'm gonna help you with a nice hot shower and a shave."

Why so amiable? He was a captive, so beaten he knew enough to go with any circumstance. Where was he? A hotel? Motel, probably. The anonymous Formica furniture of the American road. The shades were drawn, but he knew it was early morning and it did not feel like California south. Somewhere—where?—north of the Tehachapi Mountains, he felt that. They were calling him mister, that told him something. And he was alive.

310

He tried to fit the pieces. Who? Jerry? Jerry's friends? Jerry's enemies? There were a few of those in the unions and the locals, more than there had ever been; he was not the only one to observe the leader's deterioration. But why? What did they want of *him?* The big man with the high voice chirped with laughter when Burt Hammond asked his questions, how long, where, what is this place called?

There was coffee when he got out of the shower; he was able to look past the half-closed draperies to a stand of conifers across the road. He knew it had to be high enough to be at tree level wherever he was. He lay down and dozed.

He was awakened by the door opening. There stood Jerry Haggerty, alone, both palms extended. "Am I glad! You're going to be okay, kid! It's a miracle!"

Burt Hammond made it to his feet. The shower and the cold water had helped; there was no dizziness, only an empty, sickish feeling in his stomach that would not go away.

Jerry Haggerty's laughter echoed in the room. "It was the hand of God! Your number was up! Out of my hands. I mean, how foolish could you be? You got enemies. They didn't even tell me. They heard how you met privately with that little runt. It had to be a deal. They knew just how long the two of you talked."

"Who were they?" Burt asked bitterly. " 'Friends and associates,' Jerry?"

"You can't always choose, counselor. An ally's an ally. After the meet you dropped out of sight. They figured you were talking to the Task Force at a secret hideout. Like our friend Eddie Gorman. Then the hand of God reached down to protect you. God spared you. God spared me the agony of losing you."

"I haven't heard the Lord invoked so promiscuously since my mother took me to a revival meeting. What'd God do for us, Jerry?"

"He got rid of Robert Kennedy." Haggerty saw the confusion in Burt Hammond's eyes. "Of course! You've been out of it for the last two days so you don't know what happened." He told it as a man might tell a friend about a prize fight with an unexpected finish in his favor. The sweeping victory in the California primary, the most populous state in the Union, assured the nomination at the convention in Chicago. He could beat any Republican. Then a couple of pistol shots in the kitchen of the Ambassador Hotel . . .

"You mean," Burt Hammond said slowly, "Robert Kennedy is dead?"

"And your life was saved! He was your enemy too, kid. It would've been you too. The guys—everybody—knew how much you meant and still mean to me, to the Fund. But whoever came after you was running scared. We all were. Suddenly there's nothing to be afraid of."

Burt Hammond got unsteadily to his feet. "Who paid for it, Jerry? You, your friends?"

"I never ran from the guy, you know that!" Haggerty protested. "I always fought him his way. Sure, I was afraid of the runt, more scared than I ever let on, even to you. He fooled me. I'd think I had the guy figured out and he'd change on me. I'd peg him as a snot-nose trying to work himself into the big time with the McClellan Committee, a gofer for his older brother the old man was buying the Presidency for. All the time he kept playing smarter and smarter, raising the stakes, pushing for more than he'd talked about. I've played that game myself. One foot on this side of the water, the other way over there, good guy, bad guy, two worlds—all the time remaining your own man. You're like that too, kid."

"Your people had nothing to do with it?"

"Never."

After a moment, Burt Hammond said, "I believe you, Jerry." Haggerty grinned. "But anyway I'm leaving, Jerry."

"You're a little crazy too, kid," Haggerty offered amiably. "Like him, like me. People like us have to go all the way to the end of the line. You *can't* leave, know what I'm trying to tell you?"

"Sure, I can, Jerry."

"It's all going to be different. I'm ready for a fresh start. I don't need those guys anymore. I'm in the clear—"

"No, you're not, Jerry," Burt Hammond broke in. "It's still a toss-up—prison or the marble slab."

Haggerty laughed as at a well-pointed jest. "You got it wrong. It's the old Jerry Haggerty. I'll have the membership behind me bigger and stronger than ever. I'm apologizing to you as humbly as I can. I know you. You're like he was. Always ready for a tradeoff for what you've got to have right now. Okay, I'm in a trading mood."

"Another time, Jerry." He stirred as if to leave.

"Right now. I'm asking you. I need you."

"I'm going, Jerry."

"Will you come back to me?"

Burt Hammond hesitated. "Don't know."

"So I can't let you go."

"Sure you can."

"Where you going?"

"Getting married. You wouldn't stand in the way of that, would you?"

Haggerty stared at him briefly, then broke into a gale of laughter. "You're something! World falling apart, new one struggling to be born and he chooses this moment to get hitched!"

Burt Hammond could not help smiling a little himself. "So can I leave now, Jerry?"

"You want a car? You need any walking-around money?"

"I want nothing from you, Jerry, thanks just the same."

The old man's face went dead. He said no further word and moved away from the door.

Outside, the air was fresh and crisp, a salty tang to it; the ocean could not be far away. The trees stood in a carpet of brown needles that crunched under his shoes. At the end of the driveway the highway curved over a hill on its way south. He enjoyed the walking after so many days, he found the roadside fascinating, he did not put out his hand for a ride, but someone stopped and asked him if he needed a lift, and it turned out the driver was going all the way to the peninsula too. Burt Hammond was not surprised.

2

FLORA Levering, in a once-white cable-knit sweater frayed at the wrists and elbows, emerged from the greenhouse. He followed her past the huge blue-water pool and the row of unused outdoor chaises and carefully arranged marigolds, asters and daffodils that no one except the gardeners ever saw. She stopped without warning and said: "You've come too late."

"It was as soon as I could manage, Flora."

She shrugged. "Still you can help *me*. I had hoped it would happen after I died, but I've decided to be rid of Wildoaks and everything in it. The wise old men in Montgomery Street will find a thousand reasons why not. Will you handle the legal side of it for me personally?"

"Where's Courtney?" he parried. "I've come to talk to her."

"You can't."

"Is she well, Flora?"

The indomitable old lady seemed to hold her breath; a sob burst from her and she came into his arms. He had never realized how thin and fragile she was under the wools and tweeds. She was all bones. "She'll survive. She's like me. Indestructible."

At his insistence, she told what she had to, in slow, almost unwilling words. Using his sister, Kenneth Kendall had milked the estate of three million dollars. He was banking an enterprise involving the smuggling of two hundred and fifty pounds of pure cocaine from Colombia. So vast an amount had never been transported at one time before. He had partners, of course, here and in South America. Ken got in deeper than he knew. They needed his presence as much as they needed his money. Apparently they were putting up matching cash too. He was fronting a luxury cruise; drugs would be delivered among unsuspecting tourists.

Courtney had learned too much. Ken's people decided it would be unwise to let her go home. Ken Kendall kept her on as a prisoner. Of course, Flora Levering said, Courtney should not have gone with him in the first place. But he was her brother, her twin, and she could not find it in her heart to turn from a man the whole world detested. She soon confirmed what Flora said she had suspected for some time. Ken Kendall was a junkie. Which meant he was an addict. A rich addict. But still, a junkie. A junkie dealing with dealers, Courtney soon could see, is marked for destruction when his usefulness is at an end or he becomes a danger. Real dealers don't use the stuff, for obvious reasons. Fearful for her life, she tried to escape.

But she could not find the strength to leave.

The old lady paused after her voice dwindled to nothing. Burt Hammond waited until she could compose herself. "Why not?"

"She was with child."

Flora Levering picked up the thread of her narrative quickly. She told how Kenneth Kendall went into a rage when he learned of Courtney's pregnancy. He tricked his sister into taking LSD and when this did not produce the abortion he wanted, he injected her with heroin when she was unconscious. Flora Levering found herself talking to Burt Hammond's back. Her voice did not waver now, as if she had found the strength to go to the bitter end. When the heroin did not work, Ken Kendall brought in a drug-sodden physician whose main business, Flora Levering surmised, was to front for drug deals on the retail level. She believed the gentleman originally practiced as a dermatologist. "This butcher finally aborted her," Flora said.

Burt Hammond felt Flora Levering's hand touch his shoulder; he did not stir. The old lady gave no hint of pain or self-pity. These things had happened and had to be dealt with. She told of Kenneth Kendall bringing back Courtney only when she was near death. He himself was a nervous wreck. He learned his partners were freezing him out, just as Courtney had predicted, and his sister was bleeding to death. He did not know where else to go.

"I think this is as much as I can tell you, Burt," Flora Levering broke off. "I don't want to implicate you further."

He turned quickly, took her hand in a steel vise. "First of all, how's Courtney?"

"Like me. Unconquerable. Forever unvanquished. It was she who told me what had to be done and how to do it. Please, you are hurting me."

"She's okay, you're sure?"

"She has a residual problem with the drug, but our physician believes she can win there too," Flora Levering offered calmly. "She was made dependent as some hospital patients become addicted. The doctor says it can be dealt with because there is only a physical, not a psychological, need."

Burt Hammond sighed. "What was it she told you to do?"

"I will tell you what *I* did, I do not say anyone told me to do anything."

315

"Never mind playing lawyer," he said wearily. "What did you do?"

"I managed that this junkie monster who had done this terrible thing to her killed himself during an injection he was giving himself." Her voice was clear, unwavering, unbroken.

So he had come to that. Murder, and he did not care.

"I've felt more remorse at having to shoot horses who broke a leg," Flora Levering went on. "A sweet boxer dog named Max who came down with cancer at eight. A lovely red cat named Lucius who got badly mauled by a coyote. I cried then when I did what I had to to free them from their agony. But I didn't weep here." She drew a deep breath. "I've told you enough. I know it is your lawyer's duty—"

"Never mind that. You spared me the dirty work. Where's he now, Flora?"

Flora Levering turned and faced the far hills at the end of the estate where the ridge cut off the rest of the world. "Horses are marvelous. They can go where no machine can get and leave not a mark." She put somewhat blistered palms on him. "My hands have always been rough, but in a few days they will be only calloused as they always are. You see, this old woman can still dig a deep hole when she has to, my friend." She smiled wanly. "What are you obliged to do now, Burt, now that I've made you an accessory after the fact?"

"Why do people always play lawyer with lawyers?" he responded testily. "How much does Courtney know? What does she say?"

"She doesn't say, I don't ask. It ends as simply as that."

"I'd like to see her."

"I don't know if that is possible now."

"Why not?"

"She has asked me to let no one see her. She wants no pity, no remorse—"

"I want to see her."

"Stay here a few days. Perhaps she'll change her mind."

Where else did he have to go? He had almost been put to death himself. His world, the whole world, was coming to an end. He felt wearier than he ever had, nowhere to go and nothing to do, vast changes and decisions yet to be made and he was too weak to move forward or aside. "I'd very much like to stay, Flora," he declared finally.

She put him up in the pool house. He would not be disturbed there. She would have somebody see to his needs. She saw now that he himself was not entirely well and she asked him to forgive her not having noticed. "Time," she said, taking his elbow and walking beside the pool to the glass house beyond it. "Time," she said again, as she brought him inside. "Time is our best friend."

In the days that followed, he saw little of Flora Levering. Sometimes one of her rigs rode the trail that crisscrossed the fields but it sped by so quickly or was so far away he could catch only a glimpse of someone holding the reins. Courtney's presence he could only feel. He wanted to see her, if only to tell her how much he admired her for her strength and spirit, but he respected her need for privacy.

He slept badly. Where in the world *did* he belong? The deserts had proved impossible, both tamed or untamed, the Bay Area, the sprawling south. Wildoaks. Holmby Hills and Market Street, Le Printemps and Janet's cottage in the less fashionable part of Malibu. Jerry Haggerty, running wild or finally under control. Why kid himself? What mattered was that he was free, functioning, a presence. Why salve the conscience? How he had got to this point in his life did not matter; what was important was that he was here. And now of course he was implicated in a capital crime and there was no regret, only the sure sense that he could get away with murder, if only as an accessory after the fact, not a principal—and was not surprised to feel now he wouldn't even have minded *that*. Was all this because he was a prisoner of his past? He came to manhood in a world where violence seethed below the surface and blew up when the stakes became high enough. It was a time of dreams, great and small; petty violence and the murder of great dreams; a time of money, bigger money than the multitude of men had ever known, and he had come through . . .

Outside in the night he had heard the rhythmic drip of rain on the tile terrace and on the roof, a small, tentative tattoo. A chill breeze stirred the silken hangings of the great windows. He thought he had closed all the doors.

317

He started to rise to close the door. "I'll take care of it, sir."

In the dark room he saw a ghostly figure float from the door toward the bed. "My name's Courtney Levering Kendall," it said. "I believe we met at the opera."

"I vaguely remember." Burt Hammond felt her stretch out beside him. He took her into his arms and pressed her damp, chilled body to his.

"Try harder," Courtney went on. She put her mouth against his. "Note how beautifully soft the lips are. How expressive. You've never been kissed like that by anybody else but Courtney Kendall, admit it."

His hands began to move tentatively, uncertainly, over her back. He was afraid that the terrible experience she had suffered would leave a psychic mark on her, but she pressed against him, strong and eager as a child. "You'd never remember me if the light was on, sir. I've lost all the baby fat, I've got a lean, hard, absolutely gorgeous body now."

"It was always pretty fair, ma'am."

"It's changed for the better. I'm a woman now. It used to belong to a girl. Didn't you once tell me you liked women but not girls?"

"You still talk a hell of a lot, Miss Kendall."

"Sorry, sir. It's just that I'm so happy."

Tentatively he explored her throat with his mouth; he kissed her shoulders and brushed across her breasts. He could feel her stiffen when his hands sought her rump to bring her body closer to his.

"I wanted to see you," she whispered, after his hands discovered the belt that told him her body had still not got over the ordeal she had been put through.

He brought her closer. "I wanted to see *you*, Court."

"I never look behind me. Yesterday's a hundred years ago. Let me make love to you. Let me eat you, let me take you."

He found her head and immobilized it. "You don't have to, my dear. I love just holding you."

"But *I* don't. Don't be afraid because of what happened. I'm all right now, almost."

He brought her face to his and kissed her. "Courtney, I do love you."

"I hurt so badly for a time I said I would never again have sex. The very thought of it sent shivers up my back. But now I can't wait. Let me take you in my mouth, I'll be really marvelous at it, I've been reading how-to sex books." She was all over him, pushing his hands away, her mouth quickly coursing down his chest, across the belly until she cupped and encased his member, pressing her mouth to its crown and touching the nipples of her breasts to the hardness of it. "You are mine," he heard her say, "you are all mine." And then it did not matter what she said. . . .

When she awoke she turned toward him and let her fingers touch his eyes, open in the dark. "You're not sleeping," she said. "What are you thinking about?"

"Tons of shit on the streets, Courtney. All that snow, cut and recut, and recut again—and what crazies are going to do to get the bread for it."

"For me, all that's over and done with."

"You paid." He enfolded her in an embrace. "Others will have to pay."

"Why do you always have to settle scores? Life is full of unsettled accounts."

Why indeed?

"He killed my child," Burt Hammond said. "You may, I can't, forgive that."

She did not say anything for a long time. "There's nothing we can do about the past."

"That's where we differ, my dear. The present is part past, as I see it."

"Yes, you're right." He watched her get out of bed and move to the draped glass wall. "But I refuse to be manacled to my past. If I can't stop you from doing what you have do to, it'll still work out just fine. I'll be here, waiting for you whenever you want to come back."

"A prisoner." He did not tell her of her grandmother's plan to get rid of Wildoaks.

"Institutionalized. Like those happy old guys one reads about who refuse to leave their prison cells."

"But I was thinking it's time to get married, and you know how I feel about this place," Burt Hammond offered.

"Oh, we couldn't marry under any circumstances," she said quickly and brightly.

He replied as if she had meant only to tease him. "Oh, really? And why not?"

"You're going to want to have children. The doctor says it'll be highly unlikely that I'll be able to have any.

319

Don't tell me about adoptions. It's a make-do when people have to, but you don't have to, Burt. But," she added quickly, "I'll always be here for you."

"You really do look ahead, don't you?"

"And you look back. So it turns out to be a marvelous arrangement."

"I'm not looking for an arrangement."

"Then that'd be too bad for me. I wouldn't saddle you with a sterile marriage, and that's that."

He took both her wrists in firm hands and brought her full-face to his. "I'm talking about you and me, just us. I'm asking you to marry me, Courtney. You're right. I'm ready for the whole scene. So we won't be the first who can't have kids of our own. Say yes."

"No," Courtney said.

3

CHAOS IN CHICAGO
Police Battle Hippie Groups at Convention

ran the banner headline and the subhead in the *Examiner*. He had been out of touch for too long, at Wildoaks by his own choice. Five thousand Illinois National Guardsmen were on the alert, he read. Seventy-five hundred troops of the United States Army had been airlifted to Chicago from Fort Hood, Texas, to stand by in case of trouble. The International Amphitheatre, where the convention was being held, was circled by a high chain-link fence topped with barbed wire. The mayor had ordered all the manhole covers around it sealed with tar. The city's police were doing battle in twelve-hour shifts. The candidate was nominated on the first ballot, but it made no difference to the violence boiling ceaselessly on the streets and in the city parks.

A separate story told of the arrest, in Grant Park in front of the Conrad Hilton Hotel on Michigan Avenue, of seventy demonstrators. including the renowned film star and activist, Janet Morgan. The story said that she had paused to make a statement to the hand microphones held out to her by radio reporters as she was about to be taken away in a police wagon. "When the civic authorities of a great city charged with keeping public order allow its paid employees to do such things to American citizens as I have seen here today, I say one has to be afraid of growing ashamed of what is going on in our country."

The lead editorial about her was in boldface: "ASHAMED OF U.S.A."

He wondered how quickly someone would put it on the desk of Ike Ash.

Jack Anderson, who specialized in such stories and was the right place to leak the story, filed the first account of what he called "chicanery in high places." He told in a wealth of detail of the effort of the Southern Border Land Development Corporation to position itself favorably with a vast, and illegal, campaign contribution. The story spoke of financial tentacles of great corporations and the attempts by financial wheeler-dealers to manipulate government. A major scandal, Anderson called it.

Win some, lose some, Burt Hammond thought.

The biggest—to him—story of all did not appear in the papers.

He was staying for a few days in an obscure hotel on Geary Street. developing with Elmer Wright what he could about the luxury cruise Ken Kendall had sponsored, when the detective brought him word that the people on Market Street were worried. Two days before, Jerry Haggerty had been driven to dinner to a spaghetti-house called Santa Lucia in Oakland by his personal companion and bodyguard, Fats Clancy. He told Clancy not to wait; he would manage a ride home. Haggerty had not shown up since.

"He's dead," Elmer Wright said.

"That was stupid," Burt countered. "Jerry is never stupid."

"He could have been careless."

"He's facing challenges in the locals, he knows he's a target, why would he go off alone? The new man in the White House and the new Congress are going to be out for blood, dirty money, the tie-up between labor and organized crime, all of us who work the jungle section of the economy . . . Jerry symbolizes all that, and he's very careful in the face of it."

"Scared, you told me yourself."

"That's right. Cornered. Desperate. He'd fight back, not walk into a trap."

"So you think he's alive?" the detective asked.

Burt Hammond shrugged. "I know for sure he was never stupid."

Clarissa, the yacht was named. Greek registry. Built to show the world Niarchos and Onassis were not the only Hellenes to reckon with. Chartered by Kenneth Levering Kendall before going into drydock. One hundred guests carefully chosen by the eccentric young San Francisco socialite, who at the last minute decided not to go along, a touch the social columnists made much of. The guests did not let their host's absence deter their relentless pursuit of the good life. They were mostly socially impeccable freeloaders, impoverished titles, movie names that didn't mean as much as they used to, pretty girls from Dior and Mary Quant and Pucci, white, brown, Oriental. Photographers from *Oggi* and *Paris-Match* and *Vogue* and *Women's Wear Daily.* Everybody was warned. Those awful people at Customs would most certainly be going through things so do be careful about naughty cigarettes and tiny spoons. The real stash, Elmer Wright said, would turn up behind welded iron plates in *Clarissa's* hold when the ship went into drydock in Richmond, California.

Bay Shipyards and Drydock Company turned out to be Peter Goldoni, a retired state senator and one-time hopeful for the governorship in Sacramento. It was a wild surmise, the detective conceded, but since they knew for a fact dope was involved, Goldoni had to be the political connection here. The big money bought respectable fronts, abroad and here.

"They won't flood the market," the detective said. "They'll sit on tens of millions in street value. They'll do what de Beers does with diamonds—modulate supply, keep up the price. How much did your boy put into the deal?"

"Three million. All the public costs, I'd bet."

"You could get his share back, now they're home free."

"Times, say, three or four."

"Could be dangerous dealing with those people, but I daresay you could handle it, sir."

"I could. Hell, yes." Burt Hammond looked again at a file on Peter Goldoni the detective had prepared on a sheet of legal foolscap. Second-generation California family. Long list of civic and state commissions, environment, public beaches, air pollution, remedial schools. Wife, three children, charities, breeds Airedales.

"If you blow the whistle on me, Mr. Goldoni, I assure you I've made arrangements to return the favor and bust open the whole deal."

"What do you want?"

"I'm a fair man. Buy my people out for the three million right now and you can sit on your mountain of snow."

Ten million. Fifteen million. In time the drug-enforcement people would get wind of the operation, but it would be too late—what could they do, what did they have to work with? The ridge behind Wildoaks flashed before him. Kenneth Kendall was the uncertain link for all of them. Now he was dead, they were in the clear. He was in the clear.

"Break it wide open," Burt Hammond ordered Elmer Wright. "Give them all to the law."

"That means the money your man took from the estate is gone."

"A good cause. Think of it as a form of charity."

"And your lady's brother?"

"Give them all to the law," Burt Hammond repeated.

Elmer Wright grinned with relief. "You do it, Burt." It was the first time he had ever used his client's given name. "Go to the Drug Enforcement Agency. You broke it. Take the credit for it you deserve. Think of what it'll mean for you. The Feds up and down the line will sit back and think what a good man you are after all. Prove you're not this sinister character they regard you as."

"Being this character they think I am is better for my practice."

"But this is your chance to show them what you really are."

"We both know how police think. They'd start grateful but soon come to think Goldoni and company crossed me so I ratted."

"In the long run, they'd credit you."

"Once upon a time their good will mattered to me. It's too late now. You do it. Besides, isn't there a big payoff for this kind of information? They'll know better how to accept that kind of motivation."

"I'll try not to involve the sister, Burt."

"You're a good man, Elmer."

"No, sir, you are. It's been a pleasure working for you." They both seemed embarrassed even by such brief, routine sentimentality.

4

MARCO's lids lifted with surprise when he saw Burt Hammond; he rolled his eyes and left them fixed in a significant glance over his shoulder to a man sitting alone at one of the worst tables. "Here every day for almost a week," he said through a contrived, innocent smile. "Also a call every day. Texas. Won't leave a message. Hangs on twenty, thirty minutes to be sure you're not here."

Burt Hammond had a few money people in Texas but always turned down the nervous kind. "Tell the gentleman from the FBI to come over."

"You want to know about Jerry Haggerty?" Burt Hammond offered. He pointed to a place beside him.

"Would you like to see my credentials?" the agent began.

"You take mine for granted, what the hell. Are you wired? I don't mind, but if I'm to be taken down word for word, I'll have to be more precise, to spare us an embarrassment later."

"I am wired," Mr. Hammond."

"Thanks. I haven't seen the man for some time. To be exact, just after the Robert Kennedy murder. We had some lawyer-client business to resolve. He took me to some place up north. I didn't pay attention to the name. He did say he was having problems in the locals. I wasn't surprised, nor very interested. It was long overdue. Let's face it, he wasn't getting any younger and I gathered he had plans for bringing in new members by the thousands. He did not mention any names. He did not feel threatened beyond the normal problems involved with maintaining his power. He was the same old wonderful, contradictory guy. He really liked me. It's hard not to respond in kind when someone thinks you're too much so I always regarded him as wonderful.

"You people may want to know what we talked about. Let's see how I can do that for you, without violating that lawyer-client relationship, of course. Well, he wanted me to involve myself more in his day-to-day operations and, of course, I didn't want that. I don't remember if we talked of the pension fund. If we did, I told him what I usually did, that I didn't like some of his friends but then I think he didn't like some of mine, you know how those things are.

"Have I just about covered everything I'm permitted to talk to you about? Let me see. I last saw him in that motel up north. I went on to some personal affairs and that's when I heard he'd been snatched. Have you got any leads?"

The recording device strapped to the young agent's body must have inhibited him. He responded only with a shake of his head.

"There won't be any. My hunch is that it was carefully and very expertly contrived."

The agent allowed himself to say: "I wouldn't know."

"Is there anything else? Money? You'll look at Golden West's books of course. We didn't deal quite as much as some people think, but it's all there." The interview was over. Burt reached for his bottle of Evian to replenish his glass. "And now if you'll excuse me, I've got some people to talk to."

Marco saw the signal and came over to help the guest depart. "Two calls holding right now, sir," he said under his breath. "Miss Janet Morgan. And the other is that man from Texas again."

"I'll talk to Miss Morgan."

"What're you doing in that den of iniquity?" Janet Morgan sounded like she was shouting at a phone from the far end of a mine shaft.

"Where are you?"

"No place you'd know. Marvelous spot. Nothing but a sandbar and surf that won't quit. It's cold and windy. I could use a little helpful bodily warmth. Come on up."

325

"I can't break away."

"Problems because of what happened in Chicago?"

"I'm sure."

"You angry for what I did?"

"No. In fact, kind of proud of you."

"I adore you for that. Did I wreck the distribution deal?"

"Didn't help."

"I'm very low, darling. Everything I do seems wrong. I'm depressed about the way the whole world's going."

"Don't let them get you down, Jan." He did not feel very good that he could offer her nothing but a fatuity.

"Did you get yourself married?"

"Who told you about that?"

"Feminine intuition. Reverse sexism, right? Did you?"

"She wouldn't have me."

"Some ladies are dumb."

"A few are smart. You and she, for example."

"Are you happy about it?"

"No."

"Then neither am I. I have this place, nothing but a shack. I stay here whenever I want to hide out. Which is now. It's called Point Arena. Mendocino County. You have to look hard to find it. Save my film, dear, dear friend, it's my life, don't let them kill it. And go to see Rosey." He realized he had not had word of her for a very long time. "I hope she's not back on the roller-coaster. Goodbye, my love."

The phone went dead in his hand. He looked at it for almost half a minute. He thought of Janet in a place called Point Arena and Courtney Kendall in Wildoaks, each proud, indomitable, independent, self-contained. He thought of Roseanna, still alone, in and out of life.

He was interrupted by Marco putting before him a plate whose contents interested him not at all. "That other party is still waiting on the telephone, Mr. Hammond. He insists he'll hang on until he gets to talk to you even if it means all week."

"One of those. Tell you his name?"

"No, sir. Says he wants it to be a surprise."

"And one of those too. All right, let's get rid of him."

"What in the hell kind of lawyer *are* you?" the voice at the other end of the line began. "Ain't in no register. You got a license to practice, all right, but no office and no damned telephone even . . ."

He had no success in fixing the voice. He dealt with a few loan brokers in Texas, but they were Harvard Business School types and this was that vanishing breed that—

"Is this Jose-Come-September?" he asked suddenly.

"Is this Burton Z-for-nothing Hammond, *the* Burt Hammond?" the voice countered.

A surge of recall of the bond they had formed that long-ago day in the Sonora desert erased the doubts and confusions that had briefly arrested him. "Why haven't I heard from you?"

Joe Christy bellowed a laugh. "Couldn't *find* you. And anyway the A-rabs, they wouldn't let me stay retired. Kept throwing buckets of money in my direction to get me out of the country. You got a spare room up there for an old coot?"

"Got a whole house for you, Joe."

"Sure glad to hear that. I sure had a fine time with you there in the desert. You ever think about it, *hombre?*"

"Not much."

"Too bad for you. I been thinking about it a lot. Been out drilling in the Gulf near Bahrain and down there in Chiapas state again. I'm concentratin' on off-shore stuff these days. I keep tellin' everybody our Mexican cousins are sitting literally on an ocean of black gold but they're still laughin' at Joe Christy."

So that was it. The old man was back again. Lonely. Looking for a new mischief to engage him. The last time it was a pretty little *puta* in Jalisco; maybe he had the usual outlander's dream of finding an equivalent one in glamorous Hollywood. "Let me know when you want to come here, Joe." The invitation stood but at second thought he did not want to make it sound too passionate or urgent.

"Can't say just yet. What's your home number?"

"Better you call me here. I keep changing the number there every few weeks so it wouldn't be good for long."

"You in trouble, boy?"

Burt made a laugh happen. "It's how I keep out of trouble. Let me know when I can see you here."

"Sure thing." The old man sounded brought down hard; his voice went flat. "Gimme the address, friend, save me a lot of bother. You're not keepin' *that* a state secret, are you?"

Burt told him what he wanted to know and hoped the

old man wouldn't surprise him one day by showing up without warning. The desert seemed very far away in the gracious surroundings of Le Printemps. Still, there it was again, mystic and unknowable as ever, reaching out and finding him.

5

WHEN Burt Hammond reached for the switch in his quarters, someone said: "Don't turn on the lights, Burton, please."

He left the room black. "How'd you get in?" He had wondered briefly about the darkness; it was always kept lit for him. He had no doubts about the voice. "You working with the FBI now?"

"Helen and I go back a long way, Burton," Hilary Wilson Pierce said. "It also helped when I cried a little."

"What is it you want, Mrs. Wilson? Or whatever your name is."

"You." She did not let a contemptuous laugh deter her. "Your life, your career. I want to save it."

"You mean you want to save your handsome ass, lady. And maybe Ellis Griswold's." The lights went on, blinding her after her wait in iron darkness. Hilary Wilson, shading her eyes, sat in a chair beside the Louis XV table, sheathed in a close-cropped white fur over fragile silk, her straw-colored hair pulled back sleekly, the face cool with color and smooth as burnished gold. Her presence drew him to her side. "You're incredible, Hilary. How do you do it? You're even lovelier than when I first saw you." She avoided his eyes, so his hand reached out to lift her chin. "How's the husband?"

"Never mind that, Burton," she broke in. "I've come here to help you."

"I don't believe you, lady. What you want is for me to cancel that call-up of Sobordco paper, right?"

"I want to put in with you."

He had not expected that. He did not respond.

"I've got six percent of the voting stock," she went on quickly. "I have people I can count on for another two percent, I think. A stock tender is the obvious move to get control. It wouldn't work coming from you, your reputation precedes you, but I thought you working through someone on the board whom they knew, and with eight points going in—"

He laughed again, contempt mixed with admiration this time. "And I always thought you were nothing more than a marvelous partner in bed!" She got to her feet quickly. He thought she was about to strike him, but she wanted the cigarettes she had left on the table. She took one from its box and waited for him to find a light for her. "But then I never really did get to know you, did I?"

She filled her lungs with smoke. "More's the pity. Listen, calling in all the mortgage loans won't work to dislodge him. And you yourself don't have all the time in the world. You've cut very deeply in some very high places, they're out to get you and finish you."

"And yet you want to put in with me?" He watched her.

"You'll come through. You always have. And they're only politicians, you're your own boss."

"What about your sense of gratitude to Ellis Griswold?"

"Time and history have passed him by. He's a relic, a spent force. Your old-fashioned capitalist who doesn't know how to function in a new world of ecology cranks and environmental nuts and smog-conscious freaks, and people ready to die for public access to beaches—in a word, how to make do in the new world that's happening."

A rush of images blurred everything in the room suddenly. The canal, 160 acres, his father, the lights on the police cars when they found him dead, Don Pedro, even Joseph Jerome Haggerty's wide, affecting grin. He left his desk to find a chair near the window.

"You've got to work fast, Burton," she pursued him. "I know a senator who's moving heaven and earth to get you. He knows they've tried to get you in courts and couldn't find a hook. He says he'll see you before a Congressional committee. He had rather ridiculous ambitions once, and you destroyed them. So move fast. Can you manage a tender offer, maybe five dollars over the market? With the loan call-up, my hunch is we'd find a lot of stockholders would love to get out of Sobordco."

"I kind of thought the company would die of its own absurd size, like the brontosaurus."

"It'd be a cheap buy-out. Real estate's down now, but wait. Ten years from now the land we now own will be worth five times, maybe ten times what it can command now."

"And *you* take over Griswold's spot?"

"Who better?"

He grinned, with unblended admiration this time. "I did underestimate you, Hilary."

"Don't make the opposite mistake of overestimating me, my dear. I'll need you more than ever."

"We've—you've got a problem. I can call on lots of money for tax-shelter protection, cash, high and quick return, but I don't know where I can raise big long-term money for a corporate takeover."

She smiled sweetly. "I know." When she leaned over to kiss his forehead, two decades deliquesced to nothing. "The Leverings."

"You calculating bitch."

"Why, you'd be saving them, like I'm saving you and you're saving me and my money, darling. They've gone stale and flat, the old story of what happens to American big-money families two generations later. What are they doing in five-percent mutual funds and preferred stocks? Put them into the real-estate market again, Burton, what've they got to lose? And look what the name would mean to Sobordco. The Leverings! Up there with the Crockers and the Stanfords and the Huntingtons and the Matsons! Why, even a fool like Kenny Kendall would suffice to front for the job . . ."

He put the flat of his hand against her mouth, startling her briefly, but before long she read his face and she did not move to free her mouth, seeing a flicker of understanding and common purpose come to life in his eyes and in an almost imperceptible smile that creased his cheek. Her own hands reached to the hand against her mouth and held it there while she parted her lips and let him remember their softness. "We could do it, darling," she said against his fingers, pressing her tongue to the middle one. "Couldn't we?" She bit the finger with sheathed teeth.

"How long's it been with us?" he said in reply.

She unsheathed the teeth and a bit a little more, as if

to chide him. "I don't count time, as a matter of principle."

"I do. Ten years since we fucked. It was ten years before that."

"Give or take a year here or there," she conceded without enthusiasm and bit his flesh just enough to tell him not to pursue the subject.

"Sorry. Just trying to see how overdue we are for another shot in the hay. You didn't tell me, how's the old man—Sorry, there I go again, I mean, the husband?"

"Handsome. Unfortunately, boring. Fortunately, though, a jock. He's away skiing. In the summer it's Chile. He'll come back in time to go to Zurs."

"You two must be very happy."

"Divinely. He gets what he wants. So do I."

"And clearly so do I."

She sensed a sudden darkness in his voice. "Don't blame me for what happened to the girl," Hilary Wilson said quickly. "I swear I—we—no one had anything to do with what happened to her. We—I—bombed, but—"

He put his hand at the throat of her dress where it parted to reveal the rounded, perfect breasts. "You ought to know me well enough by now, Hilary." He pulled at the dress hard enough to tear it without resistance to reach her naked skin. "I've never let personal feelings get in the way of taking what I want." He ripped the fragile fabric even more. "Do you mind that I'm ruining your dress, Mrs. Wilson?"

Her warm, moist mouth found his lips. "Desolate me, destroy me, my lover . . . my pitiless young god . . ."

Time did stop here, he thought.

6

"Now you shut up a while and listen to me, counselor."

Ike Ash, tense and nervous as a Bengal tiger, paced his office from one side to another. There was no way Burt Hammond could avoid the confrontation. The studio chief's office had sent a messenger who told him when to appear, not a request; nor ready to accept an alternative appointment—a flat order. Burt Hammond expected more than the usual trouble. He himself had seen a work-print of *Eye of the Storm* the day before and he had formed his own idea of what the tough old movie mogul would think of a sensitive, beautifully photographed film about two young women from different worlds whose lives touch and change. But Ash was going to surprise him.

"You want to know the guiding principle of my life?" Ike Ash began. *"Will it make a buck?* Short of a picture showing Hitler as a jolly, misunderstood lad, or one that makes your heart bleed for a mass murderer who got that way because mama yanked away the tit too quick, there's nothing this studio won't do to show a profit. So I don't care that Janet Morgan thinks she's saving the world by getting herself arrested in Chicago. But what am I supposed to do about her picture?"

"She never said what she was quoted as saying, Ike."

"I don't care if she really sang 'America, the Beautiful'—the potential audience is now full of people who hate her guts."

"Her opinions, maybe," Burt Hammond broke in. "And those who respect her. None of that touches her talent—"

"For a would-be producer, even for a star, it was indiscreet, it was foolish, foolhardy—"

"And brave." Burt Hammond still had to fight to get in a word.

"I'll even give you that," the studio chief conceded. "But it was suicidal."

It looked like a hopeless enterprise. Hollywood had a long history of running scared when it came to unfavorable public opinion. Burt had decided that Ike Ash was a man with set opinions; Chicago was leading them nowhere.

"Let's talk about the picture," Burt offered softly.

"I saw that film," Ike Ash went on without breaking stride. "First of all, what about that song? A *sad* song over the main titles? *That's* supposed to hook an audience? It's a throat-catcher, sure, but it sounds thin, tinny and full of funny echoes. You know what? I find out this genius lady recorded it in an empty room, just her and a piano—and you know what else? It *sounds* like it was recorded in an empty room. Then the picture starts—my God, one of the heroines is black, and it turns out *she's* got more class and guts than the white one. Ain't that clever, how's *that* going to play in Peoria?"

"I found it very touch—"

"I didn't bring you here to talk but to listen," Ike Ash cut him off. "Two broads, you hear? Now you can get away with two guys, make a buddy picture and no one says, 'Hey, they could be two fags,' but *two broads?* They've got to be dykes, right?"

He paused; clearly he expected a reply to fit his argument.

"No," Burt Hammond declared flatly. He had found the picture funny and charming and sad and heartbreaking and he'd laughed and cried and he was beginning to wonder if Ike Ash couldn't, too. He hadn't the slightest idea of whether a film like it would ever get to make its negative cost back, but he was glad he'd had a part in making it happen.

"No?" Ike Ash shot back as if Burt had stuck out a leg to trip him somehow in his cavernous office. "You're goddamn right, *No*. They're two dames in trouble who could be two guys, a guy and a girl, two anybody—they're wonderful. Everything is wrong, wrong, wrong about that picture. The lighting is too low-key, the songs are so underdone I wish good old Max Steiner was still around to add a ton of *schmaltz*. And does it work? That black chick, what about her? I'll tell you. It's the only time in my life I had a hard-on and tears in my eyes at the same time. I want to sign her." He still, amazingly, had not broken his stride. "This lady is going to be the next superstar! Can you get her for me? She's so good you forget to see whether's she's black, white or polka-dot."

Burt Hammond sagged visibly. He covered his eyes with his hands. He had been on his way north when Ash's office found him. He had come prepared to fight, to deal, to compromise, to undercut the old mogul if need be, to beg if he had to, to bend his own knee or somehow bring Ike Ash to *his* knees. He felt a hand touch his back. "You all right, counselor?"

Burt Hammond looked up and smiled wanly. "You son of a bitch, I heard you were tough. You're a pussy-cat."

"Don't tell anybody," Ike Ash said. "What about the

girl? Can you get her for me? It's a deal if I've got the girl."

"She's got problems, Ike. Marital, a little upper-downer hangup, identity crisis—"

"All the usual shit, so what?" Ike broke in. "You think I just got into this business? She your client?"

"She is, as of right now."

"I'll bet she is," Ike Ash responded admiringly.

It took him the rest of the afternoon to locate Larry Marshall, holding court with four ladies in a bar around the corner from Radio Recorders whose only light came from the Budweiser neon in the window. Burt Hammond chased off the four beauties and told the barmaid to stay away. "I need your help, Larry," he began, to the man's astonishment.

Larry actually choked up several times as they went over the familiar terrain. He had failed her; he had pushed her around; he didn't know what had happened to him; he didn't know what he was trying to prove. It took the rest of the day to show him what he was, not just a husband, not a lover, not a manager, not a music business executive. He was consort to a queen who, big as she was, was now going to be bigger than ever. Burt Hammond said he expected no miracles of sudden self-enlightenment, he did not care what the gentleman did with his spare time, but that anybody who managed, in one form or another, to bring in gross sales of dollar volume in the area of two hundred million dollars in records and films and personal appearances deserved to be treated with a modicum of respect.

"I tried, God knows I've tried," Larry Marshall wailed.

"You're going to try again, remembering this time you work for her, you're married to her, but you're the consort; the lady holds the throne and you're there only because of her."

They were beyond ego, beyond hurt and humiliation. "She'll have her own film company. I want you to be its chief executive."

"She's thrown me out," Marshall sobbed.

"She needs you. Remember, you get half, that's the law in this state, so you damn well need her. But you've got to earn your money for your own self-respect. It won't be an easy buck either. But it beats washing cars, so what the hell? Will you do that?"

"Can you talk her into taking me back?" Marshall countered.

"It won't be easy." Larry Marshall grabbed his hands gratefully. The guy thought Rosey would be the problem. Burton Hammond knew better; *he* was the problem.

Larry Marshall waited in the car when he went in. Every light in the house was brightly on; the house shone on the strand that was the Malibu Colony like a spotlighted crown. The couple that took care of her had long since turned in; the paid bodyguard dozed in the small den before a Johnny Carson rerun.

Asleep in her bed, Rosey did her best to look frightful: the hair had not been brushed out, the nightgown was crumpled flannel, she had put nothing on her face to help it, the eyelids were bare of color. She was beautiful.

Something beyond words must have told her he was there, for she opened her eyes without surprise after being stared at for a long time and whispered: "What kept you, man?"

He leaned down and kissed her cheek. He was glad to see drug-free clarity in her eyes and to hear her voice so true and clear. "How do you feel?"

"Alone. I talked to Jan. Tells me it looks like the picture's going down the drain."

"She thinks the whole world's going there too," he teased.

"Ain't it?"

"The picture isn't. Remember that day in El Centro after we left the courtroom?"

"Sure, I do. But tell me anyway."

"You dreamed of owning the world. You want it, Miss Stormy Ball? I've got it for you for the taking—that is, if you really want it."

She lifted herself to her feet wearily. "That girl's dead. This one don't know what you're talking about."

"That girl's still alive," he said. He stood beside her and took her into his arms. "I know. I was there. And I'm here."

"I'm such a mess," she said, and clung tightly to him.

"Why should you be different?" he teased.

He brought her out to the terrace that fronted the house. The night was dark but they could hear the surge and return of the surf in the blackness beyond the light the house cast on the beach.

"She's not the same person, but then neither am I," Burt Hammond went on. "And she wouldn't want to be that girl today anyway." He led her to the sand, took a hand in both of his and told her that what she wanted and feared most in life had come true. "Some people say it's the worst thing that can happen, and it's happened to you. You've realized all your hopes, aspirations, dreams and ambitions."

They laughed about it, what a terrible thing to happen to anyone, to own the world, she wasn't a queen, she was more than a queen because she controlled her own life and destiny, and how many on the whole planet could say that of themselves?

They held hands and laughed even more, and later they sent out the bodyguard to bring in Larry. There were more tears and still more laughter and before he left Burt Hammond got them to agree to the formation of a new corporation, Lee, Inc., just the surname, Roseanna Lee, President, to own seventy-five percent of the one hundred shares par value, one dollar each, jointly with her husband, Lawrence Marshall, Executive Vice-President, and Burton Z Hammond, the balance, twenty-five shares, per value twenty-five dollars.

7

HIS secretary reached him at Le Printemps and began by saying he was to come home at once. Not even to finish lunch.

"You have company," Helen Mendoza said when he let himself in the door.

"Oh, Christ," Burt Hammond mumbled.

Helen's face was flushed like ruby glass. "Be nice," she said.

In the den he found Joe Christy, somewhat grayer than he remembered, but still ramrod-straight and lean. "Hiya, ol' buddy, it's good to see you." He came up to Burt Hammond and threw arms around him. "Nice place you got. Think I'll buy the one next door so's we can be neighbors."

"Good to see you, Joe. Miss Mendoza make sure you're comfortable? Do you want a drink?"

"I've sworn off the stuff, Burt." He looked significantly at Helen, a glance that Burt did not miss, surcharged as it plainly was with a heavily laid-on significance. "Don Pedro, he taught me that, said it was a crutch. Miss Mendoza here knew the man. I never knew that."

"She found him for me."

"You never told me that."

Burt Hammond glanced at her disapprovingly. He had the feeling they were holding back something from him. "She's often devious, Joe."

"Don't listen to him, Mr. Christy," Helen broke in. "Don Pedro's dead, Burt. He sent a message to you."

"Not exactly dead, at least no one knows where the body is. But I guess he's gone at that," Joe amended.

"What kind of message?"

"You'll see," Joe said. "Remember his daughter?"

"Placida. Of course."

"Passed on two years ago. I used to go up there a lot. Been drilling around Villacampo, mostly dry-holing, but I got them Pemex people pretty hyped up they're sitting on somethin' so they're supporting me all the way. Got my own pilot and a twin-engine Cessna." Joe Christy did not pause to observe the sadness that flooded Burt Hammond's eyes.

"What happened to Placida?" His voice was soft as tears.

"Some fever. Wouldn't let me help. Saw she was ailin' —coupla months later, the old man tells me she's gone to the sky beyond the sky. Last time I see Don Pedro he says *his* time has come and I have to keep a certain promise if he was not there when I flew in. I'm keepin' that promise now. It's why I busted my butt to find you and couldn't leave no messages, boy."

Burt Hammond saw him gesture to Helen. She was crying. He said: "All right, Helen, what is it?"

She went to an adjacent room. When she came back she held the hand of a boy of about ten who looked gotten up for a church social by an old floorwalker in a Neiman-Marcus who had never heard of blue jeans. The boy had wheat-colored, unruly hair which someone had unsuccessfully plastered down, blue eyes and creamy dark skin.

"Don Pedro said the boy's like you, Burt, in more ways'n one. Didn't rightly belong in one place anymore'n you do, so I was to take him to you. Here he is, your son, Burt."

Helen Mendoza sobbed: "He looks just like you." A flood of tears engulfed her.

But Hammond hesitated. He looked behind him and saw Mamacita framed under the archway at the stairs. She was crying too. His first inclination was to laugh, as one might at a vast and carefully structured practical joke. "Joe," was all he said.

"It's true, Burt." Joe Christy walked him forward. "He's a bright fella, little scared now, understandably. Talk to him."

Burt Hammond reached out and took a small but tough hand in his. "*¿Como te llamas? ¿Cual es tu nombre?*"

"Beltran."

"The nearest . . . they could come to Burton," Helen sobbed.

He looked at her with disapproval. "*¿De donde vienes, Beltran?*"

"*El desierto.* The desert," he said unexpectedly in English.

"*¿Hablas inglés, Beltran?*"

"Yes. My grandfather, he teach me . . . taught me. Make me to speak English all the time."

"You speak English very well, Beltran."

"Yes, sir. But slowly and simple. Simply. I must to learn."

"We can talk Spanish. *Hablo español.*"

"My grandfather says I must talk English only to my father."

"Do you know who is your father?"

Pausing only to turn to Joe Christy, the boy pulled off the little clip-on bow tie Joe and some salesman must have arranged for the occasion and opened the collar beneath it. He struggled for a long moment and finally succeeded in bringing out something hidden in his fist. When the fingers parted, brilliant fire without end was revealed, contained in a diamond the size of a bird's egg and held by a platinum chain. Burt Hammond turned to look with questioning eyes at Joe Christy.

"Sold it to you mighty cheap, remember?" Joe said.

"And counselor, don't tell me 'It's the stone, all right, but how can you be sure about the boy?' Look at that face, Burt."

Helen sobbed wildly. She ran to her mother. The women embraced, both awash in tears.

"Spittin' image, only prettier skin," Joe Christy went on. "It's the Indian part. I told Don Pedro that five years ago."

"All this time you knew?"

"Swore to secrecy, boy, and when Don Pedro asks you to do something, seems to me you do it."

"Come here, Beltran," Burt Hammond said decisively. The boy walked dutifully toward his father. "Do you know who I am?"

"My mother told me Tio Joe will bring me to my father."

"What else did she tell you?"

"My father is a maker of miracles. *Milagros.* Miracles. He made the lame man to walk and healed the wounds of fire and stone."

"You want to live with me?"

"Yes, Father."

"Are you certain I am your father?"

"Don Pedro said that when I am with my father I will know. I know now, *mi padre.*"

"You want to stay here in this house?"

"I don't know."

Burt laughed. "I don't know either." He fell to his knees and took the hard young body into his arms.

Helen Mendoza had prepared a guest room, two doors down from his own. He watched his son take out his old clothes and the new ones Joe Christy had bought for him. The boy treated everything with equal indifference, gravely, carefully. He seemed to have no trouble making himself at home at once in a palatial residence. Only once did he stop his unpacking and settling himself. He came over to his father and said: "Tio Joe says I must to go to school. *¿Es lejos?* It is far from here?"

"I don't know."

"Then it is surely far."

"Are you afraid, Beltran?" Burt Hammond pursued.

"Afraid?" His forehead creased with incomprehension.

"*¿Tienes miedo? ¿Temeroso?*"

"Of what, Father?"

339

"This new life. It is different from your other life, is it not?"

"Only this room and this furniture are different. My life does not change," the boy said.

8

"MAYBE his life ain't changed all that much, but yours sure as hell has, my friend." Joe Christy was restless. He inhabited the house in Mapleton Drive like a splendid hacienda-fortress, exploring its corners and discovering features its residents had not known. He and Burt Hammond found pleasure in the boy's company, teaching him to swim, to dive, to float on an air mattress, all experiences new to him. Still, Joe Christy talked of being away too long from his office down in Veracruz. The final days of the presidential election made him uncomfortable. "Only one thing in the world I know a damn about, oil, and when both parties talk about it, I wanna run," the old man said.

He was right about Burt Hammond's life. What Joe Christy did not know was that the change in his host's life was inevitable. Burt Hammond sensed rough weather ahead. Whoever came to power spelled trouble. The Teamsters might weasel out, Hoffa in prison and the anointed successor having spent mightily and wisely. Maybe, he thought, Jerry Haggerty had not been so stupid, after all.

His son pleased him. The boy was grave—understandable; intelligent, which was flattering; polite, and shy. He did not speak much of the desert, even when prompted. His eyes went dark when the subject came up; he had trouble recollecting.

Joe Christy began to wonder about the cars always parked across the street. He did his best to say nothing but silence would have been tactless. "They know something I don't?" he asked one day.

"I'd bet they know something *I* don't," Burt Hammond

countered. He had learned a lesson a long time ago. He never underrated an adversary. He could see them prepare the ground now. Stories kept recurring in the press. It was time to investigate the link between organized crime and legitimate business. Lawyers with dubious clients. The misuse of pension funds, skimming, tax dodges, the Haggerty disappearance—the moment was at hand to pull these noxious weeds, return to fundamentals, restore faith, use the power . . .

"Why do you not take Beltran to see that woman you wanted to marry?" Helen asked after Joe Christy had gone.

"You talk too much," Burt Hammond cut her off.

"You have a son now, you've lived alone too long."

"I still say you talk too much."

"If you don't marry pretty soon you'll wind up a dirty old man who thinks life is wearing a different pretty girl on the arm every day."

"Oh, shut up, Helen."

But she was right. There would be less reason now for Courtney to back away. And the more he thought about it, the more brilliant and final Hilary's plan to take over Sobordco seemed to be. Whether he could get Flora Levering to go along was something he was not wholly sure of. But the old lady would not reject the plan out of hand.

The problem was Burton Z Hammond. He was a moving target inching into range. It would be unwise to involve them.

So he stuck close to Mapleton Drive. And shut his ears to Helen Mendoza's kind-hearted nagging.

Shortly after Nixon's election, the surveillance cars disappeared. At first he thought it a bureaucratic foul-up, but the cars did not come back, week after week. Still, he refused to leave the house. *Eye of the Storm* was rushed into release to qualify it for the Academy Awards. The first reviews were handsome and the early box-office returns gratifying. Ike Ash ordered—he always ordered; he never invited—him to a party. Burt Hammond wondered what the studio boss said when he did not show up.

Janet Morgan came calling afterward. "Now he loves me, he wants me to make another picture." She took no notice of a boy's bicycle in the foyer and tossed a baseball glove she found on the den sofa to the floor so she could sit. "Will you look at the deal for me?"

He begged off but Morgan would not accept that. "Rosey tells me you're handling her, why can't you do the same for me?"

"I'm not agenting her, I'm a substantial stockholder there."

"So? Extend me the same courtesy."

He took her hands in his. "They're out to get me, Jan. And for the first time in my life, I think I can be broken."

"Don't let them."

He promised to do what he could for her. She wanted to stay the night but he begged off. She could see he was not in a frame of mind to be teased. She told him about the house in Mendocino County and said he could always stay there. He started to protest but she would not hear it. "If you need a hideout and don't use it, I'd be hurt, dear, dear friend," she said.

"I love you," Burt Hammond said when he held her in his arms.

"I love you too," Janet Morgan echoed. "Isn't it too bad love's not enough anymore?"

It rained for three days without end shortly after the new year began. The cat had problems. The station wagon would not start. Mamacita had the flu. Beltran had begun to go to school. Ellis Griswold took a full page in seven metropolitan papers challenging "insidious and dangerous quasi-criminal elements in our society" to come out into the open. The new Vice-President was saying the same things. Burt Hammond consented to meet Larry Marshall at a small fish restaurant in Santa Monica. A tour of Europe was possible; tied in with the release of the picture . . .

"Good idea," Burt said, and Marshall thought his response so quick he was interested only in ending the meeting. "Cash in on the picture, help it, and keep her busy."

"You want to look at the deal?"

"No. If you say it's okay, I'll buy it."

"I have to tell you," Marshall said. "I get the feeling you're kissing us off."

"Sorry." There was no use denying it.

It took an hour to go over all the points in the proposed

European tour and, as Burt had anticipated, no exception could be taken with any of them.

He refused a lift and took a cab to where he had been going for a number of days, the law library of the University of Southern California. The UCLA library was a lot closer to Holmby Hills, but he had the feeling he could be more easily recognized there so he always went downtown. He had a lot to read, a lot to learn about the powers of the Senate in investigative matters and its awesome Constitutional privileges. He discovered a vast area he had had no knowledge of. Even Thomas Jefferson had found it impossible to resist those sovereign powers, so what could he learn from the likes of Richard Whitney and John Pierpont Morgan, Sr., and all the targets of the late Senators Joseph McCarthy and Joseph Nye, Estes Kefauver, John McClellan? The Senate made its own law, if that was the word. What it said, went.

Yes, the weather was going to be rough.

9

A hot dry wind blew in from the desert, ending the rain and leaving the city lights diamond-sharp. In his sleep he heard the door rattle; he put it to the unseasonal Santa Ana but the noise persisted and he came to full consciousness knowing someone was hammering at his door in the middle of the night. What he saw from an upstairs window sent him racing down the steps as fast as his legs could take him.

Jerry Haggerty, grown somewhat plumper, encased in a trucker's coat two sizes too large for him, a gray carpeting of beard giving him the look of an Old Testament patriarch in a Renaissance painting, stared at him until Burt Hammond asked him in. The house was dark; Burt walked down the steps toward the street to see if the place was being covered before going in himself.

"It's okay. You're in the clear," Jerry said. "I checked first."

Burt Hammond brought him to a small library on the main floor. "I'll get you a bottle," he said, but the old man waved a finger at him. That was a surprise. He wanted nothing, responded with grunts and murmurs. Burt Hammond kept studying him for some sign, a clue perhaps, of what had driven this old man and what possessed him now. The searching eyes did not go unnoticed, but Jerry offered no comment.

"I got to sleep here tonight. You got a place for me?"

"Of course. You can stay as long as you like."

"I'll leave as soon as I can, assuming the coast's clear. Tomorrow's going to be a big day."

"Do you want to tell me what happened and where you've been, Jerry?"

"Been searching, kid."

There was a look in the eyes like none Burt Hammond had ever seen, wild, unfocused. "For what, Jerry?"

"For me, counselor. What's more, I found what I was looking for."

"And what was that?"

"I'm not crazy, so you don't have to stare at me like that. I found the old Jerry Haggerty, and that's the guy who's going to face the world and all his enemies from here on out." A torrent of words told the rest of it. One day it had come to him that win, lose or draw, his life and career were at an end. He was a prisoner of the law courts, of the congressional ferrets, of the guys he had been dealing with, of public opinion. Of his recent past. He had to break out. But how? Then it came to him, it had been right under his nose all the time, hadn't it? Hadn't he been shown how to do it? He jutted a finger at Burt Hammond. "You go off, why shouldn't I?" It was easy for others, but he was Jerry Haggerty and there were a lot of people keeping tabs on his every move. It was a time when friends and enemies were the same people, and you didn't know where any of them came from. But it was also a time to think things over. So he ran. He took his life and career back to the very beginning. Thirty-five years ago he was a raw young man and he had taken on the whole Establishment—and won! They'd tried to nail him, as they were trying today, and he had come through. Alone! Now he had a world of friends he'd come by with the help of things like the pension fund—and what was the outlook? Prison, or being gunned down in the middle of the night. Either way, death. They'd put Hoffa away and the guy still had dreams of coming back—hand-picked a man to hold the reins until he got out. Maybe he would get out, but he was through; no one was going to give him anything anymore. Could Jerry Haggerty face a future like that?

But by the same token, could he escape the inevitable Committee? Or the law court? He saw his answer in becoming again the rebel he'd once been. The country—the whole world—teemed with rebellion, the blacks, the Mexican Americans, the kids, women; in Germany, in Italy, soldiers in uniform and kids who didn't want to get into uniform—and what had he been doing, where had he been basing his strength? On the power of money, when he knew a greater power!

Madness, Burt Hammond thought; but a special madness. A few perceptions along the way were accurate, but what did Haggerty propose? He was going to reappear, a man who had found the light again and who would call on all his supporters to help him begin the search for a new and better world.

"You're asking for bigger trouble than you've got, Jerry."

"I can handle me. It's you I don't know what to do with."

The words hung in the air like an echo. There was no denying an implicit threat, the old fears and uncertainties, which Burt Hammond now knew would never go away. He made no response.

"I'll be able to handle myself," Jerry Haggerty said again. "But can I count on you?"

"Haven't you, so far?"

"You haven't been put to the fire, kid. Any day now it will happen, right this minute it's in the works, if I'm any judge, and I've been through it before, so I know, I know." He put his finger to his nose as if to indicate that a feral instinct for survival never betrayed him. "It's coming. What will you do?" Burt Hammond did not reply. "I said," Jerry's voice louder now, "what will you do? Will you talk? Will you cooperate?"

"I've got nothing to hide, Jerry."

"Don't give me that. You're thinking about *you*, what about me?"

"You were my client. I'd never talk about that."

"That won't wash, not here, not now; they'll get to me, through you, if you say one word. If you even appear. I can hide, first like I've been doing, and then behind the man I've become, the old Jerry Haggerty. Can you hide? Will you?"

Silence filled the room like a grenade tossed and waiting to explode. "I don't know if I want to," Burt Hammond said at length.

"You've got no choice, I tell you now." He paused. "If you want to live."

"That's a threat, Jerry?"

The old man shrugged. "And no more reprieves, no more luck-outs. I'm not going to wind up finished like Hoffa. And you're sure as hell not going to stay rich and comfortable while I rot." The voice was easy and without menace. "So give me your word you don't say one goddamn thing when they get to you, not one word, whatever the consequences. Me, I'll take care of myself. The old Haggerty knew how to fight the whole world, it's you who can break me. Now I'd like to go to sleep. Have you got a Bible I can read?" He broke off without warning and rose like a man with business elsewhere.

Burt Hammond found a Bible on the bottom shelf. "Thank you, my boy," the old man said. His visage was benign and he laid his hand on Burt Hammond's shoulder for support as they climbed the steps. Burt Hammond put him in a room at the far end of the hall from his own. "Bless you," Jerry Haggerty said and he let the door come closed behind him.

Burt Hammond went down the hall to Beltran's room. He sat on his son's bed and as gently as possible woke him. "Get dressed," he said softly.

The boy rose without complaint. "Where are we going, Father?"

"To see your new mother, would you like that?"

"If you would like that, it would make me very happy."

He took the wiry body into his arms and held it very tight.

10

THE boy seemed to glow with the music, so the radio was on all the way. "You are listening to the voice of the Great Central Valley," the announcer preened, as dawn broke over the broad fields; the place-names changed as the car roared north and the signals faded in and out, but everywhere local pride burned bright between the same hit songs. They did not vary. Beltran was riveted by "Mrs. Robinson." "Spinning Wheel," "Hey Jude" and "Jumpin' Jack Flash." Once Beltran touched his hand on the wheel. "I like this one, Father," he said when the announcer called the next song. Burt Hammond turned from his thoughts to hear Roseanna Lee's voice:

> "This lady and that life,
> We better come to terms,
> While we're in the eye of the storm."

In the film it had scudded across the surface of his being like a nice tune. He knew better now.

Route 5 was a straight line drawn across a flat plain; in the early morning, the sun rising higher behind his left shoulder, time was lost, space a blur, the music began to make sense to him after all, not Rosey's song alone, all of it, even Bob Dylan's whining, which he had never liked.

A glance in his rear-view mirror brought him back; it amused him that the red lights flashing on top of the pursuing car seemed unable to gain on him. But, of course, what would it prove?

"Morning," the officer said a few minutes later, when he strolled over. "That's a pretty automobile you've got. Would you mind getting out of your car?"

Damned foolish of me, Burt Hammond thought. Now there'll be a record and sooner or later, someone, somewhere, will learn that on this day and at this hour at this spot he had been seen and a traffic citation had been issued, and here, to confirm, is the signature.

"May I see your license, sir?"

The officer took the license and looked at it without comment, putting it in a clip atop the pad he opened. Burt Hammond wondered what he could do. Nothing, he decided.

"What kind of car is this?"

"It's called a Jensen."

"That like a Ferrari?"

"Not really." *There was something he could do after all.* "It's really a Chrysler 300 under the hood, the block redrilled, everything more finely tuned than a stock car," he offered amiably. "The advantage is that it can be serviced easily by any Chrysler dealer and isn't in the shop all the time like those Italian cars."

"I clocked you at ninety-five."

"Wouldn't be surprised, officer."

"Usually they say they weren't doing what I catch them at."

"Hell, with this car, this road, the weather dry, and no other cars? I was holding the beast back. I'm glad it was only ninety-five, officer."

The officer stared at him as if for the first time. "I'll go easy with you and cite you for seventy-two."

"Thanks, but you don't have to do that for me, officer. I mean, if you think I wasn't handling the car reasonably well and driving with care given these excellent road and traffic conditions, I wouldn't want you to compromise yourself."

The officer stared at him coldly. "You some kind of a wise guy, mister?"

"No, sir. I was either right or wrong. I leave it to you, sir."

The officer smiled, but his lips drew back in what could have been a snarl. He put his pad under his armpit and walked to the rear of the car as if to let his temper cool. I've offended him, Burt thought, he doesn't want to let me know it. Also, now he's going to remember me. When the process servers do not find me and the intensive search heats up, this citation by this officer will be flagged. *"Yes, I remember the guy. He was a smartass when I cited him."*

"What's the top speed on this baby?" he said amicably enough, when he returned from surveying the car.

"I've had it to a hundred and twenty and the pedal wasn't on the floor."

"One-twenty? No kidding? You don't want me to write you at seventy-two?"

"I don't want you to write me at all, officer." Burt chuckled as cheerfully as he could manage.

"I don't want to write you either. You look like you're an experienced driver who knows what he's doing, but not everybody else on the road is. Just be careful, huh?"

He saw his driver's license in the officer's extended hand. "Thank you, sir."

"What does that mean?" Beltran asked when Burt fitted himself into the driver's seat again and snapped the buckles on.

Burt Hammond shrugged. "Your grandfather would understand."

The boy slept, curled in the leather bucket like a big puppy trying to make do in a small box. Burt Hammond took the occasion to punch up some less raucous radio stations; he was now able to pull in San Francisco clearly. News was a relief from the incessant rock. The new President had coined a phrase—or some speechwriter had, surely—"the Silent Majority." Burt Hammond had trouble keeping the car at an even 70, but there was more traffic now and he saw black-and-whites cruising and he did not want to test his—what was it?—luck again, so he contented himself with five miles over.

The news from Washington began with the latest from Southeast Asia. The negotiators in Paris had resumed. The chairman of the Foreign Relations Committee had made a speech. After weeks of private, if not secret, preparations, the Senate Judiciary Committee today re-instituted—and Burt Hammond felt his foot grow softer on the accelerator as he strained to hear what he had known for so long was coming—its Select Committee on Crime and Legitimate Business. The ritual, routine words were recited again, like an old priest delivering the litany which he had first offered as a boy: inroads of organized crime, crooked unions, Las Vegas, pension funds, tax schemes, financial manipulations, corrupt lawyers, mobsters, front-men, dummy corporations, the costs in billions to the American economy.

They are looking to serve me right this minute, Burt Hammond thought.

* * *

He was headed for the parking area at the side of the house when he saw the familiar Plymouth parked in the crushed stone at the front of Wildoaks. He wheeled his car and brought it to a stop behind it. Elmer Wright must have caught him in the rear-view mirror. He was already out of the car to greet him.

"What're you doing here, Mr. Wright?"

"I was going to ask the same of you, sir. I'm trying to get word to these people, but they don't want to see me. I've been waiting since early morning."

"What kind of word?"

"There's a contract out on Mr. Kendall."

Burt Hammond coughed slightly. "What about the young lady?"

"The family has kept her pretty well insulated, but I want to tell them to be very careful with her too. There's a lot of resentment in certain circles, to put it mildly, sir."

Burt Hammond started for the stables. Elmer Wright looked with surprise at the boy running to keep up. The detective was out of breath as they passed the Carriage House, and staggering on alone when he followed them past the riding ring and the older stalls. "Flora!" he heard Burt Hammond call. The detective decided it would be wiser to sit a moment.

Flora Levering poked her head over a split door. She offered no sign of surprise or recognition. "What do you want?"

"Where's Courtney?"

Her eyes fixed on Beltran. She pushed open the door, eased past a big bay, and approached the boy. "Who's this?"

"My son."

"Didn't know you had one."

"Neither did I until just the other day."

"Looks like you."

"Skin's Indian."

"I noticed that. That makes him even better-looking than his father. What's his name?"

"Why don't you ask him?"

"I don't speak any Spanish—"

"Try English."

She was putting the boy through the usual questions when Elmer Wright came up at last. Flora stared at him balefully.

350

"This man's here to see you. You know Elmer Wright, of course," Burt Hammond said.

"They told me, something to do with Kenneth, I've no interest—"

"And Courtney. She could be in danger. Where is she?"

"On a hillside." Their eyes locked briefly in understanding. She could see the dismay in Burt Hammond.

"You'd better get her in as fast as you can, ma'am," Elmer Wright said without hesitation.

"I'll call a groom and have a horse saddled."

"I can go at once," Beltran said. "I don't use a saddle." He pointed to the bay whose ears were flicking nervously at his half-open door. "I like that one."

"Kind of big for you, isn't he?" Flora said.

"Not too big." The boy kicked off his sneakers and pulled the socks from his feet.

Flora Levering put in the bit and brought the reins around. His father lifted the boy to the horse's back and saw the animal mastered with a touch. They pointed down the path and to the top of the ridge where he could find Courtney. The horse whinnied and wheeled impatiently as Beltran brought him around. "Father." He gestured for a private word. "Is it the lady who is to be my mother?" he asked in Spanish.

"That is her decision."

"You want it, Father?"

"Yes."

The big animal pulled at the reins and pawed the ground. "*Adiosito*, Papa!" He gave the horse his head and both streaked down the path with sheer animal joy.

Burt thought he saw the old lady wipe a tear out of the corner of her eye with a bent finger. "I'm sorry," she said to Elmer Wright. "Forgive me for not seeing you sooner." She turned and walked to a stall.

When Burt found her again, she was trying to look busy in the tack room. "What the hell is she doing up on that ridge?"

"Seeding it. Heather. Stuff like that."

"I don't like it."

"I didn't either, at first," Flora said. " 'Think of it,' Courtney told me. 'In all his life there was only one person who cared about him. Wouldn't it be awful if he lost that too?' "

They walked to the house slowly. "Once she sees the boy, she'll marry you, if that's what you still want."

"If that's what *you* want, Flora."

"Why should I not, young man? And why should *I* have to want it?"

"I need about twenty-five million dollars from you, I'd say."

She stopped and wheeled toward him. "I'll be damned. A fortune-hunter."

"You talked once about getting rid of this place. Make a complete break. Come on back into the world, Flora."

"And give you twenty-five million for the privilege? You're what your reputation says, a hustler, an unscrupulous wheeler-dealer, a fast-buck artist, aren't you?"

"Yes, indeed, Flora. And you're the daughter of a robber-baron capitalist trying to fill the emptiness with a big house and creaking servants. I'm going to bring you into the twentieth century." He told her about the Sobordco opportunity, the company against the wall, swollen with assets others would sniff out soon enough, the real-estate values now stated in depressed dollars soon to be double, triple in value.

"I don't have that kind of capital," Flora Levering muttered.

"Sure you do, Flora. Once you bust open all those sterile trust arrangements and put your capital to work again."

She hesitated for a moment. "And you, what do you get out of it?"

"Nothing."

"Nothing?"

"And everything. I pick up a piece of my own heritage, you might say. Otherwise, I don't want a quarter for myself. What the hell, Flora, start by giving this house and all the art in it to the National Trust. A new Sobordco will give you something to live for again. The trusted advisors on Montgomery Street will scream bloody murder, but fire the lot of them and get yourself some hotshot lawyers."

"Meaning you."

"I'm going to have some problems of my own. Do you think you can manage for a while by yourself? Still, I've got a good operating chief for you. You know Hilary Wilson, I believe." He paused for an explosion.

Nothing exploded. Flora grinned saturninely. "That bitch? *She'll* run Sobordco?"

"No one better for our purposes right now. She commands eight percent of the voting stock going in, she's a woman, which is great public relations, she's been in the company from the inception, which will quiet the stockholders, and she'll do anything I tell her to get what she wants. And she needs us."

After a pause, Flora said: "I know your kind, young fella. You'd rather trade than eat. So long as you get what you want. My father would have liked you."

"I wouldn't have liked him, but maybe times have changed."

They heard the far echo of horses' hooves from the distant ridge and looked up to see two riders streaking neck and neck across the horizon. The old lady grinned. "That's a quarter horse she's on and the little rascal's going to beat her." She turned and did her best to express disapproval. "Plainly, he needs to be taught how a gentleman behaves."

"Won't stick, Flora."

"His father's son, you mean? Maybe there's something better than being a gentleman, at that," she conceded without any effort at consistency.

"Can you send someone to get the honors between me and Courtney over and done with, someone you can trust not to say a word until after I've gone?" Burt Hammond said.

"You're in that much trouble? You're running?"

"I need time to sort things out."

"We'll have a lovely party, just the four of us."

"Take care of my girl and boy, will you?"

They looked up to see the two horses striding neck and neck toward them. The hooves kicked up the soft gravel of the bridle path on them as the horses drove past. The riders kept laughing and urging their mounts on. It looked like they'd never stop, Burt Hammond thought.

Epilogue Is Prologue

WASHINGTON, D.C.: JUNE 14, 1970

The appearance of Burton Z Hammond before the Senate Select Committee came at a time when everything combined to make it a big story. The press, print and electronic, happened to find itself short on the news budget that week. The war in Vietnam was grinding out its usual squalid message. The administration was making a variety of proposals, public and secret, but as yet had nothing to show, so it and its minions were giving the investigation special emphasis and support. The central character in the Committee's hearing turned out to be colorful, which is to say he was young, handsome, articulate, and married to a young woman of enormous wealth. So the media went all out for a story involving so many newsworthy components. For the members of the Senate committee themselves, the moment was right as well, even without the factor of major public exposure. Two of them faced uphill reelection battles, and publicity was what they needed. The rest were serious about the legislation the chairman had lost sight of and were grateful for the chance to find out what ought to be done in the future.

Jerry Haggerty, accompanied by new counsel, a distinguished Washington lawyer known for his devotion to civil rights and for his astronomical fees, had been, as always in the past, magnificent under fire. Jerry had grown shaggy; a white beard was beginning to carpet the famous visage; even his voice was beginning to rumble like that of a prophet. His memory appeared to have come up uncertain, his hearing had become not all it should be, but goodness and generosity flowed from his heart, even for those who appeared to abuse his grace. He declared he had spent a lifetime in service to the working men and women of this nation, and the Bible he carried with him wherever he went was a token of a new, militant commitment.

Staff members of the committee fed to their friends in the working press stories about the last-minute disappearance of Burton Z Hammond. For a day or two it was rumored he had been kidnapped; murdered; somehow disposed of. His recent bride, her family's fabled estate, his affairs with world-famous artists—Burt Hammond was not only a subject for political analysts but found himself on the cover of a national weekly gossip magazine, surrounded, of course, by his ladies, past and present.

When Burt Hammond showed up in Washington, he said simply: "I've been visiting friends and thinking over what I would do here. I understand there was a subpoena out for me, but it wasn't my duty to hasten to accept it. It was theirs to find me."

Members of the financial press were quick to draw the connection between Hammond, the Levering family into which he had recently married, and the financial turmoil besetting the vast West Coast land conglomerate called the Southern Border Land Development Corporation. Asked by reporters if he was "masterminding" these moves, Burton Hammond paused in the Senate corridor and responded openly and without hesitation. "Yes. My wife's family's fortune has been socially inert for too long. It is exploring new areas in which to grow and help this country. It won't be the old Sobordco, I assure you."

The Senate committee asked if he came with counsel. He smiled ruefully and reminded the members he was a lawyer. To someone's thrust about a lawyer who represented himself having a fool for a client, he readily agreed. "But I'm the best *lawyer* I know," he added. He knew he was taking chances, but he wanted that opening laugh from the senators and the press for tactical reasons.

The Committee was hostile from the start. He asked permission to make a statement but the chairman would not have it. Burton Hammond had expected no less. He spent the first day responding in a controlled, almost inaudible voice, but responding nevertheless. When he could. Which was not always. He was a lawyer and it turned out that the Committee, itself largely composed of lawyers, wanted to know about matters Burton Hammond kept saying he was forbidden to discuss. The twin tactics of quiet openness and lawyer-privilege made the hearing somewhat less than had been hailed as and expected to be a media event. At the end of the first day, Burton Hammond was safe.

The television cameras sprang into action again when he and Courtney came out on the street. They were waiting for their rented car and its driver; each had an arm circled around the other's waist. The soundmen caught an exchange. "You were great in there," the lady said. "Tomorrow's going to get a lot hotter," the man commented.

When the car did not show up, the couple decided to walk. They were soon lost in a crowd of people heading home. They had not gone far when they heard a voice from behind call his first name.

"Goodman, Hammond . . . Oliver Hale Goodman." No hand was extended, but the old adversary from San Francisco strode toward them.

Burt introduced the gentleman to his wife and told her: "Mr. Goodman and I had some business together in San Francisco." To Goodman he said: "What're you doing here?"

"I'm with the Committee."

"Thought you'd had it with government."

"So did I. But the chance to get even with Joseph Jerome Haggerty and Burton Z Hammond proved irresistible."

"Didn't see you in there. What happened?"

"I'm in charge of the research staff. But I'm in there." Burt Hammond's face froze. "Congratulations."

"I think you ought to know your life's in danger. That's what I've come to tell you."

"Thanks very much."

"I'd be very careful, Hammond. Our sources are excellent, I assure you. Remember Eddie Gorman."

He'd read about Gorman's murder in the desert a few days before, but he offered no reaction now. "Always am careful, counselor."

"I'm only trying to be friendly, Hammond," Goodman said lamely. "I think you'd do the same for me."

Burt Hammond paused. Goodman meant well, at that. "Thanks." He took Courtney's hand and pulled her with him down the street, leaving Oliver Hale Goodman on the sidewalk, looking after them.

They were staying at a Levering family friend's place

in McLean. "We won't go there tonight," he said, while waiting in a small bar in the Madison for the waiter to bring their drinks.

Courtney said nothing until the Scotches came. "It's true, huh?" She sipped a little. "They're really out to get you?"

"Yes."

"Who's Eddie Gorman?"

"Never met him. Apparently some people think there's some connection."

"Who wants you dead?"

"How far back do you want to go?" When he drank, he took his Scotch neat; he liked it strong, smokey and unblended.

"All the way back," Courtney said.

"Then you have to start in the Imperial Valley. A man named Ellis Griswold always wanted me dead. Hilary Wilson? I've never been sure. We've given her what she wants and we're no threat. Not for now, in any case. The FBI or some rogue cops in that sainted institution? Their cops go crazy now and then, like cops anywhere. I doubt the Bureau uses the direct approach, though. Not that some guys there don't want to do everything possible to nail me; so they could be using, or helping, some outside bad guy. Heady stuff, huh?" He picked up his shot glass and emptied it. He gestured for the waiter.

"Who else?" Courtney said.

"I wish we didn't have to go to McLean tonight," he parried.

"You're begging off telling me everything."

"Somewhat." A gesture told the waiter to repeat the order. "Who knows? Haggerty. Haggerty's people, guys he doesn't even have to speak to. Lots of people. I bring out the homicidal in my adversaries, I think."

"In me you bring out the erotic," she said.

"I love you, Courtney. It sounds worse than it is." He reached out and took her hand. "Or maybe I've gotten used to it. Or good at it. I have to tell you, killers turn out to be very inept. Murder for hire as a line of work does not attract a superior kind of brain, I've observed."

"We won't go to McLean," Courtney offered. "We'll sleep in town."

"There're never vacant rooms in this hotel, Courtney."

"Wait here, my sweet." She took another sip before

leaving him. In a few minutes she came back, waving a key.

"A worker of miracles," he said.

"No, sir. They know your name and they know my name and they've got a cancelation and it's three hundred bucks for the night."

"Cheap at half the price. Let's have another here."

Courtney put a hand on his shoulder. "Upstairs and later, my darling. I want you sober and hard and now."

"Madame," he said. "Hard is never a problem with you." He had to wait for the waiter and the check before he could follow her out. She wasn't waiting.

WASHINGTON, D.C.: JUNE 15, 1970

They almost slept too late, having deliriously and joyously exhausted themselves more than once during the night. When the waiter wheeled in the table with their breakfast order, it came with a copy of the Washington *Post*. On the front page was the story of a car belonging to the Fowler Limousine Service which was found to be wired to explode on signal from a remote electronic source. A chauffer, checking an engine rattle, had taken note of something he had not observed before. He had returned to his garage where a mechanic spotted the lethal device. The Washington police were not saying yet to whom this car had been assigned. The *Post* reporter was allowed to do some speculating about names of Fowler clients, but at press time Burt Hammond's had not yet been brought in. But Burt knew it had to be his car.

By the time he reached the corridor outside the hearing room, there was no doubt it was the car that had been rented to him. "No, I don't know who'd want me dead," he told the reporters and cameramen poised to get at him.

This morning the Committee members and the staff were in no mood to be turned aside. One senator sternly lectured him on the risk to his own life, his responsibilities as a lawyer and a citizen, and the growing connection between legitimate business and dangerous criminal elements. "Do you deny involvement there?" he was asked. "Don't duck the question. Do you dare assert here that there is no connection, after this terrible thing the press

360

has reported about you?" He went on in this vein for some time before he stopped for the reply he sought.

"No, Senator," Burt Hammond said, sure he had found the opening that had been denied him the day before, "I do not deny such an involvement. May I explain?"

"Take all the time you like," the senator said.

He had won the opportunity he needed—to make a statement. "Thank you, Senator. I can only testify here from what I have in my own life learned about crime and the business affairs of this nation. In my experience, if there's a criminal element, it doesn't come from one side only of the economy. My father was killed by people who to this day regard themselves as sternly law-abiding citizens. Yet even now they are openly flouting the intention of the body you gentlemen represent in legislation passed more than a half-century ago. And you—this government, like a dozen before it—don't give a damn. I was forged in that fire." Burton Z Hammond felt good. He had paid back an obligation laid on him a very long time ago.

Burt Hammond could see staff counsel and the senators begin to stir restlessly. He kept his smile of approval to himself, and hastened to finish. "I am myself what some of you gentlemen would call a strict constructionist in legal matters. My father made me into that. This is the law. Follow it. Or change it. That's how he used to talk. All my life I've insisted my clients accept such a course of action. Now what does that mean? I always made sure what I advised was legally correct. If the law was stupid, I took advantage of it. If it could be turned in my favor, I pushed it. But I followed it rigorously. Is that bad? I'm an interested party, so I can't say. But I tell you this: We are at a stage in our history where from the very top to the bottom, the concern is not, *Is it proper?* but, *Can I do this?* Or, *Can I get away with this?* Or, *How far can we go?*

"I ask you gentlemen if you can honestly say you've never entertained such thoughts?"

A senator quickly interceded: "I do not think it behooves this witness to lecture us on law and ethics."

"With all respect to my distinguished colleague, I believe the witness is trying to respond to the question about the involvement of business and crime which was posed him." The speaker from the row of chairs where the senators sat was Gordon Eberhardt, a man Burt Hammond had known at Yale. From their very first meeting here, he had offered no sign of recognition. Burt Hammond saw nothing sinister in that. What would the world make of their connection? A payoff for campaign contributions? Mutual respect? Sympathetic hearing from an old friend? Everybody demanded simple answers, but the world had come too far and was moving too fast for the old primer-book explanations.

"Very well," the senator grumbled to Burt Hammond's former classmate. "Let us hear the witness out."

Courtney Hammond, watching her husband from the back of the room, sank a little lower on the bench. Toughness she admired. She was raised by a tough lady. She remembered unintentionally overhearing her father on the telephone when he was serving in the Eisenhower administration. His face blanched visibly when he discovered her presence in a room in which he thought he was wholly alone. "You're not ever to say anything to anyone about what you just heard, understand?" he barked at her in his characteristic way. She was a child, she had not really paid attention, it had something to do with a Navy oil reserve, whatever that was. She had not understood the panic in her father's eyes, but she knew he felt he had done something terrible. It all came back to her now. Father panicked when there was no need. Burt did not falter. The senators were taking him apart, they thought, going over the old ground about his use of cash, about his law practice with almost no files, about his way of conducting business. The alleged murder attempt. He did not apologize; he told them as simply as he could why he had to operate as he did. He had gone over this ground before with other government investigators, so he was very patient.

"*Are* you a crooked lawyer?" Courtney heard a senator snap at him.

She had once asked him something like that. Apparently she had not been the only one. "I was asked that once by a very dear friend," Burt Hammond gave in answer.

"I ask you that now, Mr. Hammond," the senator pursued. "What did you tell him?"

"Her," Burt Hammond corrected him. It elicited both a gasp and a laugh in the audience, which seemed what he sought. "It was a social conversation so I'm not breaking a client's confidence. I told this friend what I've told others who've asked me the same question." He took a long, almost theatrical, pause. "I don't know if that makes me crooked. A lot of us get called crooked. Or corrupt. I believe it even happens to public servants. Maybe we're all crooked or corrupt."

"Answer the question: *Are you a crooked lawyer?*" his questioner demanded sternly.

"Are you a crooked politician, sir?"

The chairman banged his gavel. Too many people spoke at once. Courtney Hammond heard talk of contempt, but when it was all over Burt seemed to be the only principal in the proceedings who was not emotionally aroused. There were warnings and admonitions before the witness was directly addressed again.

A senator who had not spoken before faced him. He was a small man, avuncular, with a gentle Southern twang to his speech. "Mr. Hammond," he began courteously, like a trapper used to setting his traps properly and carefully in the field, both for the sport and for the quarry he delighted in catching, "your life is in danger. From your testimony here you live in a world where there is no accommodation between disaster and success. Why do you not here and now give us the benefit of all your experience? In a word, sir, what have you learned?"

Courtney sank even lower on the bench. Flattery. The old Southern charm. The gentle hand after the mauling. She watched Burt scratch his skull with a finger, smile a little. Was he on to the old man's game? Would he be cajoled?

"I've learned how to endure, Senator, and to enjoy life." Burt was in control of himself, Courtney knew, and she smiled to herself. He would not be destroyed. She saw that, in spite of himself, even the old trapper-senator was intrigued. A grin creased the huge, jowly face as the senator leaned forward to listen. "Country boys learn how to manage in this world from the beginning, don't they, Senator?" Burt Hammond went on slowly. He would not only not be destroyed, Courtney knew, in the end he would win, even here. He would always come out ahead. There are men like that, she thought, just as there are women like that.

From the mountain ridge high above Wildoaks, the fields below were dry and golden. The distant house was a red jewel, a ruby, her favorite gem, set in gold, which she also loved. Flora Levering knew that very soon she would never again see the place from this spot. Her eyes began to mist. She heard her nickname. *"Abuelita."* She turned to face the boy whom she'd left with the horses that had carried them here. "Granny," he called to her again, this time in English, although she had made it her business to know what it was that the lad liked to call her in his native tongue. "Look at the foot of this horse. *Una lesión.*"

She came to his side, tousled his head. The leg had been superficially cut above the hoof. "He's a good, strong colt, he'll manage, Beltran," she assured him as she put down the leg.

The young man came up to where she sat again. He was too young to know many things; it could not be known to him why her eyes remained fixed on a hillside where a small cover of lilac heather flowered against the withered slope. He took a place next to her and followed the long line of her gaze. "You are sad to leave your land, granny?"

She put an arm around him. "I have seen much here, *muchacho.* Some hurt. Some pleasure. Mostly I have loved it here."

"Why do you go? Are you not happy now?"

"Sometimes one is forced off the land. By time, by things one doesn't control or understand. It is better to leave with dignity."

"Abuelo—grandfather—he told me many times if I keep the land I love here, I will never to lose it." Flora Levering looked down at Burton Hammond's son, his hand over his heart. She took him into her arms and held him very close.

Katie plunged [her hands]
into his thick, dark hair.

He had her back against the wall, and his
mouth was hard and hungry and stole her
breath. Neither of them held anything back. For
once, they gave the kiss everything they had.
She opened her lips to him. The scent of his skin
was a mingling of soap, sweat, sunshine and
sea, and she was drenched in the blend.

And then he was touching her. There was no
tentative, childish groping, no sneaky
maneuvering, not from this man. Just a sudden
and completely effective gesture of possession.
It was very flattering, and she smiled against his
lips.

He felt her smile and drew back to look down at
her. "What?" he asked.

"I like this," she said.

He wrapped his arms tightly around her. Thigh
to thigh, belly to belly, there was no mistaking
the urgency of his arousal as he buried his face
in her neck. "You're too honest." He paused.
"But I like it, too. As much of a risk as it is..."

Dear Reader,

Happy New Year! We're starting off twelve more months of great reading with a book that many of you have been looking forward to: *Times Change*, Nora Roberts's sequel to last month's *Time Was*. Jacob Hornblower aimed his ship into the past, intending to bring back his brother, Caleb, who had inexplicably decided to remain in the twentieth century to stay with a *woman*! Little did Jacob know that his own heart was about to be stolen by Sunny Stone, Caleb's sister-in-law and the only woman anywhere—or any*when*—capable of making him see the light of love! Love a little, laugh a little, as these two mismatched lovers discover that time is no barrier at all to romance.

Dallas Schulze's *Donovan's Promise* was a big favorite with readers, and now Donovan's son, Michael, has grown up. He's ready for a romance of his own, so prepare to lose your heart to *The Vow*. Like father, like son, as the saying goes, and when it comes to matters of the heart, that definitely seems to be true. Michael Sinclair is every bit as wonderful as Donovan, and his story of love is every bit as compelling as his parents' was.

The month also includes *Catch of the Day*, by Marion Smith Collins, a suspense-filled tale with a tender heart, and *Desert Heat*, by Doreen Roberts, whose luscious prose and very real characters will carry you away.

Read to your heart's content—but don't forget to come back next month for more of the best romances in town, only from Silhouette Intimate Moments.

Leslie J. Wainger
Senior Editor
Silhouette Books

Catch of
the Day

MARION SMITH COLLINS

Silhouette Intimate Moments
Published by Silhouette Books New York
America's Publisher of Contemporary Romance

SILHOUETTE BOOKS
300 East 42nd St., New York, N.Y. 10017

ISBN: 0-373-07320-8

First Silhouette Books printing January 1990

Printed in the U.S.A.

Books by Marion Smith Collins

Silhouette Intimate Moments

Another Chance #179
Better Than Ever #252
Catch of the Day #320

MARION SMITH COLLINS

has written nonfiction for years, but only recently has she tried her hand at novels. She is already the author of several contemporary romances and has no plans ever to stop.

She's a devoted traveler and has been to places as far-flung as Rome and Tahiti. Her favorite country for exploring, however, is the United States because, she says, it has everything.

In addition, she is a wife and the mother of two children. She has been a public-relations director, and her love of art inspired her to run a combination gallery and restaurant for several years.

She lives with her husband of thirty years in Georgia.

This book is dedicated
to Leslie, Shannon and Robin,
three delightful women who, I am proud to say,
are relatives of mine.
And to my cousin, Sidney,
who had the good sense
to increase the Smith family so admirably.

My gratitude and appreciation go to:
Peter Wright of the Ship's Chandler
in Destin, Florida,
and Sam Thomas and the staff
of WJTH, Calhoun, Georgia.
They were patient and forthcoming.
Any mistakes in *Catch of the Day*
are mine, not theirs.

Chapter 1

On the coast of Florida's panhandle, separated from the northern shores of the Gulf of Mexico by a peninsula, lay a pretty harbor called Welaka Lagoon. The boats anchored there were not the heavy ocean-going tankers or cargo ships that found moorings in the larger Palmetto Bay, a few miles away, but private pleasure craft and commercial and charter fishing boats.

Garden City, Florida, established as a fishing village in 1878, had grown, albeit slowly, around the lagoon. It was a small town, with a wintertime population of twelve thousand, give or take a few hundred snowbirds, the name for the people who traveled south to escape the bitter weather in the northern United States and Canada. The area was fairly prosperous, at least when the hurricanes held off until after Labor Day and the fish were biting. Tourism and fishing were the primary sources of commerce for Garden City. The strip of land between the lagoon and the Gulf was reserved for hotels and condominiums, restaurants and shops.

The tempo of life was leisurely, more related to the laid-back Florida of the fifties than the developing nineties. The residents preferred it that way.

Readjusting to the easy life-style so characteristic of her hometown was a more difficult process than Katie Johns had anticipated when she'd returned a year ago. After four years away at college and six more years in the faster-paced, more cosmopolitan business world of Atlanta, Georgia, returning to Garden City was like a step back into a kinder, gentler time. She smiled at the allusion.

A wayward breeze stirred the moss beards that hung from the huge old water oaks and picked at her khaki skirt as she stepped away from the station wagon. The crushed oyster shells that served as paving had been dumped without pattern around the trees, making this not so much a parking lot as an obstacle course, but the residents of Garden City liked their trees, too.

High-heeled shoes weren't intended for this kind of walking but there were still a number of cars around and she hadn't been able to park any closer. She straightened the lapels of the unstructured, unlined raw silk jacket— the only garment in her wardrobe suitable for a business call but not too uncomfortable in the heat and humidity of late June—and reached inside the car for her shoulder bag. As she carefully made her way across the uneven ground she checked her watch. It was a bit before 10:00 p.m., not quite time for her appointment.

She scanned the sky with a knowledgeable eye and debated going back to the car for an umbrella. After a scorcher of a day, the air was now heavy with the promise of rain. She decided that it would hold off for a while.

Heat lightning streaked between the clouds, accompanied by the distant roll of thunder. The only other sounds were the traffic from the highway, muted by distance, the wind in the trees and the whisper of water against the creosoted pilings. Though summer had arrived, bringing longer days and later sunsets, the faint light of the half moon didn't contribute much illumination to the night.

Katie checked the contents of her bag to make sure she hadn't forgotten her notebook, her pen or the sheet of figures she'd compiled for the client. It was an effort to contain her impatience as she approached the ramp leading to the docks. She seldom had to make late calls after a long day, but this one was important.

She stepped through a break in the railing. The ramp sloped gently up from the ground. To her left were the docks themselves. A wooden walkway connected the moorings, and the charter fishing boats were anchored in separate slips. Access to each slip was through a gatelike opening and under a horizontal beam upon which was painted in bright letters the name of the craft. Some of the names were funny, some intriguing, some hinted at the stories behind the names. *One-of-a-Kind. Silver Lining. Month after March. Va-cajun.*

Straight ahead and up a few steps was the public pier, jutting out into the lagoon like an accusing finger for a distance of eighty feet, or more.

To Katie's right was her destination, Harbor Grill, a superb, if vintage, seafood restaurant sitting just back from the junction of pier and docks and overlooking it all like an uneasy chaperon.

Harbor Grill was owned by Dewey O'Donnell and she was here to get his signature on a renewal contract for his daily radio spots. His advertising budget was generous and established, the sort of revenue the small station needed to survive.

O'Donnell was wavering this year. From what she'd heard from her part-time ad salesman, his argument was that during the season he didn't need to advertise; people lined up to be served. And when the off-season arrived, there weren't enough people around to hear whether he advertised or not.

Her shoes were as impractical and as much of a hazard on the docks as they had been on the shells. Though tonight the heels better fitted her image as a professional, she wished for her sneakers. She had to walk leaning slightly forward, on tiptoe, in order to keep a heel from disappearing between the planks.

As a result, her footsteps were quiet and her sudden appearance as she rounded the corner seemed to startle the two people who sat at one of the outdoor tables facing the water.

Katie recognized Louise Austen, the owner of a local boutique and wife of a Garden City car dealer.

Louise smiled distractedly, lifted a hand and Katie waved back. Louise's companion, a stranger to Katie, gave her a long, unsmiling gaze and a short nod. They continued their conversation for a few minutes. Katie wondered idly who he was.

Suddenly the man stood and said something in an undertone. He took Louise's arm, helping her to stand, then leading her toward the public pier. They passed under a safety light within ten feet of Katie. "Hi, Louise."

"Katie," Louise acknowledged briefly. She sent an apologetic smile over her shoulder.

How odd, thought Katie.

She put Louise and the man out of her thoughts when a door slammed behind her.

The owner of the restaurant appeared with a tray. "Hello, Katie."

"Hello, Mr. O'Donnell. It was good of you to see me so late."

"No problem." The breeze was more forceful here above the water. It slapped at the big apron he wore. He looked around as though aware of the weather for the first time. "Wind's picking up, I see. Maybe a storm will give us a break from the heat." He began to collect the candles in glass cups from each of the dozen or so tables on the deck and upended the ashtrays. "I have a couple of paychecks to write after I put these away. Do you want to wait out here?"

"I think so. The breeze feels good."

He nodded. "I'll be right with you."

"Okay." She smiled and wandered over to the table recently abandoned by Louise and her companion. Across the lagoon the lights of the condominiums were like a chain of jewels against the dark night. She sat down in a vinyl director's chair with her back to the view, using the time to marshal her thoughts. The argument against cancellation that she would use with Mr. O'Donnell had to be delivered very diplomatically.

She could sympathize with the man's reluctance to renew his current advertising budget. It had been a hard year for a lot of the business people in this area. They had decided years ago that they didn't want their small community to go the way of other Florida towns, eaten up by high-rise condominiums and garish strips of neon-generated nightlife, so they had instituted strong zoning laws. But they sometimes had second thoughts when the weather and the economy conspired to cut into the profits.

The sound of voices reached her over the water, drawing her gaze to Louise and her companion. They had progressed farther along the pier. Though she couldn't make out their words she recognized that they were having... not an argument, but a determined conversation.

Absently she picked up a book of matches and began to tap it on the table in a fidgety tempo. Not a nervous person, she had been uncharacteristically apprehensive about this interview ever since the salesman had returned empty-handed and said that O'Donnell wanted to talk to her.

The owner of Harbor Grill was an influential member of the Garden City Chamber of Commerce. In this small town that meant a lot; everyone belonged. If she were successful tonight O'Donnell could swing other business toward the station; if she failed to convince him, that influence could all go against her. She needed the revenue that he and the other business owners generated.

WCTZ, a small floundering station, had been purchased a year ago by R and J Communications, Inc., and was now part of their chain of seventeen stations that stretched across Florida, southern Alabama and Georgia. Katie had been recommended by her former employer as the person to turn WCTZ into a profitable link. She was young for the position and the only woman manager in the chain, but she hadn't hesitated to apply for and accept the job when it was offered. Besides the chance to come back to her hometown, this was also her chance to prove she could manage a station satisfactorily.

Mr. O'Donnell reappeared minus his apron. As he passed a table, he turned another ashtray upside down, used the heel of his hand to wipe an invisible speck from the tabletop and took a last look around to assure himself that everything was spotless.

She stood at his approach and smiled. He waved away the polite gesture, eyeing the black sky with a wary look. "I guess the rain will hold off for a while yet. Sit, Katie," he said.

She obeyed, slipping the book of matches she still held into her pocket. She pulled a file folder from a side pocket of her bag and spread her papers out on the table between them.

With a "kindly-uncle" smile, O'Donnell asked, "How's your dad?"

Though O'Donnell had known her since she was a toddler, she wasn't about to let him divert this conversation to a more personal level. She would either get this account because it was a good business deal for his restaurant or she wouldn't get it at all. "Dad's fine," she answered. She took her glasses out of the bag, put them on, and then spun without a break into her carefully prepared spiel.

"Mr. O'Donnell, I know that you've been disappointed with the performance of WCTZ. Your disappointment was justified," she said bluntly, earning herself an amused look. "But since R and J bought the station there has been a definite improvement. Let me show you the July to December figures for last year."

He listened attentively as she warmed to her subject. They continued discussing business as the lights along the waterfront slowly winked out. Listening to his tale of woe—bad business, rising prices and a lack of dependable help—Katie mustered her own statistics and cited her station's improved market share, increase in national advertising, programming changes.

The muffled sound of engines could be heard from the parking lot as, one by one, O'Donnell's employees left. But he didn't rush her and for that she was grateful. The minutes passed, the safety lights became the only illumination except for the now deserted restaurant. A sole fishing boat passed the deck, probably the last one of the night.

With her promise to prepare updated spots to replace the old, tired ones, O'Donnell agreed to renew. "You've convinced me. To tell you the truth, Katie, I was prepared to keep a token amount of advertising with WCTZ because of my friendship with your father. But I'm impressed with these sales figures and the increased ratings. You've done a fine job," he said good-naturedly. He slapped his thighs and stood. "Come on inside and I'll write you a check."

"I'd rather bill you when I bring the new spots for your approval." Katie rose and took off her glasses.

His eyes twinkled. "I may not have the money then," he teased. O'Donnell had an acknowledged reputation for poor-mouthing. In fact he enjoyed it. "Me and Jack Benny could have gone a long way if we'd been partners," he was famous for saying.

She laughed and closed the file. "I'm not worried about that," she said as she put the file away and prepared to leave. "Thanks, Mr. O'Donnell. Oh—" she stopped "—and I'll need a copy of your menu."

Five minutes later she stepped out of the restaurant onto the deck, menu tucked securely in her big bag. "I'll give you the choice times, I promise."

"You'd better. I'll leave you here, Katie. My car's parked behind the kitchen."

"Okay, and thanks again."

Mr. O'Donnell said good-night, locked the patrons' door behind her and disappeared.

Katie was grinning triumphantly. Who said you were never appreciated in your own hometown? Tonight she'd managed a very hard sell indeed and it was a terrific feeling. Now it was time for home, a hot bath and a good book. Maybe a glass of wine while she soaked.

She was practically walking on air. She forgot to watch her heels and almost fell when she was startled by the sound of a scream—a gull, surely, but it had sounded so human that her heart had jumped uncomfortably. She paused, looking around, but the direction was hard to determine. Did gulls cry at night?

She laughed at herself. In the building behind her the lights began to go off. She headed toward the parking lot, anxious to get home before the storm broke. She was soaring on the ecstatic feeling that accompanies a success.

The man who had been sitting with Louise was standing at the top of the steps leading to the pier. Katie drew even. "Hi," she said in a friendly manner. "Where's Louise?" She looked beyond him, down the length of the pier expecting to see the boutique owner. There was no sign of her or anyone else.

When Katie's gaze returned to the man she realized that he had followed her line of sight. He had a handkerchief out and was wiping his face and hands. His eyes narrowed on her as he replaced the handkerchief. Under such close scrutiny, she experienced a creeping sense of discomfort.

Up close he was a neat, slight man, dressed in a nicely tailored suit. She assumed that he and Louise must have been discussing business. His features were regular, almost handsome; his hair, a dark blond shade, was fine and straight. His shoes, out of sync with the rest of his clothes, were scuffed.

Suddenly she realized that he hadn't responded. She met his gaze and froze at the desperate expression there.

The man was terrified. And of *her*!

Movement, sound, time, all seemed suspended as they stared at each other. The moment of understanding between them was extremely personal, as though they were bound together for this instant with taut but invisible wires.

Katie tasted the first morsel of fear. Something was very wrong here. Very, very wrong.

The stranger touched the knot of his tie with his fingertips, breaking the bond. He smiled nervously, but still he didn't speak.

During the eerie exchange, which must have taken seconds but felt like forever, Katie had remained still. Her breathing was shallow, her fingers tightened around the strap of her shoulder bag. Get out of here, warned some inner voice of self-preservation. Now. She returned his nervous smile with one of her own and took a few steps beyond the junction of the pier and the deck of the restaurant toward the break in the railing.

Without warning, the man moved, quickly and lithely, to cut off her only exit.

Katie gasped aloud and stopped in her tracks. There was no mistaking his intent, not now. He was between the rapidly darkening building and parking lot, and where she stood.

With an attempt at bravado she took a step—and halted. He didn't move. He wasn't going to let her pass.

Katie wasn't a coward but, having lived six years in a large city, she was sensibly cautious, as any unescorted young woman should be. She flashed a look around the area, seeking escape. The commercial end of the docks was deserted but it was the only way open to her.

When she looked back, she realized the man had taken several steps toward her. She panicked.

Without another thought she swung away, broke into a fast walk in the opposite direction, startling the man. She stumbled once, brushing roughly against an upright. She caught the post to save herself from falling completely and glanced back at the stranger.

She had clearly taken him by surprise, but he had recovered and was following, his eyes scanning the area as he walked steadily after her.

Her eyes were searching, too, frantically, for the least sign of movement. Her pulse pounded in her ears, drowning out all other sounds. Nothing. No people, no activity, just a few safety lights. The fishermen had gone home, the boats were locked up for the night. She had retreated toward a dead end.

But wait. In the distance, dock lights were still burning in front of one of the moorings.

Without another thought Katie kicked off her shoes and ran toward the welcome beacon as though the hounds of hell were at her heels.

Joe Ryder sat on the newly washed deck with his back to the bulkhead, his knees bent. Dangling between his index and middle fingers was the last bottle of beer from the cooler. His other hand massaged the cramp in his thigh.

He listened to the roll of thunder in the distance. The weatherman on WCTZ had forecasted intermittent showers throughout the night, but from the look of the roiling clouds when he'd hit the channel an hour ago, the rain appeared to be building into a full-fledged storm.

He gave a long, deep sigh and rested his head on the wall behind him, trying to muster the energy to get up and head for the shower.

Joe hated these late-night fishing trips and rarely accepted them. His days usually began at four-thirty or five in the morning when he got the boat ready for the day's charters: fuel, bait, last-minute repairs, food and drinks stored in the cooler. By sunset each day he was usually more than ready to tie up at the dock, clean off the fish stink, have some good food, a beer or two, some music, maybe some companionship.

However, the money had been exceptionally good today. Maybe it was worth a little weariness. He closed his eyes, which were shielded from the light by the brim of an old Braves baseball cap, and lifted the bottle to his mouth. The beer was tepid. He made a face but drank it anyway; it was wet.

Gradually a sound intruded on his reverie. Footsteps, quiet ones. Quick, light ones. Running, but more slowly now. Odd, but nonthreatening.

He was the only charter captain at these docks who lived aboard his boat, so by this time of night he usually had the area to himself. Maybe if he ignored the intrusion it would go away. But the footsteps drew closer and their sound was joined by the sound of hurried breaths, quick gasps.

Lazily he opened one eye. What he saw caused him to open the other one, mildly interested. The woman's chin was thrust forward; her fists were clenched as she walked quickly toward him, swinging her free arm in exact counterpoint to her urgent stride, like a woman who was angry—or frightened. She was hanging on to the strap of her shoulder bag as if for dear life.

He did an automatic make on her: height, five-three or -four; weight, around a hundred and ten. She was young, in her twenties, slenderly, almost delicately built. And she was barefoot, dressed for success in a tailored jacket and creamy blouse, blondish hair disciplined into a strict knot at the crown of her head, but barefoot.

Katie spared one last glance over her shoulder and placed a hand over her heart to still its frantic pounding. The stranger had, indeed, disappeared. She slowed to a normal pace. The danger—if a danger it was—had passed. But there was no way she would return to that deserted parking lot by herself. Not even if she had to sleep on the hard wooden dock.

As she approached the lighted boat slip, the man she'd spotted with such relief rose slowly to his feet.

Close-up he was not the most reassuring sight. His T-shirt was filthy; his jeans, disreputable; his hair, too long. A shadow from his cap hid his eyes and most of his face. His jaw, which was visible, was strongly pronounced and covered with stubble.

As he straightened, reaching his full height, she was amazed into silence. He was tall. Standing on the dock, a good, hefty jump above the level of the boat's deck, she barely looked down on him. His shoulders were broad and solid; his biceps strained the T-shirt. Not an ounce of fat marred his midsection. The jeans, soft and fluent from many washings, fit him like a well-worn glove. He looked dangerous, thought Katie, but it was not the same kind of intimidating danger as that projected by the man she was running from. She felt no fear.

Standing hip shot as he was, the brown beer bottle dangling from his fingers, his other hand settling loosely at his waist, he was, without a doubt, the sexiest man she had ever laid eyes on.

"Something wrong, lady?" His voice was sexy, too, deep and resonant.

Katie hadn't forgotten why she was here. She put a hand to her hair, distracted, then made a small gesture in the air. "Can—would—you help me please?"

"Sure," he answered casually, tossing the bottle into a bag of trash nearby and tucking a hand in the hip pocket of his jeans. "What can I do for you?"

She looked over her shoulder. "There's a man back there..." She immediately had his full attention. Her voice trailed off when he took a step and effortlessly leaped onto the dock beside her.

His large hand closed around her upper arm in an unconscious, almost protective gesture. At this moment, Katie, who prided herself on not needing protection, who would never have accepted such a display from any of the men in her family, was absurdly grateful for it.

His casual demeanor was gone like a wisp of smoke on a hurricane-force wind. In its place was a current of attentive energy. "A man? Are you all right?" he asked first. Then, before she could answer, "Where is he?"

"I'm okay, just a little scared. He was following me, back there, near the pier," she said indicating the direction with a wave of her hand. He was younger than she'd thought at first, mid-thirties. She peered up, under the baseball cap into the deepest, bluest, most beautiful eyes she'd ever seen.

The woman had the most beautiful eyes he'd ever seen, thought Joe irrelevantly. They were wide, heavily fringed, tilted slightly at the corners, and pure gold in color. He tore his gaze away from the distraction. "You stay here," he said, dropping her arm and starting off in the direction she'd indicated.

"No, I—I'll go with you," she said, looking around at the deserted dock. It wasn't that she was scared anymore—this man would be more than a match for the other—she just didn't want to be left alone. She hurried after him, taking two hasty steps to his one long, determined stride. She explained as she went along. "He didn't say a word, but he was between me and the parking lot. He was standing by the break in the railing—you know? And he wouldn't move." She stopped long enough to pick up her shoes and had to race to catch up. "I'd seen this man earlier. He was with a woman I know. On the pier. But she disappeared." Her words were spilling out, breathlessly. All at once she stopped. "Hey," she said loudly.

He halted and turned to look at her.

"Slow down, will you?"

"Sorry," he said. His tone held no apology but he slowed his steps.

When they reached the pier they walked to the end and back. They looked into the water below. There was no sign of anything amiss.

"Whoever it was seems to have gone," said Joe after he had searched the shadows near the break in the railing. He jogged lightly to the restaurant and cupped his hands to peer through the window. He was back at her side in only a moment. "Sit down here and tell me what happened." He indicated a bench.

Katie tried to bring her thoughts into order, but as her story unfolded, she could see the skepticism forming on his face.

He pulled off the cap, wiped his brow with his forearm and resettled the cap on his head. "You didn't see your friend when you came out of the restaurant?"

She shook her head. "No, but—"

"Maybe she left while you were inside."

"Maybe, but I just have this . . . this feeling that something—"

"The man didn't make a grab for you or make a verbal threat?" he asked.

"I told you, he didn't speak at all. That was what made the encounter so bizarre." She realized that she was not communicating her suspicions well. Her sense of anxiety and distress had been so real to her, but here in the safety of this man's presence, they were difficult to describe. The story sounded garbled even to her own ears. She searched for a way to explain a threatening look, an instinct of danger. "I know it sounds crazy but he did come after me."

He sighed and joined her on the bench. He leaned forward, sitting at an angle with the fingers of his right hand spread on his right knee, elbow cocked slightly. The other hand rested on the bench between them. Katie had the craziest urge to slide her hand in under his, just for the warmth. Immediately she shrugged off the impulse.

He spoke earnestly, reassuringly. "You were frightened, I understand that, but it's very easy to misinterpret an incident like this one, particularly at night when the shadows can be deceiving."

Joe was trying to be patient. The power of those beautiful eyes as she watched him so carefully was an interference he didn't expect. "There may be a perfectly innocent explanation."

"I know what happened and it wasn't innocent," she maintained, with a sudden, stubborn angle to her chin.

He tried to keep the annoyance out of his voice. "Look, lady . . ." He paused. "What's your name?"

Katie straightened and faced him fully. "I'm Katie Johns. I manage WCTZ, the local radio station," she returned with a snap. "What's your name?"

A reluctant smile almost broke out but, Katie noticed, he brought it under control rather quickly. She wondered if he smiled often. Immediately she felt ashamed for being so snappish. She opened her mouth to apologize. It didn't matter who he was; he'd been there when she needed someone, and he'd reacted protectively before he even knew whether she needed protection or not. That was enough. But he spoke before she could get the words out.

"I'm Joe Ryder. Fisherman." He hesitated, then he added, as though he needed some kind of credentials, too, "If you need a reference, my brother is the local sheriff."

Katie forgot that she was about to reassure this man that he needed no recommendation as far as she was concerned. "Neal Patterson is your brother?" she asked, pleased beyond all rational reasoning.

"Yeah. Well, we're half brothers."

"I've known Sheriff Patterson all my life." She smiled for the first time.

If Joe had been surprised by the beauty of Katie Johns's eyes it was before he felt the sudden impact of her smile. Beautiful white teeth, soft, full lips curving into tiny dimples at the corners of her mouth, a smile that lit her whole face.

And it irritated the *hell* out of Joe. Evidently, with the mention of his brother, he was now considered respectable. He felt a long-buried sensation stir within his chest and was surprised to discover that there was still a fragment of regret in a heart he'd thought had turned to stone.

"And the sheriff knows me," Katie went on, unaware of the thoughts that had formed the frown on his brow. She only knew that she wanted this man to believe her, not to think she was some kind of nut. "He'll vouch for the fact that I don't lie."

"I didn't accuse you of lying."

"Well, you practically did. Look, I'm not telling this well, but I'm still a little shaky. Please." She lifted a hand, then let it fall back into her lap. "There *was* something menacing about that man. And I did hear a scream."

As though on cue, the wind picked up, and the cry of a bird—a gull?—split the night.

"Like that?" Joe asked dryly.

"Sort of." She waited for him to say something, watching him as he worried the side of his jaw with the knuckle of his index finger. She greeted the sight with a combination of amusement and vexation. It was a gesture she'd seen her father perform hundreds of times when he was having a serious discussion with her mother. It said that here was a man stumped by feminine logic.

Joe had been ready to escort the woman to her car, see her on her way and write off this experience. He was hungry and dirty and tired. He wanted nothing so much as to go back to his boat, grab a bite to eat, a shower, fall into bed, and forget all about Katie Johns's unusual eyes and stunning smile.

Until she admitted that she was still shaky. Somehow the idea of this lovely woman feeling frightened of anything at all continued to disturb him. He hadn't realized he was staring until she shifted uncomfortably under his gaze.

A loud roll of thunder startled them both, reminding them that the storm wouldn't hold off much longer.

She bent forward to slide her shoes on her feet. "Speaking of Neal, I think I should talk to him about this."

"Good idea."

She stood and slung the strap of the heavy purse over her shoulder. "If he tells me I'm being paranoid I'll let it drop." When he rose beside her, she held out her hand. "Thanks so much, Mr. Ryder."

Joe took her hand lightly in his own. Despite her small size her handshake was firm and strong. Like the tilt of her head, the curve of her jaw. She might appear slight and delicate, but this woman was no lightweight. When he didn't release her immediately, she tugged slightly, bringing him back from his musings.

"Well, I guess I'll be going." She turned toward the deserted parking lot, then paused. The lot was totally dark, the branches of the huge water oaks forming a black tunnel that she would have to pass through to get to her car. "Would you mind walking to my car with me?" she asked.

"Not at all. In fact if you'll wait here I'll get my keys and follow you."

Katie was surprised by the offer but not inclined to turn it down. She'd be grateful for his company. "Okay."

Once more, Joe searched the shadows. "I think whoever frightened you is gone. Still . . . Do you want to go to the boat with me?"

It was a matter of a hundred yards or so. Katie wouldn't trail along behind him like a scaredy-cat. "No,

I can see you from here." Her laugh was wobbly. "If that man comes back I'll yell bloody murder."

He nodded and took off with the same long strides as before. As Katie watched him leave, she felt a relative chill invade her bones. She sat quietly, only her eyes moving restlessly over the scene, telling herself that she was a victim of an overactive imagination. She saw movement at the last boat slip, then nothing. She waited. What was he doing? At last, he reappeared and headed back in her direction.

Joe had felt an urge to get back to her as quickly as possible, but he had taken a second to strip off the filthy T-shirt and pull on a clean one. He tossed the cap on the bed and raked his hands through his hair. He grimaced at the smell of fish and sweat on himself but there wasn't time to do more.

He grabbed his keys off the shelf beside the hatch and locked up the boat. Finally, back on the dock, he reached for the pay phone mounted on one of the posts and dug into his pocket for a coin. His conversation was brief.

When he returned she was sitting unnaturally still on the bench where he had left her. He felt a bit guilty when he saw that she was pale. He should have insisted she come back to the boat with him.

The first drops of rain fell as he approached. They were large and heavy, leaving blots on the dry wood of the planks. "Let's hurry," he said.

She got to her feet and met him at the break in the railing. He glanced dubiously at her high heels and took her arm to help her over the worst of the patches of crushed oyster shells. "I called the sheriff's department. Neal had just left and is on his way home."

Katie hadn't even thought about what she'd do if the sheriff wasn't at the county law-enforcement office. "You have a phone on your boat?"

He shook his head and urged her on. The moss-weary oaks that surrounded the parking lot provided some protection from the steadily worsening rain, but not much. "Pay phone on the dock."

"I don't know where Neal lives."

"That's okay. I'll lead the way."

"You could just give me directions. You don't have to go." The moisture had darkened his hair to black and battered a strand down over his forehead. He brushed it back impatiently.

"I'm going," he said firmly. Besides his pickup, the only other vehicle in the lot was her conservative station wagon with the radio station logo painted prominently on the doors.

"Why are you doing this?" she asked, raising her voice over the sound of the rain as he led her to the wagon and opened the door for her. Perversely she wished now that he would let her go on alone.

He glanced down at her and almost smiled again. "Could we talk about it when we get to someplace dry?" He shut the door and loped off toward the pickup truck without giving her a chance to answer.

Whatever his motives Katie wanted to get this mess over with and go home. She glanced in her rearview mirror and quickly comprehended the reason for the almost smile. Strands of her hair had pulled loose and curled in tight ringlets around her face, she didn't have a smidgen of lipstick left and she looked about twelve.

She swore, buckled her seat belt and shoved the key into the ignition, turning it fiercely. The five-year-old engine gave a protesting groan. Damn. She tried again, babying its temperamental character this time. At last it caught. She made a mental note to have the starter checked tomorrow.

Joe, keeping track of her car's headlights in his mirror, wondered himself why he felt bound to go with her. He tapped a staccato rhythm on the steering wheel in time to the cadence of the windshield wipers and made a mental list of a few reasons. She might need some moral support. He hadn't eaten; Neal's wife, Monica, was a terrific cook and was sure to have leftovers. He was curious.

Those were reasons enough. Weren't they?

The figure huddled in the shadows of a big oak tree had listened, without moving, to the grind of the engine. He had watched as the big man waited in his truck until the woman got the car going. Both vehicles finally drove away, leaving the parking lot empty, and at last the tension drained out of him.

He'd overheard most of the conversation. Now he stood there with the rain beating down on his head, wondering what to do.

He had made a mistake, a very bad mistake, when he'd chased the young woman; now she knew exactly what he looked like. He'd had no plans beyond finding out how much she'd observed until he'd seen the fear in her eyes and knew that she'd sensed some infraction, some misdeed. Then he'd felt desperate.

Still he might have left it, especially since the fisherman seemed to discount her story. But she'd managed to convince him to take her seriously enough to go to the sheriff.

Damn Louise for plunging him into this damned mess! He was out of his element, unsure what to do next, and it was all her fault. He pulled his crumpled handkerchief from his pocket and wiped rain mixed with perspiration off his upper lip and forehead. His hand was shaking. When he replaced the handkerchief he arranged it precisely.

Things would work out, he told himself. There would be no problem in finding the young woman again. He knew right where to look.

Though that, too, would be an additional complication.

Chapter 2

Joe pulled his truck into the driveway of the neat brick bungalow on Pine Drive. Katie parked on the street. She reached across the back of the seat for the umbrella she kept there.

Neal must have been expecting them because the front door of the house opened immediately. Still in uniform, he stood behind the screen door, silhouetted by the light from inside.

Katie and Joe ran through the rain, meeting on the concrete walk that led to the porch. She offered him the protection of her umbrella but he shook his head. "Too late. I'm already soaked."

"Come in, come in," said Neal holding the screen door open for them. "What a night!"

Neal Patterson had been the sheriff of this small town since Katie could remember. A man in his late forties, his appearance of solid strength had always given her a feeling of security. Neal was the one who initiated the teen

Safe Driving reward program and the antidrug lectures when she was in high school. Well respected, he continued to be reelected; seldom did anyone challenge him in a contest of any kind. He had a spotless reputation and had, at one time, served as president of the Florida Sheriffs' Association.

Now she noticed that there was a family resemblance between the two men. Not anything overt, but a similarity of bone structure and coloring. Perhaps subconsciously that was why she'd felt so secure when she'd first encountered Joe.

"Katie, it's good to see you." He greeted her with a smile and a warm handshake.

She smoothed her hair as best she could and returned the greeting.

When Neal looked at Joe his expression was more difficult to read. "The office called to say you were on your way," he said. Then he returned his attention to Katie. "I'm just wondering—what kind of trouble could Katie Johns have possibly gotten herself into?"

Katie's responding smile was distracted as she tried to gather her thoughts.

Joe, assuming that she was still feeling anxious, answered for her. "She was harassed by a man down on the docks tonight."

"What do you mean?" Neal asked, frowning.

"She was—"

"I can speak for myself, thanks," Katie interrupted sharply, without thinking. As soon as she saw his reaction she regretted it.

Joe withdrew as though he'd been struck; his expression closed as tight as a clam. "Sorry."

Neal hadn't been able to control a dry chuckle at her terse, pithy comment. "Same old Katie."

Joe looked from one of them to the other. Obviously this was some kind of an inside joke.

"I'm the one who's sorry," she said to Joe. "Neal knows I grew up with three older brothers. If I ever wanted to say anything I had to shut them up first." She spread her hands helplessly. "My defensiveness has sort of become a habit but not one I should have applied to you. Not after your help."

She turned that gaze on him, appealing silently. "Don't worry about it," he said, surprised at the softness in his voice. He shrugged, careful to keep his expression indifferent. But he couldn't look away. He felt currents between them as strong as the undertow that could pull an unsuspecting swimmer out to sea.

Neal watched the byplay between these two. They looked as though they had known each other for years, an actuality that he knew was impossible. He waited for an explanation. "Do either of you want to fill me in about this incident?" he asked when it seemed that they'd forgotten he was waiting.

His question brought them both back to the present.

Katie hoped to heaven she wasn't blushing. "I thought it was more than harassment but, viewed in hindsight, I'm not so sure my imagination wasn't working overtime." Maybe she did overreact. Maybe there was a simple explanation for the stranger's behavior. She put her hands into the pockets of her jacket and worried on the edge of the book of matches with her fingernail.

"This man chased me," she admitted, but then turned to Joe again. "I've thought of something. Louise's car wasn't in the parking lot."

"Was it there when you arrived?"

"I'm not sure. She has a red sports car. You'd think I would have noticed." She put her fingers to her temple and pressed as though she could squeeze the memory free.

"Well, whatever the two of you are talking about, let's have a seat and you can fill me in," suggested Neal.

"I'm too wet," said Joe. Katie sat in a straight-backed chair but he remained standing, looking thoughtful.

Monica Patterson entered. Her presence was like a fresh wind blowing into the room. "You certainly are," she said, viewing him askance. She carried a tray of cups and a pot of freshly brewed coffee. She kissed her brother-in-law on the cheek. "There's a clean towel in the guest bathroom. Can I get either of you something to eat?"

"No, thank you, Monica," said Katie, accepting a mug of fragrant coffee, dosing it liberally with sugar and cream.

"What did you have for dinner tonight?" Joe asked with a smile, shaking his head at the offer of coffee.

"You haven't had dinner?" Monica clucked. "Come on. I'll fix you a plate while you dry off. Honestly, Joe," she scolded. "You really should eat properly...." Her voice trailed off as she headed back toward the kitchen.

"I'll be back in a minute," Joe told Katie as he left.

Clearly Monica took a maternal, indulgent attitude toward Joe, while Katie wasn't sure what Neal's attitude was. The expression in his eyes was unreadable. "You want to tell me what happened?" he asked finally, taking a seat across from her.

She began her story. He took a pipe from the rack on a table by his chair and went through the ritual of lighting it as she talked. It was soothing to watch his routine.

There wasn't that much to tell, she realized as she explained, "The man looked almost afraid at first, Neal. Then he turned ugly." Her distress was as hard to define

here in Neal's living room as it had been when she'd tried
to explain to Joe. By the time he returned to the living
room she had reached the point where they had searched
the dock. "I don't know what I expected to find," she
finished, exasperated. "I don't like making a fool of
myself, Neal, but that man . . ." Unable to explain more
clearly, she didn't finish the sentence.

Neal had listened to the tale with a thoughtful frown.
"I think I understand. Maybe we'd better go back to the
dock and have another look around," he said getting to
his feet. He picked up his hat and pulled a set of keys
from his pocket.

Katie hadn't realized how tense she'd been until Neal's
words produced a sudden relaxation of her muscles. She
shot a look at Joe, who responded easily, "I didn't see the
car, either, but we might have missed it. The rain was
coming down hard." He gave a philosophical shrug and
smiled.

Though not full power, his smile—now that it had finally come—was remarkably potent. Katie couldn't help
staring and wondering why he didn't do it more often.
The creases in his whiskered cheeks deepened to dimples; the strong white teeth looked even whiter against his
tanned face.

A sound from Neal shook her out of her reverie.
Abruptly she rose. "Okay. Let's go," she said.

Neal took a slicker from the hall tree and handed it to
Joe. He offered one to Katie, who shook her head. He
then took another down for himself.

When the three-vehicle caravan pulled into the deserted parking lot, there was no red car in sight. This
time, Katie parked at the foot of the ramp. The men signaled to her to stay in the car and she nodded, but she left

the engine running so the wipers would keep the windshield relatively clear.

From this vantage point she had a view of the deck outside Harbor Grill, the pier and part of the docks. She could see Joe gesturing, explaining as they went along. The hooded figures of the men took on a surrealistic veneer through the blur of water and faint light.

They were back in a few minutes, both breathing hard. Neal climbed into the front seat beside her and Joe into the back. They opened the slickers and shoved back the hoods and she saw that even with the protection they were soaked through.

"Hell of a night!" Neal looked out through the windshield, searching the area, his expression growing thoughtful. "They really need more safety lights down here and maybe some private security. Our patrols come by regularly but it's pretty deserted when they're not around, isn't it?" Obviously he didn't expect either of them to answer because he went on with barely a breath, "Katie, do you feel up to answering a few more questions?"

"No, but go ahead," she said.

Joe laughed, silently congratulating her for her frankness.

Neal took her back over the same ground with no new outcome. At last he sighed. "It's a good thing Joe lives on the boat or there wouldn't have been a soul within hailing distance."

She met Joe's eyes in the rearview mirror. "You live on the boat? I didn't realize that." She wasn't sure why she was surprised. He was a different kind of man, one who would enjoy a different life-style.

"The rent's cheap."

It was a throwaway comment, but she had an idea there was more to it. "And you don't have to fight the traffic on Highway 98 to get to work."

"Yeah. Well, if you two don't need me, I think I'll hit the shower," said Joe.

Katie half turned in the seat. "Thank you very much, Joe. I appreciate your help tonight. I might have misunderstood the man's attitude. The whole thing might be a fluke but I was scared out of my shoes." She smiled depreciatively. "I do appreciate your help."

"I'm glad I was here," he said. "Well...I guess I'll see you around."

His hand rested on the seat back. She smiled and touched him gently. A casual touch, she told herself, a simple form of communication. But here in the confined space of the car, the effect on her was anything but casual. It provoked a warm, unsettling physical response even with his brother looking on. She had been aware of this man from the moment when he'd stood on the deck of his boat with the beer bottle dangling from his fingers. Aware of his movements, his magnetism, his masculinity.

As she took her hand away, she looked into his eyes— a mistake. The contrast of black pupil and clear sky-blue iris was like a contrast of intrigue and innocence. Deep within, there was an expression not easily identifiable. She read sorrow or disillusionment in the darkness but was unable to comprehend further than that.

All at once his gaze narrowed perceptively and he gave her a smile that was far too knowing.

Drat! Again she was embarrassed. Her attraction to him was probably written all over her face. She smiled her chagrin away. "Good night, Joe."

"Good night," he answered. "See you, Neal. I'll bring your slicker back." He opened the door and stepped out into the storm without another word.

Katie wrested her thoughts away from the strange, hypnotic interval and turned to Neal, forcing a lightness she didn't feel. "Do you think I should just forget this whole thing, Neal?" she asked.

Neal gave her a long look, shifting slightly in the seat beside her. The leather of his holster made a squeaky noise as the weight of the weapon resettled. "The way the man acted bothers me, Katie. You're not the type to panic. Even if Louise is not involved, I want to talk to him."

"The whole thing can be resolved in the morning when the boutique opens. I'll just drop by and ask her who he is," Katie said after a reflective pause.

"I plan to do that myself," said Neal.

She nodded. "I was surprised to hear that you had a brother," she said, changing the subject. Truthfully she wanted to know more about Joe Ryder but she didn't want to be any more obvious about it than she'd already been.

"We're half brothers," he explained. "My mother deserted my father and me when I was just a kid. She remarried some fellow in South Carolina. That's where Joe was born."

"How long has he lived in Garden City?" He wasn't here when she moved to Atlanta, but that was six years ago.

"A little over a year."

"It's strange I haven't met him."

Neal shifted again. "Joe keeps to himself," he said crisply. "It's late. We'd both better get home out of this storm."

She was taken aback by his abrupt tone. "Meaning that I should mind my own business?" she asked, chagrined.

"Meaning that Joe keeps to himself," he repeated.

Embarrassed, she sat there, fingers curled over the top of the steering wheel. "Okay. Thanks again, Neal."

"Katie . . ." He paused, seeming to want to say more. He shook his head and opened the door. Once again the force of the storm intruded. "I'll meet you at the boutique in the morning."

Katie faced the fact that, no matter how reluctantly, she'd have to carry this through. As she drove she went back over the entire incident in her mind. The sight of Louise and the man. Had Louise seemed nervous when she'd waved to Katie? She remembered the stranger taking Louise's arm, practically dragging her away at the first sight of Katie stepping onto the deck. No, that wasn't fair. Louise hadn't protested, but she had looked back over her shoulder in apology. Or was it entreatment?

That's crazy, Katie told herself. If Louise were afraid of the man she could have called out. There had been people around—Mr. O'Donnell, his employees.

Louise wasn't scared of her companion. At least not at that moment. But what about the scream? Or was it a scream? What happened? This whole thing had her head spinning. She started over.

Louise had not been afraid, not when Katie arrived. Later, fear was a possibility; the scream might have been Louise's or, as Joe Ryder assumed, it might have been a gull.

When Katie had left Mr. O'Donnell and headed for her car, the man had reappeared. Had she misread the significance of his presence?

She was certain of one thing: the man had meant her no good. But maybe that had nothing to do with Louise. Maybe he was a mugger. If so that didn't eliminate the importance of getting to the bottom of this. Neal wouldn't let muggers go loose on the streets of Garden City.

Katie finally reached her building. She parked in her assigned space then ran through the rain to the shelter of the overhang. She took the elevator to the fourth floor and when she had unlocked her door, flipped off the outside light switch. Every move seemed as if it took twice as long as normal. She put the chain on, dropped the big shoulder bag on the floor and crossed the living room to the sliding doors. The sea was as wild and turbulent as her emotions.

She slid back the door and stepped out onto her balcony. The space was covered by the floor of the balcony above but that was only protection from the direct downpour; the wind delivered an equal amount of water. But she didn't mind. Her suit was already soaked around the hem and across her shoulders.

Sometimes she liked the fierce severity of lightning as it slashed the sky, liked the tumultuous winds, the agitated clouds, the cleansing rain. She gripped the railing and leaned forward, deeply inhaling the salt air, hoping it would fill her completely and wash away the stress of tonight's incident. She didn't like feeling helpless under any circumstances.

The wind lifted the loose strands of hair that had escaped her bun, cooling her nape and her temples. For the hundredth time she blessed the depressed real-estate market that had enabled her to buy this place when she had returned to her hometown a year ago.

The members of her family enjoyed strong ties. She adored them all and she wanted to keep it that way. Living as an adult in the house a few blocks away would have strained the relationship.

Her father had wanted her to do just that, totally ignoring the fact that she was a woman of twenty-eight. Her parents had lost another daughter, their oldest child, so he was a worrier where his only surviving daughter was concerned. Her mother had finally intervened to prevent a serious clash.

Katie hoped tomorrow morning would bring an end to the puzzle of Louise Austen and her companion. She was under enough pressure right now; she had a demanding job, which left no time for distractions. Soon the owners of the station would be arriving in Garden City to evaluate her first year's accomplishments.

For the first time since she'd seen the lone stranger standing at the entrance to the pier, she felt a return of the triumph of her sale to O'Donnell. She'd have to begin early tomorrow morning on preliminary work on the spots. Wait till she told Raymond! Her assistant manager, engineer and friend, Raymond Timms, had encouraged her, while not quite believing she could pull it off.

She raised her arms over her head and stretched high. Her hands fell back to the railing and she let all her breath out, relaxing from the unbelievable day and evening, feeling the tension drain from her limbs and the thoughts ebb from her mind.

At last feeling cleansed, she went back inside. She performed her absolutions by rote. Not until she was in bed—a sheet her only cover, her glasses perched on her nose, and a book on her knee, watching the wind and rain persistently begging entrance against the glass—did she allow her thoughts to return to Joe Ryder, mystery man. *Exciting* mystery man, she amended. The kind of man who could make her blood run hot, her pulse accelerate, her lips tremble.

There was no point denying her attraction. She hadn't been so quickly affected by a man in a long time. His unsmiling, serious persona wasn't usually the type that appealed to her. With her rather traditional background she generally felt more comfortable with a pleasant, nonthreatening type of man.

Joe Ryder was as far from tame and passive as was a jungle tiger from a house cat. Katie had never played with fire in her relationships and she had a feeling that's exactly what she would be doing if she continued to think about Joe Ryder along those lines.

Maybe his appeal *was* his difference. Maybe if she knew him better she wouldn't like him.

Again she replayed the picture of him standing on the deck of his boat in his jeans and stained shirt, with the beer bottle dangling from his hand and his eyes hidden by the cap. She called up images, trying to analyze her response, explored her memory of the broad shoulders and muscular arms, the deep sexy voice.

She had a hard time falling asleep.

Joe was having a hell of a time falling asleep. His job was very physical; it was what had saved his sanity when he first moved to Garden City. He had structured his life so that at the end of the day he fell exhausted onto the big bed in the forward cabin and knew nothing until his alarm broke into his sleep. The routine of long days and short nights had provided a numbing sort of peace and was the only way he could survive.

Today had been no exception. He'd been up since before dawn. Now he lay on his back, fingers linked loosely under his head and began to breathe deeply.

He felt himself slipping toward oblivion, when suddenly that small, sharp feeling of despair that always heralded a night of dreaming pierced the quiet interlude. He knew from experience that it wouldn't go away. He could lie here and endure it, allowing himself a restless sleep; or he could open his eyes, get up and move around for a while and try again later.

Finally muttering a curse, he sat on the side of the bed, elbows on his knees, hands dangling between his legs. He knew exactly what was wrong with him—Katie Johns.

She was cute. Not his type, he tried to tell himself.

Clean. She smelled so good, so damned good. Sweet and clean and fresh. She had a drop-dead figure, slender but full breasted, very womanly and very, very feminine. Her hair looked soft and shiny and those golden eyes...he'd been around long enough to recognize when a woman was turned on. And this woman was.

Hell, she didn't know the first thing about him. If she could see into his memories she'd probably run like the devil was after her.

He slapped his knees and stood, reaching for his jeans. He'd walk for a while. The storm was no obstacle. It wouldn't be the first time, rain or not, that he had walked or jogged or run when his powers of recall wouldn't let him sleep.

He shoved his feet into sneakers and went topside. He jumped from the deck to the pier and started walking fast. In seconds he was soaked to the skin. His pace quickly progressed to a jog.

He dropped from the pier to the shore of the small harbor and the jog hastened to a dead run. His breathing was regular; his heartbeat echoed in his ears. If he could only run fast enough, maybe he could run away from his thoughts.

Joe had run, too, when he was sixteen. He had run away from home, from his father's drunkenness and beatings. He'd lied about his age, lived on the docks at Charleston, taking what jobs he could get, drinking, fighting, getting into trouble. Finally, when he was nineteen, he'd come to his senses one night—which he happened to be spending in the Charleston jail—and realized that the only ticket out was an education.

His breath was coming fast now, his joints and muscles were rebelling. He sank to his knees on the grassy verge. After a minute he twisted to lie flat on his back. The rain slackened somewhat but it still came down, wetting his face like tears. Between two dark clouds, he caught a glimpse of the benign half-moon, shining down from its orbit, reminding anyone who happened to be watching that, despite the storm, it was still there.

There had been a half-moon the night of the first shooting, too. And no moon at all the night Jerry had been shot. Jerry, who had saved his life, who had suffered because of Joe's weakness.

Where Katie Johns was clean, he was polluted; where she seemed sincere and innocent, he was corrupt. He'd seen too much, done too much. She wasn't his kind of woman.

So why couldn't he dismiss her? Why was an image of her superimposed on the moon's profile?

He answered his own question. She was his punishment, a reminder that she was from a world he could never be a part of. Memories like his were impossible to escape, a locked gate that guarded people like Katie Johns from people like Joe Ryder.

If Joe wanted a woman he looked for one who knew the score, one who would be gone in the morning. They were the only kind he allowed himself, because any other kind of woman would be horrified if she knew the real Joe Ryder.

A killer. A coward.

A killer was what they'd called him. What Olivene had called him. What he was.

Chapter 3

The boutique opened at nine-thirty. Katie didn't arrive until a few minutes later. She'd been working at home since early morning, drawing up suggestions for Mr. O'Donnell's new advertising spots. She'd finished and dropped them off for her secretary to type before she went to the boutique.

During the night the storm had blown itself out to sea. The sidewalks were crowded and she wasn't really surprised to discover the sheriff's car already parked at the side of the building. She found a parking spot on the street.

In his crisp uniform and Sam Browne belt he looked out of place in the hushed, luxurious atmosphere of Breakaway, Designer Fashions for the Discriminating Woman. Katie heard Neal's voice as she entered.

"...wondered if Mrs. Austen was planning to be in today."

Annette Allen, on the other hand, fit her surroundings as though she'd been born in the elegant boutique. Tall and lush, extravagantly made-up, her short black hair coiffed in the latest geometric style, and clothed to perfection in something fuchsia and lime, she looked like a bird of paradise and made Katie feel positively dowdy.

"I'm sorry, Sheriff," Annette answered, making no attempt to hide her curiosity. "Louise left early yesterday morning for California. She'll be gone for two weeks." She looked from the sheriff to Katie who had joined them at the desk and back again. "Is there something I could help you with?" she offered.

There was a long, pregnant pause, then Katie spoke up. "That's impossible," she said. "I saw Louise here myself, last night."

Annette shook her head. "You must have seen someone who looked like her. She left. I saw her leave," she stated positively.

"Did you take her to the airport?" asked the sheriff.

"She didn't fly. She drove."

"By herself?"

Again Annette nodded. "She wanted a few days alone. She said it would be like a vacation. She loves to drive and Dan had gotten her that new little sports car. ...I met her here, at the shop yesterday morning before she left. She had some last-minute instructions to go over with me." She laughed. "Her car was packed to the roof."

Katie swallowed any further contradiction. Obviously Annette wasn't privy to her employer's plans. She looked to Neal, who was scratching his head, his expression wary and puzzled as he studied the woman.

Annette went on, "Louise's instructions included a call to you, Katie. About the ad for our Fourth of July sale. I have a list here of the things we'd like to feature." She opened a drawer and scrambled among some papers, careful not to chip her fingernail polish.

"Thank you, Annette. I may have more questions for you later," said Neal. He replaced his hat and headed for the door.

Katie stopped Annette with a hand on her arm. "I'll come back another time, Annette. I have some things to take care of this morning."

"But this won't take a minute. If I can just put my hand on—"

Katie was already across the room. "Take your time. I'll stop by after lunch," she said, smiling over her shoulder.

She pushed through the door and headed for the area where she'd seen the sheriff's car. As she rounded the corner of the building the sight of Joe Ryder slowed her steps. A pair of dark glasses sat on top of his head, his hands were in his pockets and he was staring at the ground in front of him, listening to Neal.

At her approach he raised his eyes and looked straight at her. She saw a brief spark of reaction; his gaze heated for just a moment then cooled.

Her own reaction was disconcerted. Last night with the stubble of beard he'd looked like a potentially dangerous refugee from some cop show on television; today he was clean shaven and definitely dangerous. Again he wore jeans but these were clean and pressed to a crease. His blue oxford shirt, which he wore with the sleeves rolled back and the collar unbuttoned, was also pressed and she caught the slight scent of starch blending with his spicy after-shave. In the bright glare of the sun the lines around his eyes appeared deeper, the semblance of disillusion in his expression that she'd noticed last night, more pronounced. But he was still a very sexy man.

"Good morning, Ms. Johns," he said at last, his expression now totally noncommittal. He settled the dark glasses on his nose, hiding his eyes.

Ms. Johns? Last night it had been Katie. Hadn't it? Now that she thought about it, she couldn't remember his calling her anything—except "lady" in that rather intolerant tone.

Neal cleared his throat, reminding them of his presence.

"Good morning, Mr. Ryder," Katie answered lightly. Perhaps the formality was his version of a teasing salutation. When her gaze returned to his unsmiling expression, she knew better.

"Well? What happened?" Joe asked, looking at his brother.

Katie was jolted at the authoritative demand in his tone and waited for Neal to object.

"Louise Austen left yesterday morning for California. She was driving."

"She did not," said Katie.

Neal smiled at her inattentively and Joe nodded as though absorbing and filing some unspoken information. "What are you going to do now?" he asked his brother after a minute.

"Dan Austen's car dealership is on the edge of town. I'm going over to his office. Maybe something happened to delay her departure."

"I'll go with you," said Katie.

Both men turned to her as though they'd forgotten she was there. "Katie—" the sheriff began.

"That isn't a good idea," Joe said flatly.

"Why not? I started this whole thing; I think it's my responsibility to see it through. If Louise is there, I want to talk to her. She should know how her friend behaved."

Joe took his time responding. He exchanged a long look with Neal and leaned against the police car. He folded his arms across his broad chest and crossed his feet at the ankles. "And if Louise isn't there?" he asked with mild interest.

"Well, her husband, Dan, should know if she was in town...shouldn't he...?" Katie's voice trailed off on the last two words as she realized the situation was getting complicated. What if Louise had lied to her husband? What if she was having an affair with the stranger?

Curiously this was the first time the thought of an affair had occurred to Katie. She had assumed the meeting on the dock was in some way related to business. Now she asked herself why she'd made that assumption. Louise and her companion had been talking very earnestly, very seriously, not at all like lovers, she remembered. They'd even, at one time, seemed to be arguing. That was the only basis for her reasoning and she recognized how slim it was.

She had to ask herself another question. Would she want to be the one to blow the whistle if Louise *was* having an affair?

Joe followed the thoughts as they chased across her mind. "You see?" he offered quietly. "Louise Austen might have delayed her trip for a day without informing her husband. It has been done, you know, and it could get sticky."

"Yes," said Katie, reluctantly, thoughtfully. "But it's my fault if it does," she added. "Last night I almost convinced myself that the two of you were right but this morning...I can't forget that man or the look on his face when he chased me. He was way past the point of being furious, Joe." She raised her eyes to his, which was as surprising as it was instinctive.

Neal was the voice of authority here. Belatedly Katie shifted her gaze. "I'm worried for Louise."

Neal shot Joe a look. "Okay, you can come, but let me do the talking."

"Gladly," she answered.

"You can show me the way," said Joe, taking her arm for a moment, then dropping it immediately. "Come on. I'll bring you back for your car."

Neal climbed into the county vehicle and Katie went with Joe. She had tried without success to ignore his vital good looks, his self-confident poise the entire time she was talking to him and Neal. Her ability to think seemed to be clouded when he was near. Now it seemed she had to endure his potency for another hour whether she wanted to or not. She was annoyed. "Katie," she said beneath her breath.

"What?" asked Joe.

"My name is Katie, not Ms. Johns, not 'you,' and certainly not 'lady.' Ka-tie." She enunciated each syllable clearly. "And don't give me that bull about showing you the way. You could *ask* if I would mind riding with you."

Joe put his tongue in his cheek but he didn't look at her. "I forgot. You have two brothers, don't you?"

"Three," she answered sharply, but she had an idea he knew exactly how many brothers she had. "You don't really have to go anyway."

He didn't bother to argue. Leaving her to follow, he walked past her station wagon and down the street to where his truck was parked.

She hesitated for a minute then did exactly as he'd expected—hurried after him like an obedient puppy. She was disgusted with herself for doing it. Politely he helped her in and circled the truck to join her.

The cab was surprisingly neat—especially compared to her car. She never remembered to throw out things like parking stubs and bits of paper with scrawled memos. They tended to collect. There was a clip-on case for his dark glasses mounted on the visor—it was empty, of course—and a clipboard holding forms of some kind on the seat between them. She read the letterhead: *Mary Ann, U.S. Coast Guard Approved, charter fishing by half day, all day, and overnight, Joe Ryder.* The address and telephone number were printed below.

She wondered who Mary Ann was.

There was a cellular phone beneath the dashboard. She eyed it suspiciously. She'd fought against having one herself at her previous job, telling her boss that there had to be someplace she could escape the intrusion of the telephone.

Highway 98, which bisected the town from east to west, was the same two-lane highway it had been since it was built. In the winter, traffic was no problem. This section of Florida—the panhandle, or the Emerald Coast, as the Chamber of Commerce had dubbed it— didn't enjoy the warm winters of the southern part of the state and relatively few tourists had discovered the year-round beauty of this area. But in the summer, when the sun worshipers arrived, it was a nightmare to get from one end of town to the other.

Most of the businesses, the city offices, the bank, gro-cery stores, the radio station, the newspaper and the residential areas were north of the east-west highway. In the height of the summer it often took fifteen minutes to get from one end of town to the other, a distance of 1.3 miles.

Joe was silent during the ride. As Katie was berating herself for not concentrating on the immediate situation, she pointedly kept quiet, too.

"There it is," said Katie. The office building and maintenance facilities that served the dealership were set back from the road. Joe turned in, driving between fluttering pennants and sparkling windshields that caught the sun's reflection and threw it back.

Neal had already arrived—drivers tended to give way to a sheriff's car—and was standing at the entrance talking to Dan Austen.

Dan was a head shorter than the sheriff and outweighed him by at least twenty pounds. He was not handsome, but he was solid and dependable looking. He glanced over at the truck.

Joe put out a hand just as Katie would have opened the door. "Wait a minute," he said, looking at the two men. "Let Neal take care of telling him." As they watched they could both see that Dan was growing more and more agitated as Neal explained. At last he planted both fists on his hips and turned to glare at the truck.

With a sigh Katie gave Joe a resigned look, got out and walked across the lot to join them. Joe was right behind her.

"What's this garbage you've been telling the sheriff?" Dan demanded angrily. His face was an alarming shade of red.

Joe's hand was suddenly and unexpectedly resting supportively at her back. She hadn't anticipated needing such support but was glad for it. She opened her mouth to answer but he didn't give her a chance.

"I resent the implication you seem to have given Neal that Louise was here last night with another man. Obviously you've made a mistake."

"She spoke to me, Dan, from ten feet away," Katie said quietly.

"Louise left yesterday for a buying trip to California. This is a small town, Katie. People talk. You have no right to start a rumor like that." He was stern and un-yielding.

She was well aware of the grapevine in a small town. She wanted to reassure him about that, at least. "Dan, we three are the only ones who know about this. Except for the man who chased me."

Suddenly he was still; suddenly the scene took on another kind of menace. "What man?" he asked.

So she had to go over the story again. It was much more painful this time. She was careful to keep her voice even, not to overdramatize the incident. Invariable questions haunted her. Did she have the right to bring all this out? Didn't she have some responsibility to save Dan's feelings?

As she talked he leaned toward her. His face took on a drawn, hostile appearance. Drops of perspiration formed between her breasts and on her face. The hot sun beat down mercilessly on her head. Good Lord, the day wasn't half over and she was developing a beast of a headache.

Joe felt Katie's distress. Finally he interrupted from beside her. Dan Austen hadn't given them time for introductions so he introduced himself. "Mr. Austen, I'm Joe Ryder, Neal's brother. I was the one who was on the docks last night when Miss Johns was frightened by this man."

Dan whirled on him. "Did you see him, too?"

Joe would like to have been able to say yes if only to assuage the man's anger. "No," he answered reluctantly.

Dan dismissed him and turned again to Katie. She went on with the story.

"Dan, you can rest assured that none of this will go any farther," said Neal when she finished. "Katie was worried." He paused. "I suppose Louise calls home periodically?" He made it into a question.

Dan thrust out his jaw. "I don't know whether she will or not. I don't keep tabs on my wife, Sheriff. I trust her. When she left, she probably didn't expect to have her good name maligned." The last statement was accompanied by a furious scowl in Katie's direction. "I don't know who the hell the man was but it's a shame he didn't catch you."

Katie gasped. She raised her chin, refusing to retreat.

Joe reacted to the exchange by putting himself between Katie and the man. The move was smoothly done, not obvious, but his voice was low and dangerous when he said, "That was uncalled for, Mr. Austen."

Neal spoke up hastily. "Dan, if you hear from Louise, will you please have her call me? Then we can put this to rest."

A loudspeaker pealed Dan's name out over the lot. "I have to get to work," he said ungraciously and left.

"I'm sorry he had to find out like this," said Katie, her voice still quiet.

"Yeah," said Neal.

"Neal, I know that woman was here in town last night. So where is she now?"

"Katie, there isn't any justification for a full-scale investigation—not at this time anyway—so I can't answer you," he said. He took a breath. "I can't put out an APB or drag the harbor on supposition alone. We'll have to wait until Dan hears from her."

"Or doesn't hear. How long will you wait?"

Neal looked out over row after row of shiny cars. "A week," he said, his expression thoughtful. "Then I'll talk to him again. In the meantime I will put out a 'request for information' bulletin to the state patrols between here and California."

"I guess that's all you can do," Katie agreed.

"Let's get out of here," suggested Joe. The three of them crossed the tarmac together. Joe and Katie split off toward the truck. Joe opened the door and helped Katie into the cab.

He was about to join her when Neal hailed them.

"I don't like this, Joe," Neal said in a low voice when his brother reached his side.

Joe jammed his hands into the back pockets of his jeans. "I don't like it, either. At first I wondered but I have an idea she isn't the type of woman to fabricate a story like this."

"You're right. She isn't. And I've never seen Dan Austen so belligerent." Neal stroked his jaw, contemplating a blue Monte Carlo that Joe would be willing to bet he didn't even see. "I was thinking as we stood there how I would react if it were Monica," he went on. "And I trusted her like I do—like Dan says he does. I would be more concerned than angry. What about you?"

Joe shot his brother a tight-lipped, telling look. "I haven't been inclined to trust a woman in a long time, so I can't accurately predict how I would react," he responded coldly.

Suddenly Neal jabbed at the brim of his hat with his thumb, tipping it back. He planted his hands on his hips in a combative stance and glared at Joe. "Ah, hell, Joe. When are you going to grow up and learn you can't judge all women by our mother? Or by that woman you thought you were in love with?'' he challenged, his voice rising in irritation.

Joe stared in surprise at Neal's criticism.

It wasn't at all unpleasant to have your older brother berate you, especially when it happened for the first time in your life. It was comfortingly. . . normal. While growing up, his meetings with his brother were rare, maybe one a year, often none. He hero-worshiped Neal and had always thought if Neal had really felt like a big brother they'd have fights. He smiled slightly to himself at the memory of his adolescent fancy.

"What are you smiling about?" demanded Neal.

Joe shook his head ruefully. "When I was little I would have given anything for you to get mad and yell at me."

Now Neal stared at him as though the sun had rattled his brain. "What?"

"I guess you had to have been there," Joe replied evasively. "I agree with you about Austen's attitude," he added, jerking his head toward the building behind them, his statement bringing the conversation back to the issue. "What are you going to do?"

"Not me. You. I want you to keep an eye on her for a few days."

"No," said Joe, flatly. He whipped off his dark glasses so there would be no mistaking his resolve. He intended to say more, plenty more, but Neal stopped him with an upraised hand.

"Nothing deep," he assured Joe.

"I'm out of the business."

Neal usually gave up at this point in the familiar argument. This time he kept pressing. "The business never gets out of you. Just make sure she gets to where she's going when she's alone."

Sweat broke out on Joe's forehead. He tried to tell himself the storm last night had cleared the way for a heat wave. He wiped his brow with his forearm. "Neal, I know you're understaffed in the summer, but I've told you before, I can't—I won't—get involved in investigative work. Besides, I have charters to run. A group is coming aboard at noon."

"For a week, Joe. We'll hear something by then or sooner. You've been trained; you know what you're doing. And you're right, my men are stretched as thin as they'll go. We've got a mugger on the beach, we've got a hotel thief, we've got a hell of a traffic problem and tempers flare when the thermometer rises. Plus, Fourth of July week is coming up."

Joe planted his hands at his waist, and rolled his head to relieve the sudden tension in his neck. But he didn't argue further.

Neal drove home the last nail. "Besides, you've already involved yourself," he stated simply. "Who's crewing for you this summer?"

"Sam Mallard." Joe named a college student they both knew whose father was a retired charter captain. Joe had bought Mallard's boat, *Mary Ann*, and his business.

"Sam's a good boy. He can get his dad to go out with him for a week. And he needs the money. One week, Joe. Just a loose surveillance." Neal laid his hand on Joe's shoulder. "And I promise, I'll get mad at you whenever you want."

Joe glared at his brother but without animosity and replaced the glasses. "One week," he finally agreed, and headed for the truck.

"One other thing," said Neal. He followed Joe and, when he reached his side, spoke in an undertone. "I wouldn't mention this to her. You've seen how she feels about her independence."

Joe's mouth turned up at one side. "Yeah, I've seen."

The popular café was a hometown place, filled with restrained bustle and sounds, flatware clinking lightly against plates and cups, subdued voices, laughter. People who worked around this area of town were in and out all day for coffee breaks and lunch. It was also a place to come to share the latest news, not only local gossip, but state and national news as well.

When they left Austen's, Joe had suggested coffee and Katie had readily agreed, too shaken by the experience to return to work immediately.

"Hi, Katie."

"Katie Johns, I haven't seen you in ages!"

"Your weatherman really missed on that storm last night, Katie!"

The greetings accompanied them to their table but Katie noticed that the gazes were occupied mostly with Joe Ryder, particularly the feminine ones.

"Do you know everybody in this town?" he asked when they were seated. "Two coffees," he told the waitress who had followed them, her mouth sagging slightly, her gaze never leaving him. He had removed the glasses that hid his remarkable blue eyes.

The waitress lingered, ostensibly to write the order on the pad she held. "Anything to eat?" she asked, hopefully. Her eyes met Katie's in silent appeal.

Katie couldn't blame the woman. In the pedestrian atmosphere of the café such consummate masculinity as Joe exuded had the effect of a shark swimming through a tropical fish tank. She capitulated, mostly because he had the same effect on her. "Nothing for me thanks, Lonnie. Have you met Joe Ryder?"

The young woman tucked the pencil behind her ear and stuck out her hand. She gave him her best smile. "No, I haven't. How do you do? I'm Lonnie Duncan. Are you visiting in town?"

Conversation had died to a whisper. Joe had a strange look on his face. "How do you do? No, I live here," he said politely but without explanation as he returned the handshake.

"Well, you come in often, you hear?" said Lonnie, and spun away to get their coffee. She was back in what seemed like only seconds.

"I know most of the people who live on this side of 98," Katie said, answering his earlier question. She held the sugar dispenser over her spoon and measured— roughly—two spoonfuls into her coffee. The sunlight streamed in to paint their booth in light. "You will, too, if you take Lonnie up on her invitation."

Joe laughed softly, drawing her gaze to his. The chuckle had a rusty, unused sound, as though he didn't exercise it regularly. "So I gathered. Where do you live?"

She smiled across the table. "Oh, I've joined the condo crowd," she told him gesturing vaguely with her spoon in the direction of the Gulf. "I got a good deal when I moved back here last year. The developer had overbuilt or something and was letting the units go at slightly above cost. It was a dream of mine to live right on the edge of the water so . . ." She shrugged.

Joe took a swallow of his own black brew. "Where did you live before?"

When the sugar had completely dissolved, she set the spoon in the saucer. "In Atlanta."

He folded his arms on the table before him and leaned forward slightly. "You worked for a radio station there?"

The table was narrow. She had only to move her hand a very short distance to touch his arm. It was muscular and dusted with dark hair, tanned to a beautiful golden color. His hands were hidden from her but she was equally aware of them. She remembered plainly the feel of his strong, capable hand at her back. With his fingers stretched wide, the span of his hand had almost reached from one side to the other. She shivered at the memory. "The number one station in the city," she said lightly. "I was assistant manager."

"So you were successful." He nodded as though he'd known it all along.

"I was on the way," she hedged. More than that actually; she'd already been approached by the network about moving to a larger market, which would have meant Chicago, New York, Washington, D.C. or Los Angeles.

Joe leaned back against the padded seat. "Why did you quit?" he asked.

She found that it was easier to think and talk with those few extra inches between them. A frown settled on her brow. She wondered if she could explain all the concerns that influenced her decision. "I love what I do; I didn't really quit." She propped her chin on her hand and stared beyond him. "Well, maybe I did opt out. I started to think about what I was chasing, to wonder if there was more to this existence than sixteen-hour days, and constant stress, and the increasingly remote possibility of a personal life. I was twenty-seven years old and bought a bottle of antacid a month." She laughed, but it hadn't been funny.

She had no criticism of people who chose to live their lives on a nonstop road to the top. Her ambition to be the best at what she did hadn't diminished at all and she didn't mind going at flat-out speed to achieve that ambition; but every car had to stop, to pause for periodic maintenance.

Human beings needed maintenance, too. When her pauses occurred she wanted something to give her a lift, something beautiful to see—friends, family, a sense of community, or belonging. It was what she was accustomed to.

Joe wanted to ask if there was a man involved but he didn't. Though he wasn't ordinarily altruistic, he had begun the conversation in an attempt to take her mind off the ordeal with Dan Austen. But he found himself absorbed by this woman who knew so well what she wanted—and didn't want. It took a lot of maturity to walk away from a successful career in search of a successful life. "The fast lane got to you?" he offered with a half smile.

She made a face. "I hate the term but yes, that was the crux of it. The station here had been sold and the new owners were looking for a manager so I applied for the job." She paused. "Joe, do you think Louise was fooling around with that man?"

So much for distracting her. Joe moved his shoulders in a gesture that he hoped was noncommittal.

"I feel really badly about Dan," she said, folding her forearms. "If Louise were having an affair, I've made certain her husband knows all about it, haven't I?"

Joe watched her lift her hand and trace the rim of her cup with a rosy-tipped finger. He was struck again by how pretty, how neat, and what a normal, girl-next-door type she was. Here in her element he was seeing a whimsical, philosophical side to her, too, which was very appealing. Sitting in the sunlight with her, the smell of freshly brewed coffee, her friends nearby, he could almost believe . . .

He sighed, putting an end to the thought. "Yeah, I guess you have. But remember, Katie, you didn't start this. Louise's friend did. A woman alone at night, on a deserted dock?" He made a disgusted snort.

She laughed softly, folding her hands together, linking her fingers. "Maybe he thought I was soliciting."

He looked blank.

"A streetwalker."

Joe's head jerked at that. "You?" he snapped. His eyes grew narrow as he studied her expression. "No way," he added.

She shifted restlessly on the padded bench.

"This situation isn't the least bit amusing, Katie," he said impatiently.

She bit her lips and resumed a serious expression. "I know. I'm sorry."

Silently Joe looked at her bent head and denounced his brother. This surveillance Neal wanted would be so much easier if she were a different kind of person—or if he were.

Neal had used the justification of Joe's training to get him to agree to watch her. That training had been so intense it became a part of him. His old instincts had already kicked in, activating his powers of observation, creeping into his attitude, whether he wanted them there or not.

For instance he noted, and stored in memory, that Katie used the past tense when she spoke of Louise Austen. It was a way of expressing herself, indicating that she was convinced—even if only subconsciously—that something had happened to Louise. In her mind she had grouped the shadows, the threatening man and the scream all together.

He had interviewed hundreds of witnesses, perhaps even thousands. It was not an unusual occurrence. Most of the time it turned out to be a simple matter of "what's past is past," a way of speaking of a friend who's moved away, or someone with whom one no longer had contact. But occasionally it was a premonition based on unconscious observation of some tiny scrap of information that might be useful. The trick was to free that scrap, and possibly others.

More than once he'd caught a certain expression in her eyes when she looked at him. She was attracted to him, that much was apparent. He could make a move, ask her to dinner, give her a rush. She'd never know she was being watched, protected, whatever the hell it was he was supposed to be doing. And maybe he could pry loose the information from her subconscious.

He'd had a talent for that. *At one time,* he reminded himself. "Your motives for being in that place at that time are irrelevant. Unless the man's a fool, he had to know he was frightening you. Bullies don't get my vote, no matter how innocent they turn out to be."

"Mine, either," she breathed, settling back against the booth. "But that's a change. I was under the impression you thought I completely misinterpreted his actions."

"Maybe I was trying to convince *you* of that."

Her eyes grew wide. "Well, thanks," she muttered. He didn't want her to worry? Was that what he meant? "I think," she added, tilting her head to one side.

Again he was captured by her dazzling smile. Her gold-colored eyes shimmered with warmth. They were unique, gorgeous, mesmerizing. He remembered a book he'd read as a child that said angels had golden eyes. Joe could see, though, in the sunlight that there was a rainbow of colored flecks, aqua and green, amber and violet, upon the sea of gold. Mentally he shook himself.

Poetry, for God's sake! "Don't you have to get to work?" he asked more harshly than he'd intended.

She didn't take offense. She glanced at her watch. "Gosh, yes!" She grabbed her purse and stood.

"Wait. I'll walk you to your car." Joe pulled out a bill and dropped it on the table. He lifted his hand as a goodbye to Lonnie and received a vigorous wave in return.

"Ya'll come back!"

Katie laughed as they pushed through the door and onto the street. Her car was parked less than a block away. They reached it too soon. She wasn't sure what she wanted him to say, to do. She took out her key, unlocked and opened the door, before turning to him. "Thanks for the moral support, and for the coffee."

"You're welcome."

"Well—maybe I'll see you around," she said. She smiled and started to get in the car, but he stopped her with a hand at her elbow. "Look, Katie..." He hesitated, seeming to want to say more.

Katie waited. Her smile was encouraging.

In the end, he simply murmured, "Take care," and dropped a casual kiss onto her upturned lips.

At least it began as a casual kiss.

The moment their lips met they seemed to fuse. Katie didn't breathe, didn't move at all, for a split second until he increased the pressure. Involuntarily her lips parted slightly. He took immediate advantage, sliding his tongue along the edge of her upper lip. She felt the imprint of each of his fingers as his hand slid to her upper arm and grasped, turning her a bit so that she was facing him fully. As he tightened his hold, his knuckles inadvertently brushed the outer curve of her breast.

It wasn't deliberate, not here in the light of day, not here in the middle of the main street of town, but the contact was like fire, branding her there. Her neck felt weak; she wasn't sure it could support the weight of her head.

Suddenly Joe reached for her other arm and used both hands to push her away. His blue eyes were a stormy indigo, his breathing was raspy. "Sorry," he muttered unsteadily as he released her. And then he was gone.

Katie never knew how she started the car and drove to the station. Lucidity returned as she sat in the parking lot looking at the logo on the side of the building. She tried to deny the importance of the kiss; surely she'd imagined the sensual effect. But the taste of him that lingered on her lips, and that burning spot on the outer curve of her breast, could not be denied.

This was a small town; she was sure to see him again. And she couldn't fall apart every time that happened. He was good-looking, not handsome in a picture-book sense, but masculine in a way that was totally exciting. He stood tall but looked as though he could move as quickly and gracefully as a cat if it were necessary.

She knew other good-looking men. She dated regularly. But her sexual response had never been so intense. Not right away, not without warning.

Or left her so disturbed. She felt buffeted as though by a September storm, the kind that sometimes grew into a hurricane. The kind of storm in which the wind and rain were unpredictable, never signaling direction, just going where impulse, caprice or fancy took it.

As she sat and stared at the logo, slowly her self-assurance reasserted itself, and she made a solemn vow. Calm, even slightly cool—that would be her attitude the next time she encountered Joe Ryder.

Before the kiss she had been...interested. She had recognized the strength of his appeal and had been rather intrigued by a sense of adventure. No more. *Keep your mind on the important things.*

She entered the station briskly, took a fistful of pink message slips and the neatly typed proposal for Mr. O'Donnell from Ruth, her secretary, and entered her office. A pile of reports awaited her, centered precisely in the middle of her desk. She took off her jacket and hung it up, then hooked her purse over an arm of the coat tree and reached inside for her reading glasses. She groped around among wrinkled tissues, checkbook, billfold, lipstick. The glasses weren't there. She dropped her shoulders and looked around. Then, muttering to herself, she crossed to search the drawers in her desk, the floor, the bookshelves. Damn. She went back to the tree and looked in the pockets of her jacket.

The only thing there was the packet of matches she'd picked up last night at the restaurant. The cover was a distinctive peach color, satiny to the touch. Embossed in gold script on the front was the greeting, Happy Birthday, Louise. She didn't have to turn them over to know that on the back was the name of an exclusive restaurant in a private resort several miles down the coast. She smiled. Dan must have splurged for the birthday celebration.

A few weeks ago a date had taken her to the resort for dinner and the bill had been astronomical. She'd cooked several meals for the poor man to pay him back. She remembered at the time how amused she'd been by the personalized matches and the single rose presented to her by a stiff maître d'. Great marketing strategy, she'd decided. For only a small amount of money, the restaurant gave the impression that your evening had been carefully planned from the moment you made your reservations, when actually all it took was a hand-embossing machine in the office and a supply of roses.

The matches at their table had been embossed, too. But it wasn't a special occasion, so theirs had simply had their names in gold script.

She dropped the matches back into the pocket and resumed her search, even returning to the car. But they weren't there, either.

"Lose something?" Ruth asked as Katie passed her desk.

"My reading glasses," said Katie, impatiently.

When she got back to her desk she sat in her chair and scowled at the telephone. Would he—she didn't even have to identify *he* by name—be listed? She didn't know about cellular phones but she reached for the directory.

He wasn't. She called Neal at his headquarters and had to explain but she got the number.

"Joe Ryder," he answered tersely when she'd finally made the connection.

"This is Katie." Drat, her voice sounded breathy.

"Hi," he answered in what she perceived as a lower, more intimate level. *Fool, you're imagining things.*

If he just didn't have such a sexy voice. The sound of those bass tones was effective in undermining her will and made her feel warm and pliant inside.

Stubbornly and sternly she reminded herself of the vow she'd made just a few minutes ago, sitting right outside in her car.

He was sexy. But sex wasn't the most important thing in her life right now.

The station's ratings were important in her life. And a lot of other things, which she would catalog in just a minute. She straightened in her chair and assumed her best businesslike tone. "I'm sorry to bother you but I seem to have lost my glasses. I wonder if you would mind checking in your truck."

Her family—they were always important.

"Sure." The delay lasted only seconds. "They aren't here, Katie. Sorry."

Losing her glasses was important. She went on with her list as she fought off the responsive shivers that ran like fingers down her spine. A lot of things were more important than sex. Chocolate. Her favorite flannel nightgown, the latest Charlotte MacLeod novel waiting on her bedside table . . . picturing the recently purchased murder mystery, pristine backed, ready to open, she suddenly remembered where her glasses were. She'd worked on the proposal for O'Donnell at home this morning. Damn. "Thanks for looking. I must have left them at home."

She started to hang up but was stopped by a question. "What was the name of the man you called on last night? The owner of Harbor Grill?"

"Dewey O'Donnell?"

"Yeah, that's it."

"Why?"

"I just thought I might stop by and have a talk with him. Maybe he knew the man who was with Louise Austen."

"Why didn't I think of that?" She checked her watch. Almost eleven o'clock. "Don't go in the middle of the lunch hour. He's touchy when you interrupt his business."

"That's why you were there so late last night?"

"Yes. I had to wait until closing time. Joe, let me go with you. I'll introduce you to him."

"Hey, slow down," he protested. "This is no big deal. I was just going to stop by if I got the chance."

"Sure you were," she scoffed. "I have to go home to pick up my glasses anyway. I'll bet I beat you there."

"Katie!"

She hung up, feeling victorious for no explainable reason. She grabbed her purse and jacket and the proposals for the restaurant owner and hurried out of the office. "I have to go home for my glasses. I'll make a couple of calls while I'm out and be back right after lunch," she told her secretary.

Once again Katie was making her way across the planked deck in her high heels when a voice from behind startled her.

"Why the hell don't you wear sensible shoes?" Joe demanded. At the same time he took her arm to steady her.

"There's nothing wrong with these shoes," she protested.

"Not if you're walking on a solid surface. In fact," he said, casting a look over his shoulder to survey her shapely calves, "high heels are pretty sexy." He flashed her a quick, impulsive grin that was totally different from the rare, careful smiles he'd given her before. "But they aren't very practical here on the docks."

"I know that." Katie wasn't about to comment on her diminutive size, which was the reason she wore the shoes. "Just look on it as one of my little vanities."

"Are you self-conscious because you're short?"

"Of course not," she denied. She wasn't self-conscious, she was simply astute, she assured herself. A businesswoman who dealt with her flaws, who offered the most pleasant perspective to her clients. If she had been fat she would have gone on a diet.

"Then why do you wear them?"

She glared at him impatiently. "Because I want to be successful in my job. It's hard to be accepted professionally in your hometown where people have watched you grow up. They tend to remember you as fifteen."

"How old are you?"

"Boy, you're nosy." She hesitated. She knew she looked young; she'd fought that image of herself since she'd been old enough to baby-sit. She wanted this man to remember that she wasn't. "I'm twenty-eight, almost twenty-nine."

He raised a brow but didn't state the obvious, which sent him up a notch in her estimation. She stepped through the door to the restaurant.

The early lunch crowd had begun drifting in but only a few tables were occupied. Katie knew from experience that in an hour you wouldn't be able to move in here and all the outside tables would be filled as well. "This way."

She led him to a hallway and stopped to knock on a door. In response to an order to come in they entered Mr. O'Donnell's domain. The office had a window and an open door on the kitchen side. Mr. O'Donnell stood in the opening. He turned to look at them, then spoke to someone and closed the door. "Hello, Katie." He looked inquiringly at Joe. "Don't I know you?"

Joe extended his hand. "I'm a regular customer, Mr. O'Donnell. Joe Ryder."

"Oh, yeah, you live on your boat, don't you? Well, what can I do for you?" His glance included Katie. "It's almost lunchtime."

Katie put the file she'd been holding on his desk. "I'll leave these suggestions with you, Mr. O'Donnell. You can call me about them later." Her gaze bounced off Joe. It seemed he was leaving this to her. "There was something we wanted to ask you."

He waited expectantly. "Well . . . ask."

She was searching for the best way to proceed. They'd promised Dan that this would go no further. She should have thought it through more thoroughly. "Louise Austen was here last night. Did you see her?"

His expression closed as effortlessly as she would close a book. "Louise comes in occasionally. I don't remember whether she was here last night or not. She may have been."

Katie chose the simplest approach. "We're—I'm trying to locate the man who was with her. Do you know him?"

Mr. O'Donnell's brows knit in a scowl. "No." He'd also opted for simplicity.

"Do you mean, 'no, you've never seen him before' or 'no, you didn't see him at all'?"

"I mean just what I said. And I think you'd better stay out of people's personal lives."

Katie's brows drew together; she had hoped for more. He wasn't going to give them an inch. In addition he thought she was poking into Louise's business.

Didn't his closemouthed attitude confirm her suspicion? If things were on the up-and-up, her seeing Louise with the man wouldn't have mattered. But obviously it mattered to the stranger. Katie had no idea where to go from here. She looked to Joe for assistance.

Joe spoke carefully, choosing his words. "Mr. O'Donnell, I hope Katie didn't mislead you. We have no interest in Mrs. Austen's personal life. Or in Mrs. Austen herself. We simply want to find the man."

"Why?"

Joe hesitated. "I can't tell you that. I'm sorry. Do you know his name?"

Once more Katie was surprised at the authority and command she heard in his voice. Neal had deferred to it and O'Donnell was leaning that way. She could tell by his hesitation.

Joe would be very hard to lie to. If *she'd* been the one on the other end of his question she'd have told the truth.

O'Donnell mused for another minute. "I've seen him around a couple of times; but, no, I don't know his name," he said slowly. A noise from the other room caught his attention. He nodded to the woman who was making motions through the window. "He isn't from around here," he added grudgingly.

"Are you sure?" asked Joe.

"Yeah. He once told me the oysters were sweeter where he lived."

"You didn't ask him where that was?"

"Nah, he was talking through his ear."

When they were outside Katie asked, "Do you believe him?"

Joe sighed and ran a hand around the back of his neck. "Yes, I do. He told us all he knows. And we're faced with a dead end for now."

Chapter 4

Two days later, on Friday, Katie sat in the studio with a headset clamped on her ears and listened to a housewife protest the rather explicit wording that had been turning up recently in newspapers' personal advertising sections. This was her biweekly call-in show, five-thirty to seven-thirty on Tuesdays and Fridays. Her listeners could voice their opinions on anything from the need for a congressional pay increase to the price of Florida real estate.

This woman, a regular caller to the show, was articulate and Katie knew she could allow her thoughts to wander a bit. Her last caller had been a trial. The man had wanted to talk about himself. From experience Katie had learned that—aside from the fanatics who thought the country was hopelessly degenerate and only their ideas could save it—the self-absorbed callers were the most boring. Thank goodness she seldom had to deal with either type.

Her head ached. She put her hands up to ease the tight clamp for a second. Talk radio was popular and she would have enjoyed doing the show if she hadn't had so many other things on her mind.

Since the episode on the docks three days ago she'd been bothered by an eerie feeling that she was being watched. There was nothing substantial on which to base her misgivings, nothing she could put her finger on, but she was mindful of an itchy sensation between her shoulder blades. She didn't like the feeling one bit. She hated to be edgy and uptight.

And she hated the changes the feeling was making in her life; it was shackling her. She felt more comfortable when she wasn't alone, so she'd made it a point to be around people during the day and get home before dark each night. She would have been pleased to catch and confront whoever was following her, even assuming it was the stranger from the pier, but so far she'd been unsuccessful in even catching a glimpse.

To make it worse she hadn't heard a word about what was going on with Louise Austen. Neither Neal nor Joe had called. She told herself that she would be content to hear from either of them, but that was a lie. She'd hoped Joe would make the contact.

She was unable to get the man out of her mind. The memory of his roughly chiseled features was a constant and uncanny distraction. She'd tried setting him off to one corner of her thoughts but he always seemed to wiggle his way back to the front.

Now she forcibly directed her attention to the voice coming through the headset. "Let's hear from some other listeners on this subject. Thanks for calling in, Vicki."

Her next caller introduced an interesting extension to the topic. A number of young Florida women had been assaulted by men they'd met through personal ads, a phenomenon that was evidently widespread according to news reports.

"Women who answer personals are just stupid, Katie, just plain stupid."

She realized she had allowed the woman to ramble on for too long. "Maybe some of our listeners have had or know of someone who has had an experience like this. If you would like to call and join our discussion the number is 555-2020," she said. "Thank you for calling." She flipped a switch and moved on to the next caller.

The program operated on a five-second time delay in order to protect the station from inadvertently broadcasting inappropriate language. "I'm a first-time caller," said the man. "Your name is Katie Johns?" He spoke very slowly, very softly and his voice was breathy, as though he were exhaling with every syllable.

As soon as she heard the voice, Katie pressed another button, activating a tape to record the conversation. She wasn't sure why she did, except that the man was obviously disguising his voice. However, he sounded more nervous than menacing. Maybe her caution stemmed from a combination of things—the experience on the docks, the strange suspicion she was being followed, her general feeling of things not being quite right. He sounded . . . taut.

"Worse than answering the personals are the women who walk around asking for it."

"It? Come on now. You're not going to use that old justification that anyone who wears a bikini subconsciously wants to be raped or battered, are you?"

"There's a lot to the idea. Or these miniskirts. When they sit down you can see clear to their—"

Katie had to bleep the word—thank goodness for the five-second delay. She had her finger on the cutoff button. She didn't tolerate such calls and ordinarily would have broken the connection immediately but she was glad she hadn't when he went on in the same breathy voice.

"But they're not the only ones, Katie Johns. There was a woman hanging around the docks late at night, just a few days ago."

Katie caught her breath. The hand on the button faltered. It was *him*! "Maybe the woman had business there," she said, schooling herself to keep her voice even, to breathe deeply, though she felt like she would strangle.

"Not this one. She was looking for trouble and I was tempted to give it to her."

Was this the answer? An explanation why the man chased her? "How do you know that?"

His laugh was unpleasant. "She was minding other people's business, not her own," he continued. The nervousness she'd detected when the call began was missing now, replaced by hostility, rage—the same evolution of emotion she'd witnessed on the pier.

She could see his face before her, teeth clenched, eyes narrowed. "And if she's listening right now, she should know she'd better be careful. Maybe she ought to leave town, because I'm watching her and if I catch her alone again I might just have to teach her a lesson."

There was a moment of dead silence on the air. Katie moistened her lips. The broadcasting booth had suddenly become hot and claustrophobic. Finally she regained her voice. "This station makes it a policy never to allow threats to go out over the air. I should have cut you off but, sir, you sound like you are deeply disturbed," she said quietly but urgently. She leaned forward. "You need help. I suggest—no, I *beg*—you to talk to someone, a counselor, a minister." She winced when the phone was slammed down in her ear. She hit the cutoff button and slid a prerecorded commercial into the slot before letting her head fall forward into her hands. Her breath came out in a whoosh.

The man slammed down the phone. When he removed his hand from the receiver it was shaking violently. Damn her! Damn her!

Help? His mind screamed at the implication. He opened the door to the telephone booth and stumbled out. She was the one who would need help. She had been easy to identify, driving around in a car with the logo of the radio station on its side.

Rather than use his other resources he'd called the station. Representing a small operation like WCTZ, the secretary had been friendly and eager to supply a potential advertiser with information about its management. He'd given a false name, of course. He laughed out loud at the reaction he'd have gotten if any of them found out who he really was.

Then he sobered, straightened his tie, adjusted his lapels. That must never happen.

"I should have kept him talking. Damn! I should have kept him on the air." She spoke out loud as she made a fist and brought it down on the table.

"Katie? Are you okay?" Through the glass, Raymond was looking at her, his expression worried.

She nodded but spoke through the interoffice mike. "Raymond, do the next lead-in for me, will you? I have to make a call."

He gave her a thumbs-up and switched the controls to his booth. Katie picked up the telephone.

Neal was still on duty. She described the call quickly and felt a surge of relief when he said he was on his way.

Joe arrived first, however. Seconds after she had hung up the phone, she saw him saunter into the room adjoining her studio. At the sight of him, and without warning, she was overcome by an emotion that filled her throat. Though she hated to cry, she was helpless against the tears that welled in her eyes. She bit her lips together and waved him in.

She hadn't been able to get him out of her mind for the past two days, but she hadn't realized just how much she had missed him—missed his quiet strength—until he appeared, exactly when she needed him. As he entered the booth she held out her hand.

Joe took it, holding tight. He muttered something inane like, "It's okay" or "I'm here." He wasn't sure what he said.

Reflexively Katie checked the big clock on the wall in front of her. She didn't release his hand but she pushed a button on the mike and leaned forward. "It's time for the seven o'clock *On the Hour* news from WCTZ, Garden City, Florida. I'll be back at ten after seven for more of the *Katie Johns Show*," she informed her listeners lightly. "Don't go 'way." The required announcement helped her regain her equilibrium. The tears subsided and she smiled. "Hi. What are you doing here?" she asked, keeping her voice level. She hoped he would say something ridiculously inappropriate like, "I couldn't stay away from you."

His mouth tilted up in that quirky half grin. He answered in the same light vein. "Hi, yourself. I'm a fan of yours. I heard the show."

All pretense of a friendly exchange was gone. Her smile faded. "Then you heard the man who called?"

Joe's eyes took on an icy blue hardness. Some of the fury he'd felt when he heard the man's unctuous voice threaten Katie rushed back. He had been ready to reach out through the airwaves and grab the creep by the throat. Until he'd walked into the station and been confronted by her tears. Then the fury had been supplanted by a warm rush of protectiveness. "Yeah. I heard him."

He met her beautiful golden gaze, watered down at the moment. Her hair, pulled back in a severe bun, was probably supposed to make her look more sophisticated but if so, the style missed its mark. Instead the unobstructed, uncluttered view of her smooth forehead, her flawless complexion, her tender mouth, emphasized her freshness, her clean appearance. Tonight she wore a dress styled like a short-sleeved coat, with four large buttons down the front and a wide belt cinching her waist. It was flag-red, the same vibrant shade as her lip color.

Joe quit fighting his smile, letting it spread slowly to his eyes. "You handled him like a pro, though I doubt he'll take your good advice."

"I doubt it, too. I called Neal as soon as he hung up." She stood. "I need to get out of here for a minute."

They moved into the next room. Without asking, Joe fished into his pocket, took out some change and fed the vending machine. A can of soda was released. He popped the tab on the can and handed it to her. She took it, tilting her head back to drink thirstily. "Thanks," she said. "There's no doubt that's the same man."

"No one else was there," he agreed.

"I wonder where he's been since Monday night," she said curiously.

Neal spoke up from the door. "I'd like to know where he is now." He gave Joe a nod of greeting—or approval, she wasn't sure which—before turning to her. "Katie, I'm glad you caught me. Tell me about this man who called. What did he say exactly?"

"I taped it. You can hear it for yourself." She tossed the can into the trash can and turned to reenter the broadcasting booth and so missed seeing their startled responses to her announcement.

Joe's jaw sagged; Neal's head came up with a jerk. They grinned at each other, nodding approval, and followed her. She was already in her swivel chair, fiddling at her board.

"You taped the call?" said Joe. "How did you know to do that?"

"It's odd. I've been uncomfortable for a couple of days. I've had this feeling that I was being watched. I know it sounds crazy but I couldn't shake it off. When the man began to speak, his voice was whispery, like he was trying to disguise it. So I started the tape. Then he admitted—" She moved her shoulders. "Well, you heard him."

Joe's eyes met Neal's again, briefly. Neal held up two fingers. Joe gave an imperceptible shake of his head. No one else had been following Katie. He'd stake his boat on it.

"Quick thinking." Joe leaned across her, propped stiff-armed, hand flat on the desk, to study the workings of her control board.

It was crowded with the three of them in such a small space. Joe's hard belly brushed Katie's shoulder; his masculine scent filled her nostrils. She kept her face ahead but stared at his hand and arm. His shirt tonight was white, a stark contrast to his tan. She tried to disregard the warmth that radiated against her back.

A click denoted that the rewind was complete. The machinery spit a cassette into her waiting hand.

"You can do a great deal with a tape," Joe said. "Pick up background sounds for clues to the suspect's location or analyze regional inflections in the voice. Let's hear it."

She glanced up from the board to stare at him. Without asking herself why, she rose to let him take her place. She'd had no idea he was so knowledgeable. He slid the tape into the right slot and pushed a button.

They reran the tape several times. Joe gradually raised the volume on each repeat. What he wouldn't give for an audio forensics technician. There was a distinctive background noise but he couldn't identify it. Engines, motors, but not ordinary traffic. It fluctuated, off and on, off and on, in brief bursts.

Boats, maybe?

No.

Planes?

Possibly. He hunched over the console, his eyes narrowed in absolute concentration. His mind still occupied with the tape, he swiveled around in Katie's chair and frowned up at them.

For the first time he noticed the small smile on his brother's face, the surprise on Katie's. He quickly ejected the tape and handed it to Neal. "You'll want to send this to the state crime lab," he said abruptly.

"Make a copy first," said Katie, not even questioning his ability to do so.

When the copy was complete Neal slipped the original cassette into his shirt pocket. "I'll get it off first thing in the morning."

Joe started to tell his brother to do it tonight, but he closed his mouth on the words. He was accustomed to law-enforcement facilities that implemented his needs without delay, not even one of a few hours. He put the copy into his own pocket.

He'd listen again later. With the advent of this call, the threat to Katie had moved from the realm of speculation to full reality. Something had happened—Joe still wasn't sure what—but it was important enough to the caller for him to reveal himself once again.

Hell. He reminded himself that this investigation was not his business. He'd promised to keep a casual eye on Katie Johns, no more.

He looked at her. "Would you feel better if I followed you home?" he asked bluntly.

Katie looked down at her watch. She wondered why he was offering but she wasn't about to turn him down. "Yes, but I have another twenty minutes before sign-off," she said, giving him a chance to back out. She hoped that he wouldn't. And he didn't. "I'll hang around."

Joe parked his truck in one of the visitors' spaces. Katie had expected him to wave and drive on. Or simply to drive on, foregoing the wave. He had been uncommunicative since Neal left them at the station. She thought he probably regretted his offer. "Would you like to come in for a drink?" she asked.

Joe looked up at the sky, the stars. He smelled jasmine, gardenia. He smiled down at her. "Why don't we walk down to the beach first?"

"Okay."

This was a nice place, he thought, as they crossed manicured lawns. The building was well kept and flowered borders softened the standard Florida block-with-stucco style architecture. Floodlights illuminated the parking areas and walkways. The moon lay a path of light across the water. At the edge of the dunes they stopped to take off their shoes. Joe rolled up the cuffs of his khaki trousers. Katie dropped her purse on the sand beside the shoes and started pulling pins out of her hair.

"Trusting soul, aren't you?" he asked.

Katie shrugged and dropped the pins into her pocket. She shook her head and combed her fingers through her hair. "If you're planning a long hike I'll take it inside."

"We won't go far. I'd just like to blow the cobwebs out." When they reached the water's edge he reached for her hand, casually, as though he hadn't thought about what he was doing.

Who was he kidding? Katie Johns appealed to him on many levels, foremost of which was the sexual level. But awareness of her sensuality wasn't the only reason for his attraction to this woman. When he'd seen her in action tonight at the station, her calm in the face of the renewed threat had impressed him. Her taping of the call showed quick thinking. She was a confident lady... woman, he corrected. Yet running throughout her personality like a bright ribbon was a bit of charming naïveté, which he was sure she would heatedly deny. Right now, however, the sexual level was as far as Joe could go.

He'd avoided contact with her for two days, knowing instinctively that he could feel things, inappropriate things, like affection and tenderness, maybe other things he wouldn't even put a name to. And feelings like that would lead to an impossible situation. He'd faced the fact long ago that a traditional life-style was one he'd never enjoy.

Joe was qualified by background and skilled by training to make swift judgments about people; he could evaluate promptly, without the luxury of leisurely observation. Upon further analysis he was rarely proven wrong. Of course one of those rare times had been one too many. It had ruined his career, smeared his reputation, stolen his strength and eventually had landed him here in Garden City.

But he grew more certain that this wasn't one of those times.

"What do you think we ought to do about this man, Joe?" she asked after they had walked a few yards.

"Nothing. Tomorrow Neal will send the tape to the state lab to see if they can pick up anything. We just have to wait."

"Isn't there something we can do?"

"I'm afraid not. Waiting is ninety-nine percent of investigative work."

"You know a lot about that sort of thing?"

He shot her a look. "Yeah."

If Katie had expected him to elaborate, she was disappointed. She shuddered slightly and kicked at the water. White foam scalloped the shore like pretty edging on a petticoat. The water was warm but not as warm as his hand. "You don't know how it feels to think you're being followed."

Oh, don't I? thought Joe. He toyed briefly with the idea of admitting that he was the one following—at least the topic would distract him from his other observations, like the way the moonlight looked in her hair, the way the breeze flattened her dress against her breasts and thighs. But he dismissed the temptation. Neal had warned him that she might not be pleased. Now that Joe knew her better, he was sure she wouldn't.

He looked back over his shoulder. They'd come farther than he realized. "Do you want to head back?"

No, she didn't want to stop. She wanted to keep walking and walking, all night, all day, until she walked out of this mess with the stranger. She sighed. "I suppose so," she said.

They collected their shoes and Katie's purse and rinsed their sandy feet at a sidewalk spigot, placed at the border of the sand for that purpose.

"What about that drink?" asked Katie as she led the way to the elevator.

Joe nodded even as he told himself he should get back to his boat. "There's no security here," he said, frowning, as she pushed the button marked Four. The elevator lurched to life.

It sounded like an accusation, undeserving of a reply. "No," Katie answered nonetheless. "The association has never felt the need for it. Our building is well lighted." The car stopped and the doors opened obligingly onto an open-air hallway.

A grunt was his only response as he followed her to the recessed door, watched as she unlocked a flimsy knob lock and trailed her inside.

Joe looked around at the large room that was unusual enough to be interesting, but not so dramatic as to startle. Most of the room was white, the huge L-shaped sofa, the two upholstered chairs, the walls. Unusual was the use of the spectrums of cool greens, sophisticated blues, and all the shades in between—aqua, cobalt, sapphire, turquoise, emerald, jade—in the carpet, in pillows, a lamp and in a framed watercolor garden scene on the wall above the sofa. In the daytime the colors would be repeated in the sea and the sky beyond the windows.

The other furniture was a mix of styles and materials—polished glass and shaped iron, limed oak. Even one parlor piece, a frivolous, feminine desk of dark mahogany inlaid with light sandalwood, sat in front of a wall of built-in shelves, holding TV and VCR, stereo—a good system—books and tapes. Two large Boston ferns, one in a stand, one hung from the ceiling, softened the geometric effect.

Between two sets of glass doors a narrow section of masonry formed the support of the entire wall facing south toward the Gulf. Hung from the ceiling molding above the masonry section was a six-foot oriental scroll depicting a simple fishing scene. Beneath it was a low stool with a puffed cushion. A pair of wrinkled jeans was half on, half off the stool. Two mismatched cotton socks had been left where they landed on the floor.

The draperies on either side of that amusing arrangement were made of some light, filmy material, which would blur but not obscure her view of the water. One sneaker peeked from beneath the edge of the fabric.

A cereal bowl and a blow dryer, out of place on the coffee table, added to the gentle, inoffensive clutter. A pleasing room, welcoming and snug even in its untidiness, not pretentious. He was surprised to feel himself relax.

"I'm not a devoted housekeeper," Katie was saying as she bustled around, gathering the jeans and socks, the bowl and a juice glass he hadn't noticed. "Have a seat. Or explore if you like. What would you like to drink?" She stopped and turned a questioning gaze on him.

"Coffee?"

While he waited he took a quick tour of the rest of the condo. The plan was unique, taking the most efficient advantage of the ocean view. She had two bedrooms and two baths. One bedroom—hers—had the same view of the ocean as the living room, the other was the only room in the place that looked over the parking area. She'd turned it into an office with a desk and chair, bookshelves, and state-of-the-art computer equipment. It was as neat as a pin.

He smiled to himself. She kept her professional life in order. Returning to the living room, he held the drapes aside and looked out onto a generous balcony. A table and chairs and two loungers faced the Gulf.

He hitched his trousers and sat near one end of the sofa. He put out a finger to wipe at a dried ring of milk, left where the cereal bowl had rested. On the large square glass table in front of him was an assortment of things: current editions of all three major news magazines and a hardcover edition of a mystery novel, which he picked up absently as he looked over the remaining items.

There was a framed photo—which he presumed to be her family—of an attractive older couple bracketed between Katie and another woman, and three men who looked very much like her. The picture wasn't recent.

They were grinning into the camera, happily, as though life had been good to them and they didn't have a care in the world. He presumed the three men were her brothers; he wondered who the other woman was.

A ceramic ticktacktoe game rested on a folded newspaper. The article itself was a work of art; the board was a glazed white grid; the *X*s were represented by tiny replicas of starfish in an unlikely turquoise and the *O*s by peach-colored sand dollars.

She reentered the room carrying a tray.

"I like your place."

"Thanks. I've enjoyed fixing it up a little at a time. Do you enjoy living on your boat?"

He shrugged. "It suits me. I'm not the domesticated type."

No, thought Katie. He seemed the kind of man who wouldn't want to be weighted down with possessions. "Are you a mystery fan?" As she set the tray down she nodded to the book in his hands.

He'd forgotten he still held it. "Not enough to pay for a hardback." Or a paperback for that matter.

She joined him on the sofa, one cushion away. "I promise every time that I'll wait for the paperback version, but I always break down. I've finished that one if you'd like to borrow it."

Joe picked up a mug of steaming hot coffee from the tray, dismissing the offer. "Are these the famous brothers?" he asked, indicating the picture.

"Infamous," Katie corrected. She bit into a brownie. After she had swallowed she identified the people in the picture. "Those are my parents, Bruce and Elizabeth, my brothers, Grant, Greyson and Dallas, and me. My sister, Margaret, was a Navy nurse." Her voice dropped an octave. "She was killed four years ago, on an aircraft carrier in the Persian Gulf."

"God, I'm sorry." He was shocked. Katie Johns didn't look like tragedy had ever touched her life.

Katie looked fondly at the picture. "We miss her." The group had been photographed on the lawn in front of their house, a two-story colonial. "My dad's a doctor, a GP. Mom's the gardener. Grant and Grey are both lawyers and they live in Fairbanks."

His brows rose almost comically. "Alaska?"

"Yes, can you imagine? After living in Florida all their lives? Dallas is the only one of us who's married. He lives in Clearwater.

"They drove me crazy growing up. They tried to vet every boyfriend, tell me what I could wear, where I could go." She chuckled. "When I was little I allowed all that garbage, but by the time I was twelve, I'd learned to tell them where to go, too. I don't know why I'm boring you with this. You have an older brother," she said, licking a spot of icing from her fingers.

Joe's reaction to the sight of her tongue stunned him. He felt a surge of desire. Hot blood rushed naturally to nourish the lower half of his body. Such a compelling response was dramatic and unexpected and hadn't happened to him in years.

He deliberately allowed his lids to hood his eyes and replied carefully to her statement. "Neal and I didn't see much of each other when we were growing up," he said, but he was thinking about how she would taste—sweet, like sugar and chocolate.

Unaware of what was going on in him, she curled her feet under her. She sat on one hip, facing him; the other hip curved enticingly, flowing into the feminine curve of her thigh.

He wanted her. He wanted to run his hand over the hip, down the thigh to where the skirt ended at the knee. And he didn't want to stop until he was buried deep within her. As he watched her move—lifting her arm to sip from her cup, lower it again, tilt her head, loop a strand of hair behind her ear—his arousal became persistent.

In an attempt at composure, and to ease the pressure of his clothing, he hooked an arm along the back of the sofa and crossed an ankle over his knee. His fingers were inches from her cheek. If he turned his wrist he could touch her earlobe.

He reminded himself that Katie Johns hadn't seen the side of life he knew so well. In a word she was totally different from the women he usually dated, women who'd had their vulnerable edges rounded off by life, whose innocence had long ago been replaced by sophistication and cynicism. Not tough women, but slightly toughened, enough for self-protection anyway.

He set down his mug, the delicate china connecting too loudly with the glass table. "I'd better get going," he said and stood. Now that he had decided to leave he wanted to do it expeditiously. Wanted? Hell, he *had* to get out of here. "Thanks for the coffee. I've got to go."

Katie put her mug beside his and stood, too. She looked after him with an expression of mild exasperation. "Are you always like this?" she asked.

He had already taken two steps toward the door but at her question he turned. "Like what?" he asked.

She shook her head, waved her hand. "This wishy-washy, on-again, off-again interest. One minute you're gazing into my eyes; the next you're avoiding them. It's beginning to annoy me. I didn't twist your arm to get you to come in for coffee."

He couldn't help a small smile. He eased his hands into the pockets of his khaki trousers. "You're absolutely right. I am wishy-washy."

Katie had seen the desire in his eyes. She knew she hadn't imagined that; it gave her the necessary courage to go on. "I wish I knew what battle it is you're fighting with yourself, Joe," she admitted.

At that his face closed.

She slid her feet back into her pumps, bringing her head up to the level of his chin. "Am I too small-town? Is that it? Do I amuse you?" she asked.

He rocked on his heels and tried to think but she had advanced a step. Her scent was intoxicating. "I'm not laughing, Katie. Would you like to explain what you mean?''

"We were sitting here having a perfectly ordinary conversation, enjoyable, I thought, when all of a sudden you jump up and announce that you have to leave. You did the same thing in the coffee shop. No warning, no civilized leave-taking, just—oops, blam—I'm going. It isn't very flattering, you know. It's like, without warning, you've suddenly had all of me you can take and you have to run, to escape..."

Joe clamped his teeth together. Her scolding was mild, even refined, but to stem the gentle tide he caught her chin and tilted her face up. "You know, you ought to thank those brothers of yours for teaching you how to read men," he growled. Then he covered her lips with his.

The first time he'd kissed her he'd been shaken to his toes. This kiss was intended solely to put a brake on her words; he had to discipline himself to keep it that way. He was good at self-discipline; he'd had to be.

He raised his head and smiled gently. "Not all of you I can take. Never that. Maybe all of you I can handle with any kind of self-restraint."

"Why do you feel you have to be restrained?" she asked, disappointed that there was no tenderness, no desire, no clear feelings at all in the kiss. It was not like the kiss on Tuesday. That had been wild and hot; this was a study in iron control. But, then, he was still holding her.

His answer was confusing. "Because you're you and I'm somebody else."

Katie shook her head. "That's a cryptic statement if I ever heard one."

He chuckled with her then raked his hands through her hair and sighed heavily. "I don't mean to be cryptic. Maybe I do have the urge to run, but it's not from you,

believe me. It's from myself." He touched her face with
his fingertips. "I won't be in Garden City forever, Katie.
Hell, I won't be anyplace forever."

Katie stood still, searching his eyes. The sad, disillu-
sioned look had returned. She didn't ask why; she wasn't
sure she even wanted to know. She felt the strength in his
hand but she could pull away anytime she needed to. She
wished she could pull away from the attraction she felt as
easily. "I'm not the kind of woman who demands
promises, Joe," she said quietly.

He dropped his hand. She was wrong. Maybe she
didn't even know it, but she was wrong. "Good," he
said. "Because I'm not the man to make them."

The telephone rang while Katie was brushing her teeth.
She spat out the toothpaste and grabbed for a towel. Who
on earth could be calling this late? "Hello," she said
breathlessly, expecting the worst.

Silence greeted her.

She wiped the foam off her mouth. "Hello," she repeated.

The stranger was there on the other end of the telephone. She knew it as surely as if he'd spoken. She
couldn't deal with this, not again tonight. She hung up
and contemplated taking the receiver off the hook. Her
hand was still on the receiver when it rang again.

She almost jumped out of her skin. "Hello!" she
snapped.

"Katie, this is Joe. I hope I didn't wake you."

"No," she said, shakily. She was tempted to tell him
about the call she'd just had. No, she decided.

"Tomorrow is Saturday. Do you have to work?"

"That depends," she answered, cautious now.

"I have a charter scheduled and the boy who usually crews for me has come down with a bad case of poison oak. I wondered if you'd want—if you would like to come?"

She flipped through her schedule in her mind. Nothing was pressing; nothing that couldn't be done later. A day on the water might be just the diversion she needed to rid her mind of the shadowy keepsake renewed by the telephone call.

"Okay," she said finally. "What time?"

"We leave at seven."

"I'll be there."

Joe let his hand linger on the receiver of the handset as though to maintain contact with his mental picture of her. When he realized what he was doing he dropped his hand immediately.

He had returned to the boat to find a note taped to the window. The message had read Call Sam. He'd done so and found that Sam couldn't take tomorrow's charter.

It was too late to cancel. If he was to keep an eye on Katie, the only thing he could do was invite her to go along. He might not like it but he had no alternative. The sooner this puzzle was solved, the sooner he could get his life back to normal.

He took the copy of the tape and slid it into a portable player with an automatic rewind feature. He listened while he undressed and showered. It was still repeating when he lay back on his bed and linked his fingers beneath his head.

At last he punched the button to stop the tape. He would play it again later but now, deliberately, he cleared his mind of everything except the stranger and closed his eyes. He'd been good at this, had a talent for getting into the head of his quarry, of walking in his footsteps.

Until tonight the man had been a shadow in Joe's mind. He had a verbal description from Katie of a slender man with blond hair, nice features. The man was a nebulous figure until he heard his voice.

As he lay there he worked his way into the stranger's mind. Using all his senses he took himself back to the restaurant, sharing a late dinner with a woman at harborside. How well did he know Louise Austen? Were they having an affair?

He knew her fairly well, Joe judged. At least well enough to steer her away from any conversation with an acquaintance who showed up. According to Katie, Louise hadn't argued or protested; but why would he want to get her out of there? Because he didn't want to be introduced?

They stroll along the pier. They talk. Then she leaves. Why does he hang around? Why does he come after Katie?

Because he's nervous.

Was he simply mean as hell? He sees a woman alone and vulnerable on the docks late at night and thinks he'll get a kick, a thrill, out of scaring her to death. Then, frustrated by her escape, he thinks about carrying his terrorism a bit further.

But dammit, that didn't *feel* right.

The man fades for a couple of days. Why does he come back? And why the hell call attention to himself again by telephoning the station during her show? He could disappear forever and no one would have been the wiser. There has to be a reason, both for his chasing Katie in the first place and for the call.

Or was there another, deeper psychological problem? The man was living under the threat of revelation now and it would carry a bitter taste. On the tape the voice had sounded menacing, of course... but Joe had also sensed other emotions there, emotions like anxiety and apprehension.

God, he hoped it wasn't a random crazy.

Joe breathed deeply, and began again, taking it a step at a time. Either the stranger's motive was tangible—some evidence of his presence or evidence that a crime had actually been committed—or intangible—panic at the thought that Katie could identify him. Or both.

So why didn't he run?

Unanswered questions abounded, seeping into Joe's subconscious, making him almost a part of the man. He felt emotions, fears, anxieties as though they were his own.

The truth was simple.

The man couldn't run—he couldn't leave because he wasn't finished in Garden City.

Chapter 5

Saturday was the kind of day travel writers exulted over. The big blue bowl of sky was brushed lightly with high, meringuelike clouds, the waters of the pass were clear aquamarine, and the gulls, energized by the salt-laden breeze, dipped and swooped above the ocean-bound fishing fleet in a graceful ballet.

Joe was occupied with getting the boat safely out of the lagoon and through the channel, leaving Katie to her thoughts for a while.

Days like this one had played a large part in Katie's decision to return to her hometown to live. Yet despite her relocation, she hadn't been doing this often enough. Since she'd been back she could count on the fingers of both hands the number of times she'd spent an entire day on the water. If she wasn't careful she'd end up with an awful office pallor.

The only thing she had asked of Joe when she'd arrived at the boat was that there be no mention of the stranger today. She had told him about the second phone call last night; the call had weighed heavily on her dreams. "I need a day away from this man, Joe. Do you understand?" she'd asked.

He'd agreed without hesitation.

She leaned to her right, out from under the protection of the dark blue canvas awning of the flying bridge, and turned her face to the sun. She closed her eyes against its brilliance.

Basking in the warmth she smiled to herself, remembering the day she'd finally decided to apply for the job managing the station in Garden City. The weather in Atlanta had been awful for a week. A rare frozen rain had coated the streets, she'd had a head cold and a dripping nose, and the client she'd taken to lunch was as ornery as any man she'd ever met.

She'd made the sale, typed out the order and her application at the same sitting. Then she'd gone home to call her family. They'd been thrilled by her decision—her father had been the one who told her the job was available and urged her to apply.

She could still recall the feeling of warmth that stole through her as she'd stood at the tiny window of her apartment in Atlanta and watched the icy rain come down. Her family's love and support had always comforted her. She smiled at the memory.

"Hey, mate."

Joe's quiet call broke into her reverie. She pulled her head back under the awning. Her pupils were slow to adjust from the brilliance of the sunlight to the shade. She lifted her dark glasses and secured them on top of her head. "Yes, captain?"

He stood relaxed at the wheel of the flying bridge, completely at home on the water, only his knees flexing occasionally as compensation when they crossed the wake of another boat. His legs, below the white denim cutoffs he wore, were strong and tanned and well shaped, lightly covered with hair bleached by the sun. His scarlet polo shirt, with the name *Mary Ann* embroidered on the pocket, stretched over the well-muscled arms and torso; his long-fingered hands directed the wheel with confidence. With the dark blue awning above his head, it struck Katie that he would make a good model for a poster for the Fourth of July celebration next weekend.

Joe's boat was like him. Large and powerful but not flashy. He'd shown her around before the charter customers arrived. The boat was roomy, but in contrast to her spacious condominium, notably compact. The galley and the bathroom—head, she corrected herself—were shipshape, brightwork and stainless-steel shining, fiberglass polished. His cabin in the bow was big and comfortable, dominated by an oversize bed. Another, much smaller cabin had twin bunks. The salon was outfitted in customary marine blue with accents of cheerful yellow.

Even though she'd appeared a half hour early, there were no clothes, newspapers or coffee cups scattered about as there would have been at her place. Neither were there the small personal items she would have expected. The absence of those things added to the mystery of the man himself.

Joe had been quiet but civil as he showed her over the boat and explained her duties. He'd been polite as they boarded the charter customers, but during it all, he'd held tightly to his reserve. She'd sensed his wish to keep distance between them. And she'd not tried to encroach, merely kept up a friendly banter when it was necessary to answer or ask a question, and remained silent when it was not necessary.

As her eyes adjusted to the shade under the awning, she was struck again by the harmony between Joe and the place he inhabited.

"You might offer coffee to the paying customers," he suggested, frowning. He checked the watch on his wrist. "We'll be dropping the lines in about a half hour."

Katie knew these would be the last idle minutes of the day. They had cleared the pass, one boat in a steady stream of other fishing boats bent on the same venture, and rounded a rock jetty into the ocean. The craft separated, some heading south and east, some west, their wakes curling like butterfly wings behind them as they headed toward the open sea.

"Okay," she said amiably. "I could use a cup, too. What about you?"

"Sure," said Joe. He watched over his shoulder as she left the bridge by way of the ladder. But her image stayed with him even after she was gone.

Her white shorts weren't so tight and brief as to be conspicuous or blatant but they did show her long legs and her sweetly rounded bottom to advantage. She was pale although she had the kind of skin that tanned well. Her sneakers were the old-fashioned kind, serviceable but not fancy. They looked as though they'd been washed until the little blue rectangle at the back was ragged and indecipherable. She wore a sea-green lightweight cotton windbreaker unzipped over a baggy white shirt, tied at her waist.

Dammit, he didn't want this, he thought. Then he sighed, speculating as to how many times that thought had gone through his mind during the course of the long, restless night. He'd committed himself to Neal for a week. It would probably be the longest week of his life.

He was a private man; he'd always been a private man. The last time he'd relaxed his hold on his privacy, the incident had ended in anguish. His fiancée had left him to deal with the most harrowing experience of his life. Alone. He never intended to let anyone get that close to him again.

From below he could hear Katie as she spoke animatedly to his passengers, a father in his fifties, son in his thirties and a grandson, thirteen. Nice people. They all had variations of the same name. Edward, Ed and Eddie. A Sr., Jr. and III; a family of strong traditions. Katie could relate to that.

Edward, the senior had explained to Joe and Katie that their family had been coming to Garden City every summer since 1946, the year after the end of World War II. "While he was fighting in France my dad promised himself that if he ever got home again, he'd spend two weeks with his family in Florida every year," he'd said. "We've kept up the tradition. My wife keeps fussing about going back to Europe on vacation. We did that once. Do you know I didn't catch a fish that whole year?"

Ed, the junior, had smiled indulgently at his father's indignation. "We'll try to make sure that doesn't happen today, sir," Joe had told him.

Eddie had been swarming over the boat with the curiosity and energy of three kids. At a word from his father the youngster had apologized.

"Explore all you want to, son," Joe had said, remembering his own experience with the fishermen in Charleston harbor. He'd left Katie to get them into their life vests while he took care of the last-minute details and cast off.

A few minutes later she came back to the bridge with their coffee. The scent of the brew rose to woo him; he needed this. Although he knew it was too hot to drink, he put his lower lip to the rim and took a cautious sip, before setting the mug in a balanced holder next to the wheel. "How are the passengers?" he asked her.

"No sign of sickness. They're exchanging fish tales," she reported. "Father and grandfather exaggerating for young Eddie." She grinned. "He's a bit skeptical, like someone who's heard these stories before. Typical fishermen. You're all alike."

He smiled, too, but warily, and said the first thing that popped into his head. "What does the captain have to do to get a little respect around here?"

"Oh? It's respect you want, is it? Do I have to salute, too?"

There was that smile again. He wasn't accustomed to being the recipient of such open, affable attention from a woman. It was a personal smile, meant for him alone, one that addressed him as clearly as if she'd spoken aloud.

He admired that in her, too—in any woman—that rare talent for recognizing a mood and leaving a man to it. Another legacy from her brothers, he suspected. He knew women who would have been all over him this morning, trying to cajole him out of his testy frame of mind, and one in particular who would have pouted, demanding to know what was the matter.

The effect was predictable.

Hell, why fight it? The sun was shining; the scent of the sea was around them; he felt his mood lift and his manhood stir. "Never mind," he said, unable to resist her good humor any longer. He shook his head and chuckled under his breath.

Katie saw the change in him. Her heart took a leap.

His smile faded to a frown of concern. "You don't have much protective color. There's sunscreen in the head that's next to my cabin. You'd better use it."

"I brought some," she said.

He sat with his heel hooked on the footrest of the chair. The position elevated his knee, so he propped his elbow there and held his chin between his thumb and forefinger, watching in amusement as she dug around in the deep pocket of her windbreaker. She pulled out a lipstick, a wad of tissues, a silver-wrapped candy kiss, which she held out to him. "Want it?"

"No, thanks." He hid a smile behind his hand as she stuffed everything back and switched to the other pocket. From that one she came up with a Swiss Army knife and he gave a puzzled look at a size AA battery. Next she produced a five-dollar bill. She muttered something under her breath.

He couldn't hear her over the sound of the motor. "What?"

"Mad money," she repeated, then returned to her search, this time delving into the pocket of her shorts.

"Here?" he asked, keeping one eye on the empty sea beyond the bow and his free hand loosely on the wheel.

"It's ingrained. Inflation has set in, though. A dollar won't get you anywhere."

"Even a five won't get you far in the Gulf of Mexico," he said. "No cabs."

"I knew it was here somewhere," she said triumphantly, holding up the tube for him to see.

He nodded. "Use it."

"Yes, sir." She took off the windbreaker and tossed it in a corner of the bridge.

He watched out of the corner of his eye as she squeezed some white cream into the palm of her hand. She put a sneaker-clad foot on the back rail and bent over to apply the cream to her legs, giving him a heart-stopping view of her bottom. She worked the cream in thoroughly, with long strokes, over her calf, around the back of her knee, along the inside of her thigh, all the way to the hem of her shorts.

Exactly the trail he'd like to take with his own hands, and then his mouth. By the time she finished with that leg and started on the other one, Joe sincerely feared suffocation.

She was such a sensual creature, completely unaware of the effect her position and her action were having on him. He rolled his eyes heavenward and swallowed a strangled curse. But then he looked again.

Finally she finished. Joe began a sigh of reprieve. She replaced the top on the tube of cream, dropped it on the crumpled windbreaker and looked blankly at her sticky hands for a second.

She wouldn't. *Tissues! You've got tissues in your pocket!*

She shrugged and wiped her hands on the seat of her pants.

Joe laughed—without merriment—under his breath. The cream had left a smear that wasn't going to be easy to overlook all day.

"There," she said. "Do you need some?" she asked, returning to his side.

God, yes. Rub it all over me like that. "No, thanks. I've got a pretty good tan."

She had also found a rubber band in her pocket. She raised her arms—lifting her breasts to a seductive height at the same time—gathering her hair off the back of her neck. With a few twists of her wrist she had it confined in a ponytail.

He dragged his gaze away. "What do you plan to do with the knife?" Joe asked, trying to dredge up the image of her in a tailored suit. "Gut the captain if he makes a wrong move?"

Her lips pursed. "I thought the captain might make me clean fish. Isn't that the mate's job?"

It was a logical question and she frowned, puzzled, when he threw back his head and let his laughter ring out. The release of pressure was of tremendous benefit after what he'd just been through. He hadn't felt so good in years. Still grinning, he took her hand and turned it palm down to study it. Her skin was soft, nails bare of polish today but very well tended. "I've made other arrangements today. It would be a shame to ruin your manicure."

Joe's open, hearty laughter had transformed him. His blue eyes were clear, the disillusionment and distrust banished by his mirth. The sound, the sight, the entire experience, reached deep within Katie and warmed a spot that she hadn't realized was chilled. Suddenly she saw the man he must have been before something happened to change the light, happy things about him to dark, hungry things.

If she'd thought him good-looking before, his laughter improved her verdict to devastating. She dropped her eyes in an effort to shield them—and her—from its effect. "I'd better check on the passengers," she said hastily.

They both recognized her statement for the excuse it was. He didn't let go, instead his long fingers moved to her forearm just above the wrist. "Running?" he said softly, the smile lingering on his lips.

He was throwing back her challenge from last night when he'd decided to leave so abruptly. All at once she understood what he'd meant. "Probably," she answered with a wry smile.

He was thoughtful for a minute. "Not today," he said at last. "No running for either of us today. Okay?"

They were only a few inches apart. She could feel the heat from his body, could smell his male scent, feel the strength in the fingers on her arm. She looked at him, searched the sky blue of his eyes. A question lay there, implicit, between them.

"I still don't have any promises to give you, Katie. We're too different. But it's a beautiful day. Can't we enjoy it together?"

She touched his hand where it held her arm. "Yes, we can," she said, pleasure softening her voice.

"Then come here. I want to see you handle the wheel." He situated her between his thighs, not touching her but near enough to feel the warmth of her skin, near enough to smell her light perfume.

Neal had vouched for her expertise. He'd asked one or two of the older men whose boats were moored near his and had been assured that Katie Johns knew how to handle herself aboard, but he put her through exhaustive paces to assure himself of her competence.

The wheel felt good in Katie's hands. Her proficiency and ability came back to her quickly. The boat was wonderfully responsive. She studied the dials before her. Some of the electronic equipment was unfamiliar but she was able to identify the function of most of it. What she couldn't figure out on her own, she asked about.

When he was satisfied that she was capable of handling the large craft, he sat back in the tall swivel captain's chair. "Very good," he said.

"Thank you." She checked the compass. "How long before we reach the fishing grounds?" she asked.

He laughed under his breath. "Are you trying to discover my coordinates?"

She kept her eyes on the water but smiled ironically. "I wouldn't dare."

A professional charter fisherman's secret spots were sacrosanct. During the winter when business wasn't that brisk they loaded their boats with old furniture, junk cars and anything else that would build a haven for the fish they stalked in the summer. She'd seen the boats leave the harbor, so low in the water she'd wondered why they didn't sink. They motored slowly—out of necessity when carrying such bulky loads—to certain coordinates and dumped their cargo. The fish were quick to move in.

"How long have you been doing this?" she asked finally, halfway expecting him to cut her off with a noncommittal remark like he had done last night. To her surprise and pleasure he answered easily.

"Since I was a kid I've enjoyed deep-sea fishing. I grew up on the Atlantic coast, in Charleston, and haunted the docks." He hesitated as though he were about to elaborate. Instead he skipped over the history of the intervening years. "When I decided to change careers last year, I bought the boat and the business from Captain Mallard, who was ready to retire. He stayed on for three months. Sam, his son, crews for me in the summers. Now and then Mallard comes out with me, too."

It was the most information he had volunteered about himself in the short time she'd known him. As she listened, his deep, resonant voice sent vibrations along her nerve ends. "And did he throw in the location of his coordinates for nothing?"

Joe chuckled. "The old pirate added twenty thousand dollars to the price of the boat. Said if I didn't take it I could build my own and he'd sell the coordinates to someone else. He probably could have done it, too."

He shifted and his thigh brushed her forearm, raising goose bumps. "Do you like what you're doing now?" she asked hastily, trying seriously to keep the huskiness out of her voice.

Joe thought for just a minute about the question, one which he'd never asked himself. Did he like being a charter captain? He gave a mental shrug. It was a living.

When he'd begun a year ago, he'd looked to the sudden change in his life-style to heal some painful wounds. For the first time he realized that things *were* better than they'd been last year at this time. The wounds were still there but they seemed to be scabbing over. He didn't dare probe too hard for fear of reopening them but he could feel a definite improvement.

Diagnosis: fair. Perhaps the patient would live.

"Yes, I do like it," he answered.

Something in his voice, surprise or wonder, made her turn. With the movement her shoulder grazed his broad chest. Her face was only inches from his and she couldn't drag her gaze away. She desperately wanted him to kiss her, not the mild, colorless kiss of last night, but a mindless, numbing kiss like the one they'd shared in the middle of town on Tuesday.

He made an automatic check of the sea before them, then smiled down at her. "Hey, mate, don't take your eyes off the road," he chided, his voice a warm murmur that surrounded her as completely as the sunshine.

She turned back quickly, denouncing her own reaction. He made her forget everything except himself when he was so close.

He leaned across her and eased back on the throttle. The boat slowed, sank into a trough, rocking gently. "Time to put the passengers to work. I'll bait the hooks."

"I can bait hooks, too," she assured him, her body stiff, her gaze fixed on the bow.

Now that the boat was settled he touched her chin, turned her head, until he could look down into her eyes. "I'm sure you can but you'll handle the boat this time."

Her answer was too flippant, unlike her. She was lucky to get an answer out at all. "Aye, aye, sir. Anything the captain wants."

Without warning his blue eyes darkened, anchored on her mouth, stealing her breath, drying her throat. He touched her waist, slid his hand around until it rested flat on her midriff. He pulled her back against him, held her that way, attesting to his arousal. "I'll remember that," he growled deeply, softly.

When he was gone, Katie sagged over the wheel. He had been as sensually affected as she. He just controlled his responses better.

According to Edward, Ed and Eddie, the trip had been a roaring success. The ice chest was filled with the legal allotment of King mackerel, bedded side by side with grouper, snapper and amberjack.

Joe maneuvered the *Mary Ann* alongside a slip where for a fee today's catch would be cleaned, frozen and packed for travel back to Ohio. The Edwards left them there with promises to charter the boat again next year.

They motored slowly through the harbor traffic to Joe's slip and tied up. A lot of work remained to be done in preparation for the next day's fishing. Katie hosed off the decks and emptied the ice chest, while Joe cleaned, checked and stored the tackle. By the time they finished it was nearly seven.

Joe wiped the sweat off his brow and looked around at the sparkling deck. "Want a beer?" he asked.

"Yes," answered Katie as she collapsed in the remaining chair. She was aching in muscles she didn't even know she had. She pulled her legs up to sit cross-legged, Indian style and let her head fall back, rolling it from side to side.

Joe came out of the salon and saw her sitting like that. He felt a moment's compassion, remembering the aches and pains that accompanied his first few times out. He put the two frosty bottles down on the transom and came up behind her.

He worked the muscles at the back of her neck, across her shoulders. Her head fell forward and she moaned slightly. The sound was soft and sexy, the same kind of sound she'd make when he was inside her.

He dropped his hands. Where the hell had that thought come from? Reaching down he snared the necks of the bottles between three fingers of his right hand and held them out to her.

Katie freed one bottle and raised it to her lips. She took a long, thirsty swallow. The cold and bitter bite of the beer was just what she needed. When he'd started massaging her shoulders she'd been struck with an almost uncontrollable need to turn to him.

"Ahh. That's good," she said with a sigh. She ran the cool bottle over her heated forehead and cheeks.

Joe sat down on the deck with his back to the bulkhead, just as she'd first seen him. Sweat had plastered his shirt to his torso. She smiled as she watched him drink deeply. The brown bottle was a third empty before he took a breath.

"You did a good job today. Where did you learn?"

"My brother Dallas taught me to crew. He won the cobia tournament one year."

"I'm impressed," said Joe, meaning it. The fishing tournament for cobia, an elusive game fish, drew fishermen from all over the country. It was only one of many tournaments and rodeos held annually along this coast of Florida but it was the most prestigious.

"I knew you would be," she said, grinning.

They sat like that, not speaking, for a few more minutes. Finally Katie stirred herself. "I'd better be going."

"Are you hungry?" he asked. "Would you like to get something to eat?"

She was hungry, starving in fact, but she looked down at herself and wrinkled her nose at the smell of fish and bait and sweat. She had washed her face and hands but she needed a bath. Once she got under a hot shower she knew she would be in danger of falling asleep on her feet.

"It's been a wonderful day," she said instead of responding to his question. Working with him, laughing with him, she felt she knew him better than many men she'd known for far longer.

Joe followed her thoughts. "How does a drive-in hamburger sound?"

She brightened. "It sounds wonderful. I couldn't look at a fish tonight."

He rose with a grace she couldn't hope to match and held out his hand. She uncurled her legs, stifling another moan, and got to her feet.

As their footsteps echoed hollowly along the docks, she couldn't help remembering the stranger. It wasn't as dark as it had been Monday night and there were people around. She'd kept the blond man from intruding on her thoughts for a whole day, but now the dread was back.

Again Joe seemed to read her thoughts. He reached for her hand. "Hey," he said softly. "Neal sent the tape to Tallahassee. He'll get an answer soon."

She nodded. "I know."

"I'll follow you in the truck," he said when they got to the parking lot.

When they reached the drive-in he signaled her to stay put while he went inside. She sat in the busy lot of the Toot and Scoot, watching the crowd, teenagers mostly, move from car to car, pose and chatter and giggle, under the neon rainbows.

The drive-in had also been the hangout when she was young, a place to meet your friends after the Friday night football game, to come after school hours in hopes of stirring the interest of an older boy who wouldn't pay a gnat's attention to you in the halls of Garden City High.

Katie felt detached from the crowd, and not just because of her age—she saw a few people she recognized—but because she'd never taken the ritual here seriously enough. In those days, her primary ambition had been to escape from the small town, to do something important with her life.

Well, she'd done it. She'd escaped. And only after she'd been away for ten years was she able to face and appreciate what she'd been running from.

Joe returned minutes later with two white bags and joined her in her car. "Hamburgers, all the way, French fries and chocolate milk shakes," he announced.

"You really know how to treat a girl," said Katie, digging into one of the bags for a delicious-smelling, greasy burger. After she'd had a couple of bites, she turned her attention to the fries. She tore open a tiny envelope of catsup and squirted. "Next to a shower this is what I wanted most in the world."

Joe watched with an amused expression. "You're easy to please," he said casually. But he wasn't feeling casual at all. Her trivial reference to bathing conjured up a picture of her standing naked under a spray of water. With him. He would run his soapy hands up her beautiful legs, across her breasts and . . . ah, hell.

"I suppose I should feel guilty but I love junk food. Don't you?" she went on as she licked a drop of catsup from the corner of her mouth.

Last night . . . she'd been eating a brownie. Joe's simmering desire sparked to a full-fledged, red-hot conflagration. He wanted a thorough taste of her. Now.

He shifted in his seat, giving an offhand answer that came out as a sour grumble. She threw him a puzzled look. He took a vicious bite into the burger and chewed.

Finally replete, Katie sighed and gathered up the trash, stuffing it back into the bags.

Joe got out and disposed of them in the big plastic bin next to the driveway. He came back to her window, deciding that it wouldn't be judicious to get back in the car with her. He might teach the kids who hung out here more than they needed to know.

"Thanks again for today," she said. "I enjoyed it." She hesitated. "Can—would you like to have dinner with me tomorrow night?"

He rested one forearm on the window frame and leaned down to look at her. "I'd like that." He touched her sun-blushed cheek with a fingertip. Things were building inside him. He tightened his lips, raised his head and looked around in frustration at the busy drive-in. His gaze returned to her. "I'm following you home," he muttered.

"Oh, there's no need—"

"That's what you think. I've got a very pressing need," he grated.

Katie could not have possibly misunderstood his meaning. "All right."

He spun away and climbed into the truck. The interior light came on for a second, revealing his determined expression in more detail than the neon had done, and then it flicked off again.

But she didn't need the extra illumination. She stared at him across a space of maybe ten feet. He sat, returning the stare with an unblinking gaze, until she recovered and reached for the ignition.

Katie plunged her fingers into his thick, dark hair. He had her back against the wall and his mouth was hard and hungry and stole her breath. Neither of them held anything back. For once, at the end of a totally satisfying day, they gave the kiss everything they had. She opened her lips to his exploring tongue. The scent of his skin was a mingling of soap, sweat, sunshine and sea, and she was drenched in the blend.

Suddenly his hand cupped her breast. There was no tentative, childish groping, no sneaky maneuvering, not from this man. Just a sudden and completely effective gesture of possession. It was very flattering and she smiled against his lips.

He felt her smile, drew back to look down at her. But he didn't remove his hand. "What?" he whispered huskily as his fingers brushed over her nipple.

She tightened her fingers in his hair, noticing that his eyes looked like she felt, slightly unfocused. "I like that."

He did release her then but only to wrap his arms tightly around her. Thigh to thigh, belly to belly, there was no mistaking the urgency of his arousal as he buried his face in her neck. His breath was warm as he spoke against her skin. "You're too honest." He paused. "But I like it, too. As much of a risk as it is."

She closed her eyes; her brows knit. What was he afraid of? "I'm not a risk to you, Joe."

"The hell you're not," he said. He dropped his arms.

She came back down to earth with a little jolt.

He tweaked her nose and took a step back. "Good night, Katie."

"Good night, Joe."

Chapter 6

Life in Garden City was generally casual. Few of the habitués ever wore a jacket and tie in the evening and especially not in the summer when the temperature hovered around ninety. Only two or three resorts nearby still required a jacket for dinner. They catered to the upscale tourist trade and kept the air-conditioning thermostat set at sixty.

A tux could sit molding in a closet for years, Joe supposed, unless the Rotary Club's annual Christmas party was formal. He didn't know; he didn't belong to the Rotary Club.

He had to dig into the back of the small closet in his cabin to find a jacket. He had pulled out a dark blazer, a relic from his Washington days and an example of the work of D.C.'s finest tailor. It was a conservative navy blue and with it he wore light gray trousers and a blue pinpoint oxford shirt. His burgundy tie was subtly striped in navy and gold. His black shoes hadn't seen a coat of polish in months but when he was through with them he thought they looked pretty good.

He'd analyzed his reasons for dressing differently tonight but none of the explanations he'd come up with satisfied him. He'd completely avoided a theory suggesting this was a vintage-style, traditional, old-fashioned date.

Now, standing at Katie's door, he shifted his shoulders against the unaccustomed restriction of the jacket and checked the knot of his tie.

Maybe he wanted to show her that he could look like a civilized human being and owned more than jeans and khakis. As he approached her door, he suddenly regretted the deviation, asking himself why, in the name of God, he should care. There were more important things to worry about tonight than what he had on his body.

When he raised his hand to knock, his expression was grim.

And when Katie opened the door, hers was anxious. "Hi, Joe. Come in."

His eyes followed her bare shoulders as she turned away too quickly. He was amused to think that this dinner was as unsettling for her as it was for him. Until he saw that she had additional reason for her nervousness. A man stood behind her.

"Daddy, this is Joe Ryder. Joe, my father, Bruce Johns."

Ten to one, he belongs to the Rotary Club. Katie's father was much more of a presence than the picture on her coffee table had revealed. He was a big man with a full head of steel-gray hair, wearing a conservative suit and an ominous expression. She hadn't inherited her size from him but the color of their eyes was the same—

although his lacked the warmth and sparkle of Katie's and were a shade darker.

Bruce Johns examined him as though he were an overage deviate picking up an underage date; and, as though during the course of the evening he was going to try his best to put the make on her.

All at once the humor in the situation hit Joe and he relaxed. He was grateful, however, for the buffer of fine tailoring. He extended his hand first. "I'm happy to meet you, Dr. Johns."

"How do you do, Joe," said Bruce, unbending slightly. "So Katie's cooking dinner for you?"

"Something smells delicious, Katie. Tell me, Dr. Johns, is she a good cook?" Joe asked, man-to-man.

Bruce raised his brows, his expression relenting another notch. "Her mother's lasagna is better but she makes good key-lime pie," he answered. "I understand you're related to our sheriff, Neal Patterson. Fine man."

Joe's mind supplied the following sentence, "I'm not so sure about you." Then he cursed himself silently for being so quick on the defensive. "Neal is my half brother. We had the same mother." His voice was even with no inflection whatsoever.

"I knew her." A muscle in Bruce's jaw clenched. He didn't say anything more; he didn't have to.

Joe's mother had walked out on her first husband when Neal was just a kid. Joe knew exactly how everyone in Garden City felt about her. Hell, he'd run away from home himself. But she *was* his mother. "Did you?" he asked mildly.

"Patterson, Neal's dad, was one of my closest friends; we grew up together," said Bruce. "I wasn't particularly attached to your mother. I understand she's dead," he added. The statement was honest and probably inoffensive taken at face value but again Joe read the tone clearly: "Good riddance."

"Daddy!" Katie's protest was soft but her eyes were horrified.

"I apologize, Joe. I didn't mean to be so blunt."

Joe was surprised by the apology. Bruce Johns didn't seem like a man who would admit fault easily. "I understand, Dr. Johns. You're loyal to Neal's father." He turned to Katie who, after all, was a grown woman and could choose her own loyalties. "So you make a good key-lime pie?"

"Speaking of key-lime pie." Katie picked up a foil-wrapped plate from the small table by the door—they had gotten no farther than the entry hall—and held it out to her father. "This needs to be refrigerated for another hour or so. Goodbye, Daddy," she said firmly.

Bruce looked none too pleased at her abrupt dismissal but he took the pie.

"Tell Mother I'll call her tomorrow," added Katie.

"Nice to have met you, Doctor."

"You, too, young man," answered Bruce Johns.

Joe tried not to laugh at the appellation. He hadn't been a young man in years—if ever. They shook hands. Bruce hesitated. "I understand you bought Mallard's business. Did you get his fishing coordinates as well?"

"Yes, sir."

"I may get you to take me out one day. Mallard used to bring home some big ones."

"Anytime, sir."

He left and Katie closed the door behind him. She stood for a moment with her head bowed. Then she turned. With her back to the door, she looked at him. "I apologize. It isn't like Daddy to be so abrupt."

"He's protective. Did you tell him about the man on the docks?"

"No, of course not. You're right, he's protective. Too damned much so."

"There's nothing wrong with that," Joe said gruffly. "He didn't know me. You're a woman living alone and, these days, that can be dangerous if you're not careful."

"I am careful," she protested. "But I refuse to be paranoid." She pushed herself away from the door and brushed by him to enter the living room.

She looked different tonight. Her sundress was white, nipped at the waist, an easy span for his hands. The top was embroidered with tiny green leaves. It stopped at her knees in a swirl of skirt and more leaves. White sandals with high, delicate heels further emphasized her beautiful legs.

Her hairstyle was loose and seductive, ready for a man's hands to comb through it. She wore little jade medallions at her ears. Her whole manner was sexy as hell and . . . inviting. Maybe that was the explanation for her father's reserve.

But he wasn't going to answer the invitation. "Can I help?" he asked politely.

"Will you fix yourself a drink? I have to check on dinner." She indicated a wheeled serving cart, which held glasses, bottles and a crystal ice bucket.

"May I fix something for you?"

"Mine's in the kitchen."

He heard the oven door open, got an extra strong whiff of Italian spices. Saliva moistened his mouth in a surge of anticipation, reminding him that he hadn't eaten since wolfing down a stale doughnut early this morning. While he waited he mixed himself a Scotch and water—heavy on the Scotch. *What the hell did you expect? The man's*

*a doctor, he's a pillar of the community, rich, respected.
You're a fisherman.*

Joe had never had a problem recognizing trouble. Katie was trouble. After yesterday, his involvement had become much more than a casual one. She was becoming an obsession. And he didn't like it worth a damn.

Fuming, Katie shoved a foil-wrapped packet of bread into the oven, closed the door and checked the temperature gauge. How *could* her father have behaved like that?

She usually had Sunday night supper with her parents. When she'd called this afternoon to tell her mother she wouldn't be there, it had set off a signal as blaring as the raucous bells and flashing lights at a railroad crossing. Her mother had been pleased until Katie had mentioned Joe's brother. And her father happened to drop in minutes before Joe arrived, ostensibly for the pie she'd promised to send him.

She breathed deeply. He was *not* going to ruin this evening. Calmer now, she picked up her glass of wine and returned to the living room.

Joe stood by the bookshelves, sipping his drink, studying the titles. He moved on to her tape collection of old radio shows. "Groucho Marx, Jack Benny, Baby Snooks? You've got some collection here," he said when he saw her.

She crossed to stand beside him and slid a tape from another section of the shelf. "I've been collecting them for years; some are so old the scratches have scratches. But I love them. Do you like sixties music?"

"Sure."

She slipped the tape in the slot, turned the volume to low. Mellow music floated out.

They took their drinks to the sofa. Katie sat in her customary posture: sideways on the cushion, knees bent, feet tucked under her.

Joe's very polite, taciturn withdrawal, as well as his defense of her father, disconcerted Katie. Yesterday and last night she thought they had reached a breakthrough with each other. Dear God, that last kiss had to mean something! But when he and her father squared off, his detached look had reappeared.

Now he seemed to be making an effort to be as amiable as any casual dinner guest.

She had to do something to jar him out of this mood or the evening would end up as two overly polite people being too stiff and too formal with each other. She knew if that happened she'd never see him again. The idea was unbearable. "Why don't you take off your jacket?" she suggested. She stared at him over the rim of her wineglass.

"I'm fine." He caught the scent of spring blossoms, reminding him that he'd planned to bring her flowers. He'd forgotten that most of the businesses unrelated to tourism closed on Sundays in Garden City. He wouldn't tell her; such an admission would only be an encouragement.

She went on as though he hadn't spoken. "I've set the table on the balcony so you might as well get rid of the tie, too. It isn't uncomfortably hot but it will be warm out there."

"Later." He paused. He had some unpleasant news to deliver.

She saved him the trouble of having to introduce the subject. "Has anyone heard from Louise?"

"Yes. Neal had no answer to his state patrol inquiries about her car so he went over to see Dan Austen again."

She leaned forward, cradling the wineglass between her hands. Her eyes stirred with interest. "Tell me."

"Her first appointment in California was a dinner engagement with one of the designers on Saturday. She didn't show up; didn't check into her hotel. Austen has filed a missing person's report."

Her eyes grew wide and took on a haunted look. "So that makes it official?" she said, her words coming out on a sigh.

"It seems that things haven't been as rosy around their household as he suggested to us on Tuesday," he went on. "Now he admits he suspected his wife was seeing someone else. When he confronted her, she didn't deny it, but he says she was greatly troubled. She wanted time alone to think. That's why she decided to drive to California instead of flying. Their marriage was in a sort of limbo when she left, he said. But he also insists that he thought they would work things out. He swears he really loves her."

"Did he try to find out who she was seeing?"

"He says not. Actually if the police discover something has happened to her, and they now have reasonable cause to suspect it, Dan has you to thank for not being the prime suspect."

Katie dropped her troubled gaze, looking down into her wineglass. Light rays came in through the open drapes to simmer in the ruby-red liquid. Somehow the feeling of justification didn't sit well with her. "At least that makes up a little bit for being the one to cause the stink in the first place."

Joe tried to think of a way to make this easier for her. Nothing came to him. Finally his silence prompted Katie to raise her gaze to his face.

"Katie, the Austens' problems aren't yours. There are other possibilities. Maybe she had a wreck. Maybe she just decided to drop out but, whether Louise Austen left while you were inside the restaurant or not, she's disappeared. Something happened to keep her from her appointment. You may be the one in danger now. The man who was with her knows who you are and where you work."

"He's not going to come after me. I don't know him."

"You know what he looks like. You and O'Donnell seem to be the only ones who do. But for some reason he's focused on you. He's chased you once and you've had a threatening phone call telling you to get out of town. He's kidding himself if he thinks you're going to leave, but he was scared enough to try."

She was surprised. She wasn't sure what she'd heard was fear but if Joe... "You heard the fear in his voice, too?"

He nodded. "Yeah, I heard it. The more frustrated he gets the more unpredictable his behavior will be. Now that Austen has officially reported her missing, I want you to keep your eyes open."

She mused for a second, then asked, "What about Louise's car? It has to be around here somewhere."

"If she didn't drive it away," he persisted. Then he shrugged and grew thoughtful again. "The car puzzles me. A red sports job would be easy to spot. I don't think she would drive it to an assignation with another man; but then they were eating in a public restaurant. So what would be the point in hiding her car?"

"Because her husband thought she was out of town. During the summer not many natives eat in the tourist places, so she could probably get away with meeting him there. I remember thinking when I saw them that they must be discussing business. They weren't acting like two people in love. Driving there on the other hand would be taking a big chance. All it would take is one friend who saw the car on the street and knew she was supposed to be on her way to California...."

Joe laughed and shook his head. Once again he was struck by her intelligence and insight. "You would have made a hell of an investigator. I hadn't gotten that far. Of course all this is speculation."

"There's also Annette," she said. "Annette spent every day with Louise. You can't tell me she doesn't know about the man Louise was seeing."

"Neal had another go at Annette this afternoon. She still insists her employer has gone to California. He's inclined to agree with you that she's lying but he hasn't been able to shake her story. He's also initiated a local search for the car." He had decided to drag the harbor, too, but there wasn't any reason to tell Katie that yet.

They sat silently for a few minutes, each lost in their own conjecture, listening to the music that played softly. Finally Joe stirred, and took a sip of his drink.

Katie watched the strong muscles work in his throat. "Would you like another drink?"

He stopped her with a hand on her thigh. "No, thanks," he said, withdrawing his hand. He quickly searched for another topic. Funny, seconds ago the silence between them had been genial, musical harmony, a pleasant background for their thoughts. Suddenly he needed to fill the atmosphere with conversation. "Nice flowers," he said, wondering at his own inanity.

She smiled, dismissing the flowers in favor of looking at him. She rested her elbow on the back of the sofa and supported her head against a loose fist. "They're from my mother's garden." She sipped from the wineglass.

"I was planning—" He stopped, took a swallow of his drink.

Her brows rose toward her hairline. "To bring me flowers?"

He didn't answer.

"Thank you," she said. She leaned forward, kissing him lightly, fondly, on the cheek.

Her lips were cool, sweet. He was startled by the affectionate salute. "What for? I didn't bring them."

"For the thought," she said.

He turned his head and caught her beautiful gaze. He held his breath.... "You are something, you know that?" he murmured, letting it out on a sigh. Without releasing his hold on her eyes, he angled the upper half of his body toward her and laid his head against the cushion, smiling, openly inviting another kiss.

She smiled, too, as she answered the invitation, leaning forward to brush her mouth over his lips. The clean, minty taste of toothpaste mingled exotically with fine wine. Joe sighed again.

"Take off your tie," she repeated as she withdrew. She took another sip of wine.

Obediently Joe tugged at the knot of his tie, wondering if he were making a mistake by removing the symbols of convention between them. Ah, hell. He might as well be comfortable. He discarded the jacket, unbuttoned his cuffs and rolled back the sleeves of his dress shirt. The knot of his tie dangled loosely. He didn't remove it but he did release his collar button.

Katie thought he looked very sexy like that, with just a small triangle of his tanned throat showing.

A timer bell went off in the kitchen. "Dinner's ready." She took her wineglass with her.

Joe followed and watched from the doorway. Her movements were efficient, automatic, as she arranged the food on a tray.

"Here, let me take that for you," he said.

"Thanks." She gave him the tray and went before him to open the sliding door to the balcony.

When they were seated she shook out her white linen napkin. "Joe, I think Louise—"

"Katie," he interrupted, leaning forward to inhale the delicious aroma coming from the food. "I'm starving and this smells terrific. Can we leave Louise Austen alone while we eat?"

She was immediately contrite. "I'm sorry. Of course, we can."

Later, after the meal, they lingered over fragrant coffee and watched the sunset off to their right. Spectacular colors—from palest pinks to salmon, to vermilion, scarlet and ruby—accompanied the sinking sun and reflected on the water, painting it a corresponding shade of crimson.

The waves brushed the shore quietly, unobtrusively, as though reluctant to mark the sand. A few people were on the beach below the balcony, some sitting at the water's edge, watching the colorful display of the sunset, others walking slowly; some hand in hand, others alone. One or two joggers upset the languid rhythm but not for long.

Joe felt peace descend upon him like summer heat, a hesitant peace, but the sort he hadn't experienced in a long time, if ever. His tranquillity wasn't owed entirely to the beauty of the scene before him, or the delicious food. The woman beside him deserved most of the credit. She was easy to be with.

He glanced sideways and caught a flash of gold as she looked at him. "More coffee?" He nodded and she refilled both cups.

"I think I'm accustomed to such beauty and then along comes an evening like this," she said, her voice subdued.

He smiled and looked back to the sky. Already the colors were beginning to fade. Darkness, which settled quickly in this part of the country, would soon blot out the scene completely.

He wished it were as easy to obliterate trouble but, unfortunately, it usually hung around until you did something about it. He sighed in resignation and dragged his attention away from the sunset. "What were you going to say about Louise Austen...and her friend?" he prompted.

"Like O'Donnell, I don't think he's from around here."

Joe wasn't sure he agreed with the conclusion but was curious as to how she'd arrived there. "Why not?"

"Well..." Katie gathered her thoughts. She crossed her legs and straightened in her chair. One side of his mouth tilted in that half smile she was learning to recognize. "First of all, I don't know him. If you take the tourists away—and Mr. O'Donnell could fill in a number of those who come back every year—I know or can identify almost everyone in town."

"You were gone for years. You didn't know me."

"Yet," she responded. "Aside from the fact that I grew up here, I peddle advertising to everyone from merchants to real-estate companies to charter boat captains. I get around this town." A brief smile drifted across her lips. "Eventually I would have gotten around to you."

Amused, Joe let that one ride and joined in with her speculation. "Maybe he *was* a tourist."

"A tourist wouldn't have had enough time to develop a relationship with a woman like Louise Austen. We weren't friends but I knew her reputation well enough to know she wasn't the type to fool around on her husband. Not unless she was really emotionally involved and that wouldn't happen overnight."

Joe was struck anew by her reasoning and insight. He leaned forward, bracing his elbows on the table, ready now to play devil's advocate. "It does happen occasionally."

"Not with a woman like her. I can believe Dan if he says she was deeply troubled by the situation."

"It's a possibility," he acknowledged. "But what if your stranger owned a condo? He might have been coming here for years without becoming a regular at Harbor Grill."

She thought about that. "True," she said slowly. "But there are a lot of things that just don't *feel* right. My instincts say he's an outsider."

"On the other hand, Dan Austen could have hired the man."

She frowned at that but she couldn't resist chiding him a bit. "At one time you wouldn't even admit there was a man."

"Come on, Katie," he admonished. "I've admitted that. The first night I just wasn't certain that you hadn't misread the signals. Very intelligent, perceptive people can make mistakes like that. Believe me, I've seen it happen many times."

The statement was one guaranteed to distract her from Louise Austen for a moment. This seemed a likely time to ask some of the questions that burned on the tip of her tongue. There had been other opportunities to question him but she'd held off because she hated that withdrawn look he got sometimes.

Now he was relaxed, his long legs stretched out in front of him and crossed at the ankles. The lines around his eyes and the ones that bracketed his mouth had smoothed out until they were barely perceptible. She was reluctant to disturb his peace.

On the other hand, Joe Ryder wasn't going to volunteer any facts about himself unless she pressed. If she asked and he didn't answer, she would drop the subject. She cocked her head and tossed the question at him. "Really? What kind of work did you do before you came to Garden City?"

Joe hadn't seen it coming. Knowing her powers of observation, he should have been prepared. She'd had any number of opportunities. He'd expected the question when he was quizzing her about her career in the café the morning after the incident on the pier; he'd breathed a sigh of relief on the boat yesterday when she'd dropped the subject of his past. But he should have known it would come up again. He put down his coffee cup.

"Before I came here I was an investigator for the Department of Justice. I lived in D.C."

The words came out sluggishly as though each one had to be pushed from behind. She absorbed the information for a minute. "What kinds of things did you investigate?"

"I'm not going to tell you," he said.

"I'm not being nosy, Joe—" She stopped. "Well, maybe I am."

He laughed then and shook his head. "Yes, you are."

The laughter quickly faded, leaving his expression unreadable, but not forbidding, she noted with some surprise and much relief. He reached out and covered her hand with his. "I don't want to talk about the past, Katie. It wasn't a pretty life. Okay?" he said with an offhand shrug.

The negligible pose was an effort. She felt her heart contract. Something had hurt him badly. Tenderness washed through her and left a feeling of protectiveness that amazed her. She'd never felt protective of a man before. "Okay," she agreed softly, turning her hand over to link their fingers.

"Thanks." He brought their clasped hands to his lips. "Someday—maybe—I'll tell you about it."

"You don't have to, Joe," she assured him.

His breath was warm on her skin. She felt him smile, felt a bridge of harmony between them that hadn't been there before.

Then he touched his tongue to the back of her hand.

Unexpectedly all of her senses came stingingly alive at once; electric pixies danced along her nerve ends, their steps leaving hot sharp imprints. She tried to deny their mocking laughter.

Self-deception had never been a problem for her and now she faced the truth head-on. It was as though every other man she'd ever known before had been a training session for this one. Each relationship she'd had, a rehearsal for a relationship with Joe Ryder.

She had been firmly and positively warned off. If she got hurt she'd have no one to blame but herself. Yet even if her next breath had depended on it, she couldn't have drawn away from him.

He must have understood her vulnerable feelings; perhaps he shared some of them. Suddenly he dropped her hand. As though he couldn't help himself, he snaked his hand around the back of her neck, tugging slightly, drawing her toward his descending mouth. He stopped, his lips millimeters from hers.

Her eyes, which had begun to close, opened wide, meeting his hungry gaze. She made a small sound of protest, yearning toward him. "Joe," she whispered.

He gave her a taste of his lips, just a taste. Not nearly enough. "I want more than kisses from you, Katie," he murmured, his voice husky, his long fingers moving up through her hair to cradle the back of her head. "I want to make long, slow love with you, explore every inch of your beautiful body, feel your hands on me. I want to bury myself deep inside you until neither of us knows where we end and the other begins. If you don't want that, too, stop me right now."

She covered the infinitesimal distance herself, meeting his lips willingly, with no hesitation. He scraped back his chair and lifted her onto his lap.

The sound of the telephone from inside cut into her like a knife.

Joe voiced her feelings exactly with a string of expletives.

She leaned her forehead against his. "Hold that thought," she said with a shaky laugh. She slid off his lap and walked on weak legs to the telephone, leaving the sliding door open behind her.

"Hello."

"Katie, is Joe there?" It was Neal.

"Yes, Neal." She saw through the door that Joe was on his feet as soon as he heard his brother's name. When he joined her she held out the receiver. Instead of taking it from her, he drew her under his arm and put his hand over hers so they could listen together.

"Neal? It's Joe."

"Breakaway, Austen's boutique, has been torched. I'll have to get the fire investigators in here to be sure but I'd swear it's arson. Do you want to take a look?"

Hell, no. I want to stay right here and finish what's begun between us. Joe looked down at Katie. The moment on the balcony might have been a dream. Her face was drained of color and he felt a responsive chill. "I'll be right there," he said and replaced the receiver. "Katie . . ."

She silenced him with her hand at his lips and a small smile of regret that warmed him again. "We have plenty of time, Joe," she said. "I won't change my mind." Before he realized what was happening she was reaching for her keys and purse.

"Where do you think you're going?"

"With you." She grinned. "Just give me a minute to call my newsman."

"Hold on—"

"I'll follow in my car," she threatened.

She would do it, too. Joe muttered another expletive and said, "Hurry up."

The fire department had responded quickly and by the time Katie and Joe arrived the fire was under control, almost extinguished. But they could see the boutique was a complete loss. Plumes of water fought and subdued the last of the flames.

Just beyond the yellow tape, which marked off the scene from the public, Raymond Timms was speaking into a microphone hooked up to the cassette recorder that hung on his shoulder. Katie stood beside him, and her father stood beside both of them.

She was probably safe enough but Joe kept a sharp watch on her from inside the area that was cordoned off while he talked to Neal. A scene like this, with people milling around, he didn't know who the hell might be in the crowd. "Did you talk to Annette?" he asked his brother.

Neal looked tired, and old. He took off his uniform hat and wiped the sweat from his brow with a forearm. "Yes. We called her down here as soon as the fire was reported. Her boyfriend vouches for her. They were having dinner at the Lazy Gull when the fire started. Plenty of witnesses. She has no explanation to offer for the cause, still insists that she knew nothing about Louise's plans except that she was on her way to California. She's lying, Joe."

"Probably," Joe concurred. "Not much you can do about it."

Neal shrugged. "I hope she doesn't try something stupid, like blackmail."

So Annette was out of it for now. That left Katie. He knew better than to suggest she leave town for a while. She wouldn't hear of it. And he was the only person between her and the stranger. It wasn't enough; he wasn't good enough. "Neal, someone needs to guard Katie."

"You're—"

Joe interrupted impatiently. "Not me," he declared, waving the suggestion away. "Someone who can use a gun. I said I would watch her but this thing is heating up." He scanned the ravaged area where the fashionable shop had once stood and smiled wryly. "No pun intended, but it's certainly too hot for me."

"Nothing's too hot for you. I know your reputation, how good you are, Joe. I know—"

"Was," Joe interrupted harshly. "I *was* good. Not anymore." He looked at his brother, his expression reflecting his pain. "I can't take the responsibility, Neal. You have to free one of your deputies to take over."

"Okay," said Neal, heavily. "As soon as I can." He put his hand on Joe's shoulder. "But the equipment to drag the harbor will be here tomorrow. I need all my men. In the meantime why don't you let me issue you a gun? You may not have to use it."

Joe wavered but finally shook his head. "A gun in my hand would be useless."

"You don't know that," Neal said almost angrily. "You froze one time. One time, Joe."

Joe was angry, too, angry at his brother for his dogged persistence, angry with fate. "And it almost cost my partner's life."

"Think about it."

"All right. I'll think about it. In the meantime I want you to order her not to leave the apartment alone."

"Order her?" Neal chuckled and the anger in both of them drained away. He shook his head. "I thought you were beginning to know this woman."

"Request, then."

"You make the request. I have a feeling your appeal will carry more weight than mine."

Joe had been thoughtful on the ride back to Katie's place. He continued his silence as he walked with her to the door and followed her inside. "Fix yourself a drink if you like," she said, heading for the balcony. "I'll clear the table."

He'd forgotten that she'd left the dishes since they'd had to rush out in such a hurry.

Joe reached the door before she did. "I'll bring the dishes. You go on into the kitchen," he said.

Katie stopped in her tracks, staring up at him.

"Hey," he joked, spreading his hands. "I'm a liberated man." He tried for a smile but it didn't come off. She wasn't fooled for a minute.

"My hind leg," she scoffed. "The truth, Ryder."

He sighed and ran a hand down his face. "Okay. I don't want you standing backlit on that balcony. In fact, you should keep away from all the windows at night."

Katie's apartment faced the sea. From the balcony she could see the beach and someone on the beach could see her, but when she stepped back into the living room there was no view except of the water, the sky, the gulls and an occasional porpoise.

"I don't want you to leave this apartment, either, unless someone is with you."

Katie's jaw sagged.

"Just for a while, Katie," he urged, cajoling rather than commanding. "Neal is going to start dragging the harbor tomorrow. If the state fire investigators find what he suspects they will at the boutique, it will confirm that the situation is getting very serious, very fast."

"Oh." She turned away from the glass door. "Then you do think Louise is dead," she added quietly.

Joe didn't reply. It wasn't a question anyway. "You'll be safe inside. I'll drive you to work and wherever else you want to go until one of the deputies can take over. It won't be for long, Katie. Neal will find out who the man is. As you said, this is a small town."

"How do you know? What if they never catch him? Are you going to move in with me?" she demanded irritably, missing the sudden flash in his eyes. "I don't like to be restricted, Joe."

He took her shoulders and turned her toward him. His smile was gentle; his hands remained on her bare arms, chafing lightly. "I know. But you will be sensible, won't you?"

"Oh, sure," she replied, unable to subdue all the mockery. "I'm a very sensible woman."

They didn't speak much while they worked. When the dishes were loaded into the dishwasher and the counters had been wiped, he folded the towel he held.

His voice dropped an octave when he said finally, "I'm going back to the boat tonight, Katie. I don't think either of us is in the mood to finish what we started earlier, do you?"

A smile played at the corners of her lips. "Running?"

"God, yes." His joking reply was more than half serious. He turned her around until her back was to him with the intention of giving her a small push toward the living room. His hands slid from her arms to her shoulders. Before he released her he bent his head and put his lips to the side of her neck. "We are just postponing this, aren't we?" he asked, glad she couldn't see his expression.

She tilted her head until her cheek rested on his hand. "Yes."

"Will you wait here for me in the morning?"

"Yes, Joe." She wondered why she didn't continue her protest. What could happen to her driving to work?

"What about getting together tomorrow night? Do you like to dance?"

"I love to dance. Do you?" In Katie's experience she'd found that most men considered dancing a duty rather than a pleasure.

Joe loved to dance. It was the one positive characteristic he'd inherited from his mother. "I know a place that has a great jukebox and fresh oysters on the half shell. I'll take you there tomorrow night."

She smiled. "I'd like that." Then she remembered. "I won't be finished until nine or so. I have some book work to do. The owners of the station are coming for an inspection."

"Fine. Tim's Oyster Bar doesn't start swinging until after nine. Wear something very casual."

Chapter 7

The next morning Katie had to field calls from her mother and from her brother Dallas in Clearwater. The early-morning news report of the fire, as well as the missing person's report and her description of a stranger—*wanted for questioning in connection with the disappearance of Louise Austen*—had been picked up by other media across the state. No mention had been made of the threatening call but her mother had heard.

Katie wasn't surprised. She supposed she should be glad the story wouldn't reach as far as Alaska.

"What the hell's going on up there, Katie?" Dallas's voice sounded so good she forgave him for coming on like a big brother.

She soothed him, as she had her mother, with an explanation—not a full one, but enough to satisfy. At last, after she'd worked for a while, the shock settled in the back of her mind.

There was no shortage of casual restaurants, drive-ins, oyster bars or cafés in Garden City, but she hadn't been to Tim's in years, not since it was Pete's. She had brought her clothes to work, a pair of white cotton pants and a pale blue, scooped-neck overshirt. She decided to change before she tackled the books.

Joe found her in her office. He stood there watching her. Unaware of his presence, she worked diligently, the fingers of one hand flying over the keys of an adding machine while she made notes with her other hand. Her desk didn't quite face the door so he had a partial pro-file view. Her glasses slipped on her nose and she di-verted a finger to shove them back into place.

Her hair was loose and periodically she used the eraser end of her pencil to hook a strand behind her ear, re-vealing the soft underside of her jaw. The vulnerable sight brought a tight feeling to Joe's throat. These ten-der observations were becoming a habit.

Finally he knocked on the doorjamb.

She looked up, her expression of sudden delight as clear as a summer sunrise. "Joe," she said softly. The pencil fell from her fingers, forgotten as she rose and moved around the desk toward him. She'd obviously been marking time until his arrival. That knowledge shouldn't have made him feel taller, should it? It shouldn't have gladdened his heart and warmed his spirit. But it did. It also threw his control into a tailspin. His hands were actually shaking when he grasped her shoulders and drew her forward into a loose embrace.

She tilted her head back and smiled.

He frowned. He wasn't about to forget the unlocked door he'd found when he arrived. "Who's here with you?" he asked, his tone stern. He set her away from him but kept his grip firm on her shoulders.

She seemed surprised. "No one."

"Dammit, Katie. The door was unlocked. Anyone could have walked in here."

"Raymond said he'd lock up when he left. He must have forgotten. But he's only been gone a few minutes."

"A few minutes is all it would take. Next time you check it yourself," he directed. "You *know* how serious this is, Katie. I had a scary few seconds when I came in," he added reluctantly.

Katie's first instinct was to argue but she swallowed what would have been a snap response and gave a fleeting thought to the change in herself. Joe was worried about her. Rather than resent his concern her heart took flight at the idea. "I'm sorry, Joe. You're right, of course. I should have seen to it myself."

He'd expected her to debate the issue. When she didn't he was left without a target for his irritation. "Are you through here?" he asked. "We have a stop to make on the way."

"I'm finished. I was playing around with some figures." She picked up her shoulder bag and the bag in which she'd brought her clothes and led the way out of her office, flipping off the light switch.

He explained about their destination as he followed her to the front entrance. "Neal called a minute ago. They've found Louise's car at the airport."

Katie, who had been digging in her bag for the keys, was astonished. She stopped short. "At the airport?"

Joe was right behind her. He put a hand to her waist. "Watch it."

"At the airport in the city?" she added. Had Louise flown to California after all?

"At the Garden City Airport," he explained. "He asked me to take a look. Do you mind?" he asked belatedly.

She preceded him outside and locked the door behind them. "Of course not. A private plane," she mused, dropping her keys into her purse.

The drive to the city's tiny airport was a short one. They bypassed the concrete-block building that housed the offices and Joe waved to one of Neal's deputies, who was standing by his car near the building. The man made a move to intercept them, but he must have recognized Joe, because he stopped in midmotion and lifted his hand.

Joe looked around the area, then continued on a track that ran parallel to the runway, which was just long enough to accommodate a private jet. "Neal said the car was in an old hangar off by itself."

Katie pointed. "That one over there, I'll bet."

The airport had been expanded and modernized during the seventies, when the resort business was thriving. There were a number of hangars clustered near the end of the runway but Joe passed them and turned off toward the older building that was in a bad state of disrepair. The road leading to it was overgrown with weeds.

The truck's headlights shone into the open bay, illuminating the rear of the red sports car. He shoved the truck into gear and reached behind the seat for a heavy-duty flashlight. "You can wait here for me if you want to. This won't take long."

A soft laugh was the only answer she gave him as she got out.

"Don't touch anything," he cautioned. "They haven't dusted for fingerprints."

The inspection was a disappointment because there was nothing to see. The car had simply been driven inside and parked. Joe ran the light over the car and then turned it into the far corners of the building. There were a few ominous scratching noises. Rats. Katie shivered.

A lot of people made use of the small strip but, evidently, no one used this building. Weeds grew up between the cracks of the concrete floor. Dust balls had gathered against the walls. She didn't know what she'd expected to see but there was nothing here, no signs of a scuffle, nothing. She cupped her hands and looked in through the windows of the car.

"Careful," reminded Joe.

They returned to the airport office. The manager was cooperative but he had no idea when the car had been left there. He went home at six or thereabouts, he told them. The airstrip wasn't guarded; landing lights were left on all night. Anyone who landed after dark could tie down his own plane. There was even an outside phone booth for calls.

It was a casual arrangement, like any one of a thousand other small-town airstrips all over the country. The manager agreed to make copies of the logs for Monday, Friday, and Sunday, the times they knew the man had been in town, and have them for the sheriff in the morning. They had to try everything, of course, but Joe didn't hold out hope that the log would be of help.

Katie repeated her description of the man. She realized that it could have fit a number of men arriving at and leaving the airport during the peak season—husbands and fathers joining, on weekends, wives and children who moved down for the summer. They thanked the manager and left.

Joe was discouraged and frustrated. He threw the truck into gear. "Hell, let's go eat."

Tim's Oyster Bar was deeper within the harbor, out of the way of the boat traffic, among the buildings that housed the support businesses for fishermen, motor rebuilding, ship repair, chandlers and fitting merchants.

Dockworkers and commercial fishermen spoke loudly over the sound of the jukebox coming from a back room. There was a large bulletin board above the cash register, crowded with business cards and notes, some curled at the edges by age.

Ceiling fans stirred the smoke in the air. The food smells mingled, but not unpleasantly—the spicy scent of boiled shrimp, the dusty odor of hops from steins of beer and lager, the crisp aroma of freshly fried foods: shrimp, oysters, fish, potatoes.

The bar was a stretch of Formica-covered counter that reached from a point near the entrance to the opposite wall. Dowels dropped wicker-shaded lights every three feet along its length. The floor was worn linoleum; the stools, sturdy oak and backless. Arranged on the walls, neon advertisements provided a colorful backdrop. There were four sets of tables and chairs hewn from the same strong wood, all empty. A couple of booths against the wall were occupied but most of the customers seemed to prefer the bar.

A man and a woman worked behind the counter as though to an unsung rhythm, moving between the long bar and the huge refrigeration unit, the stove and grill, the taps.

Joe introduced Katie to the couple who were working. They were the owners, Tim and Denise Little. Tim was a big-bellied, muscular man in his mid-fifties who nodded and held up the wicked-looking oyster knife he was using to open a heap of wet, dirty gray shells. "I won't shake hands," he said.

Denise glanced over her shoulder. With a smooth motion that was evidence she'd done it many times, she raised a basket of French fries from a tank of hot oil, hooked it on the side of the reservoir to drain and wiped her hands on her butcher's apron before she smiled and shook hands. "Glad to have you," she said. She turned to Joe. "The oysters finally came in today. We've only been waitin' since the weekend." As Denise spoke her eyes skidded distastefully over her husband.

Both Tim and Denise were cordial and welcoming, but anyone could have sensed the animosity between the two of them. One of the patrons caught Joe's eye and grinned as he threw up a hand. "Howya doin', Joe."

Joe returned the man's casual greeting with a grin of his own. Another man, eyeing Katie curiously, moved aside, leaving two adjacent stools free. "Thanks, Lem."

Joe gave Katie an assist and straddled his stool like he was mounting a horse. "We'll start with a dozen each," he told Denise. "And two draft beers."

Then he remembered. He turned to Katie with a sheepish smile. "Sorry. What will you have?"

Katie laughed. "Draft is fine."

As the older woman moved away, Joe leaned toward Katie's ear to whisper. "They've been married for twenty-five years and fight like cats and dogs most of the time. When they make up the food's lousy."

"Why?" asked Katie.

"Because they get distracted and can't keep their minds on what they're doing. They'll stop to cuddle, burn the fries and forget to put salt in the shrimp."

Katie chuckled. I can sympathize, she thought. Joe's warm breath in her ear was distracting. His muscular forearm rested on the counter inches from hers. She wanted to lean closer to touch her arm to his, to feel his lips on her ear. After last night . . .

"Joe!" The musical voice came from the door, but the lovely blonde to whom it belonged was across the floor in an instant. She linked her arms around Joe's neck and pulled his head down for a kiss. Then she drew back to look up at him. Though her glossy lips formed a pout, she was clearly delighted to see him. "Where have you been, honey? I haven't heard from you in almost a week."

Joe had the grace to look embarrassed. "Dolly," he acknowledged. "It's good to see you."

"Good to see—?" Her voice broke off as her eyes met Katie's across Joe's shoulder. "Ahhh," she murmured in understanding. She smiled and withdrew her arms. "I'm Dolly," she said, extending her hand. She didn't look annoyed. "I'm . . . a friend of Joe's."

Katie took it. "I'm Katie," she said. "I'm a friend, too."

Joe shot her a smoldering look. Denise plunked two round, battered metal trays down in front of them, breaking into the moment. The man who had vacated his stool for Katie spoke around her. "Hey, Dolly, come over here and give one of those kisses to a real man." With a last knowing look at Katie and a glance for Joe, Dolly moved away.

As Denise brought their beer from the huge refrigerator, Katie stared down at the plump oysters, resting on a bed of ice, arranged in a circle around a container of red sauce and lemon wedges. -

Joe took a handful of napkins from a dispenser and gave Katie half of them. "She is just a friend," he said, his voice only lightly emphasizing the word *just*. He passed a basket of cellophane-wrapped crackers. "Taste the sauce. It may be too hot for you," he said as he added horseradish to his.

A friend. Okay. She dipped her fork into the container and touched it to her tongue. It was hot but not uncomfortably so. She speared an oyster from its shell and bathed it in the red sauce while she unwrapped a cracker.

The oysters were fresh and sweet. "Umm, delicious," she murmured.

Joe was digging into his own. "They're the best on the coast."

"Why don't I ever come here?"

Joe shrugged. "It's not exactly your kind of place, is it?"

Katie paused with her fork halfway to her mouth. "What do you mean by that?"

"Do you see anyone here in a suit?"

Katie replaced her fork on her plate. "Are you implying that I'm a snob?" she asked amiably. "If you are, may I make an observation of my own?"

"Certainly." If he was disconcerted by her attitude he didn't show it by as much as a flicker of his eyes.

Katie put her elbows on the counter, linked her fingers and used them to prop her chin. "You have a tendency to be a bit of a snob yourself," she said, careful to keep her voice breezy.

Despite her efforts, his brow darkened, his eyes took on a brooding look. She went on before he could object. "A reverse snob. From the very first you've repeatedly reminded me how different we are. Every time we seem to be getting close to understanding each other you shove that between us. I don't see those differences as clearly as you do."

"Your father wouldn't agree."

"My father was unforgivably rude to you last night. But it wasn't because he doesn't consider you worthy of me—" she shook her head and laughed softly "—God, that sounds so Victorian. He thought he was being loyal to his friend, Neal's father."

"I understand loyalty," he reminded her. "Let's drop it." More likely Bruce Johns knew he had left his last job under a cloud. He turned his attention to the oysters.

"Okay."

Katie noticed something else about Joe while they ate. He was well liked by his friends, had almost a charismatic effect on them. Because she was with him, she was accepted. When they moved to the back room, where the jukebox and small dance floor were, a number of people came to their table to ask his opinion about something, or tell him a bit of family news. More than one woman looked at Katie with a hint of envy.

He took time for them all, listening attentively, answering earnestly. It was as though the clock that regulated his relationships had been turned to slow and patient.

He was a wonderful dancer, too, she realized as soon as they stepped onto the floor. He was sure in his movements. The beat of the music seemed to match his mood. She'd scanned the songs on the jukebox and found that its list was punctuated with a number of fast ones; but tonight the slow songs were the only ones that played.

It was nearly midnight when Katie excused herself. Dolly followed her to the rest room as though she'd been waiting. She reassured Katie that she and Joe really were just friends and explained that Joe had helped her out of a sticky situation one time with a man who thought that macho meant cruel. They lingered for a few minutes and when Katie returned to the table she was laughing under her breath.

Joe stood and took her hand, leading her onto the dance floor. Another slow song had just begun. He pulled her close. "I saw Dolly follow you in there. What are you laughing about?" he asked, his mouth tilted in a half smile.

"I wondered why no one had played any fast songs. Dolly said you probably bribed them."

His fingers spread at the small of her back, bringing her in closer contact with his hips, his thighs. "Yeah? Maybe I did."

"I'm glad. I like the slow music better." Katie fitted her head between his jaw and collarbone. "Dolly also told me that if you didn't light my fire, my wood was all wet."

Joe laughed, drawing every eye in the place. He ignored them and whispered into her ear. "Do I light your fire?"

She raised her head and looked at him. "You know you do," she said softly.

The lights of the jukebox were the only illumination in the room; they painted his face red and gold and silver. It was too dark to see the color of his eyes but the expression of controlled desire in them was unmistakable. No one could see when he slid one hand between them to cover her breast in a brief caress.

The first recording faded away; another love song took its place. The languid mood intensified, leaving Katie in a lazy haze of yearning. Each time his thigh brushed hers, she felt the heat; each time he tightened his arm to guide her in the dance, she felt her body grow warm and heavy against his muscular chest. She wanted to be even closer than they were. She heard a hungry sound emerge from her throat.

With a small smile of understanding and accord, he lifted their clasped hands to his shoulder and left hers there, while he wrapped his other arm around her waist, bringing her flush against him. His palm traced circles at the small of her back; he spread his legs slightly and she felt his arousal hard against her belly. When their hips moved in a parody of lovemaking, her breathing grew shallow and her eyelids so heavy that she could barely keep them open at all.

"Katie?" he whispered, his lips taking little nips at her earlobe between the words.

"Mmm?"

He chuckled, the sound vibrating through her as though it were her own laughter. She shivered in delight. Neither of them had spoken of it but they both understood that tonight they would make love, tonight they would begin where they had left off last night.

"Last dance?"

"Yes."

They danced this time with their eyes locked together. It was hypnotic, mesmerizing, totally enthralling. And it wasn't just affecting her. He, too, wore a rather confused, dazed look. When the dance was over he stood with his arms around her as though he wasn't quite sure what to do next.

She smiled lazily up at him. "Can we go to your boat? I've never made love on a—"

The word was cut off by a devastating kiss. His tongue plunged inside her mouth, swirling, tasting, taking possession. His arms tightened until she could barely breathe. "Let's go," he said huskily.

"To the boat?"

"Yes, if I can wait that long."

In the truck he sat her close beside him. Their thighs touched from hip to knee and her shoulder was wedged behind his. His arm brushed her breast each time he moved. He drove slowly, carefully, and by the time he parked at the dock she felt that her skin would surely melt from the heat radiating from his body and hers.

He parked and got out, holding the door for her to slide out behind him.

She hesitated. "Ah, Joe..."

He waited. She fumbled for her bags, both of them, and handed them to him. "I—uh—brought my tooth-brush."

Joe held both bags in one hand and stared at her, his pulse vibrating like a drumbeat in his head. He was completely unprepared for her statement and he had an idea that if he laughed she'd make him take her home. No way. He covered his mouth for a second, then he held his other hand out to her. "Good," he said. "I hope you didn't bother with a nightgown."

The scene was familiar, the scent and taste of the night air the same, the whispering sounds of the water as it kissed the hull of his boat and the wind off the sea were unvarying; but the atmosphere was also unexpectedly foreign, influenced by the unexplored, exotic flavor of their changing relationship.

Fingers entwined, they walked quickly to the boat, their eyes cutting to each other and shifting away, their emotions contained by a slender thread. Neither of them spoke as he jumped lightly to the deck and turned to lift her aboard. He hesitated, his hands at her waist. Then he took her hand again and led her through the salon, past the galley and into the master's cabin. The light coming in through the cabin windows was enough to see by, so he didn't turn on the lamp.

Not until the door was closed, not until they were enclosed in privacy, did Katie allow her lungs to empty of the sigh that had been building.

The effect on him was instantaneous. He closed his eyes, his brow furrowed by emotion, as he folded her in his arms, his mouth seeking her lips blindly, hungrily. She circled his neck with her arms, holding tight. His fingers dug into her bottom and he lifted her against him. His hair smelled of shampoo and smoke.

He broke off the kiss suddenly; she felt him fight for control, taking long breaths. "Katie, Katie," he murmured softly against her cheek. "I can barely speak, I want you so much."

"Me, too. I do," she whispered unsteadily. Somewhere in the back of her mind she knew her words sounded crazy but he didn't laugh.

Gently he released her and pulled his shirt over his head. She'd always considered undressing the awkward part of lovemaking but his eyes spoke encouragingly. She lifted her arms for him to remove her top. Without waiting for him to perform the task she reached back to unhook her bra.

Holding her shirt in his big hands, he watched, his eyes dark. She stopped, suddenly unsure what to do with the bra now that it was off, and looked at him.

Joe smiled slightly and held out his hand, pleased with this small evidence that she was a bit self-conscious. She smiled, too, handing him the bra. And then his eyes dropped.

His fists clenched in the soft fabric of her clothes as he had his first glimpse of her naked breasts. They were beautiful, firm and full. Slowly he tossed the clothes aside and, reaching out, lifted her hands to his shoulders.

Katie forgot to breathe as, hands at her waist, he brought her body into warm, delicious contact with his. "Oh, babe," he whispered, moving her against him. The slight friction was unbearably erotic. "You feel so good."

Her body began to ache with desire in all her sensitive places. Her face was against his skin, and she inhaled deeply of his masculine scent. She brushed her cheek against his shoulder like a cat seeking to be petted.

His hands moved with restless abandon over her back, stroking from her hips to her shoulders, from the fabric of her slacks to her bare skin and back again. His warm touch on her skin excited her. "So do you," she whispered. She was unable to keep her head erect.

He slid his fingers up into her hair, tangling them there to hold her for his kiss. She moved her hips with instinctive desire and felt his immediate response. As though of one accord, they separated to dispose of the rest of their clothes. They acted by feel alone as they unzipped, unbuttoned, discarded; their gazes, locked, burning with hunger, each of them with attention completely focused on the other.

At last they came together again beside the bed. This time they hesitated, as though agreeing mutually to stretch the anticipation to the last electrifying moment.

Joe extended a finger to brush back a tendril of her hair. Katie smiled and laid her palm over his heart, feeling the rapid beat there. Her fingers moved on, testing the texture of his skin, lightly dusted with hair, the hard muscles of his chest. She found a puckered scar running down his side. She heard him catch his breath. "Does that hurt?" she asked softly.

"No."

And then they were wrapped together on the down comforter, sinking into its soft depths, legs tangled, lips fused. His hands were on her breasts, her stomach, the backs of her knees, the insides of her thighs. Wherever his hands touched her, stroked her, his eyes were there, caressing, too, and his mouth explored, tasted.

Katie felt like she was flying. He touched her intimately, possessively, gently at first. And then, when he realized that her need was as strong as his, he touched her more demandingly. Her nails raked the strong muscles of his back.

Slowly, carefully, he entered her.

She knew she was being completely filled for the first time in her life, that no matter what happened she would never feel this complete again. There was a depth to his passion, to his lovemaking that she'd not experienced before. She'd never known that a man could be so strong and so tender at the same time. His features blurred under the force of her emotions and she opened her eyes wider, afraid to lose sight of every nuance, every expression on his strong face. He moved above her with unshakable confidence, urging her, with soft murmurs of encouragement, with the movement of his body, to follow, to lead, to reach for the stars.

When she reached for, and caught, the sensation that was the ultimate of feeling, he was there with her, ready to reach, too. They climaxed together, the firmament exploding in a thousand vivid colors.

At last, Katie could breathe again. She looked up at him, propped on his elbows above her, his breath coming hard. He covered her face with kisses, affectionate kisses, gentle kisses, that held just a hint of recklessness. He rolled to his side with a soft moan, holding her close in the crook of his arm. She curled a leg over his thigh, not only to keep a tangible hold on reality but also to offer comfort to him.

What an odd thought, that this man, so strong, so intelligent, should need comfort. She wondered where the idea had come from as her eyes closed, her breathing became regular.

Joe lay awake long after Katie had fallen asleep, aware that he had given a part of himself that could never be reclaimed.

The man waited outside Katie's condominium, watching. Where the hell was she? With that damned fisherman probably.

He stepped out of the shadows to check his watch then melted back into the niche he'd found from which he could watch her unit. 1:00 a.m. Was she planning to spend the night on the boat? He cursed under his breath.

Then he stopped, reminding himself not to let his emotions run away with him. Everything would work out. He wiped sweat from his forehead and ran his fingers over his jaw. His shirt was a wrinkled mess. He needed a shower and a shave.

He'd give her another hour.

Chapter 8

Katie's consciousness stirred behind the curtain of sleep but she fought it back and snuggled deeper into the co-coon of warmth that surrounded her. In her dreams her intuition warned her to be very cautious. The feeling persisted even as she stifled a yawn.

At last full consciousness would be deferred no longer and she opened her eyes. She was lying on her back. Joe was on his side, his body curved around her, his arm across her stomach. Early-morning sunlight, dancing off the water, reflected on the ceiling above her.

The intuition, premonition, whatever it was, was right. Her emotions were a turmoil of mixed impressions, anxiety and amazement, worry and wonder. She'd given freely, completely of herself, holding nothing back. And now she worried that Joe would feel trapped by the ex-cess of emotion she'd shown. He'd encouraged her, urg-ing her on with his hands, his lips, his body, urging her to reach for heights she hadn't known existed.

She couldn't blame her anxiety over Louise Austen, or the beer; she hadn't had that much. She was in this relationship...love affair...whatever it was, very, very deeply. She squeezed her eyes shut again, trying to hold tightly to the memory of Joe's loving. She had touched the stars and the moon, knowing it would feel like this.

Joe had not lied to her. She knew that he wasn't going to awaken this morning and declare his eternal love. He didn't make promises. He'd made it clear the first time he'd been in her home that it was nice but domesticity wasn't for him. He always maintained that he was in Garden City temporarily, that sooner or later he would be moving on. He had no ties, except for the rather loose one with his brother, and he had no desire for them. After one night of lovemaking she didn't expect him to change his outlook, his philosophy. So why was she feeling so fragile?

Because she had lied to herself. She had thought she could settle for a brief romance, at least until her infatuation had burned itself out. With the coming of the dawn she faced the knowledge that her feelings were neither transitory nor were they an infatuation. She was falling in love with this man about whom she knew so little and so very much.

She took mental inventory of exactly what she *did* know.

He was thirty-six years old. He was the brother of a man she admired and their relationship seemed congenial though they hadn't grown up in the same home. He was a former investigator with the Justice Department in Washington, and he could dress either like he'd stepped out of *GQ* or off a tramp steamer. He was a fisherman. Those were the tangible things.

On an intangible level she knew his friends had a great deal of respect for him. She'd seen that demonstrated last night at Tim's. He was diplomatic and charismatic, though she doubted he was aware of those attributes. He was a wonderfully tender lover; and, when you peeled away some of his layers of reserve, he had a warm sense of humor. Those layers might be peeled back for a glimpse but they would never be stripped off completely. They were there to protect him from something. She wondered what it was.

She knew that he had been deeply wounded.

Had his pain been caused by a woman? She didn't think so. There may have been a woman involved but whoever she was, she had added to his pain, not precipitated it. Katie didn't have a logical reason for reaching that conclusion but she'd reached it anyway. He wouldn't have quit his job for a woman. No, whatever had wounded Joe was of his own making and it was related to his former profession.

She didn't even consider asking Neal. Unless Joe decided to tell her himself, she would never know. He might tease her about being nosy but she wouldn't let her curiosity come between them. She would take him on faith for however long their relationship lasted.

Joe's breathing was relaxed and rhythmical. She cut her eyes to the clock. Almost seven. She thought momentarily about sneaking out, then dismissed that idea.

As she lay in the warm curve of his body, however, she realized that she had to erect some self-protective barriers of her own. Clearly he felt a sense of responsibility toward her because of the man on the pier. Whatever emotional strings accompanied that responsibility must be cut. After the pressure was lifted, after the situation had been explained, then she would discover what his true feelings toward her were.

If he had any true feelings toward her. Time, that was what they needed. Time and space. And she had to figure out a way to ask for time and to give space.

Suddenly she knew he was awake and watching her. She hadn't heard the rhythm of his breathing change; he hadn't moved. But all at once her nerve endings sent the message to her brain. She turned her head on the pillow and met his steady gaze. Her nose was inches from his; she smelled the scent of passion, of desire, of man. "Good morning."

Joe felt relaxed, at peace with himself. Last night Katie had helped him shut the door on a lot of the dark places in his mind and opened him to the sunlight that was in her golden eyes. If he'd met her a year ago they would never have reached this point. During that time he'd been doing a lot of healing, of both his body and his mind, but he hadn't known until now.

He could lie here all day looking at her pretty face. Last night she had given more of herself than he deserved or expected and, surprisingly, he wanted to give something back. He was a man who didn't let go of his control, but this morning he was as open as he'd ever been. He yearned to do the things with her he'd never done when he was young—to walk in the rain, to hold hands in a dark movie theater, to lie on the beach and study the stars.

He felt so damned *good* and all his fantastic feelings were because of this woman. "Good morning," he said softly, grinning as he rubbed a knuckle across her cheek.

Joe's smiles had begun to come more easily and more often than when Katie had first met him. She was accustomed to seeing them, to being warmed by them. But this one was different. If it hadn't been, Katie might have thrust all her misgivings away and responded to her feelings instead. His eyes sparkled knowingly, and in her eyes, his grin was . . . cavalier.

Her own smile barely reached the surface of her mouth. She glanced at the clock. "Goodness, I didn't realize it was so late. I have an early appointment this morning."

Joe was suddenly immobilized; the warm blood coursing through his veins became icy. He saw her expression as an attempt to dismiss the importance of what had happened between them; he felt the interlude and his tranquil feelings dissolve.

Well, what the hell had he expected? Hadn't he warned her to be wary? His face closed; all signs of feeling, all his tentatively budding emotions drew back into that dark, safe place where he kept them hidden.

His disenchantment took the form of grief—grief for something that was an illusion, had always been and would always be a fallacy.

He knew she cared, in her way. He'd forgotten that he didn't need or want anyone to care about him. He'd forgotten and it had cost him. He'd thought—well, to hell with the rest of what he'd thought. God, if it hurt this much to leave himself open, he was better off remaining like he was—self-protective.

"You have time for breakfast?" he asked noncommittally.

Katie hesitated. Something had happened between one minute and another. She'd seen him close her out as surely as if he'd closed a door between them. "Sure," she said, her voice determinedly light. "Let me get dressed first. Then we can see how the time runs." She wished

they were at her place. In her own familiar surroundings, she could have managed. Here, she wasn't sure.

Joe gave her a last probing look. "Okay," he said. "I'll
put on a pot of coffee while you shower." He swung his
legs off the opposite side of the bed and stood.

Katie caught her breath at the sight of his backside.
The powerful shoulders and arms, the long muscles down
his side, his narrow waist and tight buttocks, his strong
legs. A captain's job was physical and required a healthy,
robust body. She wondered if he had been this well toned
when he worked in Washington. Probably. An investigator probably had to be.

He looked over his shoulder and caught her staring. An
unpleasant smile curved his lips. "I thought you were in
a hurry," he said.

When she emerged from the shower a few minutes later
she heard voices. She brushed her hair, applied a minimum of makeup and dressed quickly in the matching
blue skirt and blouse she'd put into her bag along with
her toothbrush. When she entered the salon Joe was
alone.

"I thought I heard someone out here with you."

He pulled a dish of cinnamon rolls from the microwave and put them on a trivet in the middle of the table.
"Sam Mallard and his dad. They're taking my charter
today."

"Really?" She reached for the coffeepot and filled
both the mugs on the counter. But he shook his head
when she brought them to the table. He had broken off
a roll and he was eating it standing up. "I'll shower while
you eat. I don't want to hold you up."

She searched for sarcasm but didn't hear any. "Joe,"
she said. She had a terrible feeling that she'd handled
things all wrong. To keep him from thinking she would

try to tie strings on him, she had a feeling she had come across as uncaring. Misunderstanding had grown into animosity from less. She couldn't bear that. "A few minutes won't matter. Sit."

To her surprise, he sat, but his face was closed to her.

She wasn't sure how to approach him in this mood. She wasn't even sure what his mood was. She cleared her throat and touched his forearm where it rested on the table. "Joe, let's talk."

He raised a dark brow and peered at her over the rim of his cup. "About what?"

"About us. About last night."

When he didn't react she plunged on. "Last night was wonderful . . ."

Joe heard the implied "but." He'd never known how to verbalize tender feelings. Hell, he'd never *had* many. Now he was frustrated by his lack of skill, but he had to try. He set his mug down and took a deep breath. "Look, Katie, I'm pretty much of a loner so I'm not very good at talking about my feelings." It was the most he'd ever admitted about himself to a woman. He felt as though he were traversing a thin precipice.

"Neither am I, Joe. That's the thing. I don't want you to feel responsible for last night. I'm a big girl now. And I don't attach a lot of importance to . . ." Her voice trailed off.

"Sex?" he supplied.

"No. Yes. Oh, darn." She raked her fingers through her hair and rested her cheek on her open palm. "Sex is important, of course it is. I guess what I'm trying to say is that I'm not accustomed . . ." She groped for the right phrasing and finally gave up. "I don't sleep around," she said abruptly.

"I didn't think you did," Joe said, feeling his tension ease slightly, until she spoke again.

"I believe we need some space. We've been thrown together a lot because of circumstances. Last night was...well, it happened too quickly. And just because we made love, we don't have to make a commitment, too, do we?" Argue with me, she demanded silently. Tell me I'm wrong.

Joe had this crazy urge to reject her question out of hand, but he stopped to think. She was pushing him away. If he argued she would push all the harder. It was her nature.

He had no choice but to give her the distance she requested. "This will be over soon. When Neal can free one of his deputies to take over, you'll have me out of your hair."

"I didn't say I wanted you out of my hair. I simply asked for breathing room." Her brows drew together. "What does Neal's deputy have to do with you and me?"

Joe hesitated. "Neal asked me to keep an eye on you until the situation is resolved or he can free a man to take over. I'm the one who's been following you." He saw the disbelief on her face change to hurt then, swiftly and subsequently, to anger.

"You?" she breathed. "You have been following me? After—" She stopped to think, scraping her fingers into her hair. "Last week, after the phone call, when I told Neal . . . it was you?"

The accusation in her eyes hardened his resolution. He shrugged. "Hell, I didn't want the job. Why do you think Sam and his dad are taking my charters? They've done them all, except for the one Saturday."

Katie felt like laughing and crying all at the same time. "You never really cared about me at all, did you?" she

demanded, her voice rising. "You were just doing a job."
Her eyes stung unexpectedly; her stomach hurt. So this
was the reason for his interest. She should have known;
he'd told her that she wasn't the type of woman he usually was attracted to. The only rational thought to emerge
from her reeling senses was relief that she hadn't revealed how deep her own feelings were.

"Well, it will be a relief when it's over, I'm sure. All
this—" she waved a hand in the air "—trailing . . . is that
what you call it?"

"Tailing," he supplied impassively. A muscle jumped
in his jaw.

"Well, it must have eaten into your social life as well."

"Katie, I didn't say—"

"Why didn't you tell me?" she interrupted, furious
now. "You knew I was uncomfortable."

He ran the knuckle of his right forefinger along the left
side of his jaw. "We, Neal and I, didn't want to frighten
you."

"That's the most ridiculous reason I've ever heard. I
was already frightened."

"Yeah," said Joe. "I agree. It was stupid not to tell
you."

"And I won't have any more of it."

His head came up at that. "Any more of what?"

"I won't have you following me around. You can just
quit."

"Actually that was what Neal said you would say." He
leaned back in his chair, hooking an arm over its stile. A
smile played across his lips. "What are you going to do?
Complain to the sheriff?"

"That isn't funny."

He leaned forward crossing his arms on the table before him. "I know. I'm sorry," he said. "And I'm too

tired to play games. Maybe you're right, maybe last night was a mistake; we've certainly gotten off to a bad start this morning. But I'm not going to stop following you. I'll try to stay in the background, but I will be there."

She clenched her teeth helplessly. She needed to stomp out of here, but she didn't have transportation. She could wait on the deck, though. "Fine. When you're ready you can take me to get my car." She picked up her bags and headed for the ladder.

"Aren't you going to eat?" he asked, then realized how inane the question sounded.

She shot him a look. "I'm not hungry," she said shortly and left the room.

He headed for the shower. Shucking his jeans he stepped into the stall and turned the taps with a ferocity that surprised him. The cold water hit him in the face. He stepped back, waiting for the water temperature to rise.

Damned woman used all the hot water! He bent his forehead against the wall and closed his eyes.

Face it, Ryder, you're a washout when it comes to relationships with women. Where sensitive feelings are involved, you're about as functional as Bigfoot at a fancy dress ball.

But that was the way he'd survived, wasn't it? And his pride wouldn't let him beg. There were too many strikes against them anyway. Her father didn't care for him and her family was very important to Katie. Oh, she might rail against the doctor's cool reaction to Joe when they met, but she'd never let herself get really involved with anyone he didn't like. He would do just as he'd promised. He'd stay in the background.

When he joined her on the deck a few minutes later, her golden eyes were bright and clear. Too bright, too clear.

Joe felt like the last of the grubby bums.

"Ready?" she asked spiritedly.

"Yeah."

When they reached her condominium he pulled up beside her car. Yesterday he'd had her on the seat of his old pickup, close to him, close enough for him to enjoy the scent of her perfume and listen to her pretty voice, close enough for her smile to warm him.

Today she was hugging the door. The smile she turned in his direction didn't come close to reaching her eyes. "Thanks for the ride."

Damn his quick tongue. Damn his pride. "Katie," he said quietly. "I didn't mean to hurt you."

"You didn't," she said quickly. "We both knew going in that this was temporary, didn't we? I was only angry because you and Neal didn't let me in on your plans. But I'm all right now."

He gave her a skeptical look. He nodded. His gaze followed as she got out of his truck and into the station wagon. Maybe he should give her time to cool off before he tried to talk to her again, give her the space she'd asked for.

The day was longer than Katie had ever imagined a day could be. She wanted it to end. Like a hurt animal she needed privacy to lick her wounds.

But privacy wasn't available. There were advertisers to call on, further arrangements to be made for the owners' visit, her regular Tuesday-night show to do, and the ever-present truck in her rearview mirror to remind her of the man she'd seen on the pier and Louise Austen, missing person.

Still there, she noted that night at eight o'clock as she swung into the parking lot of her condominium complex

and breathed a heartfelt sigh of relief. She switched off
the engine, removed the keys, gathered up her purse and
a file she'd brought home to work on, and got out of the
car. Her footsteps were slowed by weariness and she
didn't spare a glance for the truck. All she wanted at this
moment was a long hot bath and bed.

Her anger had long since faded; she wasn't one to dwell
on resentment. During the day, when her mind wasn't
fully occupied with her job, thoughts of Joe and this
morning's confrontation kept intruding. She realized at
last, now that it was too late, that when she woke this
morning, she should have kept her mouth shut.

She also realized she knew Joe better than she'd
thought she had. He was skittish and proud. From things
he'd said she knew, too, that he hadn't had a traditional
upbringing; neither he nor Neal seemed to harbor much
love for the woman who had borne them. Perhaps Joe
was afraid of emotional ties rather than wary of them.

Underneath his strong exterior was a man who had
found it necessary to build defenses. What she had to
decide was whether she was brave enough to try to batter
them down. And she couldn't make such a decision when
her brain was fuzzy from fatigue. She inserted her key
into the lock. Home—and alone—at last.

She flipped the switch that would illuminate the liv-
ing-room lamps. And froze where she stood.

Joe sat slumped in the front seat of his truck, looking
up at Katie's doorway. A few residents came and went as
he sat there but most of them were in for the night. Some
of the windows glowed with the characteristic blue radi-
ance of a television set. A man left the door open on a
ground-floor unit, spilling light across the tarmac as he
carried a bag of trash to the Dumpster.

Katie was a creature of habit and he knew the pattern by heart. She would turn on an inside light, close and lock the door behind her, and flip off the outside light. Then he would make a last circle around the grounds before leaving.

Any minute now.

The light didn't go out. Another light flashed on instead. He recognized it as coming from the small second bedroom she'd fixed up as an office. Surely she wasn't going to work this late. He was bone-tired and she must be, too. He remembered the file she'd taken from the car.

He got out of the truck and circled the building. When he got back the light was still burning. He could leave; she was inside and safe. She'd probably gone to sleep with the lights on. But something about the alteration of the pattern disturbed him.

He stood there with his hands on his hips, his head thrown back, staring up at her door. Hell, the last thing he needed was another confrontation with her tonight. But he couldn't leave until he knew, beyond a shadow of a doubt, that she was all right.

Ignoring the elevator, he took the steps two at a time. He was going to feel like a fool if he woke her.

He knocked, softly so that if she were asleep she wouldn't be disturbed. After a minute, someone inside fumbled with the latch and the door was thrown open.

"Come in," Katie said expressionlessly.

"What the—" The room was in shambles. Drawers pulled out and dumped, sofa cushions thrown aside, chairs overturned. The watercolor that had hung over the sofa lay aslant against the gateleg table, its glass shattered and a piece gouged out of the frame. Books were tossed, and tapes...dear Lord, her tapes of the old shows that she loved so much. Some had been stomped on, others pulled from their casings. A fern had been over-turned, spilling dirt on the carpet.

He took a quick look into the kitchen and bedrooms; the scene was the same. The whole damn apartment had been trashed. When he returned to her side his gaze roamed over the mess. Anger, fear, panic overcame him and he demanded, "Why didn't you get the hell out of here? Don't you realize he could have been waiting for you?" When she didn't answer immediately he swung around to look at her.

Her beautiful golden eyes were filled with tears; she was trying hard not to cry. The sight caught him in the gut. "Ah, Katie, I didn't mean to yell, babe," he said, pulling her into his arms. "I'm sorry."

Katie went willingly, drawing strength from him, grateful for his warm, tight hold. "Why me? Why did I have to be the one to see him, Joe?"

It was the age-old cry of the victim and Joe didn't have an answer for her. All he could do was hold her, to give her his physical support. He wished he could comfort her, wished he could come up with the right words, the help-ful thing to say to heal this hurt. Neither of them thought to question their assumption that the man on the pier was responsible.

When Katie felt steady again, she pulled back to look up into his face. There was compassion there and ten-derness, but there was something else as well—an expression in which she took fiendish, diabolic pleasure. She almost laughed aloud.

Fury burned deep within his eyes and matched her own. Fury that someone could violate her this way. It made him her champion again. "Thank you, Joe."

"For what?"

"For being as mad, as furious over this chaos as I am."

Joe tipped her head back and wiped the tears away with his thumb.

Until that minute Katie hadn't been aware that she was crying. "I'm just so angry," she added, quick with her explanation, earning herself a tilted smile from Joe.

"I know," Joe said, holding her tightly against him. God! He was shaking like a leaf in a winter wind. He didn't want to let go. "I know, honey."

The strain between them was set aside; neither of them referred to it. She burrowed more deeply against him, needing his nearness to sustain her. She was too angry and too tired to think. "I thought you'd gone," she said, her voice muffled against his chest.

His arms tightened, his lips were in her hair, he rubbed her arm briskly. "I wouldn't have left, not until your lights went out. And not because it's a job, either." It was the only mention he'd make of the morning's quarrel.

When Katie had entered to find the destruction in her home, she'd been stunned by the sight. Even after she'd recovered somewhat she had still been unable to decide what to do. She didn't want to call Neal. He would send Joe back and she would not have him feeling obligated to her again. She didn't want to alarm her family, either. So she'd locked the door, put the chain in its slot and started cleaning up.

"How did he get in, Joe?" she asked.

"I don't know. I'll look around."

She didn't want him to release her, not yet. She fluttered her hand against his chest. "I didn't get very far with the mess."

"Come on." He turned her in the direction of her bedroom.

When they reached the doorway he paused, noticing for the first time that the clock radio on her bedside table was emitting static. The intruder must have left it on, as Joe had done in his truck, tuned to WCTZ to determine what time her show was over. It gave the man leisure to search thoroughly and be gone from the condo in plenty of time to escape discovery.

"You'll feel better after a bath," he said.

Joe offered the solution like the English offer tea, as a panacea for trouble. "A bath? I don't want to take a bath," she declared, as though he'd lost his mind. "I have to clean this up."

"Not until Neal has seen it," said Joe. "You might think about what this man was looking for, because he's clearly looking for something."

With Katie still under his arm, Joe continued through the mess in her bedroom. They both tried to ignore the message that had been scrawled across her mirror in lipstick. "Get out." In her bathroom there was less disarray because there was only the cabinet beneath the sink to search.

Muttering angrily under her breath she bent down to scoop up rolls of toilet paper and cleaning supplies and shove them back out of sight. The towels still hung neatly from their bars. Except for one washcloth and a hand towel that were thrown carelessly across the edge of the sink.

Katie ceased her muttering, suddenly in the middle of a word, as though her voice had been cut off from a spigot. She sat on her heels staring at the towel that dangled in front of her eyes. He could see the spirit literally drain out of her, leaving her motionless. "Honey, what..."

She recovered quickly. From a still, frozen figure, in seconds she became insulted, outraged, vital. She leaped to her feet. "My towel!" she shrieked. "The son of a bitch used my towel and washcloth!'' She scooped up the towel and flung it toward a trash can with such vigor that the can tipped over.

If the circumstances hadn't been so abhorrent, Joe would have laughed at the sight of the small vengeful tornado that had erupted like a whirlwind in the confines of the small room. By the time he recovered she was tossing things about with a frenzied abandon. ''My soap, my towel. My glass!''

Joe hadn't noticed the glass on the counter beside the lavatory. He moved quickly, before she could pounce. Grabbing her, he pinned her arms to her sides. ''Don't touch it!'' he ordered. ''Don't touch anything else.''

She struggled for a moment, then seemed to collapse in his arms. ''But, Joe...'' Her cry was plaintive and sent a stab of pain through his heart. ''He used my things.''

For some reason this affected her more than the destruction of her living room or the scrawled threat on her mirror. ''I know, honey. I know. C'mon.'' He bent to pick her up and left the room.

He paused when he got to the guest bathroom and looked in. Nothing seemed to have been disturbed in here. He set her on her feet and took a clean glass from the chrome holder.

''What are you doing?'' asked Katie, watching as he washed it under the faucet and dried it vigorously with a towel.

''Take this in your hand. Use a firm grip. Neal will need something with your fingerprints.''

''Oh.'' The reminder that strange hands had touched her things brought on another swell of anger. ''My family's fingerprints will be all over, too.''

"Yeah, I know. Neal will have to get samples. Who else?" He took the glass from her hand, still holding it with the towel.

"You," she went on. "A lot of people." She put a hand to her head. "I can't think. The exterminator. Millie, a cleaning lady who comes once every two weeks."

"When was she here?"

Katie looked up in surprise at the subdued excitement in his voice. "She was here yesterday," she explained. "She has her own key."

"I hope she's thorough. It may help to narrow things down a bit."

"She's very thorough."

"When Neal has been and gone I'll help you clean up."

"But—"

"No 'buts,'" he interrupted, backing out with his hand on the knob. He hoped to hell he wasn't messing up any more prints.

Katie put a hand on her hip. "Joe?" she asked wryly.

He stopped at the first sign all day of her pretty smile, strained as it might be. "What?"

"Do you mind if I get my bathrobe?"

Something flashed in his eyes but was gone before she could identify it.

Chapter 9

Neal arrived in less than ten minutes. His expression was grim when Joe opened the door to him. He stood still, hands on his jean-clad hips, and took a long look around the room. "This man's beginning to aggravate the hell out of me, Joe. We've got a nice, quiet little town here. Most of the time being the sheriff's just another steady job, until along comes somebody like this son of a bitch to whip up trouble."

"Yeah," said Joe. "That's what Katie called him, too." It occurred to him that he seldom saw his brother out of uniform anymore. It also occurred to him that despite his attempted quip, Neal was feeling the pressure from this case. He held himself rigidly and the lines that cut from his nose to the corners of his mouth were severe.

"Greg will be along in a minute," Neal added, speaking of one of his deputies.

Joe had discovered a broken pane in the narrow window to the side of the door, which explained how the man had gotten in. He pointed it out to Neal.

"I saw that when I came in. She needs a set of bars there."

"Yeah," said Joe dryly. "You want to tell her? By the way, she knows about my surveillance."

Neal gave him a grin. "It was only a matter of time. How did she take it?"

"Not well. But she'll go along." He planted his hands on his hips, his posture unconsciously mimicking his older brother's. "Especially now."

They went through the rooms together. When they reached the bedroom Neal stood looking for a long time at the message scrawled on the mirror.

"Evidently the man decided to make himself at home. He washed his hands—or something—in here," said Joe, moving to the bathroom. "He may have used the glass."

That got Neal's attention fast. His head jerked up. "What the hell?"

"When Katie saw it she blew up. She threw the towel and washcloth at the trash basket. A couple of other things, too, before I stopped her."

Neal bent down, touched the articles. "Dry as a bone. When did this happen Joe? You were following her."

"I figure it happened sometime last night or tonight before the station went off the air." He explained about the radio being tuned to WCTZ.

Neal was quiet for a minute. The silence threatened to stretch into discomfort before he spoke again. "And where was Katie last night?" he asked finally.

"She was with me. On the boat. This morning I dropped her by to pick up her car. I didn't come upstairs."

Neal lifted a brow but made no comment on the admission. He sighed and went back into the living room. "What if she'd walked in on him?"

"Maybe he was hoping for it," said Joe quietly. He plunged his hands into his pockets and turned away. Neal's question was the same one that had haunted him from the moment he'd walked through the front door.

It didn't look like anything was missing. They'd have to have Katie check but the TV, stereo, all the things that thieves usually went for, things that were easily fenced, were still here. Except for the framed painting nothing was broken. So it was a trashing. And a threat. Or had the intruder been looking for something?

Neal took a deep breath and blew it out when they reached her office. Here things had been searched, thoroughly searched, but oddly there wasn't the destruction here that there was in the rest of the condo. "I wonder what he was looking for?"

Before Joe could speculate, the doorbell rang. Greg, Neal's deputy had arrived.

"I'd best get started," he said after a quick glance. He picked up the small fingerprint kit he'd brought with him and opened it.

Joe roamed about the place, looking for a small detail, something, anything that would give him a feel for the man. He kept returning to the bathroom off her bedroom. He picked up the towel, held it to his nose and inhaled deeply. Nothing there to stimulate his senses, except the smell of Katie's soap. He dropped the towel and bent forward at the waist, studying the glass carefully where it sat beside the sink. Then he turned his attention to the cake of soap resting in a small, dried residue of suds. The manufacturer's name was deeply carved into its white surface.

Suddenly his eyes narrowed. He straightened and turned to the spilled contents of the trash can. He went down on his haunches. Careful not to touch anything he searched carefully until he found what he was looking for. The wrapper off the new cake of soap. He called to Neal and Greg.

By the time Katie emerged from the hot shower she did feel better. She donned pajamas and wrapped herself in a thick terry robe before emerging from the bathroom.

Neal and his deputy were at work on the fingerprints.

Joe caught sight of her as she stood in the doorway watching. "Hi," he said gently. "Are you okay?"

"I'm fine," she answered, tightening the belt on her robe with a decisive jerk.

Neal glanced up from the work he was doing near the entrance. He carefully pulled off a strip of wide tape and stored it in a glassine bag. But he didn't look encouraged. "We're getting prints from one spot on the door frame, Katie, but they're probably yours. This kind of lock isn't the safest, by the way, and you need bars on the window by the door. That's how he got in."

Joe smiled to himself at the smooth way Neal inserted the suggestion and went on without interruption, "You'll have to tell us if anything has been taken."

Katie hadn't missed the mention of bars. She set her mouth and crossed to the window, pushing back the opaque curtain to see the damage. Simple, all he had to do was reach inside and open the door. "I didn't even see this," she said, wondering at her own oversight. "I can't believe I didn't see it. I hate bars."

"Yeah, I figured you would. It looks like he remembered to wipe his prints off the frame," Neal continued, indicating the area around the window that was now covered with gray dust. "Joe did find something."

Greg had joined them. "Nothing on the glass but . . ." He held up another bag. Katie recognized the wrapper off her favorite brand of soap. "Was this a new bar?" the deputy asked.

She nodded. "I hadn't even opened it."

"Then this may be a break. There are a couple of good clear prints here."

Neal thanked the deputy, helped him pack his equipment, then dismissed him. "Go home and get some sleep, Greg. We have a long day ahead of us tomorrow."

When the deputy had left, Neal turned to Katie. "If this man has ever been arrested or served in the armed forces we'll get an ID on him. If not, at least this is evidence to take to court."

"I hope you catch him soon," said Katie feelingly.

Joe opened the door to the balcony and stepped outside. Her eyes followed his movements.

"No more than I," said Neal, drawing her attention back to himself. "Come on, walk through with me and see if anything has been taken."

Nothing had, not that she could see. They paused in front of her dresser mirror. She shivered.

Neal seemed to hesitate. "Katie, Joe told me you knew that we were keeping an eye on you."

She nodded. "He also told me that he hadn't wanted the job," she said lightly. She smiled, trying to keep the bitterness out of her expression.

Neal must have seen it. "Maybe you ought to ask him why. It has nothing to do with you, you know."

"No? Then why?"

Neal scratched his head. "That's all I can say. Maybe I shouldn't have said that much." He hesitated. "Would you like to go to your folks' house for the rest of the night?''

She thought for a minute, combing her hair back with a distracted gesture. "No, Neal. I'd rather stay here."

"Then I'm staying with you," said Joe from the balcony door. His expression was unreadable.

Her eyes flew to his, flickered to Neal, and back again. She didn't want to rehash their argument in front of his brother.

"Your sofa looks comfortable." It was the one place she'd restored to some kind of order.

Neal nodded. "Good. Katie, I don't want you to go anywhere alone until we find out what happened. And I'd rather you didn't mention this break-in, at least not out in public, for a while."

She winced at the thought, but spoke calmly. "Don't worry, Neal. I want to get it cleaned up and forget it ever happened."

"Good." He squeezed her shoulder. "I'll see you in the morning, won't I?" he said to Joe.

"Sure. I'll walk out with you."

Joe stopped at the elevator. Neal pushed the button and turned to him. "Joe, are you sure you won't let me deputize you? You're not going to let anyone else look after her now, anyway."

Joe's eyes met his brother's. "I didn't know I was so obvious," he said. Finally he shook his head. "No, Neal. I'll stay with her, but I won't be deputized."

"She doesn't know the whole story, does she?"

"No." He shoved his hands into his pockets and his gaze fell to the floor in front of his feet. He added quietly, "There's no future for us, Neal."

"She's a strong lady. You might try being honest with her."

"I have been honest," Joe protested.

"There are lies of omission. Tell her, Joe," he urged. "Tell her the whole story."

The elevator arrived and Neal held the door with one hand, waiting for an answer that he didn't get.

Neal sighed heavily but he didn't prod further. He stepped into the elevator. "My office? About nine?"

Joe nodded.

After Neal had gone, and Katie and Joe were left alone, she immediately felt self-conscious. "Well..." Her voice trailed off; she avoided his eyes. She bent and picked up a magazine, then stood holding it in front of her with her arms wrapped around it like a protective shield. "You really don't have to stay. I can—"

He fixed her with his gaze. "I'm not leaving you alone, Katie," he said firmly.

She pressed her lips together. She'd be glad of his presence—she didn't really want to be alone tonight and she didn't want to go to her parents' house. She was grateful for the way he'd handled everything but gratitude wasn't enough to completely erase her hurt.

He started to pick up the broken glass from the painting. Avoiding his eyes she took the frame and picture and put them behind a door.

He stopped her as she passed, touched a strand of her hair, tucked it gently behind her ear. "Katie," he said quietly. "Honey, don't look like that. I said I'd sleep on the sofa. We need to talk; I know things between us can't be settled in bed. Tonight's not the night for the kind of discussion we have to have. You're tired." His thumb traced the dark smudge under her eye.

She looked up at him with a hint of a smile. "You're tired, too, Joe. Why don't we leave this mess? I can ask Millie to come back."

"Then get me a pillow and let's both get some sleep."

Sleep wouldn't come. Katie opened the sliding door to the balcony hoping the chant of the sea would relax her. Then she got up and closed it again. Her bed looked as though a monkey had slept in it. She would love a glass of iced tea. She had closed the shutters across the bar, so if she could get to the kitchen, the light wouldn't disturb him. But she would have to cross the living room to get there.

She kicked the covers aside, then a scant minute later, pulled them back to her chin. She'd been exhausted. What in the world was wrong with her now? An overdose of apprehension seasoned with adrenaline? Or Joe's presence in her living room? Memories of his tender lovemaking haunted her; each time she closed her eyes images formed on the inside of her lids like a motion picture. Vivid images, stirring images.

Finally she muttered a word that was not normally a part of her vocabulary, threw off the covers yet again and tiptoed to the door. It didn't make a sound as she eased it open. Her footsteps made no sound, either, on the thick carpet.

"I'm not asleep." When the strong male voice came at her through the darkness, she almost jumped out of her skin. She put a hand over her heart to quell its rapid beat.

A click and the lamp beside the sofa came alive, illuminating his broad, tanned torso. He withdrew his arm and rested on his elbows, his mouth curling slightly in sympathy. His hair was mussed, his eyes bloodshot. "I don't suppose you've got a cigarette around here, have you?"

"No, I don't smoke."

"Neither do I but right now I feel like I could use one."

Katie felt unsure standing there in her robe and looking down at him. His jeans and shirt were thrown carelessly over a chair. He was covered from the waist down by a quilt her grandmother had made, a particularly feminine design, which, oddly, emphasized his masculinity.

She didn't know why she should feel this way. Last night they had explored each other in as many ways as a man and woman could. There probably wasn't an inch of her he hadn't seen and she had touched and tasted and kissed the broad chest, including the angry scars.

A ready-made cure for her insomnia was right there in front of her. She could shed her robe; he would lift a corner of the quilt; she would crawl in beside him. His body would be warm and hard and smooth...she turned away. "Would a glass of iced tea do just as well?" she asked, moving toward the kitchen.

Joe squinted at the wall clock. "Sounds good. I can't sleep anyway."

Katie prepared the teakettle, spooned instant tea into a pot, filled glasses with ice, then remained in the kitchen trying to decide whether she was unwilling or unable to go back into the living room. Joe joined her a minute later. He'd pulled on his jeans and was barefoot.

He leaned back against the counter, his hands beside his lean hips, his fingers curled over the Formica edges, his legs crossed at the ankles and watched her. It was a deceptively easy stance, but she could feel the tension radiate from him even before he spoke. "Katie—" One hand went up to rake through his disheveled hair. "Since neither of us seems to be able to sleep anyway, maybe this would be a good time to talk."

She shrugged.

"I'm not very good at explanations, and I sure made a mess of things this morning, but I want to try again. I think the time has come to be completely honest."

She leaned against the opposite counter, mirroring his stance. The harsh overhead light shadowed the lines around his eyes, deepening them and giving him a harassed look.

"I was feeling exposed this morning, Joe. I suppose I overreacted." This was important to him. She wouldn't make the mistake again of passing this relationship off as negligible just to save her pride. Pride had interfered before. "You've been honest from the beginning. I never questioned that."

"You should have questioned. You should have questioned everything about me," he said harshly.

She started to tell him that he didn't owe her any explanations but he interpreted her thoughts correctly. "I have to explain, Katie," he said very softly, before she could speak. His eyes were blue enough to drown in. "And I think we both know why. There's no use trying to ignore it." He shook his head ruefully. "We've known each other barely more than a week, but we could probably fall in love, couldn't we?"

"Probably," she acknowledged after a moment.

"It would never work. Believe me. If I were a different man . . . if we'd met a decade ago . . ."

She was looking at her hands but at the unmistakable regret in his voice her gaze sought his. "If we'd met a decade ago I would have been fresh out of high school," she said with some asperity.

The kettle let off a shrill whistle. "I think I need to sit down for this." She stirred water into the pot. When it had dissolved she poured it over the ice, listening to the crackle as hot met cold. She handed him one of the glasses and led the way out onto the balcony.

The sky was dark; the moon had set hours ago. The only light spilled out from the kitchen. The ocean, at low tide, had grown calm emitting only a brush of sound against the shore. They seated themselves at the table across from each other.

Katie waited for him to speak first. When he remained silent she picked up the thread of conversation herself. "I don't see that when we met matters, Joe." She looked across the table. "Unless you're married or something."

His mouth curved but he faced forward. "No. I came close once. We lived together, we were planning to be married but..." He sighed heavily. "We didn't quite make it to the altar."

"Then I can't accuse you of being unfaithful."

When he spoke his voice held no trace of emotion. "I've been called much worse... I've been called a murderer and a coward."

She inhaled sharply. Joe felt his heart grow as heavy as a log in his chest. He dreaded this, the emotions he would see in her eyes, aversion, contempt, disgust—the withdrawal. But she surprised him.

"Who in the world would make such an accusation? That's ridiculous."

For a moment, just a brief, fleeting sliver of time, he felt his heart swell, thankful for her sudden, unexpected allegiance. Then he sighed. "No, it isn't ridiculous," he said heavily. "I did everything I was accused of."

Joe hunched forward in his chair, turning the glass in his big hands and staring out through the railing at the dark ocean beyond. His shoulders were rounded as though under a physical and psychological burden too heavy for any human to bear.

Katie felt the heavy weight as though it were her own. Her instincts told her also that there was something askew here. Joe might have killed in the line of duty but he was no murderer. As for cowardice—she didn't believe it for a minute. "Go on, Joe," she encouraged quietly. "Maybe it will help you to talk about it."

Joe set aside his tea and surged to his feet. Gripping the railing he continued to stare into the night but the scene playing before him was not framed by the sky nor the peaceful rhythm of the waves.

"It happened about two years ago. I was working undercover, investigating a connection between organized crime and the racing circuit. We were about to unravel a tangle of bribery, blackmail, extortion, and corruption that had been going on for years. We had caught some small fish but we needed one more piece of evidence in order to take on the big guys, the people in charge. Then I got a message from my boss at the Justice Department. They had reason to suspect that my cover had been blown. He ordered me to wind up my mission, gather whatever proof I could, and be back in Washington the next day. That night I got a call I'd been waiting for for months, to meet an informant at the track. The man was a driver for one of the bosses. He was going to give me a secret account book, one the accountants didn't even know about. In exchange we were going to place him in the witness protection program.

"I couldn't resist this one last try. We had worked for so long to get inside the operation...I should have seen...it was all a setup." He shook his head to clear his mind of remorse.

Joe remembered everything about that night. He remembered how the wind stirred the palms at Hialeah into an incessant rustling, making the high-strung Thoroughbreds fidgety. From the minute he'd set foot in the paddock, something had smelled wrong. But he'd still been confident he could handle the situation if he could find his informant. He was cocky, too damned cocky; but God, how he'd wanted to get the bastards. He'd been on this case for almost a year. He was determined not to walk away empty-handed.

The few lights that were left on at night were suddenly extinguished. The night was as quiet as death and black as the devil's heart. He froze, temporarily blinded by the abrupt darkness, but his remaining senses were alert. He began to move, carefully, quietly, toward the designated meeting place.

It had only taken a moment for him to realize that he was being followed—no, more like herded—by two people behind him and one off to the side. They were heading into an area under the grandstand. He decided to let himself be maneuvered, up to a point. He drew his gun and melted into the shadow of a concrete support column.

Then the shooting had started. Automatic fire was coming from all sides. At the sound of the first shot Joe had hit the ground rolling and come up firing. But the action hadn't saved him. He'd taken a bullet in the side.

The gun battle lasted less than a minute. He could still hear the ringing in his ears and the rush of running footsteps through the startling, inexplicable silence.

"When somebody finally turned the lights on I discovered that the only person I'd shot was not only carrying a toy weapon, but—" Joe had to pause a minute before he could go on "—he was retarded, Katie, and a kid, only eighteen years old. I knew him; he hung around the track." His head sank beneath the level of his shoulders. "He didn't die right away. He looked at me like a child who's fallen down and hurt himself. He wanted me to make it better." Joe shook his head. "There was no accusation in his eyes, he didn't even know I'd been the one who had shot him." Joe couldn't forget the boy's expression as he looked up from the dusty ground, puzzled and hurting and not able to understand why.

"Dear God," breathed Katie. She wanted to go to him but despite the vulnerability of his stance, something in the rigidity of his spine, the forbidding angle of his shoulders transmitted the stark message that her sympathy wouldn't be welcome. "What happened?" she asked, when it was evident that he wouldn't continue unless she prodded. "Did you have to go to trial?"

Joe straightened. "It didn't come to a trial, but it was a close thing." He shook his head. "They were thorough, I'll give them that. They didn't want me dead, just discredited. The Racing Commission would have raised hell with the Justice Department for interfering in their jurisdiction, enough to provide an effective smoke screen anyway. But they made one mistake.

"I wasn't supposed to be wounded, you see. I was supposed to be found alone there with the kid and the toy gun, making it look like I was trigger-happy. I never thought I'd be grateful for a bullet gone astray.

"The informant I was to meet that night was caught three days later boarding a plane for the Bahamas. He finally admitted the whole scheme, that they'd gotten wind of an infiltrator in their organization and that the young man I shot was a plant to smoke out my undercover status and frame me. I was vindicated in the departmental hearing,'' he told her.

It was apparent to Katie that he hadn't forgiven himself.

''After I got out of the hospital, and after the hearing, I took a leave of absence. The department shrinks pronounced me cured.'' A sharp bitter laugh escaped him. ''There's always a manpower shortage in the Department. They said I was ready to return to duty but I knew that someday a situation was bound to arise....''

Katie knew, at that moment, that she was in love with this man. Because his emotions were hers; because she felt his pain and sorrow, his remorse. His tears. She felt, too, his sense of hopelessness. She managed to keep her voice steady. ''Go on.''

''I was waiting for it, dreading it. Sure enough, a year later my partner, Jerry, and I ran into a hostage situation where I should have used my pistol. The man had already killed three people. I had the piece in my hand, pointed at the perpetrator, and I couldn't squeeze the trigger.'' He looked down at his palm, fingers outstretched, as though it belonged to someone else. Then he gripped the railing again. ''No one was any more surprised than I was when it happened. I froze as surely as if I'd been turned to stone. Jerry was wounded but managed to save both of our lives.

''There is no way on God's green earth I'll ever be able to forgive myself.'' He could rationalize the use of firearms all the other times during his career when it had been necessary, but he would never be able to fire a weapon again. Never.

He worked his hands into the pockets of his jeans, rocked on his heels but he didn't turn to her. ''I turned the weapon in; I haven't touched one since. The life I have is all I want. My boat, a reasonable relationship with my brother, a few friends."

"And the woman you lived with? What happened to her?"

"When she found out her hero had feet of clay, she split."

He lifted one shoulder, as though to shrug off a memory, a need. "I never blamed her. I'm a bad risk for a relationship. She taught me that I'd rather be an observer than a participant." He didn't add that it was all he'd ever be able to manage. "Do you understand, Katie? If things get too complicated, I'll leave Garden City."

His words held a poignancy, a yearning for more, that he didn't even hear, thought Katie. She felt very, very sad for both of them. She shook her head, unable to speak, unable to give him the reassurance he asked for. She loved him.

To always hold people at arm's length, to distance himself from the warm, loving relationships of life, that was not something she could relate to. She might be fiercely independent but she also cared deeply for her family, her friends, for Joe. She couldn't imagine a life without people to love.

Katie understood a lot of things now that she hadn't understood before about this complicated man. This incident from his past haunted him, heaped guilt on him; but first, his upbringing had made him wary.

He was wrong about something, though. He might deny commitment because it meant letting himself be vulnerable to his feelings. But he was committed whether he would admit it or not. She'd seen his caring side at Tim's, where people asked his advice, valued his opinions, appreciated his help. She looked over at his magnificent chest, at the scars along one side; and she realized that he was scarred as well, by something other than a weapon.

Her eyes burned with the desire to cry. For his sake, for the unpredictable situation in which he'd found himself embroiled, for what, in his eyes, was a failing that he had to live with forever.

But she wouldn't cry, wouldn't do that to him. He would interpret tears as pity. Maybe, soon, he would realize...

"Katie?"

"Yes, I understand," she lied. "Does Neal?"

"Hell, no. He's been making noises about hiring an investigator—me—ever since I got to Garden City." Joe returned to his chair and they sat there for a time, not speaking. But the silence wasn't uncomfortable.

The tension that had surrounded him like an aura seemed to have slackened with the telling of the horror tale. It was true that a future for them was as unlikely as a flight from this balcony railing. But he did need a friend to love him. Maybe, in time, he'd need a woman with tender feelings, too.

She yawned with no effort at all, and put her hand over his. "Do you think you might sleep now?" she asked.

Joe looked across at Katie, remembering the first time he'd seen her, flying barefoot down the dock, her eyes wide with fright, but her slender body strong with determination. He'd thought she was cute.

Now the light from behind them illuminated her tangled hair, her delicate profile, her sweet smile. Now when he looked at her his breath stopped at the sight of her exquisite beauty, the kind of loveliness that shines from within.

He sampled the deep regret that would be his companion for years to come—regret deeper than he'd felt when he left home at sixteen, deeper than he'd felt when his career had turned to ashes, deeper than he'd felt when his fiancée had turned away from him and his disgrace. He rose and used his hand to pull her up. "Maybe we both can sleep."

Back on the makeshift bed Joe watched the sky turn from black to dark gray. He was unaware of a tear that seeped from the corner of one eye and trickled down into his dark hair.

Chapter 10

The next morning Katie called Millie, who said she could come after lunch. Katie tried to prepare her but gave up after a minute. She hoped the woman wouldn't quit when she saw the havoc.

She had picked up her clothes, which had been strewn everywhere, the night before and had scooped them all in a pile to be washed or cleaned. She could barely stand to touch them. She found one clean bra and two pairs of panties in a drawer he hadn't dumped.

Finally she gave up and dressed for work. What Millie didn't get to, she would finish tonight.

She and Joe were walking out the door when the telephone rang. It was Raymond Timms. "Katie, could I have a ride to work? My car won't start. I'm afraid it's the alternator again."

She smiled. "That sounds serious."

If Joe thought the smile looked a little brittle, he didn't mention it. She'd been quiet this morning as she'd tried to do what she could to straighten up while he cooked breakfast for them both.

"It is serious," Raymond replied. "The garage here doesn't have one so they'll have to order."

Katie paused. "Hang on a minute, Raymond." She put her hand over the phone and turned to Joe. "This is Raymond from the station. He's having car trouble. If you're going to drive me anyway...?" She didn't have to finish; he was already nodding. "Raymond? I won't need the car for a day or so. Suppose I drop it off at your house on my way to the station."

"Great, Katie. Thanks."

Joe rode her bumper all the way to the north part of town where Raymond lived.

Raymond came out the front door of the bungalow as soon as he saw them pull up to the curb. He took the keys from Katie. "I'll be at the station in about ten minutes, as soon as I drop the kids at school," he said.

Raymond's wife, Gloria, commuted to her job in the city every day. "Okay. See you there. And don't worry about the car. Keep it as long as you need it."

"Thanks, Katie." He waved them off.

Joe dropped Katie at the station. "What time is your meeting?" he asked.

She had a meeting this morning with several members of the Chamber of Commerce and the mayor. Fourth of July weekend was almost upon them and they needed to finalize the last of the publicity for the special events that would mark the holiday. "At eleven-thirty."

"I'll be here."

"I could get used to having a chauffeur," she said three hours later when she climbed into the truck beside him. He had dropped her at work and returned to the boat to shower and shave. Now he was dressed in lightweight khaki slacks and a conservative pale blue-and-pink striped button-down shirt. His cuffs were rolled back to his elbows.

She sighed. "But I'll never get used to the reason. I wish this was over."

He reached across the seat for her hand. "Neal's making progress. Your tape of the phone call, finding the car, the prints on the soap wrapper...it's all coming together. He'll have a lead on this dude anytime now."

"And you? Are you going to help him?"

He shrugged. "I'm doing what I can."

"You could do more. With your background you could be a great help. You could let Neal make you a deputy."

"Look, I'm not much of a bodyguard without a gun; I'd be a hell of a deficient deputy." He dropped her off at the Chamber office without saying another word.

The meeting was over a few minutes after noon. The group was more worried about the forecast of rain for the holiday weekend than about anything else. Katie reassured them by admitting, though it provoked her to do so, that her weatherman had been wrong before. She was going to have to do something about the man. He hadn't even predicted the bad storm a week ago.

Joe was waiting. "Lunch?" he asked.

"Please. I'm starving," she answered as she climbed into the cab of the truck.

He took her to an open-air, seaside café. She rid herself of her jacket with a sigh of relief. When they were seated, she with her back to the sunlight, Katie had her first chance to study him head-on. All morning she had wondered what the effect of last night's revelations would be.

She caught her breath at what she saw in his expression. Their conversation last night seemed to have altered his frame of mind considerably. The sunlight reflected in his eyes rendering them a brighter, more optimistic blue. There was less constraint, less rigidity about his features.

He caught her staring and grinned. "Confession is good for the soul, it seems."

She grinned back. "I'm glad."

Over a salad and grilled shrimp, she broached the subject of his charters. "Joe, I know you can't continue to act as my bodyguard. You have a business to run. And didn't you say you have one charter you have to take out yourself? Is that tomorrow?"

"No, it's not until Friday. Maybe I'll get you to crew for me again."

"I can't. Friday is the big day, make-or-break, opening night, for the manager of WCTZ. The station owners are coming down to go over the 'book.'" At his questioning look she went on, gesturing with her fork as she talked. "Every May the results of the ratings for the previous year are published. It's called the 'book' and it's the bible of radio advertisers. A station with good ratings gets more advertising from national sponsors and it's easier to sell ads to the local merchants, too, if they know they're reaching a respectable audience."

Joe speared a shrimp off his plate. "And how are your ratings?" he asked around a bite.

Katie shrugged. "Okay, I guess," she said and continued to eat.

"Just okay?" he scoffed. "I can't imagine Katie Johns being satisfied with 'okay.' Tell me."

A tiny spot of dressing was on her lower lip; she caught it with her tongue. He should be used to it by now but it still played sudden and unexpected havoc with his libido. He shifted on the hard wooden seat and forced himself to concentrate on what she was saying. "The partnership that owns the radio station also owns sixteen others. They've been studying the book to evaluate how good a job I'm doing as compared with the other managers."

"And you're doing well," he suggested.

"I think so," she finally conceded. "Now it's a question of degree. When they bought this station last year and hired me to make it go, the programming had been allowed to slide along with the advertising. It's better than it was before. But it isn't as good as it could be." She crossed her fingers in her lap. "I hope it's enough for the owners. In another year I could really make a difference." She raised her glass of iced tea to her lips. "I'll know Thursday."

"Do you mean you could lose your job?"

"Nothing that drastic. But they might bring in another manager over me, someone with a lot of experience. I wouldn't like that." Katie tried to set her concern aside. There wasn't any use in worrying about it. She had done a good job. Either she won or she lost. "So that's why I can't crew for you and your charter."

Joe nudged his plate away and crossed his arms on the table. He'd been aware all along that she'd had job pressure to deal with as well as the threats from this man, but he hadn't known how intense that pressure was. She'd downplayed the importance of her situation to him and it made him feel guilty to think that he'd taken so much from her—her empathy, her understanding, her compassion—last night.

"Maybe by Friday it will be a moot point anyway. Neal's sent the prints to Washington. We both went through the airport logs this morning. He's assigned one of the state's investigators to do the interviews."

"If the man logged in," she reminded him.

"Yes. If. It's worth a try. Maybe they'll come up with something. Do you have any appointments away from the station this afternoon?"

"No. But I did want to meet my cleaning lady and try to explain why there's fingerprint powder all over the condo. I hope she doesn't quit when she sees the mess."

Joe reached for his wallet.

Katie was startled when she realized the waitress was standing there. She hadn't heard the woman approach. She'd felt a little nervous all morning.

"I'll talk to her. I'm meeting the locksmith and the glazier at your place at four," he said. She had agreed with his suggestion that she have a dead bolt added to her front door; she was still unsure about the bars but it seemed she had no choice.

"It might take them a while to fix the window, install the bars and the dead bolt. Will you wait for me at the station?"

She nodded her agreement and, picking up her purse and jacket, prepared to leave. "I have plenty to do."

Midday heat rose in heavy waves from the pavement in front of the restaurant. "Damn," said Joe. "I should have left the windows down in the truck. Wait here in the shade for a minute.''

He opened the door and, fighting an even hotter blast, reached in to start the engine. He returned to Katie's side. "Let it cool off in there. You couldn't sit on that vinyl. Your weatherman wasn't kidding when he said we were in line for the season's first heat wave."

"I'm glad he got something right," she said wryly as she propped her shoulder against a wooden post. "Whew," she said, fanning herself with her hand. "As long as the sea breeze can get to you, you're okay."

Joe smiled down at her, shoving his hands into his pockets. Then he turned away to scan the area.

Or that was what she thought he was doing. When he spoke again she wasn't so sure. His voice dropped an octave. "Katie—" he waited for a group leaving the café to pass "—I want to thank you for listening last night."

Katie didn't know what to say. She wished he would turn around and look at her. "I hope it helped to talk, Joe."

He rubbed the back of his neck with his hand. "Yeah, it did. You were a terrific listener." He returned his hand to his pocket. "I've never told anyone else the whole story."

Katie traced the line of his broad shoulders, solid and strong beneath striped broadcloth, with her eyes. She longed to comb her fingers through the shining clean hair that brushed his collar. On impulse she slipped a finger through the locker loop on the back of his shirt and tugged. "Gotcha."

He looked over his shoulder, a surprised smile beginning to curve the corners of his mouth. "What?"

She smiled and moved a step closer to his back. It was the nearest she'd been to him all day and she was hit suddenly by the tangy scent of his after-shave, mingling with perspiration and that indescribable male smell. Her smile was a secret one. "I like for someone to look at me when they're telling me I'm terrific."

Joe laughed out loud and turned too quickly for her to release her finger. It twisted in the tiny strip of fabric and her arm was over his shoulder. Her toes barely touched the ground. "Gotcha," he said, snaking a hand around her waist and lifting her fully against him. Their faces were inches apart.

Her smile faded. "Joe, you know what you said last night?"

"I said a lot of things," he answered.

"About us...that we could be falling in love..." she whispered.

He inhaled sharply. "Katie, dammit—" He would have released her, would have turned from her again but she held on.

"Shut up. Just shut up and listen," she said firmly. "I didn't ask you for anything, did I? I don't expect you to do anything about it. I just thought you needed to know that somebody cares for you. Now you can let me down."

She held her breath, waiting, feeling her heart pound wildly against his chest.

He smiled but it was a smile with no humor. As though he couldn't help himself, his head blotted out the sun; his mouth came down softly to cover her parted lips, his tongue darting inside to taste her.

She wrapped her other arm around his neck, murmuring his name softly into his mouth.

The jarring sound of a giggle broke them apart. Joe didn't spare a glance for the group emerging from the restaurant. He rested his forehead against Katie's for a minute. The skin there was damp; his breathing was shallow and ragged. "Katie, I don't know..."

She stopped him with a hand on his mouth. "No promises."

"Let's go," he said huskily. He set her on her feet and turned so she could free her finger from the loop on his shirt.

The air-conditioning had done its job. The truck was wonderfully cool. Katie lifted her hair off the back of her neck and hung her jacket over the seat between them. "I think I'll leave this here," she said. "I'm through being an executive for the day."

"I'm glad to hear it." Neither of them said anything about the kiss or her ambiguous declaration but in each of their minds was a question about what would happen between them tonight.

By the time Joe picked her up that evening, Katie had berated herself a hundred times for blurting out her feelings. She waved through the window when she saw him pull in. "I'll be right out," she mouthed.

He jammed the gearshift into park, glared at her and got out of the truck, slamming the door behind him. He looked—irritated. If his expression was anything to judge by, whatever was bugging him was her fault. And she was very much afraid she knew what it was. Despite her reassurances that she wasn't asking for a commitment, she'd placed a burden on him that he didn't want.

Her eyes narrowed at his expression. She'd seen that look on Joe's face before, the most recent time being last night when he'd walked in to find her condominium trashed, but it had never been directed toward her. It was a bit daunting. Something had changed drastically since lunch. She put her hand to her stomach and waited.

Joe hit the swinging glass door with the heel of his hand, strode through the reception area and down the hall to Katie's office. He was disgusted and fighting hard against anger, a battle he was losing.

Katie had taken up a position behind her desk. Her golden eyes were wide with wariness but he was beyond caring. He stalked straight over and threw something down in front of her. "Would you like to explain this?" he demanded in a dangerously quiet voice.

Her eyes fell to the object and her heart sank to her toes. There on the blotter before her was the book of matches she'd picked up the night Louise disappeared. "Oh, no," she breathed, stricken by her lapse. They had been in the pocket of her jacket. "Joe, I'm sorry. I picked up the matches off the table that night. I forgot about them."

"Forgot?" he mocked. "You *forgot*?"

She straightened, squaring her shoulders.

"Son of a bitch!" he whispered, taking long, deep breaths in an effort to control himself. "Katie, we have been over and over every step you took that night. How the *hell* could you possibly forget something like this?" His voice had gotten louder.

Her own tone rose to compete with his. "I just did! Okay?"

Raymond stuck his head around the door. "Hey, ya'll are gettin' pretty noisy. Everything okay in here?"

"Everything's fine," said Katie, coming out from behind the desk. "He wants to break my neck—and justifiably so—but I don't think he will."

"Don't be too sure," said Joe, shaking his head, but a wry smile was growing on his face. He rarely lost his temper; but this situation was beginning to wear on him. He'd been on his way to pick her up at the station. When he'd stopped the truck at a red light her jacket had slid from the back of the seat where she'd hung it, and he'd started to straighten it to keep it from wrinkling. The matches had fallen out of her pocket. Happy Birthday, Louise had leaped at him from the shiny peach cover.

Now he held out his arm and she went to him unreservedly.

"I'm so sorry. Do you really think it would have made a difference if I'd remembered earlier?"

Joe hugged her, then he lifted her by the waist and sat her on a corner of her desk. "Now tell me, who smoked, Louise or the man?"

Katie put a hand to her temple and closed her eyes, trying to remember. "Let me think. I didn't really pay much attention until later... wait!" Her eyes flew open, excited now, she went on, "They were sitting there at the table, talking. He pulled out a cigarette but he didn't have a light. You know how a man will pat his pockets."

"What happened next?"

Katie stared at a spot over his shoulder, but she was seeing the two people at the table. "She took the matches out of her purse. He lit his cigarette and started to put them in his pocket. She said something. She was smiling but he wasn't. I think—but I can't be sure—he returned them to her. Oh, damn! Why can't I remember?"

"You did good," said Joe. He planted his hands on either side of her hips and leaned forward to kiss her. The sound of Raymond whistling in the hall stopped him. He lifted her off the desk. "Let's go."

Raymond met them by the entrance. "I'll get the door," he said, taking out his keys to lock up. "See you tomorrow."

Inside the truck Joe hooked a hand around the back of her neck and pulled her to him for a hard, slow kiss. "Kissing you is getting to be a habit and it's been a long time since lunch," he murmured against her lips. He felt her smile.

In the back of his consciousness Joe heard the engine of the station wagon turn over—and turn over—but it didn't catch. He released Katie and put the truck in gear but before he moved, Katie stopped him with a hand on his arm.

"Just a minute. Let's make sure he can get that thing started."

The blast hit while she was still speaking. It threw the hood of the station wagon upward and back, against the windshield. The ground beneath them shook like an earthquake.

Joe exploded into action; ramming the truck into parking gear, he was out of the cab in an instant. As he raced for the blazing vehicle his mind, his powers of observation, kicked into overdrive, registering things he didn't even consider until later.

He wrenched open the door on the driver's side, released the seat belt and grabbed Raymond's left arm all in a quick fluid movement that took no cognizant thought. He tossed the man over his shoulder and ran, making a desperate dive to put distance between them and the car before the flames reached the gas tank.

That secondary explosion, following only seconds later, was the dangerous one. He turned his head, frantically searching through the nightmare of smoke and flame. "Katie!" His cry reached out toward her.

The impact of heat and concussion hit them like a wall. As he watched, Katie, half out of the truck, was thrown to the ground by the force of the impact as thoughtlessly as a bored child would toss a doll aside. But away from the destruction, thank God.

The car was destroyed in an instant, disappearing completely in an incredible inferno. A column of black smoke surged up to merge with the night sky. Bits of debris and metal rained down on them as Joe covered the injured man's body with his own.

Katie was at their side immediately, on her knees. Joe grabbed her arm; he had to touch her, to assure himself that she was all right. Tears were streaming from her eyes; her lips were moving; but the violent explosion had assaulted his eardrums, leaving him momentarily deaf to everything but the clanging in his ears.

"Joe! Oh, dear God, Joe." Katie squeezed the hand that had reached for her and ran her fingers anxiously over his face, his shoulders. She slapped at his smoldering sleeve. "Raymond—is he—"

Joe read her lips. He levered himself up on an elbow and looked at the man on the ground beside him. He placed his fingers on a pulse point on Raymond's neck. "Pulse is strong, but rapid. He might be going into shock. We've got to get him to the hospital." His ears were clearing but the words still sounded as though they'd been spoken by someone else, at a distance.

Raymond's eyelids fluttered, lifted. At first he merely looked dazed and confused but then he must have realized what had happened. He groaned and his eyes fell shut again.

"The truck will be faster than an ambulance." Joe got to his feet, picked Raymond up bodily and hurried to the truck. "Open the tailgate," he ordered tersely. "You'll have to ride back here with him."

Katie complied, fumbling only slightly with the chains. She hopped onto the bed of the truck and held out her arms.

A man from the service station next door came running up. "I called the fire department. What happened, Miss Johns?"

"Call the sheriff, too, Willie," said Katie, ignoring the man's request for information.

"Don't let anyone get near that car until he comes," added Joe. "Tell him we'll wait for him at the hospital."

At the note of authority in Joe's voice, the man nodded vigorously and took off to follow his command.

When Raymond was arranged as comfortably as possible Joe touched Katie's arm. "Hang on. I'll try to drive carefully."

"Are you all right?" she asked, eyeing his shirt sleeve. "Can you drive?"

"I'm fine."

The trip to the hospital, only a few blocks away, seemed an eternity to Joe. He pulled in under the harsh lights of the emergency entrance, jumped out of the truck and ran through the swinging doors.

The emergency room was almost deserted. Two teenagers sat across from each other, their eyes swollen and faces glowing a ruddy red. Too much sun was a common complaint in the summer, especially along this coastline where the sand was an extremely reflective white.

A uniformed nurse looked out from a treatment room where Joe could see a doctor stripping off gloves. Another teen was sitting on the side of a paper-covered table. At the sight of Joe's smoke-smeared face the nurse spoke in a quiet voice to the doctor and came right over.

Joe didn't wait for her to speak. "An explosion. There's a man outside in my truck."

The nurse spun on her heel and caught a wheeled stretcher by the handle, pushing it before her through the still flapping doors. The doctor was right behind her and Joe followed him.

"What happened?" the doctor asked as he pulled down the tailgate. He made a quick, cursory examination of Raymond's injuries before helping the nurse to maneuver the injured man onto the stretcher. He spared no glance for Katie.

"A car explosion," said Joe.

The man raised a brow and looked suspiciously at Joe. "Gasoline burns?" He and the nurse pushed the gurney between them with no wasted motion.

"No. It wasn't a gasoline fire," said Joe succinctly. They were back in the emergency-room lobby. "The sheriff's on his way."

"And your names?"

Katie answered before Joe could. "Katie Johns and Joe Ryder. This man is Raymond Timms. He works for me. It was my car that blew up."

The doctor looked at her then. "Sorry. You'll both have to wait out here."

"I'll call his wife," said Katie. "What can I tell her, Doctor?"

"I don't know yet," answered the doctor. He shut the door in their faces.

Katie fumed as she dropped a quarter into the telephone on the wall and dialed Raymond's home number. Joe joined her there. When she looked up at him, the enormity of what they'd just witnessed suddenly dawned on her. Her hands and voice started shaking. Still holding the receiver she stepped into his arms. "He acted like we were the guilty ones and he didn't even mention your burns," she said with quiet fierceness.

"I'm not hurt."

In response Katie took his arm and turned it over. The skin there was an angry red. She would have said more except the phone on the other end of the line was picked up. "Gloria, this is Katie." Oh, Lord—how to word this. "I'm at the hospital. Please don't get upset but there's been an accident and Raymond's being treated."

"Raymond? I'll be right there," Gloria said.

Katie was extremely grateful for the woman's calmness. Raymond had always been a perfect foil for his wife's mercurial temperament but when balance and stability were necessary, Gloria seemed to find them.

As soon as she put down the phone, Katie turned again into Joe's embrace. His arms were there for her, hard and tight and infinitely comforting, chasing away the shadows for her.

A sharp, hurtful image of Katie, lying on the emergency-room table instead of Raymond, formed in Joe's brain. He bent his head, burying his face in her neck, to inhale her scent, to taste her skin. *You were meant to be in that car. Oh, God, Katie.*

Though he didn't speak she absorbed his horror like a reverberation through her body. She buried her fingers in his smoke-scented hair, rocking him in her arms, giving as well as receiving comfort now. Finally she pulled away, touching his face gently. "Joe, you have to have your arm looked at."

Another nurse spoke from the admissions counter. "Dr. Villana is on his way from X-ray," she said in terse tones. "Would you both step over here for a minute, please?"

Joe had become still under Katie's gentling caress. He seemed preoccupied and strangely quiet. He gave Katie a gentle shove toward the counter as he said, "Take care of this, will you? I think I hear my brother coming."

True enough, the sound of a siren that Katie had only noted subconsciously grew louder. Joe covered the distance to the doors with long strides as it reached an ear-splitting crescendo.

"Sir?" said the nurse.

Katie watched him for a minute, then turned to the woman. "He'll be back."

The woman had a sheaf of papers to be filled out and a number of questions to be answered. Katie made an effort to keep her mind on the answers but she was distracted not only by her worry for Raymond, but also by Joe and Neal talking together in a corner of the waiting room. Contrary to what she expected, Neal looked pleased. She couldn't imagine anything in this situation to be pleased about.

Joe was saying, "Neal, I want in. All the way in."

His brother lifted a brow. "All the way? As in a badge and gun?"

"Yes. A badge and a gun." Joe was angry, fiercely, frantically, ferociously angry, as he described the explosion to Neal. Katie was supposed to be in that car. At the idea that it might have been her lying injured and unconscious—or worse—in the treatment room he had felt physically sick. He had to swallow the bile that rose in his throat.

Raymond was bigger, stronger than Katie. The blow, a result of his head hitting the side window at the force of the explosion, would render him unconscious. It might have snapped her neck. He was wearing a shirt and jacket, which had given him some protection from the blast. The short sleeves of Katie's light cotton dress would have been no protection at all.

A deep, empty feeling spread through Joe at the thought that he might have lost her forever.

He nodded in response to his brother's question, clenching his jaw. He would never be sure he could use a weapon until it was too late to think of an alternative, but maybe a gun would serve as a deterrent. Especially since the man was an amateur.

He explained to Neal what had happened. "The explosion was a botched job. If he'd been a pro, Raymond would have been dead. I didn't take time to examine the wreck but I noticed a few things. One, the explosion blasted outward. The hood flew up and the force went out and up from underneath. Two, it looked like a dynamite blast."

Neal nodded, confirming Joe's suppositions.

"I thought so. It didn't act like plastic," Joe mused. "A pro would have had access to plastic but an amateur probably would not." Thank God. Plastic explosives did more damage and all you had to do was slap them into place.

"Even so he has to have some knowledge of explosives."

Joe agreed but he was more interested in the man's motive. "He would have been nervous, hanging around the station for long enough to wire dynamite. He's getting agitated, Neal; he's pushing. And there's a reason for it, one that we haven't seen yet. He can't run. Something holds him here. If we only knew what the hell it is."

The arrival of Gloria Timms interrupted their conversation. Neal and Joe joined Katie in answering what questions they could.

At last the doctor came out of the treatment room. "He's going to be all right."

Katie sagged against Joe. The doctor went on, "He has a granddaddy of a headache and I'd like to keep him here overnight but you can see him now."

Katie followed Gloria and the doctor into the treatment room.

Neal watched them go then said quietly, "I have a badge and gun in my trunk. Walk out with me."

"You were sure I'd change my mind about this?" Joe asked as he accepted the holstered weapon and the folder with the badge of sheriff's deputy. The badge he shoved into his back pocket; the weapon he put in the glove compartment of the truck then locked the vehicle.

"No. I wasn't sure. I was hopeful that after you had time to think last night, the break-in might spur you to take an official part in the investigation. Things are breaking quickly. I've been promised an answer by tomorrow on the prints."

"I've got something that might even be quicker than that." He handed Neal the matches and explained where they had come from. "I've got a feeling about these matches, Neal. If Dan wasn't the one with her . . ."

Neal nodded, turning the packet over in his fingers to read the name of the resort. "I'll ask him. If not I'll get in touch with the manager out there. And hope the jerk made reservations."

"I was planning to spend the day with Katie at the station. But I can't just sit on my hands, Neal. If you'll put a man with her—"

Neal nodded again. "We're narrowing down the area of the dragging operation so I can spare a man to be there all day."

"When and where do you want me to start?"

"Tomorrow. I want you to go by Annette's place." He tore a page from his notebook and handed it to Joe. "Here's the address. She knows more than she's telling but I can't get her to open up. Maybe you'll have better luck."

Joe glanced at the slip of paper, folded it and put it in his pocket. "I'll try. Maybe the news about the blast will help her remember."

As he was speaking a frown spread over Neal's brow. "What the hell—" He caught Joe's arm and turned it over as Katie had done. Then his eyes came up to lock with Joe's. His expression was solemn and pensive. "Look, Joe, you're my brother. My only brother and I love you. Take care of yourself, too. Please."

Joe met his brother's eyes. He couldn't speak. Katie first . . . Neal . . . his brother had never said anything like that to him. He was affected, deeply affected.

But he didn't know how to respond. Affection, compassion, sentiment, were all emotions that were so foreign to him.

Frustrated by this flaw in himself, he dropped his eyes to his arm and swallowed hard. "It looks worse than it is, but it's beginning to burn." Actually it was hurting like blazes. "I'll get something to put on it before I take Katie home. And I'll call you in the morning after I've seen Annette." He hesitated. "Thanks, Neal," he said, his voice sounding gruff. He started back toward the swinging doors.

"Hang on," said Neal.

Joe swung around.

"Haven't you forgotten something?" asked his brother with a small smile that included understanding.

Joe couldn't think of anything he'd overlooked. He was anxious to get started. There was nothing to do until morning. Protecting Katie was his first priority right now. He hated for her to be out of his sight for this long. "What?" he asked.

Neal sauntered over, the smile spreading to a grin. "Raise your right hand and repeat after me..."

Chapter 11

The bars were in place. Shiny new locks were on her doors.

Katie looked around her living room. Except for the blank place on the wall where her watercolor had hung and her ferns, which had been beyond salvage, the room looked as it had two days ago. Still she couldn't escape the feeling of being somehow—violated. She crossed quickly to the bedroom.

Joe sauntered along behind her, watching but not commenting until she was satisfied.

The closet looked bare with the few clothes left hanging there. The cleaners had picked up most of her things. Her shoes were lined neatly on the floor; they looked as though they had been polished. The mirror was clean. She sighed. "I feel like it's home again," she said finally when they were back in the living room. She collapsed on the sofa.

Joe headed for the door. "You're not leaving?" she asked stupidly. When he didn't answer immediately she apologized. "I'm sorry, Joe. It's none of my business."

He smiled slowly and leaned over the back of the sofa, sliding his fingers into her hair at the nape, working the tense muscles there. "It's very much your business and you know it. You may as well know, too. I'm an official deputy sheriff."

She rolled her head under the pressure of his fingers. But at the last statement, she became very still, hope blossoming in her chest, hope that he was making the first move to put his past behind him. She twisted her body so that she was looking at him across the back of the sofa. His hand fell away from her neck. "What coercion did Neal use this time?"

Stiff-armed he bent forward to cover her lips with a soft kiss. "I volunteered."

Her heart leaped. She strained toward him, returning the kiss. "You did?"

"Yeah, I did. Can you believe it?" He laughed to himself; then he sobered. "When I saw that car go tonight, and knew that you were supposed to be in it, I knew that I couldn't stay on the outside any longer."

She had to be careful not to read too much into this. She placed her hands on the sides of his face. "You haven't been outside since that first night, Joe. You've been involved from the first, whether you'll admit it to yourself or not. Because whatever you say about being an observer, you're not one. You care about the people you know. I saw that the night we went to Tim's."

He stared at her and straightened. "Yeah, well, maybe," he said as though he didn't believe a word of it.

"I left something in the truck," he muttered. "I'll be right back."

While Joe was gone, Katie, energized by this breakthrough, went to the kitchen to see what she could come up with for dinner. Neither of them had eaten since lunch. Lunch. Lord, it seemed an eternity since they'd eaten that meal on the porch of the small seafood restaurant.

When Joe returned he found her leaning over, peering into the refrigerator. He came up behind and slid his arm around her waist.

She jumped, letting out a small scream. "Don't *do* that!" she snapped, then apologized immediately. "I'm sorry but, Lord, you scared me to death."

Joe shook his head. "I should have known better," he said. Katie might present a brave front but deep down she was frightened.

"You've been busy," she observed dryly. Inside her refrigerator were steaks, potatoes, lettuce, mushrooms, celery, several bottles of salad dressing, and a magnificent strawberry cheesecake, which she recognized as being from a New York-style deli downtown, as well as several kinds of cheeses, bacon, eggs.

"Yeah, well, I checked. Aside from leftover lasagna, key lime pie and a carton of milk with an expired date, your refrigerator was empty."

"How did you know what to buy?"

"Your cleaning lady helped me make a list and I went shopping while she cleaned the place," he told her. "She said you like steak. Besides it's the only thing I can cook."

Millie had no idea about Katie's preference in food. More likely he made the list and asked if she thought

Katie would like what was on it. Millie, being a woman, probably agreed without ever looking. She chuckled softly. "Generous of you. All this looks interesting but isn't it a bit late to cook such a big meal?"

"We could just graze and have the steaks tomorrow night." He took a banana from the fruit bowl he'd filled earlier and started to peel it. He crossed his legs at the ankle and leaned a hip against the counter as he ate. "Have some."

"Thank you." They each ate a banana and a peach, but Katie demurred when he offered her a bunch of grapes. She pushed the hair back from her face with a tired gesture. "That's enough for me. I'm going to have a bath and get ready for bed."

"Okay." Joe watched her go. He finished off the grapes and poured himself a big glass of milk. The telephone on the wall rang. He could hear the sound of the shower so he shrugged and picked up the receiver.

"Hello."

There was silence on the other end, such a long silence that Joe felt the tension build in the muscle at his jaw. Was this the man? Just before he let loose a few choice words, he heard a sound, like someone clearing his throat.

"This is Joe Ryder, isn't it?"

He recognized the voice immediately. The tension drained away leaving him as deflated as a balloon. "Yes, it is. I'm sorry, Dr. Johns, Katie can't come to the telephone right now. May I have her call you back?"

"That won't be necessary." He paused. "Not since I know you're with her." Another pause. "Her mother and I didn't like the idea of her being alone." The man seemed to be having difficulty with this conversation. "I finally got the whole story out of Neal. Joe...thank you for being there for Katie. She's very special to us.''

"She's very special to me, too, Dr. Johns," he said in a low voice.

"Well, tell her to call if she needs anything."

"Yes, sir. I will."

"Goodbye."

Joe blew out his breath over his lower lip. Then he took the gun from behind his belt and gazed at it for a long time. Finally he entered the living room and searched for a place to put the damned thing.

He was still looking when Katie entered the room. The sight of the gun in his hand stopped her in her tracks.

"I was looking for a place to hide it," he explained quickly. He struggled to disregard her clean, shiny face, her long legs under the knee-length robe and the mingled scents of soap and toothpaste. He stared down at the weapon as though he'd picked up a snake. "You know," he said thoughtfully. "For years one of these was a constant companion. I used it a few times and I felt as naked as a baby if I didn't have it with me. Now I feel like I've never even held one."

Katie swallowed the dry lump in her throat. It wasn't as though she'd never been around guns. Her father and brothers were hunters. When she was younger she'd done some target practice herself. But seeing Joe holding this one, and in her living room, was a shock. "Is that part of the official uniform?" she asked.

"I guess so."

Clearly he wasn't happy having the gun in his hand. There was a long silence. At last Katie broke it. "Well, I'm ready for bed. Good night, Joe," she said, starting to turn away.

"Katie?" She halted. "Your dad called while you were in the shower. He said to let them know if you needed anything."

A smile of pure amusement formed on her lips. "Did you tell him I was in the shower?"

"Of course not." Joe blushed. Joe Ryder actually blushed.

"Did he give you a hard time?" she asked.

The color receded. "No. As a matter of fact he was gracious, said he was glad I was with you."

She sighed heavily. "I suppose Neal told him everything."

"Yeah, he did."

Her brows rose. "And Daddy didn't say he was coming right over to get me? That's progress." She smiled again. "Well—good night, Joe."

The idea of being alone was suddenly difficult. "Don't go to bed yet," he said. Joe stowed the pistol in the drawer of the lamp table beside the sofa and sat down, patting the cushion next to him. "Sit with me for a while."

She hesitated briefly. "Okay, if you lend me your shoulder." She curled her feet under her and leaned against him. They sat quietly for a minute. At last she tilted her head back against his hard shoulder. "I really feel dumb for forgetting about the matches, Joe," she said softly.

He rubbed her arm, reassuring her. "Honey, I'm not angry. But if you think you can stand it, I would like to go back over that night one more time. Maybe there's something else."

Katie went over the story again, explaining about the

matches. But the telling of the story reactivated her dread. Her muscles began to tighten; her nerves to sing. She *hated* the feeling.

Joe noticed. He reached for her clenched fist and gently opened her fingers one by one. Her beautiful eyes bewitched him. "At least now we know why he trashed your apartment."

"You think he was looking for the matches?"

"I'm sure of it. There had to be something that would lead back to him. And when he couldn't find them he became more desperate. The car bomb was a reckless measure and reckless men make mistakes. We're getting close."

"Close isn't good enough, is it?" she asked on a tired sigh. He shook his head. Her eyelids drooped and she lay her head on his shoulder again. "I just hope we can get through this without anyone else getting hurt."

Joe lifted her hand to his lips. It was a courtly gesture, totally uncharacteristic, and it surprised him. The tension was there between them, ebbing and flowing as relentlessly as the tides. "Go to bed," he ordered softly.

"Good night. Thank you for the locks and bars and groceries." He laughed. She kissed his cheek, smiled a sleepy smile, rose and left the room.

When he was alone Joe raised a hand to pinch the bridge of his nose. He sighed, linked his fingers behind his neck and rested his head on the back of the sofa. The matches, an errand he'd take care of tomorrow if Neal didn't have any luck. He'd go out to the resort and ask a few questions. But first he had to see Annette. He'd get the story out of her this time.

His eyes fell shut. He'd be glad, too, when this was all over. He was almost asleep when a sound intruded, a soft domestic sound. Katie was moving around in her bedroom. The soft footsteps roused him. He surged to his feet, scraping his hair back with a hand that shook and headed for the guest bath.

The toothbrush she'd provided for him was in the holder. Last night hers had hung beside it; she refused to reenter the bath off her bedroom until after Millie had cleaned it. He muttered a gutter word; it made him feel better.

When he came out of the bathroom a few minutes later he turned left instead of right as though a magnet pulled him in that direction. He just wanted to see her, he told himself.

"Joe?"

"I didn't mean to wake you. I wanted to see if you were all right."

Katie smiled into the semidarkness. "Come here," she whispered.

"No. I'm beat and I know you are, too." But he approached the bed. The mattress tilted as he sat beside her. Her scent, the sweetness of wildflowers, reached his nostrils. She reached for his hand. "Katie...I'm warning you..."

Katie laughed and lifted the sheet invitingly. "Don't worry, I won't jump you. That sofa can't be comfortable and you're too tired to do anything but sleep tonight."

And, dammit, it was true. He shucked his slacks, lay down beside her, reached out to gather her close and slept.

"Katie, I mean what I say. Don't open this door until I get back."

"Yes, sir." She thought she had concealed her smile but obviously not. He was grumpy this morning. It was barely six o'clock. They had slept together, curled up like spoons in a drawer. It was one of the most satisfying experiences Katie had ever had.

He'd awakened first and eased out of the bed. He had brewed the coffee and dressed before he woke her with a cup and a cautionary word to wait for him to return.

"There isn't one funny thing about this situation," said Joe.

The smile faded immediately. When she spoke her voice was quiet. "I understand that, Joe. I know it's inappropriate for me to feel—" she searched for a word to describe her feelings "—light-headed. Maybe it's a reaction to the things that have happened. I feel like we've won a skirmish with this monster." She lifted a hand and let it fall to her side. "I'm relieved that Raymond is all right, and you're all right."

Joe noted that, despite her words, the hand she used to gesture was shaking. He sat on the edge of the bed and pulled her off the pillows and into his arms. "And you, Katie," he said huskily. "And you." He held her for a while. It would have been wonderful to stay all day with her right here in this bed. He wanted to hold her sweet body and make long, slow love to her, but first things first. He had a lot to do, things that would help keep her safe. Her safety was more important than his desire.

As though she read his mind, she murmured, "I won't open the door until you get back, I promise. Having you around gives me a sense of security."

For a moment Joe was taken aback by the comment. At last he tilted her chin up and covered her mouth with his. "I'll see you at eight-thirty," he muttered huskily when he released her.

When Joe arrived at the address Neal had given him, he found a clean but modest quadraplex. According to the address the apartment number was 1-B. The door to 1-A was labeled Manager and moved imperceptibly as he entered the foyer. He rang the bell to Annette's unit but got no answer. Finally he crossed the hall and pushed the button for the manager's apartment.

"Can I help you?" The woman, who peered with one eye over the chain, was wary. Despite the early hour she was dressed.

"Yes, ma'am," said Joe with a reassuring smile. "I'm looking for Annette."

"Oh, she's moved out. Just yesterday."

Moved out? Had she run? "Would you by any chance have her new address?"

The woman eyed him keenly with both eyes now. "I don't think I should give that out to just anybody that comes looking."

"Of course." Joe thought of the warning he'd delivered to Katie a short while ago. He thrust his hand through his hair. How was he going to get the woman to open up? Suddenly, chuckling to himself, he remembered the badge in his pocket. He was legitimate he realized with some surprise—a status he'd never expected to repeat again. "Here is my identification. I'm a deputy with the sheriff's department." He smiled.

The woman was charmed. "I'm Mrs. Marvin. Come in, Officer." She slipped the chain free and opened the door. "Have a seat. May I get you something? Coffee or tea?"

Joe didn't correct the misnomer. He sat on a Victorian sofa that was as hard as a concrete bench, refused the offer of coffee or tea, was surprised and tempted when she added the offer of a beer, but turned that down, too.

Finally he got the address, and recognized it as being in an expensive high rise. Quite a step-up. How could she afford such a jump now that she was unemployed? He rose to leave but stopped for one more question. "Mrs. Marvin, did Annette have a lot of visitors?"

She pursed her lips. "I'm sure I don't know," she said huffily. "I don't keep watch on the tenants' comings and goings."

Joe smiled again, more warmly this time. "I didn't mean to suggest that you do. I just thought you might have noticed a strange car parked in front."

"No, her latest friend didn't have a car."

Joe held his breath. "Really?"

"He came on foot. I thought that was strange, too. He was very well dressed. Not that there's anything wrong with walking, he just didn't seem like the type who would want to. He was always in a hurry, you see."

"Do you remember what he looked like?" asked Joe, his heart thudding in anticipation.

The description jibed with Katie's. Why had Annette lied? Joe asked the woman for permission to use her phone and called Neal to report the move. His brother had a sobering bit of news for him, too. He got out of there fast.

He'd been correct about the step-up. The landscaping around the building was lush and extravagant. This apartment was more geared to tourists and weekly rentals than to permanent residents. He found the apartment and rang the bell.

Annette was not alone but the man who lounged casually on the plush upholstered sofa in his bathrobe definitely wasn't the man Joe sought.

He'd been hoping to catch her off balance by appearing so early but there was nothing uncertain about her demeanor. She stood in the doorway with her hand on one thrust-out, leotard-clad hip. This wasn't the Annette they had met the day after Louise had disappeared. That Annette had been sensual but ladylike; this one was a siren. "Mr. Joe Ryder, right?"

"That's right," said Joe. "I presume Mrs. Marvin called. May I come in?"

She shrugged as though she didn't care one way or the other and sauntered away, bestowing upon him a prime back view of swinging hips. The man on the sofa didn't move when she introduced him as her fiancé, Steve Sutton.

"Perhaps we should talk in private," suggested Joe.

"I don't have anything to hide from Steve," said Annette as she joined Sutton on the sofa.

Joe looked around. Expensive, he noted, very expensive. Hi-tech and glass; chrome and leather. There was nothing here that hadn't been selected by a decorator. It lacked the warmth and charm of Katie's condominium. "Nice place. Quite a step-up."

"Yes, I inherited some money recently."

"Annette, you're playing with fire."

She shared a secret smile with the man beside her. "I don't know what you're talking about."

"Then let me enlighten you." Though he hadn't been invited, Joe took a seat at right angles to them. He leaned forward, elbows on his knees, hands linked loosely between his legs. "Last night a man was injured in a car explosion that was meant for Katie Johns. You may know him, Raymond Timms. Luckily the attempt wasn't done very efficiently or he would be dead." He paused to give serious weight to his next disclosure. "Louise Austen wasn't so lucky. They dragged her body up from the harbor at dawn this morning."

When he'd called from Mrs. Marvin's apartment, Neal had informed him of the grisly discovery. At that moment, Joe had realized just how much he'd hoped that this whole thing was an aberration, that Katie had made a mistake, that the call to the station, the vandalism, the explosion, everything connected was somehow a horrible coincidence. But he'd learned long ago that there were no coincidences in this business.

It was a lesson he shouldn't have forgotten.

Annette gasped at his disclosure but Joe ignored her and went on. To enhance the shock effect, he spoke conversationally, deliberately letting the mildness of his voice contrast with the horror of his words. "Louise's husband, Dan, is at the morgue right now trying to identify her remains. It won't be easy. Do you know what a body looks like when it's been in the water for a week or so? The fish won't have left much flesh on the bones but what there is will be bloated and discolored.

"Now," he said, leaning back in the chair. "Do you want to tell me about the man who visited you in your old apartment?"

"I don't know what you're talking about," she whispered. Her face was parchment white in contrast to her fuchsia leotard. Sutton looked sick.

But Joe was unable to shake their story that they knew nothing. Finally he shook his head and wearily got to his feet. "You're really stupid, you know it?" he snapped.

"A smart person doesn't blackmail a killer and expect to get away with it." He breathed in and out in a concentrated effort to calm himself. "You are in grave danger, Annette. You, too, Sutton if you're in on this. More important to me is Katie Johns. The man might not have been successful with a car bomb, but there are a lot of ways to kill. I'd be careful if I were you."

Annette's eyes flicked to her fiancé; he gave a small shake of his head.

Joe took one more stab at it. "You might decide to leave town suddenly. If you remember something after you're gone, here's my number." He took out his wallet and gave her a card, one of the ones he gave out to his charter customers. He looked at them both for another minute; then he left.

Katie dressed comfortably in a cool wraparound skirt, a tailored shirt in matching aquamarine, and slid her feet into flat-heeled sandals. She didn't intend to leave her office today except to make sure the maintenance men had done their job and that every inch of the station was spotlessly clean and the grounds neatly mowed and shrubbery trimmed.

Most of the station's accounting books were in order but there were other small jobs to be done. She had the weekly check of the EBS, Emergency Broadcasting System, equipment today. The file of public letters, both critical and complimentary, had to be updated for the second quarter of the year. Everything had to be ready and perfect for tomorrow.

She'd been watching for Joe's truck from her spare-room window. When he pulled into the parking lot, she waited obediently for him to come to the door for her.

"Did you see her?" she asked as soon as he entered.

He ran a frustrated hand around the back of his neck. "Yeah. She still won't open up." He described Annette's new condominium.

"Good Lord, Joe! That's the most expensive building on the beach. The owners of the radio station are thinking about buying a unit there, and they're very rich."

He hooked an arm around her neck, throwing her off balance for a second. His expression was distracted and he held her solidly against him.

She wrapped her arms around his waist. "Speaking of the owners, I've got to get to work." She started to withdraw.

"Wait." He tightened his arm across her shoulders and looked down into her eyes. She met and held his gaze, realizing that he had something to tell her and the news wasn't good.

For a long moment they didn't speak. Slowly, magnetically, his mouth was drawn to hers.

Katie might have been mistaken but it seemed to her that when their lips finally met, the kiss held a tender promise. But his expression remained deeply troubled.

She knew before he spoke what was coming. She closed her eyes to prepare herself, then she opened them again. "Louise?"

He nodded.

Held within his strong embrace she could handle anything, she thought.

"Honey, they found her body this morning."

She was wrong.

"Did you find out anything about the matches?" she asked when Joe picked her up that night.

"Dan didn't take her to the resort for her birthday, which was in March. The reservation book for March is in a storage building. They'll have to find it tomorrow.

"Tonight you're coming back to the boat with me," he went on with a single-minded resolve.

Too much was happening at once. She had an armload of files. The media had the full story now and her secretary had fielded most of the phone calls and visits but Katie still hadn't finished everything she had to do in preparation for tomorrow.

"All right," she answered.

"We'll stop at the condo to pick up your clothes and take the steaks with us, too."

"Fine."

"And we'll sleep together again."

"Mmm."

Joe slanted a look at her. "What does 'mmm' mean?" he asked.

He was nervous, she realized. Joe Ryder didn't like to ask. She'd bet he'd never asked a woman in his life. How could he be nervous about that? She'd already all but admitted she was in love with him.

But his shoulders were braced as though for a blow.

Keep it light, she told herself. This man would take a lot of convincing. Slowly she found a balance she'd needed all during this long, hellish day. Her mouth curved into a sly, teasing smile. "It means I have a lot of work to do but I'll try to fit you in."

Joe visibly relaxed at her tone. His mouth curved up at one corner. "You're a hard woman, Katie Johns," he cracked. "You'd better get started. I'm not a patient man."

"I'd say you were very patient," she said.

"What time do these people arrive in town tomorrow?"

"They're already in town. They're staying in the condo I told you about this morning. But I don't have to be at the studio until eight-thirty, if that's what you're asking."

"That's what I'm asking." His smoldering gaze was a distraction but when she would have moved forward into his arms, acknowledging the sexual tension between them, he deliberately held her off. "Let's get going."

The boat looked like home to her as they walked the length of the docks toward his slip. Her small sandals, his deck shoes made soft slapping sounds on the weathered wood. Joe carried her files in one hand against his hip and held her hand with his other.

She was reminded of a time when she was young, walking home from school with Billy MacDougal, her first boyfriend. They'd swung their clasped hands, filled with joy and the elation of first love.

She looked up at Joe's profile. Not a boyfriend, not a boy. A man. All man. Suddenly she put their hands in motion, swinging them forward. By the time they reached the backswing he'd recognized what she was doing and laughed, the sound seasoned with both affection and poignancy.

They probably looked ridiculous but she didn't care. They needed simplicity tonight, a healthy, fresh atmosphere. She fought off the image of Louise that had brought tears to her eyes regularly all day long.

"This reminds me of when I was fourteen. Except I never carried any girl's books home," he admitted.

Amazing. He *had* read her mind. Or their thoughts were so attuned they followed the same wavelength. "The girls probably carried yours," she responded tartly.

He didn't answer, just smiled that maddening, mysterious little smile.

The boat gave a gentle lurch as they jumped aboard. Joe handed her the files and said, "Go on below. I'm going to move us."

"Move the boat? Where?"

"Out next to the channel buoy." When she still looked puzzled he explained further in a tender, gentle tone. "Anyone walking along these docks could just step on board, honey. I don't want to be taken by surprise."

Katie's pleasant mood drained away like air from a child's balloon. "Sure, I guess you have to," she said softly, so softly that she didn't think he'd heard.

"I wish I could encourage you to forget your worries for good, Katie, but you've got to be on your guard every minute," he said seriously.

She looked up at him, the golden gaze wide, admitting what he already knew. "When I'm with you I'm safe."

Joe had pondered her brand of trust earlier. He'd tried to deny—and asked himself whether he could handle—the responsibility. He still wondered but found he was basking in her faith. Whether or not the faith was deserved was another question, one which he wouldn't know the answer to until, possibly, it was too late.

But he knew he would do everything that was humanly possible to prevent harm coming to her. Including carrying the damned gun. Whether or not he could use it was the big uncertainty.

He patted her rump. "Scoot," he ordered, and climbed quickly to the flying bridge.

Occasionally over the next couple of hours, she would look up to find him watching her with an absorbed gaze. Each time she would relax against the back of her chair, feeling her heart melt within her, ready to put aside thoughts of anything other than him.

Joe continued to steer her gently back to work, insisting that she finish with every detail. He helped her organize her presentation. He also cooked the steaks in the small galley and allowed her time to eat. Finally she tossed down her pen and lifted her arms over her head in a long stretch of tired muscles. "That's it. I'm done. If there's any statistic I haven't memorized..." She shrugged and let her hands fall to her lap.

The smile that had begun on his face as he watched her wind down spread to illuminate his blue eyes with hunger and banked fires.

A corresponding ribbon of heat curled within her.

Without a word he stood and came to her.

"Is it unfeeling to want you as much as I do? When Louise..." She choked on the words and held out her hands blindly.

Joe scooped her up from the chair into his arms. "No, by God, it isn't," he said, his voice strong, convinced.

The smile had vanished; his eyes blazed with a profound emotion that was so close to love, so very close. Katie held on to his shoulders as he strode through to the cabin in the bow. "Then tonight we celebrate life. I'm aching for you," she whispered as he let her feet slide to the floor.

Their clothes seemed to melt away. He kissed her, touched her, charting her body like a blind man. Every move he made was gentle and slow, but underlying his tenderness was a simmering intensity that encouraged her growing excitement.

Each one of her senses was finely, delicately attuned to him. His voice, a husky whisper murmuring encouragement, seemed to surround and fill her, traveling along the nerves beneath her skin, then surfacing to meet the caress of his mouth, his tongue. Her swelling hunger was underscored by his scent; her ache, spreading out from the center of her desire, smoldering like a fire banked, magnifying until she couldn't tell where he touched her, where his body ended and hers began.

Then he was inside her. The universe dipped and paused and swayed, held its breath and burst into a thousand shards of shimmering light. Her nails dug into his shoulders as her body pulsated in climax.

Joe didn't think he would ever breathe again. He held himself rigid, waiting, until the last shudder radiated from her body. Then he finally loosened the slender thread of control he'd been able to maintain. And the world exploded around him. He bucked wildly, the storm of his release driving her deeper into the soft mattress. He muffled his shout in the soft skin of her neck.

He raised himself on his elbows. He brushed the damp hair back from her forehead. "Oh, babe, did I hurt you?" he gasped.

"No, oh, no." She opened her mouth, pulling his head down. Their tongues reached, tasted, savored.

Holding her hips to keep their bodies joined, he turned. She lay over him, his hands moved in long, sweeping caresses from her thighs to her shoulders and back again.

Later, when they could breathe again, and speak, Joe repeated his concern. "Are you sure I didn't hurt you? God, I've never lost myself like that."

"I'm sure I left some scars myself," she answered softly, soothing his shoulders with her fingertips. She raised herself to kiss the spot. The action scraped her breasts across his chest, her smooth thigh against his hair-roughened one.

She felt him stir within her. Her lips parted in a small smile of pleasure and inquiry and satisfaction. "Joe...?"

Joe sifted his fingers through her hair, holding it away from her face. His eyes were hooded but a half smile met hers. "With a woman like you . . . anything's possible."

Chapter 12

Mrs. Anita Nelson, née Anita Rayburn, and her partner, Neil Jones, were the heirs to the partnership of Rayburn and Jones Communications, Inc., or as the company was more commonly called, R and J Communications. Established by their grandfathers, the company had grown slowly but consistently.

A beautiful woman in her forties, Anita was the younger but more forceful of the two partners; and she was the one to please, as Katie had quickly perceived during her job interview a year ago.

Neil Jones was a quiet, retreating man, who looked like a cuddly bear and was always accompanied by his equally quiet wife. He was content to let Anita take the lead in most of the fiscal decisions. But it was he who came up with innovative suggestions for programming.

Katie liked Neil unreservedly; she was wary of Anita

even though she respected the older woman's shrewd business sense.

They arrived at 9:00 a.m. After coffee and pastries were served by a nervous Ruth and attended by all the staff—both full-time and part-time, a total of eight—Katie waited for a signal that the partners were ready to begin the business of the day. Neil looked expectantly at Anita, who checked her watch again.

Finally she sighed. "My husband was planning to join us. However, we won't wait for him."

Anita swept her way into Katie's office and sat behind Katie's desk. Katie pulled a straight chair in from the hall leaving the two, more comfortable ones, which faced her desk, for Mr. and Mrs. Jones. She smoothed the skirt of her black linen two-piece dress and waited expectantly.

Anita certainly knew what she was doing, thought Katie as the morning progressed. Both she and Neil were generous with their praise of the progress Katie had made in the year since the partnership had purchased WCTZ. They had seen the figures from "The Book," which had come out in May and covered ratings for the previous calendar year, and the slow but steady increase in revenues since Katie had taken over managing the station last June. But Katie had more current figures to show them, including the sharp advertising jump in March.

"The new programming schedule has been most effective, it seems," said Anita.

"Neil's suggestion for expanding the weather and fishing reports has gotten a positive reaction from all our sponsors," she said. "They seem to appreciate our giving extra time to information that affects their jobs so directly."

Neil piped in. He had a high voice that amazed Katie. "How is your idea for the out-of-towners show going?" he asked.

In January she had initiated a program aimed at the people who moved here temporarily every winter. "The snowbirds seem to like it," she said. "I've replaced it for the summer with a country/rock music show that should appeal to teenagers."

At a raised brow from Anita, she went on, "It was a marketing decision. The Chamber of Commerce has done a study. In the winter most of the money spent with Garden City's merchants is spent by the older generation, and in the summer, by the kids."

That satisfied both of them—about the running of the station, at least. Over a working lunch, which Katie had arranged to have catered, she had explained in more detail about the murder of the boutique owner and the destruction by arson of the woman's shop, the break-in at her own apartment, and the destruction of the station wagon.

Anita's expression grew more horrified with each disclosure. "Well," she huffed. "I certainly hope this will be over soon. It can't help the reputation of the station to have its manager mixed up in something like this."

At the tactless statement, Katie merely smiled. She had been unnecessarily nervous about this meeting, she realized. Looking over the statistics from an objective viewpoint—which she'd been too close to the job to do until now—she realized that she had a lot to be proud of.

The realization lifted her spirits. If the owners didn't appreciate the long hours and hard work she'd put in, it was their loss.

She couldn't worry about her job right now; she could always find another one. According to circumstances, she had to worry about her life.

The deputy patrolling on foot outside the station had made them restive, fidgety. Katie could sympathize; Greg's presence made her restive, too, when he'd first arrived yesterday morning. But she would have been a lot more uncomfortable without him there.

The charter trip seemed interminable. Neal had a man at the radio station and Raymond had promised to stay until Joe got there, but Joe was still uneasy. The man was getting reckless, desperate.

All through this long day, images of Katie had played through his mind—images of her beside him on the flying bridge, pictures of her laughing, of her face flushed from their lovemaking, of her beautiful eyes filled with warmth, affection, generosity...love, unreserved love.

Sometime during the wee hours of this morning he had finally understood just how profound his feelings for her were. He was deeply in love. Joe Ryder, in love. Unbelievable, almost laughable, except he didn't feel like laughing. He felt joy and exhilaration and excitement—and he felt apprehension.

He didn't know whether or not he deserved her love, but he knew damn well he was going to take it. He'd never felt like this before. Olivene, the woman he'd lived with for a year, had loved him, he supposed, in her way. But, as it proved, hers wasn't the kind of love that survived, that built on itself, not the kind that could stand up under adversity. Katie's was. He looked at his watch.

The sky was just overcast enough for the fish to bite well. Joe's clients, a group of businessmen from Birmingham, were overjoyed as they hauled in blackfin tuna, bonito and their limit of the protected King mackerel.

As soon as they returned to the dock, Joe called Katie. He hadn't admitted how anxious he was about her safety until he heard her voice.

"I'm on my way," he said gruffly. "You can help me clean the boat later." He looked over at the young boy he'd paid to do that job.

"Thanks a lot," she answered wryly. The sound of her soft laughter sent frissons of excitement and anticipation through him.

"How did things go?"

"Well, they weren't too happy about the police hanging around." He heard her voice drop to a quiet level and recognized her effort to contain her excitement. "But, Joe, they were pleased, really pleased, with the progress I've made."

He laughed. "Hey, that's great. I'll spring for champagne."

"Deal," she replied immediately. "If you and Neal can find this man soon, my life will return to normal." She paused and now there was a teasing note there. "Well, nearly normal."

"Katie—" He opened his mouth to tell her that he loved her. And closed it again. Not over the phone. He wanted to see her, hold her, when he made the admission.

"I'll wait for you," she said softly. "Hurry."

He touched the plunger hook one time, got a dial tone and called to check in with Neal. He knew his brother would have called him on the ship-to-shore if there had been any significant developments but he wanted a progress report.

When Neal answered he sounded harried and there was the distinctive click of call-waiting. "Joe! I'm glad you called. Hang on a minute, will you?"

Neal switched to the other line before Joe could say he would call back later. Joe sighed and sat down on the edge of the railing. A few other fishermen were performing the chores that marked the end of the day's work. Hoses were connected to spray salt water off the decks, rags and mops were out, bait boxes were dumped and the gulls swooped down to scavenge what was left after the fish were cleaned. There were several empty slips, affirmation that he hadn't been the only one to have a successful business day.

He waited—and waited—and thought about hanging up. He wanted to get to Katie. He wouldn't feel comfortable until he had her by his side...for the rest of their lives.

Damn, that sounded good!

But Neal might have news about the matches. He'd been holding the line for ten minutes when Neal finally came back on. "Joe, that was Annette calling from police headquarters in Atlanta. She knew who he was all right. She had an appointment with him for tonight, but after you told her that we'd found Louise's body she left town in a hurry. She swears she didn't know anything had happened to Louise but she's singing like a bird about everything else."

Joe felt his emotions rise to meet Neal's exuberance and his brother went on, "The name was confirmed by the resort as well. We've got him. We have a name and address. And an explanation for his excessive interest in Katie.''

''Who is he?''

''He's Calvin Nelson, the husband of Anita Rayburn Nelson. She is one of the owners of R and J Communications, out of Tampa. The partnership owns the radio station, Joe. They're even buying a condo in Garden City.''

''I know. The owners were here today. Katie's been busy getting ready for their visit.''

''That fits with Annette's story. I'll meet you at the radio station first. Then we'll pay a call on the Nelsons.''

Annette hadn't shown up for their meeting. The blond man, Calvin Nelson, had waited almost an hour for her, his alarm growing with each minute that passed. Tears stood in his eyes; he didn't *want* to hurt anybody. He'd never wanted to hurt anybody. But circumstances always seemed to conspire against him.

He'd thought the money, a lot of money, would keep Annette quiet—she was greedy—but she'd double-crossed him. Now he had to silence Katie Johns *and* Annette, somehow.

Louise had mistaken a careless fling for true love. He let out his breath in a snort of derision. She was foolish, sentimental. Saving that book of matches from her birthday dinner was the sort of indiscreet, emotional garbage she liked to litter up their affair with.

He laughed, a dry sound. The stupid fool had actually expected him to leave Anita and marry her. This was all her fault.

Leave Anita? Anita was his wife. He was truly stunned by Louise when she'd announced that she was pregnant. She had already begun to make plans. She'd gone on and on about where they would live, what they would name the baby, how happy they would be. Until finally he'd had to hit her to shut her up. She'd screamed as she'd fallen against an upright post. He'd heard her neck snap.

He hadn't meant for her to die. It was an accident, a horrible accident. But after she was dead it was so easy just to roll her body into the water. He'd remembered the matches. He searched her purse before throwing it in the water, too. Then he'd returned to the table. But the matches were gone and the only person who could have them was the woman on the pier. If he could have caught her that night and gotten the matches back all this could have been avoided. He didn't know what kind of records the resort kept and he had made the reservations in his own name that night—an incredibly stupid thing to do. He *had* to find those matches.

Now events were closing in on him. The shock of discovering that the woman on the pier was Katie Johns, who worked for his wife at the radio station, had only been the beginning. She had seen him with Louise and she had the matches. He'd called, he'd threatened, he'd searched her condo and come up empty. She wouldn't be scared off. Where the hell *were* the damned matches?

The bomb didn't work. Hell, he'd even caught the wrong person in the station wagon. Besides, what did he know about bombs? Nothing that couldn't be found out in the public library.

Anita was suspicious, too, about all the hours he'd put on the Cessna lately, ostensibly for business. What business, she demanded to know. His explanations had satisfied her for a while. He was good at talking himself out of trouble—always had been.

He bit into his lower lip, wiping his wet palms on his trousers. He stayed out of sight and watched as the deputy made another round of the building. Each time, the man stopped to try the back doorknob, and checked the lock of the one window on the otherwise windowless wall. On the next circuit he was going to have to make his move.

"You go on home with Gloria, Raymond. You weren't even supposed to work today." She eyed the strip of bandage at his left temple with renewed guilt. "I mean it. Go home."

"I'm fine, Katie. Thanks to Joe. I couldn't let you face Rayburn and Jones without support." Raymond shook his head stubbornly. "And I'm not leaving you here alone," he argued.

"I'm not alone. Greg is right outside. He's been walking circles around this building all day long."

"I promised Joe—"

Katie interrupted. "Joe called ten minutes ago. He'll be here any moment to pick me up." She reached for her purse to demonstrate that she would soon be leaving, too. "All the doors are locked except for this one. Go," she ordered.

"He's on his way?"

She nodded.

"You'll lock up behind me? You won't decide to wait outside?"

"Do you think I'm crazy?" she teased. Actually she was nervous enough without his reminder.

"Okay," he said reluctantly. He waited on the other side of the plate glass entrance door until she had turned the key in the lock. He spoke to the deputy who was just rounding the corner of the building. Then he waved and climbed into the car that had been idling outside the entrance. Gloria and their daughter, Gina, were waiting for him.

Katie watched the car leave the parking lot. Despite her brave words she felt a sense of overwhelming loneliness seep into her as soon as the rear lights disappeared. The deputy had disappeared again, too. She wished he would come back around; she'd ask him to wait inside with her.

Suddenly, in the light of the lobby, she felt exposed. She moved back toward her office and pulled the drapes. Where was Joe, she wondered. It didn't take this long to get from the docks to the station.

If he'd called her as soon as he docked, there could have been a dozen details to clear up. The unloading of the fish, icing down, settling the fees—any number of things could have caused the delay. But he'd said he was on his way.

She put down her purse and keys and looked at the clutter on her desk. At least something had gone right today. As she'd told Joe, Mrs. Nelson and Mr. and Mrs. Jones were pleased with her presentation and the additional advertising revenue the new standings would bring in. The insurance company had been cooperative and they should be getting a brand-new station wagon soon.

Tonight she and Joe would celebrate more than her success. Their relationship had taken a giant step forward last night. She wasn't sure how she'd reached that conclusion but she was certain. More than certain, she was positive. She smiled, wanting him to hurry, wanting to touch him, to be enfolded in his arms again, to be kissed.

The smile froze on her face as she suddenly found herself standing in a dark and silent office. Between the edges of the drapes she could see that the streetlights were still burning. This wasn't a power failure. Momentary confusion was replaced by dread, visceral and profound dread. *Oh God, he's come for me.* Where was the deputy?

She opened her mouth to call out but then, almost on the heels of the blackness, came a sound from the rear of the building, a sound of shattering glass, and a muffled curse. She fought down her fear and the urge to panic. Instead she got angry. *You animal. I hope to hell you cut yourself . . . badly.*

She wasn't going to let this monster win. Joe would be here any minute to help her. Joe. The thought of him made her gather her resolve as she slipped out of her shoes and stood very still, almost afraid to breathe.

Oh, God. Joe.

If anything happened to her Joe would take his revenge personally. He was just beginning to get his life back in order; that mustn't happen. Suddenly she felt in control, calm. Her brain, fueled by adrenaline and fear for the man she loved, went to work, taking over from her emotions. She knew this floor plan like the back of her hand. That was an advantage. She was alone and without a weapon. That was a disadvantage. The darkened corridors of the station were both a refuge and a trap. She had to get out of here. But she had to move carefully.

She searched her mental image of her office for something—anything—she could use to protect herself. There was nothing, not even a letter opener or an umbrella. Escape was the only way.

The keys were on the corner of her desk. She groped for them.

The feeble musical chime they made when she picked them up stayed her hand and she caught her breath. If he'd heard the sound, her position was pinpointed. He'd come right for her. She listened. Nothing. The noise had been slight. Maybe he hadn't heard.

By feel she found what she hoped was the right key and took one step toward the door.

Another furtive sound reached her ears. Nonsense, she reproved herself. The carpet would muffle her footsteps. She'd head straight for the front door, open it and run out. The hall that led from her office to the lobby was pitch-black. In her office the crack between the draperies had provided, if not light, at least a lifting of the darkness. She trailed her fingers along the wall.

When she reached the corner where the two corridors intersected, the illumination coming through the entrance door beckoned, but she didn't make the mistake of rushing forward. Instead she carefully inventoried the lobby, paying particular attention to the shadowed corners.

She could see nothing. The only sound was the pounding of her own heart.

It was now or never. She was about ten feet from the door. Ten feet equaled about three long steps. She had to make the move, had to take those last steps that would lead to freedom, and Joe.

Concentrate on Joe, on being in his arms again. She inhaled, flooding her system with oxygen, and took the first step. And the second. She held the key out in front of her, extended toward the lock. The third step was just a finish of the quick journey.

Though the scene seemed to be playing in slow motion, she actually almost flew toward the door. Metal scraped against metal; she turned the key and reached for the handle. A smile of relief was growing on her face when suddenly her mouth was muffled by a hand, her arms were pinned to her sides by a strong arm and she was dragged back into the shadows.

Joe knew something was wrong as soon as he turned the corner. The building was veiled in darkness. None of the spotlights were on.

Fear descended upon him like an icy shroud. Katie! Dear God, where was Katie? His emotional impulse was automatic. Turn into the parking lot, jump out of the truck and break in the door. At the last minute his training and expertise took over from his emotions. *Oh, God, please let it be enough.* He wrenched the wheel back into alignment and drove on for half a block until his truck was hidden from the station by a high hibiscus hedge. Then he jumped out and doubled back on foot.

The edge that kept him alive hadn't been honed in a long time. The balance had shifted, the balance between hard and soft, between civilized and savage.

He tried to revert to the man he had been. That man had a chance of saving Katie. He must think coolly and logically. She knew he was coming. She was depending on him and he wouldn't, couldn't, let her down. As he started toward the darkened entrance of the building, he heard sounds of a scuffle from around back.

The noise was enough to jump-start the skills he'd prayed for. He reached under his jacket and felt the reassuring grip of the revolver planted in the small of his back.

Without a conscious thought he drew the weapon and rounded the corner, his body in a crouch, both hands on the grip, finger poised over the trigger.

The blond man was wrestling with a wildly struggling Katie, *his Katie*, trying to get her into the open trunk of a car parked there. The deputy lay unmoving on the ground.

"Let her go," said Joe in a low voice, metallic in the warning he conveyed.

The man's head snapped up. His eyes were wide with terror. He sought and found Joe in the shadows with the instincts of a cornered animal. He jerked around, keeping Katie in front of him and clumsily yanked a gun from his pocket. "Stay back!" he yelled, waving the gun. "Stay back or I'll kill her, I swear to God! I'll kill her right now."

Joe felt the blood chill in his veins at the same time cold sweat broke out over his body. From the way he held the weapon Joe realized at once that the man wasn't familiar with firearms. And a novice was even more dangerous than an expert in a situation like this.

Katie's beautiful eyes were fixed on Joe.

"Let her go," he repeated. "You can't escape, Nelson. Annette is in Atlanta. She has told the police everything. We found the matches and we know you made the reservation at the resort. The sheriff's on his way."

As though to prove Joe's statement, a siren sounded in the distance and startled the man who held her. And at Joe's mention of his name, she felt the intensity of reckless action in the body behind her. That damned gun was aimed at Joe, *her Joe*. Could he fire in return? Of course he could, if he had the chance. But he'd be afraid of hitting her.

She had to do something. She had continued her struggles in an attempt to take advantage of the man's distraction. She'd tried to hurt him but her scratching and clawing had been ignored completely as though the man couldn't feel pain. Suddenly, her adrenaline rose. Desperation gave her the power and strength she'd lacked up until now.

She clamped down hard with her teeth on the fleshy part of the man's palm and tasted his blood. It gagged her but she continued to bite as she raked her nails over the arm around her waist.

He made a noise of pain in his throat and thrust her aside. "Bitch!" She fell to the ground beside Greg, who moaned.

He pointed the gun at her head and she waited.

It was the opening Joe had been waiting for. Without hesitation, he fired.

The bullet took the man in the shoulder. The gun he had been holding spun into the air behind him. He spared one glance for his lost weapon and turned to run, but Joe was on him before he could move.

He pinned the injured arm behind the man and hauled him to his feet. He had his fist cocked for a blow to the jaw—he wanted to beat this monster to a bloody pulp—when he heard the sobs and saw the tears streaming down the man's face. His bloodshot eyes darted about in panic and he cringed, as far as he could move, away from the fury on Joe's face.

"Hell! You aren't worth it!" Joe said, looking at the pitiful creature in his grasp. All the fight, all the desire for revenge, went out of him. He shoved Nelson against the side of his car, whipped off the man's belt, and bound his arms behind him.

The deputy groaned and rolled to his feet, holding his head. He viewed the scene before him and groaned again. He took over from Joe, whipping out a pair of handcuffs, which he added to Joe's handiwork.

Katie sat where she was, holding her breath, until the man had been completely immobilized. Then she was hauled up and into Joe's arms. She wrapped her arms around his neck and held on as though she would never let go, holding, being held tight against his pounding heart.

They remained like that, touching each other, whispering desperate loving phrases to each other, until Neal's car pulled in, illuminating them with its headlights.

The man on the ground began to talk as soon as he saw the sheriff's uniform. "I wasn't going to hurt her. I just wanted to scare her into keeping her mouth shut. That's all I ever wanted to do to Louise. Her death was an accident, I swear! She fell and hit her head on the pier. I know I should have called an ambulance, but it was so easy to roll her body into the water.

"My wife would have left me, you see," he went on, grasping his injured shoulder. "Don't you understand, she would have left me?"

Neal turned the man over to another deputy, who read him his rights, put him into a second department car and drove away. Then he joined Katie and Joe. "Are you both all right?" he asked, his voice thick with emotion.

Joe turned to his brother, keeping Katie under his arm. "We're okay," he said meeting Neal's eyes straight on.

A smile, reminiscent of Joe's, spread on his brother's face. The resemblance between them was amplified by the expression. Neal reached out to hug them both. "You're more than okay, aren't you?" he asked Joe.

"Yeah," Joe drawled. A deeper, unspoken communication passed between them. "Both of us."

Neal turned to Katie. "You're gonna let him speak for you?" he asked mildly.

Katie grinned. "Anytime."

"Good. I'll see you two at the sheriff's department, won't I?"

"Tomorrow," said Joe.

Neal shook his head regretfully. "Now, Joe. You know the procedure. We'll have to have a statement."

"I'm a deputy, aren't I? I'll get the statement."

"Signed."

"Signed, sealed and delivered," promised Joe. "Tomorrow."

"Do you think Nelson was sincere when he said he didn't mean to kill Louise?" Katie asked later that night. She lay against Joe's side on the big bed in the bow of the boat, her cheek against his heart.

She had changed into jeans and a shirt while Joe had moved the boat into the channel and they'd watched the fireworks over the water. Firecrackers, soaring rockets in red, white and blue, heralded the beginning of the Fourth of July weekend festivities.

Afterward, he'd returned to the slip. They had talked a lot but not about the important things.

Joe's hand stroked her upper arm meditatively before he answered. "I have my doubts. But it's up to a jury to decide."

They were both fully clothed, a complication Katie hadn't counted on. She had spoken to her parents; they were reassured. She and Joe had eaten a take-out supper during the fireworks display. Neal had called twice on the ship-to-shore radio to keep them up-to-date on the man's confession.

In between Joe was chronicling all the changes he intended to make in his life in order to be worthy of asking her to marry him. He never mentioned the word love, not once in his discourse.

Finally Katie could stand it no longer. She sat up, swung her legs off the bed and headed for the door.

"Where are you going?" asked Joe, pained by the sudden loss of her next to him.

"Home. There's no more danger to me so I might as well sleep in my own bed."

"You can't leave. We're talking about getting married, for Pete's sake!"

She turned at the door to look at him. "No," she said softly. "*You're* talking about it. For the past hour you've barely allowed me a word in edgewise. You're telling me how you're going to transform the man I fell in love with into some paragon, a completely different person, someone I might not recognize, a new man." She forced a smile. "Who knows? I might not even love the new man if he does all that changing."

She almost made it to the ladder before his arm caught her around the waist. She couldn't control her wince as his arm touched the bruise there.

Immediately he was all concern. "Katie, oh, babe. Did I hurt you?" He cradled her in his arms and took her back to the bed. "Let me see." He pushed up her blouse and saw the discoloration across her rib cage. His face twisted. "I should have killed the son of a bitch."

Katie touched his cheek. "I'm glad you didn't. I'm not forgiving him for what he did. But when he started to cry..." She shook her head. "He looked pitiful, didn't he?"

His mouth lifted in the characteristic half smile that always stirred her blood. "Not half as pitiful as I'm going to look if you walk out on me." Joe planted his hands at her sides. He looked down at her, his expression full of wonder.

"Why?" Katie breathed in softly.

"I love you very much, Katie Johns, more than I ever thought it was possible to love anyone," he said with no hesitation. "I want to marry you and live with you for the rest of my life. Will you take me as I am?"

Katie let her breath out. Her eyes fell shut, then opened again, brimming with happiness, with elation, joy. Her emotions spilled out like generous golden tears, bringing a lump to Joe's throat. "That was worth waiting an eternity for. I love you, Joe."

The fireworks that lit the night sky—a clear sky—over the channel were nothing compared to the fireworks between them.

* * * * *

A compelling novel of deadly revenge and passion
from bestselling international
romance author Penny Jordan

Eleven years had passed but the
terror of that night was something
Pepper Minesse would never
forget. Fueled by revenge against
the four men who had brutally
shattered her past, she set in
motion a deadly plan to destroy
their futures.

Available in February!

SPP-1A

DIAMOND JUBILEE CELEBRATION!

It's Silhouette Books' tenth anniversary, and what better way to celebrate than to toast *you*, our readers, for making it all possible. Each month in 1990, we'll present you with a DIAMOND JUBILEE Silhouette Romance written by an all-time favorite author!

Welcome the new year with *Ethan*—a LONG, TALL TEXANS book by Diana Palmer. February brings Brittany Young's *The Ambassador's Daughter*. Look for *Never on Sundae* by Rita Rainville in March, and in April you'll find *Harvey's Missing* by Peggy Webb. Victoria Glenn, Lucy Gordon, Annette Broadrick, Dixie Browning and many more have special gifts of love waiting for you with their DIAMOND JUBILEE Romances.

Be sure to look for the distinctive DIAMOND JUBILEE emblem, and share in Silhouette's celebration. Saying thanks has never been so romantic....